EX LIBRIS

READER'S DIGEST
CONDENSED BOOKS

READER'S DIGEST CONDENSED BOOKS

VOLUME 3 • 1973

THE READER'S DIGEST ASSOCIATION
PLEASANTVILLE, NEW YORK

CONTENTS

Illustrated by John McClelland

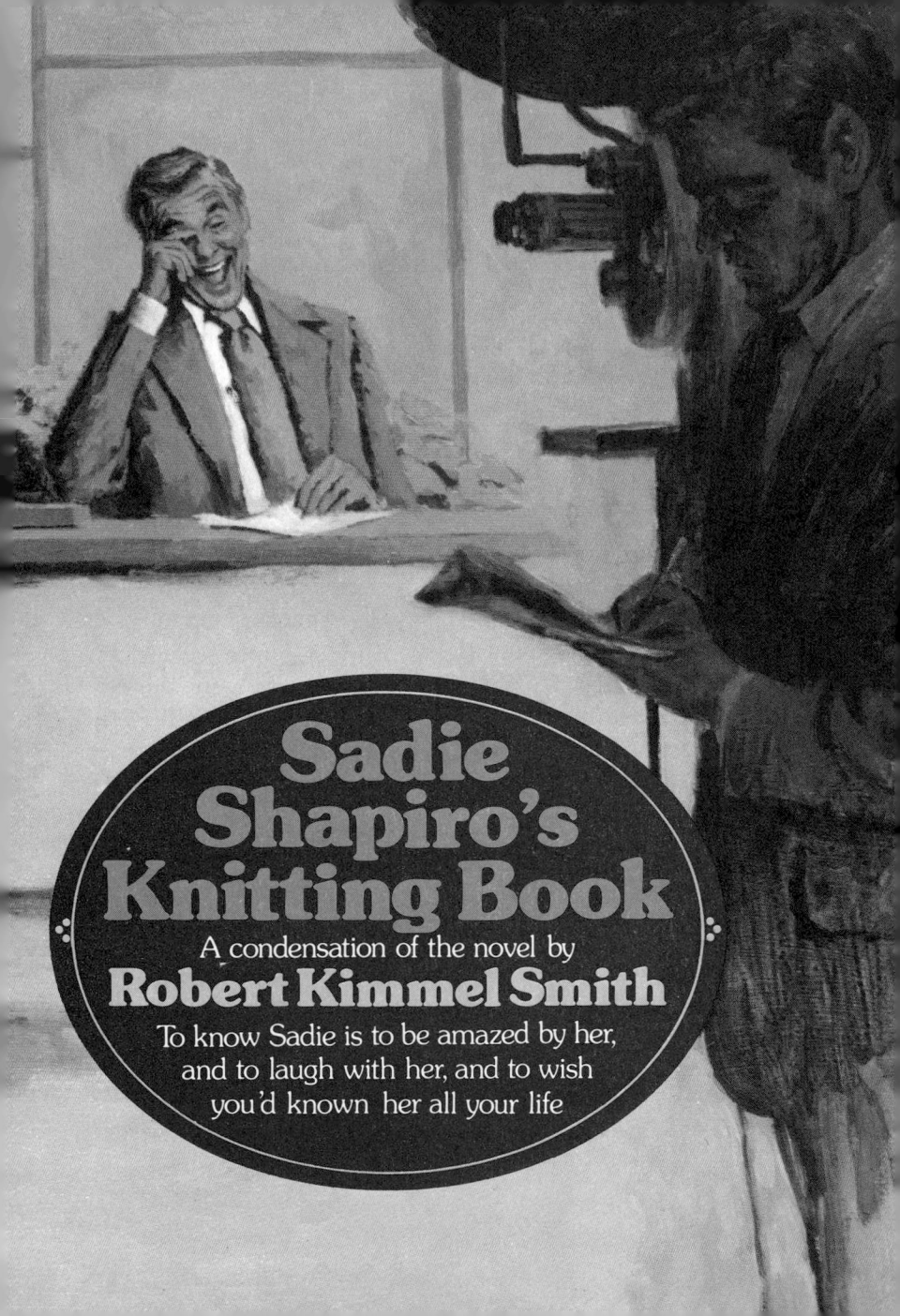

Sadie Shapiro's Knitting Book

A condensation of the novel by
Robert Kimmel Smith

To know Sadie is to be amazed by her,
and to laugh with her, and to wish
you'd known her all your life

SOMEWHERE on her desk there had to be a pencil.

Marian Wall held two fingers in the margin of the black-bound manuscript while she searched through a litter of galley proofs, ashtrays, business cards, the remains of a liverwurst sandwich on rye toast, five envelopes containing bill payments she had meant to mail last week, and assorted scraps of paper scribbled over with ideas. There had to be a pencil. She opened the center drawer of her desk. Underneath a jumble of emery boards, tissues, paper clips, plastic spoons, and packets of sugar, a spot of yellow indicated a well-worn Mongol #2. Now for a scratch pad, bottom left-hand drawer. Now what was it she wanted to note?

Sighing, Marian put the pencil between the pages to hold her place and closed the manuscript. I have been working on too many gothic novels, she thought. After a while they all tend to become one in your mind. The brave young heroines in danger, the old rotting mansions set in bleak landscapes, the mysterious (but handsome) young men who would either threaten or fall in love with the heroine, and sometimes do both.

Turning in her swivel chair, Marian looked into the oval mirror that hung on the smudged cream-colored wall. Thirty-three years old, she thought, and I hate my hair. She peered at the strands of gray. Does she or doesn't she? She doesn't, and it shows. Next

week, a color rinse, a new dress. She blinked at her image, tears just behind her lashes. Stop kidding yourself, she decided.

When the telephone rang, she was happy for the interruption. "Is that you, Marian?" a soft male voice asked.

As Marian answered, she heard a quiet chuckle, which instantly identified the caller. It was the oddball admirer who had been phoning her at home and in the office for months. Heathcliff was the secret name Marian had given him. "Oh, sweet Marian," the voice was saying.

"Please," Marian interrupted, "I don't have time right now."

"I will be there tonight, and when you open the door . . ."

I must call the supermarket, thought Marian, tuning the caller out. She looked at her watch.

" . . . and you'll be wearing something special . . . all white, with just a small diamond clip at your throat . . ."

Retrieving the pencil and losing her place in the manuscript, Marian began to make notes on the margin of the title page. Butter, eggs, Velveeta, a package of Ring Dings, a honeydew melon because Laura, her eleven-year-old, liked it.

" . . . and I'll sweep you into my arms and hold you close. Then I'll step back and look at you. I could do that for hours, you know that, don't you, Marian?"

"What?"

"How much I love to look at you. Did I tell you?"

"I think so, yes. When we were dancing on the George Washington Bridge. Last week."

There was a moment of silence. "I said that?" Heathcliff asked.

"Yes. You had them stop the traffic for the evening, remember? And there were just the two of us, dancing on the George Washington Bridge—except for the New York Philharmonic providing the music, of course."

"I must be having a breakdown," Heathcliff said. "I don't recall saying any of that."

"Take my word for it," Marian said as the telephone rang softly. "Hold on, I've got another call." She punched the lighted button and Jack Gatewood was on the line.

"Hey, Marian," he began, "it looks like this knitting thing is coming up to bat. Arnold likes the samples and is talking full speed ahead. Could you meet me in his office?"

"Look, Jack, I don't want to edit that book. I told Arnold—"

"Tell him again," Jack said. "We tee off in five minutes."

"Oh," Marian groaned. The knitting book. Now where had she put the correspondence file and the patterns?

"Where was I?" Heathcliff asked as Marian punched in his line.

"Standing back and admiring me."

"Right. And I'll be wearing tails, of course, and I'll whisk you out the door . . ."

Damn the knitting book. They would gang up and stick her with another arts and crafts book to edit, another thankless, demanding job. Because she was a woman, right? That's why she'd get stuck with the knitting book, as she had been commandeered for the crewel book, not to mention her all-time hate: *Redecorating With Wallpaper*. Gothics and handicrafts, that was her lot at Harbor Press. A woman's place is in the office, editing books for women.

" . . . in the back of a hansom cab, clip-clopping through Central Park, holding you in the curve of my arm—"

"I've got to hang up now," Marian said—

"Come on," Heathcliff protested, "I'm just getting started."

"Really, I have to go."

"Well, I'll call you at home."

"Will you just look at these marvelous creations?" Arnold Hawthorne held aloft a brightly colored sweater knitted in an allover paisley pattern. The portly publisher of Harbor Press ("Books for the Millions") winked at Jack Gatewood, his editor-in-chief. "I smell a big seller here, Jack, don't you agree?"

"It just could be," Gatewood said, smiling at Marian, who sat beside him on the nubby tweed couch.

"And to think it came from slush," Hawthorne went on. "Over the transom, from nobody." He shook his head in wonder. "Whoever created these items is an absolute genius." He held up a small

knitted oblong with three white buttons sewn on its upper surface. "Now this is fantastic, isn't it?" he said. "What the hell is it?"

I'm going to be stuck with it, Marian Wall thought sourly. "It's a glove, Arnold," she said, getting up and putting it on her small hand, "a child's mitten. These three buttons on top are the eyes and nose of an animal, see? And when the child opens its hand, like this, you see the animal's mouth, here on my palm, and the little pink tongue inside."

"Wonderful," Hawthorne said. "Are the other patterns this person submitted as good?"

"I don't know," Marian said. "I've never knitted a stitch in my life. All I know is that the package came to you. You sent it to Jack, who sent it to Eustace, who shoved it on to Mace, who left it on my desk. Inside the package were fifty knitting patterns with instructions, and these samples. The sweater, the mittens, and these." She held up a pair of children's slippers knitted in heavy blue wool, with an elegant bow tie worked in across the instep. "Plus the note, which you've already read."

"Have you contacted this Mrs. Shapiro?" Jack asked.

"I haven't tried," Marian said. "Not until I was sure we were interested in the book."

"By all means do, then," said Hawthorne, waving a heavy hand. "The market for craft books is booming these days."

"Arnold," Marian said slowly, "I don't want to edit it."

"Marian, Marian," soothed the publisher.

"I mean it. All I ever seem to work on around here are gothics and handicrafts, and it's not enough. I'm a complete person, Arnold, besides being a woman, I mean. Give the book to Eustace Fielding. Give it to Mace Masterman. Every good novel I find you give to them, anyway. Who first read *Memoirs of a Painted Lady?* I did. And who got to work on it? Eustace Fielding."

"And how many copies did it sell?" said Hawthorne. "Nine hundred and forty."

"Marian, sweetie," Jack put in, "you've been carrying this operation on your back. You're our strength, our heavy hitter."

"I'm more like your dishrag," Marian said, folding her arms.

Hawthorne regarded the bare spot worn into the carpet in front of his desk. "Marian, those books of yours and Jack's sports books are what keep us going. Do you know how many copies of *Redecorating With Wallpaper* we've sold? Fifty-three thousand at nine ninety-five a copy. And two book clubs have taken it."

"If it weren't for you, we'd already be in porno," Jack said.

"Or worse," echoed Arnold Hawthorne, nodding. "Is there something worse than porno?"

Silent, Marian stared for a long moment into Jack Gatewood's gray-green eyes, looking for a sign. But that perfect sun-bronzed face was passive, as it almost always was. It was the face of a tennis pro, an Austrian ski instructor. No, more than that, it was the face of a movie star who would be cast in those parts.

"All right," she said with a good-loser's smile, "you win again." She knew she would do the knitting book because she was and always would be Marian Wall—the girl who had begun as a switchboard operator at Harbor Press and worked her way up.

"I knew you'd agree," said Hawthorne, beaming. "Find this Mrs. Shapiro and sign her." He made an expansive gesture with his hand. "Give her anything she wants for an advance—up to seven hundred and fifty."

Marian collected the samples and walked slowly to her office. Why do I always get to the point of threatening to leave and never say it? she asked herself. In the next instant came the answer: You know you can't afford it. And what's more, you're afraid they'd let you quit. If that happened, who would keep you and Laura afloat while you looked for another job?

Back at her desk and feeling depressed, Marian reread the note that had accompanied the samples and patterns. "I don't know why I'm sending you this except I'm maybe one of the best knitters in America and maybe sometime you want to put out a book on knitting so we could get together. These are my best 50 patterns and if you don't like them just say so and I'll quick send you 50 more. Patterns I got and all of them original too. So let me know. If you don't like them we'll still be the same friends and you'll send me back and I'll pay the postage." The signature read:

"Mrs. S. L. Shapiro," and below that was an address in Queens and a telephone number. Also a P.S.: "I know about Harbor Press from reading *Redecorating With Wallpaper*."

Marian dialed and waited through four rings before the phone was picked up. "Hello. Mrs. S. L. Shapiro, please."

"You'll have to speak up, I don't hear too good," a woman said, "and besides, they're all playing bingo. We never disturb them in the bingo room except an emergency. A person needs maybe one number to make bingo, you know, and you can get your head handed to you you call them away."

"Is there a Mrs. S. L. Shapiro there?"

"S. L.?" the woman said. "Oh, you must mean Sadie."

"Sadie?" said Marian. "Look, my name is Marian Wall and I'm with Harbor Press. Can you have Mrs. Shapiro call me back?"

"Ooops! There's the dinner chimes. I got to go now."

"Wait!" said Marian. "Who am I talking to? Is this a residence or a business firm?"

"You could say both. It's the Mount Eden Senior Citizens Hotel, and I don't want to be late for dinner."

JUAN OTERO sang softly to himself as his taxi crawled slowly along the Long Island Expressway. Stop and go, stop and go. Juan mopped his wet brow with a gray-yellow handkerchief. June, hot, and a parkway that was solidly bumper to bumper.

"Will it take much longer?" Marian asked.

"A year, maybe two," said Juan. He looked into the rearview mirror and regarded the passenger he had picked up near the Grindl Building in Manhattan. Cold, he thought, very cold. She does not know of love or of passion. He caught the woman's eyes in the mirror and flashed her a smile. "A curse of God because we dare to invent the automobile." His comment brought no more than a glassy stare from the brown-haired lady. There were some people who did not know a joke even when it tickled them under the chin. He sneaked another look. Not a bad chin, he thought, nor was her mouth forbidding. And the rest of the face, especially the upturned nose, could almost be called pretty.

"Maybe you ought to get off the expressway," Marian said. "We don't seem to be moving."

"If you like, I get off," said Juan. He swung the taxi sharply into the right-hand lane, provoking an angry chorus of horns and some shaken fists. "Do you know Queens?" he asked, turning onto the exit ramp that led to Queens Boulevard.

"Not at all."

"Good. Then we get lost together."

"Forty-seven twenty-five Hollis Avenue," Marian said. The mountain is going to Mohammed, she thought bitterly, for a knitting book no less. Why wouldn't the mysterious Mrs. Shapiro come into the city, have lunch, and discuss the project as any normal person should? And why, on the hottest June day the world had ever known, was she dragging herself to the Mount Eden Senior Citizens Hotel located in God-knows-where, Queens? Would Mace Masterman, or any other editor in his right mind, make such a trip? He would not. Only you, Marian Wall. What a horrible way to make thirteen thousand dollars a year. Less withholding, Blue Cross, city and state taxes, and F.I.C.A. (whatever that was). Publishing. Ech! How did a bright young girl, Barnard, magna cum laude, get into publishing? I just drifted into it because, well, what else does an English major do?

She looked at the house numbers on the tree-lined street. They were at nine hundred and falling. "Are we near Hollis Avenue?"

"Who knows?" Juan shrugged. "Is a foreign country."

An English major. How those words had affected her life! She remembered that day, so long ago, in the coffee shop of the United Nations Building. The man, handsome but for his hawk nose, looked at her over his coffee cup as she transcribed notes for the thesis she was writing. "And what do you do?" he asked as she looked up, his eyes a muddy brown that matched the river flowing by just outside the window. Blushing like the schoolgirl she was, she stammered, "I am an English major."

"And I," he said smiling, "am a French colonel."

Jean-Claude de Lattre Wall was indeed, as it turned out, a colonel, and also a diplomat—but not too diplomatic to take her

hand and hold it in his. Nor to read her fortune and future in his quiet voice, tracing the lines with a finger. And the days that followed were as golden as his hair and filled with the tenderness of first love.

They were married in the small chapel at the United Nations, and when graduation time came Marian was already pregnant under her flowing black gown. But even before their daughter, Laura, was born, the marriage had begun to come apart. Jean-Claude's true love, Marian sorrowfully discovered, was alcohol in any form. Under its influence, which was almost constant, the gentle colonel was transformed into a monster of anger who thought nothing of striking her or throwing things against the walls of their tiny apartment. Shortly after their final argument, the colonel disappeared into the Congo. Marian soon learned that his diplomatic status made it impossible to force him to support Laura. So with only one more rent payment left in the bank, Marian began working as a switchboard operator at Harbor Press. A year later her divorce from Jean-Claude became final.

"I THINK we are getting there," Juan Otero called, bringing Marian back to the present. They were riding under an arch of green shade trees that bordered what appeared to be a park. On the side of the street opposite the park were small frame homes, and from the numbers painted on the garbage cans that lined the sidewalk, Marian saw that forty-seven twenty-five lay not far ahead. "Are we on Hollis Avenue?" she asked.

"No," said Juan, "but I think it cannot be far away." He pulled to the curb at the next corner. "We ask someone, okay?"

Through the window Marian could see coming toward them a strange figure. A woman? Yes, a woman, in a shaggy suit of bright pink. A *sweat suit?* Yes, it was a sweat suit, and the woman was jogging, or at least bouncing slowly up and down, as she made slight forward progress. A tiny wisp of an old woman, with gray-white hair peeping out from under her matching pink tam, and on her nose a pair of silver-rimmed sunglasses.

"What is she doing?" Juan asked. "Is she loco?"

"Jogging, I think," said Marian. "I'll ask her for directions," she said as she stepped from the cab. "Excuse me—"

The old woman drew abreast of the taxi and held up a small hand. "Wait," she managed to say between gasps. The pink sweat suit was knit, Marian observed, and beautifully designed in an overall diamond pattern. On the back of the loose-fitting jacket an emblem had been worked into the design. On closer examination, Marian saw that it was a kind of wheelchair. Under the spokes of the wheels were the letters M.E.S.C.H.

"Forty-seven twenty-five Hollis Avenue," Marian said. "Is it near here?"

The old woman managed to nod. "Hold on a second," she said, her small chest heaving. Drawing a handkerchief from the sweat suit's side pocket, she mopped her brow. "A mile and a half I jogged," she wheezed, then consulted her wristwatch. "In only an hour and ten minutes." At this the woman smiled broadly, then suddenly took a step backward, staggered as if she would fall, and draped herself across the taxi's front fender in a half swoon.

Marian bounded to her side, as Juan hastily scrambled out of the cab to help. "Are you all right?" she asked anxiously. She fanned the air above the old woman's face with her patent leather handbag.

"Don't be afraid," the old woman said haltingly. "It's only my heart and maybe my liver." She ran her free hand across her midsection. "Of course, my gallbladder isn't what it used to be, but that's an old story, already." She began to lift her head, then thought better of it and reclined across the fender. "Then again," she went on, "it could have been the fatty pot roast for lunch. My worst enemies should have to eat what they give you. And then you go out and jog a mile and a half on top of a meal like that, you got to have your head examined, right?"

"And in this heat." Marian nodded.

"Heat, shmeat." The woman lifted her head, looking somewhat stronger, and managed to sit half-erect upon the fender. "You let a little heat stop you, or a little cold or rain, you know what happens? You end up sitting in a chair by the window, that's what.

Who else is going to take care of your body if you don't? Rockefeller? Just sitting around and playing bingo, you don't stay healthy. Believe me, a lot of people my age are dead already. Help me down," she said, extending a hand to Marian. With Marian gently tugging, the old woman managed to get off the fender and on her feet.

She suddenly thrust her hands skyward, took a deep breath, then plunged toward the ground. Alarmed, Marian reached out to her, and then stopped as the woman performed a perfectly respectable deep knee bend and came back to her feet, smiling. "All right," she said, "good as new. Thank God I won't have to jog again until the day after tomorrow."

"Are you sure you're all right?" Marian asked.

"Fine, fine. As good as a person seventy-two or seventy-five years old has a right to feel." She clutched Marian's arm and squeezed it gently. "Don't worry, and thanks for being so sweet to me. Not everyone shows feelings, you know. You could drop down dead on the street today and people would just step right over you, and that's your America." Adjusting her tam, the woman prepared to march off.

"Wait, lady," said Juan. "I'm looking for the Mount Eden Senior Citizens Hotel."

"Next street over and around the corner." A sudden smile brightened her face as she looked at Marian. "There's a woman coming to see me today. From Manhattan . . . a book publisher."

Oh, sweet heaven, Marian thought, please don't let it be. "Are you . . . Sadie Shapiro?"

18

"The same," said Sadie Shapiro, "and you must be Marian Wall." Taking off her sunglasses, Sadie favored Marian with a broad smile, the corners of her bright blue eyes crinkling. "Pay off the cabman, cookie," she said, "we can walk it from here. Unless . . . you wouldn't want to jog a little, would you?"

THE MOUNT Eden Senior Citizens Hotel was a three-story, modern-looking, whitewashed structure set in a grove of stately elms on a quiet street. Only when one got close were the cracks in its façade visible. A concrete loggia projected over the building's circular driveway, and in its shade a group of elderly men and women sat talking among themselves as Sadie and Marian approached. Marian was acutely aware of their eyes and the unabashed way they looked her up and down.

"So, Sadie," one of the women called, "how far today?"

"A mile and a half."

"Is that a normal person?" a man in a wheelchair remarked.

"Listen," said a woman with blue hair, "you know when she'll be happy? When she kills herself, then she'll be happy." This remark precipitated a general clacking of tongues among the group.

"Keep moving," Sadie confided as she led Marian toward the doorway. "One word and we'll be here all day."

The lobby was frigidly air-conditioned and circular in shape. A clutter of overstuffed chairs and French provincial divans, all slip-covered in yellowing plastic, were arranged in conversation groups. The floor was terrazzo inset with shiny brass fleurs-de-lis. The central focus was an immense crystal chandelier, its ropes of beads set off by brass cherubs, each carrying a flame-shaped electric bulb on his back.

"How do you like it?" Sadie asked with a small smile.

"Interesting," said Marian, hoping not to offend.

"The Fountainblue *North*, we call it."

Across the lobby was a tall, spare man, wearing white slacks and

a blazing red golf shirt. Spotting Sadie, he waved and came walking up, a king-sized cigar clenched in his teeth. "So," he said, "how far did we jog today?"

"A mile and a half. In an hour and ten minutes."

The man's thick white eyebrows raised, and he took the cigar from his mouth long enough to flick an inch of ash to the floor. "Terrific," he said. "Next year, the Olympics."

With a wide smile Sadie turned to Marian. "Marian Wall, I'd like you to meet Mr. Sam Beck, a special friend of mine."

"Who would like to be even more special and a lot more friendly," Beck said, grasping Marian's hand. "You must be the publishing lady. I used to be in publishing myself."

"Really?" Marian said, smiling.

"Had a newsstand on Broadway and Seventy-second Street. So tell me, have you made Sadie an offer yet?"

"Not yet. But we intend to publish Mrs. Shapiro's book. I'm here to work out the details."

"Ah-hah," said Beck. He nudged Sadie's elbow. "I've been trying to work out the details with Sadie for two years now."

"Sam," cautioned Sadie, "behave yourself."

"I'm seventy-seven years old," Beck said. "There's no percentage in behaving myself." He winked at Sadie. "Light of my life, I hear there's going to be a full moon tonight. You want to come up to my room and listen to Artie Shaw records?"

"We were just leaving. By, Sam," Sadie said with a flirtatious wave as she led Marian away. "The sweetest man in the whole place. So full of life, and he keeps himself so nice. You wouldn't think he had a prostate five years ago, would you?" she asked. "Come on, I'll show you around."

They walked across the lobby and into a large dining room that looked out onto a garden. "Where the elite meet to eat," said Sadie.

In an adjoining room a dozen women sat at card tables. "The bridge club," Sadie whispered. "They only take time out to eat and sleep." A connecting door led them back to the lobby. "You've spoken to Bertha," Sadie said, pausing in front of the reception desk. "Bertha!" she shouted in a voice so loud it startled Marian.

A face that might have been Grandma Moses's peeked out from behind the switchboard, a telephone headset crowning the gray hair. "Hello, Sadie," Bertha said, smiling.

"This is my friend, Marian Wall," Sadie shouted. "Bertha Maloney, our telephone lady."

"How do you do," nodded Marian.

"Anytime," said Bertha Maloney.

"Poor woman," said Sadie as they walked toward the elevators. "She makes up a little on the rent here by working the switchboard."

"Are there other tenants who—"

"Guests," Sadie corrected. "Adolph Hitler insists we call ourselves guests, not tenants."

"Hitler?"

"Max Adolphus, the so-called manager." The elevator doors creaked open, and an aged man wearing an antique uniform held the doors as Marian and Sadie entered. With a shaking hand he closed the elevator gate and started the car upward with a jerk.

"You see, Marian," Sadie said, "everything at Mount Eden is a clique. They have a grandmothers' club and all they do is sit around and tell stories about their grandchildren. You saw the bridge club downstairs. Then there's your mah-jongg group, and your bingo group, not to mention canasta and kalooki. The same women all the time, playing the same games, and saying the same things."

"And you don't play cards?"

"What I do mainly is stick to my knitting."

The elevator jerked to a stop and Sadie showed Marian down a narrow hallway. She paused at her door and then opened it. To Marian, the room appeared to be straight out of a Holiday Inn. Except for the hospital-type beds and the oxygen and paging plugs on the wall. "Make yourself comfortable," Sadie said, indicating an upholstered chair. She took a housecoat from a sliding-door closet and disappeared into the bathroom. To the accompaniment of the sound of Sadie's shower, Marian explored the cramped double room. Why had Mrs. Shapiro chosen such a life? Or had it been

chosen for her? On a dresser was a color photograph. Two young children were on a beach with palm trees. Florida, perhaps? Behind the children was Sadie, seated on a deck chair, and next to her sat a man and a woman, the children's parents judging by the smiles they displayed. Sadie's son? It was possible. His eyes narrowed at the corners as Sadie's did, and there was an overall shrewdness about his face—in his strong mouth and sharply defined nose—that bespoke a Shapiro inheritance.

Marian looked toward the door as Sadie stepped confidently from the bathroom, the brightly printed floral housecoat wrapped about her small figure. "Why are you standing?" she said to Marian. "Sit down, relax."

Sadie stretched out slowly on a bed. "A half hour on my back and I'll be myself again. There, that's better." She turned to Marian. "Now we should talk over about the knitting book, right? So fire ahead, I'm nothing but ears."

Marian opened her attaché case. At that moment Bessie Frankel, Sadie's roommate, came into the room. She smiled at Sadie, who introduced her to Marian.

"They should all drop dead, right?" Bessie immediately demanded of Marian. "Three daughters, you give them a lifetime, they end up packing their mother off like a steamer trunk. Is this right, I ask you?"

"It's not right," said Sadie. "They don't deserve your little pinkie."

"They should be like a chandelier," trumpeted Bessie. "Should hang in the daytime and burn at night."

"You're a hundred percent right," agreed Sadie.

"Such a heartache from children I wouldn't wish on anyone," Bessie said. She smiled in a satisfied way, then sighed heavily.

"Bessie, darling," Sadie began, "I'd like to talk over something important with my friend, Mrs. Wall. So maybe you'll be an angel and go downstairs to the garden for a while?"

Bessie's eyebrows rose. "So who would stay where she's not wanted?" She sniffed and, turning on her heel, left the room.

Marian looked questioningly at Sadie. "Does she really resent her children?"

"Resent them?" Sadie smiled. "She *loves* them. If they asked, she'd move in with any one of them in a minute."

"But the way she went on and on."

"Only a habit. In fact she forgot one of her favorites today. About they should live to lose all their teeth but one, and in that one tooth they should have a terrible toothache. It's like a regular routine. But when her children come to visit, Bessie is the happiest person in the world. Of course, as soon as they leave she starts talking about them again."

"I don't understand."

"Listen, darling," Sadie said patiently, "you can make a federal case out of it, or you can live with it. I lived with my son Stuart and his wife for three years after my Reuben died, he should find eternal peace. And what happened? My daughter-in-law and I drove each other crazy. I'm a neat person. I wouldn't exactly call her a slob, but the best housekeeper in the world she isn't. By me you don't wash a floor with a mop. After all, if God didn't want us to scrub floors, why would He make scrub brushes? So what was the answer? To fight like cats and dogs forever, or to move out and let her live the way she likes, and me to be myself also? So I moved up here to Mount Eden, and believe me, my daughter-in-law and I have been the best of friends ever since. And since she and my Stuart moved to Coral Gables, we've been even closer.

"Meanwhile, I'm happy here. After all, a person like me, seventy-two or seventy-five years old, she doesn't have to do her own cooking anymore, or cleaning, or shopping. And if she wants to spend the whole day on her knitting, who is there to say no?"

At the word "knitting," Marian realized that from the moment she had met Sadie she had not spent one second talking about the business that had brought her to Mount Eden. "Mrs. Shapiro," she said, "we want to produce your knitting book. All of us at Harbor Press are convinced of your skill. But that's only the beginning." She gazed at Sadie's recumbent figure and felt a sudden weariness. The myriad details of preparing a complicated book for publication, the months of work, and the dozens of meetings she would have to live through with Sadie Shapiro towered before her.

"Listen, you know who you're talking to?" Sadie was saying. "Maybe the best knitter in America, that's all."

"I'm sure," said Marian.

"A Sadie-come-lately I'm not. It's maybe fifty years I've been knitting. I started when I was carrying Stuart. I wanted to make him something—booties, maybe a little sweater—and with my Reuben working nights, what else was there to do without a TV or even a radio? I started out buying every pattern I could find—there wasn't a lot—but I made them all. Hats, gloves, sweaters. I made matching coats for the baby, Reuben, and myself in a powder blue wool. I remember the color of it to this day. I made tea cozies, afghans, lap robes. I'm telling you, I became some crazy knitter. Pretty soon I began to make up my own patterns. Carriage covers, fancy tablecloths, slipcovers. More hats, gloves. sweaters—new ones, my own designs. I made neckties for Reuben, and knitted shirts. Knitting was my magnificent obsession—if you remember that picture, which I'm sure you don't because you're only a young girl."

"Mrs. Shapiro—"

"Listen, if I had been smart enough to open a knitting store, I would be a rich woman today."

"—we have a lot to discuss."

"The money I spent on wool alone, your best friends, Marian, should have such money."

"*Please, Mrs. Shapiro,*" said Marian more loudly than she had intended. A look of surprise crossed Sadie's face, but she stopped speaking. "I'm sorry," Marian continued, "but you must let me go on for a few minutes without interrupting."

Sadie sighed heavily. "From this minute I'm as quiet as a carp."

"Fine," said Marian. Speaking at twice her normal rate, she explained the serpentine series of steps involved in creating the book and bringing it to market. Through it all Sadie lay quietly on the bed, eyes bright, lips grimly sealed. "We had in mind an advance payment of seven hundred and fifty dollars. Two hundred and fifty dollars on signing the contract, the balance upon delivery of an acceptable manuscript. Is that satisfactory?"

Sadie said nothing.

"Mrs. Shapiro? Sadie?"

"Now I can talk?" Sadie asked, an angelic look on her face.

"Yes," Marian said, her voice under control.

"Seven hundred fifty dollars?" Sadie said. She sat up and swung her legs off the bed. "Believe me, Marian, forty-four cents would be enough. Nothing even!" She pointed a manicured index finger and wagged her gray head. "You know what I say to money? I say phooey to money!" Sadie got to her feet. "Why did I send you my patterns?" she began rhetorically as she paced the room. "Why did I collect knitting ideas ever since I was a young girl? It's a long, long story."

And it was.

SADIE walked to the desk of the Mount Eden Senior Citizens Hotel. "Bertha!" she called out three times. The telephone operator's smiling visage peeked out from behind the switchboard. "Did you get the mail?" Sadie shouted. "Letters?" She mimed opening an envelope.

"Oh, yah," said Bertha, brightening, "you got a big one this morning." She handed a bulky envelope across the counter.

Sadie looked at the return address. "Hey! It's from Harbor Press." She opened the envelope and withdrew a five-page document bound in blue paper.

"It's my contract! Oh, boy! I got to show this to Sam Beck." Whirling with delight, Sadie trotted into the dining room.

At his usual table near the garden windows, Sam Beck sat sipping coffee and smoking a cigar. Seated with him were Bessie Frankel, Sadie's roommate, and Abe Farkas, Beck's friend.

"Here it is," Sadie announced, drawing up a chair. "My contract. From Harbor Press." She waved the document in the air.

"Calm down before you drop it in my coffee," Beck said. He took the contract from Sadie and, putting his glasses on the end of his nose, began to read. "How do you like that?" he grinned at Sadie. "It's a real contract." Sam lifted his coffee cup in a toast. "Congratulations, my author. This is wonderful."

"I know," said Sadie. "I'm so excited I'm jumping up and down."

"Lots of luck," Abe Farkas said.

"Mazel tov," said Bessie from behind a spoonful of farina.

"Who's got a pen?" Sadie asked. "I want to sign this right away and send it back before they change their minds."

"Not so fast, Sadie," Abe Farkas said, wagging his head. "Forty-seven years in dry goods, I learned one thing. Contracts can be tricky. Don't sign anything without reading it."

"He's right," Sam said. "I'd have a lawyer look it over before I signed it." His eyebrows furrowed with concentration as he drew on his cigar. "Wait a minute. We've got a lawyer right on the premises. Rosenbloom. The little guy, sits over in the far corner of the dining room. He walks with a cane and he's on a salt-free diet. I was talking to him the other day, while we were handicapping the horses. If I remember right, he said he used to be on Wall Street. He's your man, Sadie." Beck put the contract in the inside pocket of his blazer. "Leave it to me."

But two sticky weeks later, the matter of Sadie's contract was still unresolved. Rosenbloom proved to be Harold R. Rosenbloom, former head of the contract department of Weymouth and Lazard, a giant industrial holding company. There were "one or two minor points" that might be negotiated, he had told Sam Beck after reading the contract.

Thus it was that Marian found herself once more on the way to Mount Eden, a journey she had promised herself she would never make again. The parties involved were waiting for her in the library, and Sadie made the introductions.

"I'm very happy to meet you," said Harold Rosenbloom with a courtly half bow. The diminutive lawyer was wearing a conservative charcoal gray three-button suit with a vest. "I'm sorry if we've inconvenienced you by making you take another trip out here. Our points of disagreement are small, as you know."

"That's all right," said Marian, calling upon reserves of patience she did not know she possessed.

"In two minutes we'll be finished and then we'll all have some iced tea," said Sadie brightly.

"Let us hope so," Rosenbloom said with a small smile. He took up the blue-bound contract and began to read it aloud.

I can't believe he's going to read the whole thing, thought Marian. She looked at Rosenbloom, whose pince-nez perched upon his bony nose. The man was so thin and frail that she could almost see his bones. He continued through the contract for the next thirty minutes, and Marian found herself spellbound. His grasp of the alien field of publishing was amazing. As he explained each item to Sadie in clear terms, Marian learned things about the Harbor Press contract she had not known were there. It was a brilliant performance.

At last Rosenbloom finished, apologizing to Marian for taking so much time. "I'm far from an expert on book contracts," he said, "although twenty years ago when Mr. Weymouth wrote his memoirs, I did make a study of the field. There is one last item that still concerns me. I'm thinking of commercial rights."

"Please tell me what's a commercial right?" Sadie asked.

"Manufactured items inspired by a book," said Rosenbloom.

"They could be anything," Marian said. "Mickey Mouse T-shirts, for example. Or in your case, Sadie Shapiro T-shirts."

"My face on a T-shirt." Sadie grinned. "Who would buy such a thing?"

"Me," said Sam Beck. "I would be the first customer for a Sadie Shapiro T-shirt."

"I think publishers should publish books, period," said Rosenbloom, ignoring him. "They have no right to exploit ideas or characters. Sadie's face and personality belong only to herself. If you have no objections, Mrs. Wall, I'd like to insert a clause saying: 'All rights not herein granted to the publisher are reserved for the author.' Is that agreeable?"

"I'll have to check with Mr. Hawthorne," Marian said. "Is there a telephone I could use?"

"This way," said Sam, showing Marian to the door. "Right down the hall." As she left, he turned to Rosenbloom. "You're doing a terrific job, Harold. You must have been a helluva lawyer."

"In my time," Rosenbloom said, a strange half smile on his face.

"I'm really having great fun this afternoon. My first legal work in eight years. Thanks for asking me, Sam."

"I'll bet you really enjoyed your work," Sadie said.

"It was my life, Sadie. The practice of law, the give-and-take, the hidden traps and sudden maneuvers. How I miss it!"

"How come, if you liked it so much, you decided to retire?"

Rosenbloom's laugh was humorless. "The tick of a clock did me in, Sadie. One day I was the head of a contract department of ten men and the next day I was sixty-five years old. Which meant I was out. We had a mandatory retirement policy. It's funny. I helped draft that policy when I first went to work for Weymouth and Lazard, forty years before. Who knew that I was hoisting myself with my own petard?"

Sadie shook her head in sympathy. "What's sixty-five? Sixty-five is a kid."

For Marian, it was proving to be a long summer. The ten-year-old air-conditioning unit in her office window broke down. Sweaty and harassed, she worked on through July and August, her red pencil crawling across endless pages of typescript that described bleak moors and country houses. On top of this there was the problem of Laura. Summer in New York was no festival for an eleven-year-old whose mother worked forty hard hours a week and brought manuscripts home on the weekend as well.

And Sadie Shapiro. Oh, God, Sadie Shapiro! Now that the contract was signed and Sadie was knitting sample garments to be photographed, the pride of Mount Eden would debate colors and wools with Marian over the phone every day, each conversation beginning with, "So how is it going?"

The plain truth was it was going much too slowly. Sadie had managed to knit only ten samples, which, with the original three, meant that there were still thirty-seven items her flying fingers must complete before all the photographs could be taken and the knitting book put to bed. The slow pace was having its effect upon Arnold Hawthorne. More and more frequently Jack Gatewood would visit Marian's office, asking her to put pressure on the

old girl. So we don't get left at the starting gate, Jack would say.

Poor Jack, Marian thought, he was much too nice to be an editor-in-chief. Whenever he was called upon to apply pressure, his manner would grow ever more bluff and the sports clichés would leap from his lips. His swift rise in the business had begun with *Dribble to Glory*, the biography of a basketball star who had been Jack's roommate at Ohio State. Once launched into the sports area, Jack had become an editing-writing factory. Scores of athletes began to keep diaries, and he turned their almost illiterate products into fast-selling, highly promotable books.

But what about the real Jack Gatewood? After nine years of working side by side with Marian, he remained a mystery to her. Their relationship, so perfect in the office, ended with the close of the working day. And yet under his blazing virility and his actor's face, Marian felt certain, there was a part of himself Jack kept carefully hidden. More than once, before going to sleep, Marian found herself thinking about Jack Gatewood.

It was on a Friday in late September that Sadie's slow progress brought on the crisis. Jack came into Marian's office, his face set, and sat down in the chair opposite her desk. "Prepare yourself for a shock," he began. "Arnold wants to back out of doing the knitting book. There are eight major publishers bringing out knitting books next fall. Arnold says if we don't publish the knitting book in the spring, forget it. If you get hold of all the samples in two weeks, we can just make it."

"Two weeks is impossible and Arnold knows it," Marian groaned. "It will break Sadie's heart."

"We'll honor the contract, of course. She'll receive the rest of the advance we promised."

"That's not the point," said Marian with some heat. "She's an old woman. This book has become her whole life."

"I wish I could help," said Jack, avoiding Marian's eyes. "Unless the samples are in the house and ready for photography in two weeks, the book will be killed."

"The book is dead already, Jack. Thirty-seven samples in two weeks—it can't be done."

"I'm sorry," Jack said, getting up from his chair. He stood for a moment, his pale eyes fixed on Marian. "I never get the chance to bring you any good news, do I?" he said with a sad smile. "I guess you'll have to break the news to her." His face once more a mask, Jack Gatewood retreated quickly, leaving a fuming Marian behind him.

"Damn!" she exploded, banging one knee against her desk and tearing a hole in her dollar seventy-nine panty hose. How was she going to tell Sadie?

She was still thinking about it when the phone rang. "We are approaching Venice by moonlight," Heathcliff began. "Behind us, the gondolier is—"

"Not now!" said Marian. "I don't have time."

"But I have plans about Venice," said Heathcliff.

"I'm hanging up," said Marian, hanging up. She held a trembling hand on the receiver for a moment and then dialed Mount Eden. I'll just jump right in and tell her. And then she'll start crying and I'll start crying and . . .

It took eight rings before Bertha Maloney answered, and a long five minutes before Sadie got to the phone. "Sit down, Sadie," Marian said after exchanging greetings. "I have some very bad news about the book."

"You lost the samples," Sadie said, "or you didn't get the latest batch I sent—five pieces—the dirndl, the paisley shawl, one wide-pleated skirt, plus the two A-line shifts?"

"Sadie," Marian interrupted, "it's not the samples. It's the whole book. Arnold Hawthorne says if you don't have all the samples finished in two weeks, there isn't going to be a book."

There was a long and chilling silence in which Marian's heart sank slowly into her sling-strap sandals. "Sadie? Are you there? Speak to me, Sadie!"

"Boy, oh boy, that's some little joke you just made there."

"Sadie, it's no joke. Lots of other publishers are bringing out similar books. We have to publish in the spring or not at all. I'm sorry to break it to you this way, but—Sadie? Hello?"

"I'm here, don't worry. Tell your Mr. Hawthorne if I wasn't a

lady I'd say something that would make even me ashamed. Two weeks he gives me, to finish thirty-two samples."

"I know it's impossible—" Marian began.

"Who said impossible? Did I say impossible? Believe me, from this mouth you didn't hear that word."

"But Sadie, it can't be done and I don't want you killing yourself trying to do it. Please, Sadie, it's only a book."

"Excuse me, Marian, but with me it's already a lot more than a book. It's my whole life. If God could make the whole world in only one week and still get a day off besides, then maybe I can do the job also."

"But Sadie—"

"Never mind 'but Sadie.' Boy, if you were on that ship with Columbus, we wouldn't be standing here in America today."

"You can't do it, Sadie."

"I *can* do it, Marian. A Shapiro never quits. Two weeks, the man says, and two weeks it'll have to be. If I have to work night and day. In fact, if you don't mind my saying, I shouldn't be standing here talking when every minute counts. So you'll excuse me, please."

"Wait!" Marian cried. "Sadie?" But there was no reply. All she heard before the connection was broken was Sadie saying, "Fingers, get ready to do your stuff."

"OH MY!" exclaimed Marian as she stepped into the taxi. "It's you again."

"You called the radio cab service, no?" said Juan Otero as he turned around to look at his passenger. "*Caramba!* It is the lady who goes to see the crazy old woman." He surveyed Marian for a moment. "We going to Hollis Avenue again?" he asked.

"For the last time, I think," said Marian. She could not remember a worse two weeks. At home she snapped at Laura and in the office things were more frantic than ever.

She'd called Sadie every day, but the old woman had not deigned to come to the telephone. "Sadie says to tell you," the old switchboard operator wheezed, "that a certain person is too busy to speak to another person when she is knitting her fingers to the bone, especially if that other person works for a slave driver like Arnold Hawthorne, who shall be nameless."

Poor Sadie, Marian thought as the taxi crawled along the expressway. She opened her handbag and looked at the check. The book was now officially dead and all that remained was to get Sadie to take the money.

Eventually Juan pulled the taxi to a halt at Mount Eden's driveway. "Next time you call cab service, ask for Juan," he said as Marian stepped from the cab.

"I'll do that," she said, and closed the door.

Unlike the way it was on her previous visits, there was no small crowd of Mount Edenites sitting under the porte cochere. Where is everybody? Marian wondered as she made her way through the empty lobby to the reception desk.

Bertha Maloney's aged gray head peeped out from behind the switchboard. "Aha, the editor lady, tool of the sweatshop bosses." Marian looked into a pair of unquestionably hostile eyes. "For a handmaiden of the capitalist exploiters, I shouldn't do favors. But if you want Sadie, she's upstairs. Sixth floor, solarium."

"Well, thank you very much," Marian said icily. Turning on her heel, she strode briskly to the elevator.

"I heard everything, you shouldn't be upset," the old operator confided in a shaky whisper.

"What's got into that woman?" Marian asked.

The old man smiled grimly. "Commonist," he hissed. He put a spastic hand on the controls and the car began to rise. In a few moments it jerked to a sudden stop. "You want Shapiro. Down the hall to your left."

Marian walked slowly down the corridor and approached a door marked SOLARIUM. As she came closer she heard a strange clicking sound from within. Marian opened the door and stopped short. The total population of the Mount Eden Senior Citizens

Hotel was gathered before her. Seventy or eighty men and women sat in deck chairs, bridge chairs, and wheelchairs arranged in a rough circle. And every single one was knitting!

In the center of the circle, on her feet and talking a blue streak while knitting furiously, was Sadie Shapiro. "Terrific, Mendelson," Sadie was saying, "you go like that for three more rows. Easy, Smolowitz, you're going to bend the needle. Courage, Meyer, you're looking good. Abe, wait for me, I'll show you how to do the next line."

I don't believe it, thought Marian.

Turning to inspect the corps of knitters behind her, Sadie caught sight of her editor. "Marian!" she shrieked. "Not yet! The two weeks isn't up until tonight! Mr. Hawthorne, he should get a carbuncle on his big toe, said two weeks. A bargain is a bargain. By tonight you'll have it."

"I'll have what?"

"Everything!" Sadie said. There was a look of pride in her bright blue eyes. "Thirty-two samples, cookie, knitted and fitted and finished complete. In all the colors we agreed." A triumphant smile lit Sadie's face as Marian stared. "Funny how sometimes you don't know about people. There I was, knitting my fingers off, knowing that no person in this world could possibly meet that deadline. And it turns out all I had to do was ask for help.

"I told Sam Beck and Bessie Frankel the spot I was in. Sam blabbed it around the dining room, and we were off to the races. The bridge group, the canasta people, and the mah-jongg circle came in. So all of a sudden I had ten, maybe twenty, experienced knitters and about sixty others just dying to help out. And then we got organized.

"Each good knitter took ahold of about ten of the others and showed them how to hold the needles, what to do, and like that. We laid out the patterns and instructions and divided up the work. The more experienced took the specialty items. The beginners we gave the easy things, the straight going.

"Sam took charge of the assembly line—he's a terrific organizer. And meanwhile, Bessie got after the knitting store on Jamaica

Avenue—a customer like me they don't get every day—and they started sending over the needles and the wool and the whatnot, and before you could say Jack-be-nimble, we were halfway finished. Believe me, Marian, it's been a wild and woolly two weeks around here."

Marian leaned over and kissed Sadie gently on the cheek. "Sadie, I do believe Harbor Press is going to be publishing a knitting book next spring."

Sadie nodded, her small face serious. "We got a big problem, though. You know up front in a book, where the writer says 'to my dear wife' or 'to my children'?"

"It's called the dedication page."

"Right. Well, on that page, Marian, I made a few promises. Do you think we can fit in about eighty names?"

Before Marian could answer, Max Adolphus waddled into the crowded room, his round face flushed with anger. "What is the meaning of this?" the manager demanded of Sadie.

"A few friends get together and knit a little bit," Sadie said blandly. "That's all."

"Come off it, Shapiro," the manager said. "This thing is organized, I can smell it. And if it's organized, it's unauthorized." Turning away, he quickly scanned the crowd. "I see some people here who should be down in therapy."

"But isn't this therapy, of a sort?" Marian said.

"Who are you?" Adolphus asked belligerently.

"We're publishing Mrs. Shapiro's knitting book," said Marian.

"A knitting book," Adolphus said slowly. "I see. That's also unauthorized. Conducting a business enterprise on the premises without permission is strictly against the rules. You know that, Shapiro. I'm putting you officially on notice. One more infraction and you are out of here. O-u-t, out."

"I'm sorry, Sadie," Marian said as she watched the manager depart. "I guess I talked out of turn."

"Forget it, cookie," Sadie said, squeezing Marian's arm. "He had to find out anyway. And from that Omar the Tentmaker I'm not afraid."

34

"But Sadie, suppose he does force you out of here? What would you do? Where would you go?"

"Don't worry"—Sadie shrugged—"a Shapiro will always get by."

By now Marian knew that the woman who called herself Sadie Shapiro and dwelt in Mount Eden's somewhat tarnished splendor was something more than your average little old lady in tennis shoes. There was an elemental quality about Sadie, a life-force that made things happen.

The knitting book shaped up quickly in the next few months, and production flowed without a hitch. The only hang-up was over the title.

Arnold Hawthorne's wife had come up with "Knits—Neat and New!" Marian argued against this and Jack Gatewood agreed. Jack's contribution was "The NEW Knitting Book." This presupposed, of course, that there was somewhere an old knitting book under the Harbor Press aegis.

Sadie, of course, knew all along what the title of her knitting book would be. As she told Marian over the telephone when the search had reached crisis proportions, "Darling, stop fooling around with crazy titles for my book. The name of the book is going to be 'Sadie Shapiro's Knitting Book' by Sadie Shapiro. Not because I got a swell head, but because my name happens to be Sadie Shapiro and this is a knitting book written by me, so it's only logical, right? And besides, there probably hasn't been another woman named Sadie Shapiro who ever wrote a knitting book, so no one would ever confuse it."

A few moments later Marian was trying it out on Jack Gatewood. "It just won't do," he said, swiveling in his big black leather chair. "It . . . ahh . . . mmm."

Sensing doubt, Marian plunged ahead. "Try it, Jack. Go ahead, repeat it to yourself a few times."

" 'Sadie Shapiro's Knitting Book,' " Jack said. "Ridiculous." And yet, even as he dismissed it, a smile played at the corners of his lips. " 'Sadie Shapiro's Knitting Book,' " he said very slowly.

"You see?"

A grin crossed Gatewood's actor's face. "It does have a ring to it. 'Sadie Shapiro's Knitting Book.'" Jack laughed. "I'll be damned," he said, "now you've got me liking it." He stood up and smiled. "Come," he said, "we're off to see the wizard."

"'Sadie Shapiro's Knitting Book,'" Jack said, pacing before Arnold Hawthorne's desk.

"Insanity," Hawthorne said. "You've both been drinking."

"'Sadie Shapiro's Knitting Book,'" Marian said happily. "Try it, you'll like it."

"'Sadie Shapiro's Knitting Book,'" the publisher said. "'Sadie Shapiro's Knitting Book,'" he said again, more slowly. "Incomprehensible. And yet . . . 'Sadie Shapiro's Knitting Book.'"

"He's hooked," Marian said.

A dazed smile crossed the heavyset publisher's face. "'Sadie Shapiro's Knitting Book'!"

"You see?" Jack said. "That's what happened to me. It's very hard to hate a title like that."

"Done, and done," said Arnold Hawthorne, shaking hands with himself. "And whose brainstorm is it?" he asked Marian.

"Who else?" she said, raising her shoulders in a shrug that was unaccustomed, and yet oddly familiar.

THE day Sadie Shapiro's book was officially published dawned bright and clear. The sun lifted over Jamaica Bay and rose in the polluted gray sky to warm the city. For the people at Harbor Press, and for Sadie Shapiro, it was Publication Day, always a time of joy and hope, and simple but dignified ceremony. But Pub Day means more than that, for it is also the day on which the book in question is officially offered for sale in the nation's bookshops. No matter that half the bookshops have not received the work, and the other half have chosen to display it in some dark corner behind a post.

So as Marian Wall sat in her cramped office awaiting Sadie's arrival for a good-luck lunch with her and Jack Gatewood, she pushed aside the gray nubbins of failure already associated with the book. Four book clubs had rejected it. It had been overlooked

by the trade journal, *Publisher's Weekly*. But it was Pub Day, and failure had no place at the table.

At the appointed hour Sadie arrived, her face aglow with excitement. She was wearing a shiny black satin dress with a corsage of gardenias pinned at the shoulder, a gift from Sam Beck, who had seen her safely into a taxi. Sadie looked absolutely lovely, at least to Marian, and the two women exchanged warm hugs. Then Marian led Sadie on a short tour of Harbor Press, ending in the office of the publisher. "This is our editor-in-chief, Mr. Gatewood," said Marian.

"Call me Jack," said Jack, extending his hand.

Sadie stopped and stared, putting a bony hand to her chest. "A Greek god," she said, "a Hollywood actor. I can't believe that he can also be an editor-in-chief." The color rose in Jack's cheeks. Sadie nudged Marian. "So handsome," she stage-whispered. "Why didn't you tell me?"

At this awkward moment Arnold Hawthorne, stepping carefully over the bare spot in his carpet, came forward and shook Sadie's hand. "I've looked forward to this moment for many months," he said, beaming.

"So you're the famous Arnold Hawthorne," Sadie said, leaning backward as if to get a better view. "You look a little bit like my Reuben, may God let him rest, except, of course, my Reuben wasn't as bald as you are, Mr. Hawthorne, and he was maybe a good twenty pounds lighter." Hawthorne grinned weakly, the color in his face rising to match Jack Gatewood's.

"Cake and bread," Sadie said, nodding sagely. "Deadly enemies." She poked a gentle index finger at Hawthorne's beltline and then brought it up to shake at him. "I'll bet you're a naughty boy at the dinner table, right?"

"Speaking of food," Jack said weakly, "how about lunch?"

After a twenty-minute cab ride crosstown, they were greeted at the restaurant by Pietro, the elegant maître d'. "Good afternoon, Mr. Gatewood. I have a table for three overlooking the garden." With a sweeping half bow, he led the trio to their table, which sparkled with glassware and snow-white napery.

"Now then," said Jack when they were seated, "what shall we have to drink? Sadie?"

"Water will be fine. I'm not a drinking person."

"Come now, it's Publication Day. I think a small celebration would be in order."

"All right," said Sadie. "What the heck, I could be dead any minute, anyway. But nothing strong, please."

Jack beckoned to the hovering waiter and ordered Marian's usual Scotch, a light aperitif for Sadie, and a Beefeater martini for himself.

When the drinks arrived, Jack raised his glass. "To *Sadie Shapiro's Knitting Book* and the charming lady of the title."

Sadie smiled, waited while the others drank, then ventured a sip of her own libation. She smacked her lips. "Not Manischewitz Concord," she said, "but not too terrible either."

Pietro quietly materialized and handed around the enormous menus. Marian and Jack ordered *moules vinaigrette*.

"What is this?" Sadie pointed to an item on her menu.

"Prosciutto and melon, madame," said Pietro suavely. "Smoked Parma ham, slightly peppered, over slices of ripe Persian melon. Would you care to try it?"

"Of course, but without the ham and pepper, please."

Pietro made the notation on his pad without the slightest hesitation. "And for the main course I would suggest the *vitello tonnato*, milk-fed veal with a light tuna-fish sauce." He kissed his fingertips. "Today, it is for the gods."

"Sold," said Marian.

"Me, too," said Jack.

"Tuna-fish sauce," Sadie said, shivering, "you know what this is to a gallbladder?"

"I sympathize," said Pietro. "I, too, suffer from this complaint since two years now."

"You eat something a little fatty or a little cole slaw, you might as well make out your will?"

"Ah, yes, you know it well. Just yesterday, I ate only a mouthful of *bœf à la mode*. Half the night I could not sleep."

"A young man like you," clucked Sadie. "You took your Gelusil?"

"It did not help. Nothing helped."

"I usually try to sleep sitting up. You ever try that? Take two pillows and lay back kind of sitting up?"

"Interesting," said Pietro. "It sounds like it may be a good idea."

"Couldn't hurt. So I don't have to tell you what to bring me," said Sadie with a smile.

"Leave it to me," said Pietro. "I will bring you what I set aside for my own luncheon." He turned and glided away.

"I don't believe it," said Jack. He stared at the retreating Pietro. "Five years I've been eating here and the most he's ever said to me is, 'Nice weather we're having.'"

"Listen," said Sadie, "you just have to know how to talk to people."

"How dare you burst into my laboratory this way!" Philip Sidney, third earl of Worcestershire, demanded. He stood before Marian, barring further entry into the dimly lit chamber, his rounded lips set in a hard line that displayed his strong jaw to full advantage. "Get out, you little fool, before you see too much."

"Wa-wa?" said Marian Wall as the ringing telephone cut short her dream. She fielded the receiver on the third ring.

"We are standing atop the Eiffel Tower, my darling," Heathcliff began. "It is dawn, and the City of Light is at our feet."

"What time is it?"

"Ten after seven."

"Yipes! I've overslept! Thanks for waking me. Talk to you later." Marian hung up and shuffled off to the shower.

Some moments later she was greeted by a flurry of pistol shots and clanging gongs as she joined Laura in the kitchen. "Turn the radio down," Marian said. "I can't stand that awful rock before coffee."

"Shhh, Ma!" Laura shushed. "That's superduper hit one."

Marian opened the cabinet and took down the six bottles of vitamins and minerals that supplemented her unbalanced diet. She quickly gobbled a vitamin C pill, two E's, a multivitamin

with iron, another with niacin, several wheat-germ-oil capsules, and a Unicap for good measure. Pouring a glass of orange juice, she stood for a moment, her back against the refrigerator, and surveyed her daughter. Laura came within twenty pounds of being beautiful, Marian thought, and a diet was definitely in order. The girl's eyes were almond-shaped and huge, and the rest of her features were fine. But all of this was hidden by her weight. There was something sick about the way Laura attacked food. "What are you doing?" Marian asked the child, busy at the table.

"Flying an airplane," Laura said, sighing a little and fluttering her eyes at the ceiling.

"Laura!" Marian said in a cautionary tone.

"I've got a butter knife in one hand and a doughnut in the other. What the hell do you think I'm doing? I'm buttering a doughnut."

"See here, young lady," Marian countered, "don't speak to me that way."

"I'm sorry," Laura said, "it must be the way I've been brought up." She took a snapping bite of the doughnut and exchanged a high-velocity glare with her mother. Marian turned away and covered her emotion by searching for instant coffee in the cabinet.

Does every mother have a communications problem with her daughter, she wondered, or am I the only one? Trying to keep her voice under control, she said, "Why do we have trouble talking?"

"I don't know," Laura said. Her finger was making small designs on the dusty table. "Maybe I need a father."

"You had one," Marian said. "It didn't work out."

"Maybe *you* need something, then."

Right in the heart, thought Marian. "Maybe," she said, shrugging. "If you find out what it is, let me know."

Laura downed the rest of her milk in one swift swallow and went off to collect her school books.

THE monthly sales figures that were waiting on her desk did not improve Marian's mood. The knitting book was not doing well. Just a month after publication, and after the two small ads had

run in support, Harbor Press had shipped less than two thousand copies. For a project as costly as Sadie's, it was just short of disaster. Damn and double damn, thought Marian. With a few lucky breaks Sadie's book might be up at the top.

She hurried off to Arnold Hawthorne's office. "Arnold," she said, seating herself next to his desk, "I demand a promotion!"

A look of pain crossed his face. "Look, Marian," he said quickly, "I know you're expecting a raise, but business is awful."

"Not me," Marian corrected. "Sadie's book. It's had a poor start, but the potential is there *if* we help it happen."

"I saw the figures," said Hawthorne, rolling his eyes. "We've already run two big ads," he added.

"A quarter of a page each."

"Which is what the budget will allow," said Hawthorne. He shook his head. "I won't throw good money after bad, Marian."

"Arnold, don't you see? A little money spent right now is what's needed. Sadie's book is unique. No one's ever seen anything like those little mittens with the animal faces on them. Somewhere there's a feature article for the women's magazines; I can feel it in my bones."

"I agree," said Hawthorne, "but we seem to be overlooked when it comes to publicity. Harbor Press is a small outfit and we just can't afford publicity people."

ACROSS the East River, at that very moment, the problem of promoting Sadie's book was also under consideration. Seated at a sunny table in Mount Eden's back garden, the author listened closely as Sam Beck held forth. "They're not doing enough, Sadie, not by half. Those two ads in the paper were piffle. If you looked fast you were sure to miss them."

"Sam's right," Harold Rosenbloom said. "I think we ought to pool our collective brains and consider the problem. Surely, between us we have some contacts who might prove useful. Think."

"Twenty-five years I belonged to the Knights of Pythias," said Sam. "Maybe I could fix it so Sadie could give a knitting talk at the next wives' night."

"All right," Rosenbloom said, "that's a start." He took a gold pen from his breast pocket and made a note.

"Excuse me," Bessie Frankel said. "My son-in-law Myron, a wart should grow on his earlobe for putting me here, could maybe help."

"What does he do?" Farkas asked.

Bessie hesitated, moving her head from side to side. "I'm trying to think. Myron once said something about being an interviewer. It's a program, late at night on television."

"A television show?" Rosenbloom said slowly.

"Right," she said, nodding to herself. "My Rosalie's Myron, that's what he does. He picks out the people who go on this program. Something on NBC . . . with a Johnny somebody on it."

"Carson?"

"Oh, you know it?" said Bessie. "Right. What Myron does is pick out the people who go on the Johnny Carson show. Do you think it would help if I asked Myron to put Sadie on?"

JOHNNY CARSON's Green Room was actually painted a deep blue and was kept at a cool 72° F. Her hair neatly combed, her face smoothed by layers of deep tan TV makeup, Sadie Shapiro sat quietly in a club chair next to Marian while three young production assistants hovered nearby in a state of constant attention. To Marian's wondering eyes, Sadie was easily the calmest person in the room. In fact she had maintained the same calm through the two pre-show interviews.

"You know what to say?" Marian asked.

Sadie nodded. "Mr. Carson will ask me questions, and I'll answer them. Then he'll ask me to knit, and I'll do a few lines, and then I ask him if he wants to try it, and I pass him the needles, and he'll try it and get all mixed up, and it'll be funny."

"Perfect," said Marian. "Just remember, don't be nervous."

Sadie patted Marian's arm. "What have I got to worry?" she said. "They're going to kill me if I don't make a hit?"

The two women settled back to watch the large color TV set in front of them. "The Tonight Show" had just begun and Ed Mc-Mahon was running through the guest list: playwright Mel Brooks, New York Jets football star Joe Namath, singer Sarah Vaughan. Sadie's name, of course, was last, and the only one not spelled out in white letters on the screen. Then the show's assistant producer came into the Green Room. He squatted down in front of Sadie and Marian. "Mrs. Shapiro," he said, "there's been a change of scheduling. Instead of putting you on last, Johnny wants you first. You can do your bit with him, we'll cut away for a station break, and you can leave."

"Whatever," said Sadie.

The assistant producer conducted Sadie and Marian into the wings. In a few moments he whispered, "Smile," and then, with a cheery wave, Sadie walked toward the curtain as Carson wound up her introduction.

". . . the author of *Sadie Shapiro's Knitting Book*, one of the world's best knitting instructors, won't you greet Sadie Shapiro."

As the applause rose and Sadie emerged from behind the curtain into the lights, Marian found that her fingertips were in her mouth. She looked at the monitor to see what the world was seeing: an elderly gray-haired woman, slim, small, and rather spry, her face set in a wide smile, walking very slowly, and carrying a JAMAICA AVENUE KNITTERY shopping bag. Marian took her fingers from her mouth and crossed them.

Johnny Carson shook Sadie's hand as she seated herself in the guest's chair. "Well now," he said, "I don't think we've ever had a knitting instructor on with us before . . ."

Sadie turned to grin at Bessie Frankel, who was seated in the audience with Sam Beck, then turned back to the host.

". . . but your book is so unusual, we decided to have you on." Carson smiled at Sadie, who smiled right back. But she didn't say anything, and for a moment she was in full close-up, a grin set on her face.

"Scared out of her mind," the assistant producer whispered to Marian. "She'd better not freeze."

Carson picked up a copy of the knitting book as the camera zoomed in close. "*Sadie Shapiro's Knitting Book* is the title and it's published by Harbor Press. Well, now, Mrs. Shapiro, how long has it been since you first began playing with needles?"

Sadie looked at the ceiling, thinking. "I started," she said, "I think when I was carrying Stuart and I wanted to make a pair of booties. So it's like maybe fifty-one, fifty-two years already."

"I see," said Carson. "Stuart, I take it, is your son."

"Correct."

"And you began knitting as a hobby when you were pregnant."

Sadie's mouth dropped open. "Oooh," she said, "like that you talk on television?"

Carson grinned. "You mean 'pregnant'?"

"Ayee, you said it again!" cried Sadie, provoking a gust of laughter. "Listen," she added, "in my day we didn't talk like that. A word like you used we wouldn't even say in the parlor, not to mention on TV."

"*Well,*" said Carson in his Jack Benny voice, "I won't mention it again, Mrs. Shapiro. By the way, may I call you Sadie?"

"Of course. And I'll call you Mr. Carson."

There was a light in Sadie's eyes as she grinned slyly at Johnny. "The old lady's coming on," the assistant producer said to Marian.

"Do you mind, Sadie, if I ask how old you are?"

"Of course I mind," Sadie began, getting a laugh, "but I'll tell you anyway. This year, God willing, I'll be seventy-two—"

There was instant and loud applause with Carson leading it. When it died down, Sadie added, "—or seventy-five years old." She knocked wood on the desk as the audience laughed wildly. Ed McMahon doubled over with laughter.

"You mean," Carson said as the tumult subsided, "you don't really know how old you are?"

Sadie nodded. "Listen, when I was born it was olden days, remember. Not like the kiddies today, ipsy-pipsy in a brand-new hospital—the minute they're born they got already a footprint, a fingerprint, a birth certificate, and a Social Security card. When I was born, they just knew there was another person in the house.

44

My father and my mother weren't exactly thrilled, to tell the truth. And what with getting out of where they were and coming to America, who could remember anything anyway? My mother always said I was born the year they had the measles epidemic, which would make me seventy-two. My father insisted it was the year Uncle Theodore went away to Kiev, which would make me three years older."

"I see," said Carson, "and when is your birthday?"

"April eighth or July thirty-first."

That little snapper resulted in pandemonium. Carson rocked with laughter and rubbed tears from his eyes. It took almost a minute for order to be restored.

"Let's see," said Carson finally, "that makes you an Aries and a Leo."

"What are you talking?" said Sadie. "I'm Jewish!"

The audience went around the bend again. "My God," the assistant producer said to Marian, "the woman's a natural. You sure she isn't a professional actress?"

"I'm really not sure what she is," said Marian, looking at the chaos around her. Platoons of assistants were scurrying hither and yon, relaying instructions. Sarah Vaughan's song was the first casualty, quickly followed by the film clip showing Joe Namath in action. The little lady in the guest chair was quietly bringing down the house, and Carson shrewdly gave her her head. She told tales of her life and hard times, the words rolling off her tongue in a zany reverse English that was warm and endearing. Sadie was golden, Sadie was real, and completely unexpected.

Finally Sadie was offering to make a sweater for Carson, getting him to remove his jacket while she measured him and McMahon wrote down the figures. She showed him various kinds of wool and made him choose a color and style. With all this she never got to show Carson how to knit, which was all she was expected to do in the first place.

"You are a beautiful person," Carson said as he kissed her cheek. "Please come back soon."

"Got to," said Sadie. "I'm making you a sweater." With a cheery

wave, she started off as the applause built, then hustled back to retrieve her shopping bag, grinned sheepishly, and jogged off into the wings. In thirty-two minutes, give or take a handful of commercials, Sadie had knitted a place for herself in the fabric of American folk myths. The little old lady who had walked onstage an unknown, came off a star.

A cluster of excited backstage folk surrounded Sadie and shook her hand. A crusty old stagehand leaned down to peck at her cheek. "I think I love you," he said. Sadie adored it.

"We want her back next week," the assistant producer said to Marian, "and I'd like you to lay off the other shows until Sadie is on again with Johnny."

"What other shows?" asked Marian.

The assistant producer laughed. "The ones who'll be calling you tomorrow morning. Every talk show in America is going to want her, Mrs. Wall, and what's more, you're going to sell a jillion copies of her book."

When they were alone for a moment, Sadie said, "Marian, let's be honest. I was a big hit, wasn't I?"

"Sadie, you were a smash."

"That's what I thought." There was a weak smile on Sadie's face. "So tell me, Marian, why do you look so worried, and why don't I feel too good?"

Marian regarded the old woman for a long moment. "I think you're on the brink of fame and money, Sadie. And I think it may change your life. Perhaps in some ways you won't like."

Sadie nodded. "All right," she sighed, "I'm going to cross the Ruby Kahn. What happens after that only God can say."

Stepping off the elevator in the lobby of the RCA Building, the two women found Sam Beck. Surrounded by a cloud of blue cigar smoke, he stepped forward to greet them. "Well, well, if it isn't the divine Sadie, her hairdo, and her orchestra."

"Hi, Sam." Sadie smiled.

"How do you like that? She talks and everything, just like a regular person. And she still remembers me. I thought, after being buddy-buddy with Johnny Carson, you wouldn't know me."

"Where's Bessie?" Sadie asked.

"Bessie is in the midst of reconciliation number twenty-three with Myron and Rosalie. They were kissing and crying all over each other. She's spending the night at their place."

"Wonderful."

"The best of both worlds," Sam said. "She still has a pair of daughters and sons-in-law to cuss out when she needs to. Now let me kiss you, my TV star." Stepping forward, he engulfed Sadie in his arms and held her for a long moment.

"She was magnificent, Mr. Beck," said Marian. "They want her back next week."

"That's what I was afraid of," said Sam sadly. "Poor old Sam Beck won't stand a chance anymore."

"For Sam Beck there'll always be a chance," said Sadie, smiling. "Not a good chance, but a chance."

Outside, Marian watched as Sam helped Sadie into a cab. He settled back, his long arm making a cradle for Sadie's head to rest on. As the taxi pulled away, he was kissing Sadie's cheek. How heartwarming it looked, and how lonely it made Marian feel. Maybe I'll be lucky, she told herself. Maybe Heathcliff will call tonight and at least I'll have someone to talk to.

On the morning following Sadie's first television appearance the telephones never stopped ringing at Harbor Press. By ten o'clock the first of what would become a bushel of telegrams arrived. By eleven Marian, Jack, and Arnold Hawthorne were working furiously in the publisher's office, trying to keep pace with a veritable flood of orders for Sadie's book. They worked into the night without a break. Two days later Hawthorne declared a moratorium on phone orders so that the staff could process those already in the house, a matter of some twenty thousand copies.

"How are we doing with production?" a shell-shocked-looking Arnold Hawthorne asked.

"We've been guaranteed twenty-five thousand bound copies by the middle of next week," Jack said, "with an additional twenty-five thousand on standby."

"Not enough," said Hawthorne. "Make that fifty thousand and fifty thousand the following week." The publisher leaned back in his chair. "How are the television bookings coming?"

Marian consulted her clipboard. "Next Wednesday she goes back on 'The Tonight Show.' The following morning she's on 'Today.' She's going to knit ties for Frank McGee and Joe Garagiola. The next week she's on with Dick Cavett, and there's a David Frost special. The week after it's Mike Douglas and Merv Griffin."

"Very good. What else?"

"About thirty women's shows want her. Some are produced locally and syndicated nationwide. That means we'll have to send Sadie on the road. We ought to coordinate luncheon-club appearances and bookshop autographing parties. Which means booking hotels, laying on transportation, and getting someone to travel with Sadie for three or four months."

"I guess you know who that's going to be," Hawthorne said. He looked at Marian's sad eyes and smiled. "We're at the beginning of a once-in-a-lifetime publishing dream. We've got to punch all the right buttons. I want you to supervise Sadie personally. Keep her happy. Hold her hand, rub her back."

'She's seventy-two or seventy-five years old, Arnold," said Marian. "I hope she's strong enough to take all this."

"Nonsense! Couldn't you see that light in her eyes on the Carson show? Sadie will thrive on becoming a star."

"He's right, Marian," Jack said. "When she went jogging off into the wings, I thought she could run for miles."

"All right," said Marian, "let's say Sadie has enough energy. What about me? I have a daughter at home. I just can't go charging off into the hinterlands."

"Take Laura along," said Hawthorne. "It will be educational. I promise there'll be no scrimping on the expenses. Eight or nine weeks in New York should handle all the nationwide media. Then you and Sadie go on the road."

"Oh, I almost forgot," said Jack Gatewood. "The Arts and Crafts Book Club wants Sadie's book. They'll pay ten thousand dollars as a guarantee."

48

"Great!" Hawthorne said. "But I think we should resubmit Sadie to the Book-of-the-Month Club and the Literary Guild and let them fight it out."

IF YOU were one of the few people who missed Sadie Shapiro's second appearance on "The Tonight Show," you surely must have heard news of that rare evening by now. Many newspapers carried stories about it the following day. Sadie was the number one topic of discussion around the country. People talked about the fantastic sweater she had knitted for Johnny Carson, complete with the letters NBC and the network's multicolored peacock resplendent on a field of bright puce, and about how Carson had spent the rest of the evening hosting the show in Sadie's sweater.

Later that evening Sadie was booked for five more appearances on "The Tonight Show." By Friday of that week confirmed orders for twenty-five thousand copies of *Sadie Shapiro's Knitting Book* had been received by Harbor Press. At eight dollars and ninety-five cents a copy that meant that Sadie's royalties (less her seven-hundred-and-fifty-dollar advance) came to almost twenty-three thousand dollars.

By now the rest of the media were beginning to have a field day with Sadie. *Sports Illustrated* printed Sadie's design for a knitted Olympic Games patch that could be worked into almost any garment. *McCall's* scheduled an interview with her son, Stuart. *The New York Times* featured one of her favorite recipes on the women's page, and made her the focal point of an article about the aged.

At Mount Eden, mail began to arrive for Sadie from all over the country; at first only a trickle, then mounting to as many as fifty letters a day. Harold Rosenbloom sorted them, using the small neglected library as his office. Requests for autographs were routinely handled, but other letters were more difficult.

"'Dear Mrs. Shapiro,'" Harold read, as Sadie knitted quietly in the armchair near the desk. "'Last year I lost my husband after forty years of marriage. Since he's gone I can't eat or sleep. All I can think of to do is to kill myself. Please tell me what to do.'"

"Write her like this," said Sadie, without missing a stitch. "You should be ashamed of yourself for what you wrote me. I also know the sadness of losing someone near and dear. But life doesn't go away if you just sit and stare at it. Life *is*, whether you like it or not, and you better like it because without it there's nothing. You must be a young woman still. Who knows what's ahead? Get yourself out, see people. Give it a year, two, maybe five. To kill yourself there's always time, but never after that."

"Sadie," Harold said, "I don't think you have to answer every letter. It's beginning to take up a lot of your time."

"In my book, when a person writes to you, you answer back."

"I thought you'd say that, so I have a proposal. Let me handle your mail for you. The routine ones I'll take care of, the crazy ones I'll throw away, and the ones you really ought to see I'll give to you to answer."

"Sold," said Sadie. "Only promise me you won't throw away letters that ask for help, because if I can help a person even a little, I'd like to."

"Agreed," said Rosenbloom, "although sometime soon—"

Before Rosenbloom could go on, Sam Beck thrust his head in the doorway. "Sadie, come quick. There's a whole women's needlepoint club outside and Farkas is holding them in the driveway. Head them off before they get inside and Adolphus spots them." Sadie put down her knitting and jogged off to intercept her fans.

Sam Beck went outside and stood watching as Sadie signed autographs. Sadie had become a star now, and clearly, her life was no longer her own. The trouble was, there was less of her life to be shared with someone named Samuel Joseph Beck.

JUAN OTERO's taxi was waiting as Marian came dashing out of the Grindl Building in mild disarray. "We going to Mount Eden?" Juan asked, and as Marian nodded, "*Bueno,* I have a good shortcut by now."

Once in Queens, Juan cut off the expressway and drove through quiet, tree-lined streets instead. "That is some *pistolera,* that Sadie," he called back to Marian. "When she chases the big McMahon the other night, I thought my Carmelita would fall off the bed. She going to do another TV show soon?"

"A David Frost special later today. Oh, damn!" Marian suddenly cried. "'Wide World of Sports' is taping Sadie jogging this afternoon and I forget to tell her! Hurry, Juan."

Juan's cab rounded the corner of Hollis Avenue and came rolling up to Mount Eden. Parked in the drive was a station wagon marked ABC NEWS, and blocking the drive was a small mob.

Marian pushed through to the lobby entrance only to find her way barred by the ancient elevator operator. "Nobody gets in without they have a pass," he said, arms folded across his chest.

"It's me, Sadie Shapiro's editor."

"Oh, yes," the old man said, his eyes focusing. "You I got orders to let in. Report to the manager's office across the lobby."

Marian found Sam Beck sitting with the manager. "Here's Mrs. Wall, Sadie's editor," Beck said. "Tell her what you told me."

The manager turned his small eyes on Marian. "Mrs. Wall, there are rules here at Mount Eden, and they are meant to be followed. I insist that Mrs. Shapiro end this disturbance at once. I cannot permit Mount Eden to be overrun by this—this—*public relations circus!* Cameras and flashbulbs everywhere you turn. The last days of Pompeii!"

"I'm sorry things have gotten so out of hand, Mr. Adolphus," Marian said lamely. "I'll try to make other arrangements for her next interviews."

"That's not good enough," Adolphus said flatly. "There are to be no further interviews at Mount Eden. Furthermore, I demand that you get rid of that crowd of curiosity seekers. At once."

"You mean those people in the street?" asked Marian. "Surely you must see that we have no control over them."

A smile played over Adolphus's lips as his fat fingers drummed busily on the desk top. "There is a way," he smirked.

"You mean you want Sadie to leave?"

"You said leave, Mrs. Wall, I didn't. And now that you mention it, I think it's a perfectly wonderful idea. Say this afternoon sometime, before six."

"Now I know where Martin Bormann went," Sam Beck observed.

"Now see here, Mr. Adolphus," said Marian, "that's unfair."

"I am perfectly within my rights," the manager purred. "When she came to Mount Eden, Mrs. Shapiro signed a rental agreement which gives me the power to dispossess her at my discretion. And she has violated five or six different rules."

"Where are you, King Kong, now that we need you?" groaned Sam Beck.

"Six o'clock, Mrs. Wall," Adolphus said stiffly. "If she leaves by then, I won't sue her for the madhouse she's turned this place into." With that, the manager waddled swiftly from the room, slamming the door behind him.

For a brief moment Marian and Sam Beck exchanged glances. "What a mess," Marian said.

"I don't know about that," Sam observed, looking at the end of his cigar. "It could be the biggest break I ever had."

"THERE she goes," said Howard Cosell into the microphone as the television crew snapped into action. "That woman you see jogging past our ABC camera . . . that seventy-two- or seventy-five-year-old woman who has captured the heart of the nation . . . Sadie Shapiro . . . inspiration to the world . . . her short, choppy strides a textbook picture of perfect jogging form."

Sadie bounced along toward home. Ahead of her, people lined the curb. Crazy. Coming out to see an old woman in a sweat suit. And the camera crew on top of the station wagon. Sadie darted down the alley into Mount Eden's back garden.

Mrs. Bradie, a resident, called out to no one in particular as Sadie slowed to a walk, "What's the matter, big shot, you're not in the mood for autographs today?"

Sadie kept going, her proud head erect. Bradie had turned sour, like many of the others. Sadie had become much too famous for their liking.

53

From the doorway that led into the back garden, Marian and Sam Beck stood watching Sadie approach. "Look at her, Marian," Sam sighed. "Is my Sadie a fine figure of a woman or not?"

"Your Sadie is a woman without a home at the moment, Sam. Who's going to give her the bad news?"

But before either could speak, Sadie did. "Marian, Sam, I just decided something. I'm leaving Mount Eden. Any place that doesn't want me, I don't want."

"Funny you should mention that," said Sam. He took her arm. "Take a little walk with me in the garden, Sadie. I got something important to say, and I don't think it can wait."

Sadie's eyebrows arched, but she allowed herself to be led away down the garden path. Sam held his cigar at arm's length and contemplated the tip of it. "What you just said, about leaving Mount Eden. That's been on my mind for some time, Sadie. And one thing I got to say—if you go, I go."

"Congratulations. So there'll be two less for dinner."

"Sadie," Sam said, squeezing her arm, "what I mean is this. Until you moved into Mount Eden I thought everything was over with me. Seventy-seven years old, Sadie, and I was going out of my mind waiting for the end.

"But the minute you got on the scene my whole life changed. Peppy, Sadie, I had forgotten about peppy. That's the way I used to be until my wife, let her rest, passed away. You showed me that if you let yourself go you can turn into a vegetable. Compared to you, don't you see, that's what I was. A turnip. Maybe a rutabaga.

"But you were my example and I woke myself up. However much time I got left, let me live it like a person—that's what you showed me, Sadie. And from that minute until now I stayed as close to you as I could. And now you're going to move and that's why I'm talking. Because I can't let you go without I tell you what's laying here inside on my heart. I need you, I want you, I probably even love you, Sadie. So let's move out of here today. We'll go to a hotel. And then we'll find a little apartment, and that'll be it. Sadie Shapiro and Sam Beck, together at last, now and forever."

Sadie turned to face Sam. "You're going to marry me, Beck?"

Beck coughed and a puff of blue smoke flew out of his mouth. "*Who* married? Did I say anything about marrying?"

Sadie shook her head. "A proposition like yours I could hear on the street. I don't need it from an old friend."

"Sadie, please, marriage for people our age is out of the question. Who's going to say anything if we live together? We each have a little money. And with our Social Security we can have a life."

"Hah!" said Sadie. "Always you're after moofki-poofki."

"All right, a little moofki-poofki. It's only natural, I'm not a Stonewall Jackson. But you know about my prostate."

"Hold it! Don't talk dirty."

"Come live with me and be my companion. Sadie, please."

Hands clasped behind her back, Sadie walked a few steps away and then paced back. "Not until the ring is on the finger, Sam Beck," she declared. "I am a woman who never slept in the same bed with a man who wasn't her husband, and I'm certainly not going to start now. So if there's a decent proposal somewhere on your lips, Sam Beck, I'm all ready to hear it."

"I swore on my wife's deathbed I would never marry again. It wouldn't be right. Besides, I'm not a rich man, but a little money I got, and a lot of insurance. I also got two kids and four grand-children. Believe me, they've spent all that money already. I can't marry you, Sadie. Please don't ask that."

"What is this with money? Did I ever mention that word in your presence? I'm talking principle. Sam Beck, you're a fine man, and I probably love you a little. But until I hear from you a few words that begin, 'Will you marry me?' I'm not going to be listening." She stepped forward and kissed him squarely on his lips. "So good-by, Sam Beck," she said, and walked away.

As Juan's cab pulled away from Mount Eden's doorstep, Sadie looked back at the few people who had gathered to say a quiet good-by. Sam Beck was not one of them, and that hurt most of all. "You never know what's around the corner in this life, do you?" Sadie said. "So now it's good-by, Mount Eden—hello, Manhattan, and who can tell what's going to happen tomorrow."

"Something wonderful, no doubt," said Marian, making an effort to be cheerful. She had never seen Sadie so distraught. The sparkle was gone, that inner glow that made Sadie the special person she was. Rather too quickly Marian turned the conversation to the book's latest sales figures. Fifty thousand copies were now in print, and sales were running ten thousand copies a week.

None of this news seemed to cheer Sadie. "At my age, to have trouble with a man," she said, shaking her head. She turned and looked closely at Marian. "Marian, would you sleep with a man who wasn't your husband?"

Marian smiled, thinking of the absence of men in her life. "I'm no expert when it comes to love, Sadie."

Sadie sighed and shifted in her seat. "I'm going to miss him. A man like Sam is no Tom, Dick, or Harry. Still, when you live your whole life according to certain rules, it's very hard to change. What Sam wants I couldn't do in a million years. And especially not tomorrow." Sadie's eyes met Marian's. "Oh, Marian, when I went on that show with Johnny Carson, who knew that people would be running after autographs from me, a woman who never got past the eighth grade! I'm telling you, this is some crazy America we're living in."

"It's winner take all, Sadie."

Brightening, Sadie reached over and clasped Marian's hand. "I'm lucky I've got a good friend like you, Marian. Are you sure you have room to put me up until I find a place to live?"

"I'm positive," Marian said. She squeezed Sadie's hand. "With all the interviews coming up, it'll make sense for us to be together. And I'm sure you'll be comfortable in my study."

"I'm sure, too, Marian. Meanwhile, tell me about your Laura. What's she like?"

Marian chuckled ruefully. "I wish I knew, Sadie. She's eleven and living with me, but I can't say we get along. I think she has just realized that most families come equipped with a father, and she resents not having one quite terribly."

"If a marriage doesn't work out, it's between a man and a woman. It's not for children to say."

"Of course, Sadie. But still . . . there it is. And I think, because of this, Laura wants to punish me. So she purposely does things that will make me angry. She has a weight problem, too, and I suspect it stems from this underlying frustration."

"Trouble with a child is like a stone in your heart. Sad, very sad. And how big are her feet?"

"Her what?"

"Her feet. I thought, on the way to the studio, I would knit her a pair of slippers. Pass me my knitting bag, and then tell me all about that David Frost person I'm going to meet."

Some hours later, Sadie threw the studio audience, and the affable David Frost too, into fits of laughter. Most of his British circumlocutions were lost on Sadie, and he could not easily follow Sadie's words. In the confusion, only one question and answer stood out. It came when Frost, as is his custom, asked Sadie for her definition of love.

"Love," Sadie said, "means never having to say you're sorry, but you say it anyway, because if you love someone you don't want to hurt their feelings so you say it whether you mean it or not, because a human being is a human being, and we each have our own ways, and if you don't have respect for each other, then what do you have?"

"I don't know," said a puzzled Frost. "What does one have?"

"Me, you're asking?" shrugged Sadie. It ended the interview and Frost invited her back for another appearance on his show.

Outside the studio, as Sadie and Marian walked to Juan's cab, Sam Beck stepped in front of them. "Well, well, if it isn't the star herself and her friend, Clare Boothe Luce."

Sadie's heart leaped, but she held herself in check. "Sam, what are you doing here?"

"Just passing by," he said coolly. "By the way, starting tomorrow I'll be looking for an apartment. I wondered if there was any neighborhood you preferred."

"Yes," said Sadie, adopting Beck's cool tone. "Near City Hall, where the marriage licenses are."

He looked despairingly at Marian. "Would you believe a woman

seventy-two or seventy-five years old is worrying about her virtue?"

"Don't talk to Marian," Sadie cut in. "This is between you and me, Beck. Now I've got to run. I don't like to stand on street corners talking to strange old men."

Beck handed the women into the taxi. Closing the door, he bent down to look in the open window. "Take care of yourself, Sadie, and remember—Sam Beck has just begun to fight."

It was after nine o'clock of a long and trying day before Sadie settled herself at the dinette table in Marian's apartment. Her fingers, as always, operated in top gear as she reached down to free a loop of green wool from the basket at her feet. In another few hours, Virginia Graham would have a pantsuit à la Shapiro. Across the table Marian sat reading a manuscript. From time to time a pair of tortoiseshell "work" eyeglasses, perched on her nose, would slide down and her hand would flash up to hold them in a graceful, unconscious gesture.

Laura, not yet in bed, was playing records at peak volume. Marian winced as a new number was introduced by shrill guitars. "Is that too loud, Sadie?" she asked.

"What?" asked Sadie. "I couldn't hear you, the music's so loud."

Sighing, Marian walked into Laura's room and closed the door behind her. Sadie heard a few shouted words between mother and daughter, and then Marian returned. The stereo was silent.

Obviously upset, Marian went back to her reading. Laura was apparently everything that Marian had said, and perhaps a little more. Eleven years old, Sadie thought, was a difficult age.

Marian put down her pencil, took off her glasses, and closed the top manuscript on the pile. She ran a hand across her eyes. "Would you like a cup of tea, Sadie?"

"No, thanks. I was only staying up to keep you company."

"Don't wait for me. I'm going to be at this for hours."

"Must be important," said Sadie.

Marian shrugged. "It's editing. Two more gothics."

"Aha! Editing. At last I'll find out what that is."

Marian laughed. "It's not that easy to explain, Sadie. Sometimes

I do little more than read a manuscript and say, 'Very good.' That's rare, though. Mostly it involves cutting a story down to size."

Sadie nodded. "Sounds like a terrifically hard job."

"Sometimes. But it's often very exciting. Take our biggest gothic, *Hardcastle Castle*. When I got that manuscript it was actually a contemporary romance set in Yugoslavia, about a woodcutter and a young girl. The last four hundred pages, as I recall, were a strong plea for Serbo-Croatian unity."

"But who would read that?"

"Exactly. So I suggested the locale be changed to nineteenth-century England, that the hero be a local baron who owned a useless coal mine, and the love interest become a young governess whose father had just patented a new sort of miner's lamp. It worked like a charm."

"They must pay you a lot of money for what you do."

"Arnold Hawthorne isn't widely known as a big spender," Marian said. "Maybe some of it is my fault. Harbor Press is the only place I've ever worked in publishing. I suppose Arnold looks on me as a switchboard operator who made good."

"I knew I didn't like that Arnold Hawthorne the minute I saw him. If you don't get respect at Harbor Press, why don't you go work somewhere else? A girl with your brains, your looks. I'm going to call Arnold Hawthorne and tell him a thing or two."

"Sadie, don't," Marian said sharply. "Hawthorne is my problem. And so is Laura."

"Laura's problem is fifteen pounds. She'd be a different child if she lost some weight."

"Maybe. And maybe it's me."

Sadie looked closely at Marian. "If you don't like what you are, then change it. You should get a raise and a promotion, and men should come flocking to your door."

"The only man in my life is a voice on the telephone," said Marian. "And the only reason I talk to him is because I'm so lonely."

Sadie reached over and held a warm hand on her shoulder.

After she'd had a good cry, Marian said, "Oh, Sadie, I feel better than I have in a long, long time."

"How MUCH longer is she going to be around?" Laura asked between bites. With a heavy hand, she spooned a mound of marmalade onto a scrap of toast and crammed it into her mouth.

Marian took a sip of her bitter morning coffee. "Mrs. Shapiro is our guest," she said, "and she's only been here a few days."

Laura mumbled something between bites. Marian decided to let it pass. "In just a few weeks, you and Sadie and I will be starting our cross-country trip—and we'll have lots of fun, Laura, I promise." A smug smile turned the corners of Laura's mouth skyward.

Marian's throat tightened. Whenever she held out her hand in friendship to Laura, it got bitten. Starting very soon, she told herself, I become strict.

"Good morning, everyone," came a cheery voice. If Sadie had heard Laura's question, her face did not show it. Looking fresh in her bright floral housecoat, she was the essence of cheerfulness.

"Can I make you some breakfast, Sadie?" Marian asked.

"No, thanks. I already know where the saltines are, and my cottage cheese I picked up the other day. I'll put up some water for my tea." She drew some water and put it on the stove to boil, then seated herself at the table next to Laura. "So don't say good-morning, sleepyhead, see if I care," she said, winking.

"Good morning." Laura took a large bite of her cupcake.

"A cupcake with chocolate icing," Sadie mused. "All sugar and no protein. Every cupcake puts about half a pound on you. What else do you like?"

Laura reached out to the box on the table and put another cupcake on her plate. "Pizza, mostly. And frankfurters, and peanut-butter-and-jelly sandwiches."

"That's quite a little list," said Sadie.

Laser beams shot out of Laura's eyes. Marian jumped into the breach and reminded her of the time. With dark looks and much slamming of doors and drawers, Laura collected her school books

and came back to stand in the kitchen doorway. "Is Mrs. Shapiro going to be here when I come home from school?" she asked, her chin upraised in Mussolini fashion.

"Yes," said Marian, looking her daughter straight in the eye. The girl left the apartment without another word.

For a few moments there was only the sound of water coming to a boil on the stove. Sadie rose and went about the business of making tea. Marian sipped her coffee and stared at the wall. "Now you know everything," she said.

"Well, maybe I shouldn't have started up with her," Sadie said, sitting down with her tea. "I think Laura doesn't like herself too much, so maybe it's hard for her to like anyone else. Sometimes developing a shape like a pear can also give you a chip on your shoulder."

"Could be," Marian agreed, "but diet days are coming. I've made up my mind."

"Good."

"And I've been thinking about our talk the other night. I'm going to beard Arnold Hawthorne in his den. I'm tired of being underpaid and overlooked. Yipes!" she said, glancing at the clock. "I'm late. I'm going to hop into the shower and then scoot."

Alone in the kitchen, Sadie sipped her tea. Maybe there was a way to help Marian with Laura's weight problem? She couldn't interfere too much between mother and daughter. And yet, since she was living here for a while, she might lend a hand.

The sound of the telephone interrupted Sadie's thoughts. She went to the living room and picked up the phone. "Cortina d' Ampezzo at twilight," said Heathcliff, "with the snow falling gently on your hair. The two of us at the top of the ski lift . . ."

It must be my bad ear, Sadie thought, because I can't be hearing what I'm hearing. She shifted the receiver.

". . . grasping you to me, I whisper in your ear—"

"Whoa! Whoa!" said Sadie. "Say no more. Who is this?"

There was a sharp intake of breath on the other end. "I'm awfully sorry," the voice said. "Excuse me."

Shaking her head, Sadie put the phone down as Marian, her

head wrapped in a towel, peeked out of the bathroom door. "Was that for me, Sadie?"

Sadie stared at Marian, then smiled. "Marian, if that was for you, we're both in a lot of trouble."

AFTER Marian had left for the office, Sadie wandered about the small apartment. She felt lonely and deserted. Come on now, she told herself, you know what to do. Keep your head and your hands busy. So saying, she showered and dressed. Then, like a pint-sized dynamo, she whirled about the house making beds, straightening books, dusting the furniture. She then took up her knitting bag and polished off a cap and scarf for Laura.

Laura . . . What to do? She walked into the girl's room and sat on a chair near her desk. Make believe you are Laura Wall, she thought. What would make you start behaving yourself—would even make you go on a diet?

From above Laura's bed, poster faces stared down at Sadie. David Cassidy smiling, Bobby Sherman eating a popsicle. Dozens of other young faces cut from magazines plastered the wall.

Of course. When Laura wasn't thinking about food, she thought about boys. With long hair and guitars. Singers, musicians. The people who played that music she was all the time listening to.

No doubt about it, thought Sadie, what keeps a girl in shape is a boy. She walked to the phone and dialed Bessie's son-in-law Myron.

"Hello, Sadie, famous TV personality and author," said Myron. "And how are you today?"

"Needing a favor, Myron."

"For you, anything. Shoot."

"Myron, do you have on your program any of these—what do you call 'em—rock-and-roll singers?"

"We have them, sure. What's up?"

"Is anyone on tonight?"

"Yeah. Tonight we have Ronny Porter and Canned Fruit."

"Canned Fruit? This is the name of a person?"

"No," said Myron, laughing. "It's a group."

"Would an eleven-year-old girl know them?"

"Every eleven-year-old in America knows Canned Fruit."

"All right. Now here's what I want you to do," and she explained her idea.

"I can't ask them to come over to your place today," Myron protested. "They're busy people, stars."

"Just a courtesy call, Myron, from one star to another. If you don't help me I'll have to ask Johnny Carson. So please, Myron, you'll call these Canned Fruits like a good boy?"

"I'll try, Sadie, but I can't guarantee a thing." Ten minutes later, Myron called back. "You're amazing. They said yes. They'll be there just before three."

"Oh, Myron, you're a doll. Thanks."

"Don't thank me," Myron said. "They all want to meet you, Sadie. Ronnie Porter's mother is your biggest fan."

WHEN the doorbell rang just before noon, Sadie thought it might be Laura, returning home early from school. To her surprise and delight, it was a tired-looking Harold Rosenbloom. She fell on him with affection and pulled him into the apartment. "Can I make you some lunch, Harold?"

"A cold drink, perhaps," he said, mopping his face with a snow-white handkerchief. While Sadie went off in search of refreshment, he walked painfully to the living room, leaning heavily on his cane, and sank down on the couch.

"To what do I owe this treat?" Sadie asked when she had handed Rosenbloom a glass of icy lemonade and seated herself.

"Business, Sadie. And pleasure, on my part, to see you again. Mount Eden is not the same place with you gone."

"I'm beginning to miss Mount Eden, too," said Sadie.

Rosenbloom took a sip of his lemonade, opened his briefcase and withdrew a sheaf of letters. "Now then, to business. Your mail is fascinating, Sadie. You've been getting the most amazing offers for tie-ins with your book. For instance, the Minnesota Vikings would like you to design new warm-up suits for them."

"And what are the Minnesota Vikings?"

"A professional football team. The only specification they make is that the suit be knitted in the team colors, purple, white, and gold. After you design it, they'll arrange for a manufacturer to produce them. They also plan to sell facsimiles to their fans. They're offering quite a bit of money for the design, plus a royalty."

Rosenbloom held up another paper. "Now here's an interesting offer. A company wants to open a chain of shops across the country on a franchise basis. They want to use your name—Sadie Shapiro's Knitting Shops—and the fee they're offering is substantial."

"My name they want?" She shook her head in disbelief.

"How about this? It's from some moneymen in Dallas, in the franchise food business. Would you believe Sadie Shapiro's Drive-in Restaurants? Featuring something called a knitburger?"

"Harold, you're joking. Don't tell me any more. I wouldn't give my worst enemy a knitburger."

"I have about a half dozen other offers here, Sadie. You're a hot property, and lots of people want to use your name. There's a bundle of money out there, just waiting to be scooped up."

"Who needs money, at my age. With Social Security and Reuben's pension, I've got enough to get by."

"No one turns his back on an opportunity like this, Sadie," said Rosenbloom. "I'd do the work. All you'd have to do is say yes or no once in a while, and sign some papers."

"All to make money. It's crazy, Harold. Listen, if I wanted to be rich, I could have married Al Rosman, don't think I didn't have the chance. The man was in the dairy business and he was crazy about me. The Prince of Pot Cheese, they called him, with money running out of his ears. But was he kind, like my Reuben? Did he love me the way Reuben did? Why, I wouldn't give you a dime for a Rockefeller next to my Reuben. There's more to life than money, Harold."

Rosenbloom reached for his drink. "How about if I make it a non-profit corporation? A charity, if you like. The Sadie Shapiro Foundation. And all the money it makes, you can give away."

Sadie looked at Rosenbloom. "Is it you, Harold, who needs all this money?"

Rosenbloom chuckled softly, shaking his head. "No. I'm very well provided for." Slowly, pain showing in his face, Rosenbloom crossed one leg over the other and put his head back against the couch. With his eyes closed, he went on. "I want to do this, Sadie, because I want to do it. I made a big mistake when I turned sixty-five. I should have opened an office for myself and kept my hand in. I'm like a piece of machinery, Sadie, left out to rust in the rain. I'm a sick man, I know that, but all I've done for years is sit around and listen to my arteries hardening. With you as my client, I'd be back in it. I would work for you for the pure joy of doing it well. I'd be making deals again."

"You really need to do this, don't you?" Sadie said.

"Like I need air to breathe."

"If you don't mind my saying, you look terrible, Harold. I'm not sure it's such a good idea, working hard again."

"Every day that passes, I'll never live again," he said. He opened his eyes and she saw tears in them. "I have to do this, Sadie," he said. "And you have to let me. Please, don't make me beg."

"I didn't say no, yet," said Sadie softly. "Tell me again how it works."

Speaking very slowly, Rosenbloom explained the steps involved in setting up a nonprofit charitable foundation. There would come into being a corporation, he told her, and a board of directors. Sadie would head that board, with himself, Sam Beck, and Marian taking the other seats. "I'll send some papers along for you to sign in a few days," Rosenbloom said. "You won't be sorry, Sadie. I promise you."

"I hope so, Harold, for your sake as well as mine."

"The Sadie Shapiro Foundation," he said, smiling. "I can't wait to get started."

"Myron sent us," the voice in the hallway said. A tumult of color and texture leaped to Sadie's eyes the moment she opened the door. She stared at their wild, shoulder-length hair, shaggy beards and mustaches, faded Levi's dotted with bright patches, vests of curly animal hide. "Like, wow," the tall one in front said.

"The real Sadie Shapiro. I'm, like, Ronnie Porter, and these guys are Canned Fruit."

"Come right in, Mr. Porter . . . and Fruits."

The singing group slouched past Sadie into the living room. Canned Fruit put down the alligator guitar cases they were carrying and looked around. "Man," one of them said, "like straight America, U.S.A."

"Wow," said Porter, flashing a wide, lopsided grin. "My mother thinks you're aces. She, like, watches you all the time on the box, ya know?"

"That's nice. Tell her I think she's got a very handsome son."

"Oh, wow," said Porter, "you're beautiful. Like, even at your age, doing your thing, knitting and everything, with wool and all."

"Hey, man, ask her if we can smoke," one of the others said.

"Of course, Fruits," Sadie said. She watched Canned Fruit take crumpled cigarettes from their vests and light up.

"Tell me about this gig, Mama," Porter said. "Myron said we didn't have to play or anything. What's up?"

Sadie seated herself next to Porter and told him about Laura, her weight, and her general state of unhappiness. "So I figured," she summed up, "to me she wouldn't listen, but to you she would."

Porter's face grew serious. "Heavy," he said.

"Exactly."

"Okay, I'll do it. When does the chick get here?"

"Any minute."

Almost at once they heard the sound of a key turning in the front door and Laura came in. She walked into the living room and stopped dead in her tracks, her mouth open.

"Laura," Sadie said, getting up, "we have some visitors. This is Ronnie Porter, and those are Canned Fruits. I'd like you to meet Laura Wall."

"Oh, wow," said Laura.

Porter grinned at Laura and stood towering over her. She seemed rooted to the floor. He helped her off with her knapsack. "I've heard a lot about you from Sadie, here. So like, hello."

"You *know* Sadie?" Laura's voice rose a few octaves.

"We're old friends. In show biz, and all." He turned and winked at Sadie.

Like a zombie, Laura let Porter lead her to the couch and sat down beside him. "Oh, wow," she said.

"Oh, man," said Porter, "look at them eyes. She's like a Madonna. How about this chick, guys?"

"Yeah," said one Fruit.

"Oh, wow," said another.

"Like, if we needed a chick in the act, you would be it, Laura. Stand up and turn around slow. Let me look on you good."

Still looking dazed, Laura stood and modeled for Porter. "You remind me of Mama Cass," he said, and Laura's face fell. She bit her lip. "Yeah, that's the way you come on. Like Cass Elliot. A little doll face on top of a big body. Beautiful."

Laura stared at Porter, her face working. Then a tear rolled slowly down her cheek.

"Hey, Laura, did I say something wrong? I mean, I figured you want to look the way you look, don't you?"

"No-oo-oo," she said, covering her face with her hands. Then she really started crying. Sadie drew Laura to the couch, cradling the little girl in her arms. She stroked her hair and made soothing noises, clucking into her ear.

"Oh, wow," said Porter, "like, I'm sorry. I mean, I figured maybe fat was your thing."

As these last words hit home, Laura began to wail. "I don't want to be this way. I don't! I don't!"

"This is an ugly scene, man," one of the Fruits said.

"The worst," said another.

"Hey, Laura, listen," Porter said. "If you don't want to be fat, hey, then don't be. Like, stick with the real things and lay off the chemicals. That's body pollution. You know, pick up on yogurt and wheat germ and nuts. Things like that, Laura, and it won't take long to get straight. You'll see."

"Hey, man, let's split," said a Fruit.

As Laura took her face from Sadie's shoulder, Porter flashed her a grin and a V sign. "Good-by, Laura," he said. "Sadie, you keep in

touch and let me know how she's doing." Gathering the Fruit, he led them out the door.

"Oh, Sadie," Laura cried, "I don't want to be fat. But what am I going to do?"

Sadie held her close. "Laura, I thought you'd never ask."

ONE of the major changes wrought by the runaway success of *Sadie Shapiro's Knitting Book* could be seen in the carpet at the foot of Arnold Hawthorne's desk. The old rug, bare spot and all, had been torn out by the roots and replaced. The publisher also now sat behind a three-thousand-dollar imported teak desk that all but dwarfed the room. "All right now," he said as Marian and Jack Gatewood seated themselves on the couch, "let's get the weekly Sadie Report up-to-date. Jack, why don't you fill me in on the sales picture?"

"Right. Sales are holding at about seven thousand copies a week. Sold to date, sixty thousand. Back orders, fifty thousand. The only problem we have is producing books fast enough."

"Splendid. What about the book-club, foreign rights, and reprint sale, Marian?"

"Both the Book-of-the-Month and the Literary Guild took it, as you know. In addition, the Arts and Crafts Book Club will make it a major selection next month. It's been sold in England and France, and we have three German publishers bidding for it even as we speak. I've had nibbles from four paperback publishers. Those rights should bring us between one hundred fifty and two hundred thousand dollars more. By the way, Arnold, about how much has Sadie earned thus far?"

"Oh, I'd say offhand about a hundred thousand dollars," said Hawthorne, smiling. "Now then, tell me about Sadie's promotional tour. When do you leave?"

"In two months. The first stop is Cleveland, and then we'll work our way west. We'll be coming back to tape some TV shows in

New York from time to time. And pick up some clean underwear."

"Very good," Hawthorne said. "We'll miss you, Marian."

"There's something I'd like to take up with you," Marian said. "A promotion and a raise, not necessarily in that order."

"Jack, I think you'd better leave us," Hawthorne said.

Jack said, "Give him hell, Marian," and closed the door softly behind him.

"Now then, Marian, what's on your mind?"

"Money, first. I make thirteen thousand a year. It's not enough. I want twenty-five."

"Twenty-five!" the publisher exploded. "Are you crazy?"

"Just waking up. And I want to be made a vice-president."

Arnold Hawthorne's face had gone sallow and he slumped in his chair. "My dear, loyal Marian, stabbing me in the back."

"Between the eyes, Arnold. And I'm not your dear, loyal Marian. I've grown up now. I don't handle the switchboard anymore or go downstairs for coffee, remember? I've been carrying this place on my back for years without being paid for it."

The publisher shook his head. "Twenty-five thousand dollars. It's absurd. I don't know what's got into you."

Marian threw back her head and laughed. "I think I know what's got into me, Arnold. A little of Sadie Shapiro. Some of her spirit and energy and confidence. Work side by side with Sadie and some of it begins to rub off on you. A lot of people have been calling me lately. Editors, publishers—for the first time in my life, I'm in demand. Twenty-five thousand, Arnold, not a penny less."

The publisher swallowed hard. As he slowly nodded, his face looked gray.

"And the vice-presidency. Yes or no, Arnold."

"You win," he said, raising both hands in surrender.

Marian swooped down on him and kissed his cheek. "You won't regret it, Arnold. And now I've got to run."

THE two figures rounded the corner of the track alongside the reservoir in Central Park. The older one jogged along in perfect form. The young girl in the matching sweat suit seemed to bounce

rather than jog, and her straining face had turned bright red. "Just a little more, Laura, we're almost home," Sadie said.

Laura groaned and wiped the rivulets of sweat from her face with the back of her hand. "Sadie," she puffed, "I think I'm dying. When I take a step, everything bounces."

"But that's good. Every bounce is breaking up the fat. Think of it that way."

"I can't think," said Laura, slowing down.

"All right, let's walk a little."

"Sadie, don't get mad, but this jogging is making me hungry. What's for dinner?"

"Food is your enemy, remember that, Laura."

The girl swallowed hard. "No dinner, okay."

Sadie laughed and threw an arm around Laura. "Of course you'll have dinner. Dieting doesn't mean fasting. It only means starving a little. Tonight you'll start off with a big dish of carrot and celery sticks, followed by a plain broiled hamburger with lettuce and tomato salad. And for dessert, cottage cheese."

A look of pure pain crossed Laura's face.

"What do you think, skinny comes easy?" Smiling, Sadie bounced up and down on her toes and put herself in gear. "Let's go. Last one across Central Park West is a rotten egg!"

"WHAT are all those papers you're signing?" Marian asked one evening several weeks later. "They look very official."

"From Harold Rosenbloom. He makes X's and I sign my name. It's for the foundation. You should have heard him on the telephone today. He was laughing and telling jokes. He's in his glory, Marian. Two days a week he goes to Wall Street. He met with those football people today. The Minnesota Vikings, they call them."

"I love your design for their warm-up-suits. And while we're on the subject of designs, I think it's time to start thinking about a sequel to the knitting book."

"I already have," said Sadie. "At least, I got a title. 'Sadie Shapiro's OTHER Knitting Book.' What do you think, cookie?"

"Perfect." Marian grinned.

As the women smiled at each other, Laura came into the living room, ready to have Marian see her to bed. After a few weeks of dieting, her cheeks no longer ballooned and the heavy swell of her waist was fast disappearing. She kissed Sadie and went off to her bedroom with Marian.

Where are you, Sam Beck? thought Sadie as she sat alone in the living room. You haven't called me in two weeks. I'd like to take a walk with you, or go out to a movie, or just sit and talk.

Just then the phone rang and Sadie answered it. "Just you and me," the voice began, "and the sound of waves breaking on the shore. I turn and take you in my—"

This time Sadie didn't hesitate. "Is that so?" she exploded into the phone. "You should be ashamed of yourself."

There was a cough on the other end and a quick intake of breath. "Oh, I did it again," Heathcliff said. "Forgive me. Look, would you please call Marian to the phone?"

"I should call Marian to the phone to talk to a maniac?"

Sadie stared at the telephone in her hand. This is altogether a strange person, she thought, and maybe even worse. She was hesitating, holding the phone at arm's length, when Marian came back into the room. "It's that crazy person from the other day, Marian," Sadie said. "Now he even knows your name."

Marian dropped her eyes, blushing. "I'll take it in my bedroom," she said, running and closing the door behind her.

Sadie heard Marian pick up the extension and begin to exchange some words with the caller. Unbelieving, Sadie listened for a moment before putting down the phone. Marian not only knew the man on the phone, she had spoken with him before.

Marian's face was flushed when she finally emerged from the bedroom. She lit a cigarette and sat down in the armchair that flanked the couch. Clearing her throat, she looked sidewise into Sadie's staring eyes. "Sadie, let me explain."

"Wouldn't budge an inch from here," said Sadie, as if speaking to herself. "This has got to be some terrific explanation. Talking to a madman and you're going to explain that?"

"He's not a madman. He's just . . . sort of . . ."

"He's just your ordinary sex fiend, that's what he is. And you, Marian Wall, a mother and an *editor* no less, want to talk to him? I don't understand."

"Well . . . you see . . . I've been getting calls from him for over a year now, Sadie."

Sadie seemed to levitate from the couch. "Over a year! Marian Wall, are you out of your mind? Call the police! Why do you want to fool around with a man who makes crazy phone calls? Why, Marian? Tell me."

Marian chuckled without mirth. "Well, there aren't a lot of men exactly chasing me at the moment. Not for years, if we're speaking the truth. And this one—I call him Heathcliff—is the only man in my life. Perhaps it's silly, but I've sort of gotten used to speaking with him. And I like the fact that he's so romantic. The things he's always saying sound as if they came right out of a book."

Sadie groaned and put her head back against the couch.

"It sounds mad, Sadie, but he's harmless. In fact I think he's warm and creative, and I don't mind humoring him. I couldn't call the police after all this time."

Visibly upset, Sadie rose. "So as far as you're concerned, you'll go on talking with him as long as he's interested, right?"

"Right."

"Hmm," said Sadie, thinking out loud, "then there's only one thing left to do, Marian."

"And what's that?"

Sadie grinned. "Invite him up, of course."

For Marian, the next day passed with glacial slowness. As she worked, her mind kept picturing the scene that might take place that very night. What would he look like? Tall, dark, handsome? What if he wasn't? What would she do if a short, ugly, pathetic-looking Heathcliff appeared in her doorway? Forget it, she told herself, he probably won't show up at all.

For Sadie, the approach of dusk made her more and more uncertain. What had she done? What would happen if a masked intruder

rushed in when they opened the door? Just to be on the safe side, Sadie inveigled Laura into spending the night with one of her school chums. Alone in the apartment, she looked through the kitchen's assortment of knives, then rejected them. No, she said, you live by the knitting needle, and if you have to die by it, so be it. So she took the precaution of finding her very longest and strongest needle and having it handy.

At dinner, neither Marian nor Sadie ate with much appetite. "He probably won't call," Marian said, her voice edgy.

"He'll call."

"I suppose so. He almost always does." Marian lit a cigarette. "He probably won't come here, though."

"He'll come."

Marian swallowed hard. "Listen . . . ah . . . I don't suppose you'd want to talk to him? I mean, just to ask him over?"

"You're the one who's experienced with maniacs, Marian," Sadie said. "I mean, with me he's not a personal friend."

As the telephone rang, they both leaped up. Marian disappeared into her bedroom at top speed, closing the door behind her. A sudden weakness buckled Sadie's knees. They were going to let a maniac into the apartment. And it was all her idea.

She heard Marian calling and headed toward the living room. Her face an off-white shade, Marian stood in the bedroom doorway. "He'll be here in ten minutes."

With a whoosh of escaping air from her lungs, Sadie sank into an armchair. Had her heart really stopped beating?

"Sadie!" Marian rushed across the room and knelt before the old woman. "Are you all right?"

"Not to worry," Sadie said. "I'm fine. It only happens maybe once or twice a year. Mainly when I get scared to death. In another minute I'll be a hundred percent. Meanwhile, tell me what he said when you invited him over."

"It was very strange, Sadie," Marian said, her head cocked to one side. "I had the feeling he must have been hoping for that invitation for a long time. I just told him that I was waiting and to hurry over. And he said, 'Oh, I'll be right there.'"

"How did he sound?"

"As if he were in a trance. Very calm."

"Oh, boy," said Sadie, "that's a bad sign. When a maniac gets very calm you're in big trouble."

Marian stared briefly at Sadie. "I was thinking the same thing."

"Marian, maybe this wasn't such a terrific idea."

"Now you tell me," said Marian.

Sadie rummaged in her knitting bag and found the needle she had selected. "I'll be standing behind the door with this. One false move . . ." She made a long thrust with the knitting needle that drew a smile from Marian.

"Whatever you do, Marian," Sadie counseled, "don't let the maniac see how scared you are. It makes them crazy."

"I'll remember that," Marian said. "It's funny. Half of me wants to get a hatchet, and the other half wants to put on more perfume."

Marian had just lit another cigarette when the doorbell rang. Springing up, she exchanged a terrified look with Sadie. On tiptoe, Sadie gingerly approached the front door and flattened herself to the wall alongside it.

Trembling, Marian walked to the door. "Who is it?" she asked in a voice that was barely a whisper.

"The telephone man," came a voice from the hallway.

Marian took a last look at Sadie and then unlocked all three locks. She opened the door a crack and peered out. "Oh, no!" she cried, stepping back in anguish and shock. "No!" With a strangled cry, she turned and ran to her bedroom.

Summoning all her courage, Sadie drew herself to the doorway and looked out. Standing there, eyes downcast, hands nervously working the brim of a straw hat, was a man she had met many times before. "Mr. Gatewood!" Sadie gasped. "It's you." She stared openmouthed. "But you're . . . you're an *editor-in-chief!*"

A grim smile played about Jack's mouth as he looked away. Sadie stepped aside and opened the door halfway. "As long as you're here," she said, "you might as well come in."

Jack slowly walked into the living room. He seated himself on the couch, and then she settled into an armchair beside him. The

ensuing silence seemed to go on forever, broken only by the sounds of Marian's sobbing.

Sadie stared at Jack, trying desperately to make sense where none was apparent. Such a handsome man, she thought. Always dresses neat. Fingernails clipped and clean. A perfect gentleman.

Jack cleared his throat loudly and brought his eyes up to meet hers. "I'm sorry about this," he said in a controlled voice. "More than you can possibly know. Forgive me, please."

"Forgiven," said Sadie. "Don't bother your mind with it."

"Thank you," Jack said. "Well, I'd better be leaving. Will you tell Marian that I'll resign from the firm. She and I can never work together again now that she knows—"

"Not so fast," countered Sadie. "If anyone is the injured party, it's Marian. And she hasn't said two words to you yet. First, let's get this whole thing straight. You *are* the person who's been calling Marian, aren't you?"

Jack's eyes dropped to the rug. "Yes," he said, barely audibly. "I'm so ashamed I wish I were dead."

"I just wanted to make sure," said Sadie. "But let's keep deadness out of this. We're all people in this world and we all have our own ways. Of course, some are crazier than others." She smiled at Jack but he was looking away.

"Tell Marian I'll disappear from her life," he said. "I'll go somewhere. Australia, perhaps."

"Oh, boy," said Sadie, "that's some solution, to run away. Mr. Gatewood"—she waited until Jack's eyes came up to meet hers—"wherever you're going to run away, remember: you're still going to be Mr. Jack Gatewood. So stay here, at least until I talk to Marian, please. . . ."

Moving slowly, Sadie retreated to Marian's bedroom door. Marian lay face down on her bed, crying softly. "Why did it have to be Jack?" she sobbed.

"It's not the worst thing," Sadie said. "At least the crazy person is someone you know."

Marian groaned. "Tell him I never want to see him again. Tell him I resign."

Sadie sat on the edge of the bed and took Marian in her arms. "The poor man. He's sitting there like a lost soul, just waiting for you to say a kind word to him."

"Never," Marian sobbed. "Make him go away." Sadie got up from the bed. She turned to rejoin Jack, and paused before opening the door. Think, she commanded herself. Shapiro, do your stuff. A man like Jack doesn't call a girl like Marian for months without feeling something for her. And Marian would not have gone into conniptions on seeing Jack if she didn't hold him in some special place in her heart. Something was definitely doing between the two of them.

Sadie's face was the picture of cheer as she rejoined Jack. "Marian's having a good cry," she reported. "Won't take two minutes, she'll be here to say hello. Look, I got to ask you a question. What do you feel about Marian? Maybe it's not my business, but I have to know."

Jack looked at Sadie. When he spoke, he looked even more handsome than before. "I love her, Sadie. I adore her. I have from the moment I saw her, nine years ago."

Sadie's grin was triumphant. "I knew it. Of course you love her. Why else would you call up and talk nutty? So there's no problem. You love her, and I think she cares a little for you. So what's a few insane phone calls between friends? I mean, these things can be forgiven."

"It's not that easy, Sadie. You see, I have great difficulty in—"

"Wait a minute," Sadie said. "Take a rest. I want to talk to Marian." Quickly she slipped into Marian's bedroom. "Hey, cookie, guess what?" she said brightly. "Jack just told me something that'll make you feel terrific. Marian, he's in love with you."

As if a magic button had been pressed, Marian began wailing once more. Sadie fled to the living room.

"All right," she said, sitting down and rubbing her hands together briskly, "I think we're making progress. Now you were telling me something you can't do, right? What is it?"

With a look of great pain, Jack began to speak. "I can't tell Marian I love her. I can say such things to you, or to Marian over

the telephone, disguising my voice and pretending I'm someone else. But I can't say it to Marian directly."

"I don't understand."

"Neither do I," said Jack, "but when I look at Marian something just turns off my brain and I'm speechless. There are so many things I want to say and I can't say any of them. I'm all right with other women, Sadie. There's never been a problem until Marian came along. I knew she was different as soon as I saw her, and the more deeply I came to love her, the harder it was to tell her.

"The crisis began more than a year ago. I knew Marian was unhappy over her work, and I feared she might leave Harbor Press. I knew I had to say something about how I felt, but I couldn't. One night, after I had been walking the streets for hours, I went home and dialed Marian's number. When I heard her voice I panicked and it was as if another person possessed me. The voice I spoke with was not my own. The words I was saying . . . I don't know where they came from."

"Like a Dr. Jekyll was hiding in you," said Sadie.

"Marian didn't refuse to speak to me," Jack went on. "She listened, and even spoke back to me."

"Is that a wonderful girl?" Sadie said. "She's an angel."

"And so I kept calling. Once a week, in those days. More frequently as time went by. I even had another telephone installed in my office so I could call her during the day. Once I even called her on both phones at the same time. I was Jack on one and her lover on the other."

"Love comes out in funny ways," Sadie observed. "I had a friend once, her husband used to punch her on the arm every day before he went to work. If a few days went by and he didn't give her a good smack, she used to worry."

"When Marian asked me to come here tonight," Jack said, "I was ready. Somehow Marian had to know that that person on the telephone was me—another part of me, perhaps, but me all the same."

"You were very brave," Sadie said, getting up. "Don't go away."

Marian was quietly sitting on her bed, smoking a cigarette, when Sadie came in. Sadie quickly summarized her conversation

with Jack. "Believe him, Marian. He loves you. A little mixed-up, maybe, but in his heart for nine years is only you."

"And in nine years he's never even hinted it. Except on the telephone, posing as someone else."

"Who knows what's laying there in the hearts of men," said Sadie, looking for the moment like an Oriental sage.

"I just can't accept a secondhand love, Sadie. Why hasn't he spoken before now?"

"Marian, please don't expect miracles. I know, every girl thinks about a Sir Galahad comes riding along on a white horse. But where does that happen, except in books? My Reuben, let him rest in peace, never looked like Clark Gable. But an honest, good man he was, with a lot of wonderful ways. In books they never tell you when it's cold out, a man gets up and puts an extra quilt on you, you shouldn't be cold. A Romeo never gets involved in that. Believe me, what you should be thinking about is tenderness, kindness, and consideration, and on the phone he's very passionate."

Marian's look was scornful. "And what do we do when it's time to make love, Sadie? Does he call me long distance?"

"You got a point there," Sadie conceded. "I'll be right back."

"Everything is ipsy-pipsy," she reported to Jack, "except for one little thing. She wants you to go in and tell her how much you love her."

"I thought as much," he said, inspecting the rug. "I've lost, then. It's all over."

"A Shapiro never gives up," Sadie said, rolling up her sleeves. "And neither should a Gatewood."

Jack stared at Sadie.

"Off the couch," she commanded. Half pulling him to his feet, she marched him swiftly across the room. "Pick up that telephone," she ordered.

Jack picked it up. His mouth opened but no words emerged.

At top speed Sadie circled the room and extinguished every lamp. In almost total darkness she felt her way back to Jack. Clapping a small but strong hand on his shoulder, she exhorted him, "Start talking."

There was a moment of silence and then a low laugh. "I'm holding you at arm's length, looking into your lovely eyes, feeling the warmth of your skin, the sweet curve of you molded into my—"

Quickly Sadie pushed him to Marian's door. "Keep talking," she said. "Whatever you do, don't stop talking."

"I feel possessed by you. I want to keep kissing you forever."

"He's talking, Marian," Sadie said, running into the bedroom, half dragging a reluctant Marian toward the door. "He's saying things to you."

"I won't listen."

With a strange cry, Sadie ran to the bed and snapped off the lighted lamp. Finding her way back in the dark, she forced Marian to the door. "Marian, you've got to listen," she whispered. "You only get one chance, now grab it."

"No," Marian's lips were saying, but her ears were tuned to the sweet music that came through the half open door.

Fifty years of knitting gave strength to the small hand that reached through the doorway and grasped Jack Gatewood by the end of his tie.

Twenty years of jogging gave strength to the lean body that pulled him, still talking, through the doorway and into Marian's open arms. There was the sound of a sharp intake of breath, a quiet sigh of pleasure, and then Sadie was in the darkened living room, her back against the firmly closed bedroom door. She listened to the silence for a moment, and smiled.

THE next morning, dressed in a sweat suit of lavender, Sadie crossed Central Park and began circling the reservoir. The air was clear, the morning sun bright. As she jogged, feeling strong and free, her mind went over the events of the evening before. She still felt twinges of guilt. Against their will, she had forced two people to do something she, herself, had never done. It was wrong, she knew, but was it? Jack was made for Marian, and vice versa. But the vice in that versa was what troubled her. Why was something that was right for Marian not right for herself?

What did she really feel for Sam Beck, she asked herself, and

what about her firm ideas of chastity? Thinking hard, she rounded the corner of the reservoir and began jogging toward home. Central Park was abloom in the bright spring sunshine. Young men and women walked their dogs, and a few nannies sat with baby carriages.

Sam Beck. Living with a man again. Sleeping in the same bed with a man who was not her husband. What would she feel in her heart about it?

She wanted terribly to be with Sam, to hear his jokes, to share his sunny disposition. She wanted to feel her hand on his arm when they were out walking, to smell the rich scent of his cigar, to see the shine in his soft, brown eyes when he looked at her. Love—it can make even a smart person crazy.

On Central Park West, down the block from Marian's apartment house, she found a bench in the sun and sat down to think. If what Marian and Jack had found last night was right—and she thought in her heart it was—then could not Sadie Shapiro and Sam Beck find the same?

All right, suppose they took an apartment. A few bright, sunny rooms overlooking the park. A cozy kitchen for tea and talk, a few comfortable chairs, and a good light for knitting and reading. And what would the name on the mailbox read? Beck/Shapiro? Two adults, living together as man and wife, except that she would not be a wife. What would she be, then? A concubine, at her age? All the ancient words she had heard her mother use with scorn flashed through her head.

A faint breeze stirred the leaves of the tree above her head and tears filled Sadie's eyes. How could she live with Sam when she could not live with her conscience? How could she not live with him when being apart caused so much heartache?

The door to the apartment house swung wide and she saw Marian, smiling, step out into the sunshine. Behind her, the door swinging closed as he followed, stepped Jack. Hand in hand, they waited in the sun while Jack hailed a taxi. As it pulled away, Sadie saw Marian's head turn to Jack. They were kissing in the back seat as the taxi turned into the park.

Upstairs, Sadie showered and lay down. Mercifully, she slept until noon. Waking, she wandered about the apartment, the heavy weight of her conscience giving her no peace. A dozen times she walked to the phone to call Sam and a dozen times she could not. On her next trip the telephone rang even as she had it in her hand. She head Sam's voice, but it sounded very far away. "I have bad news," he said. "Sadie, Harold Rosenbloom is dead."

SLOWLY the crowd of people who had come to mourn filed into the chapel and seated themselves on the polished wooden benches. Holding fast to Sadie's arm, Marian guided her down the aisle and to a bench near the front. Sadie's face was pale and drawn, reflecting a long, sleepless night.

Marian had never seen Sadie this way. The old woman's spirit had been crushed by the events of the previous day. She blamed herself for Rosenbloom's death, repeating over and over: "I did it. I should never have let him go back to work." No matter how hard Marian tried, she would not be comforted. The guilt she felt was overwhelming.

Two rows behind Sadie sat Sam Beck, Abe Farkas, and Bessie Frankel. Many other Mount Edenites were seated throughout the chapel. Down front, Rosenbloom's family filed into the first row. A young, clean-shaven rabbi mounted the altar as the casket was wheeled into place. As he began chanting an ancient prayer, Sadie bent her head, weeping. Marian's arm went around her shoulders and she pressed Sadie's trembling form to hers.

Twenty minutes later they stood on the sidewalk outside the chapel. Limousines were drawn up at the curb for the trip to the cemetery. Out of the crowd stepped the tall figure of Sam Beck. Wordlessly, he took Sadie's arm and helped her into a limousine, then stood aside as Marian, Bessie, and Abe Farkas entered. Throughout the drive he held Sadie's hand and stroked her hair as her friends tried to give her comfort. By the time they stood beside the grave, Sadie was beginning to look and feel better.

The prayers and benedictions were recited, a few last words were spoken, and Harold Rosenbloom's body was lowered to its

final resting place. As the mourners walked slowly down the grassy slope that led back to the road, Sam Beck drew Sadie aside.

Holding her hand, he led her through a grove of trees to a shaded knoll and sat down with her on a marble bench. "I have a little visit to pay," he said. "You'll wait for me here." Beck squeezed Sadie's hand and walked a few steps back up the hill. In front of a simple headstone, Sadie saw him pause, his head bent. She saw his lips moving. Then, handkerchief in hand, he wiped at his eyes. Keeping his head averted, he adjusted the lapels of his suit coat and fussed with his tie. When he rejoined her, he was once more composed.

"Listen, Sam," Sadie said slowly, "I've been doing a lot of thinking these last twenty-four hours."

"I know," said Sam as he sat down beside her. "So have I."

"I'll always think about what I did to Harold," Sadie said slowly. "How I sent him out to work again, a man so sick—"

"Please, Sadie, let it go. You gave him happiness in his last days, and that's what you should remember. I was with him every day these last few weeks. I know how pleased he was to have something to do. He was a different Harold, laughing and joking."

Nodding, Sadie reached out and took Sam's hand. Their eyes met and then she was in his arms, hugging him close with all her strength. "Sam," she whispered, "I got something to say."

"Wait," he said, breaking the embrace and holding her at arm's length. "Let me speak first."

"No, Sam, please. It's been on my mind. I know you got all kinds of good reasons why you can't marry me, which I don't understand at all. I mean, there's children to be thought of, and you already told me about your insurance and your will, which I never thought was a good reason, but maybe I'm a little bit in the wrong too. Who says because you hold an idea in your head for seventy-two or seventy-five years that idea always has to be right?"

"Are you finished?"

"No. Only getting started. Sam, I made up my mind. I don't care if I'm breaking a law or people will talk about us or that the mailman will know we're living together and we're not a man and

wife. Because who knows how long it'll be, or God forbid, how short the time is that's left for you and me to be together. I only know that my heart is filled up with your goodness and your kindness, with that smile that gives me such a feeling inside I want to hug you whenever I see it. I love you, Sam Beck, and I don't care who knows it or what they say—their tongues should get heavy if they say a word to me—but I don't care about anything except being with you forever and making you happy, and if that's a sin, then call me sinner, because from this very minute I'm not going to let you out of my sight."

As Sadie paused for breath, Sam smiled. "Are you all finished now?" he asked gently.

To Sadie's surprise, she was.

"Now I'll have my say." Dropping to one knee, he took her hand and pressed it to his cheek. "Sadie," he said, "let's get married."

AND they did.

Not on "The Tonight Show," which was the master publicity stroke Arnold Hawthorne fought for. And not without an anxious moment along the way.

There were many arrangements to be made, and only two weeks before Sadie's promotional tour. There were blood tests ("An old woman like me they're worried about VD, they should be ashamed," Sadie kept saying) and marriage licenses to be arranged. Not to mention the matter of the dresses to be worn by the bridal party. Sadie, of course, wanted to sit down and knit them at once. But on this occasion she took Marian's advice to buy a dress, especially when Marian forced Arnold Hawthorne to move forward his royalty payment to Sadie—a little matter of $147,987.03 to be precise.

Several days later, on a warm, clear Sunday afternoon, Sadie Shapiro and Samuel Joseph Beck were married in the back garden of the Mount Eden Senior Citizens Hotel in Queens, New York. The bride wore a cocktail dress of bright blue silk that matched her eyes, and carried a bouquet of pink roses and maidenhair fern. She was attended by her daughter-in-law, Mrs. Stuart Sha-

piro of Coral Gables, Florida, Mrs. Marian Wall, vice-president of Harbor Press, and the flower girl was Miss Laura Wall of New York City.

The ceremony completed under a canopy of white gardenias, the wedding party was sped in a fleet of limousines and one yellow taxi driven by Mr. Juan Otero to the Fifth Avenue Presbyterian Church, where the newly joined Mr. and Mrs. Beck stood up for Marian Wall and Jack Gatewood.

A joint wedding reception was held at the Hotel Pierre, and media coverage of the dual nuptials was extensive. A host of show-business luminaries attended the reception, and "The Tonight Show" orchestra provided music for dancing.

The following day both wedded couples and Laura set off for Kennedy Airport to embark on a combined honeymoon and publicity tour.

As the United Airlines 727 taxied down the runway and prepared to take off, Jack and Marian sat holding hands, so happy they hardly knew where they were. Directly behind them Sadie and Sam were similarly engaged.

Gathering speed, the jet aircraft thrust itself noisily into the afternoon sky. Up, up it rose, over Jamaica Bay, still higher over the apartment houses of Jamaica, before beginning its turn to the west over the streets of Queens. Far below, as Sadie looked down in awe, the whitewashed brightness of Mount Eden was clearly visible. Laughing, Sadie looked at Sam and gently squeezed his hand. An Eden is where you make it, she thought to herself, and it really could be anywhere.

Then she reached below her seat and took up her knitting.

Robert Kimmel Smith

Contrary to what she told Johnny Carson, Sadie Shapiro, heroine of *Sadie Shapiro's Knitting Book*, was born two years ago in a Chinese restaurant in New York's Chinatown. Robert Kimmel Smith, his wife, Claire, and another couple had just started on the egg-drop dumplings when the two women—both in publishing—fell to talking about the big boom in craft books. Smith, who at forty had abandoned a Madison Avenue advertising career to see if he could write, listened as the publishing shoptalk got around to a new knitting book that needed a title. The best the two women could come up with was "So-and-So's Knitting Book," which everyone around the table agreed was terrible. Out of the blue, Smith heard himself mutter, "It's no good for a knitting book—but what a great title for a novel."

From then on Sadie Shapiro—the world's greatest knitter— had Smith locked in a full nelson. He took Sadie's name from his mother, Sally ("Sadie") Kimmel, Sadie's pithy speech from various maternal aunts, and her knitting prowess from an aunt of his wife's, addicted to knitting slippers for the two Smith children. But Sadie's gusto, energy, and thirst for new experience—along with her jogging skill—are all Smith's own.

"You should take chances," Smith says in Sadie's authentic voice. "I didn't know if I could write, but I had to try. When I sold my first story"—a suspense novel called *Ransom*—"on the strength of the first hundred pages, I knew I could do it. Then when the Eugene O'Neill Memorial Theater took my first play, which I wrote in two weeks as a practice exercise, I thought, I must be a playwright, too. I expect to spend the next forty years shuttling back and forth between comic novels and funny plays."

If a movie is made of *Sadie*, Smith would love to see Barbra Streisand play her. "Think about it," he advises. "It'll get you."

Of course, he is now writing *Sadie Shapiro's OTHER Knitting Book*. We'll tell you only that Marian Wall is having a baby and Sadie's foundation has bought Mount Eden. As for Sadie herself? "Full of bounce," Smith says with a grin. "Even if she is seventy-three or seventy-six years old."

The Years of the Forest

A CONDENSATION OF THE BOOK BY

Helen Hoover

PAINTINGS BY NITA ENGLE

In *A Place in the Woods*, which delighted so many of our readers in 1969, Helen Hoover wrote about the unexpected trials and rewards of wilderness living.

Now, even in the remote north country, things have begun to change. The trees of the forest have been bulldozed to bring in electricity. The road has been improved and nature's balance threatened. Civilization, which the Hoovers fled earlier in their lives, has made its relentless way to their doorstep in the woods.

How they face this new and most dangerous of intruders is not only a nostalgic re-creation of woodland life as it once was, but a story of survival of a different kind.

Having mastered living with unpredictable nature, they now must learn to coexist with their entirely predictable fellowman— or abandon the one place on earth that won their hearts.

1956—Cut Wood

It was early afternoon near the beginning of May. I sat by the lake on a pink granite slab, looking through the clear water at the gray, green, and brown submerged rocks. A crayfish poked his claws tentatively from between the stones. A giant water bug departed at speed. Maybe he had seen the crayfish and was taking precautions. A school of tiny fish flirted by, and out from the shore there was a plop and a series of expanding rings where a big fish had broken the surface. I was amazed, as I always was, at the adaptations that made it possible for so many creatures to live comfortably through the bitter winter in the water under the ice.

A loon laughed a cheerful *ho-ho-ho-ho*. I dabbled my fingers in the water. It was still very cold and, as it rippled its way from the Minnesota shore to the low hills of Canada, it turned indigo in color. Above the hills, black-green with spruce and browny-gray with bare aspen tops, the sky was pale. It darkened gradually to deep azure at the zenith, where little clouds like bunny tails lay motionless. I sat up, shook the drops from my fingers, and rubbed the cold from them.

The ice had gone out only a few days earlier, and dirty patches of snow lingered under the swirled roots of cedars, beside boulders, and on the north side of our log cabin.

Spring was here, though, in the air—damp and soft and scented

by the earth. The pussies on the willows were a month old and bedraggled. Soon slender pale leaves would appear. The red squirrels had finished their amorous chasing through the pines, and mothers-to-be, showing smooth red summer fur where patches of their gray winter coats had fallen away, were carrying grass and leaves to secluded nurseries. A crow, back from the south since mid-March, swooped over me and circled, cawing an alarm.

The forest year in the North Woods had begun, full of rising life and a surge of what, in men, would be called optimism or hope. In wild creatures it comes as naturally as breathing. Man-made standards of good and evil are unknown to the forest, and its innocence and strength are such that it has, given Ade and me understanding by merely allowing us to watch its activities.

The sun had passed the highest point. Ade would soon be back from his six-mile round-trip walk from our log cabin to the Lodge for the mail, and such a hardworking husband would be hungry. I stood up and noticed a crack starting across the slab on which I had been sitting. How long would it take endless freezing and thawing to break the great piece of granite? As I walked up the path I wondered if I would still be here when that happened.

IN THE cabin I pulled open a deep, heavy drawer under the kitchen counter and looked through the items remaining from last fall's shipment of groceries. The choice for lunch seemed to be limited to a lone envelope of dehydrated vegetable soup. I also saw an abandoned mouse nest. I emptied the drawer to take it outside for washing, and found a crumpled piece of paper caught behind it. It was a list of things to do that Ade must have jotted down right after we had bought the log cabin as a vacation spot two years before, in the spring of 1954. I added water to the soup, put it on the wood range, and then went into the living room to sit by the window and read my find:

Clear brush and paths	Running water
Clear trash	Inside toilet
Remodel icehouse	Clear small cabin

Lay hardwood floor	Get another car
Build dock	Cut wood
Fix roof	Make a living
Finish inside	Take a vacation
Install wiring	

I went to my desk and drew a line through "Build dock." A boat had come with the log cabin, and we had hastily constructed a skid instead. I also crossed out "Remodel icehouse" and "Lay hardwood floor." Ade had done a fine job converting the icehouse into a studio for himself, but the building had been ruined by fire five months ago. As the hardwood for the floors had been stored in it, the fire had taken care of that, too.

"Cut wood" was one of our ever-present chores. "Get another car" and "Make a living" had surely been tacked on following a collision last year on the snow-narrowed blind hilltop, which had not only left us without transportation but had prevented Ade's getting to Duluth to sign a contract for artwork, which in turn left us with no income. "Take a vacation" could have been written in at any one of a thousand times when Ade must have felt as weary and hopeless as I had.

My eyes followed a blue jay through the trees to the partly charred icehouse—now euphemistically called the work building—and I remembered how hectic the weeks after the fire had been.

The sound of Ade's boots squelching in the spring mud brought me back to the present. I put the list in the center desk drawer for future reference and rushed to stir the soup.

That night I lay awake a long time thinking of the past and hearing the east wind breathing, resting, breathing again through the trees and in the chimney. This kind of wind meant a soaking three-or-four-day rain.

I let my mind wander to the winds that dry the sodden ground of spring and whisper through new growth, that howl as gales to topple dead timber. That frustrate and aid both the hunted and the hunter. I thought of the water from the clouds, that is the savior of life and sometimes its taker. And of rain roaring in tor-

rents to wash debris from the earth and freshen the streams and raise the lake levels; or rain that drizzles in silence to fur every leaf with silver, green the mosses, and soak the duff until mushrooms pop up like elves in big hats. I remembered the sound of rain, pattering like the feet of many mice.

My mind went again to the wind, returning to steal the diamonds left by the rain. Drowsily I thought of the utter dependency of every living thing on mother earth, and drifted from my fantasy of jeweled leaves into sleep.

NEXT morning Ade and I stood together at a window and looked out on a dim and dripping world. Ade sighed and stretched. "Glad the mail was yesterday. I'd better get at the new notepaper designs, if we're going to make any money selling them next fall."

I went to my typewriter to write an order, and he settled at his drawing board.

After the long soaking rain, the clearing turned green as if by magic. The birdsongs grew fewer as the birds nested, and not many animals came near the house because they, too, were preparing to bear young. But the *chip-chip* of the red squirrels was there for company, and a pileated woodpecker came, with his vivid red crest and shining black back, to drum his mating call on a hollow cedar tree.

The mosquitoes and black flies were out in full force, ready for their task of fertilizing the flowers, and they bit so ferociously that we gave up outdoor work. I cleaned in corners that had not looked dirty during dim winter days, and Ade whittled plugs to fill the knotholes in the floor.

Early in June, Ade went up the hill to the Lodge to get oil for the lamps and came back with Ernie Witmanski. Ernie was a young engineer at the ball-bearing factory in Chicago where I had been production metallurgist until 1948.

We had a gay and noisy reunion. Suddenly I wondered aloud what he was doing in the woods, and Ade followed with, "How did you find us?"

"I've a troop of boy scouts with me at the Lodge. Brought 'em

ack from a canoe trip . . ." His voice died, and he turned red under his tan. Self-consciousness in Ernie was incredible.

"Whatever's the matter with you?" I asked.

"I—I wouldn't want to hurt your feelings . . ."

"I'm really a very touchy type," I said, and Ade snorted.

"Well . . . O.K. then. I saw 'Hoover' on one of the mailboxes. I remembered how you told me you'd spent the first third of your life in a small town, the middle third in a big city, and you wanted to spend the last third in the wilderness. So I asked a couple of people at the Lodge if you might be my friends from Chicago. Someone said it wasn't likely—that you were a couple of kooks who claimed to be an artist and a metallurgist. And another one laughed and said, 'The guy has cooties in his beard.'"

He stopped because Ade and I were doubled up with laughter. This was the second summer after Ade had lost his razor blades and had let his beard grow. It was waist-long and thick, giving him the appearance of a Biblical prophet in a windstorm. And this was the time of the "beat" generation, with bearded young men and sad, disheveled young women drooping over guitars. The contrast between the beats and us, both forty-six, puffing about at full speed to keep alive, would tickle me for years.

After Ernie left I noticed that the birdsongs and squirrel talk were stilled. There was a sense of waiting which told me a storm was coming. I hurried to bring in half-dry socks and shirts from the clothesline, and Ade moved tools to shelter.

The storm came just after the sun set. Lightning forked above the hills. The first gentle rain gave way to hail that rattled on the roof and slashed at the earth. It passed in a few minutes and I opened the door to a scent as clean as that of new-mown hay. The little balls of ice lay in glassy piles, and blue jays dropped down to eat them like candy.

Such weather told us it was time to move Ade's pet rooster, the Crown Prince, and his majesty's two hens, Bedelia and Tulip, to summer quarters. Their winter home, a slope-roofed and tarpaper-covered house, had a heater devised by Ade from an old railroad lantern, and a perch. Though it could be kept warm at forty

below, it did not give them enough room for wing stretching.

Chickens being unpredictable, Ade opened their door only partway. The Crown Prince fell to the ground, picked himself up with dignity, flapped his wings, and settled on Ade's arm. Tulip followed him after a cautious survey of the outside.

But when Ade reached in to pick up Bedelia, she shot past him to a branch overhead, where she exploded into frenzied squawking.

"You take Prince and Tulip," Ade directed, settling them on my arms. "I'll nab Bedelia."

I walked slowly through the woods to the summer house—our first home when we moved north—smiling at the way the two turned their heads from side to side like tourists catching a scenic view as they drove by. I released them in the big run that Ade had built, wire-mesh-covered as a protection from hawks. Hideous squalls announced the approach of Ade and Bedelia. Ade let the beleaguered hen fly through the gate into the run, and shortly peace descended as all three scratched eagerly in the dirt.

They were jet-black Minorcas. Tulip and the Prince were large and gracefully formed, and their scarlet combs were spectacular. Bedelia was small, with a haphazard comb and the expression of someone who smelled something forgotten in the refrigerator. On the credit side, she laid bigger eggs than Tulip, maintaining her eccentricity by crowing instead of cackling to announce her accomplishment.

Once they were comfortably settled, we moved ourselves to the summer house, trotting back and forth for a day with such necessities as food, typewriter, blankets, and books. It was a stimulating change because the summer house had large rooms, high ceilings, big light-filled windows, knotty-pine walls, a double fireplace, a bright kitchen, our good furniture, a piano, and a screened porch for relaxing. I typed on the porch when it was warm, inside by a fire when it was chilly, and in all weathers except pouring rain spent some time in the majestic old forest between the cabins.

This kind of remote forest whispers of creation and the timeless things—life, death, eternity. I wandered under the green roof, looking at mossy mounds that covered long-fallen trees and

at scrolled bark on mighty birches; smiling at young saplings taking advantage of patches of sunlight. In the evening when moonlight touched the pillarlike trunks at the forest's edge, the spaces between the trees were great, arched doorways.

The garden south of the summer house was flooded with sunlight and with a dismaying number of raspberry runners that were thrusting up vigorous canes. While removing them, I yanked at a tough one buried in moss at the top of a low stone wall. The whole mass came out, to reveal a horrified chipmunk staring up at me from an unroofed tunnel. Hastily I smoothed back the earth, went for bread to put on the wall for the disturbed tenants, and retired inside to watch from the kitchen window.

Five minutes later the small householder poked her nose out from a crack between the stones, climbed the wall, and patted down the displaced pad of moss. Then she went to the bread, sniffing, ate two pieces, and carried the rest home.

Within a week, homemade bread on the wall had attracted so many chipmunks that we had to take corn from the chickens' supply. Eventually a daring individual took corn from my hand, and after that, the adventurer and what must have been all his relatives and friends rushed to the door whenever Ade or I went out, and sometimes one hopped onto a boot toe to look up in a most appealing way.

One day a chipmunk jumped into the chickens' feed pan. The Crown Prince bent down and the chippy sat up, so that they were almost beak to nose, staring at each other. I held my breath, because the rooster could surely kill or seriously injure the little animal with one peck. Instead he seemed pleased— maybe he thought this was a baby chicken—and made pleasant clucking sounds.

When the squirrels got wind of the corn supply by the kitchen door, the peace was sadly disturbed, so I left corn for them outside the front porch, which was near their tree homes. The squirrels were as effervescent as champagne and as sputtery as strings of firecrackers.

The chipmunk youngsters stayed out of our sight until they

could hardly be distinguished from the adults, but by July there were wide-eyed squirrel children everywhere. They hopped stiff-legged. They crept under grasses, tails twitching, until they could leap out at a brother or sister and roll and wrestle. I once saw triplet sisters playing train—the front paws of the rear two tight around the hind legs of those in front, while they hopped ahead with many falls and readjustments.

WE BOTH worked hard that summer, and by October, when we moved back to the log cabin, the knotholes in the floor were filled, and Ade had hammered protruding nailheads flush with the wood. I had written and sold some articles. Ade's new notepaper designs had been patiently hand cut on stencils, and I addressed his advertising mailers while he was mimeographing and packing the paper for sale. By and large, it had been a productive summer.

Now the hairy and downy woodpeckers were busy around the woodpile, hunting insects under the bark, so we asked the butcher to send suet with our next order. Ade hung a suet cage on one of the cedar trunks and the woodpeckers then breakfasted there, hunted in the bark during the day, and had a suet snack before dusk. A week later a young bear yanked the cage down. Even though we sympathized with the little bear, we put the repaired feeder away that night. At dawn we were awakened by a hubbub of cackling and drumming. The woodpeckers wanted their suet. Ade dragged himself out and hung up the feeder, waiting half asleep until the birds had fed to bring it in. From then on, the first one who heard the birds went through this process until the bears had retired for the winter.

One day when Ade was making more feeders, he got his beard tangled in the wire. While I laughed myself to tears, he reached for the scissors, saying, "I'm going to get rid of this right now, before I get hung up in the brush somewhere."

It was then that his hair, uncut for months and well below his collar, caught my attention. "You could let it get a little longer and braid it, pioneer fashion," I suggested.

"Or go across the lake and get Awbutch to cut it."

We stood by the boat skid, looking at a scene that does not come often. The water was completely still, and the hills across the lake, brilliant with the gold of late-turned aspen leaves, were so perfectly reflected that a photograph would not have differentiated between the real hills and their mirror image.

Ade slid the boat into the water, and we moved toward the far shore. Awbutch was waiting as we glided in to her dock. She caught our painter and tied us up with expert brown hands. "Company's good today," she said. "Mother's out in the woods, so I'm all by myself."

"How old is your mother?" I asked.

"Seventy-five maybe."

"Seventy-five? In the woods by herself?"

She laughed. "You forget. She's been in the woods all her life." Awbutch went into her cabin and brought out a chair. While she worked with scissors, comb, and clippers, I thought that our old friends would think it very strange that Ade should go by boat to Canada to have a Chippewa girl cut his hair.

"I'd ask you to stay for supper," Awbutch said, "but Mother says there will be wind on the water before dark. I don't know how she knows, but she does. If you don't hurry, you might knock a hole in your boat on those rocks by your house."

As we moved out from shore, we felt the slow rise and fall of the water ahead of the coming wind, and Awbutch's voice followed us. "I'll come and see you after the lake freezes over."

At Thanksgiving my aunt had sent us the wherewithal for dinner. Afterward Ade hung the turkey carcass on a cedar trunk for the birds, and tacked a large piece of browned skin to a feeding bench outside the cabin door. We were reading one evening while snow whispered against the windows and piled up in Christmas-decoration fashion at the corners of the small panes. Ade put down *Plutarch's Lives* and went to the kitchen to rummage for something to eat. I followed and opened the door to see how much snow there was. I sensed movement on the feeding bench beside me.

The little animal clutching the turkey skin tight to his furry breast was unmistakably a flying squirrel. His tail hung down like a flat plume, and I could see folds of fur at his sides. His enormous eyes were like shiny black moons, now filled with terror. I backed inside and he seemed to vanish, so swiftly did he spring away. We left suet and broken graham crackers on a shelf in the shed. Soon the flying squirrels accepted us and we could watch them feed by dim lantern light.

SHORTLY before Christmas we got an unpleasant surprise in the mail: a big bill from the grocery. The store did not give credit. They sold books of coupons to people who rarely came to town. The books were kept in the store, and when the coupons were almost used up they sent a note to the customer. We had not ordered since Thanksgiving, and the bill was dated December 8. We investigated and discovered that someone had used our name and our winter budget of coupons to get free groceries. There were not enough coupons to cover the order, so they had made an exception and billed the remainder.

"What'll we do now?" Ade wondered.

"We'll have to use some of the fire-insurance money to pay the bill. I don't like it, but we can't let it get around that we're deadbeats. We'll make do somehow. We don't have perishables, but we've plenty of staples, and Bedelia and Tulip can be counted on for a couple of eggs almost every day. Thank God we've enough food for them."

We had a diminishing store of canned vegetables; plenty of margarine, baking powder, and yeast; enough coffee to last until spring if we were careful; some tea, brown sugar, chocolate, and powdered milk; one small can of salted peanuts; potatoes, flour, and sugar in hundred-pound sacks; smaller sacks of corn-meal, oatmeal, and dried beans; partially used cases of spaghetti and canned mushroom sauce; and, outside in our freezer made from an old barrel stove, there was a little cheese and part of a slab of bacon.

Trying to create a Christmas dinner out of these materials

would use more than we should at one time. And nothing was going to turn up as it had the year before, when Awbutch's brother had come after the fire and invited us to dinner. We had snowshoed across the frozen lake and had a glorious day with his family—Awbutch and their mother and two cousins.

Bother a Christmas feast! We would do nicely without one. Ade's notepaper had done so well that he had been trying to find time between chores to prepare for some anticipated repeat orders. He could do that. I'd write something—and I'd better find a subject good enough to keep my mind off roast turkey.

It was very late on Christmas Eve when I heard the faint howling of a wolf, and stepped out into the falling snow to listen. The sound came nearer as the animal moved along the Canadian shore. His wild voice rose and fell, beautiful and deep-toned. As he moved on, one long cadence lingered and faded, like the voice of the wilderness saying, "Noooooo-eeelll!"

When Christmas night came, cold and star-filled, Ade had his notepaper done and I had a Christmas animal fable ready for final typing. It had been a satisfying day after all.

In January and February, the months of deep winter, an increasing number of birds and animals were looking for handouts. Every morning a pair of whisky jacks were at the door. I cooked seven pancakes: four for Ade, two for me, and one for them. I went out with a piece of pancake on each palm. They came, one to a hand, and settled down to warm their feet on the cake while picking around its edges. Then each tore off a section and flew with it to the woodshed roof.

These birds are often called gray jays, or Canada jays, but the local name, we were told, was derived from an Indian word for them which sounded like *wiskijon*.

One day Ade brought Tulip in. "The chickens have no way to wear their beaks down," he explained, "and the upper part is so long they can't pick up feed. I'll have to file 'em."

With her feet tucked between his knees and her wings restrained by his arm, Tulip submitted, complaining, though the

treatment was painless. I shall draw a veil over Bedelia's performance except to say that she had to be confined in a straitjacket devised from a towel and safety pins. The Crown Prince behaved like a gentleman. He sat on Ade's lap, making comfortable sounds, and did not object even when Ade trimmed his spurs, grown so long that he locked them when he walked and occasionally fell down.

Because we felt the effects of our unbalanced diet not only in hunger and weakness but in lowered resistance to cold, we were thankful that we still had plenty of wood to keep us warm in the worst weather.

THEN, one day in March, Ade was hit by an excruciating attack of facial neuralgia, an illness he had had on and off for years. After five days the pain subsided enough for him to take some soup. Soon he fell asleep. I slipped out with the toboggan to bring more wood from the diminishing supply in the carport by the summer house. But I just could not get the logs properly balanced, and the whole thing upset every time I met a ridge in the snow. I have no idea how many times I piled and repiled the logs on the toboggan along the winding path.

Next day Ade was still pale and weak. He was giving me a futile argument about being quite well enough to do his chores when there was a knock on the door.

The man who came in after kicking the snow from his boots against the doorsill was a distant neighbor. He had learned from the mailman that Ade had not come for his mail. "So I came to see if anything was wrong and I could help."

And help he did, bringing another toboggan-load of wood and filling every container we had with water, after chopping open a hole in the ice that had frozen over the lake. After we had tea and bread and margarine, with Ade sitting up wrapped in a blanket, the man left, saying that he would bring our mail next Saturday, so that Ade would not have to make the long walk.

Then Ade and I talked of the night during our first winter when Jacques Plessis, a strong-bodied, big-hearted woodsman

who was now our staunch friend, had first come to our cabin near exhaustion from a long trek out of the woods. Of how the man just gone had returned to us the help we had given Jacques. And of how there was always someone who, when he came on the little signs that all was not well, took the time to do whatever was needed.

1957—Install Wiring

IT WAS mid-May before the ground thawed enough for us to consider the garden, and almost July before we had normal June weather, and since our growing season is at best about a hundred days, we gave up the garden until the following year.

Warmer weather brought a blaze of dandelions to the clearing, which supplied us with summer greens. Our wild chives grew two feet tall, and we sautéed them as a vegetable.

Late one afternoon I went for a walk in the woods, and it was almost dark when I returned to the cabin. I wondered why Ade had not lighted a lamp. As I came in, he said too loudly, "I'm all right. Just a nicked finger."

He had grazed the side of his right forefinger with an axe, slicing away the skin from palm to tip. I lighted the lamp and got bandages and disinfectant.

"I was a little tired, so I started to chop with my left hand," he explained.

"It's time to get an oilstove. Your drawing hand is more important than saving money."

We sat late that night studying catalogues. After three evenings of planning, all was ready for me to write an order for the stove, another for notepaper supplies, and a third for our winter groceries. And we had managed to leave enough to buy oil at bulk prices from the tank truck, plus the necessary tank.

LATE in August we were almost buried by cartons when the freight truck brought our orders. We dined sumptuously that evening on canned corned-beef hash, tomatoes, and wax beans, and

felt considerable satisfaction in knowing that we had twenty-three more cans of hash and also twenty-four cans each of chili and salmon.

Once fed and rested, I became entranced by the stove. I could see hours of time freed for both of us. Now all we needed was a tank and some oil.

It had been a happy summer, alive with birds. Robins' cheerful songs filled the air, and a pair of rose-breasted grosbeaks nested near the log cabin. The chipping sparrows brought their young to pick cracked corn from the paths. Whenever we could, Ade and I left our work to listen to the song of the olive-backed thrush—its rising tones, clear and thrilling, going away in a delicate spray of music.

On a September afternoon we went for one of our rare boat rides and were drifting home when Ade, who was looking shoreward, blurted, "My God!" The oil truck was on the road, going out. You couldn't mistake that bright yellow.

We had completely forgotten about getting a tank and oil for the winter.

"Will he be back up the Trail?" I asked. "We've got to have oil. To move the wood stove back and go after wood now—"

"The Lodge closed Labor Day, but the mailman told me that fellow who bought the Greenfields' cabin is staying the winter. I'll walk over and find out if he's getting oil later."

When Ade returned, he grimly pitched his cap across the room and dropped into a chair. "The man says the truck doesn't come up the Trail in the winter. He also says he'll sell us oil in cans at retail price. That's resort price—and high. *If* I take the cans up there and bring them back."

"Up and down those hills? He's got a truck, hasn't he?"

"Sure. And he goes past here every time there's mail. I don't understand this," Ade said. "We've never had any trouble getting along with people, and I can't believe the ones up here are less accommodating than anyplace else."

"They aren't, but you've forgotten. Over a year ago someone

told Ernie we were kooks, and not a soul but the man who came to help when you were sick and the deliveryman has knocked at this door since. We've been too busy to think about it, but we're different and therefore suspect."

Ade stretched and grinned. "Oh, well, we can go easy on heat and watch the pennies, as if that's anything new."

He hurried to patch the leaks in the roof before the gray days of cloud and rain. My rosy begonias overflowed two containers made by cutting an oil can in half lengthwise. Every night I brought them in against the possibility of frost, every day took them out into the light, hoping this would strengthen them against the long winter on a windowsill.

A wind from the south brought the pine needles down in clouds. It was Indian summer, when the squirrels and chipmunks paused in storing seeds to relax in the sun, and the wild geese went high overhead in their trailing wedges, their cries like distant trumpets.

Then the rain came. Ade and I, gratified that there was only one small leak in the kitchen ceiling, went to work on the notepaper mailer and had it ready to go when a north wind cleared the sky and dropped the afternoon temperature to thirty-eight. The next morning the flowers were blackened, and maples showed their first gold.

In the evening we had the fun of lighting our new oilstove. I crossed out "Cut wood" on Ade's list with deep satisfaction.

The October days were bright-leaved and warm, the nights frosty but not very cold, so that we needed heat only a few hours a day. Freed from woodcutting and stove tending, we filled increasing numbers of notepaper orders, and I wrote two articles in response to interest from magazine editors.

One day the sun was so pleasant that I went for a walk without my jacket. The next day I paid for my sojourn by nursing an aching jaw and neck. A week later I knew from the throbbing that I had an abscessed tooth. Then Ade made a trip for oil, and came back grinning. Jacques would come by to take me to town.

The morning we went, the snow from the last fall had not been touched by the wind and lay velvet-smooth on the branches that reached above the little road. At the top of a long, steep hill I saw two giant spruces, sentinels that had watched when the road had been a foot trail, years before a white man had seen it.

In the Village, Ade and Jacques went off to shop while I faced the coming extraction with my usual craven attitude. This was foolish because the tooth was so loose that I hardly noticed its coming out. I drowsed all the way back to the cabin.

The next morning I woke with a severe headache, and by evening I was hot with fever. The thermometer showed 104.5 degrees, and I knew that infection had spread from the tooth. Ade was frightened but I was not. I lay there, as much under the control of natural forces as a tree in a gale. If my fighting power was the stronger, I would recover. If it was not, I would become part of the earth from which I came.

A week later, when I woke feeling hungry, I knew that I had gained an acceptance of death and an understanding of the natural laws that govern the steady renewal of life and growth. The circumstances that opened my mind to this came from our isolation, but the knowledge came from the forest.

Just before Christmas, when I was strong enough to walk, Ade escorted me to the lake, which was still open. There was frost in the air, like sparse snow, cool against my face. Almost at the moment of sunset the moon rose like a colorless sun behind the veiling crystals. It was a wonderful welcome back to the winter woods I love so well.

After we had returned to the cabin, Ade handed me a frosty parcel. "Two pounds of ground beef," he said proudly. He had hidden it in the barrel-stove freezer, as a surprise.

"Meat loaf!" I shouted. "Meat loaf for Christmas!"

As he opened the door to return the package to its storage place, he said, "It sounds idiotic, but I think of heaven as a pound of hamburger these days."

NEW YEAR'S EVE CAME on still and cold. I dragged out a carton and sat on the bare floor, cleaning the neglected records we had brought from Chicago. We had given our player to a friend there because it would be useless here without power. Handling the records only made me long for festive music to celebrate the coming year. And we surely needed something to make the night festive. Feeling depressed, I put the records away and sat by the window, watching the last light fade from the sky, hoping that perhaps a deer might cross the hill in the dusk.

Then I heard the sound of an engine running—it was not a car. I was about to call Ade, who was in the work building, when the cabin blazed with light. I was confused, then knew that he had finally gotten the light plant working.

Remembering Ade's list, I excitedly yanked open the desk drawer and had just crossed off "Install wiring" when Ade came in, all smiles. He reached past me to turn on our table radio.

We switched all over the dial. We could get New Orleans and North Carolina, but not Duluth. News reports were not much different from those we had left behind three years before. Commercials, once annoying, were now funny as we considered the utter unimportance of some of the things being touted. But music was still music, and attractive to both of us.

"You know," I said, "if I could hear Louis Armstrong sing 'Blueberry Hill,' I'd walk to town in my bare feet."

"You can do it tomorrow, then," Ade said. "Listen!"

And there was the well-loved gravelly voice coming across the miles with the song that I always feel brings me good luck.

Just how lucky it was, I would rather not say. Six weeks later the two articles I had written in October and which we had expected to pay our taxes and insurance, came back, rejected. I rewrote them for other magazines and sent them out again.

ON THE first of March heavy snow came on a driving wind. Deep drifts and fallen trees blocked the road. It was a week before the plow came through. The oil diminished rapidly, and Ade left to get more as soon as the road was cleared.

When he returned, he looked so discouraged that I heated some coffee before I asked what was wrong.

"He's leaving until May," Ade said wearily. "I tried to suggest he might lend me a key to the oil tank, but he said he was almost out."

We drooped in our chairs, staring at the wall. Suddenly I sat up. "We've been going along with the idea that we've been living an independent life, haven't we?" He nodded. "Well, the thought comes a bit late, but our independence has been a dependence on people who happened to be near."

"That's what everyone says—up here people *need* each other."

"That's true sometimes. But when something goes wrong we ask for advice. It's a bad habit. When we had a fire, there was nobody around, so we put it out. From now on we think first of what *we* can do."

Ade sat up as abruptly as I had. "And the current problem is how not to freeze before it warms up," he said. "First, let's consider the fuel we have left."

We still had some wood, but drifting snow had frozen over it so deeply that Ade doubted if he could break it free. If we were very careful, we would have oil for enough low night heat to prevent our food from freezing.

"It will help some," Ade said, "if we stop the drafts between the floorboards. Newspapers are perfect insulation, and there's a big stack left."

"And those shag rugs we dragged from Chicago can go over the papers."

"And the wood stove's still set up and it'll burn anything. I've a lot of combustible trash piled here and there. . . ."

"And there are those old clothes."

For the next three weeks the wood stove simmered and wheezed under its load of damp wrapping paper, torn boxes, moldy rags once intended for a braided rug—you name it. You can get a lot of heat from an old overcoat, but it is a good idea not to open the stove door because of the stink of burning wool.

We were constantly plagued by uncertainty. New snow fell.

The temperature seemed fixed below freezing. We were delighted to make use of the trash, but always there was an underlying feeling that we might have to start burning furniture.

In mid-March crows flapped overhead. Not long after, the crying of gulls drifted to us. They had come to fish in our lake. Then one day there were chipmunk tracks beside a hole in the snow. I put out corn, and the next day the chippies were dashing back and forth from their burrow, storing it.

In April the little brown house sparrows came. I had seen none since we left Chicago, where sparrows are a uniform dust color, even the male's black bib being hidden by dirt. Two weeks later there was a small flock of purple finches, their feathers ruby-bright in the sun. It was warm that day, with dripping icicles and leaves starting to show on the willows, and Ade went to see if he could dig out some firewood.

I decided to wash my winter-dull, stringy hair. A bit later Ade, returning with the wood, yelled, "Geese!" and I dashed from the cabin with soapsuds flying. We stood on the shore while the faint cries grew louder and the thin, shifting line of flyers passed high above the gray and rotten ice—calling, calling in high clear voices of opening waters and the death of winter.

After I finished the interrupted shampoo, I ran to the kitchen window to see hundreds of juncos in the trees and on the ground. I looked to see if one special junco might be there.

I had first seen him on an April morning a year before, when the whirring of many wings had brought Ade and me to the window. While Ade had put out corn, the plump, lively little birds argued in their twittery voices about who would get to the grain first. One flew to the windowsill and pecked at some crumbs left by the chickadees. "*Twit, twit-twit, twit,*" he said in an unhappy-sounding voice. He held his right leg awkwardly, and I opened the window a crack and spread corn on the outer sill. The injured bird flew only a short way, then returned and fed hungrily.

We named him Mr. Twit. When the flock moved on two weeks later, Mr. Twit was unable to go. He settled down with our summer birds and sang hopeful, coaxing songs.

Then one morning another crippled junco hopped into the yard, dragging a left wing that had stiffened in a spread position. Although she could not fly, she made long, hopping glides with the help of her good wing.

Mr. Twit courted her in his best manner and she soon became Mrs. Twit. The pair disappeared and we knew they were nesting, but where? One day Ade went out to clear away a pile of brush. He was met by a wildly fluttering Mr. Twit, who was prepared to defend his brush pile against all comers. It was as dense as a brier tangle and as safe as any place nearby. Soon we saw Mrs. Twit feeding two black-streaked fledglings.

When the aspen leaves were lying like gold coins on the brown duff, the fall migrants arrived. When they went, only Mrs. Twit was left, hopping forlornly on the first light snow.

We made friendly overtures and she soon accepted us. She stayed in her nest in the brush pile, where the thick mat of twigs held the snow, an excellent insulator. All had gone well until after a soggy snowfall, when overhanging balsam fir boughs dropped great clumps of snow and buried the nest.

Ade and I dug frantically. When we found Mrs. Twit, she seemed lifeless. We hurried her inside, wrapped her in warmed bits of wool I had saved to patch Ade's underpants, and waited. A half hour later her beak opened and closed, and I dropped water into it from a spoon. She swallowed some, then seemed to drop off to sleep. Fearfully I felt inside her coverings. The heartbeat was strong and steady.

Ade suggested that we look at her injury before she regained consciousness. The wing was probably broken and badly healed, but maybe something could be done. Very carefully I felt along the bones. On the underside of the main joint, a bit of twig was wedged under the skin so that it acted as a brace to hold the wing outspread. Ade held Mrs. Twit while I snipped the twig with a wire cutter and pulled the pieces out with tweezers. The joints had stiffened and the muscles wasted, but the wing otherwise was sound. There was a chance that she might fly again.

We decided to keep her inside until she was stronger. One

day I noticed that the stiff wing was slightly folded. It was time to begin its exercise. Mrs. Twit did not mind my slow and gentle flexing of her wing and it improved rapidly, but she did not move it herself. We tried dropping her a short distance onto a cushion, but she used only her good wing to break her fall. She was conditioned to being a bird with one wing. A week later a dog barked outside, and she *flew* to the top of the corner cupboard. Instinct had done what training could not do.

When the spring's big cloud of juncos came down from the sky, a lone bird with a crooked right leg flew above the brush pile, making coaxing sounds. There was a flash of gray and white, a swoop of wings, and Mrs. Twit was sitting on the brush, almost bursting her throat with song. Mr. Twit perched beside her. Then, singing and circling each other, they rose into the air.

They left with the flight, when the last snow was melting and violet leaves were green. We were not to see them again.

1958—Clear Brush and Paths

I was not very lively during the transition months from winter to spring. I came to the conclusion that, because of the lack of iron in our food, I was probably anemic. I had headaches, and muscular cramps and pains. Then, as I brushed my teeth, I saw blood on the brush and felt the looseness of my teeth.

Shocked, I knew I had scurvy. It was hard to believe, but I remembered Great-aunt Anne telling me of the "spring sickness" that was all too common among her forebears. I had sneakily given Ade a big half of our vegetables and canned meat because he needed strength for his hard labor, and malnutrition had caught up with me.

What I needed was vitamin C. Lemons. It was Wednesday and the mail truck was due to come up the Trail because an experimental twice-a-week schedule was being tried. So Ade took a little of our ready cash and went to mail it, along with an order, to the grocery store.

On Saturday the parcel came with a note. Since Ade had sent

too much money, the grocery had used the excess for a pound of ground beef, which they said was specially priced. They also enclosed a large chunk of suet, Jacques having once told them we fed birds.

"I've a feeling Jacques told them more than that," Ade said.

Those lemons were delicious. I even ate them in segments like oranges, without noticing the sourness.

While I was recuperating, I sat up in bed and tried to find some expenses we might cut to allow more food money. In 1957 we had spent $1,464. Taxes and insurance $352; oil and gasoline $160; food $480; household supplies $30; shipping for the last two items $90. These essentials took our total earnings of $1,112. The balance—for notepaper supplies, postage, six flashlight batteries, repairs to Ade's worn boots, a small box of aspirin, and the newspaper—came from our fire-insurance settlement.

We could drop the newspaper and let the taxes go temporarily, trusting we might be able to pay them before we lost our property. As a last resort, the fire insurance could lapse.

Ade and I had come to the forest believing that we would have to work harder than we had ever worked. We thought the depression years had prepared us, but they had been comparatively easy. Here we were poverty-stricken—cold, hungry, ragged, sick, and touched by flashes of paralyzing terror at the thought of never having some small pleasure or physical comfort or a moment free of worry.

And yet we found moments of joy in this innocent forest. The wild creatures were our hosts, our friends and companions, our teachers, our entertainers, the source of the material for our livelihood. That we should kill them for food was unthinkable. Instead, we helped them as we could and cherished the environment that was their home and ours.

NEAR the end of May I was myself again, and was kneading bread one day when someone shouted outside. I opened the door to the oilman, who said, "Did your oil hold out? I knew you'd be O.K. on gas—" He stopped at my blank expression.

Ade came from his workroom, saying, "I got the impression you didn't come up during the winter."

"Of course I do. Lots of places have tanks too small to carry through."

Ade then described our means of getting fuel for the past nine months. The driver offered to sell us oil at 18.8 cents a gallon—as opposed to the 30 cents we had paid—and pump it into a tank. He shook his head. "You don't look it, but there's a little city not rubbed off you yet."

Two weeks later the tank was installed and filled. We were set for summer and well into the coming winter. We moved to the summer house as soon as the sun was supplying daytime heat through its big windows. As we went back and forth between the houses, we watched the destruction of needles on our balsam and spruce trees by caterpillars, which the local paper identified as budworms. In less than three weeks the trees were almost completely bare.

Since there was nothing we could do about the worms, we went on with our work. Ade wanted to plant vegetables, and I wanted to try some flowers, just for fun. When the seeds and plants we'd ordered arrived, he planted in the plots we had prepared the year before, and I yanked out rough grasses and set my begonias out for the summer, planted some wild buckwheat vines around the cabin, and experimented with dahlia seeds.

Late in June we decided to use Ade's birthday and the week after to unkink our muscles and plan our work well ahead. Leisure was so nearly unknown to us that this took on the glamour of a celebration. Ade amused himself by working on the radio from our 1937 Chevy, damaged in the collision and still sitting in the carport. I settled on piano practice, which went well in spite of a number of keys stuck by dampness.

At the end of the first day we were reading in bed when a series of bumps came from the chicken coop. "Bear!" Ade yelped. We jumped up, grabbed the lantern, and ran out. The lamplight showed me the Crown Prince lying limp, very pale of comb and wattles.

"Did the bear hurt him?" I asked.

"No bear. I think he fell off his perch," Ade said.

I wondered if chickens ever had heart attacks. I slid my fingers under his breast feathers and felt his heartbeat—weak, slowing, faltering. Then nothing.

Ade said, "He's not hurt—what's wrong?"

I turned away so that I would not cry. It seemed too cruel that Ade should lose his pet on his birthday.

We buried the Crown Prince in the morning and decided that the best way not to listen for his vanished crowing was to go to work on the log cabin. I scrubbed the kitchen linoleum, while Ade climbed onto the roof to do what little he could about the many new leaks. Later I stepped out just in time to hear him swear and see his glasses slide off the eave and shatter on a stone.

He insisted that he could get along without them. I reminded him that reading was one of his most important diversions, to say nothing of his drawing, and that headaches from eyestrain would add no joy to his life. I clinched the argument with the local paper, which contained the name and address of a Duluth oculist who had spoken at a meeting in the Village. Secretly, I felt the trip might cheer him. Two weeks later, looking very strange in city clothes, Ade left to hop a ride with the mailman to town, and take a bus from there to Duluth.

I determined to make the best of my days alone by completing my sample chapters for a possible nature series for children. The second afternoon was brightened by a visit from the man who had been so kind when Ade had been laid low by neuralgia. He had heard that Ade was in town to see a doctor, thought I might need assistance, and incidentally brought a bag of grapes. After he left I put a bunch of them in a plate on the kitchen table.

That evening, before I settled to read, I went for my grapes and was puzzled to find strips of skin in a pile on the plate. I got another bunch for myself, left a lamp turned low in the kitchen, and sat in the darkened living room where I could watch for the arrival of the grape peeler.

A mouse appeared, seemingly from nowhere. He nipped one grape from the stem, peeled it carefully, adding the strips to the pile on the plate, then ate all the flesh and departed with the seeds, presumably to be stored.

Ade returned from Duluth with new glasses in time to watch the kitchen mouse go through his nightly routine. A few days later we saw another mouse investigating the inside of the piano. This was much too lavish a home for even the most discriminating mouse so, after making sure no felt had been chewed and no nest started, I closed the piano.

In August the mail brought a long-delayed IRS refund that we had both forgotten about. It was a check for $547.90, almost twice what we had expected and a small fortune to us. If my $600-a-year average from writing and Ade's notepaper business held up, we could eat better and relax a little during the winter.

A week later another envelope returned one of my stories, asking for hasty revisions as the magazine wanted it for their forthcoming December issue. They also liked the nonfiction nature pieces I had sent, and would start the series next summer. As if this weren't enough, the Metal Treating Institute, to whom I had sent an article based on a metallurgical project I had done in Chicago, forwarded a check several times larger than I had received for any previous writing. I celebrated mildly by ordering yards of red denim, on sale at a mail-order house, to replace the old drapes.

The garden produced erratic crops. Ade saved the plants from the hares, and the hares from being poisoned on rhubarb leaves, by improvising ramshackle fences from ends of chicken wire, old window shutters, and boards. The lettuce flourished and was attacked by slugs. The onions went to tops, but we found these flavorful. The chard did fairly well, and we left some plants to supply seed, which we could gather later. We got a few small potatoes that we ate in two meals. We could count on a good crop of salsify and carrots for winter.

Along about this time I crossed "Clear brush and paths" from

Ade's list. I could see by fall that they were going to continually revert to flowers, and so would never be finished. And almost everything growing here produced useful berries or blooms, or provided cover for our small neighbors.

One day in October I stopped to listen to the distant whine of chain saws. Ade said, "They're cutting the right-of-way for the power line."

"Where?"

"Along the Trail and up this road. Not actually along our road, but a quarter mile south of it, I think. The thing is, do we want power?"

"We probably can afford it, but I'm not sure it'd be worth it. Let's wait and find out what they'd want to do."

A week later we sat with a representative of the power company, reading the easement we would have to sign if we took the power. ". . . And to cut down from time to time all dead, weak, leaning, or dangerous trees that are tall enough to strike the wires in falling . . ."

"How do you determine 'dangerous trees'?" I asked.

"Any tree that's within its own height of the line," the man said casually. "Could start a fire if one fell on the line."

Many of our trees in the area where they would cut were more than a hundred feet tall. Signing this would mean that they might clear all the virgin timber on a swath two hundred feet wide, which would be a third of our property.

Ade smiled slightly. "We don't want it."

The man said, "Everyone but you will have power. It will add thousands to your property value."

Ade's eyes were on the forest. He said, "Sorry you've had your trip for nothing, but we'll live without commercial power." It was now almost dark, and snow rattled against the window panes. Ade added, "Something big's coming out of the northwest. If you don't want to be stranded, you'd better get on the road quick."

If the power salesman thought he was being ordered out, he

changed his mind before he had driven the three miles to the Trail. The snow came slanting thick on a high wind. By morning the chain saws were stilled and the land was white and soft and very clean.

Then the jays came, and the chickadees, and the nuthatches, and the squirrels—and Ade and I swept and shoveled to uncover their buried feed, while snow thumped down from the branches and now and then a tree fell under its burden with a long, tired, splintering sound. Winter had come.

IN DECEMBER a check came from my aunt for our Christmas dinner. We hastily sent an invitation to Jacques, and mailed the grocer an order for a feast with all the trimmings.

The next Saturday Ade dragged the big carton back on the toboggan. We found the bill on the bottom, along with more suet and a scribbled "Merry Christmas" attached to a bag of old-fashioned hard candies.

The feast was a success, from the turkey to the chocolate coconut pie. While Ade and Jacques leaned back and looked as stuffed as the turkey had been, I went to the window and gazed across our clearing.

A deer stepped out of the forest, headed straight for the Swiss-chard seedstalks that still protruded above the snow, and began to eat. He was so thin that every rib stood out, and I could see the bones of his flanks. His legs trembled as he pulled the stalks loose. When I beckoned, Ade and Jacques came to stand by me, and the buck looked up at us. His left eye was bluish, half-closed—blind. He jerked as though to run away, then dropped his head again to the seeds.

Jacques named him Peter and told us how to feed him. That night we saw him come stumbling to bury his nose in the cedar Ade had cut fresh for him. And later I saw him curled to sleep in the snow under the cedar tree, in the place that was to be his for the rest of his life—and beyond, as long as Ade and I may be alive and remembering.

We felt that his coming was part of some plan we could not

yet know, and that our task was to see him as strong and sleek as he once had been. We did not notice the difference when I took the cornmeal from the morning pancakes and cut the oatmeal portions in half so that Peter might have the cereals. It was enough to see him holding his head higher day by day. When the oilman, who had learned about Peter from Jacques, arrived in January, he brought three sacks of feed "for the chickens"—he thought we would not want word of our buck passed around, for his safety.

Except for helping Peter learn to look to the left with his good right eye, we did nothing to train him. Instead, we let him show us what *he* wanted. And so we learned truly to live with the forest; to understand the animals instead of trying to make them understand us; to leave them wholly free in the use of their all-important protective instincts.

When the snow melted, Peter began to roam, looking for his own new green. And when he left on an April morning, he was fat and strong and handsome. We did not know that his coming had been one of the most important events in our lives.

1959—Clear Trash

THE spring was late. I had paid little attention to the crunching and grinding of the lake ice, so it was almost a surprise one afternoon when the sheet buckled and rumbled and broke up with a roar. While the loons and gulls voiced their ancient calls above the freed blue water, the thick slabs of ice piled up on the shore and began to melt. The buds of calypso orchids were showing, and soon their yellow-touched, tiger-striped cups and lavender crowns would be bright against the duff.

Shortly after that we started gardening. Our garden tools, by the way, consisted of a bent shovel, a nicked hoe, and a partly tineless rake, passed on to us by a very old and kind man, who had been caretaker for the former owners of our summer house and who must have used the tools for thirty years.

The warm light showers brought out the budworms, which

denuded the trees even more quickly than the previous summer. The infestation was spreading; the hills across the lake showed an ominous brown.

When the snow was melting off the previously planted beds, we saw green shoots—carrots. Ade dug and found those we had not been able to get the previous fall in perfect condition. The salsify had also survived the winter. We left the plants and were eventually rewarded with a tall green row, topped by purple flowers that opened and closed as the sun came and went.

One day Jacques came whistling down the hill with the good news that he was going to set up camp for the winter within walking distance. The cutting of timber for the power line had left many good logs lying where they fell, and he was going to salvage the wood. He invited us to go to town the next day, and we accepted with enthusiasm.

After Jacques left, I made a list of perishable groceries, then turned to the wholesale catalogue. We had kept our profitable work going over the summer and might end the year in the black for the first time since our move. This meant more and better winter staples. I ended up ordering ten cases of groceries.

Next afternoon Jacques dropped us at the post office and went off to buy supplies. Glancing through the mail, we walked to the grocery and placed our order, then to the harbor, where we sat on a dock by Lake Superior, watching hundreds of gulls crying as they circled above a fish house.

WE HAD planned a lot of outdoor work for the remainder of August, but teeming rains came and fungi sprang up in quantity. There were mushrooms with white concave tops large enough to hold a quart of water. Others were pale green and deep violet. Under the pines were ranks of slender, dull yellow clubs. Lifting from the duff were fragile red and yellow and white parasols no wider than a thimble. The earth was dotted with white puffballs, and clusters of honey mushrooms grew from the cedar roots. Both of these latter were edible, and greatly enjoyed by us.

The few clear days were enlivened by blasting on the road, which jarred the cabin and tossed pieces of broken rock into the clearing.

Near the end of the month, various people called on us to suggest that we would surely want a phone when Northwestern Bell ran their lines in. They told us that would mean taking power also, because the power poles would carry the phone lines. We knew by this time that explanations about our trees would be met either with lectures or blank stares, so I said that neither power nor phone was any novelty to us and that we would continue to live without them.

One day Mr. and Mrs. Conrad, who had built a new lodge to the east of us, came to call for the first time. They were also from Chicago and thought we might like them to bring us something when they returned in the spring. Martha looked at the yards of red denim on the table and asked how I was going to make it up. I said by hand. And—miracles do happen—she said she had a treadle sewing machine, and would I like to use it for the winter. With visions of curtains, patching, sheets and such going through my head, I accepted.

On their way out, just after Labor Day, Oscar Conrad brought the machine, a turn-of-the-century model, its cabinet elaborately inlaid. It would even be a pleasure to look at.

The weather was perfect and Ade went to work on the trash heaps. The worst of them was the former owner's dump, filled with old clothes, bottles, cans, and assorted junk. Ade got it all ready to haul—on some distant day—to the dump maintained by the Forest Service. He salvaged an undamaged three-pound can of coffee, which came in handy because we ran out while waiting for our groceries. Things happen to coffee that has been repeatedly frozen and thawed for a few years, but the brew was brown and hot, even though it tasted like stewed wood chips. I crossed "Clear trash" from the list in the desk drawer.

The garden had repaid all our efforts. We had eaten tender rhubarb very early and fresh peas almost as soon as lettuce. The Kentucky Wonder beans had climbed fifteen feet into the trees

and we gathered thirty-five pounds. We had pulled small carrots all summer and still had a bushel of big ones for winter.
Our zucchinis weighed in at from two to eight pounds.

We had just tucked away the carrots when the mail brought
me an announcement that I had won a national metallurgical
award with the article I had sold the year before, and an invitation to the presentation of the plaque at the annual dinner of
the American Society for Metals in Chicago. A sizable check
was enclosed. It would be fun, I thought—to meet old friends, to
talk shop again. Then I looked at Ade's frayed shirts and my navy
blue pants, past mending and full of holes, and mailed an order for
clothes. This was more satisfying than traveling such a distance
for a few people I would never meet again.

LATE on the night of December 1, I was writing at the kitchen
table, but stopped short, chilled by the sound of a knock at the
door. An accident? Someone lost? I pulled aside the curtain and
looked straight into Peter's face. When I opened the door, he stood
waiting, his antlers almost as wide as the doorway, tapping with
his hoof, bobbing his head to ask for supper. Everything was
brighter because he was with us again.

And later, when the doe, Mama, came, Peter taught her that we
were safe for her and her twin half-year-old bucks, whom we
named Pig, for his appetite, and Brother, for his gentleness.

Ade walked miles every other day, cutting high branches of
cedar from well-separated trees, so that he would not harm any
single one. I tried not to go out when the deer were near because I did not want them to get too used to any human.

As the snow melted, they browsed separately more and more.
Mama was growing heavy with her fawns to come. When the
ground was bare and Peter went away to his special summering
place, Mama and the twins stayed on while the hurrying showers
of wet spring snow gave way to rain and the ice rotted. Then there
were the tracks of only one deer, and finally one day the corn we
put out for Mama was untouched. She had gone to the place
where her fawns would be born.

I CRAWLED out of bed and into pants and shirt, socks and moccasins, and flipped the top sheet on my desk calendar. "May Day," it said, in fancy type encircled by spring flowers. I pulled the red denim curtain and looked out—at a foot of new snow!

I touched a match to the fire Ade had laid, and put on the coffeepot. As I reached in the breadbox for a loaf of bread, the cabin shook under a blast of wind and the downdraft forced smoke out of every crevice in the stove. I flung the door open and rushed outside coughing.

Then I saw that water was running off the roof. The sun was warm, the thermometer read fifty degrees, and spring was really here. I brushed snow off a stump and set my begonias, drooping from the long winter, out in the sun.

Suddenly I noticed a snowshoe hare eating the begonias. At my outraged squawk, the hare fled and Ade came out as to a fire. As we carried the plants inside, I asked if he could make some kind of conservatory for them.

Soon afterward Ade built a small screened enclosure on a platform supported against the cabin, with the window forming the back. In warm weather, when this could be left open, the flower box made the room look spacious.

Then the forest presented us with a perfect day to do our first outdoor washing. Our old washer was powered by a gasoline engine that belched fumes and left the cabin smelling of oil and gasoline. So the space in front of the woodshed became the Sylvan Glade Laundry. Ade hauled out the machine, filled it with water, and coaxed and threatened the ancient engine until it started with a roar. I popped in the soap and the first load, set the machine to work, and we settled on the step under a delphinium-blue sky.

The one disadvantage of using the machine was that we had to haul endless buckets of water from the lake. However, we bought a secondhand water system cheap—a pump, a small gasoline engine, and a stock tank. Ade set the tank near the laundry, fitted

it with a cover, and bought some plastic hose, which could be used to fill the tank, water the garden, and fight fire.

Perhaps I cheated a little when I crossed "Running water" off Ade's list and wrote "six" for the years it had taken us to accomplish this, but I knew it was as near as we would ever come to a city water system.

In June the hot weather favored the budworms—they ravished the balsam and spruce. The newspaper reported that ninety-six thousand acres were affected and that trees completely defoliated for three years would die. Ade and I knew that the damaged species would not be lost because I had found little trees up to two feet tall that were untouched. But the sounds of chain saw and axe rose as people cut down their "dead" spruce and balsam trees, all they had of the original stand.

We learned that budworm attacks had come many times during the life of the big trees, the last severe one in the area having been in 1912. It was perfectly clear that if all the spruces had died at that time, there would be no two-hundred-year-old spruces left. We had counted rings on some that had fallen and were sure of their age. We decided to wait and see.

When Ade next went for the mail, he returned to announce, "We'll have a refrigerator in about a week." At the mailboxes, a summer neighbor on the lake had offered Ade a refrigerator he had just replaced with a larger one. When Ade said we had no power, the man grinned. "That's fine. This one's gas."

"How much?" I asked.

"Nothing."

I was silent. What can one say about such friendliness?

On the first of July the refrigerator was installed, and working. Ade went up to the Conrads' to arrange for returning Martha's sewing machine, now that she and Oscar were settled for the summer, and brought back two bottles of Coke, a pound of ground beef, and a half-gallon of strawberry ice cream. With ritualistic care we made the meat into patties and stored them to freeze. Then we filled two ice trays with ice cream and sat

down to eat the rest. Believe me, it tasted like a cone used to when I was ten years old.

In September, when the first yellow leaves were showing, Ade and I stood outside the cabin, looking at the high tops of the surrounding trees. The pine and cedar were full of promise, but the spruce and balsam were brown and barren. However, as we went on into the forest dimness, we saw unexpected patches of light and color, where the sun shone through the stripped branches to spatter like golden rain on the forest floor. In the newly brightened places, maple and honeysuckle had sprouted. We knew that, given time, the natural forces would overcome the worms and build another balanced forest.

In the languor of Indian summer, while the days were full of the smoky scent of decaying leaves, Mama brought her new does—Pretty, pearl gray, long-legged, and serene; and Fuzzy, short and chunky, with a face so hairy that she looked a little like a buffalo calf. Then Peter came to tap on the step before he followed Mama into the quiet places to mate.

THE snow fell, soft as down, on Thanksgiving Day. Deer watching and mail took up my time through December. Ade, when not scattering feed or shoveling snow, was putting together something which he kept a dark secret. On the last day of the year a letter came from a publisher asking me to write a sample based on a book I had suggested. After dinner that evening Ade brought out his surprise—a windup record player made of old phonograph parts left in the cabin, with pickup and needles bought by mail, and it played all speeds with only an occasional wail when it needed rewinding in the middle of a long-play. We got out our records. I made sandwiches and got the coffeepot ready. Then we settled to enjoy ourselves.

It was a sentimental night, a night of looking back. Ade found a record of a tune called "Geechee Stomp," an organ solo by one Thomas Waller before he became the famous "Fats." Glen Miller's theme song smoothed the wrinkles out of the day. Eddie Duchin's singing fingers performed for us, and Bing Crosby was

young again with "Good Night, Sweetheart." The thunderous chords of Beethoven were too much for our speaker, but Enrico Caruso filled our little house with *"Celeste Aïda"* and Alma Gluck sang *"Aloha Oe"* to the passing year.

On the stroke of twelve we went out into the night, dim lit by stars and the faint green glow of the aurora. Ade let the lantern beam swing, and glowing eyes told us that Mama and her fawns were coming for feed and Peter was lying under his tree. The merrymaking of past New Year's Eves seemed empty beside this one with our deer and our music and our forest.

IN JANUARY the cats arrived, a lynx and a bobcat traveling together. We saw the lynx first, clawing and spitting as he tried to chew grease from a drip pan put out for the chickadees. His haunches were almost skin and bone, and his ribs showed. He had come into the dangerous daylight, and the presence of man, because he was starving. The sun broke through the clouds and, as the warmth touched him, he lay down wearily and dozed. His fur was like ruffled gray plush, and he had a reddish snub nose, luxuriant whiskers, and upright black tufts almost as long as my thumbs on his ears.

Then he turned his head and we saw the bobcat stepping from behind Peter's tree to take his turn at the pan. This cat was thin, too, but showed his still-good condition by supple movements and a sleek, rust-colored coat. He had a tiger-cat face, tufted ears shorter than the lynx's, and a similar stubby tail.

This companionship between two usually competitive species was even more surprising to the game manager I wrote to for information than it was to Ade and me. We could not discover the bobcat's sex, but the lynx was male. We do not put aside the possibility that our cats were a mated pair. When together, they treated each other with the greatest consideration. We named the lynx Big Cat and the bobcat Tiger.

Ade and I, remembering our own times of hunger, were filled with pity for them. So we put out two piles of suet, bones, and ground beef about ten feet apart. As soon as we were inside, the

two animals came and ate quietly. After a short rest for whisker licking, they crept between the logs that supported the storage building. Underneath there they were sheltered, and this became their den while they were with us.

Our deer learned to feed when the cats were in the clearing, as long as a careful watch told them where the carnivores were. The cats were wary of the deer, too, and made no attempt to move near them and their sharp, slashing hoofs.

One moonlit night as I stood outside under a cedar enjoying the cleanness of the air, I suddenly heard rustling in the branches overhead. Snow fell, and Big Cat dropped into the drift beside me, longer than I was tall. He turned his golden eyes up to me, then blended into the shadows. He could have dropped onto my back and killed me with one snap at the base of my skull—but he did not.

We were running low on scraps and had decided to order something from town when Ade returned with the mail and the news that some ice fishermen had seen the cats cross the ice from Canada. This meant that almost everyone who came to our area would be looking for them to collect the bounty. If we ordered a large quantity of meat scraps, word might leak out.

So we ordered twenty-five pounds of bargain short ribs, canned boned chicken, some canned cat food, and our usual supply of suet and scraps. Everything was well-received but the cat food, which neither Tiger nor Big Cat would touch. Even the whisky jacks passed it up, and it was eventually eaten by some ravens. When we heard later that it was the newest thing to bait bobcat traps with cat food, we were pleased no end.

It was March and the snow was melting. The cats were hunting now. They were back to the beauty and weight and strength that had been theirs normally. Big Cat made three trips across the ice to Canada and back in ten days, as though he might be checking on conditions there. Finally the cats disappeared, and the deer were frisky, as if in high glee.

On the morning of April 11, when there had been no sign of the cats for eight days, I went to the lakeshore. There I saw a

double line of tracks on the ice, still clear—the neat, four-toed marks of a bobcat and the big snowshoe ones of a lynx. My eyes followed them to the far shore. Tiger and Big Cat, fat and rested and strong, had gone home.

1961—Make a Living

AT THE beginning of May the lake ice was still thirty inches thick, though water was moving beneath it. At night it boomed as it refroze, and Ade said it reminded him of big guns he had heard off the China coast. Then, on a morning when a warm wind was soughing through the pines and spruces, there came a sound like the grinding of a giant's teeth. The ice was moving eastward in a pack. By evening the lake was blue and clear.

Three days later the spring fishermen arrived. This year, due to the widening of much of the Trail, the men towed in cartop boats and cruisers fit for interisland service in Hawaii.

The weather brought the budworms earlier than before, and there were hysterical demands for spraying with DDT in high concentrations. Rachel Carson's *Silent Spring* was still a year in the future, but there was already plenty of evidence of DDT's dangerous potential. I wrote to the local paper and got a number of letters saying, in effect, "Get out of the county, you crackpot, or you'll regret it." I wrote the Forest Service in Washington and received a "There, now. You just let us look after the fish for you." From a forest insect laboratory came two entomologists, who said most of our trees were still in good shape and suggested that we pray for cold, wet weather.

We had the bad weather at the end of May and on into June. The tops of the big trees stayed green, and Ade and I rejoiced.

Soon Mama, Pretty, and Fuzzy appeared, and in mid-June the forest offered us a share in one of its most beautiful happenings. One day Mama brought her wobbly new fawns, Starface and Little Buck, to stay with us. She may have been influenced by a drought and by the scent of smoke from forest fires in Canada. We had a brook where one might drink, underground springs that kept the

surface growth green, and our land bordered the lake where one might, in case of fire, plunge in and survive. The Fourth of July passed with few visitors to the area. Word of the danger was spreading.

Day and night we smelled smoke, and the sun set red behind the murk. One afternoon after hearing on the radio that one hundred fifty-seven fires were burning north of us in Ontario, I sat by the lake and watched smoke rise just behind the hills of the far shore. It was a little fire—yet. Then great white puffs came up. Steam. Special planes carried water from a nearby lake and dumped it on the blaze. This one, at least, would not spread.

It could have been depressing without the animals. Their need of assistance in the days of almost nonexistent seeds and moist greens, and their confident gathering around the cabin, diverted our thoughts from the fires.

We had the deer with us off and on all summer. The twin fawns, Starface and Little Buck, rolled in the tall grass, drank together from a tiny spring, reared on their slim legs to box. Mama watched complacently.

Then one September day a sandy-haired young man in the green uniform of a forest ranger came to the cabin. While I put the coffeepot on, he introduced himself. His name was Chuck Martin and he brought us the news that Hurricane Carla, after devastating the Texas Gulf coast, had veered north and was due to pass over us in a few days. I could feel myself turning pale as he said, "With this virgin stand beside you, you'd be fools not to get out. I came to tell you that I'll be back in plenty of time to take you to town, along with some others. In fact, I'll come in now and then in the future—for some more good talk and coffee. Or you can drop me a line if you need something."

The radio was at its rasping worst for two days. Then a voice slipped through from Duluth, reporting that the storm would pass over Lake Superior, miles east of us. That afternoon the sky turned black. There were five-and-a-half inches of rain in an hour, and eight inches more during the night and the next day. All that time we heard the deep rumbling of continuous thunder

and could see the blue and purple of lightning far away to the south and then the east, as the great storm moved by. Our only damage was road washouts, a small price to pay for the end of the drought.

In October the mail brought a letter from the publisher to whom I'd sent sample chapters. He liked them and asked if Ade would do the illustrations for the book. A contract was enclosed. Two weeks later Pig and Brother returned, and I received the first installment of the advance on the book.

With the yard full of deer, our purse full of money, and my head full of ideas, I tried to start the book but was too excited. A good walk usually set me straight, so I went out on the road.

I walked a long way that Friday afternoon, hearing the last calls of the crows, breathing in the rich scent of autumn earth. A man drove along and stopped when he saw me.

We talked a bit, and he asked if we'd seen any deer.

"Just our old doe and her kids," I told him. "And the young bucks she brought with her. They're really beauties."

His shaggy eyebrows raised. "I thought you had a big buck with a fine head."

"Oh, you mean Peter. He doesn't come in this early."

I turned homeward with the sun in my face and joy in my heart. The long, hard pull was over, and we could earn a living, not lavish, but all we needed for the homely life that had brought us fulfillment.

Deeply content, I came back to our clearing. Pretty, Fuzzy, Pig, and Brother were lying on the bank. Little Buck and Starface stood near Mama, nuzzling her neck. Bedelia was taking the last dust bath of the season, while Tulip watched from the hen house. Ade stood with an empty feed pan, watching the deer.

As I slowly became part of this scene of peace, I thought of the words of an ancient king:

> *He maketh me to lie down in green pastures:*
> *he leadeth me beside the still waters.*

Some sound woke me the next morning in the gray light before sunrise. I sat up, listening, but there was nothing now save the chittering of two squirrels. I dressed, stepped out into the woods just as the first rays of the sun touched the treetops, and saw tracks with the edges still crumbling that told me Pig and Brother had just come this way.

Suddenly the crash of a rifle racketed through the woods, then another, not a hundred feet from me. I realized with a shock that deer season had begun, and started toward the hunter who was shooting within sight of the summer house.

Then I heard a man's voice. "Listen! There's another one!" I stopped, suddenly cold. I was in dark clothes, on a deer trail. I dropped behind a ledge, then slithered twenty yards to the road, just in time to glimpse a car with an out-of-state license disappearing around a curve.

I was shaking and felt sick, so I sat down on a rock and closed my eyes. But I could still see the antlers of a deer slung across the trunk of the car.

When I had inspected the scene and returned to the cabin, Ade sat me down and poured me some coffee, saying, "You're white as death. What happened?"

After I got over the attack of jitters, I gave him a rough summary. ". . . And they got Pig and Brother—both of them."

"You can't be sure."

"Yes," I said. "A car and a truck had parked at the summer house. The tire tracks were plain. They knew where to come. I'm sure now what woke me was the shot that got one of the deer. It was before the sunrise opening time. And the truck was gone when I got there. It carried the first deer."

The rest of the nine-day hunting season was a horror. We heard shots everywhere, which gave me fits of muscular cramps and vomiting. Working on the book was out of the question. We could only hope that Mama, being old and wise, had gotten her family safely away when she heard the first shot.

Several days later an old friend from Minneapolis knocked at the door. He hunted but was outraged at anyone who would

kill a half-tame deer or shoot on posted land. After a good look at me, he said, "So you know about your two young bucks."

"Yes. And I know it wasn't accidental," I said, and told him about the tire tracks. "I don't understand how they knew they were here. Bucks aren't usually hanging around houses in the rutting season."

"They were tipped off."

"Who?"

He mentioned a name I'd never heard of. But then I remembered my conversation with the man who stopped in his car the Friday afternoon of the day before the season opened. "Stupid, trusting, bigmouthed me. I told somebody about the deer."

Our friend sighed. "It figures."

"I don't get it," Ade said. "We've had no deer hunters before."

"There are more hunters now," our friend said. "And the local people know a lot of 'em won't come back to spend their money if they don't get their buck. The road, the power, the phone—they bring these guys who are too green to find a deer in the woods." He looked from Ade to me. "You've kept civilization out of here—and I'm with you a hundred percent. But it won't stay away from you any longer."

THE next night Starface returned, bleating pitifully for his mother. He ran from us and would not eat until Pretty, limping from a bullet in her right hindquarter, came cautiously back to her old feeding place and adopted Starface.

Then, to our relief, Mama came in during a snowstorm and Starface ran to her. She licked him on whatever part she could reach as he leaped around her. And, at last, our beloved Peter stepped out of the forest, unharmed.

For a while they came for food only at night. When we heard Mama's *stomp-stomp*, we went out with their grain. When they ventured into the yard by day again, all four vanished at the sound of a car or a strange voice. We were touched at their trust in us, but this did not take away my painful thoughts of Pig and Brother, whom I had inadvertently sent to their deaths,

nor of Fuzzy, who loved people, and of Little Buck, not six months old, who must also have met the bloody hand of man.

Then, in January, Peter, too, went to meet his destiny. Judging by the tracks we found, a wolf followed him and killed him. Something rare and irreplaceable was gone from us. But as I saw Starface growing more like him every day, I knew that I was part of the endless cycle of life, from which nothing is ever lost.

Shortly after that I found Tulip dead on the floor of the hen house. Like the Crown Prince, she had simply died.

This intensified the lingering shock from losing Peter and the others. Worst of all was my growing uncertainty about the people we knew. During the years surrounded by the innocence of the forest, I had forgotten the duplicity that can dwell in man. I could not forget that my peaceful walk and a few words spoken in misplaced trust had brought man's violence to scar the Eden that Ade and I had labored for years to attain.

We could still try to keep our place in the woods. But we could no longer plan on its remaining a sanctuary for the animals and for ourselves.

1962—Get Another Car

In May unseasonably heavy cold rains washed out most of the budworms. After the rains came hordes of squirrels—thin, patchy-coated, clawing, desperate with hunger. They had eaten the budworm pupae, but their staples for winter are the seed-laden cones of balsam, spruce, pine, and white cedar, along with dried mushrooms. The weakened balsam and spruce had produced no cones for four years, and now drought inhibited the mushroom crop. I cooked up some "squirrel cakes" of flour, dry milk, cheese, and sweet chocolate; and Ade cleaned Bedelia's house, scraping up a thin layer of grain embedded in droppings. The squirrels snatched eagerly at this unusual supply of minerals. Soon they were spirited and smooth-coated, but their matings were sterile. In other parts of the forest many squirrels died.

The interlinked changes were endless. The reduced squirrel

population affected deer, because cedar cuttings they brought down as they harvested cones were important food to deer. The wandering grosbeaks and crossbills, who eat evergreen seeds, did not appear, and there were fewer evergreen seedlings.

I WAS spending many hours at the typewriter, and when I felt mentally stale, I groundhog watched or took walks or fed Bedelia. She ate heartily, laid two or three eggs a week, and paid little attention to events outside her domain.

When the book was roughed out, I roamed the forest with field guides, double-checking my observations for accuracy. Sometimes I sat at the base of a big pine or spruce, closed my eyes, and just listened.

I learned to tell the movement of a mouse in dry leaves from the sound of a breeze stirring them. I learned to tell temperature by the feel and sound of snow under my boots. I could sense rain coming by the scent of earth on the wind, and be ready for frost when there was a certain tightening in my nostrils. I found that air can have taste, as when the "showers of sulfur" from the pines gave it a different savor from that brought by pollen falling from the deciduous trees. Once in a rare while I had the feeling of being watched, and turned to see a deer tensed at the edge of the brush.

THE day after Labor Day, when the rush of boats was over and the forest could again relax, was still summer, a summer of days bright with butterflies and nights when great moths bumped and fluttered against our lighted windows. It ushered in a time of unusual wild plenty. The balsam-fir tops were purpled by cones so frosted with resin that they glistened in the sun. The white cedars were so laden with little wooden flowers that their branches bent low enough for our deer to munch the leaves, although I hoped they would stay away until after the hunting season.

Ade put up additional "no hunting" signs. There was shooting in our yard from the opening of the grouse season, though. This

so disturbed my concentration that I started to work on the book at night, from ten until dawn. I finished the revision and typed steadily on the final draft in spite of a shortage of sleep, a dull awareness of the approach of the deer season, and a fear that our deer might return any day.

Then, on the afternoon before the season opened, it began to snow and Pretty brought her firstborn fawns to the feeding bench. They were little does as beautiful as their mother, nervous and eager, twitching snowflakes off their noses, leaning against Pretty when she bent her head to lick an ear. Ade and I stood at the window, and I could feel myself quivering.

"We'll have to get them out of here," Ade said, "and soon, so the snow can cover their tracks. But if the fawns see that we're threatening, they may never be at ease here. And Pretty won't understand it either."

I began to think. "I know how. I'll take grain out and put it under one of the big pines. You get the automatic. When they move toward the feed, slip out and stay behind the cabin. I'll tap on the window when they're through eating."

When the deer had eaten and moved some distance away, I stood for a moment, bitter at the thought of destroying the peaceful scene, then signaled to Ade. Through the roar of the big gun, echoing from hill to hill, I heard the thud of hoofs dying away. Pretty's confidence had been damaged, but if she did not connect the gun with us, she would bring her family back.

I flopped into a chair as Ade cleaned the pistol. "If Mama and Starface are anywhere near, they heard that," he said.

The next morning the snow lay thick, and there were no hoof-prints. Ade went for the mail, and I was at my desk when I heard a car stop, and then voices. I went out and saw the hunters.

I went in, picked up the automatic, slid in the clip, and started toward the road. A pair of hunters were just about to climb over a fallen tree and into our woods.

"What are you doing?" I asked.

They looked surprised. "There's deer down there," the tall one said. "Nobody lives there."

I pointed to our posting and down the hill. "If you look through the brush you'll see a house."

"Yeah—some old shack," he said indifferently.

"There're no deer around. You'd see the tracks if there were. And my husband and I live in that house."

"But we were sent here."

"Who sent you?"

He was opening his mouth when the other man, who suddenly seemed to sense something wrong, pulled at his arm. "Let's get out of here."

"Yes," I said. "Let's."

The first speaker got truculent. "You can't keep us out."

Smiling, I flipped the big handgun from behind me, thumbed the safety down, and said, "You think I can't?"

They went, with great speed, and I eased down the hammer of the automatic.

That evening our ranger friend, Chuck Martin, dropped in and asked abruptly, "Did you have some trouble down here today?"

"Not exactly," I said, and explained.

Chuck looked very amused. "Do you know Jack Wickersham? No? Well, I was up at the Wickershams' place this afternoon, and he told me there was a crazy woman down here, running around with a gun. He described you pretty well, and I just said, 'Oh, that's Mrs. Hoover.'"

Slowly the laughter grew. Finally Chuck wiped his eyes and said, "I figure it'll keep some of these heroes out of here. Just in case, I'll drive down the road when I come up the Trail. There's nothing like an official car to put a damper on things."

One ploy or the other must have worked, because we passed the following eight days without hearing a shot.

THE days slipped quietly into December, and I stuck doggedly to my manuscript, although I was uneasy until the deer came back. Mama arrived first, and Starface followed in a couple of hours; then Pretty with her now very timid twins.

We celebrated Christmas with Jacques, who came over from his house trailer for dinner. His truck was giving him trouble, so he took Ade down to his place to see what he could do about its innards. I had my typescript ready to mail when I heard Ade returning. I paused in the act of typing the label when he came in, looking rather dazed.

"What's the matter?"

"Nothing—only Jacques has given me his car."

I almost collapsed, not being used to people who gave away cars as they might a nice trout for supper.

"But what'll he do— Oh. Use the truck, of course."

"It's another Chevy," Ade said in a distant voice. "Not new, but not too old. It needs repairs, but I can handle most of them. Still there's insurance and the cost of gas and oil—"

"I can't think of a better way to use the rest of the second book payment."

After more than eight years, being on wheels again would be an adventure. I pulled Ade's list from the drawer and marked off "Get another car." I crossed out "Make a living," too. Only five items remained.

On January 8 Ade went to town to take his driver's test. On April 22, 1963, we made our first trip to town under our own power since November 1, 1954. It was exciting to arrange in person for our groceries and to help load them in the back seat. And, best of all, we no longer had to feel that an emergency of ours might lead to inconvenience for someone else.

1963—Clear Small Cabin

MAY began with soft warm air, fruiting mosses, and thickly needled evergreens, recovering now from their seige of budworms. The area once buried under wood-chopping debris repaid Ade's patient clearing with a blanket of bunchberries, their white blooms opening slowly across the patch as the afternoon sun reached farther every day. I found a secluded spot where fifty calypso orchids, rare in our area, were in pale purple bloom.

Ade and I, with our transportation, had prepared to get around and have some fun before the summer people arrived. But this was not to be. The midmonth mail brought a batch of editorial queries on my manuscript.

We did manage to squeeze in one picnic by the lake. We lay back on the sand against a driftwood log and watched three gulls bathing, until a boat swung in toward shore and the birds flew away. Our relaxed mood had gone, so we ate and went home.

While I was deep in paper work, Ade removed the trash from the storage building and hauled it, load by load, to the dump. With a vicarious feeling of accomplishment, I marked "Clear small cabin" from Ade's list, feeling that nine years to do it was not too long, considering the obstacles and more urgent tasks.

In the middle of October I looked out one day to see a grouse with one chick. While her single child fed, the mother stood on a stone and never stopped turning her head, searching for danger. At the same time a small doe slipped cautiously out of the woods with a single fawn to take some grain from the bench under the cedar tree. I heard, faintly, the far-off sound of a shotgun: a grouse hunter. The two wild mothers listened but, when the sound was not repeated, went back to carefully watching their young.

I felt that I had had enough of shooting around our home and sat down to write a letter to the local paper about it. It was a pretty stiff letter, but it was printed, and may have been responsible for our not having any grouse hunters near us that season.

Toward the end of the month the mail brought us the first copy of the new book, *The Long-Shadowed Forest*. And one of the people from the grocery, his wife and family drove out to show us a plug for the book they had come on in a magazine. I was touched, and thrilled, because this was the first published comment on my work I had seen.

Then it was the eve of the deer season, and I restlessly watched the yard. But whether it was my letter to the paper or the publicity attending the book publication, we neither saw nor heard hunters during that deer season.

EARLY IN DECEMBER Mama strolled across the snow with her well-grown new twins. Then the young mother and child who had come to the yard in October returned. We named her Little Doe, and her fawn Fatso. On Christmas morning, very early, I heard the squeaking of hoofs on the snow and looked out to see Starface standing where we had first seen Peter. He had brought a friend. This new buck was tall, unusually dark brown, and wore an expression that caused us to name him Wistful. Finally, on January 5, in thirty-below cold, Pretty came back at dusk, her fawns frisking beside her. She had been shot again, this time a graze from the rear along her left hip. She stepped carefully, but did not limp. I wondered if her brighter-than-most coat made her an easy target.

That winter with the deer was full of apprehension, because wolves moved into the vicinity for the first time in years. Long before we heard wolf songs in the hills, the deer told us they were around. They gathered in the yard, restlessly listening, bodies tense and ears moving.

So began a twenty-four-hour job which we divided between us until the wolves left. We could not use shots to frighten the wolves because this would also send the deer away from their food. Instead, we reversed our policy of quiet and were as noisy as we could be when we went outside by day. The deer came only on every third or fourth night, and we flashed lights and shouted near the cabin on nights when we felt the deer would not come. The wolves did not care for this, and several times we saw them pause on the lake ice, then run for Canada when they heard or saw us.

Our care in trying not to tame the deer paid off. Deer tamed and fed at other places for the entertainment of observers were less wary of natural danger, and thus became easy prey.

One day we saw a wolf pack of seven running on the lake ice. The pups had outgrown the spiky tails and awkward, oversized feet of babyhood and were almost as large as the adults, but whirled off, wrestling and rolling, to explore snow ridges. One started to investigate the wooden cover on our water hole, but the father

gave an authoritative bark. The nosy pup hastily left the man thing and took up a place behind his sire and mother. This discipline and obedience is characteristic. No animal works harder to provide for his family than the dog wolf, nor shows greater patience with his pups, even if they chew his ears when he is trying to enjoy an afternoon nap.

I received many letters from persons who had read my book, and most said something like, "How can you defend a creature as cruel as a wolf?" I answered all such letters more or less as follows: "No wild animal is cruel, because the word implies consciousness of inflicting pain. Predators feed as instinct directs, and their killing is guiltless. Only man has the power to understand what he is doing, and so only man can be cruel."

Shortly after the wolves finally left, heavy snows deepened the layer on the ground, burying the deer's natural food. So many strange deer came in to feed with ours that Ade went to town and brought back a hundred pounds of corn—all he could get, because so many other people were feeding birds and deer. So we wrote an emergency SOS to Chuck. The day he came the area around the cabin was full of deer. But by the time he walked down the path, there was not a sign of deer except tracks.

"I brought eight hundred pounds," he said, warming his fingers on a cup of coffee. "Too much?"

We assured him that it was not, while he looked out of first one window and then another. Finally he said, "All I can see is tracks. Where are they?"

I laughed. Ade pulled on his cap and jacket, and went out, saying, "Watch." He picked up the tree pruner and, as he walked up the path, three brown oblongs that looked like boulders lifted their heads, stood up, stretched, and followed him. He stopped under the first big cedar tree and clipped a small branch from high above his head. The three deer were at the nourishing leaves before Ade had walked on to another cedar. As the pruner kept snapping and more branches fell, deer appeared as if by magic, from behind trees, over little ridges, seemingly from the snow itself, and joined those already trailing Ade.

1964—Finish Inside

SOMETIMES people who see the forest only in summer, when its tallest evergreens are dark, its brush thick and full of shadows, find it somber, even depressing. I wish they could see it as it was that spring, when all its growth was touched with lightness and fragility. The little maple leaves were as serrated as snowflakes, and against their yellowish masses the new cedar looked more blue than green. The ground was arrayed in a varicolored multitude of shiny leaves that moved in the mercurial breezes to fill the open spaces with shimmering. The webs of ground spiders, dew-covered in the morning, added glimmer to the brightness. Then the ice opened and a few boats moved on the lake.

Some weeks later Ade brought me the first royalty check from the book. It was several times what I had expected, and the book was a reasonable success.

Ade stared at it, looked upward, and said, "Roofing at last!"

We were headed for town in fifteen minutes. Shortly after our return Ade retired joyfully to the roof. To the sound of pounding and the smell of tar, I sorted boxes of lists and notes, reminders of our struggles to make the cabin livable and attractive. They might give me an idea for another book. I could clearly recall the cabin as it was in 1954 when we moved in—water and smoke-stained fiberboard ceilings; floorboards so rough and splintery they could neither be swept clean nor effectively scrubbed; walls water-streaked and unfinished; gaps around the floor edges, openings between the logs—everything dark and depressing.

The little house was now convenient and comfortable. Ade built a storage cupboard in an empty kitchen corner. Once this was done and the wood cookstove replaced by a three-burner gas plate, with a large, heavy kettle that did duty as a Dutch oven, the cabin interior was settled. It was with something like complacency that I crossed "Finish inside" from Ade's list.

As the summer ended, I grew stale and cross in my futile

efforts to get an idea for another book. To clear my muddled thoughts, I went to town with Ade one day. The maples were almost bare already—hard frost had come early. The pines were shedding tufts of needles like thin, tawny shuttlecocks. And there were mallards everywhere that there was water. At one point, where the road passed close to a small lake, we stopped the car and were surrounded—ducks in front, behind, on both sides, even ducks underneath.

When we got to the Village, the harbor was full of ducks. They crossed the road in long strings, going to the back door of a restaurant for refreshment. I asked a friend where they all came from. She said that the departure of summer people had left the tame ducks to fend for themselves, and many had made their way to town, apparently looking for people to feed them.

We bought four hundred pounds of corn, all we could load into the car, with the intention of making sure that any mallards who came our way would be strong enough to take off when it was time. When we got home, our yard was dotted with ducks. Three days later there were more than a hundred.

It was a joy to go out with feed. Ducks came in a waddling crowd, to walk over my feet, stand on my toes, and look up at me eagerly. There were black mallards and mixed varieties among them. The lake was in an uproar all day as the summer's young splashed and paddled, lifted, and soared higher and higher with every trial.

When our supply of corn began to run low, we called the forestry office, and Chuck arranged to bring us some more. The night before he was to come we had a storm. Before dawn the rain and wind was so loud it woke me and, thoroughly alarmed, I got up and looked out the west window. Below a cloud of utter blackness the rain was turned greenish by an ugly light. I saw the big pines and spruces whipping and bending like saplings. I woke Ade when the roaring began, so that we could get to the strongest part of the cabin in case one came down on it. It was the sound of trains in a subway, magnified to fill the forest. I heard a tree cracking, the sound thin and sharp against

the hideous background of noise. I forced myself to stand still, and wait. The roaring swelled as it moved from the west, was deafening almost overhead, moved on toward the east—then dropped abruptly to an earsplitting whine and was gone.

"What on earth was it?" I finally asked.

"A tornado. I heard 'em when I was a kid in Missouri. But it's all over," he added consolingly. "Let's look outside."

The inky cloud was disappearing in the northeast, and blue sky showed above the western hills. The biggest spruce at the edge of the clearing was down. The yard was almost flooded—and full of ducks.

"You'd think there'd be more damage," I said.

"I'd say it went up the lake as a waterspout. We're very lucky. And so are the ducks. All we got were the side winds. They'd be mostly dead except that they sleep onshore." He looked closely at me. "You're kind of pale."

"I feel fine," I said blithely, "maybe a little featherheaded."

Later our neighbor, Martha Conrad, came over. "The road's all fallen trees, and the power and phone are out of service. I hope you have some corn."

"Not much," I said.

"What can we do? There're more ducks than ever."

"It's a guess when Chuck'll be able to get through now," Ade said. "We'll divide the fifty pounds we have left."

"And we can bake extra bread," I added.

He loaded the corn into her canoe, and we watched her paddling home through water ornamented by ducks.

Some days later Chuck came down the hill.

"We're checking damage to the timber," he said. "When I saw the state of the road, I wondered if you people had been hit, so we cut our way in. A twister went through toward town. Thousands of trees toppled."

Then Chuck's mouth fell open. He was staring toward the shore, where a solid sheet of ducks moved toward us. He smiled. "It's a good thing I had your corn in the truck before the storm hit. My cargo will really be welcome." He and an assistant brought

our corn. Then the rangers went on to clear the road to the Conrads' and take them half the grain.

As the days grew colder and sleet mixed with the rain, ice laid plates of crystal along the edge of the water. We could hear the bell-like music of their breaking as the water moved them against each other. Fewer and fewer ducks came for food each day.

On the Saturday after the end of deer season, the first staying snow came, as softly and gently covering the earth as a mother wrapping her firstborn against the drafts of winter. Ice was thickening along the lakeshore, the ducks were gone, and the quietest time of the forest was near.

The hardier cabin owners, who had stayed on to enjoy Thanksgiving under the big trees, left when the snow came. Proprietors of lodges that would be open during the winter were spending Christmas elsewhere. Ice fishermen would not arrive until the lake was frozen over. Ade and I loved these few weeks because they brought back to us the quiet that had been winter-long when first we came.

Ten days after the end of the hunting season, Mama slipped cautiously into the yard, followed by Pretty and Pretty's sister of another year, Eyebrows. Little Doe came with Fatso, rounder and more coppery than ever and looking very young for his spike antlers. And there were two young does with fawns, new members of Mama's entourage. Some days later Starface came.

I had decided that my next book would be the story of Peter, and with the deer outside the windows and the stillness unmarred by man sounds, the days flew by and the pages swiftly stacked up. By Christmas I had things well enough in hand that we could do something special. The day was clear and not very cold, and the snows had surrounded us with a Christmas-card forest. All of which said: Go for a drive.

We idled along through a forest entangled, tufted, swathed in glittering white. Some of the windthrows left by the tornado were so buried in snow that they could hardly be distinguished from outcroppings of granite. We came to the edge of a frozen lake overlooked by a bluff. There we ate sandwiches and drank

coffee from a thermos, while the clear sky misted over with mother-of-pearl and a slim moon appeared. Then a black wall of cloud rose to steal the color from the sunset mist, to silhouette the trees in white, and to engulf the moon.

We arrived home in the dark, just as the big cloud began to deliver its snow—thick flakes, feathery, floating, and gleaming in our lantern beam. And down the hill, one small lamp had glowed all afternoon in a window to light us home.

The night after Christmas was windless, faintly lighted by the frost-dimmed moon, bitingly cold. I became aware of movement through the snow-muffled woods—rustling as branches were touched, the faint creaking of steps on the snow. From the window I saw Mama nosing in the yard for grain. When I opened the door, deer moved all around the house, bounding into the brush, flowing in liquid grace through the shadows. These deer were strangers. Only Mama stood firm, stomping under a tree.

All night long the strange deer fed, and then moved westward. From their number I knew we had witnessed a mass movement of deer. This might be a migration to a wintering yard, in which case the herd would return to their original location in the spring. Or it might be a permanent move. Our section of forest was now too old and tall-grown to supply good winter browse. A new home amid the brush of a recently lumbered area would be better for them.

On a St. Patrick's morning without any new green, Mama's far-flung descendants came back to the place where they had wintered as fawns. They trampled the snow into a playground where the fawns leaped and flung up their heels, while the does stood quietly watching. The bucks were shadows behind the clustered stems of the brush. Mama rested in the sun on a cushion of dried horsetails, and I had the feeling that she was gradually moving farther away with every year. While the deer were all around me, I wrote the final paragraphs of my book about Peter's legacy.

Then, with the melting of the snow, the deer went away as gently as mist on a summer morning.

1965—Inside Toilet

THAT April Alvin Tresselt, my juvenile editor, came to the woods to work with me on a book to be made from my children's nature stories. He was an Easterner born and bred, and everything around us was new and different to him. So it was a pleasure, when he had settled in the cabin, to hear him say that he had had a mental picture from my letters and writings, and was afraid that the reality would destroy the image, but that it had not. He explored a bit, and as the days passed, the book grew almost without effort. Alvin titled it *Animals at My Doorstep*.

Ade and I were conscientious about reminding him to watch for bears, and I am sure he thought we were having fun, until he opened the door one morning to see a bear, almost full-grown, strolling toward the house, along the path from the storage building, looking larger than life and very black.

Very early one morning after our guest had gone, I heard a faint shuffling in the shed. Through the door panel I saw a full-grown male bear carefully pulling the paper from the shelf where we fed the flying squirrels. When it fell and showered his face with the remains of the oatmeal, he backed away in alarm. After cleaning his fur and eyes, he used his nose to push a bucket he had knocked over into its original position. I could hardly believe my eyes. Bears simply are not neat, but this one seemed to want to leave as little evidence of his visit as possible.

He walked a few feet in a beginning drizzle and lay down under the cedars, so relaxed that he did not bother to move when the rain increased. Why should he, with his furry coat? Instead, he rolled onto his left side—a six-foot-long storehouse of power—stretched his four legs straight out, and wriggled his toes! Then he rolled on his back, gave it a wonderful scratching, flopped onto his side again, and dozed. A half hour later he flipped upright, combed his face and head carefully, and went away with a bouncy walk that was almost a dance.

Friends came in one afternoon and said they also had noticed

the big bear's careful investigations and, because he was so polite, had named him Gentleman Jim. While we were talking, a mother bear and her new twins and her yearlings walked in single file past the window—and five bears make quite a parade.

This was definitely a bear year, which people said was due to the rain and the promise of a good berry crop. I do not think anyone really knows why though, except the bears. The rains kept on, the greenery was lush, and berry bushes bloomed everywhere. By late summer, however, the continuing downpours and the prevalence of clouds had ruined the wild berry crop, and the bears came by the dozens to hunt for food in garbage dumps near lodges and towns.

When we saw a cub licking up the cracked corn we had put out for the chipmunks, Ade changed their feeding place to a spot some distance from the cabin. The next night the big garbage can where he kept the feed was knocked over. Two days later I opened the door and faced a full-grown female, sitting on the step within handshaking distance. The following afternoon I looked up from my typewriter to meet the eyes of a four-hundred-pound male, standing outside my window. After dark he smashed a window of our storage building and ate some ten pounds of feed.

And so started the noises in the night. *Clang,* as an oil can was tossed aside. *Thump,* as a log was flung out of the way. *Bang,* as our washing machine was overturned. And there was the hair-raising rustle of thick fur rubbing against the door, the snuffling of noses that left smudges on our windowpanes. We tried everything humane we had heard of to discourage the bears, including ammonia, which stings their eyes and noses. But they were so hungry they braved even that. It was only a matter of time until we should find a bear in the house.

Both of us grew haggard from loss of sleep. Ade was trying to do a set of urgently needed book illustrations, but could not draw with shaky hands. So we packed a bag and drove to a motel by Lake Superior where Ade could finish the job in peace. Oddly enough, at night when all was quiet, I found myself listening, and knew that I missed the bears.

THAT SUMMER THE INFLUX of people increased steadily; the road was seldom free of cars. I tried to work on my book, but strangers kept knocking on the door. One afternoon I opened the door to see a woman and two children huddled behind a man, who had just kicked a red squirrel through the air. It landed heavily on the edge of our doorstep. I picked up the terrified, whimpering animal and felt for broken bones, while the trespassers insisted that the squirrel had attacked one of the children and tried to climb his leg.

I gave the squirrel a graham cracker from my pocket and let him escape up a cedar. Then, suddenly, I had had it. I yelled at the man. The group fled.

Little by little my frustration built up, and near the end of August I woke in the small hours with a very sick stomach. I fled to the privy, not bothering to wake Ade. At dawn Ade found me on hands and knees at the doorstep, too weak to knock for help.

Ade said, "We are going to get an inside toilet!"

I did not argue because such a sick spell would have meant death by freezing if it had struck on a cold winter night. I did say that the project seemed impossible without piped-in water.

Whereupon Ade handed me literature he had obtained earlier, about a gas-fired toilet operated by electricity. It sounded fine, so we bought one from a mail-order house, and he installed it. I checked "Inside toilet" from his early list.

Ade came back from getting the mail one day in September with the news that a phone cable was to be laid along our road. We had not wanted a phone in the days when our place was almost inaccessible and, therefore, safe. But the flood of traffic on the Trail had changed all that. I wrote immediately. A prompt reply said the cable would not be installed until summer, but that we could have a phone any time by the placing of a drop line from the main line along the edge of our property. Ade went to the Lodge at once and called the office.

By the end of the week we had a telephone. Even though it was on a party line, where conversations might be overheard and

which might be busy when we wanted to call, it brought back the feeling of being able to cope that I had enjoyed during earlier woods years.

After our neighbors left for the winter, I dug in on the book, going ahead through the falling of the leaves and the rains that wet things down before the coming of the snow. My stomach felt as though inhabited by bats as the deer season approached, but when two days of it had passed without incident and there was no sign of our deer, I began to relax. Then, late in the afternoon there were two shots nearby.

Ade took a pair of recently purchased binoculars, went out, and returned with a license number. He picked up the phone, listened, hung it up. "There's a phone off the hook," he said.

Three days later, after numerous trials of the phone, we knew that the line was being intentionally blocked. To know that anyone near us was so callous to the needs of others as to deliberately isolate them frightened me.

Six days later, when the sun had gone down to end the season, I went for a walk. I had only been out a minute or two when there was a shot so near that I saw the brush shake as the deer fell and the hunters ran to it. I heard four voices, then the slam of our door and Ade calling, "Where are you?"

At that moment there was another shot. The bullet passed so near my head that my right ear rang, and I heard the slug *thunk* into the ground somewhere back of me. Ade dropped down beside me.

"I'm all right," I managed. "Are they gone?"

"Yes. I heard them run back into the brush. Where did the shot go?"

"There," I said, pointing to the telltale hump where the slug had gone in.

He dug with his fingers and exposed the .30-caliber bullet. He looked at me, at it, then in the direction from which it had come, his face distorted by fury and horror. "Great God! If you'd been a few inches to the right—or standing—"

"I was," I said flatly. "Both. I moved just as the shot came."

151

He put the bullet in his pocket, held out his hand to me, and without another word we went back to the cabin.

We sat close together on the sofa and, after a long silence, he said, "We can't stay here through another deer season. We might as well be in a war."

Perhaps I am not very brave, because I was so relieved that we would not be here for the deer season next year that working on the book became easy. It was helped as our deer returned. Mama arrived first, bringing one of Pretty's fawns—a lively dark little doe we named Orphan Child. Starface was more than ever an image of Peter. I finished typing my manuscript on the bitter cold afternoon of New Year's Day.

It was a good way to start a new calendar year, but now I had the problem of marketing the book I had just finished. Unlike the first book, I had written it as a labor of love and wanted it to be changed as little as possible. I mentioned my quandary in a letter to a writer friend, who sent me the name and address of her agent. I mailed the script to New York and shortly after had word that the book had been sold.

1966—Fix Roof

SHORTLY after the sale of my book, titled *The Gift of the Deer*, I went to meet my agent in Duluth.

Ade met me in the Village when I returned. He had picked up our mail and, while we waited for lunch, I opened an envelope and took out my share of the book's advance payment. We decided to buy a new car. "Have you given any thought to the kind of car you'd like?" I asked.

"Well, yes. There's one in the window of the Ford place—good lines, but smaller than anything we had in Chicago. They call it a Mustang." I looked and was lost. So we went home laden with color charts and accessory listings.

Then one sunny July afternoon Mama slipped into the yard. She was less agile than she had been. From the window we watched her eat and then go to her favorite spot on the bank

to lie down and chew her cud. I hardly left the window until it was dark, because I felt that we would not have old Mama's company much longer.

Late in the night we heard her stomp for corn, and after Ade had fed her, she vanished in the brush on the hill. Then we heard a thud and a tinkling sound.

"She's been hit," I said, starting toward the road. We ran.

A man's voice said, "It's a damn deer. I've smashed my grille. Let's get out of here before somebody spots us. Bring the deer."

We had almost reached our entrance when the car backed past—a dark, heavy sedan, running without lights and with its powerful engine tuned to whispering perfection. Our dear, faithful Mama was gone.

The galley proofs of the deer story came in the next mail and, with Mama's death so soon past, I checked the proofs with a tight throat and tears behind my eyes. I heard every car that went by, and knew that where once there had been one, there now were a dozen. Human voices from the road and lake competed day and night with the sounds of breezes and birds. Our once-safe haven was no longer safe at any season.

When Ade went after our new car a month later, I was stuck at the cabin to wait for a foreign phone call; a friend in Oslo hoped to visit us on a trip to the United States. Some hours later I heard a strange auto horn blowing Ade's initials in Morse code, and rushed up the path to view our burgundy Mustang. I admired the black upholstery, got in and out a few times, sniffed the newness, and regretted that I could not go for a ride because the call had not yet come through.

Then one rainy day a young man came to the cabin to ask if we would sell him the 1937 Chevy. He was not the first person who had wanted it, but he was the first who had a real feeling for old cars and did not think of them as something to be used only to make a fast buck. I made a pot of stew and dumplings for all of us, after which our visitor rushed home during a lull in the rain, saying he would return.

While I washed the dishes, Ade leaned against the fridge and

stared—at me, at the ceiling, back to me, and again to the ceiling.

After some minutes of this, I asked, "What *is* the matter?"

"Nothing, except that this is the only heavy rain we've had for months and you aren't very observant."

This made no sense to me and I said so.

"The roof," he said. "I finished it when you were in Duluth. Do you realize that this is the first rain in twelve years that hasn't dripped down our necks?"

That night I crossed "Fix roof" off the list.

In October, when the leaves were bright, we stood by the road to watch the old car being towed away, to be renewed and eventually join the parade of antique cars. I sighed and Ade said, "There's another loose end tied up."

ONE evening in late January, when I went out to check Bedelia's lantern heater during the night, I found her coughing. I brought her inside and fixed her a box in the kitchen. By early morning her comb was hot with fever, and I could hear gurgling in her chest. Pneumonia—or something very like it. We dissolved our last penicillin tablet in water, and it eased her some.

I called a druggist, who said I must have a prescription. "For a hen?" I asked. He hung up. I couldn't locate a doctor. Then I thought of a Chicago friend who knew how we felt about Bedelia and who was employed by a world-famous pediatrician. I reached her and explained. Two days later the mail brought an antibiotic specifically for pneumonia, but it was too late. Like an elderly person weakened by severe illness, Bedelia faded until her heart stopped.

We buried her near the Prince and Tulip. I found myself still saving bits of apple for her, and every time Ade went outside, he started to check on her and her heater. She had been a living link with our first spring in the woods, and remembering not to do all the little things for her was difficult and distressing.

We were still depressed as winter moved toward its end. Ade thought that if the rising pressure of civilization should eventually force us to find a new place, it would be a good idea to

make a scouting trip as soon as the vegetation was in condition to feed our deer. We could return before the end of May, refreshed by a look at the Southwest, which he wanted to see as much as I did. He did not mention it but, after all, we had not had a vacation in thirteen years.

1967—Take a Vacation

BUT we were not able to get away that spring, or that summer, and in the early fall a driveway was built from the road to the lake, across the land adjoining ours on the east. It passed little more than a hundred feet from our cabin door.

Ade and I again talked over our situation. The owners of the land were not the kind of people to annoy anyone and had a perfect right to do as they pleased with their property, but once a road is built, curious strangers will roam the immediate area. Having no roadway into the nearby forested land had been an important safeguard for animals near the cabin in the past.

When we bought our place, we knew that changes were in the offing, but it seemed to both of us that they had come sooner and with farther-reaching effects than we had expected. Power and improved roads meant more building. Clearing increased runoff water and silting of the lakes; more cesspools stimulated algae growth in the clear water, as the privies of the old days had not done. More planes, snowmobiles, and boats added their oil films to the lake. Many users of the Trail thought the forest so far removed from civilization that no rules of sanitation and behavior applied in it, so they polluted the water, cut trees for the fun of it, left campfires burning, and littered their trails. A few highly commercialized establishments had so changed their locales as to destroy the wilderness character there.

So we sat in our hard-earned home, discussing our uncertain future.

Ade sighed. "There's only one thing to do. Get out and look around. We've agreed to go during the hunting season, and there isn't anything to stop us, with Bedelia gone and a good wild crop

for the squirrels. The Conrads are staying the winter, and Martha told me she wanted to try feeding some deer. And we've a car good enough to take us anywhere for as long as we please. It's strange how it's all worked out."

"Yes. All we have to decide is when to go."

"We aren't going forever, you know."

"Of course not—but something *has* gone forever from here."

THE time of the turning of leaves had come and with it our departure date. I opened my desk drawer, crossed the last item, "Take a vacation," from Ade's list.

I stepped out into the woods while Ade made a final check of the cabin.

The clear sunset light picked out every needle of the pines and spruces against the paling sky. I looked up the path toward the road where the Mustang, touched by the light through the maple leaves, waited for our bags. We had not wanted to leave until this perfect day was over.

I walked very slowly down the moss-edged path to the lake. The twilight spread lemon and Nile green and mauve across the sky. The melodious voice of distant loons reached me, to be immediately drowned out by the roar and splashing of a plane returning from some fishing lake in Canada.

I touched the water. It was faintly warm on the surface and still clear, and there was light enough to see the drowned rocks covered with algae, resembling brown fur.

I ran my fingers over the granite slab, looking at the crack I'd seen when first I had come here thirteen years before. It was a wide break now. The earth was patiently making soil from its rocks, undeterred by man.

I hurried to the car while Ade was warming the engine. When I turned around, the little cabin was still visible, lonely and almost hidden by the shadows. I looked up at the great trees standing tall against the dim sky, the guardians of our very special place. I commended our wild friends to the care of the forest, whispered, "We'll be back," and got into the car.

1971—Epilogue

WHEN we came back after our sixth trip of exploration, there was such a dense fog that turning into the Trail was like taking a road into limbo. I rolled down my window so that I might better see in case Ade needed guidance.

We talked of places we had seen. The Plains, golden with wheat, dotted with cattle. The Lower Sonoran Desert, accented by scarlet-tipped ocotillos, tracked by peccaries and horned lizards and sidewinders. The Rocky Mountains, white with lingering snows, whose peaks might truly house the gods. We had seen marvels—but had found no place for ourselves.

"Well," Ade said, "something'll turn up. Anyway, the fog's thinning."

He swung into our side road. It had been widened, and the moss and ferns of the south bank had been bulldozed, leaving bare and eroding earth. The forest will cover the scars, I thought.

After we passed the Lodge, we saw small roadside clearings with power poles, freshly opened driveways, piles of cut trees and brush. The changes seemed to have gained size and speed like an avalanche. I had known it would happen, but actually seeing it was depressing, and the drizzle that began added to my state of gloom. I had hardly looked around when Ade pulled up at the familiar cut-in.

"You stay here while I get the cabin door open," Ade directed. "It'll probably be stuck again, and you'd get soaked waiting down there. *I* brought my raincoat."

I waited, trying unsuccessfully to shake off my depression. Then I heard thuds, silence, more thuds—heavier the second time. The door must really be stuck.

So I opened a letter to pass the time. A university student, Gary C. Brown, had written: "War, hate, death. That is all I seem to read today. All this news about how man is *not* relating to his environment. What I want are positive books, books that tell how man *can* relate to his world—as you have."

I read it again. Just how *had* we done this? After considerable pondering I decided that, first, we had not tried to live off the land. We caught no fish and killed no game, because we knew that man can take freedom and life from living creatures, but he cannot give these birthrights. We cut no living tree and, aside from the produce of our garden, we ate only leaves and mushrooms—the gathering of which did not injure the plants.

Second, we had tried to leave as little trace of our passing over the earth's surface as possible. Our path had been a driveway when we bought the place, but after a cloudburst washed it out we let the forest cover its gravel and mud. The tall trees reminded me of those sacrificed for new power lines. When we did not want to use our limited power plant, our oil lamps gave plenty of light for reading and typing. Cleaning them had been a small price for virgin pines just outside a window.

As I was thinking that the trick was to find the simplest way of handling the larger necessities of living, Ade poked a plastic raincoat through the open car window. By the time I was waterproofed and had lifted my bags out of the car, he was halfway to the cabin with his larger load. I followed slowly through a woods so leafless that it might have been fall instead of spring.

The clearing was empty of deer. The door of the tiny chicken house was closed, and the run where Bedelia had once dust bathed had been dismantled two years before. I wondered what had become of the feed pan Ade had held in his hand on those past and lovely days. And suddenly the old feeling of shock and disillusionment came to increase my feeling of emptiness, as it did each time we returned from our wanderings.

Ade's voice came across the clearing. "Pete's sake, hurry up! I'm hungry."

I gathered my wandering emotions and hurried, envying him his recuperative powers, for he had loved our peaceful, gentle time as much as I had.

In the cabin, the blended smell of wood, mildew, and mice was comfortingly familiar. I lighted a match and turned on a stove burner. No gas. I went out to the woodshed to turn on the valve,

listened, shook my head vigorously, and opened the valve. I must have imagined that a deer stomped within a few feet of me.

As I turned to go in, I looked toward Peter's tree—and saw him standing in the shadows. I was frightened, for I knew that Peter was dead. Then the deer stomped again and, as he stepped forward, the clouds parted.

Sunlight fell on him, and I saw the white spot on his forehead. This was Starface, Peter's last son, so like his father that he had made me think I was seeing a ghost. Ten years old, he still remembered his first feeding place, although there had been no corn under the tree for four winters. The cedar's lowest branches were nibbled clean—while we were gone he and no doubt other deer had come to eat and rest here, in their own place.

I knew at that moment that this always would be our place, too. No amount of surrounding changes could take it away, because such a place is more than a piece of earth. It is where you find the fulfillment of your deepest needs, and you find it only once, if you are lucky enough to find it at all. But once you find it, you never leave it entirely and you never lose it, because it has become a part of you for as long as you live.

Starface stomped again. I called softly to Ade. He looked out the kitchen window, smiled at me, and filled a can from the small store of corn we always had waiting for our return. He handed me the feed, and I saw a squirrel watching me as he groomed wet fur.

As I took the can toward Peter's tree and Starface stepped back a discreet distance, I knew that I had found what all men seek— my place in the world of my time.

Helen Hoover

The Years of the Forest, Helen Hoover believes, completes her series of books about the years she and her husband, Ade, lived in the North Woods. Condensed Books readers shared their experiences in *The Gift of the Deer* (Volume 4, 1966) and *A Place in the Woods* (Volume 3, 1969).

The Hoovers still have the cabin. "We'll continue to live there all our lives," Mrs. Hoover says. But—for now—it will be a time of wandering. Her latest book was written in Ranchos de Taos, New Mexico, because Mrs. Hoover could find the quiet there that was beginning to disappear from the rapidly developing North Woods. She worked in a rented hundred-and-fifty-year-old adobe house— "warm in winter and cool in summer"—and she remembers most fondly the kindness of the villagers. "Gary Brown, who wrote me a fan letter in *The Years of the Forest,*" Mrs. Hoover recalls, "visited us in Taos. He said the Spanish people here were the friendliest, most warmhearted people in all the world. I'd like to double that."

Now the Hoovers will begin to travel. First, perhaps, to Florida; after that, it could be Mexico or Switzerland, although Mrs. Hoover has a hankering to see the Amazon. "We're just going to wander," she explains. "It may be productive of heaven knows what. But if we're ever to see the world, it must be now. We're both sixty-three and we've worked hard all our lives. It's good to feel footloose, and our only tie is the cabin."

This past summer was the first the Hoovers have not spent in the North Woods for twenty-five years. But Mrs. Hoover says she was not sorry to miss the thirty-day hunting season that followed. "I think they got Starface," she says. "I haven't heard for sure yet, but he hasn't been seen."

In time, of course, the Hoovers will return—but the important things now are voyages and long vistas. "I am going," Mrs. Hoover says, "to clear my mind after reliving, in the telling, all the years. I don't expect to be homesick. Perhaps inner security is the only kind, and I feel at home anywhere."

THE TAKING OF PELHAM ONE TWO THREE

A CONDENSATION OF THE BOOK BY

JOHN GODEY

ILLUSTRATED BY SANFORD KOSSIN

As the clock ticks off the minutes to disaster, a great city mobilizes to face the consequences of a crime so daring, so unthinkable, that no emergency plans exist to cope with it.

A subway train has been hijacked and held for ransom. Unless one million dollars is delivered in an hour, one hostage will be shot every sixty seconds.

With chilling expertise John Godey reveals exactly how the hijackers work, and takes you inside the most guarded arenas of city government as well. The politicians, the financial giants, the police, and the men of the Transit Authority all emerge as individuals caught in the same spiraling tension that ensnares the reader.

The result is a rare novel of suspense and adventure in which the supercrime of the decade becomes a fascinating reality.

Part One

STEEVER

Steever stood on the grimy southbound local platform of the Lexington Avenue line at Fifty-ninth Street and chewed his gum with a gentle motion of his heavy jaws. His posture was relaxed and at the same time emphatic, as if a low center of gravity and some inner certitude combined to make him casually immovable. He wore a navy blue raincoat, neatly buttoned, and a dark gray hat tilted squarely over his eyes. His sideburns and the hair at the back of his head were white, unexpected in a man who appeared to be in his early thirties, dramatic against the darkness of his complexion. The florist's box he carried was outsize, suggesting an opulent burst of blooms inside, designed for some once-in-a-lifetime anniversary or to make amends for an enormous betrayal.

Steever did not show any sign of anticipation or even awareness when the train approached. Four-eyed—amber and white marker lights over white sealed-beam headlights—Pelham One Two Three lumbered into the station. Brakes sighed; doors rattled open. Steever faced the center door of the fifth car of the ten-car train. He entered and walked to the isolated double seat directly facing the conductor's cab. He sat down, standing the florist's box between his knees, and glanced at the back of the conductor, who was leaning out of his window, inspecting the platform.

165

The train started with a lurch thảt tilted the passengers first backward, then forward. Steever, without seeming to brace himself, barely moved.

RYDER

Ryder withheld the metal subway token for a fraction of a second before dropping it into the slot and pushing through the turnstile onto the Twenty-eighth Street platform. Walking along the platform, he examined his hesitancy. Nerves? Nonsense. A concession, maybe even a form of consecration, on the eve of battle, but nothing else. You lived or you died.

Holding a brown valise in his left hand, a heavily weighted Val-A-Pak in his right, he walked to the platform's south end. He stopped by a placard bearing the number 10 that indicated, he knew, where the front of a ten-car train would stop.

He eased back against the wall and set his suitcases down, one on each side of him, just touching the edges of his shoes. His navy blue raincoat brushed the wall lightly. He pulled the brim of his dark gray hat decisively lower over his gray eyes, set deeply in bony sockets, which didn't seem in harmony with his rounded cheeks and the puffiness around his lips.

A rumbling sound heightened to a clatter, and an express train whipped through on the uptown track, its lights flickering between the pillars like a defective movie film. A man pacing impatiently near Ryder stopped at the edge of the platform, bent at the waist, and peered back down the track. Ryder heard the sound of an approaching southbound train and saw the leaner retreat. The train swept into the station, and its front end stopped precisely where Ryder stood. He looked at his watch. Two more trains to go. Ten minutes. He watched the tail of the train whip out of the station, then leaned against the wall, between his suitcases, and looked casually along the platform. A figure in blue was walking toward him—a Transit Authority cop. Ryder noted details: one shoulder lower than the other so that he seemed to be listing; bushy, carrot-colored sideburns curling down to a point an inch below the earlobes. A car length away the TA cop stopped,

saw Ryder looking at him. He faced front immediately and straightened his back. It brought his low shoulder up and improved his posture.

BUD CARMODY

As soon as a train cleared a station, the conductor was expected to step out of his cab and provide information and other assistance requested by the riding public. Although Bud Carmody was well aware that too few conductors followed this regulation, that wasn't the way *he* ran the job. He *liked* presenting a smiling countenance and answering dumb questions. He regarded his affection for the railroad as a matter of inheritance. One of his uncles had been a motorman for thirty years. Right after high school Bud took the Civil Service test. Now, when he became eligible by serving six months as a conductor—only forty days more to go—he would take the motorman test.

Meanwhile he was having a good time. He had taken to the job right from the start and had even enjoyed the training period— twenty-eight days of school, followed by a week on actual runs under the tutelage of an experienced man. He didn't exactly disbelieve the atrocity stories all the old-timers told him, but other than some verbal abuse, he had had absolutely none of the bad experiences they kept dwelling on, such as being spat at, beaten up, robbed, stabbed, mobbed by school kids, or hit in the face by someone on the platform as you leaned from your window when the train pulled out of a station. It was the last that worried conductors the most.

"Fifty-first Street, this station is Fifty-first Street."

He spoke into the mike in a clear, cheerful voice, and it pleased him to know that it was heard simultaneously in all ten cars. He inserted the necessary keys in the bottom of the panel and pressed the buttons to open the doors as soon as the motorman stopped the train. He leaned far out of his window to check the passengers getting on and off and shut the doors—rear section first, then front section. He checked his indication box, which was lit up to show that the doors were all closed and locked. The train started again,

and he hung out the window for the regulation three car lengths, to make sure that nobody was being dragged. This was where a lot of the old-timers cheated, with their morbid fear of being assaulted.

"Grand Central station next. Next stop Grand Central."

He then stepped out of the cab and took up a position against the storm door. He folded his arms across his chest and studied the passengers. It was his favorite pastime. He played at trying to figure out from their appearances what kind of work they did, how much money they made, where and how they lived, even what places they were headed for.

He braced himself against the roll of the train (he liked his ability to adapt to it the way a sailor developed sea legs) and focused his attention on the man sitting facing the cab. He was striking for his size—breadth, really, he wasn't all that tall—and his white hair. He was well dressed in a dark raincoat and new hat, and his shoes were highly polished, so he was certainly no messenger, in spite of that large florist's box. That meant he had bought the flowers himself and was delivering them to someone in person. Looking at that tough face, you wouldn't have thought of him as somebody who bought flowers. But you couldn't tell a book by its cover, which was what made life interesting.

The decelerating train dragged under Bud's feet. He set the pleasant puzzle to one side and went into the cab.

"Grand Central station. Forty-second Street. Change for the express. This is Forty-second Street, Grand Central."

RYDER

Over the years Ryder had developed two theories about fear. The first was that it had to be handled the way a good infielder played a ground ball; he didn't wait for it to come to him, he went to meet it. His second theory was that people in tight situations showed stress because they wanted to. They were appealing for mercy for their harmlessness, as a dog did that rolled on its back for a fiercer dog.

Ryder's theories were offshoots of the simple philosophy that

ruled his life and that he rarely talked about. Not even under pressure. He remembered a conversation with a doctor in the Congo when he had walked bloody-legged to a forward aid station. The doctor, a major, was an Indian, with an elegant, amused air, who plucked the bullets out of his flesh with a flourish of the forceps. A man with style, which didn't at all explain what he was doing serving in a crazy war between two highly disorganized African factions. Except money. Except? It was a good enough reason.

The doctor held the bloody metal up for him to view. "Are you not the officer they call Captain Ironass?"

"Excuse me," Ryder said. "You're looking at it. Is it iron?"

The doctor packed the wound. "Just curiosity. You've developed a bit of a reputation for fearlessness. Or recklessness. Opinion is divided. I'd be interested in hearing your own judgment of the matter."

"You've probably seen more than I have, Major. I defer to you."

"No such characteristic as fearlessness. Recklessness, yes. Not caring, yes. Some people wish to die."

"Meaning me?"

"Can't really say, not knowing you. You can put your trousers on now. I am not a psychiatrist. I'm merely curious."

"Not me." Ryder put on his steel helmet. "I'm not the least bit curious."

The major gave a sporting smile. "I do think I've gained an insight to why they call you Captain Ironass. Take care."

Watching the unhappy profile of the Transit cop he had stared down earlier, Ryder thought, I could have given the Indian doctor an answer, but he would probably have misinterpreted it and concluded I was talking about reincarnation. You live or you die, Major. It didn't mean you courted death or saw no mystery or loss in death. It just reduced the principal uncertainty of life to a workable formula. The stark profundity of yes or no: You lived or you died.

A train was coming into the station. Near the Transit cop, a leaner was bent so far forward that he appeared to have over-

committed himself. Ryder tensed and almost moved to pull him back to safety, thinking, No, not today, not now. But the man drew back at the last moment in a belated reflex of fright. The train stopped, the doors opened. The Transit cop stepped in. Five minutes to go, Ryder thought.

The train started. The designation of this one (since headway between local trains was five minutes at this time of day) would be Pelham One One Eight, according to the simple system that identified a train by the name of its starting point and the time of its departure. Thus, having left Pelham Bay Park station at 1:18 p.m., this train was Pelham One One Eight. On the return trip from Brooklyn Bridge-Worth Street station it would be something on the order of Brooklyn Bridge Two One Four. At least it would on a normal day. But today there would be some considerable disruption of the schedule.

WELCOME

Two stops north of where Ryder waited at Twenty-eighth Street, Joe Welcome had been on the Grand Central platform for fifteen minutes, while Pelham One Two Three, responding to the hold signal, waited for the next express train to pull in. He was restless and edgy as he checked the arrival of southbound locals against his watch. Fidgeting, he had walked an erratic sentry post of thirty or forty feet, alternately eyeing the women on the platform and himself in the mirrors of the vending machines. The women were all crummy. He derived more satisfaction from his own image—the handsome, reckless face, olive skin a shade paler than usual, the dark eyes glowing with a strange fire. Now that he had gotten used to the mustache and the sideburns, he kind of liked them. They were a hell of a good match with the soft glossy black of his hair.

When he heard Pelham One Two Three coming, Joe Welcome walked back along the platform so he would enter the last car. He was jaunty in his navy blue raincoat, slightly suppressed at the waist. His hat was dark gray, with a narrow, curled brim and a bright yellow cockade flowering out of the band. When the train

stopped, he went in through the last door, banging his valise, brown and tan in wide alternate stripes, against the knee of a young Puerto Rican girl trying to get out. She gave him a resentful look, started to say something but, assessing the malice of his smile, changed her mind. She stepped out of the train. Across the platform the express train came in. Welcome glanced into the rear half of the car, then began to walk toward the front, looking at the passengers on both sides of the aisle. He passed into the next car; the train started with a sudden jerk, throwing him off-balance. Recovering awkwardly, he walked on, his eyes sweeping the passengers. No cops, nothing that looked like a hero. He walked with confidence, and it pleased him to see so many eyes turn up to him. It pleased him even more to stare them down, mowing a whole row of eyes down like ducks in a shooting gallery. Bang, bang, down they went. It was his eyes. Violent eyes, and he knew how to use them, he knew how to scare the vinegar out of people.

In the fifth car he flicked a look at Steever, but Steever ignored him. He brushed by the conductor, a young stud neatly dressed in pressed blue, the golden Transit Authority badge on his hat brightly polished. A pale string bean, Welcome thought; if you hit him right you'd probably break his jaw like a piece of china. The image of a jaw fragmenting like a fragile teacup struck him as funny. Then he frowned, remembering Steever sitting there like a chunk of wood with that flower box between his legs. Dumb ape. Plenty of muscle, but *just* muscle; upstairs was an empty room. Steever. With the flower box, yet. He hurried on and reached the first car as the train decelerated for Thirty-third Street.

A few passengers got off; a few entered. Welcome picked out Longman, sitting opposite the motorman's cab. He was quite a distance away. The car was seventy-two feet long, right? Seventy-two feet, and it had forty-four seats. Big deal, making him learn that junk.

As the doors started to shut, a chick bumped it back with her shoulder and slipped in. He looked at her with interest. Short-short miniskirt, long legs in white boots. So far so good, now let's see the front view. He smiled as he checked her out. Big eyes,

171

heavy fake lashes, wide gorgeous mouth, long black hair falling straight down out of one of those sexy soldier hats with the brim curved up on one side. An Anzac hat. She took a seat in the front half of the car, and when she crossed her legs, the little skirt climbed halfway up to her neck. Nice.

"Twenty-eighth Street." The conductor's voice, singing out like an angel. "Next stop is Twenty-eighth Street."

Welcome wedged his hip securely against the brass handle of the rear storm door. Twenty-eighth Street. Okay. He made a rough count of the seated passengers. About thirty or so, plus a couple of kids standing up, looking out of the front storm door. About half of them would get the boot. But the chick in the funny hat was staying, no matter what Ryder or *anybody* said. Crazy? So he was crazy. But she would provide, like they say, the love interest.

LONGMAN

Longman sat in the seat in the front car that corresponded to Steever's four cars back. It was directly opposite the shut steel door of the motorman's cab. His package was covered in heavy wrapping paper and marked in black crayon: "Everest Printing Corp., 826 Lafayette Street," and he held it between his knees as Steever was holding the flower box.

Longman had boarded Pelham One Two Three at Eighty-sixth Street to make certain that sometime before Twenty-eighth Street he would find the seat opposite the cab unoccupied. He was the one who had been stubborn about that seat. He had won his point.

He watched the two boys at the window of the storm door. They were about eight and ten, round-faced, and intent on their game of driving the train through the tunnel. He wished they weren't there, but it was inevitable. On any given train, at any given time, there was sure to be a kid or two romantically playing motorman. Some romance!

When the train reached Thirty-third Street, sweat broke out all over him, as if a heat wave had suddenly swept the car. For an instant the train bucked, and he felt a heart-stopping surge of hope. Something wrong with the motor. They have to cut the

power, lead their passengers to an emergency exit, and haul the train away to the yard. . . .

But the buck disappeared, and Longman knew—as he had all along—that the train was okay. And so, out of desperation, his mind sought out other possibilities. Suppose one of the others had suddenly taken sick? No. Steever wouldn't have the brains to *know* he was sick, and Ryder . . . Ryder would get off his deathbed. Maybe Welcome, feisty and crazy as he was, had gotten into a fight over some fancied insult. . . .

He looked back to the rear of the car and saw Welcome there. I'm going to die today.

The thought came unbidden to his mind, accompanied by a flash of fire through his body. He felt suffocated and wanted to tear his clothing off and give his burning body air. He fumbled at the neck of his raincoat and worked the button half free before stopping. Ryder had said they weren't to open any part of their coats. His fingers forced the button back, and his legs began to tremble. Were people staring at him? He didn't dare look up.

"Twenty-eighth Street. Station is Twenty-eighth Street."

He was up on his feet, still trembling, but moving well enough, dragging his package after him. He stood facing the cab door, bracing against the rapid deceleration. He glanced at the rear of the car. Welcome had not moved. Longman watched the people move forward on the platform, waiting for the doors to open. He saw Ryder leaning against the wall, very relaxed.

DENNY DOYLE

Somewhere on this run, Denny Doyle had spotted a face on a platform that reminded him of someone. It kept tantalizing him until, just as he was pulling out of Thirty-third, it popped into his head. It was one of those bony, black Irish faces you always saw in pictures of dead members of the IRA. The person it reminded him of was that *Daily News* reporter who had come snooping around to write an article on the subways. The TA Public Relations Department had made Denny available to him as "a typical veteran motorman." He had asked a lot of questions,

some of which seemed ridiculous at first, but were pretty smart when you thought about them.

"What do you fellows think about when you're driving the train?"

For a wild second Denny thought it was a trap, that the reporter had somehow latched on to his secret, but that was impossible. He had never breathed a word of it to a living soul. So he had handed the reporter a deadpan answer. "A motorman don't have time to think about anything except his job. There's a lot to it. I watch the signals, the switches, the doors, I try to give the passengers a smooth ride, I keep an eagle eye on the rail. We have a saying, 'Know your rail.'" He *did* know his rail, so damned well that he hadn't made a serious mistake in twenty years. He knew more than his rail; he understood how the trains worked. He knew that each car was driven by four 100-horsepower traction motors, one for each axle; that the third rail fed in 600-volt direct current through the contact shoes; that moving his controller into power position sent a signal to each car's motor control unit. He even knew that the cars cost almost a quarter of a million dollars apiece, which meant that when you were operating a ten-car train, you were in charge of two and a half million dollars' worth of equipment!

The truth was that you did do almost the whole job automatically, without thinking about it. Take the holding lights back at Grand Central. He had known they were up without really seeing them and known when they went off. Now, heading for Twenty-eighth, he knew he was at the right speed for the red to turn amber ahead of him, and knew that if he did have to hit the brake he could do it without shaking up the passengers. You didn't have to think about all that; you just *did* it.

Peg had asked him, one time, the same question the reporter had. She said, "What in hell do you think about all day?"

"I think about God, Peg," he had said solemnly, and she had told him to save that for Father Morrissey. But what could he do—tell her that he added up weight? You had to do *something* or flip your lid. He was willing to take a bet that plenty of other motormen played games. At least his pastime was not sinful.

He added up weight. At Thirty-third he had dropped about twenty riders and picked up maybe a dozen. A loss of about eight. At 150 pounds per passenger, the net loss was 1200 pounds, giving him a current total of roughly 793,800 pounds, including the weight of the cars. Naturally, he could never tell *exactly* how many people got on or off, so it was really just an educated guess. But he was pretty good at it, even in the rush-hour mob scene.

According to the Transit Authority, the top limit you could squeeze into a car was 180, but at times, especially when there were delays, you got at least another 20 per car—all 44 seats filled and a good 155 to 160 standing. So you could believe the old story about the man who died of a heart attack at Union Square and had to travel into Brooklyn before enough passengers got out so he could fall down.

Denny Doyle smiled, thinking of one rush hour a few years ago when a main had burst and flooded the tracks. By the time the trains got moving again, there was a sea of humanity on every platform. That night, at one point, he had been hauling well over a million pounds!

He was still smiling as he swept into the Twenty-eighth Street station.

TOM BERRY

Eyes shut, sprawled in his seat in the front section of the first car, Tom Berry gave himself in trust to the train, soothed by its predictable rocking and yawing. He made no effort to keep tally on stations slipping by. He knew he would rise at Astor Place, prompted by habit and that sixth sense, somehow allied to the instinct for survival, that New Yorkers developed. Like animals in a jungle, like plants, they adapted, mutated toward specific defenses created to cope with specific threats.

He smiled at his conceit and lingered over it, refining it, even working up the casual phrasing he would use in telling it to Deedee. It occurred to him, not quite for the first time, that he was *zeroed in* on Deedee. Nothing counted unless he shared it with her. It might be love. At least that was one possible label to put on

the complexity of crazy and contradictory emotions they were tangled up in.

His brows formed a frown as he considered yesterday afternoon. He had half run to her freaky pad with his heart beating high in the excitement of seeing her. She had opened the door to his knock and immediately about-faced and left him standing, his mouth unhinged on an aborted smile. Even in this moment of dismay and approaching anger she knocked him out, and never mind the uniform that worked overtime at disguising her beauty: the denims raggedly cut just above the knees, the steel-rimmed glasses, the shiny brown hair dragged back at the sides of her head and then allowed to fend for itself.

Her voice floated to him. "I'm not going to see you anymore."

He had expected it and had gauged the exact tone. "I think you ought to change your name," he said.

He meant to throw her off-balance with an irrelevancy. But as soon as he spoke he recognized the ambiguity of his words.

"I don't believe in marriage," she said, turning. "Even if I did, I'd sooner shack up with a . . . an anything . . . than marry a pig."

"I wasn't proposing marriage. I meant *your* name. Deedee. It's too cute. Revolutionaries should have no-nonsense names. Stalin, Lenin, Mao, Che. What *is* your right name?"

"What's the difference? I detest it." She shrugged. "Doris."

She detested a number of things besides her name: the establishment, male dominance, wars, poverty, cops, and, especially, her father, that eminently successful accountant who had provided an education at an Ivy League college and who almost—but not quite—understood her, and from whom, to his extreme distress, she would now accept money only in the direst straits.

Her lack of consistency bugged Tom. If she hated her father, she shouldn't take money from him, and if she hated cops, she damned well shouldn't be seeing one. But she was flushed at the moment, and very pretty, and somehow defenseless. He said gently, "All right, what have I done?"

"You *brutalized* an innocent black man."

"Oh. Oh, yes. Is that what I did?"

"Two friends of mine saw it all. On St. Marks Place. Not a half hour after you left here, you beat the life out of a black man who was doing absolutely nothing wrong."

"He wasn't exactly doing *nothing*. He was urinating on a woman. She naturally objected."

"So you beat him to a pulp."

"Did I?"

"My friends recognize police brutality when they see it."

"Look," Berry said patiently. "You weren't there. Did your friends see him pull a knife on me?"

"Exactly the kind of thing I *expected* you to say."

"Your friends didn't see that part of it? And they were there, right? Well, I was there, too. I intervened—"

"By what right?"

"I'm a cop," he said in exasperation. "I'm being paid to maintain order. That punk's rights weren't being infringed upon—the woman's were. The Constitution gives everybody the right to freedom from being used as a dog's lamppost. I intervened on behalf of the Constitution."

"Above all, don't try to be funny about it."

"I pushed him away from the woman and told him to get the hell off the street. He pulled a knife and went for me."

"You didn't hit him or anything?"

"I gave him a shove. A nudge, to get him moving."

"Ah. Excessive force."

"*He* used excessive force. He came at me with a knife. I took it away from him, and in the process I broke his wrist."

"Breaking a man's wrist isn't using excessive force?"

"He kept trying to stab me. I'm not ready to go that far for the sake of community relations." She was silent, frowning. "Or," he said deliberately, "to please my girl and her half-baked ideas."

She moved with astonishing speed, hurling herself at him. "Get out of here! Get lost, you pig! Pig!"

He underestimated the force of her rush. It slammed him back against the bookcase. Laughing, protesting, he tried to catch her hands, but she surprised him again. She doubled up her fist and

hit him in the stomach. When he straightened up, he grabbed her and began to shake her. Her teeth rattled. He saw a look of pure rage come into her eyes, and she tried to knee him in the groin. He twisted away, then caught her knee and imprisoned it between his thighs. Suddenly she stopped struggling.

And so to bed. He smiled reminiscently. The train stopped, and he opened his eyes a slit to check the station. Twenty-eighth. Three more stops. He ached to see her.

RYDER

Waiting at Twenty-eighth Street, Ryder looked about him incuriously. Then Pelham One Two Three came on as subway trains always do, with the appearance of going too fast to be able to stop. But the first car halted smoothly in front of Ryder. He picked up his bags, holding them both somewhat awkwardly in his left hand, and walked without haste toward the motorman's cab, his right hand in the pocket of his raincoat on the grip of his gun.

The motorman was leaning far out of his window, watching the passengers board. He was middle-aged, with a ruddy face and silvery gray hair. Ryder rested his shoulder against the side of the train and, in the same moment that the motorman became aware that his view of the platform was blocked off, Ryder placed the muzzle of the gun against his head.

Denny Doyle jerked his head back in a violent reflex and struck it against the window frame. Ryder crooked his hand inside the window and this time carefully placed the gun against the motorman's cheek, directly under his right eye.

"Unlock your cab door," Ryder said. His voice was flat, uninflected. The motorman seemed dazed. Ryder leaned on the gun, feeling the man's soft cheek give to the pressure. "Pay attention to me. Open your cab door or I'll kill you."

The motorman nodded, but didn't otherwise move. He looked paralyzed; his high-colored skin had turned gray.

Ryder spoke more slowly. "I'm going to tell you this just once more. Then I'm going to shoot your face off. Open that door. Don't do anything else. Don't make a sound. Do it *now*."

The motorman's left hand slid blindly along the steel door until it felt the latch, and Ryder heard the tiny click as the lock disengaged. The door was pulled open, and Longman, who had been waiting inside the car, edged into the cab, pulling his package after him. Ryder then tucked his gun back in his coat pocket and carried his bags into the train. The moment he was inside, the doors shut.

BUD CARMODY

A voice said, "Turn around, I got something to show you."

Bud Carmody was hanging out the window of the conductor's cab, observing the Twenty-eighth Street platform. The voice came from directly behind him. Something hard jarred the base of his spine. "This is a gun. Come in and turn around slow."

Bud pulled his head in. As he turned, the gun remained in contact with his body and ended up nested weightily in his ribs. He was nose to nose with the florist-box man.

Bud said in a pinched voice, "What's the matter?"

"Do exactly like I tell you," the man said. "If you don't, I'm going to hurt you." He twisted the gun slightly. The front sight pinched the thin skin over Bud's ribs, and he almost cried out with the pain. "You going to do what I tell you to?"

"Yes," Bud said. "But I haven't got any money. Don't hurt me." He tried not to look at the man, but he couldn't avoid it. The man's face was large and dark-complexioned, but his eyes were light and they seemed to have no expression and no depth. There was no entrance in them—as he had heard eyes spoken of—no entrance to the soul.

"Go back out the window; check your rear-section cars, and if the platform is clear, shut them up. Just the rear section. Keep the front cars open. You got that?"

Bud nodded. He wasn't sure he could speak if he tried.

"Then do it," the man said. And Bud, with the gun shifted back to his spine, put his head out of the window, pressed the button, and saw the rear doors shut.

"Stay right where you are," the man said, and then put his head out of the window beside Bud's. It was a tight squeeze. He looked

toward the front, and Bud felt his breath on his cheek. Someone was talking into the window of the motorman's cab. It looked natural enough, but Bud knew there was a connection with the man in his own cab.

"The second he gets on the train, shut the front doors," the man beside him said. "Okay, *now*. Close them up."

Bud pressed the button hard. The front doors shut. The indication box lit up.

"Announce the next station." The gun nudged him.

Bud spoke into the mike. "Twenty-third Street, Twenty . . ." His throat was tight and dry and he couldn't finish.

"Do it again," the man said. "Do it better this time."

Bud wet his lips. "Twenty-third Street next."

"Good enough," the man said. "Now walk through the train until you get to the first car. I'll be following with the gun in my pocket. If you try to pull something, I'll shoot you. In the spine."

As Bud edged out of the cab, his hip brushed against the florist's box, and he reached out instinctively to steady it. But it was surprisingly stable and hardly moved. He didn't hear any footsteps behind him as he went forward, through one storm door after another, but he knew the man was behind him, ready, as he had promised, to crack his spine like a dry twig.

The train began to move.

LONGMAN

Longman felt light-headed, almost dizzy, as he waited for the motorman's door to open. *If* it opened. He grasped at the possibility in desperation.

The two boys were looking at him, smiling shyly, seeking his approval for their game. Their innocence and trust touched him, and he found himself smiling at them, although a moment ago he would not have thought himself capable of it. For an instant, matching warmth with warmth, Longman was at ease—until he heard the hand sliding along the inside of the cab door and the tiny click as the lock disengaged.

He fought a panicky impulse to run. Then he picked up his

package and opened the door. As he pulled it shut behind him, he saw Ryder's arm and gun disappear back through the window. Awkwardly he reached for his own gun—remembering guiltily that it should have been in his hand when he entered the cab—and pressed it into the motorman's side. Denny Doyle was pouring sweat. Between us, Longman thought, the cab will stink like a locker room.

He said, "Move over to the window," and the motorman obeyed with almost comical speed. He heard a light tap on the door and slipped the latch to let Ryder in, noticing as he did so that the indication box was lit up: all doors closed, ready to go. Ryder piled his Val-A-Pak and valise on top of Longman's package and squeezed in. The cab was crowded now.

"Go ahead," Ryder said.

Longman crowded against the motorman so that he could square off in front of the panel. His hands went toward the controls, then stopped. "Don't forget what I told you," he said to the motorman. "You touch that mike pedal and I'll shoot your foot off."

All Denny Doyle was trying to do was stay alive so he could collect his pension, but Longman had spoken for Ryder's ears. He was supposed to have warned the motorman earlier about the foot pedal that activated the radio microphone, but had forgotten it. He glanced toward Ryder for approval.

Ryder's face was impassive. "Get started," he said.

Like bike riding, Longman thought, it was one of those things you never forgot how to do. In the most natural way his left hand found the controller, his right the brake handle. But touching the brake handle made him feel guilty. A brake handle was a very personal thing. Every motorman was issued one his first day on the job, and he kept it from then on, carrying it to and from work. In a way, it was like his badge of office.

"You don't know how to drive it," the motorman said, scared.

"Don't worry," Longman said, "I won't wreck you."

Pressing down firmly on the controller to nullify the deadman's feature—the pressure-sensitive safety device that automatically stopped a train, if the motorman were suddenly stricken and he re-

leased his hand from the controller—Longman nudged it to the left into switching position, and the train began to edge out of the station. He crawled into the tunnel at five miles an hour and checked out the signals without even having to think about it. Green, green, green, amber, red. With a sudden sense of exhilaration he thought how exciting it would be to ram the controller up through series position into multiple, and rocket through the tunnel at fifty with the walls zipping by, the signals obliging him so that he wouldn't have to touch the brake until he slammed into the next station.

But they were only going for a short ride. He estimated three train lengths out of the station, then knocked the controller off and eased the brake to the right. The train rocked to a halt. The motorman looked at him.

"Smooth stop—right?" Longman said. "No jerk, no snap, no pull." He felt fine. And Denny Doyle, responding eagerly to the tone of his voice, smiled broadly.

Ryder's voice brought Longman down to earth. "Tell him."

Longman said to the motorman, "I'm taking the brake handle and the reverse key, see? I want your cutting key." He held his hand out. The motorman looked uneasy, but fished the cutting key out of his pocket. "I'm leaving the cab now," Longman said, and was pleased at how calm he sounded. "Don't try anything."

"I won't," said Denny Doyle. "I really won't."

"Better not. And remember what I said about the radio." Longman felt a sense of superiority over the motorman. An Irishman, but not the fighting kind. He was scared silly.

Longman put the brake handle and the bulky keys in his raincoat pockets, squeezed by Ryder, and walked back through the car. The two boys stared at him in awe. He gave them a smile and a wink. The passengers barely glanced at him.

RYDER

"Turn your back to me," Ryder said. "Face the window."

The motorman looked at him apprehensively. "Please . . ."

"Do as I say."

The motorman faced about. Ryder removed his right glove, hooked an index finger into his mouth, withdrew pads of medical gauze from beneath his lips and then from inside each cheek. From his right pocket he took out a cut-down length of nylon stocking. He removed his hat, pulled the stocking over his head and, after adjusting the eye slits properly, put his hat on again.

The disguises had been a concession to Longman. Ryder had argued that, with the exception of the motorman and conductor, nobody on the train would notice them before they put on their masks. And even if they did, it was a fact—the police were the first to admit it—that untrained citizens were notoriously unreliable in their descriptions of people. But he had not disputed Longman's point except to reject anything elaborate. What the disguises boiled down to were Longman's eyeglasses, Steever's white wig, Welcome's false mustache and sideburns, and the gauze pads to fill up the hollows of his own face.

"You can turn around now," he told the motorman.

The motorman glanced at the mask, then averted his eyes in a pointed demonstration of his lack of interest in what Ryder looked like. It was, Ryder thought dryly, a friendly gesture.

He said, "You'll be getting a radio call from Command Center before long. Ignore it. Don't answer. Do you understand?"

"Yes, sir," Denny Doyle said earnestly. "I promised the other man I wouldn't touch the radio." He paused. "I want to stay alive. They can call all they want to. I'm deaf."

It would be a minute or two before Grand Central Tower, becoming restive, would contact Command Center with the advice: "All signals clear in area, train laying down." For Ryder it was a dead interlude. Welcome, he knew, was guarding the rear storm door of the front car; Longman was on his way to the cab of the second car; it was a safe assumption that Steever and the conductor were moving forward. He trusted Steever implicitly, although he had less brains than either of the others. Longman was intelligent but a coward, and Welcome was dangerously erratic. They would all be fine if everything went smoothly. If not, their weaknesses would begin to show.

"Command Center calling Pelham One Two Three. Command Center calling Pelham One Two Three. Come in, please."

Ryder tuned the voice out of his consciousness. By now Longman would have the brake handle, the reverse key, and the cutting key emplaced in the second car. Severing the cars would take less than a minute.

"Dispatcher calling Pelham One Two Three. Do you read me? Please report, Pelham One Two Three. Come in."

The motorman looked at Ryder with open appeal as his sense of duty struggled with his fear. Ryder shook his head sternly.

"Pelham One Two Three! Where in hell *are* you?"

LONGMAN

As Longman went to the rear of the car, he didn't dare look at the passengers, despite Ryder's assurance that he would have to fall flat on his face to be noticed. Welcome was watching his approach with a crooked smile. The mere sight of him made Longman nervous. A weirdo, a maniac, a man who had been fired by the Mafia because he misbehaved? He stood there squarely in front of the storm door. For an instant Longman was convinced that Welcome wouldn't budge, and panic began to rise in him like the mercury column in a thermometer. But then, with that mocking smile, he slid the door open. Longman took a deep breath and went through.

Between the cars he paused, visualizing, beneath the steel threshold plates, the thick electric cables that transmitted power from car to car, and the neat grasp of the couplings. Steever was holding the door to the second car open, and Longman saw the frightened conductor standing beside him. Steever handed over the door key, which he had taken from the conductor. Longman went into the cab, locked the door after himself, and proceeded to· arm the panel, so that the train could be driven forward or backward from this car. Then he put the cutting key in place.

Except in the yard, a motorman rarely had occasion to cut a train, but it was simple enough to do. Longman turned the cutting key, and the coupling between the first and second cars unlocked.

He set the reverse key in reverse position. Then, pressing down on the deadman's feature, he edged the controller into switching position. The open couplings disengaged smoothly, and nine cars of the train moved backward. He estimated a distance of about one hundred and fifty feet and gently applied the brake. The train stopped. He removed the brake handle and the two keys, stuffed them into his pockets, and stepped out of the cab.

A few passengers squirmed with impatience at the delay, but it didn't seem to bother anyone that they had moved backward. It would bother the Tower, all right, though. Longman could just imagine what must be going on there.

Steever held the storm door for him while he jumped down to the concrete roadbed. The conductor followed, then Steever. They walked quickly through the tunnel to the first car. Welcome, crouching, extended a hand to help them up.

Longman was relieved that he didn't try to fool around.

Part Two

CAZ DOLOWICZ

Fleshy, his belly straining the buttons of his jacket, Caz Dolowicz moved with deliberate speed through the crowds in the Grand Central terminus of the crosstown shuttle. He belched at almost every step, bringing a measure of relief from the painful accumulation of gas that pressed upward against his heart. As usual, he had eaten too much lunch.

A few steps past the Nedick's stand, he pushed through the inconspicuous gate with its sign reading To Super's Office. Dolowicz was amazed, as always, that the unlocked gate didn't tempt the curiosity of passersby. Just as well—they could live without civilians wandering into the Tower and asking stupid questions.

Walking on through the tunnel at his heavy, steady pace, Dolowicz caught here and there the glint of an eye—one of the army of cats that lived in the tunnel preying on the rats which infested it by the thousands.

Directly ahead, a train charged at him head on. Smiling, he

walked straight toward it. It was the northbound express, and in a moment it turned away. On that first day, twelve years ago, nobody had warned him about the northbound, and when it came thundering toward him, he had flung himself into the trough in terror. It was still one of the simple pleasures of his life to escort a new man down the tunnel and watch it happen.

Dolowicz climbed the steps and entered the control center he ran for eight hours a day. Actually its technical name was Interlocking Plant, but nobody ever called it that. It was the Tower Room, or simply the Tower, named after the old-time towers raised above tracks at key points.

Dolowicz took in the scene. What made the Tower beautiful was the model board, stretched high across one wall, recording in colored slashes of light the routes and movements of every train that passed through the sector, all of it superimposed on a map showing the tracks and the stations. His towermen were all busy at their flashing consoles, watching the action on the model board as they spoke to desk trainmasters, dispatchers, and towermen at adjoining key points. His eye went to Jenkins. A woman. A woman towerman. And black, yet. He couldn't get used to the idea, even after a month. Well, he had better; the talk was that a lot more women were taking the towerman test! What next—motorwomen? Not that he had any complaints about Mrs. Jenkins. She was quiet, soft-spoken, competent. But still . . .

Marino was beckoning to him. Dolowicz walked over and stood behind him. On the model board a southbound local was standing between Twenty-eighth and Twenty-third.

"He's laying dead," Marino said. "Couple, maybe three minutes."

"Well, get onto the squawk box to Command Center."

"I did," Marino said, aggrieved. "They're trying to raise the motorman now. He don't answer the radio."

Dolowicz could think of a number of reasons why the motorman wouldn't answer the radio, the chief being that he wasn't in the cab, that he had climbed out onto the track to reset a tripper that had accidentally cut him dead, or maybe to fix a hung door. If he needed more serious repair help, he'd have radioed in for

a car knocker. But whatever the trouble, he was required to report to Command Center by radio.

"Unless he's a jerk," he said to Marino, "the reason he didn't call Command Center is because his radio is probably busted. And the lazy bum won't exert himself to pick up a telephone."

When he had joined the system, there was no such luxury as two-way radios. If a motorman got into trouble, he would walk the track to one of the telephones placed at five-hundred-foot intervals and report in. The telephones were still there.

"The bum's going to get written up for this," Dolowicz said, forcing a belch. "What train is it?"

"Pelham One Two Three," Marino said. "Hey, he's starting to move." Then his voice rose in astonishment. "I don't believe it. He's moving *backwards!*"

RYDER

When Longman rapped on the cab door, Ryder held him up for a moment while he unlocked the brown valise and took out the submachine gun. The motorman gasped. "Put your mask on," Ryder said to Longman as he let him in. "Get your weapon out and shut the door after me."

He squeezed out of the cab, the tommy gun held vertically along his pant leg. In the center of the car Steever was pulling his gun from the florist's box. At the rear Welcome was grinning, his tommy gun trained down the length of the car.

"Attention," Ryder said in a loud voice, and watched the passengers turn toward him. He held the gun in the crook of his right arm, the fingers curved around the trigger. "You will all remain seated. Anyone who moves will be shot. There will be no further warning. If you move, you'll be killed."

He braced himself as the car began to move slowly forward.

CAZ DOLOWICZ

The red slashes on the model board in the Grand Central Tower began to wink. "He's moving," Marino said. "Forward."

"I can see that with my own eyes," Dolowicz said.

"Now he stopped," Marino said in a hushed voice. "He stopped again. About halfway between the stations."

"A pure mental case," Dolowicz said. "I'm going down there and see what the hell's going on. And I don't care *what* his excuse is, I'm going to have that motorman's—" Suddenly he remembered Mrs. Jenkins and stopped before he mentioned the part of the motorman's anatomy he intended to have. Cripes, he thought, if I have to watch my language, I'm going to pack it in. How the hell could you run a railroad without swearing?

As he opened the door, a raging voice blasted through the speaker. "What the hell is going on with that crazy train?" It was the desk trainmaster, screaming into his mike from Command Center.

"Tell his nibs supervision is on the way," Dolowicz said to Marino, and hurried down the steps into the tunnel.

RYDER

The submachine guns represented a substantial outlay of money —sawed-off shotguns, which were terrible enough weapons, were much cheaper—but Ryder considered these a sound investment. He didn't particularly care for them as weapons, but used them for their psychological effect. Even the police, who were aware of the tommy's limitations, would show some deference for a weapon that could spew out four hundred and fifty lethal .45-caliber rounds per minute. Most of all, it would impress the passengers, with their standard movie-inspired image of submachine guns cutting people down in rows.

The car was hushed as Longman eased it slowly through the tunnel. Steever, in the exact middle, faced Welcome at the far end. Both were masked. Ryder now took account of the passengers in the front half of the car: two small boys, saucer-eyed, probably more fascinated than frightened. Their young, plump mother, hung up between two conventions—fainting or protecting her cubs. A hippie-type young man with shoulder-length blond hair and beard to match, wearing a Navajo poncho and thonged sandals. Comatose. Bombed out or sleeping off a high. A flashy, dark-haired girl

in an Anzac hat. A high-class hustler? Five blacks: one of them a militant type he'd seen on the platform; two of them almost identical boys carrying packages—long, bony, sad faces, with huge eyes; a middle-aged man, handsome, well turned out, holding an attaché case—maybe a lawyer; and a stout, placid woman, probably a domestic, wearing a coat with a patchy silver fox collar. Then there was an old white man, tiny and alert, duded up in a cashmere coat, a pearly Borsalino hat, a foulard silk tie; and a female derelict, color indeterminate, a wino, layered in coats and sweaters, unimaginably grimy, snuffling in a semiconscious daze. A burly man in a tweed jacket and a rumpled shirt. And others. Figures in a city landscape. Only the black militant stared at him in direct challenge. Good enough, Ryder thought, they were simply cargo. Cargo with a fixed value.

The car dragged under his feet, bucked, and came to a stop. Steever turned inquiringly. Ryder nodded, and Steever cleared his throat and spoke. His voice was heavy, monotone, muffled.

"Everybody in the back half of the car," Steever said. "Up on your feet. Be quick about it."

Ryder, anticipating the stirring in his half of the car, said, "Not you people. Sit fast. Anybody who moves will be shot."

The black militant moved with measured defiance. Ryder trained the gun on his chest. He moved again, wriggling his hips, and then subsided, content with his demonstration. Ryder, too, was content; the challenge was ceremonial, it could be ignored.

"Everybody up. You understand English? On your feet!" This was Welcome getting into the act.

The cab door opened and Longman came out, prodding the motorman ahead of him with his gun. Longman spoke softly and the motorman nodded and fell heavily into a seat alongside the stout black woman. Longman, at a signal from Ryder, bent to unlock the front storm door. The two boys were in his way and he put his hand between them, not roughly, and separated them.

The plump young woman cried out. "Brandon. Robert. Please don't hurt them." She jumped to her feet and took a step toward the boys.

"Sit down," Ryder said. The woman's mouth shaped a protest. "Don't argue. Sit down. The kids, too."

The woman drew the boys to her convulsively, planting them between her knees. As Longman stepped out the door and dropped to the tracks, Ryder checked off his passengers, shifting the muzzle of his gun from one to the other, deliberate, intimidating. The girl in the Anzac hat tapped her foot restlessly on the filthy floor. The hippie was nodding, smiling, his eyes still closed. The militant black, with his arms folded across his chest, was staring with accusatory stoniness at the well-dressed black with the attaché case. The boys were squirming with embarrassment in their mother's scissors hold. The passengers at the rear were now facing the door three abreast, with Welcome worrying at them like a sheep dog.

Without warning the lights went out and the emergency lights blinked on. The passengers looked alarmed. The power was now out in the sector between Fourteenth and Thirty-third streets on all four tracks, local and express, northbound and southbound.

Ryder said, "Conductor, I want you to walk all of those passengers back down the track."

Bud Carmody said, "Yes, sir."

"Collect all the passengers in the other nine cars of the train, too, and lead them back to the station."

Bud looked worried. "What if they won't leave the train?"

"Tell them their train isn't going anyplace."

"Sir?" The mother, craning over the heads of her boys. "Please, sir. Please? Can I leave? My children are very high-strung—"

"Nobody in this end of the car leaves," Ryder said.

The old man in the cashmere coat said, "I'm not asking to leave, but shouldn't we be informed what's going on?"

"Yes," Ryder said. "What's going on is that you're being held by four desperate men with machine guns."

The old man smiled. "I guess if you ask a foolish question . . ."

"Could you give us some idea of how long we'll be detained?" the girl in the Anzac hat said. "I'm in the theater and I've got a terribly important audition."

"That's enough," Ryder said. "No more questions."

Longman came in through the front storm door brushing grime off his hands. It was probably years since the emergency power box had last been used. Ryder gestured to Longman to train his gun on the front passengers while he went to the rear of the car to cover the departure of the conductor and his flock. Bud Carmody jumped down to the roadbed. The passengers followed awkwardly, with Welcome speeding them on, using his gun as a prod. Ryder, satisfied, went back to the cab. Ahead, the tunnel lights, which were on DC, had gone off. But the signals and emergency lights, on AC, still worked. Close by, there was a single blue light indicating an emergency telephone, and then an unbroken procession of green signal lights.

Ryder lifted the microphone from its peg and felt for the black button which would activate the transmitter. But before he could press it, a voice filled the cab.

"Command Center to Pelham One Two Three. What the hell is on? You cut the power? Without phoning Power Central to explain? Are you *reading* me? This is the desk trainmaster. Come in, Pelham One Two Three."

Ryder flicked the button. "Pelham One Two Three to Command Center. Do you read me?"

"Where the hell have you been? What's *with* you? Why didn't you answer? Come in and start talking."

"Pelham One Two Three to Command Center," Ryder said. "Command Center, your train has been taken. Do you read me?"

TOM BERRY

Tom Berry told himself—had been telling himself—that there was absolutely no point when he could have taken suitable action. Maybe if he hadn't been daydreaming so hard about Deedee, he might have sensed that something suspicious was going on. But by the time he opened his eyes he could count four submachine guns, any one of which would have turned him into a side of bloody meat before his hand even touched his gun. So with a .38 in his belt, he had simply sat on his reflexes. If it was any conso-

lation, he was alive and well, and probably at the end of his career as a cop.

He had been trained and sworn to uphold the law, to enforce order, not just stand by like the public he was pledged to protect. Cops were not expected to snooze through a crime or reckon the odds against them too finely. Not even cops in plain clothes like him; or cops off duty. If they got killed for their pains, it was in the highest tradition of police work.

Who would have mourned for him, he wondered. Deedee? Would she remember him beyond tomorrow except in terms of a missing person in her bed? Or would she wake up to a realization of what "off the pig" meant in terms of spouting lifeblood and shattered bone and ruptured organs?

The heavy presence of the .38 against his stomach allowed him no comfort. It kept reminding him that he had neglected to become a brave corpse. Deedee would understand. She would even congratulate him on his liberation from being a witless instrument of the repressive society. But his superiors would take a different view. There would be a departmental trial, dismissal. All cops would despise him. Even those who were blatantly on the take were not so corrupt that they would fail to get themselves killed uselessly.

One ray of sunshine: You could always get a new job. Getting a new life was tougher.

CAZ DOLOWICZ

Dolowicz ran down the steps at the Twenty-eighth Street station. He flashed his identification card at the change-booth clerk and charged through the gate. A train was standing in the station with its doors open. If Pelham One Two Three was still lying dead, the signal blocks would hold up this one, Pelham One Two Eight. He realized suddenly that the train was lit only by the dim battery-operated lights. He hurried on to where the motorman was leaning out of his window.

"When did the power go?"

The motorman was an old-timer. "Who wants to know?"

"Caz Dolowicz, the Grand Central Tower trainmaster, wants to know."

"Oh." The man straightened up. "A couple of minutes ago."

"You radio Command Center?"

The motorman nodded. "What's up—man under?"

"I'm going to damn well find *out* what's up." Dolowicz went on to the end of the platform and descended to the roadbed. He was always in favor of seeing things for himself. Spurred now by anger and anxiety, he began to trot. His gas pains slowed him down some, but pain or no pain, he trudged on steadily through the tunnel until he heard voices. He stopped and, with narrowed eyes, peered through the dimness at a bulky wavering shape coming down the track. It looked like a crowd of people.

LONGMAN

Longman had been as cool in the tunnel pulling the emergency switch as he had been cutting the cars and driving the train. He felt fine when he was doing the technical things. But the moment Ryder disappeared into the cab he had begun to sweat again. It brought home to him how secure he felt with Ryder, even though the man scared him stiff half the time. He hadn't established *any* kind of relationship with the other two. Steever was efficient, but a closed system, and Welcome was not only cruel and kinky, he was probably a certifiable maniac.

The submachine gun seemed to vibrate in his hands, as though it picked up the agitated beat of his own blood. He shifted his eyes anxiously to the cab door, but at the sound of a low warning whistle from Steever he focused again on the passengers in the row of seats to his right. They were his responsibility. The left row was Steever's. Ryder had arranged it that way so they wouldn't be in each other's line of fire.

The rear section of the car looked abandoned. Welcome was profiled toward the storm door, his machine gun pointed down the track. He looked to be spoiling for action, praying probably for something to go wrong so he could kill somebody.

Longman strained for some sound from behind the cab door,

but could hear nothing. So far the operation had gone without a hitch. But it would all go down the drain if they balked at paying. Ryder had assured him that they had no reasonable alternative. But suppose they decided not to be reasonable? What if the cops got hard-nosed? Well, in that case a lot of people would die. Including themselves.

Ryder's credo: You live or you die. It was an abhorrent thought to Longman, whose own credo, if he had ever verbalized it, would have been: Survive at any cost. Yet, of his own free will, he had signed on at Ryder's terms. Free will? No. He had drifted into it in a sort of dream state. But wasn't it his own idea? Hadn't he himself brought it out into the open and then refined it from a game, a playfully vengeful fantasy, into something criminal and profitable?

He had long ago stopped thinking of his first meeting with Ryder as accidental. The word was "fate." They had met at the state unemployment office on Sixth Avenue and Twentieth Street. He had noticed Ryder several times—a tall, slender man with black hair and fine, intense features. Not what you would call a man's man exactly, yet somehow suggesting depths of hidden strength and a quality of controlled confidence. But that assessment had come later. Actually Ryder wasn't extraordinary, and in any other place than that line of dejected boys and girls and beaten-down middle-agers he wouldn't have stood out.

Sometimes people struck up conversations on the lines, but Longman usually picked up a *Post* on his way and never talked to anybody. But when, a few weeks after he had first seen him, he found himself directly behind Ryder, he had begun a conversation with him. He had been hesitant at first, because Ryder was obviously someone who might freeze a man out if he didn't want to talk. But finally he had started it by showing him the headline on his *Post:* ANOTHER 747 OFF TO CUBA.

"It must be catching, like a disease," Longman said.

Ryder nodded politely, but said nothing.

"I don't understand what they get out of it," Longman said. "Once they get to Cuba they're either thrown in the clink or they

have to go out in the sun and cut sugarcane for ten hours a day."

"I couldn't say." Ryder's voice was unexpectedly deep and authoritative. A boss's voice, Longman had thought uneasily, and something else he couldn't quite put his finger on. His silence suggested that he had no interest in the subject. Ordinarily, Longman would have pulled back at that point. But in some way he didn't understand, he wanted to win this man's approval. And so he went on and uttered the words which, in the long run, were to prove prophetic.

"If there was something in it for them, a lot of money, say, I could understand it. But to take all that risk for nothing . . ."

Ryder smiled. "Everything is risk. Taking the next breath is a risk; you might inhale something poisonous. If you won't take a risk, you have to give up breathing, too."

"You can't," Longman said. "I read someplace that it's impossible to stop breathing voluntarily, even if you try."

Ryder smiled again. "Oh, I think you can manage it if you go about it the right way."

Longman went back to his *Post*, feeling that he had made a fool of himself. So a week or two later he was surprised and flattered when Ryder came over to join him at a coffee-shop counter and afterward walked with him to the unemployment office.

Longman felt enough at ease to try to take up the thread of the first conversation. "I noticed there was another one of those plane hijacks this week. Read about it?"

Ryder shook his head. "I'm not much of a newspaper reader."

"This one never made Cuba. An FBI man shot him dead."

"It beats chopping sugarcane."

"Being dead?"

"Being dead is an improvement on a lot of things I can think of. Trying to sell mutual funds, for example."

"Is that your line of work?"

"I tried it for a few months." He shrugged. "I was a lousy salesman. I guess I don't like asking people for things. I prefer telling them what to do."

"You mean being a boss?"

"In a way." Which was all the explanation he offered.

Longman's curiosity was aroused, but he didn't pursue it. Instead he talked about himself. "I was on a construction project, small houses out on the Island. The builder ran out of money, and I was laid off." Ryder merely nodded, and Longman went on. "That's not my trade. I was a subway motorman."

"Retired?"

"I'm only forty-one."

Ryder said politely, "That's about what I figured. That's why I was surprised at the idea that you might be retired."

It was a gracious apology, but Longman wasn't fooled. He had a worn look, a grayness, and people usually overstated his age. "I quit the system a few years ago."

Ninety-nine out of a hundred men would have followed up by asking why he had quit. Not Ryder. Annoyed, Longman asked a counterquestion which he would otherwise have avoided.

"What was your line? I mean your regular line?"

"The military. I was a soldier."

"That's a pretty good deal, I guess. What was your rank?"

"My last grade was full colonel."

Longman knew that men of thirty, which was what he reckoned Ryder to be, did not get to be full colonels. He hadn't figured Ryder to be a bull slinger. He nodded, disappointed.

Ryder said, "Not the American army."

The explanation didn't allay Longman's suspicion; it simply deepened the mystery. What army *had* Ryder served with?

He stepped up to the counter to have his book processed, then waited for Ryder to complete his turn. Outside, they fell in step again. "Going anywhere in particular?" Longman said.

"Thought I'd take a walk."

"Mind if I tag along? I haven't got anything to do."

They walked up Sixth Avenue to the Thirties, impersonal again, until Longman could stand it no longer. While they waited for the light at Thirty-fourth, he blurted it out. "What army *were* you in?"

Ryder paused for so long a time that Longman was on the verge of apologizing. But then Ryder said, "The last one? Biafra."

"Oh," Longman said. "Oh, I see."

"And before that the Congo. Also, Bolivia."

"A soldier of fortune?" Longman read adventure novels.

"That's a fancy name for it. Mercenary is more accurate."

"Well," Longman said, thinking not so much in terms of fighting for money as killing for money, and somewhat aghast at the idea, "I'm sure the money was secondary to the adventure."

"The Biafrans were paying me twenty-five hundred a month to lead a battalion. I wouldn't have touched it for a penny less."

"Bolivia. Where that Che Guevara was? You weren't on his—"

"No. I was with the side that killed him."

"I didn't exactly think you were a Commie," Longman said with a nervous laugh.

"I'm whatever I'm paid to be."

"It sure as hell sounds exciting. What made you quit?"

"The market dried up. No job opportunities. And no unemployment insurance. Would you like a beer?"

After that, the walk and the beer became a weekly custom. At first Longman was puzzled that someone of Ryder's class bothered with him, but he was shrewd enough to guess the answer. Like so many people in the city, Ryder was lonely. And so they became companions, of a very impersonal sort, for an hour or two a week.

Then, one day, it changed.

Once again it started with a newspaper headline. They saw it at a bar where they'd stopped for a beer: Two DIE IN SUBWAY SHOOTOUT.

Two men had tried to stick up a change booth at a subway station in the Bronx. A Transit cop had shot them both dead. A picture showed the robbers sprawled on the station floor. "Addicts," Longman said. "Nobody else would go for the money in a change booth."

There the matter would have ended—as Longman so often reminded himself—if he had not, bartering for Ryder's esteem, taken his fantasy out of its hiding place.

"If I wanted to perpetrate a crime in the subway system," he said, "I sure as hell wouldn't hold up a change booth."

"What would you do?"

"Something sensational, where there'd be a big payoff."

"Like what?" Ryder's interest was merely courteous.

"Like hijack a train," Longman said.

"A *subway* train? What could anyone *do* with a subway train?"

"Hold it for ransom."

"If it was *my* subway train, I would tell you to keep it before I paid to get it back." Ryder was amused.

"Ransom for the passengers," Longman said. "Hostages?"

"I don't see how it could work," Ryder said.

"Oh, it might. I've thought it out, just for laughs."

He *had* thought it out for laughs, the bitter kind. It was his revenge against the system.

Ryder turned on his stool to face Longman squarely. In the voice of command, as Longman now understood it to be, he said, "Why did you leave the subway system?"

It took Longman unawares. "I got the boot," he blurted.

Ryder kept looking at him, waiting.

"I was innocent of wrongdoing," Longman said.

"What were you charged with?"

"I wasn't *charged* with *anything*. It was only insinuations, but still they forced me out. You sound like a district attorney."

"Sorry," Ryder said.

"Hell, I don't mind. The beakies had to find a victim—"

"Beakies?"

"Special inspectors. Undercover men. They go around in plain clothes, checking up on trainmen. Sometimes they even dress up like kids, you know, long hair. Spies is what they are."

"They're called beakies because they're nosy?" Ryder smiled.

"That's what everyone thinks. Actually they got their name—like the bobbies in London—from the first chief of Security Services on the old IRT, way back. His name was H. F. Beakie."

Ryder nodded. "What did they accuse you of doing?"

"Some gang was supposed to be passing dope," Longman said

defiantly. "You know, giving it to some motorman downtown, and then someone picking it up in Harlem. The beakies tried to pin it on me. But they never got any evidence. How could they, if I didn't do it?"

"They tried to frame you?"

"They did frame me, the bastards. Do *you* think I'd do something like that? You know me."

"Yes," Ryder said. "I know you."

KOMO MOBUTU

Komo Mobutu had kept his cool. The event was not his business *at*-tall. Somebody could rip off the subway twice a day, and he wouldn't blink an eye. If it didn't have to do with the revolutionary aspirations of the black people, it wasn't *here*.

Mobutu sat very erect, facing a fancy white fox in an Anzac hat. When the old dude next to him had spoken, he didn't even turn his head. But now, from the corner of his eye, he dug those two black boys across the aisle. Good African types, maybe seventeen or eighteen. Serving the master, carrying the white man's packages for him. What burned him up was what they were doing with their big brown eyes, rolling them around like marbles.

Suddenly he was standing, shouting in a fury. "You stupid niggers, you too *young* to be Tomming. Get your *eyes* straight, you hear? Look the man in the eye!"

Every eye in the car was now on him, and as he stared at one after the other of them, he lingered on the well-dressed *Nee-gro* with the attaché case. A white nigger, not worth the bother. But the two boys . . . it might be worth putting on a demonstration for them. Turning to face the man with the gun, but addressing the boys, he said, "You don't have no cause to be scared of *no* white jackass, brothers. Someday soon we are going to ram that gun down his peeg throat!"

Steever, bored, said, "Shut your damn mouth."

"I don't take orders from no ofay peeg!"

The man gestured with his gun. "Come here to me, loudmouth."

"You think I'm afraid of you, peeg?"

"I just want you over here," the man said. "Come on over."

Mobutu walked to the center of the car and stood before the man, his back very straight, his hands clenched in anger. "Go shoot me," he said. "But I warn you, there are thousands like me, and we promise to cut your peeg throat—"

Effortlessly, without passion, the man smashed his gun on a diagonal across Mobutu's left temple. Mobutu felt a stunning pain, a red rain in his eyes, and he reeled backward, thumping to the floor in a sitting position.

"Go sit down, and never open your mouth no more."

Mobutu heard the man's voice dimly. He stood up, then fell back into his seat beside the old dude, who put out a hand to steady him. He shook it off. The car was hushed.

"He asked for it," the gunman said. "Don't nobody else."

Mobutu pressed his handkerchief to his mashed eyebrow. Through his other eye he focused on the messenger boys. Their eyes were still bugged. He thought, I took a blow for nothing. Everyone was studiously avoiding looking at him, even those who might ordinarily be fascinated by the sight of blood.

FRANK CORRELL

The headquarters of the Metropolitan Transportation Authority, commonly called the TA, is located in a large, granite-faced building at 370 Jay Street in what is known as downtown Brooklyn. It is a comparatively modern structure, and the TA's administrative functions are spread throughout.

On the second floor the TA Police Nerve Center occupies extremely cramped quarters, in marked contrast to the prodigal amount of third-floor space available to the Trainmasters' Office, better known as Command Center. Each of the three divisions of the subway system occupies its own large enclave at widely separated spots.

IRT, the A Division, the oldest but smallest, has four dispatchers assisting the desk trainmaster. Each one sits at a steel desk with an electric console through which he can speak to every motorman's cab.

The desk trainmaster is the boss of the dispatchers and of the minute-to-minute operation of the division. His console allows him to reach every one of his motormen. He is responsible for keeping the trains running smoothly and on time. He earns his pay on any day, but particularly when an emergency threatens the functioning of the division. Then his job is to work out a flexible emergency schedule, or "flex," to keep the trains running: switching locals to express tracks and vice versa, or from the East Side line to the West—any of a variety of improvisations designed to maintain service even in the face of major catastrophes. To keep passengers advised of any schedule change or emergency, Command Center has a Communications Desk, which records its messages on tape and cassette and relays them to the stations. When there are major delays or emergencies, the desk gets in touch with the media—newspapers, radio, and television—and keeps them abreast of developments.

Frank Correll, one of three desk trainmasters who functioned in shifts around the clock, knew all of this as well as he knew himself—though he couldn't have described it. If you asked him how he lifted his arm, he would scowl and say, "You just lift it," meaning there are some things you don't have to think about.

A good desk trainmaster develops a sort of psychic divining rod that helps him smell out serious trouble. Frank Correll's sixth sense had told him something bad was wrong with Pelham One Two Three. After telling Grand Central Tower to get the lead out, he took over from the dispatcher, trying to raise the train from his own console. But even he was not prepared for what he heard when Pelham One Two Three at last came through. He lapsed into a short and very uncharacteristic silence. Then he let out a roar, and all over the vast area of Command Center men broke into grins. Even among desk trainmasters, traditionally the hard-bitten, mercurial stars of the TA who act their roles to the hilt, Frank Correll was famous. Wiry, loudmouthed, charged with a superfluity of energy, he was perfectly cast. And so nobody, hearing his outburst, had reason to suspect anything out of the ordinary.

Correll banked the fires of his temper and said quietly—for him, "I heard you. What do you mean *taken the train?* No. Wait a second. Why did you cut the power? Why haven't you reported it to Power Central? Come in, and you better make it good."

"Do you have a pencil, Desk Trainmaster?"

"What kind of damfool question is that, Motorman?"

"This is not the motorman. Listen to me carefully. Pay attention. Do you have a pencil?"

"Who the hell *is* this? Identify yourself."

"Listen to me, Desk Trainmaster, I don't like to repeat. Your train has been taken by a group of heavily armed men. The power has been cut, as you know. So has the train. We are in the first car of the train. We are holding sixteen passengers and the motorman hostage. We will not hesitate to kill all of them if it becomes necessary. Over."

Correll cut out and hit his six button which, among other things, automatically cut him in to Transit Police. His hands were shaking with fury.

CLIVE PRESCOTT

One of the TA chairman's secretaries phoned from the thirteenth floor to Lieutenant Clive Prescott of Transit Police on the second floor to inform him that the distinguished visitors from Boston, back from lunch with the chairman, were at this moment on their way down, and please to remember that they were *personal* friends of the chairman and were to receive preferential treatment.

"I'll have the red carpet out as soon as I finish vacuuming it," Lieutenant Prescott said. He hung up and went out to the information desk guarding the approaches to Nerve Center and waited for the elevator to discharge its precious cargo.

They were politicians, and Irish—and what else was new?—one guarded, one hearty. Their names were Maloney (hearty) and Casey (guarded). Their almost identical sharp blue eyes took in Lieutenant Prescott's sharkskin suit and boldly striped red-white-black shirt. Their handshakes were at the same time crisp and warm—the grips of men who shook hands as a way of life.

It was protocol to go first to Operations, but Prescott decided to steer them toward Teletype and the Roll Call Unit. Relaxed, a casual lecturer to an elite class of two, he explained the clattering machines. "We're wired up with the New York Police Department going and coming." He paused, and in the silence the NYPD Teletype clicked steadily and placidly. "As you may know, the strength of the TA Police Force is approximately thirty-two hundred men. Actually we rank among the first twenty-five police forces in the entire country. Our beat is a vast one—two hundred and thirty-seven miles of track, four hundred and seventy-six stations—about sixty percent of it underground."

Maloney said, "You don't say." Casey stifled a yawn.

Prescott decided to skip Roll Call Unit. "And now," he said, "we'll go to Operations, the heart of the Nerve Center." They entered a large room, cut up by glass dividers into a maze of squares and rectangles. Naturally enough, the visitors zeroed in at once on the huge police map covering the far wall.

"We call that the status board," Prescott said. "It pinpoints the disposition of all the men in the field." Prescott had never seen the section deader. "I wish you could have been here yesterday," he said. "We had a bomb scare, and we were really humming. Over there we have Records. Records of all the activities of the day—summonses, arrests, injuries."

Behind him he heard Garber, the Operations lieutenant, let out a shout. "Roberts, wake up. Some gang has hijacked a train on A Division. Armed with automatic weapons. Bring in all units on Lexington Avenue line in vicinity of Twenty-eighth Street."

"Hijacked a *subway* train?" Casey was suddenly wide-awake and laughing. "What would anybody do that for?"

"Where'd the information come from?" Prescott asked Garber.

"Desk trainmaster," Garber said. "He's talking to the hijackers in the cab of the train."

"Gentlemen," Prescott said to the visitors, "I believe the chairman is expecting you." He hustled them out to the elevator, and as soon as he had sent them on their way to the thirteenth floor, he ran upstairs to Command Center, on the floor above.

Waiting in the cab for the desk trainmaster to return to the radio, Ryder acknowledged the greatest hazard of the whole operation; he would be spending a great deal of time in the cab and not in continuous personal command of his force.

It was something less than an ideal army. Longman a coward, Welcome undisciplined, Steever steady but in need of guidance. It left a good deal to be desired, but so had all his commands in the past. The perfect soldier, it occurred to him, would be a combination of Longman's intelligence, Steever's discipline, and Welcome's dash. So—depending on how you did your arithmetic—his force consisted either of three flawed soldiers or one complete one.

"Pelham One Two Three. Come in, Pelham One Two Three."

Ryder pressed the transmit button. "Are you ready with a pencil, Desk Trainmaster? I want you to write down exactly what I tell you. *Exactly*. Do you read me?"

"I read you. You're off your rocker."

Ryder said, "I'm about to give you seven items. Point One: Pelham One Two Three is completely in our control. We own it. Have you got that?"

"What *are* you people? Panthers?"

"Point Two, Desk Trainmaster. We are heavily armed with fully automatic weapons. Check me."

"I check you, you madman. You can't get away with this."

"Point Three: We have no scruples about killing. Don't take us lightly. Check me."

"Do you know you're screwing up the whole damn East Side?"

"Check me, Desk Trainmaster."

"Go ahead. Let's hear the rest of this garbage."

"Point Four: You will not attempt to restore power until we instruct you to. If you do, we'll shoot one of the hostages. And we'll shoot one every minute until the power is pulled again."

"Idiot, the cops are going to be all over you."

"Point Five," Ryder said. "If anyone attempts to interfere—cops, anyone—we'll kill all the passengers. Do you read me?"

"You are something *else*."

"Point Six: You will contact the mayor at once. Inform him that we demand a million dollars for the release of the car and the passengers. Check me."

"Keep dreaming."

"Point Seven: The time is now two thirteen. The money must be in our hands in one hour. That is, no later than three thirteen. For every minute past the deadline we'll kill one hostage. Have you got that, Desk Trainmaster?"

"I got it all. But if you expect me to do anything about it, you're even crazier than I thought."

You devised a strategy based on the logical reaction of the other side, Ryder thought, or it was worthless. But rank stupidity could wreck you. "Listen to me, Desk Trainmaster. I want you to patch me in to Transit Police. At once."

"Here's one now, gangster. A cop. Have a good time."

Ryder waited, and a new voice came on, slightly out of breath. "What *is* this?"

"Identify yourself," Ryder said.

"Lieutenant Prescott, Transit Police. Identify *your*self."

"I'm the man who stole your train, Lieutenant. Ask the desk trainmaster to let you read his notes. Be quick."

Waiting, Ryder could hear the lieutenant's breathing. Then: "Prescott to Pelham One Two Three. I read it. You're crazy."

"So I'm crazy. Is it a reason for not taking me seriously?"

"Look," Prescott said. "I take you seriously. But there's no way you can get away with it. You're in a tunnel."

"Lieutenant, at precisely three thirteen we'll begin executing hostages, one each minute. I suggest you contact the mayor."

"I'm a Transit Police lieutenant. How do I get to the mayor?"

"That's your problem, Lieutenant."

240 CENTRE STREET

Although Transit Police has a direct line to Police Headquarters at 240 Centre Street in Manhattan, the call advising of the hijacking of Pelham One Two Three was fed into the 911 line, the emer-

gency system designed to speed up police response to urgent outside calls.

Granted that stealing a subway train wasn't an everyday occurrence, nevertheless the police dispatcher who received the call didn't get excited about it. When you dealt constantly with catastrophes, the alleged theft of a subway train was nothing to write home about. The dispatcher followed routine procedure.

A computer readout informed him which of the dozen or so patrol cars in each of the bordering precincts, the Thirteenth and Fourteenth, were available. He radioed two cars, Thirteen Boy and Fourteen David, to check out the incident and report back at once. In less than two minutes Fourteen David reported.

At the same moment another report was being transmitted on an elevated level. Lieutenant Prescott had contacted Chief Costello of Transit Police, who had in turn phoned the chief inspector of the NYPD, with whom he was personally acquainted. The chief inspector, who was practically out the door to catch a plane for a vital Justice Department conference in Washington, turned the matter over to Planning, ordering a major mobilization of manpower. Then, regretfully, he left for the airport.

Patrol cars from the Thirteenth and Fourteenth precincts converged on the affected area to control traffic and open up passage for all other arriving police units. The Tactical Police Force was ordered out to handle the inevitable crowds. A police helicopter was ordered into the air.

Members of the Special Operations Division were issued machine guns, submachine guns, shotguns, tear gas, rifles equipped with scopes for sniper use, bulletproof vests, searchlights, bullhorns. Much of the ammunition would be .22 caliber, to minimize the danger of ricochet casualties among police and bystanders.

A number of the division's trucks sped to the scene. These vehicles are awesome arsenals of weapons, rescue equipment, and specialized instruments, including keys for the opening of subway emergency exit grates.

Except for a few detectives, all forces would be uniformed. The officer in overall charge of the operation was the borough com-

mander. His rank was assistant chief inspector, and his head-quarters were in the Police Academy on East Twenty-first Street, a brisk walk to the scene of the incident. However, he rode to the scene in an unmarked four-door chauffeur-driven car.

In all, more than seven hundred police personnel would be involved.

WELCOME

With the Thompson gun hanging down along his right leg, Joe Welcome looked out the window of the rear storm door. The stillness bugged him and he was itchy for action. When Ryder was spelling out the assignments, he made "sole responsibility for securing our rear" sound important. But it turned out to be dulls-ville. Steever, up front, at least had had a little fun beating on the spade's head.

Since then the passengers had hardly moved. He'd like it better if they tried to pull something. Not that they had a chance. They would be chopped meat before they got six inches off the seat. Steever would see to that. Maybe Longman would zap them, too. Maybe not. Longman was supposed to be a brain, but he was a creep. Steever had guts, but he had sawdust where his brains belonged.

He turned back to the tunnel. Nothing. A few green signals on the uptown side. What was taking Ryder so long?

Ryder. You had to give him two things: He was a good or-ganizer, and he had guts, for sure. But he was a cold stud. Even in the organization, where they also had this thing about disci-pline, they weren't *cold*. You don't need any book to interpret screaming Sicilian curses. Ryder never raised his voice.

Not that he liked Italians that much either, or he wouldn't have changed his name. He remembered the judge asking him if he knew that Joseph Welcome was an exact translation of Giuseppe Benvenuto.

An assault rap was dropped a few weeks before he pulled the stunt that got him fired. The organization had ordered him to mess up a couple of guys, but instead he offed them. Not that

they gave a damn about the guys he killed, but he had disobeyed orders. Discipline. Instead of promising to be a good boy, he gave them a lot of guff, and next thing he knew he was out. Fired by the Mafia!

Well, who needed *them?* If this deal came off he would have a hundred thousand out of it, and that was more than a lot of ginzos in the organization made in ten years.

He returned his attention to the deserted track. But it wasn't deserted. In the distance—he squinted his eyes—in the distance someone was walking the roadbed, coming straight on.

ANITA LEMOYNE

The machine guns were freaky, but Anita wasn't frightened by them. Nobody was going to hurt her. Now and then she met a man she couldn't turn on, but not every day. Tough as these gunmen might be, they weren't about to destroy a commodity whose value they appreciated, if only objectively. But if this crazy thing didn't wind itself up pretty soon, it was going to cost her money. It was beginning to make her fidget. The john she was on her way to see was a hundred-and-a-half trick, and he didn't like people being late.

Her foot, which up to now hadn't stopped kicking to the rhythm of her impatience, suddenly froze. Could she con one of those four creeps into letting her go? Hadn't the one at the rear been eyeballing her ever since she got on the train? She could recall what he looked like before he put on the mask: a ginzo, a pretty Latin-lover type.

He suddenly began to shout. He had the rear door open, with the machine gun stuck through it, and he was beating his gums at a high-decibel level out into the tunnel.

LONGMAN

First blood. That was the traditional railroad term describing the first time an engineer killed someone on the tracks. Longman had applied it, erroneously, he realized, to Steever's hitting the loudmouthed black with his gun. Steever's blow, so calmly de-

livered, had tuned up his sense of disbelief. How could he ever have let Ryder hypnotize him into this—out of his living mind?

But *was* that what happened? Had he meekly followed Ryder *against* his own will? Standing here with the submachine gun an alien weight in numb hands, he admitted he had been conning himself when he pretended it was all fun and games. Ryder's probings were serious efforts to decide whether the hijack was workable. They were all leading up to a decision for or against commitment, and Longman knew it. Why, then, had he gone the route? Well, for one thing, Ryder was a natural leader, he a natural follower, perhaps even a hero-worshipper.

He recalled his surprise, the week following the first mention of the subject, when Ryder began to ask practical questions. He had found himself sweating out the answers. For example, when Ryder had pointed out the difficulty of keeping passengers in all ten cars under control, Longman had come up with the solution—cut the first car out of the train. Ryder had nodded. "Yes, a dozen hostages give you as much leverage as a hundred."

He was not always so successful. At every point in the plan Ryder probed for weaknesses, making no effort to solve the problems, simply stinging Longman's invention into activity.

One day Ryder said, "Determined people could probably succeed in taking the train, but I'm not satisfied they could get away."

"I admit it's tough," Longman said casually. "Very tough, but I think I know how it can be done."

"Tell me," Ryder said.

It spilled out of him eagerly and proudly, and when he was finished, he looked at Ryder in triumph.

"Another round," Ryder called out to the waiter. Then he said to Longman, "Let's do it."

Attempting to match Ryder's nonchalance, Longman said, "Sure, why not?" But he felt suddenly dizzy. It was as if his whole life reared up before him, dreary, squalid, gray, friendless. At forty-one he was at best doomed to a succession of inane dead-end jobs. What probably convinced him to make this last desperate pitch

for a better life was the harsh memory of his brief period as an apartment-house doorman. Holding doors for people who never really acknowledged his existence, even those who condescended to greet him; dashing out into the rain to whistle up cabs; relieving strapping matrons of their bundles; walking dogs; smiling and groveling and pulling at the bill of his cap. A flunky in a monkey suit.

It was a powerful memory, and it sustained him through all the preparation, though he never shook off a sense of foreboding.

Joe Welcome's voice shattered the silence with the terrifying force of an act of sudden violence. A car length away, he was squared off in front of the door, screaming into the tunnel. Longman knew that Welcome would fire, that whoever was out there would die. The firing was almost an anticlimax. Before the echo died Longman was pounding frantically on the cab door.

CAZ DOLOWICZ

Like a thin, somber Pied Piper, Conductor Carmody stood at the head of a line of passengers that straggled far back on the roadbed into the dark damp of the tunnel. He was sweating; worry lines were embedded in the smoothness of his forehead.

Dolowicz was shouting, "I don't give a damn if they were armed with cannons. You aren't supposed to leave your train."

"They *made* me. I didn't have any choice. They had machine guns!" Bud Carmody croaked, turning for corroboration to the passengers.

Several nodded gloomily. A voice called out, "Let's go, let's get outta this dump." Other voices picked up the refrain, and Dolowicz realized the danger of panic.

"Okay," he said to Carmody. "Get these people to the platform. There's a train in the station. Use its radio to tell Command Center what you just told me. Tell them I'm investigating."

"You're going *down* there?"

Caz Dolowicz brushed by Carmody and started down the track. His anger renewed itself at the sight of the nine cars that had been cut away, standing uselessly, hulkingly, their weak emer-

211

gency lights giving them a pathetic half-life. He plodded on for maybe a hundred yards. When he looked up and saw the pale illumination in the first car of Pelham One Two Three, he fell into a trot. As he came closer, he saw the silhouette of a man standing in the rear storm door. It occurred to him to approach cautiously, but the warning flashed by, leaving cold rage in its place. Bastards! Daring to monkey with his railroad!

"Stay where you are, Johnny." It was a loud voice, echoing through the tunnel. Dolowicz stopped, outraged.

"Who the blazing hell are *you* to give orders?" he shouted back. "I'm the trainmaster, and I'm coming on board." He started walking again.

"I warned you, stupid!" The voice was almost a scream.

From a distance of a dozen feet Dolowicz looked up, and in the same instant that he realized the man was pointing something at him, he saw the sunburst flash and felt, with a surge of fury at this new indignity, a sharp, intense pain stitch across his stomach. Dead, he staggered two paces backward before collapsing across the polished rail.

ARTIS JAMES

As Transit Patrolman Artis James started down the station-entrance steps, it didn't occur to him to bemoan the fact that he was leaving the sunlight. The underground was his element, as the sea was the sailor's. He was waving to the change-booth clerk before he remembered that he had turned his radio off when he had gone to buy cigarettes. He switched on, and a call came through at once. He cleared his throat and acknowledged.

"Where the hell have you been?"

"Sorry, Sarge, I had to go outside, I had an 'Eighty—"

"That's no reason to go off your radio."

"I had to help this 'Eighty into a cab," James said glibly. "She was so weak I couldn't hear her voice. To hear what her address was I had to turn down the radio."

"Some story. Never mind. Where are you now?"

"Twenty-eighth, southbound platform, just going in."

"Help maintain order there. Platform very crowded?"

"I can handle it," Artis said. "What's the problem?"

The sergeant said, "Look, don't react. Train has been hijacked. Don't react. Help on the way. Maintain order."

At the south end of the platform Artis saw a boil of people climbing up from the roadbed. He hurried forward. Half a dozen people started babbling in high excitement. Shrillest of all was the young conductor with them. "The train is hijacked," he said. "Get through to somebody. Armed men, with machine guns—"

Artis held up his hand to stem the flow of hysteria. Into his radio he said, "Patrolman Artis James calling Nerve Center."

"Come in, Patrolman James."

"There's at least a hundred passengers coming up off the tracks."

The conductor was screaming at him. "—down the track. To the train. I told him, but—"

"Hold on," Artis said into the radio, and then to the conductor: "Say that again."

"The Grand Central trainmaster went down the track."

"Sarge, the conductor says the Grand Central trainmaster went down the track a few minutes ago," Artis reported. "Come in."

"He's nuts. Look, James, you better go after him, fast, and turn him back. But don't in any way get involved with the criminals. Exercise *extreme* caution. Acknowledge."

"On my way. Over and out."

Artis James had been on the roadbed just once before. The tunnel was haunted by shadows, and he was heading toward a band of heavily armed criminals. And all on his own.

The lights of the cars of Pelham One Two Three came into view. Skirting the dead train, he began to run. He was puffing by the time he made out a wavering shape some distance in front of him on the roadbed. He bent over for concealment, and the trainmaster took on bulky definition. Suddenly there were voices in the tunnel, angry and echoing. He kept on, but more prudently, taking shelter behind one pillar before advancing to the next.

He was sixty or seventy feet from the car, behind a pillar, when a staccato burst of gunfire reverberated through the tunnel.

Blinded by the muzzle flash, his heart pounding, he pressed himself into the ungiving metal of the pillar.

It must have been a minute before he risked peering around. Two people were looking out of the back door. The trainmaster was sprawled on the track. He thought of trying to work his way back to safer ground, but the danger of being seen was too great. He unslung his radio and, in a whisper, called Nerve Center. "They shot the trainmaster."

"So far as you can tell he's dead?" The voice was dispassionate; it was collecting facts.

"They shot him with a machine gun. He must be dead."

"You sure he's dead?"

"You expect me to go up there and feel his pulse?"

"Take it easy. Go back to the station and await further instructions."

"If I move, they *see* me," Artis whispered urgently.

"Oh. Then stay where you are. But take no action, *no action* without specific instructions. Check me."

"I check you. Stay put, and no action. Right?"

"Good enough. Over and out."

RYDER

A dead soldier, Ryder thought. The other side has suffered a casualty. The body might have been a fat kewpie doll, its upturned cheeks tinged green in the reflection of a signal light.

"I wasted him," Joe Welcome said. "I stitched him right across the belly."

Ryder looked out past the body—it was no longer a threat, if it had ever been—at the terrain: the roadbed, the burnished tracks, the grimy walls, the pillars that might conceal a man. There was no movement, only the becalmed darkness.

"I got the action started," Welcome said. He was taking short, shallow breaths. "I got us on the scoreboard."

He was all revved up, Ryder thought, his blood mixture enriched by a killing. "I want you and Steever to change places."

"How come?" Welcome said. "What for?"

215

"The passengers know you shot somebody. They'll be easier to handle because they'll be intimidated. Play it cool; they'll behave themselves." Ryder went back to his observation of the tunnel. Steever came up behind him silently.

"Take over back here," Ryder said. "I want Welcome up closer to me so I can keep an eye on him."

Steever peered up the track. "It going okay?"

"On schedule. I predicted it would be slow at the start. They're still stunned on the other side. But they'll catch on."

Steever nodded, content. He was a good soldier, Ryder thought. He took a chance and would accept any outcome, not because he was a gambler but because his uncomplicated mind understood perfectly the terms of his employment. You lived or you died.

Ryder went forward. Against the center post Steever had vacated, Welcome had taken up a widespread stance, and the passengers were scrupulously looking in another direction. He stood beside Welcome and spoke without preamble. "Before, some of you asked for information." He paused as the passengers turned toward him. "The information most important to you is this—you are hostages."

There were one or two groans, and a suppressed scream from the mother of the two boys; others exchanged questioning glances, as if, uncertain of how to react, they sought guidance. Only the black militant and the hippie seemed wholly unaffected. The black's right eye, showing around the edge of his bloody handkerchief, was a hard, disciplined blank. The hippie was smiling beatifically down at his wriggling toes.

"If we get what we want, you'll be released unharmed. Until then, you will do exactly what you're told."

"And if you don't get what you want?" the old man said.

The other passengers avoided looking at the old man, as though to disavow complicity; he had asked the question none of them wanted answered. Ryder said, "We expect to get it."

"What do you want?" the old man said. "Money?"

Welcome said, "That's enough, grandpa. Button up."

"What else is there?" A smile twitched Ryder's mask.

"So. Money. And if you don't get the money?"

"We'll get it," Ryder said. "What should concern you all is that we won't hesitate to kill you if you get out of line."

Ryder went down the aisle to the front of the car.

Longman stepped out in front of him. "I think we got a cop," he whispered.

"What makes you think so? Which one?"

"Take a look next to the hippie. Ever see anybody looked more like a cop?"

He was the bulky man in the tweed jacket and rumpled shirt.

"Let's frisk him." Longman's whisper turned into an audible croak.

When the question of frisking the passengers had arisen, weeks ago, they had decided against it. Even if anyone did have a gun, only a fool would attempt to use it against such enormous odds. But now, partly to quiet Longman, Ryder said, "Okay. Cover me," and walked back up the aisle again.

He stopped in front of the man. "On your feet."

Slowly, fixing his eyes on Ryder's, the man stood up. Next to him, the hippie was industriously scratching himself under his poncho.

TOM BERRY

Tom Berry caught the word "frisk." The tall man, the leader, seemed to be studying him, briefly weighing some proposition advanced by the whisperer. A wave of heat swept over him. Somehow, they had made him. The heavy Smith and Wesson .38 was snugged firmly in his belt beneath the concealing poncho. And what was he going to do about it?

The question was urgent. By the terms of your training and conditioning and oath, your gun was a sacred object, and no man could be permitted to take it from you. You defended it as you would your life. So you didn't give it up unless you were the kind of poltroon who wanted to live at any cost. Well, that was exactly the kind of poltroon he was.

And so he had chosen dishonor over death. But then the leader

of the hijackers started toward him, and all his training, conditioning, brainwashing, whatever you wanted to call it, spat squarely in the eye of his intellect, and he became a cop who believed all he had been taught. He slid his hand under his poncho and began to scratch himself, moving his hand steadily across his stomach until the fingers brought up against the hard wooden butt of the .38.

The leader loomed above him, his voice at the same time impersonal and threatening. "On your feet."

Berry's fingers had already closed on the butt when the man at his left stood up. And so Berry didn't really know, and was relieved of the burden of having to know, whether or not he would have drawn. His coppishness, he thought, blinked on and off like the sign on a Chinese restaurant.

Funny, Berry thought, the man does look like a cop. The leader was frisking him efficiently. When he was satisfied there was no weapon, he took the man's wallet and went through it quickly. "Newspaperman. Ever been told you look like a policeman?"

The man was sweating, but his voice was steady. "Frequently."

"You're a reporter?"

The man shook his head. "No. I'm a drama critic."

Almost playfully the leader said, "I hope you like our show."

Berry suppressed a laugh. The leader went back to the motorman's cab. Berry began to scratch himself again, his fingers retreating from the revolver. He folded his hands across his chest and grinned vacuously at his toes.

RYDER

In the cab Ryder was remembering a bright, sunny day that accented rather than softened the tawdriness of the city streets. Longman had suddenly stopped short and blurted out a question that must have been plaguing him for weeks.

"Why is a person like you doing this? I mean, you're smart, and young; you could have a life . . ." Longman paused. "You're not really a criminal."

"I'm planning a criminal act. That makes me a criminal."

"Well, okay. But what I want to know is *why*."

There were several answers, each partially true, which was to say partially untrue as well. He might have said he was doing it for money, or for excitement, or because of the way his parents had died, or because he didn't feel things quite the way other people did. And perhaps any of those would have satisfied Longman. Instead he said, "If I knew why, I probably wouldn't be doing it."

Ryder was aware that he had plucked this answer out of the air, not because he believed it but because he had no interest in the question. He knew the facts of his life, and that was enough for him. Whether you drifted with the current or tried to fight it, you reached the same destination—death. It was a matter of indifference to him what route he took, except that he preferred something scenic over something expedient.

He had learned much about the value of life from the example of his parents, who had died of accidents within a year of each other. His father's accident consisted of a heavy glass ashtray that had come sailing out of a window, thrown by an irate woman at her husband, who had ducked, so it smashed his father's skull instead. His mother's accident was cancer.

He was fourteen that year. He had acknowledged the losses without mourning, perhaps because he had already cultivated an unusual detachment derived from the sensed absence of love in his parents' marriage, which more or less included their only child. But he had never held it against them. It wasn't only the love things that were missing, but the hate things as well.

He went to live with a schoolteacher aunt in New Jersey, and according to some whimsical last wish of his mother he was enrolled at a military academy near Bordentown and rarely saw his aunt. In the summers she placed him in a boys' camp in the Adirondacks while she went off on an annual European vacation.

He regarded his school as inane. Although he had quick reflexes and was quite strong for his weight, sports bored him. Academically he was in the top ten percent. Socially, by choice, he was a loner. He had two sexual encounters, which he enjoyed

219

so little that he eliminated sex from his schoolboy curriculum.

Nothing in military school or two years of ROTC at college prepared him for his discovery of a métier once he went into combat. It was in Vietnam, in the halcyon days when Americans were "advisers." Second Lieutenant Ryder had been assigned to an ARVN major on some ill-defined mission to a hamlet northwest of Saigon. They were ambushed and would have been wiped out to a man if the Vietcong had been better disciplined. But when the ARVN unit turned and ran, the ambushers broke cover and chased them in the open.

The ARVN officer had died in the first volley. With the help of a sergeant who spoke some English, Ryder rallied the troops and mounted a counterattack, discovering in the process that he was fearless—or, more accurately, that the thought of death did not in any way affect his competence.

He fought frequently after that. If he didn't precisely take pleasure in killing, certainly he found a measure of satisfaction in his cool efficiency. At the end of his tour he was reassigned as an instructor of infantry in Georgia, where he remained until he was mustered out.

He took his accumulated pay to make a tour of Europe. In Belgium, at a bar in Antwerp, he met a cheerful, hard-faced German who recruited him as a mercenary. When the market for mercenaries dried up, he knocked around in Tangier for a bit, turning down opportunities to do some smuggling. Eventually he returned to the States, to live in Manhattan.

A few weeks after he began working as a salesman of mutual funds, he drifted into an affair with a woman client who professed to be in love with him. Perhaps she was. He was a skillful enough partner, but he had no compelling sex drive. The day he was fired from his job he stopped seeing the lady. Neither event stirred him.

He could not have said why he accepted Longman's friendship, except that it was offered. Nor could he explain to himself why he was willing to embrace a criminal venture in Manhattan. Perhaps it was because the strategical problems appealed to him. More probably because the money meant the end of having to

earn a living in uncongenial ways. Certainly the high risk appealed to him. But, finally, motivation didn't matter, only the action leading therefrom.

CLIVE PRESCOTT

Lieutenant Prescott's boss, TA Police Captain Durgin, called Command Center to report the news about Dolowicz. Prescott reached over Correll's shoulder and took the phone.

"Stay put, Clive," the captain said. "Maintain contact with the train. Are they saying anything?"

"They've been silent for the last few minutes."

"Tell them we reached the mayor. Tell them we need more time. Any questions?"

"Yes," Prescott said. "I'd like to get in on the action."

"That's not a question. Stay right where you are."

Trainmasters and dispatchers from the other parts of Command Center were now surrounding the console.

"Gentlemen," Prescott said. A dozen faces turned toward him, cigars twitching. "Gentlemen, this console is now in effect a police post. I'll have to ask you to clear out." He stared sternly at the group; then, expressionless, cigars rotating, they began to drift away. "Frank, see if you can raise the train."

Correll, the desk trainmaster, jumped to his feet. "How do you expect me to keep the line running if you take my console away?"

"Use the dispatchers' consoles." Prescott slipped into Correll's chair and activated the boom mike. "Command Center calling Pelham One Two Three."

"If I was handling it," Correll said, "I'd go storming in there with guns and tear gas and manpower."

Prescott deactivated the mike. "You're not handling it, thank God," he said. "Why don't you start working out a flex to keep the line running?"

"That's another thing. I'm stuck with a mile-long gap, all four tracks out, right in the center of the city. If you just gave me power on two tracks, even *one* track."

"We can't give you any power. Try relaxing. You'll have your

railroad back in an hour or so, give or take a few minutes—or lives."

"An *hour!* You realize we're creeping up on *rush hour?*"

"Calling Pelham One Two Three," Prescott said into the mike.

"Pelham One Two Three to Lieutenant Prescott at Command Center. I'm looking at my watch, Lieutenant. It reads two thirty-seven," Ryder said.

"You're not giving us enough time," Prescott said.

"You're down to thirty-six minutes. Check me."

"I check you. But a bureaucracy moves slowly."

"Time it learned how to move fast."

"You know, we don't have a million dollars just lying around."

"You haven't agreed yet to pay it. The money isn't hard to raise—not if you're serious about it."

"I'll be in touch. Just don't hurt anybody else."

"Else? What do you mean by *else?*"

A blunder, Prescott thought. They didn't know a TA patrolman on the track saw Dolowicz's death. "People back on the station heard gunfire. We assumed you might have hurt a passenger."

"We killed somebody out on the track. We'll kill anyone else we see in the tunnel. *And* a passenger. Keep that in mind. Any infraction and we'll kill one hostage."

"They are innocent people," Prescott said. "Don't hurt them."

"Thirty-five minutes left. Contact me when you have word."

"Check. I ask you again—don't hurt those people."

"We'll hurt as many as we have to."

"Back to you soon," Prescott said. "Over and out." He slumped back in the chair, wrung out with suppressed anger.

"To listen to you pleading with that punk," Correll said, "it makes me ashamed to be an American."

"Go away," Prescott said. "Go play with your trains."

HIS HONOR, THE MAYOR

His Honor, the mayor, lay abed on the second floor of Gracie Mansion with a stupefying headache, aching bones, and a temperature of 103.5°. The floor beside his bed was littered with offi-

cial business which he had discarded unread. Someone else would do the work of the city. He had issued orders that no calls were to be put through, barring a major disaster such as Manhattan Island slipping off into the bay, a circumstance he sometimes prayed might come to pass.

It was the first morning since he had taken office that he had not left the mansion at seven sharp for City Hall, and he felt both truant and disoriented. So when the phone buzzed, he struggled to focus his attention and lunged for it. The voice at the other end, speaking from downstairs, was that of Murray Lasalle, one of his deputy mayors, the man referred to by the press as the "spark plug of the administration."

Lasalle said, "Sorry, Sam, it can't be helped."

"God's sake, Murray, I'm about to die."

"Postpone it. We've got a crisis on our hands."

"Can't you handle it? I feel genuinely awful, Murray."

"Sure I can handle it, like I handle every other nasty job in this stinking misbegotten city, but I won't."

"Don't ever let me hear you say won't. There's no such word in the lexicon of a deputy mayor."

Lasalle, who had a cold himself, said, "Don't give *me* lessons in politics, Sam, or, sick as you are, I'll remind you—"

"I'm kidding," the mayor said. "Sick as I am, I have more sense of humor than you have or ever will have. What's the calamity? It better be good."

"Oh, it's good, all right," Lasalle said. "A gang of men have seized a subway train." He overrode the mayor's voice. "*Have seized a subway train.* They're holding sixteen citizens and the motorman as hostages, and they won't release them unless the city pays a million dollars in ransom."

For a moment, in his fever, the mayor thought he had misunderstood. But Murray Lasalle's voice was gratingly clear.

"Hell and damnation," the mayor said. He had led a sheltered childhood and never learned to swear convincingly, but because he regarded it as a social grace, he never gave up trying. "Why do people think up such things to torment me? Can't we let them

keep the damn subway train? We'll never miss it." He sneezed. "The city hasn't *got* a million dollars."

"No? Well, you'd better find it. Somewhere. Even if you have to liquidate your Christmas Club account. I'm coming right up." The phone slammed in the mayor's ear.

POLICE COMMISSIONER

From the rear seat of his limousine, speeding uptown on the Franklin D. Roosevelt Drive from 240 Centre Street, the police commissioner spoke on his radio to the borough commander at Twenty-eighth and Lexington.

"What's it like there?" the commissioner said.

"Murder," the borough commander said. "As usual, they came out of the woodwork. I estimate twenty thousand spectators, and more pouring in all the time. I'm praying for a hailstorm."

The commissioner leaned to his right for a glimpse of the clear blue sky over the East River. He straightened up at once. He was an incorruptible and intelligent man who had come all the way up from patrolman, and although he understood that the luxurious black limousine was a valid, even necessary prerogative of his rank, he could not sit in it comfortably.

"Got barriers up?" he said to the borough commander.

"Certainly. And muscle, courtesy of the Tactical Police Force. We're holding our own, and trying to push new arrivals off into the side streets. We're not going to be winning any new friends."

"Traffic?"

"I've placed a patrolman at every intersection from Thirty-fourth to Fourteenth, and crosstown from Fifth to Second."

"Your second-in-command?"

"Deputy Chief Inspector Daniels of Special Operations. He's breathing fire. He wants to go in and clean those bastards out. So do I."

"Don't let me hear that kind of talk," the commissioner said sharply. "Stand by, take up tactical positions, and wait."

"Yes, sir, that's exactly what we're doing. All I'm saying is that it goes against my grain."

"Never mind your grain. Do you have all the emergency exits manned up top?"

"Both sides, as far south as Fourteenth. I've got about fifty men in the tunnel—north and south of the train, well concealed. All wearing vests and armed with machine guns, riot guns, tear gas, the whole arsenal. And a half dozen snipers with night scopes. We could fight a war down there."

"Just make sure it's understood that nobody is to move. Those people will kill. We're taking all their threats seriously. Did you interrogate the passengers they turned loose?"

"Yes, sir, as many as we could latch on to. They're contradictory witnesses. But the conductor, a nice Irish kid called Carmody, is helpful. We know how many took the train, and how."

"A dozen?"

"Just four. Wearing stocking masks, armed with Thompson guns. Dressed in black raincoats and black hats, according to the conductor, and familiar with subway operation."

"Yes. You might put somebody on the files of discharged Transit employees. Not that it will help at the moment."

"I'll ask the Transit Police to take it on. There are a few hundred of *them* here, too. Including Chief Costello."

"I want him treated with the utmost respect."

"Communications are awkward. TA Command Center at Jay Street is the only direct contact with the hijacked car. The DCI is set up in the motorman's cab of a train standing in the Twenty-eighth Street station. He can use its radio to talk to TA Command Center, but not to the hijacked car. And he can't hear the hijackers' end of a conversation. I asked the hijackers, through Command Center, if they would allow us to communicate with them by bullhorn in the tunnel. They refused. They *like* it complicated."

"Who is the person in direct contact with them?"

"A TA Police lieutenant. Prescott. Seems sharp. But what reason would those people have for not agreeing to bullhorns?"

"Psychological, I guess. Show us who's boss. I'm signing off now, Charlie. Keep everything cool, and I'll be in touch."

The limousine swung into the Gracie Mansion drive. The driver

came to a lurching stop behind three other black official limousines. The commissioner jumped out of the car and started on a trot for the verandaed front of the house.

The television stations put the news of the hijacking on the air within seconds of receiving the story on their tickers. Most of them broke into ongoing soap operas to make the announcement. Several, less willing to offend their faithful midday audiences, ran a slow-moving strip across the bottom of the screen, thus making it possible to enjoy fact and fiction at the same time. The news departments sent mobile units winging off downtown. Universal, the largest of the networks, sent, in addition to their unit, Stafford Bedrick, news superstar, in person. Ordinarily Bedrick covered only the most dignified news events, but he had volunteered for this assignment, sensing its vast potential in human interest.

Some camera crews commandeered offices in buildings overlooking the scene, and through their windows shot panoramic views of the crowd. Other crews circulated at street level. Most of these, frustrated in their efforts to reach the police command post which had been set up in a parking lot on the southwest corner next to the subway entrance, kept themselves occupied with man-in-the-street interviews.

Stafford Bedrick, however, knew how to use his famous face and voice as instruments of his will. They cut him a path to the very center of things: the police command post in the parking lot. His entourage followed, beasts of burden laden with cameras, cables, and sound equipment.

"Inspector? Stafford Bedrick. How are you?"

The borough commander whirled, but outrage was nipped in the bud by instant recognition. Almost by reflex, he smiled.

"You won't remember," Bedrick said with transparent modesty, "but we've met before. When those hoodlums tried to set fire to that Russian outside the consulate?"

"Sure," the borough commander said, and prudently turned his smile off; the commissioner regarded intimacy with the media

as a subtle form of corruption. "I'm pretty busy, Mr. Bedrick."

"I realize this is not the ideal time for an interview, Inspector—I hope to have that pleasure on my regular show—but perhaps a few words of reassurance that the police are exerting every precaution on behalf of the unlucky hostages?"

"Exerting every precaution."

"The burning question, of course, is being settled a few miles upriver at Gracie Mansion. Is it your opinion, Inspector, that the decision will be to pay the ransom?"

"Up to them."

"If the decision were yours, would you pay it?"

"I do what I'm told."

"Discipline. Of course. Sir, would you care to comment on the rumor that this is the work of a revolutionary group?"

"I haven't heard any such rumor."

"Inspector," the borough commander's uniformed driver called from his car. "Radio, sir, the commissioner."

The borough commander abruptly made for the car, followed closely by Bedrick and his crew. He slammed the door and rolled up the windows. Reaching for the hand mike, he saw a camera lens pressed against the window. Turning his broad back, he faced the opposite window. Another camera appeared.

Within five minutes of the announcement of the hijacking on television and radio, the news desk of *The New York Times* accepted a telephone call from a man who said he was Brother Williamus, minister of sabotage of BRAM, Black Revolutionists of America Movement. "I desire to inform you," he said in a rich, jovially menacing voice, "that hijacking that underground flier, you know, is a revolutionary sabotage action of BRAM. You know? Striking swiftly and ferocious, a storm unit of BRAM have use this means to convey upon the white downtrodders the aim of the movement to hit Charley where he live. The money obtain through this revolutionary act will be used to further the aspirations of BRAM toward the black brother, wherever he may be. Right on?"

In all, the *Times* received over a dozen calls from such claim-

ants, the *News* an equal number, the *Post* a few less. In addition, each paper was besieged by people offering clues to the hijackers' identities and plans for overcoming them; opinions on the philosophical, psychological, and sociological motivations of the hijackers, and, above all, on the wickedness of the mayor.

The switchboard at City Hall was inundated. Public relations men, clerks, and even secretaries were detailed to handle these calls, with instructions to make no commitments and to avoid irritating the callers to the detriment (the qualifying word "further" was tactfully omitted) of the mayor:

"If the city pays these bandits off, it will be an open invitation to every crook and crackpot in the city. I don't want my money used to coddle criminals."

"What's more important, human lives or a few paltry dollars? If one of those passengers suffers death or injury, you can tell that fine mayor of ours that I will dedicate the rest of my life to exposing him for the monster he is!"

"Call out the National Guard. Send them in there with fixed bayonets. I volunteer my help even though I'm eighty-four. Things like this didn't go on when I was a boy."

"Can you please find out if my brother is on the train?"

"God bless the mayor. Tell him I'm praying for him."

"Pass this on to the police. All they have to do is flood the subway tunnel."

HIS HONOR, THE MAYOR

In ordinary circumstances His Honor, the mayor, might have enjoyed sitting above the battle while his subordinates debated the merits of a given subject, each astride his own hobbyhorse of bias and self-interest. But now, light-headed with fever, he feared that his judgment would be impaired and that he might make a faulty decision, which is to say one that would be politically unprofitable. Not that he was so unprincipled as this might suggest, because he undoubtedly would—as he always did—temper expediency with decency, a fatal human failing he was helpless to rectify. Present at his bedside, in addition to the police commis-

sioner, the comptroller, the chairman of the Transit Authority, the president of the City Council and Murray Lasalle, were his wife and his physician.

Propped up on a pillow, struggling to keep his rheumy eyes open, His Honor permitted Murray Lasalle to moderate the conference with his usual mixture of sharp intelligence, impatience, and gutter toughness.

The mayor knew that Lasalle had already arrived at a decision and expected him to support it. For a rarity, political advantage and the mayor's best instincts coincided. The *Times* would gravely support him on humanitarian grounds. The *News* would grudgingly approve, yet contrive to blame him for the hijacking. The well-to-do would say aye, the taxi driver nay, the black community would be indifferent. Nothing ever changed. He knew for a fact that the city had already chosen up sides on the propriety of his having the flu.

"The issue," Lasalle said, "and we have no time to waste, is whether to pay the ransom. Everything else—whether we can legally offer the money, where we're going to get the cash, whether we can catch the hijackers and recover it—everything else is secondary. And we can't discuss it at length, or we'll have seventeen corpses on our hands. I'm going to allow one fast round of argument, five minutes' worth all told. Ready?" He nodded to the police commissioner.

"Well, we're mobilized to the fullest extent," the PC said. "I could go down in there and wipe them out. But I couldn't guarantee the safety of the hostages."

"In other words," Lasalle said, "you're for paying the ransom."

"I hate to give in to criminals," the police commissioner said, "but to slaughter the innocent with the guilty—"

"Vote," Lasalle said.

"I abstain."

Lasalle turned to the TA chairman. "You're up."

"My entire concern is with the safety of my passengers. A refusal to pay up would cost us the faith and trust of our passengers. We must pay the ransom."

"With *what?*" the comptroller said. "*Your* budget? I advise Hizzoner to make no financial commitments until we know where the money is coming from."

"I take it your vote is nay," Lasalle said.

"I haven't expressed my philosophy," the comptroller said.

"No time for philosophy," Lasalle said.

"But I don't doubt there's time for *her* philosophy?" the comptroller inclined his head stiffly toward the mayor's wife, who had once spoken of him as "a Scrooge without hope of redemption."

With a curling lip, the mayor's wife registered a vehement aye.

"Thank you, Madam Mayor," Lasalle said. He nodded to the president of the council. "Your turn."

"I vote nay for the following reasons—"

"Okay," Lasalle said. "One abstention, one aye, and two nays. I vote aye, and that makes it two-two. Sam?"

"Wait a minute," the president of the council said. "I want to explain my decision."

"No time," Lasalle said. "People's lives are at stake. The deciding vote's up to Hizzoner. Sam. Will you wrap it up, please?"

"Arrange for the payoff, Murray," the mayor said.

Lasalle pointed at the commissioner. "Pass the word to the bad guys that we're paying." To the comptroller: "What bank do we do the most business with?"

"Gotham National Trust. I hate to do it, but I'll phone—"

"*I'll* phone," Lasalle interrupted. "Everybody out. Let's move."

"You're full of the stuff of humanity, darling," the mayor's wife said.

"He's full of it, all right," Lasalle said.

RYDER

Even with the light in the cab turned off, Ryder knew he presented an easy target. He didn't doubt there were police in the tunnel, or that several of them would have him squarely centered in their sights. But unless they decided to fight it out instead of paying the ransom—in which case he would simply be the first of many to die—he was running no greater risk than the other three

in their more sheltered positions. His cover was circumstance, and it gave him reasonable protection. As in battle, he asked no more and would accept no less.

He had little patience with romantic concepts of war. Such descriptions as "held out to the last man," "fought with utter disregard for their safety," "against overwhelming odds" struck him as being the pathetic rallying cries of losers. He knew the classic examples, most of them monuments to inept planning, idiot pride, or miscalculation: the Light Brigade, the Alamo, Pickett's charge, Thermopylae. All military mistakes. Holding out to the last man meant you were wiped out; disregard for safety multiplied your casualties. He accepted the idea of sacrifice for his command, but only for tactical advantage, never for glory.

His "command"—what a name for his little band of misfits! Except for Longman, he hardly knew them; they were bodies chosen to fill the ranks. Only he was a volunteer; Longman was a reluctant draftee. In a way, Ryder realized, he had enlisted Welcome and Steever to balance the imaginative but cowardly Longman. He had found them through the man who had sold him his armament, like himself a former mercenary. Now he was a dealer in weapons, with a warehouse in a run-down area of Newark and a hole-in-the-wall office on Pearl Street. His blind was a business in hides and skins. His office contained a phone, stationery, and floor-to-ceiling bins of merchandise that he dusted once a month for appearance' sake.

Submachine guns were no great deal for him to supply. If you wanted them badly enough, he could even get you two-man submarines complete with torpedoes. When the arrangements for four Thompsons were completed, the dealer fished up a bottle of whiskey, and he and Ryder refought some old battles (including a number in which they had been on opposite sides). At one point the phone had rung. "One of my boys," the dealer said when he hung up. "Crazy as a coot. I wish somebody would take him off my hands and save me the trouble of killing him." He looked at Ryder with morose humor. "Maybe you'll do it?"

"Do what?"

"I don't know what. You're buying four tommy guns. So maybe you'd be interested in this maniac?"

"You don't make him sound like attractive merchandise."

The dealer shrugged. "This boy happens to be a square peg in a round hole. I've got him running my warehouse, but he's bored. If I was ripping something off, I'd hire him. If I had a submachine gun that needed a shooter, I wouldn't hesitate to put him behind it. Guts to burn."

"But crazy."

"Only a *little*. I don't mean psychotic. Wild, say. But tough and—" He cast about for a word. "And honest," he said with surprise. "*Honest*. I mean he's not a double-crosser, he won't sell out."

"That's a consideration, unless he's *too* honest."

"Nobody is *too* honest. Can it hurt to take a look at him?"

Ryder had taken his look at Joe Welcome the following week. The boy was cocky and tough and too intense for comfort, but these weren't serious drawbacks. The question was whether he could take orders. Ryder brought up the organization. "I understand you left them to go into business for yourself. But you're working for somebody."

"That's a bunch of crap. I quit them because they're a bunch of old ladies, they got old-fashioned ways. I hope what you got in mind ain't old-fashioned."

"I wouldn't say so. In fact, I don't think it's ever been done before. You could get killed." Ryder watched the boy closely.

"I didn't expect you were offering a hundred gees for something where you couldn't get hurt. I don't scare."

Ryder nodded. "I believe you. Can you take orders?"

"From you? I'll be honest," Welcome said. "Right now I can't promise. I don't know you, you know?"

"Fair enough," Ryder said. "We'll talk again."

"You're a quiet stud," Welcome said. "But quiet don't have to be bad. The boss told me you had a career. I respect that."

The following week, not entirely without misgivings, Ryder signed Welcome on. Meanwhile he had met Steever, also through the weapons dealer, and about him he had few reservations. In

the caste system of the underworld, Steever was a heavy, as opposed to a Longman type, who would be classified as a brain. He was from the Midwest, had graduated from petty theft to armed robbery, and served time once. He had been arrested seven or eight times after that and brought to trial twice, but had no additional convictions. Ryder did not doubt that Steever would take orders.

"If it works," Ryder said, "you'll make a hundred thousand dollars."

"That's a big score."

"You'll earn it. It's a high-risk job."

"It figures," Steever said, meaning, Fair enough, I don't expect something for nothing.

And so, for better or worse, he had his army.

MURRAY LASALLE

Murray Lasalle allowed his secretary to look up the number of the bank for him, but warned her that he wanted to initiate the call himself. The secretary, an old Civil Service war-horse, was miffed at this expropriation of her rights and became even more so when Lasalle, sitting on the edge of a desk in the historic downstairs room that had once been Archibald Gracie's salon, urged her to "move it." She withdrew, muttering.

Lasalle dialed the number with impatient flicks of his finger and told the switchboard operator that the mayor's office was calling, that it was an emergency, and that he must be put through to the chairman of the board immediately. He was connected with the chairman's secretary.

"The chairman is on another phone," the secretary said. "He'll be happy to speak to you as soon as—"

"I want to speak to him right this very instant."

"He is engaged in an overseas call, sir," she said smoothly.

"Don't back-talk me, sister. This is life or death, seventeen lives, *minimum*. City emergency. So you break in."

"I'm not permitted to do that, sir."

"Look, if you don't get yourself inside his office and get his at-

tention, you're going to be prosecuted to the full extent of the law for criminal obstruction."

Her voice faltered. "I'll see what I can do, sir."

He waited, drumming his fingers on the desk, and then a plummy voice filled his ear, "Murray! How are you, old man? Rich Tompkins here. What's the flap, Murray?"

"How the hell did I get *you?* I asked for the boss, damn it, not his lousy press agent."

"Murray!"

Protest, terror, a prayer for mercy were contained in those two syllables, as Lasalle had known there would be; he had struck at the soft underbelly. Rich Tompkins was vice-president in charge of public relations for Gotham National Trust, a position of importance and dignity. He was a conservative pillar of the banking community, but he had a skeleton in his closet—for five mad months after graduating from Princeton he had worked as a movie press agent. It was the equivalent, in his world, of having been a priest or a Jew, and he lived, as Murray well knew, in a permanent state of fear that his secret would be revealed and destroy everything: hundred thou salary, Greenwich estate, forty-foot yacht, lunches with governors of the Stock Exchange. He had been a scholarship student at Princeton and had no ancestral fundament of family or finances. Stripped of his position and its perks, he was wiped off the face of the earth.

Coldly, Murray said, "What are you doing on this phone?"

"You see, I was in the chairman's office when Miss Selwyn came in. Murray, in any way that I can possibly help—"

In three sentences Lasalle informed Tompkins of the situation. "Unless you can authorize the transfer of a million dollars, I want you to break into that old windbag's conversation. Immediately. Do you read me?"

"Murray, I can't. He's talking to Burundi."

"Who the hell is Burundi?"

"It's a country. In Africa? One of the newly formed under-developed African republics? We *finance* them."

"Who is *them?*"

"I told you. Burundi. The whole *country*. So you see—"

"I see only a former movie flack obstructing the city government. Get him for me in thirty seconds, or I'll blow it, Rich."

"Murray!"

"The countdown has begun."

"What can I tell him?"

"That he's got a most urgent local call waiting."

"Murray, it takes *four days* to get a Burundi call through."

"Fifteen seconds, then I tip the media. Republic Pictures, pimping studs for hard-up actresses—"

"I'll get him. I don't know how, but I'll get him. Hold!"

"Good afternoon, Mr. Lasalle." The chairman's voice was grave and measured. "I understand the city has an emergency?"

"A subway train has been hijacked. Seventeen people are being held hostage. Unless we deliver a million dollars in less than a half hour, those seventeen people will be killed."

"A subway train," the chairman said. "What a novel idea."

"Yes, sir. You understand about the haste, sir? Is there any problem about that much cash being available?"

"Through the Federal Reserve Bank, none whatsoever. We are members, of course."

"Good. Will you arrange for us to be given it at once?"

"Given? How do I take *given*, Mr. Lasalle?"

"Lent," Lasalle said, his voice rising. "We want to borrow a million. The sovereign City of New York."

"Borrow. Well, you see, Mr. Lasalle, there are technicalities . . . authorization, terms, duration of loan."

"We haven't got time for all that, with all due respect."

"But *all that*, as you put it, is of importance. Our directors and officers and stockholders will ask—"

"Look, you ignorant son of a bitch," Murray screamed, and then paused, awed by his own unspeakable audacity. But it was too late for apology or retreat, and in any case they were not his style. He plunged on, his voice an open threat. "You want to keep our business? I can take it around the corner, you know. And that's only the beginning. I'll find violations on—"

235

"No one," the chairman interrupted in slow wonderment, "no one has ever called me by *that* epithet before."

It was an opportunity to make generous amends, but Lasalle pushed on recklessly. "Well, I'll tell you something, Mr. Chairman. If you don't get started on that money this instant, it's going to be on *everybody's* lips."

CLIVE PRESCOTT

The decision at Gracie Mansion had been relayed from the police commissioner to the borough commander, from the borough commander to Deputy Chief Inspector Daniels in the cab of Pelham One Two Eight in the Twenty-eighth Street station, and from the DCI to Prescott at Command Center. Prescott called Pelham One Two Three. "We'll pay the ransom. Repeat, we'll pay the ransom. Acknowledge."

"I read you. I will now give you further instructions. You will obey them to the letter. Confirm."

"Okay," Prescott said.

"Three points. First: The money is to be paid in fifties and hundreds, as follows: five hundred thousand dollars in hundreds, and five hundred thousand dollars in fifties. Check me."

Prescott repeated the message slowly and clearly, for the benefit of the DCI who was hearing his end of the conversation.

"That works out to five thousand hundred-dollar bills, and ten thousand fifty-dollar bills. A total of fifteen thousand bills. Point Two: These bills are to be put up in stacks of two hundred bills each, bound with a thick rubber band lengthwise and another widthwise. Confirm."

"Five thousand hundreds, ten thousand fifties, in packs of two hundred bills, bound fore and aft with rubber bands."

"Point Three: All the bills will be old bills, and the serial numbers will be random. Check me."

"All old bills," Prescott said. "No serial sequences."

"That's all. When the money arrives, you will contact me again for additional instructions."

Prescott signaled Pelham One Two Eight. "I picked it up," the

DCI said. "The message is on its way to the mayor. Get back to them and try to get us more time."

Prescott called Pelham One Two Three. "I passed on your instructions, but we have to have more time."

"It's two forty-nine. You have twenty-four minutes."

"Be reasonable. The money has to be counted, stacked, brought all the way uptown. It isn't physically possible."

"No."

The flat, unyielding voice left Prescott stunned. "Look," he said, "give us another fifteen minutes. Is there any point to killing innocent people?"

"Nobody is innocent."

God help us, Prescott thought, he's some kind of lunatic. "*Fifteen minutes* is worth slaughtering all those people for?"

"All?" The voice sounded surprised. "Unless you force our hand, we have no intention of killing them all."

It's the madman's first near-human reaction, Prescott thought. "So give us the time."

"Because if we killed them all," the voice said calmly, "we would surrender our leverage. But if we kill one or two or even five, the leverage remains. You will lose one passenger for each minute over the deadline. I won't discuss it further."

Prescott wavered on the edge of rage, hopelessness, a willingness to demean himself in any way that was necessary, but he knew that all of it, any of it, would come up against an implacable will. And so, fighting to control his voice, he shifted his ground. "Will you let us pick up the trainmaster? The man you shot? We'd like to send a stretcher down."

"No. We can't allow that."

"He may be suffering."

"He's dead. But if you insist, we'll put a half dozen rounds into him to put him out of his misery, if any."

Prescott folded his arms on the console and slowly lowered his head. When he looked up again, his eyes were streaming with tears. He balled up a handkerchief and pressed it deeply into each of his eyes in turn, then signaled the DCI. He said, in a

disciplined voice, "No time extension. Flat refusal. He'll kill a passenger for every minute we're late. He means it."

The DCI, in a voice as inflectionless as his own, said, "I just don't think it's physically possible."

"Three thirteen," Prescott said. "After that we can start scratching passengers, one per minute."

FRANK CORRELL

Hyped up, noisy, leaping from console to console, Frank Correll devised a flex to keep the entire line from being paralyzed. For instance, Lexington Avenue line trains departing from the East Bronx were diverted to the West Side tracks at 149th Street and Grand Concourse. South of Fourteenth Street, some trains were run off into Brooklyn, some sent around the loop at City Hall or South Ferry, which brought them northward to Bowling Green, where they began to pile up. Buses were commandeered to portage riders to other lines in the midtown area.

It was a messy improvisation, but at least it avoided a catastrophic standstill. "Like the show must go on," Frank Correll shouted, "the railroad gotta keep running."

MURRAY LASALLE

Murray Lasalle assaulted Gracie Mansion's handsome staircase two steps at a time and entered the mayor's room. His Honor was lying on his face, rump in air as the doctor hit it with a hypodermic. The mayor flipped over and pulled up his pajamas.

Lasalle said, "Get out of bed and put your clothes on, Sam, we're going downtown."

"You're out of your mind," the mayor said.

"I will not permit His Honor out of bed," the doctor said.

"Nobody asked you," Lasalle said. "I make the political decisions around here."

"Murray, I'm sick as a dog. What's the sense of this?"

"The sense of it? Seventeen citizens in jeopardy of their lives and the mayor won't even *appear?*"

"What's the good of appearing? So I can get booed?"

"Look, Sam, all you have to do is go down and talk to the hijackers on a bullhorn, then you can go to bed again."

"Will they listen to me?"

"I doubt it. But it has to be done. You want the other side to plead for your citizens' lives?"

"They're not sick," the mayor said. He sat up, swung his feet over the edge of the bed, and pitched forward. Lasalle caught him. "This is crazy, Murray. I can't even stand up. If I go downtown, I'll get even sicker." His eyes widened. "I might even die."

"Worse things can happen to a politician than just death," Lasalle said. "I'll help you on with your pants."

RYDER

Ryder opened the cab door and walked out to the center of the car. He took up a position slightly in front of Welcome but off to one side, to keep Steever's field of fire clear.

"Your attention, please."

He watched the faces turn toward him, reluctantly or in a sudden almost spastic reaction to his voice. Only two met his eyes: the old man with grave but lively interest, the militant black defiantly over the blood-dyed handkerchief. The motorman's white lips were moving silently. The hippie kept his dreamy zonked-out smile. The mother kept touching her boys, as if to commit them to memory. The girl in the Anzac hat was sitting erect, a calculated pose to bring her breasts forward, to accentuate the curve of her thighs.

"I have further information for you," Ryder said. "The city has agreed to pay for your release."

The mother drew her children to her compulsively. The militant's expression remained unchanged. The old man clapped in soundless applause.

"If everything proceeds according to schedule, you will be released unharmed to go about your business."

The old man said, "By 'according to schedule' you mean what?"

"Just that the city keeps its word."

"Okay," the old man said. "I would like to know, just from curiosity, how much money?"

"A million dollars."

"Each?"

Ryder shook his head. The old man looked disappointed. "Sixty thousand apiece is all we're worth?"

"Shut your mouth, old man." This was Welcome's voice, but it was uninterested. Ryder saw why: he was playing games with the girl. Her pose was for his benefit.

"Sir." The mother was leaning toward him, crushing her boys together. "Sir, the instant you get the money, you'll let us go?"

"No, but soon afterwards."

"Why not *then?*"

"No more questions," Ryder said. He took a backward step toward Welcome. "Stop fooling around with that girl," he said in an undertone.

"Stop worrying," Welcome retorted. "I can handle these slobs and that broad at the same time."

Ryder frowned, but said nothing. He went back to the cab, ignoring Longman's anxious look. There was nothing to do now but wait for the deadline. The next move was out of his hands. He didn't even bother to look at his watch.

TOM BERRY

As soon as the leader returned to the motorman's cab, Tom Berry put him out of mind and resumed thinking about Deedee—how he had met her, and how she'd affected his head. Not that he hadn't been entertaining some vaguely uncoplike thoughts on his own, but Deedee had made him examine his assumptions seriously.

He had been on plainclothes patrol in the East Village now for three months. He didn't know why he had stuck his neck out for this detail, except that he had been bored witless by duty in an area car with his partner, a fat-necked type who hated Jews, blacks, Poles, Italians, Puerto Ricans, and almost everyone else, and was violently in favor of war—the one in Vietnam, as well as

all others past and future. So he had let his hair grow down to his shoulders, raised a beard, put in a supply of ponchos, headbands, and beads, and gone down among the motorcycle freaks, street people, radicals, acid heads, teen-age runaways, and dwindling hippie population of the East Village.

The experience had turned out to be kooky, but not boring. He had gotten to know and like some of the hippies, also some of the hustlers in hippie clothing (in a way he was one of those himself), and some of the sharp black men leading a joyous existence on the strength of a skin color that was high fashion in those purlieus. Then through Deedee he had met several highly motivated revolutionary kids who were refugees from middle-class comforts and the elite campuses of Harvard, Vassar, Yale, and Swarthmore. Not that he would want to run a revolution with them in the ranks or that Mao would be particularly crazy about them, either.

He had met Deedee during his first week, when his instructions had been to acclimate himself to the community. He had been studying the titles in the window of a bookstore on St. Marks Place when she came out of the shop and stopped to look at the window display. She was standard nonconformist: denims and T-shirt, hair streaming over her shoulders, no bra or makeup. But the hair was lustrous and clean, the denims and T-shirt laundered, the figure willowy, the features open and just missing beauty by a shade.

She became aware of his scrutiny. "The books are in the window, baby." It failed of toughness because her voice was not a street voice but soft, well modulated.

He smiled. "I was digging the books pretty good until you came along. You're prettier."

She frowned. "You're pretty, too, but I didn't try to demean you by saying so, did I?"

He recognized the polemics of Women's Lib. "I'm not into the male chauvinist bit. Honest."

"You may *think* you're not, but you gave yourself away."

She walked off, in the direction of Second Avenue. For no

particular reason he trailed along. He said, "Buy me a coffee?"

"Buzz off."

"I'm tapped out."

"Then go uptown and panhandle." She looked at him sharply. "Are you hungry?"

He said he was. She bought him a sandwich. She took it for granted that he was a member of the movement—that amorphous search-for-a-better-world flux of young people that was sometimes political, sometimes social, sometimes sexual, sometimes a form of mimicry, and often a combination of all of those—and she grew quickly exasperated at his ignorance. He found her charming and irritating at the same time, and he didn't want to arouse her suspicion. So he said, "Look, I only copped out recently, I'm just beginning to learn what the movement is all about."

"You had a straight job?"

"In a bank, would you believe it," he said glibly. "I hated it. Finally I got around to chucking it, to doing my thing."

"You don't quite know what your thing is yet, do you?"

"But I really want to learn," he said, and looked away from her in a situation that called for a long, meaningful glance into a girl's eyes. He was, at least, learning about *her*.

"Well, I can help you."

"I appreciate it," he said gravely.

They met the next day, and she began his ideological education. The following week she took him to her pad, and they shared a stick of grass and went to bed, already half in love. He had to do some sleight of hand with his gun to keep her from seeing it. But a few days later he was careless, and she spotted it. Her eyes were huge with shock as she pointed to the short barrel of the .38. "What are you doing with a pig gun?"

He found that he didn't have the stomach to lie to her. "I'm . . . well, Deedee, I happen to *be* a pig."

She surprised him by hitting him on the jaw—a closed-fist punch that staggered him, and then she sank to the floor and cried, heartbreakingly, like any bourgeois chick. Later, after recrimination, accusation, confession, and protestations of love, they

decided not to break off, and Deedee vowed secretly—though she didn't keep it a secret for very long—to dedicate herself to the liberation of a pig.

LONGMAN

Longman had never been convinced of the necessity of a stringent time limit, and he had argued vehemently against the forfeiture of the passengers' lives as a penalty.

"The moment they stop believing we mean what we say we're through," Ryder had said. "We intimidate by setting a tough deadline, and we convince by killing when we threaten to kill."

Ryder's arguments always went directly to the success of the operation, and on those terms you couldn't question his logic, bloodcurdling as it might be at one moment, and conservative the next. On money, for example, Longman had been for demanding five million dollars.

"Too much," Ryder had said. "They might balk at it. A million has a ring to it, it's the kind of sum people can understand, tolerate. You stand to end up with four hundred thousand, tax free. It's all the money you'll ever need. It's a big improvement on unemployment benefits."

The matter was settled, but the conversation left Longman wondering just how important the money was to Ryder; whether, in fact, it wasn't secondary to the adventure itself and the challenge of leadership.

Ryder had certainly not counted pennies buying what he called "matériel," and had financed everything himself. Longman knew the submachine guns had come high, not to mention the ammunition, handguns, grenades, money belts, the specially tailored raincoats, and finally the curious metal construction they referred to as "the Gimmick" that he'd designed under Ryder's prodding.

Suddenly Longman became aware of Welcome and the girl in the Anzac hat. If two people, separated by ten or fifteen feet, could be said to be making out, they were. It was queer, kinky. Not that he was a prude. He had done it all—simple and fancy—and enjoyed it. But not in public!

ANITA LEMOYNE

Anita Lemoyne gave the creep a long, passionate look to keep his fires burning. It was a rotten life. If she reckoned what she had to put out just to make the rent in that fancy high-rise she lived in (not to mention greasing up doormen and supers and renting agents and cops), it added up to a hell of a lot of tricks with no return. If there were some way to do it, she would blow the city and find a little house with a yard in the suburbs or even the real deep country. Sure—and live how?

The creep was still zeroed in on her, his eyeballs practically popping out through the holes in his mask. He was preening himself, God's gift to women. One thing for sure—he had to be a wacked-out character to be thinking the way he was right in the middle of ripping off a subway train. And what about herself? Well, she was a pro, and she couldn't help reacting in a professional way. Besides, it was a scary situation, and she'd decided a while ago it wouldn't hurt to make a friend. She still didn't think they'd deliberately harm her, but with so many guns around—well, she had seen pictures on too many front pages of innocent bystanders lying in their own blood. I don't want to be no innocent bystander, I got to get out of here!

KOMO MOBUTU

Mobutu's wound had bled itself out, although it still seeped somewhat into his saturated handkerchief. I blew my cool. I took a hit for a couple of dumb niggers who'll never know from nothing. I would not mind shedding my blood, every pure black drop of it, if it would help to set my people free. But face it—sometime it do not avail, it simply do not avail.

He felt a tap on his arm. The old dude beside him was offering a large folded handkerchief. "Take it," the old man said.

Mobutu pushed the handkerchief away. "I got my own."

"Go. Take my handkerchief. We're all in the same boat."

"Old man, you are in your boat, and I am in my boat. Don't sell me no same boat deals."

"Okay. But take the handkerchief anyway. Please."

"I will take nothing from a white peeg, old man."

"White—granted." The old man smiled. "Pig—you happen to have the wrong religion. Come on, young man, let's be friends."

"No way, old man. I am your enemy, and one day I will cut your throat."

"That day," the old man said, "*I'll* borrow *your* handkerchief."

Mobutu's handkerchief was too wet to absorb any longer. The old man had surely bought his handkerchief with profits wrung from the blood of black brothers and sisters. It therefore truly belonged to him. It was a small enough reparation. He reached for the handkerchief.

COMMAND CENTER

The Communications Desk of Command Center was busy sending out bulletins directed toward clearing all station platforms in the area affected by the power cut. Played over the PA systems, they urged passengers to leave the platforms for alternate routes— "a short walk to the BMT, IND, or West Side lines." Each message contained an adjuration to "clear the stations, please, by order of the New York City Police."

Although a number of people responded, the majority refused to budge. ("It's the way they are," the TA Police chief said to the borough commander. "Don't ask me why.") To avoid a battle, the police made no effort to clear platforms by force. Instead, they mounted guards at the street entrances to keep newly arrived passengers from descending. This measure proved effective, except at the Astor Place station, where a group of passengers, under inspired leadership, rushed the entrance, overwhelmed the guards, and stormed down the stairs to the platform.

THE CITY: OCEANIC WOOLENS BUILDING

In the lobby of the Oceanic Woolens Building on Park Avenue South near Twenty-eighth Street, Abe Rosen was enjoying the most fantastic business of his life. Spectators streamed from the streets into the lobby, gathering four deep in front of his stand. As fast as his candy bars disappeared he would open new boxes. He was

sold out of cigarettes in a half hour, then the cigars began to go, and finally his newspapers and magazines. The lobby had become all but impassable as people stood there smoking, eating candy, and inventing rumors.

Sooner or later Abe Rosen heard them all:

"A dozen ambulances . . . they turned the third rail on . . . some passengers were on the tracks. A million volts . . ."

"Castros. A bunch of Cuban Commies. The cops chased them into the tunnel and they commandeered a train. . . ."

"This cop outside told me they gave them an ultimatum. If they don't surrender by three o'clock, the cops are going in and blast them out. . . ."

Abe Rosen kept saying, "Yeah, yeah, yeah." He sat on his scarred wooden stool with nothing to sell and nothing to do and a sense of bewilderment and loss. Through the lobby doors he could see the crowd waiting patiently for God knew what—a body carried out on a stretcher, helpless feet sticking up; the sound of gunfire; somebody with blood on him.

Suddenly he remembered Artis James, who had gone back to duty right about the time it all started. Could Artis be involved? Nah, he answered himself, with thousands of police on hand, did they need a subway cop?

CLIVE PRESCOTT

Lieutenant Prescott, who had been the best basketball player in the history of his college in southern Illinois, had not been quite good enough for the pros. He had been chosen late, worked hard during his tryout, but been dropped. He was essentially what he would have called, if he didn't think it pretentious, a man of action. His desk job did not suit him, although he recognized that it was highly privileged and, for a black man, distinguished. Lately he had been thinking of trying for something else, even if it meant less money, but he knew it was hopeless because of his four hostages to fortune—his wife, his two kids, and his pension.

He sat staring at the desk trainmaster's console, feeling sorry for himself and for the captives on Pelham One Two Three. He

held himself in some measure responsible for both. He should in this case have been able to persuade the hijack leader to extend his deadline. With twelve minutes to go and the money not even on its way, there wasn't a chance. And he had no doubt that they'd keep their word and kill a passenger as penalty.

Across the room, Correll was shunting trains here and there, haranguing motormen and towermen, hysterical and happy. A contented man, Prescott thought sourly, a man who adored his work, who throve on the ultimately solvable adversity.

Prescott jumped to his feet and made three mindless circuits of the console, then sat down suddenly and signaled the DCI on Pelham One Two Eight.

"Yeah, what is it?" DCI Daniels said briskly.

"Sir, I'm checking to see if the money is on its way yet."

"Not yet. I'll let you know."

"Good," Prescott said. "It's on its way. I'll pass the word to Pelham One Two Three. Over."

"I said *not yet!*"

"Yes, sir," Prescott said. "And it's just a question of how long it takes to run it uptown?"

"Look," the DCI said irascibly, "I'm telling you the money isn't—" He stopped abruptly, and Prescott thought, The old buzzard has finally remembered that Pelham One Two Three can hear my end of the call but not his. "Okay," the DCI said. "I think I know what you've got on your mind. Go ahead."

Prescott called Pelham One Two Three. "Lieutenant Prescott. The money is on its way."

"Yes." The leader's voice was uninflected.

"We're cooperating," Prescott said. "You can see that. But it's physically impossible to get through city traffic in eleven minutes. Do you read me?"

"Ten. Ten minutes."

"It can't be done. It's the condition of city traffic. Will you give us a ten-minute extension?"

"No."

"We're moving as quickly as we can," Prescott said. He heard

the pleading in his voice and knew that just beneath it lay rage. "All we need is a little more time. Give us a break."

"No. The deadline is three thirteen." It was flat, deadly.

Prescott kept trying. "All right. It's out of the question for us to get the money to you by three thirteen. But suppose we can get it to the station entrance by then. Will you change the deadline from delivery to you to arrival at the station? Will you do that for us, at least? Come in. Come in, please."

After an interval that was so protracted that Prescott had decided to call again, the leader's voice suddenly came back. "All right. I agree. But no more concessions. Do you understand?"

Prescott's breath tasted sour. "Okay. I'll pass the word."

"Call me as soon as the money arrives. Over and out."

So I took action, Prescott thought. I bought a few minutes of time. The only trouble is, it won't do any good.

ARTIS JAMES

TA Patrolman Artis James was uncomfortable. At a distance of about sixty feet from the rear of the hijacked car, scrunched behind a steel pillar, he was covered only if he didn't move. His muscles were stiff and aching, but aside from that he was beginning to feel spooked. The tunnel was gloomy, and the wind that blew through it carried all sorts of imaginary whispers.

Not that *all* of them were imaginary. He knew police were in there—twenty, maybe fifty, armed with all kinds of guns, all trained on the car or, to put it another way, aiming in his general direction. Furthermore, he couldn't be sure they had been advised of his presence; it was the kind of detail the brass overlooked in their concern with the big picture. A bad situation. Not only did he have to avoid being seen by the hijackers but he had to worry about arousing the suspicions of cops behind him.

His right wrist, pressed to his side, felt the cigarettes he had bought from Abe Rosen, and he had a sudden unbearable craving for smoke in his lungs. Then it occurred to him that if things went badly, he might never smoke again, and the meaning of death took shape: not being able to eat again, or sleep with a woman.

The whole idea was so painful that he waved it away with a sharp gesture, then froze as he realized that he had exposed his hand. Nothing happened, but he was shaken. Why didn't somebody help him, out here in no-man's-land? He was one forgotten black man. If, on the other hand, he were a white man, his face and hands would shine out in the darkness. So maybe there was some virtue in his color after all. The thought made him smile, but he didn't smile for long. He snapped his mouth shut, thinking: My damn teeth are lily-white!

HIS HONOR, THE MAYOR

Tires squealing, the police commissioner's car swung down the incline from the mansion. The commissioner sat directly behind the driver, with Murray Lasalle in the middle and the mayor, huddled under a plaid blanket, at the other window. As the car straightened into East End Avenue, the mayor produced one of his most explosive sneezes.

"Use a tissue," Lasalle said. "You'll make us all sick."

"This is crazy, Murray."

"I don't do things without reason," Lasalle said coldly.

"Going down into that damp, windy tunnel—that isn't crazy?"

"Bundle up nice and warm," Lasalle said.

The commissioner was speaking on his confidential radio line. The mayor said to Lasalle, "What's he doing?"

"Telling them you're coming. Look, all you have to do is get on a bullhorn and make a dignified plea for mercy."

"Suppose they shoot at me?"

"They have no reason to shoot at you."

Sick as he was, the mayor got off a joke. "You mean they're out-of-towners?"

"Relax," Lasalle said. "Do your turn, and we'll drive you home and you can go back to bed. Think of it as a benefit appearance."

"If I thought it would actually help—"

"It will."

"The hostages?"

"No," Lasalle said, "you."

The borough commander sat in his command post in the Twenty-eighth Street parking lot with his eyes on his watch. The minutes were ticking off anarchically, like unmanageable cancer cells. "Three oh three," he said. "Ten minutes, and they haven't even started yet."

"If they kill somebody," the TA Police chief said, "I'm for going down there in force and wiping them out."

"I'm for doing what I'm told," the borough commander said. "They kill one, there's sixteen left. If we go in shooting, they'll all get killed. You want a decision like that on your head?"

"So far," the TA Police chief said, "nobody has asked me to make *any* kind of decision."

"Sir—" A sergeant, sitting in the rear of the car, held out the handset. "It's the PC, sir."

The police commissioner's voice said, "Fill me in."

"The money isn't started yet. I can't see how it can get here on time. The next move is theirs. Unless my orders are changed."

"They're not," the commissioner said. "I'm calling from the F.D.R. Drive. We're on our way down. The mayor is with me."

"I'll hold the crowd for him," the borough commander said.

The commissioner's breathing was audible. "His Honor will make a personal appeal to the hijackers."

"Anything else, Commissioner?"

"That's all," the commissioner said heavily. "That's all there is, Charlie."

THE FED

There is little doubt that never before in the sixty-year history of the Federal Reserve Bank had the chairman of a great member bank of the stature of the Gotham National Trust inquired about so undignified an amount as a million dollars. In the normal course of events, requests for cash deliveries are made through regular channels, much as the ordinary depositor makes a withdrawal from his neighborhood bank—although the figures are astronomically larger. The Fed checks the authorization for the

member bank, then counts out the money, dumps it into a canvas sack, and signs it out to the armored-car service dispatched by said member bank.

That's really all there is to it, and that's why the Fed, in its homespun way, refers to itself as a bank for banks. On a more sophisticated level, of course, the Fed functions as an extragovernmental agency in controlling the flow of money in order to keep the national economy in equilibrium. That is to say, roughly, it increases the supply of money in periods of recession and unemployment and decreases it in periods of prosperity and inflation.

The Fed does not ruffle easily; in fact, it is virtually unflappable. Yet it underwent a mild case of nerves in the wake of the call from the chairman of the Gotham National Trust to its president. Not because of the call, however unique it might have been, but because of the tradition-flouting instructions concerning the handling of the money. The Fed ordinarily has one way, and one way only, of packaging the huge levies of cash it services to its member banks: it is put up in packets of one hundred bills each, which are bound by a strip of paper widthwise, and then collected into packs of ten. These are tied with string and known as bundles. New, mint-fresh bills come wrapped in paper, are known as a brick, and resemble a ream of inexpensive bond.

The Fed *does not* put bills up in packets of two hundred; it *does not* bind them in rubber bands; and it *does not* select used bills to order. Normally it makes up its packages randomly from whatever bills are available at the moment—usually a mixture of both new *and* used.

But, of course, when the order comes from its own president, the Fed *does* do what it normally *does not*.

All cash is handled on the third floor of the Federal Reserve Building, an impregnable fortress at 33 Liberty Street in New York's great financial district. The visitor to the third floor—there are not many—enters through a massive gate watched over by an armed guard and, as long as he remains, is scrutinized by closed-circuit television cameras. After passing through another gate, he finds himself in a corridor, long, rather ordinary, containing a few

wooden trunks on wheels; these are used to transport sums of money to and from the vault. Armed guards stand about. On the visitor's left, behind gates, are the security elevators, in which money is taken down to the loading platforms on the Maiden Lane side of the building. Farther along the corridor, behind grilled windows, is Paying/Receiving and, behind panes of glass, Sorting/Counting.

Receiving clerks accept and sign for incoming sacks of bills sent to the Fed by member banks, then pass them to Sorting/Counting, across the aisle. Paying clerks make up the packages that are going out to member banks, sack them, and turn them over to the bank's armed guards for delivery.

Sorting/Counting processes the money that comes into the Fed from its member banks. The counters are mostly men. Immured in individual cages, they break open the seals on the canvas money bags and count the number of packets in each bag, but *not* the number of bills in a packet.

The sorters, most of whom are women, occupy a large office of the bullpen type. The sorter's technique consists of taking a batch of bills, creasing the whole batch lengthwise, and then, almost faster than the eye can see, distributing it according to denomination into various slots in a machine which counts the bills fed into it. Despite their dazzling speed, the sorters spot worn and damaged bills and mark them for destruction and even pick out counterfeits, which the tellers at the member banks are supposed to spot, but frequently overlook. The bad bills are known as mutts.

The special order for a million dollars requested by the chairman of the Gotham National Trust was filled by a Paying clerk in just a few minutes. Suppressing his annoyance at the unorthodox departure from procedure, he selected ten bundles of fifties (ten packets of one hundred fifties in each bundle); and five bundles of hundred-dollar bills (ten packets of one hundred hundreds in each). He then cut the strings of the bundles and proceeded to tie up pairs of packets with thick rubber bands. Each of these packets now contained two hundred bills and was approximately an inch thick. The total pile of fifteen thousand bills made a

block approximately twenty inches high and twelve inches deep.

When he was finished, the Paying clerk put the block of bills into a canvas bag and pushed it through his raised window to two guards. The guards hurried out with the money bag, which weighed about twenty-five pounds, and rode a security elevator down to the Maiden Lane loading platform.

PATROLMAN WENTWORTH

Cops in the Special Operations Division were not unaccustomed to improvisation on a grand scale, but Patrolman Wentworth, sitting behind the wheel of an NYPD small truck parked at the loading bays of the Federal Reserve on Maiden Lane, was nevertheless impressed by the lavishness of this occasion. His partner, Patrolman Albert Ricci, was shocked into silence by it, which Wentworth accounted a blessing. Ricci was a nonstop talker with one theme: his large and volatile Sicilian family.

Wentworth looked with pleasure at the eight men of the motorcycle detachment sitting astride their bikes, occasionally goosing their engines with a little touch of the accelerator. His own engine was running, too, smooth and powerful, but it was nothing to compare with the deep stutter of the cycles.

A voice came over the radio, important and impatient, demanding to know whether they had the money yet. It was the fifth call in five minutes. "No, sir, still waiting, sir," Ricci said. The voice cut out, and Ricci, shaking his head, said to Wentworth, "Something. Really something."

Pedestrians negotiating the narrow old street kept glancing at the truck with the motorcycle escort. Most of them moved on, but one little group had formed across the street. They carried cases chained to their wrists, and Wentworth figured them to be runners, with maybe millions in securities in their cases. He saw a couple of kids stop and talk to the motorcycle cops, eyeing their bikes with awe. But they were met with cold, stony silence.

"You feel honored having the Gestapo for an escort?" Wentworth said to Ricci.

"Something," Ricci said. "Really something."

"Plus a cop at every intersection all the way uptown," Wentworth said. "Don't say 'Something, really something.'"

Ricci looked at his watch. "What's taking them so long in there? We can't make it. It's a physical impossibility. Even if they was to come out right this minute—"

Two guards came running out of one of the bays, each holding an end of a canvas bag, each with a drawn gun. Ricci opened his door and they tossed the bag into his lap and slammed the door shut as Wentworth gunned his motor. The motorcycle sirens were already building volume. "And away we go," Wentworth said. He heard Ricci reporting on the radio.

At the corner a cop waved to them and they turned right into Nassau Street, one of the narrowest thoroughfares in the city. But cars had been pulled up on the sidewalks, and they sailed through, past John Street, Fulton, Ann, and Beekman, and shot up Park Row past City Hall on the wrong side of the street. Wentworth laughed with exhilaration as they roared against stopped traffic, the bike cops opening everything up with shrieking sirens. He had only half believed that there would be a cop at every intersection, but it was true. The number of cops tied up in the operation was staggering. Muggers in the rest of the city must be having a field day.

"Don't spill the money, Al." He was shouting to make himself heard over the medley of sirens and roaring motors.

"We can't make it," Ricci shouted back. "No way."

"I'm not even gonna try. Next corner, as soon as the bikes clear it, I'm turning left, and keep on going, and you and me, we got ourselves a million dollars."

Ricci shot a look at him, combining uncertainty, fear, and— Wentworth was certain of it—wistfulness. "You realize how many tons of pasta half a million would buy?" he went on. "It could feed that dumb dago family of yours for the rest of their lives."

"Look," Ricci said. "My sense of humor is as good as your sense of humor, but I don't like racial slurs."

Wentworth grinned as another corner and another guardian cop went by in a blur. The broad avenue ahead was Houston Street.

BOROUGH COMMANDER

At three oh nine the small truck containing the ransom money reported an accident crossing Houston Street. To avoid hitting a pedestrian who was defiantly crossing in front of them, the two lead motorcyclists had swerved sharply and sideswiped each other. Both riders were thrown. Before they had stopped rolling, Ricci was on the radio. Communications signaled the borough commander. Instructions? The borough commander ordered two cyclists to drop off to help the injured policemen. Everyone else to keep going. *Keep going.*

A roar from the crowd caught the borough commander's attention. The helmets of the TPF cops began to bob anticly, and he could see them straining to contain sudden bulges in the crowd. Rising on his toes, he caught a glimpse of the mayor, bareheaded, but wrapped in a blanket. He was smiling and nodding his head, and the crowd was booing him. The commissioner was by his side, and they were heading toward the command post with the help of a half dozen TPF cops.

The borough commander looked at his watch: three ten. And the sweep-second hand was racing at high speed. He looked southward down the avenue and then at his watch again. "They can't make it," he muttered.

A hand tapped him on the back. It belonged to Murray Lasalle. Beside him, the mayor was smiling, but his eyes were tearing and he was leaning against the commissioner.

Lasalle said, "The mayor is going down into the tunnel with a bullhorn to make a personal appeal to the hijackers."

The borough commander shook his head. "No can do."

Lasalle said, "I wasn't asking for your permission. All I want you to do is to make the arrangements."

The borough commander looked at the commissioner and read his blank expression as a hands-off policy. Good enough.

"Sir," he said to the mayor, "I appreciate your concern in this matter." He paused, marveling at the diplomacy of his language. "But it's out of the question. Not only for your own safety but for the safety of the hostages."

He saw the commissioner's head nod. The mayor, too, was nodding, but possibly only from sheer physical weakness.

Lasalle eyed the mayor. "Mr. Commissioner," he said, pointing to the borough commander, "order this man to comply."

"No." It was the mayor, his voice firm. "He's right. It would only louse things up and maybe get me shot in the bargain."

Lasalle said ominously, "Sam, I warn you—"

"I'm going home, Murray." The mayor fished a scarlet woolen stocking cap out of his pocket, pulled it down over his ears, and started to walk off.

Lasalle chased after him. "Sam, have you flipped? Since when does a politician wear a hat with a hundred thousand people watching him?"

The commissioner said, "Carry on, Charlie. I'll see them off and be right back. You're running the show."

The borough commander nodded, remembering that it was the mayor, not the commissioner, who had scotched Lasalle. He would have felt better if the commissioner had been faster on the draw. He looked at his watch: three twelve. "That TA Lieutenant Prescott had the right idea." He turned to the walkie-talkie man. "Signal the DCI. Tell him to get word to the hijackers that the money has arrived."

CLIVE PRESCOTT

"Pelham One Two Three. Come in, Pelham One Two Three." Prescott's voice was vibrant with emotion.

"Pelham One Two Three to Command Center. I read you." The leader's voice, as always, was calm and unhurried.

"The money has arrived. Repeat, the money has arrived."

"Yes. All right. You made it just on the tick."

A flat statement. No emotion. Prescott was outraged. The man had ice water for blood. He had to be psycho. "And if we went a tick further," Prescott said, "you'd have knocked off an innocent person?"

"Yes. I will now give you instructions for delivery of the money. You will follow them to the letter. Acknowledge."

257

"Go ahead."

"I want two policemen to walk down the track. One to carry the money, the other a lit flashlight. Acknowledge."

"Two cops, one with the money, one with a flashlight."

"The one with the light will swing it continuously from side to side. When they reach the car, the rear door will open. The other man will toss the bag into the car. Then they will turn and walk back to the station. Acknowledge."

"Check. That's it?"

"That's it. But keep in mind that the ground rules remain in full effect. Any wrong move and we'll kill a hostage."

"Yeah. I could have guessed that part of it."

"You have ten minutes. If the money isn't delivered—"

"Yeah," Prescott said. "You'll kill a hostage. It's getting monotonous. But they can't walk it that fast."

"Ten minutes."

"Give us fifteen," Prescott said. "It's a hard walk on the roadbed, and one of them will be carrying a heavy package."

"Ten minutes. No further discussion. When we have the money in hand, I'll call you back with final instructions."

"For what? Oh, the getaway. You'll never pull it off."

"Check your watch, Lieutenant. I've got three fourteen. That gives you until three twenty-four to deliver. Over."

"Over," Prescott said.

PATROLMAN WENTWORTH

Patrolman Wentworth, flooring the accelerator, passed Union Square at 3:15:30 and pulled up in a rubber-burning stop in the Twenty-eighth Street parking lot forty seconds later. Wentworth recognized the borough commander lumbering toward them. From the side of his mouth Wentworth said, "We're in fast company, Al. I figure he hands us a two-grade promotion on the spot."

The borough commander, breathing hard, yanked Ricci's door open and shouted, "Throw that bag out!"

Ricci, flustered, gave the bag a heave. It struck the borough commander and buckled his knees. He picked it up and tossed it

to two cops who were standing by—a TPF patrolman in blue helmet and a TA sergeant. "Take off," he shouted. "You got about eight and a half minutes."

He watched the sky blue helmet and the serge cap disappear down the stairs, then turned to Wentworth and Ricci. "Don't hang around here," he said. "We got too many cops. Report to your dispatcher and get back to work."

Wentworth put the truck in gear. "Inspector Gracious," he said to Ricci. "He sure has a heartwarming way of saying thanks."

"Jumped two grades," Ricci snorted.

"Now you wish I made that turn, like I said, and run away with all the money?"

"I wish," Ricci said gloomily, and reached for his microphone.

"Not so much as a well done or thank you," Wentworth grumbled. "I'm sorry we didn't boost a few packages, I mean it. I wish I was a criminal, so I could win a little respect from somebody."

SERGEANT MISKOWSKY

TA Sergeant Miskowsky had only been on the track once before in his eleven years on the force, chasing a couple of drunks. He remembered being scared stiff about falling into the third rail. The power was off now, but the hairs on the back of his neck were prickling. The tunnel was dark and should have been very quiet, but it wasn't—there were odd rustlings. After they passed the nine empty cars of Pelham One Two Three, he knew that the tunnel was crawling with cops. A couple of times he could have sworn he heard several of them inhale at the same time. Spooky as hell. He held his five-cell flashlight tightly in his hand—they would be in one beautiful jam if he dropped it—swinging it slowly from side to side. They were making good time, but he was beginning to suck wind. Not the TPF cop, loping along as if the money slung over his shoulder were weightless. He was breathing like a baby.

"There she is," the TPF cop said. "Look. Somebody in the rear door of the car. See him?"

"I hope he knows it's us," Miskowsky said. "I hope he don't get confused and start shooting."

"Not yet," the TPF cop said.

"What do you mean, not *yet?*"

"Not till he can see the whites of our eyes." He laughed.

ARTIS JAMES

Artis James felt as if he had been behind that pillar forever. The tunnel had become his element, like a fish's element was the water—an underground ocean, dark, damp, whispering.

He did not dare look behind him for fear of what the shadows might contain. Even the car ahead was more reassuring, because it was a known quantity. He put his eye to the edge of the pillar and saw half of someone's head and one shoulder come into view. The figure remained for about ten seconds, then withdrew. It kept returning every minute or so, and Artis knew it was the rear lookout checking the track, his submachine-gun muzzle pointed forward like an exploring antenna. It occurred to Artis that against the light in the car that head made a good target for somebody. Granted, the revolver was inaccurate at that distance, except for an especially good shot. Like himself, for instance. Given time to aim carefully, he could pick it off.

He tried to remember the exact orders he had been given by the Operations sergeant. Stay put. And no action. Something like that. Still, if he could offer a dead criminal as an apology, could they penalize him for not obeying orders to the letter? When the figure next showed itself, Artis took up firing position and lined it up in the sight of his revolver. Next time the head came into alignment he squeezed the trigger.

With the safety off he would have had himself one dead criminal. After the figure withdrew he flicked the safety on and off a few times, for no good reason. He held the gun at his side the next time the figure showed. After it disappeared he lined up on the doorway, and this time, for kicks, he flipped the safety to fire.

When the figure reappeared, it lined up in his sight as if by appointment. Artis drew a deep breath and squeezed off. The shot echoed through the tunnel like a bomb explosion. The figure pulled back sharply and he knew he had scored a hit. Then the

tunnel became a madhouse of racketing gunfire and muzzle flash bouncing off the walls. He dug in behind his pillar as bullets spanged toward him, and he was sure that if he weren't killed by the hijacker he would catch it when the cops in the tunnel returned the fire.

SERGEANT MISKOWSKY

"They're shooting at us," Sergeant Miskowsky screamed, and dropped to the roadbed, pulling the TPF cop down with him. He buried his head in his arms as machine-gun fire crackled around them. The TPF cop pushed the canvas sack in front of them. "Not that it would stop anything," he whispered. "A million bucks, and a bullet would sail right through it."

The firing stopped abruptly, but neither of them moved. "What do we do now?" Miskowsky whispered. "You feel like getting up and walking into that firepower?"

"Hell, no," the TPF cop said. "We wait and see."

The tunnel seemed twice as dark as before, the silence more profound. Miskowsky was grateful for both.

RYDER

As Ryder started down the aisle, the passengers, following him with glazed eyes, seemed stunned by the violence of the gunfire. The window of the rear door had collapsed. Welcome stood facing it, half exposed to the tunnel, his feet braced on the floor in a litter of shattered glass. The muzzle of his gun moved in a slow circle, probing the tunnel like the antenna of some malevolent insect. Steever sat on the isolated seat, and Ryder could see the dark wet patch on his sleeve, just below the shoulder. He paused and looked down at him inquiringly.

"Not too bad," Steever said. "I think it went right through."

"How many shots?"

"Just one. I let go a few rounds." He tapped the gun lying across his lap. "I guess I got mad. Couldn't see nothing, so there wasn't no sense to it. Then this one"—he nodded at Welcome—"come running and ripped off a burst."

Ryder edged up beside Welcome. Through the glassless door the tunnel was still and shadowy, an underground forest of dun-colored pillars. There were men out there, but they were perfectly concealed. Welcome was quivering with tension, and his breathing was shallow and rapid.

"You left your post without orders," Ryder said. "Get back to the center of the car."

Welcome said, "Drop dead."

"Go back to your post."

Welcome whirled suddenly, so that the muzzle of his gun pressed Ryder's chest. Through his raincoat Ryder could feel the hollow ring of the bore, but he didn't shift his eyes. He kept them focused on Welcome's, glowing darkly in the slits of his mask. "Go back to your post," he said again.

"Shove your orders," Welcome said, but Ryder knew by some subtle change in the eyes that he was backing down. The confrontation was over. For now. Ryder waited as Welcome strode stiff-legged back to the center of the car before he sat down beside Steever.

"You're certain there was just a single shot?"

Steever nodded.

"No answer after you fired? Or after Welcome fired?"

"Just the one shot, that's all."

"Somebody got nervous," Ryder said. "It was just some individual stupidity. But we can't let it pass."

"I'm not mad anymore," Steever said.

"Mad's not the point. We have to keep our promise. Everything depends on their believing we mean what we say."

"Knock off a passenger?" Steever said.

"Yes. You want to pick one out?"

Steever shrugged. "They're all the same to me."

Ryder bent toward the bloody sleeve. "As soon as it's done, I'll take a look at your shoulder. Okay with you?"

"Sure."

"I'll send one back. Can you handle it?"

"I'm fine," Steever said. "Send him back."

Ryder stood at the center of the car. Which one? The old wino was probably the least loss. . . . No. It wasn't his business to make judgments, just to designate a casualty.

"You." He pointed at random. "Come here, please."

"Me?" A wavering finger touched a chest.

"Yes," Ryder said, "you."

DENNY DOYLE

Denny Doyle was daydreaming. He was driving a subway train, but on a very strange line. It was underground, all right, but it had scenery—trees and lakes and hills, all bathed in sunlight. There were stations, but he wasn't required to stop. It was a perfect ride.

The daydream dissolved with the first shattering shot from the roadbed. And then the machine gun answered. Denny pulled his head into his shoulders. When he saw the wetness on the heavy man's raincoat, he almost became sick. He couldn't stand the sight of blood. If the truth had to be told, he was a physical coward, an unnatural sin for an Irishman.

At first, when the leader of the hijackers pointed, he was going to refuse to get up, but he was afraid to disobey. He stood up on trembling legs, aware that all the passengers were looking at him. His legs were rubbery, and that gave him the idea of purposely collapsing. But he was afraid the leader would see through it and get angry. So he moved to the center of the car with the help of the straps. Then he reached for one of the center poles and held on with both hands, looking up into the gray eyes that showed through the leader's mask.

"Motorman, we have something for you to do."

Denny had to swallow twice before he could speak. "Please don't do anything to me."

"Come along with me," the leader said.

Denny clung to the pole. "I have a wife and five kids. My wife is sick, she's in and out of the hospital—"

"Stop worrying. They want you to move those nine cars back there when the power comes on."

The leader took Denny's arm and walked him to the rear of the car. The heavy man stood up to meet them. Denny averted his eyes from the bloody sleeve.

"Walk to the first car," the leader said, "and wait for instructions from Command Center. I'll help you down to the track."

Denny watched the leader slide back the storm door. He hung back. "The controls," he said. "How can I work the train without the keys and the brake handle?"

"They're sending a full set of tools."

"I hate to use somebody else's brake handle. You know, every motorman has his own brake handle."

"You'll have to make do." For the first time there was a note of impatience in the leader's voice. "Let's go, please."

Denny stepped to the door and stopped. "I can't do it. I'll have to go past the dead body. I can't look at it."

"Just shut your eyes," the leader said. "Swing down now."

SERGEANT MISKOWSKY

"What are we supposed to do," Miskowsky said, "start walking like nothing happened?" Behind the money bag his cheek was pressed to the filthy roadbed.

"Damned if I know," the TPF cop said. "Whoever fired that first shot is going to catch it, I'll bet on that."

"So what do we do?" Miskowsky said.

"You're the sergeant. What *do* we do?"

"I ain't *your* sergeant. Anyway, what's a sergeant with all this brass around? I want orders before I move."

The TPF cop was peering over the top of the money bag. "There's two guys at the door now. No, three."

"Yeah. They just opened the storm door, they're talking—" The sergeant stiffened. "One of them just jumped out."

Miskowsky watched the shadowy figure straighten up, look back at the car, face about again, and slowly start walking.

"He's heading for *us*." Miskowsky's whisper was hoarse. Focused on the walking figure, he never saw the big shape loom in the open doorway. There was a flashing stab of brightness, and

265

the walking figure reached upward and then crumpled. The tunnel repeated the shots in a series of echoes.

"My God," Miskowsky said. "It's war."

BOROUGH COMMANDER

A Special Operations Division sniper in the tunnel reported the shooting. The borough commander's first reaction was bewilderment. "I don't get it. We're still under the delivery deadline."

The commissioner was pale. "They've gone ape. I thought they'd at least stick to their own rules."

The borough commander remembered the rest of the sniper's message. "Somebody threw a shot at them. That's it. Reprisal. They are sticking to their rules."

"Who fired the shot?"

"I doubt we'll ever know. The sniper says it sounded like a pistol shot. But the message of this killing is clear. They're telling us they're men of their word and we'd better act accordingly."

"Where are the two men with the money?"

"The sniper says they're about fifteen feet away from where he is. They hit the deck when the machine gun went off."

The commissioner nodded. "What's your next move?"

My next move, the borough commander thought, but knew he'd have liked it less if the commissioner had given him an order. "There are sixteen hostages left, that's still the prime consideration." He picked up the walkie-talkie and called DCI Daniels on Pelham One Two Eight, instructing him to contact the hijackers through Command Center and inform them that the ransom money would be on its way again, but that more time was needed because of the delay owing to the recent incident.

"You hear all that?" the borough commander said. "You ever hear a cop kowtow to murderers like that before?"

"Easy," the commissioner said.

"Easy. They call a tune, and we dance to it."

"Cool it!" the commissioner said sharply.

The borough commander looked at him and read a mirror reflection of his own anger and misery. "Sorry, sir."

"All right. Maybe we'll have a shot at them later on."

"Maybe. But I'll tell you something, sir—after this I'll never be the same man again. I'll never be as good a cop."

"Cool it," the commissioner said.

ARTIS JAMES

The man who gunned down the motorman was the one Artis James thought he had hit. He didn't connect the two events; at least, not yet. He peeked out from behind his pillar just as the motorman—he could make out the pinstripe overalls—was climbing down to the roadbed. When the man in the doorway fired, Artis ducked again. By the time he thought it was safe to take another look, the motorman was a motionless hulk a few feet from the other motionless hulk that used to be the trainmaster.

Artis turned carefully, putting his back against the pillar. He switched on his radio and signaled TA Headquarters. He had to repeat three times before headquarters came in.

"I can barely make you. Speak up, please."

"I can't speak louder. I'm too close, they'd hear me. This is Patrolman Artis James. In the tunnel. Near the hijacked car."

"All right, that's a little better. Go ahead."

"They just shot the motorman. They put him out on the tracks, and they shot him."

"Mother! When did that happen?"

"Maybe a minute or two after the first shot."

"*What* first? Nobody was supposed . . . Did somebody shoot?"

It struck Artis all at once and left him numb. Oh, God, if he had something to do with killing the motorman . . .

"Come in, James," the radio voice said impatiently. "Somebody shot at the train."

"I told you," Artis James said. You did it, baby, he thought, oh, God, you did it. "Somebody shot at the train."

"Who, damn it, *who?*"

"Came from behind me someplace. Maybe scored a hit. Shot came right out of the tunnel behind me."

"The motorman. Dead?"

"Not moving. Don't mean he's dead. What do I do?"

"Nothing. For God's sake, don't do *anything*."

"Right," Artis said. "*Continue* not to do anything."

RYDER

By the time Ryder had picked up the first-aid kit from his valise in the motorman's cab, Steever had his raincoat and jacket off and folded on the seat. Ryder helped him with the money jacket and then peeled the bloody shirt sleeve down over his arm, leaving Steever stripped to the waist, his torso massive, dark-skinned, matted with hair.

Ryder sat down beside Steever and examined the wound, a neat round hole oozing blood. The underside of the arm, where the bullet had emerged, was somewhat mangled.

"Looks clean," Ryder said. "Painful?"

Steever tucked his chin in to look at the wound. "Nah. I never feel pain too much."

Ryder rummaged for the antiseptic solution. "I'll use this and then bandage it. It's the best we can do now."

Steever shrugged. "It don't bother me."

"It might get stiff after a while," Ryder said.

"No problem," Steever said. "I can't hardly feel it."

When Steever was fully dressed, Ryder picked up the first-aid kit and left. He noted the continuing interplay between Welcome and the girl in the Anzac hat. His jaw hardened, but he didn't stop. At the front of the car Longman stepped toward him. "The motorman?"

"The motorman is dead." Ryder went inside the cab and shut the door. Someone was calling frantically on the radio. He activated the transmitter.

"Pelham One Two Three to Command Center. Come in."

"Prescott here. Why did you kill the motorman?"

"You shot at one of my people. I warned you."

"Someone disobeyed orders and fired. It was a mistake. If you had checked with me, you wouldn't have had to kill him."

"Where is the money?" Ryder said.

"About a hundred yards down the track."

"I'll give you three minutes to deliver it. Same procedure as before. Acknowledge."

"I'd like to meet you sometime. I'd really like that."

"Three minutes," Ryder said. "Over and out."

SERGEANT MISKOWSKY

A voice came out of the darkness. "Hey, you two guys."

Miskowsky, gun in hand, said hoarsely, "What?"

"I'm over here behind a pillar. I got orders for you from the borough commander. Resume delivery of the money."

"They know we're coming? I mean, they won't shoot?"

"They got the welcome mat out for you. Why not, with a million in cash? The order is move it fast."

"I wish to hell I was someplace else," Miskowsky said, falling in beside the TPF cop, who was already moving.

"Into the valley of death," the TPF cop said.

TOM BERRY

Tom Berry watched the leader wedge the rear door open and then take his place beside the heavyset man on the isolated double seat. Both of them trained their guns on the open door. Then Berry saw the flashlight on the tracks and knew what it signified. The city was paying off. The light was moving closer at an almost liturgical pace, which, Berry thought, was the way he would walk himself if he had to advance toward a couple of machine-gun muzzles. He made out two figures. He couldn't see whether they were cops, but what else could they be? He felt a sense of agonized empathy with those two out there, and then, for no good reason, the image of his late uncle obtruded on his thoughts.

What would Uncle Al have said about a pair of cops meekly delivering a million bucks to a gang of hijackers, or crooks, as he'd have called them? Well, Uncle Al wouldn't have believed it, for starters. Uncle Al, or his superiors, would have barreled in shooting. Fifty, a hundred cops with guns blazing, and in the end the crooks would have been dead, and a half dozen or so cops, and

most of the hostages. In Uncle Al's day cops were crook catchers, not crook payers.

In Uncle Al's time everything was different. People might not have been wild about cops, but they feared them. Try a word like "pig" and you knew where you'd wind up. In Uncle Al's *father's* time police work was even simpler; most problems were solved by a beer-belly Irish cop hauling off and punching some harmless kid. Well, the policeman's lot had undergone quite a change in the third generation. Now, people called cops pigs and nobody laid a hand on them.

He could imagine how horrified Deedee would have been by Uncle Al, not to mention Al's corrupt old man. On the other hand, she would probably take satisfaction in the idea of cops serving as messenger boys to thieves, viewing it as some kind of service to the people. Oh, well, Deedee. There were quite a few things Deedee had backward. Not that he had such a clear idea himself of what *frontward* was.

Two faces appeared at the rear door. One belonged to a blue-helmeted TPF cop, the other to a TA sergeant. The TA man shone his light into the car and the TPF man flipped a sack from his shoulder onto the floor. It landed with a soft thud. The officers, their faces red but unemotional, turned around and walked away.

Part Three

LONGMAN

Longman watched the money dump out as Ryder held the sack upside down—dozens of green slabs, neatly tied up with rubber bands. A million dollars—everybody's dream—tumbling out onto the filthy composition floor of a subway car. Steever took off his coat and jacket and Ryder checked the ties on his money jacket. Four money jackets had cost Ryder a pretty penny to have made up. They were on the order of life jackets, fitting over the head and tied at the sides. Each one contained twenty pockets, front and back in two tiers, evenly spaced. All together there were seventy-five packets of bills, which figured to eighteen and three-quarter pack-

ets per man. Not that they were going to split it that finely. Three of them would have nineteen; one would have eighteen.

Steever stood like a mannequin, hands at his sides, as Ryder inserted a package in each pocket of the money jacket. When he was finished, Steever changed places with Welcome. Welcome kept gassing while Ryder methodically but swiftly filled his jacket, then signaled to Longman. Longman's heart began to thump. But Ryder started shucking his own coat and jacket, and Longman felt a pang of resentment. Why was he last? After all, whose idea was it in the first place? But his feeling of pique vanished at the touch of the money. Some of the packets he was pressing down firmly into the slots of Ryder's jacket were worth ten thousand each, others twenty thousand!

"All this money," he whispered. "I can hardly believe it."

Ryder was silent, turning so that Longman could get at the rear pockets of the jacket.

"I just wish the rest of it was over," Longman said.

Ryder's voice was icy. "The rest of it will be fun."

"Fun!" Longman said. "If anything goes wrong—"

"Get your stuff off," Ryder said.

When Ryder was finished with him, they all returned to their places. Longman felt weighted down, although he knew his eighteen packages didn't add up to more than five or six pounds. It amused him to see some of the passengers look at him with envy, as if wishing *they'd* had the guts and brains to pull off something like this. He smiled broadly, stretching the mask. But when Ryder went back inside the cab, he stopped being amused. The getaway was going to be the hairiest part of all.

Suddenly he was convinced that it wouldn't work.

RYDER

Ryder said into the mike, "Pelham One Two Three calling Prescott at Command Center."

"Come in. This is Prescott."

"Have you got your pencil, Prescott?"

"Yes. How's the money, leader? All in order?"

"I remind you that these instructions must be obeyed to the letter. The hostages' lives remain in jeopardy. I'm giving you five items. Write each one down and acknowledge. Point One: At the end of this conversation you will restore power to the entire sector. Acknowledge."

"I read you."

"Point Two: You will then clear the local track from here to South Ferry station. By that I mean switches properly set, all trains between here and South Ferry cleared out, and all signals green. I emphasize the signals. They will be green. We are not to be tripped by a red signal. Repeat, please."

"Local track cleared to South Ferry. All signals green."

"If we see a red signal, we'll kill a hostage. *Any* infraction and we'll kill a hostage. Point Three: All trains, local and express, *behind* us are to lay dead. And nothing is to move *northbound* between South Ferry and here. Check me."

"Okay, I've got it."

"Point Four: You will contact me as soon as the track is clear to South Ferry and the signals are all green. Acknowledge."

"Contact you when track is clear, signals green."

"Point Five: All police personnel in the tunnel are to be removed. If this is not done, we will shoot a hostage. Absolutely no police personnel are to be on the South Ferry station. If this is not done, we will shoot a hostage."

"I check you. Can I ask a question?"

"About your instructions?"

"About you. Are you aware that you're insane?"

Ryder looked out at the empty track, peopled with shadows. "That isn't relevant," he said. "You have ten minutes. You will then contact me again for final instructions. Over and out."

CLIVE PRESCOTT

Prescott was relieved when the NYPD high command agreed to comply with the hijackers' instructions. Not that they had an alternative, but he knew how the pressures of frustration could warp judgment. Cops were, after all, human beings. Of a sort.

He jumped up from the console and ran across the room. Frank Correll, occupying a dispatcher's desk, was shouting into his microphone. Prescott tapped him on the shoulder and he whirled around, glaring.

"Listen to me," Prescott said. "I have new instructions—"

"I don't give a damn about your instructions!" Correll shook Prescott's hand off his shoulder and turned back.

Prescott folded back the flap of his sharkskin jacket with his left hand, and with his right drew his service revolver. He cupped Correll's chin, pulled his head back, and placed the muzzle of the revolver in Correll's eye.

BOROUGH COMMANDER

From his command post in the Twenty-eighth Street parking lot, the borough commander issued orders for compliance with the hijackers' new instructions, but also arranged for plainclothes detectives to be on the South Ferry platform and for a saturation of police in the area aboveground. Then, baffled, he consulted with TA Police Chief Costello.

"What have they got in mind, Chief?"

Costello shook his head. "It beats the hell out of me. Myself, I wouldn't have picked a tunnel to have to make a getaway from."

"But they picked it. Which presumes they have a plan for getting out. They want the power back on and the track cleared. What does that suggest to you?"

"That they're going to run their car, obviously."

"Why did they specify South Ferry?"

"Damned if I know. The Lex local doesn't even run there at this time of day; they'll have to be switched at Brooklyn Bridge. Could they have a boat in the harbor? A seaplane? I just can't imagine what they're up to."

"South Ferry comes after Bowling Green. What happens *after* South Ferry?"

"The track loops around and comes right back to Bowling Green. There are trains standing in Bowling Green station now, they'd simply be blocked."

The borough commander thanked him and glanced at the police commissioner, who looked worried but profoundly neutral. *He's giving me my head, displaying implicit trust in his subordinate. And why not? There won't be any glory out of this.*

"We can tail them in another train," the TA chief said. "I know we promised not to—"

"Don't the signals turn red after their passage, and wouldn't our train be stopped by trippers?"

"On the local track, yes, but not on the express track," the chief said. "Maybe they won't think of that."

"They'll think about it," the borough commander said. "They know too much about subways. Maybe we *can* tail them, but if they make us, they might kill a passenger."

"We can also follow their progress on the model board at the Grand Central Tower—as far as Brooklyn Bridge station. After that, Nevins Street Tower takes over southward into Brooklyn."

"That tells us exactly when they move?"

"Yes. And where they are every moment they're on the tracks. Of course we'll have TA cops on all the platforms, too."

"Okay," the borough commander said briskly. "Let's set it up. Your Tower to track their movements. An express train to follow behind. Is it possible to turn off all its lights?"

"Yes."

"Okay." The borough commander shook his head. "Hell of a thing to stalk somebody with—a subway train. I'll put DCI Daniels in charge of it. Patrol cars will follow on the surface. The big problem is communication. Tower to here to Communications to patrol cars? It stinks. Better place two men at the Tower on separate phones, one to me and one to Communications, so a dispatcher can pass it on directly to the cars. I want every car we've got on this. Every cop. NYPD and TA, both. Cover all stations, all exits. How many emergency exits are there, Chief?"

"About two to a station."

"Just one thing." The commissioner broke his silence. "Every care must be taken. We don't want any more dead hostages."

"Yeah. They're still calling the shots." The borough commander

suddenly felt chilled. Shadows had closed in; the crowd seemed to be congealed; his cops looked like frozen sticks of blue. It was true, he wouldn't be the same man after this was over. It had taken the mickey out of him.

TOM BERRY

The sudden return of full lighting in the car caught the passengers unawares, and they blinked in confusion. The bright neons showed up stresses the emergency lights had softened: tight, trembling mouths, lines of strain, eyes dulled by fear. Tom Berry observed that the girl in the Anzac hat showed mileage; the dimness had been kind to her. The handkerchief the militant black held to his face was shockingly red. The hijackers seemed bulkier and more menacing. Well, Berry thought, they *were* bulkier, by a quarter of a million dollars each.

The cab door opened and the leader stepped out. "Ah," said the old man, who seemed to have appointed himself spokesman. "Here's our friend, now we'll find out what's next."

"Your attention, please." The leader waited, poised and patient, and Berry thought, It's almost professional, he's used to handling people. "All right. In about five minutes we're going to move the car. You will remain seated and continue to do as you're told."

The emphasis on *will* snatched at Tom Berry's memory. The army. Of course. "You *will* wear Class A uniforms. . . . You *will* fall out at oh eight hundred hours." Okay, small mystery solved—the leader had given orders in the army. So what?

"We expect to release you unharmed in a short while. But until then you are still hostages. Conduct yourselves accordingly."

The old man said, "Since you're moving the train, if it's not too much trouble, can you drop me off at Fulton Street?"

The leader disregarded him and went into the cab. Some people were glaring at the old man, disapproving of his levity.

And so, Berry thought, the ordeal was almost over. Before long the passengers would be taking deep drafts of the polluted air of the surface and plying the police with inaccurate and widely divergent eyewitness details. All except for Patrolman Tom Berry,

who would offer a disciplined version, despite the contempt his fellow officers would make no effort to conceal. When he walked in on Deedee after the interrogation, he would all but officially be unpigged. What would he do then? Marry Deedee and settle down to a life of revolutionary bliss?

The smaller of the two boys began to whimper. Berry watched his mother try to silence him. "No, Brandon. Quiet."

The boy said loudly, "I'm tired, I want to go out."

The woman's whisper was fierce. "The man said quiet!"

GRAND CENTRAL TOWER

When the trains south of Pelham One Two Three began to move and the red slashes twinkled on the model board in Grand Central Tower, a cheer rose from the dispatchers. Marino, frowning, glanced over his shoulder, knowing that Caz liked quiet in the Tower Room. But of course—Caz was dead. Which, it occurred to Marino, made him senior man. Well, *he* liked it quiet, too.

"Let's keep it down," he said, and realized he was using Caz's favorite phrase. "Let's keep it down in the Tower Room."

Marino was holding a telephone pressed tensely to his ear, connected to Communications at Police Headquarters on Centre Street. Next to him, her brown face impassive, Mrs. Jenkins was connected to Operations at Transit Police Headquarters.

"Nothing yet," Marino said into his phone. "They have begun to clear the track to South Ferry." He gestured to Mrs. Jenkins. "Tell him Pelham One Two Three is still laying dead."

Marino's eyes returned to the model board and focused on the red slashes that represented the position of Pelham One Two Three. It was very still in the Tower Room.

"Right now it's us who's carrying the ball. So keep it down." Marino said sternly. "Just as if Caz was still with us."

DCI DANIELS

DCI Daniels led a picked squad of thirty men along the roadbed to Woodlawn One Four One, which lay dead on the express track five hundred feet north of the Twenty-eighth Street station.

The motorman saw them coming and hung his head out of his cab window.

"Unlock your door," the DCI said. "We're coming aboard."

"I got no orders to let nobody aboard," the motorman said.

"You just got orders," the DCI said. "What do we look like, the Russian Red Army?"

"I guess you cops all right." The motorman appeared at the storm door with his key. "I guess you got the authority."

"You're a good guesser. Give me a hand." Daniels clambered up off the track, grunting. Half of the thirty or so passengers in the car crowded forward. He held up his hand. "Back up, folks. You're going to move back into the other cars." He crooked his finger at four of his cops. "Move them."

The passengers gave ground grudgingly and the rest of the police piled aboard. Daniels took a grip on the motorman's arm. "We're going to chase a train," he said. "I want you to turn off all your lights, then separate this car from the rest of the train."

"Man, I am not allowed to do any of that."

The DCI tightened his hold. "I want *all lights out*, inside and out, and I want this car cut off."

Increasing pressure on his arm disposed of the motorman's arguments. With the DCI half pushing him, he went into the cab and gathered up his brake handle and reverse and cutting keys.

The DCI assigned a man to accompany the motorman and they hurried to the rear of the car, where the last of the passengers were being herded out like animals through a chute. Carrying rifles, shotguns, tear-gas guns, the main body of policemen shuffled awkwardly into the seats. The DCI went into the cab. Through the front window the tunnel was brighter than before, but it was still a gloomy place, the endless procession of pillars looking like a forest of denuded trees.

RYDER

Ryder opened the cab door and beckoned to Longman. "Go ahead," he said.

Longman edged the controller forward. The car began to move.

"It's scary." Longman spoke nervously, with his eyes fixed on the track ahead, on the signals, green as far as the eye could see. "Knowing there are cops hidden out there."

"Nothing to worry about," Ryder said. Nothing to worry about, he meant, as long as the other side had to accept the terms of the strange warfare whose rules he himself had formulated. But Longman seemed reassured. His hands were steady on the controls. This was his element, Ryder thought; this was his strength. Everything else was weakness.

"You know exactly where we're stopping?"

"Exactly," Longman said. "On the dime."

GRAND CENTRAL TOWER

When the little red blips denoting the position of Pelham One Two Three began to flicker on the model board in the Grand Central Tower Room, Marino gave a hoarse shout into his phone. "She's moving!" He waved excitedly at Mrs. Jenkins, but she was already speaking to TA Police Headquarters. Her voice was level and carefully modulated. "Pelham One Two Three has begun to move southward."

"All right," the police dispatcher on Marino's line said. "Continue to report as she moves, but calm down."

"Moving pretty slow," Marino said. "But not stopping."

"Keep talking. But keep it cool. Okay?"

NERVE CENTER

At Transit Police Headquarters, Operations Lieutenant Garber listened to Mrs. Jenkins' calm voice on his phone.

"Okay," he said. "Hold it for a minute." He turned to a dispatcher. "They're moving. Alert every available man. Patrol cars, too. NYPD is tracking them, but so are we. Make sure men on the Twenty-third Street station get the word fast." He looked at his watch. "Damn it, they jumped the gun. They're up to something."

The Operations Room was bustling. Wouldn't it be beautiful if *we* got them, Lieutenant Garber thought. *Us*, TA, and not the NYPD.

At Command Center there was a flurry of excitement when a dispatcher at an IND desk casually remarked that he had figured out how the hijackers planned to make their getaway.

"They're gonna use Beach's old tunnel."

His announcement drew the immediate attention of his fellow dispatchers. For the benefit of those among them who wanted to know what the hell Beach's old tunnel was, he shifted his cigar to speaking position in a corner of his mouth and expounded. In 1867, one Alfred Ely Beach rented a basement in a building at Broadway and Murray Street and proceeded to construct New York's first subway, a tunnel that ran a distance of three hundred and twelve feet to Warren Street. He brought in a single railroad car and blew it back and forth through his private tunnel by means of compressed air. The public was invited for a ride, but showed scant interest, and the project died.

"The Lex local goes right by where that old tunnel is," the dispatcher said. "These fellas go into that tunnel and hide—"

The IND desk trainmaster, who had been listening, put his own cigar in speaking position and said, "That old tunnel has been gone since they started to dig the first real subway back in 1900, thereabouts."

"You got proof?" the dispatcher said.

"Proof," the desk trainmaster said. "Some of the original bricks of Beach's old tunnel are built right into the IRT wall. Look out the window, just past City Hall, and you'll see the old bricks."

"I never looked out a subway window in my life. What's to see?"

"The bricks of old Beach's old tunnel."

"Well, it was an idea," the dispatcher said.

"Better go back to work," the desk trainmaster said.

RYDER

Longman said, "Can I push it up a notch?"

"No," Ryder said. "Steady as it goes."

"Are we past where the cops were hidden by now?"

"Probably," Ryder said. "Keep it steady."

"Calling Pelham One Two Three. Prescott here."

Ahead, Ryder saw the long spread of brightness that was the Twenty-third Street station. He picked up the microphone. "Come in, Prescott."

"How come you're moving? The track isn't clear to South Ferry yet, and we've still got five minutes. Why are you moving?"

"A slight change of plan. We decided to remove ourselves from all those cops you had hidden in the tunnel back there."

"Hell," Prescott said. "There weren't any cops there. Look, if you keep on as you are, you'll run into red signals. I don't want you to blame us if you're tripped."

"We'll stop soon and wait for you to clear the track. You still have five minutes."

"How are the passengers?"

"The passengers are fine, so far. But don't play any tricks."

"*You* crossed *us* by moving."

"You have my apology. Instructions remain the same. Over and out."

Longman said, "You think they know anything? I mean—all those questions?"

"No," Ryder said. "The questions are natural ones. They're thinking as we want them to."

"Look at them hanging over the edge of that platform," Longman said. "When I was a motorman, I had nightmares about a dozen of them tumbling in front of my train."

As the car entered the north end of the Twenty-third Street station, they could hear shouting from the platform. Fists were shaking, and at least a dozen people spat at them as they passed.

BOROUGH COMMANDER

The commissioner's limousine pulled out of the Twenty-eighth Street parking lot and swung down Park Avenue South. The commissioner and the borough commander sat on the rear seat. At Twenty-fourth Street, a cop was frantically trying to clear cross traffic out of their path.

"We might make better time by subway," the commissioner said.

The borough commander looked at him in open astonishment. In all the years he had known him, he had never heard the commissioner make a joke.

When the driver turned on his siren and shot through the intersection, the borough commander spoke into the mike. "Still moving?"

"Yes, sir. Slowly, in what they call switching position."

"Where are they?"

"Almost to Twenty-third Street."

"Thank you."

The commissioner was peering through the rear window. "We're being followed. A television truck. Maybe two."

"I should have given orders to impede them. They're a pain."

"Freedom of the press," the commissioner said. "We're going to need all the friends we can get after this is over."

The radio crackled. "They're entering the Twenty-third Street station, sir, speed still about five miles per hour."

"Some sort of traffic jam up ahead," the commissioner said.

The radio voice said, "Not stopping. Going right through Twenty-third Street station."

"Open it up," the borough commander said to the driver. "Make that siren sing."

DCI DANIELS

In the cab of the darkened front car of Woodlawn One Four One, the DCI watched impatiently as the motorman placed his instruments on the panel.

"Now," he said, "you understand what I want you to do?"

"Follow that train. Right?"

"But not too close. I don't want them to see or hear us."

The motorman nudged the controller into series. "See is one thing. Hear is another. No such thing as a quiet subway train."

They sailed past the Twenty-eighth Street station, empty now except for a handful of patrolmen. When Twenty-third Street became visible in the distance, the DCI said, "Slow it down. Keep your eye peeled for their lights. Crawl."

"Red signal there on the local track," the motorman said. "Means they went by here not too long ago."

"Slow," the DCI said. "Crawl. Don't make a sound."

"You sure asking a lot out of one old subway car, Cap'n."

THE CITY: STREET SCENE

The crowd's antenna, an organ tuned to a permanent wavelength of suspicion, evaluated the departure of the commissioner's limousine as a prelude to breaking camp. In a matter of minutes the crowd ceased to exist as an effective entity. A few hundred idlers or romantics remained, clinging to the forlorn hope of a shootout in front of their eyes. Philosophers and theorists held seminars in small clusters:

"What about that mayor! Who needed *him* down here?"

"They should of gone in with their guns blazing. You start coddling crooks and they take advantage. A good crook knows his psychology."

"If it had of been me, I would of got *ten* million."

"The police commissioner? He don't even *look* like a cop. How can you respect somebody who don't look like a cop?"

"You know how they're gonna get away? I figgered it out. They're gonna fly that train to Cuba!"

RYDER

The emergency exit north of Fourteenth Street was an opening in the tunnel wall containing a ladder that led to a grate in the sidewalk on the east side of Union Square Park near Sixteenth Street. Ryder watched as Longman stopped a hundred feet short of the white light marking the exit.

"Right?" Longman said.

"Fine," Ryder said.

Longman was sweating, and Ryder became aware for the first time of how badly the tiny cab smelled. Well, he thought, when did a battlefield smell like a field of daisies? He put his hand into the brown valise cautiously, took out two grenades, and inspected their pins. From the first-aid box he brought out the spool of ad-

hesive tape and tore off two long strips. He wound one strip loosely around each grenade.

"Those things make me nervous," Longman said.

"Everything makes you nervous," Ryder said factually. "They're safe as tennis balls as long as the pin remains in and the lever is not released."

"Do you *have* to?" Longman said. "I mean—suppose they *aren't* following us on the express track?"

"In that case we took an unnecessary precaution."

"But if they *aren't* following us, then eventually an innocent express train will come along—"

"Don't argue," Ryder said. "I want you to start working as soon as I leave. You *must* be finished by the time I get back, so we can move the train immediately."

"Command Center calling Pelham One Two Three. Lieutenant Prescott, Command—"

Ryder pressed the transmitter button. "Pelham One Two Three. Track clear yet?"

"Not quite clear yet. About two to three minutes more."

"Be quick about it. And no police on the track, anywhere, or we'll react. You understand *react*, Lieutenant Prescott?"

"Yes. We're complying with your instructions, there's no need to hurt anybody. Acknowledge, Pelham One Two Three."

Ryder hung the mike back on its hook. "Don't answer," he said to Longman. "He'll quit after a while. Get started."

He turned the latch and went out of the cab. Welcome was lounging against the center pole, the submachine gun dangling from his right hand. Ryder suppressed a twinge of anger. Steever stood up and slid the rear storm door open. "Cover me," Ryder said, and dropped lightly to the roadbed. He straightened up and began to trot northward between the gleaming rails.

TOM BERRY

As the leader came out of the cab, Tom Berry caught a glimpse of the smallest hijacker straining to lift some kind of heavy metal construction out of what looked like a Val-A-Pak. He saw the leader

speak to the heavy man at the rear door, then jump down to the track. And now, Deedee, Berry thought, will I take advantage of his absence to storm the Winter Palace? No, Deedee. I will do no such thing. Ah, by what right do I mock you? Right or wrong, you believe in something. But who am I? Half cop, half doubter. If I believed in being a cop, I would probably be dead.

And now as long as I'm being selfish, Berry thought, I hope the hijackers make a nice unmessy getaway so I don't die accidentally in a crossfire between trigger-happy hoods and trigger-happy cops. Not that a getaway seemed possible, given that the hijackers were bottled up in a tunnel with all exits plugged by cops. Still, it was reasonable to suppose they had figured out a happy ending for themselves, wasn't it? Well, that's their problem.

DCI DANIELS

"*Shshsh.*" The DCI was peering through the front window. The motorman applied his brake suddenly and the DCI's nose bumped the glass.

"There she is," the motorman said. "She's laying dead. If you strain, you can see her."

The radio crackled, and the DCI listened intently to Command Center's end of an attempt at conversation with Pelham One Two Three, but the car was obviously not responding. "They won't answer. Arrogant murderers!"

"What we do?" the motorman said. "Stay like we are?"

"We can't get any closer or they'll spot us. I never felt so helpless in my entire life."

"You see something out there on the bed?" the motorman said.

"Where?" The DCI stared. "I don't see a thing."

"Looked like a man. Might be I could been mistaken." The motorman took his eyes off the track and looked at his watch. "Except what happened, I'd be home right now. Got me working on overtime, time and a half, but I rather be home."

"Keep watching."

"Time and a half don't mean much. Taxes get it, anyhow."

"Just keep watching."

The parts of the Gimmick were neatly arranged in the Val-A-Pak and, except for the weight of the shaped iron piece that fitted over the controller, it was all as easy as it had been in rehearsal. Yet he could remember when the crucial problem, eventually solved by the Gimmick, had seemed hopeless, and their entire plan had appeared doomed.

The problem was that you couldn't possibly drive a train without a motorman, because a deadman's feature was built into the drive mechanism. If something happened to the motorman and the controller was pushed forward into drive position, the deadman's feature would come into action and stop the train the minute the weight of the motorman's hand was taken off. Longman had been in despair.

Yet, they found a solution. The heart of the Gimmick was a heavy iron mold cast to fit the controller like a rough glove. Set in place, its weight substituted for the pressure of the motorman's hand and kept the deadman's feature deactivated. Simple and beautiful, Longman thought, and grunted as he hefted it out of the Val-A-Pak and fitted it on.

The rest of it was equally simple: three lengths of pipe to be joined together—the first, less than six inches long, to fit into a slot at the front of the Gimmick; the second, about three feet long, to angle downward toward the tracks; the third, also three feet long, to be angled toward the tunnel wall. These pipe pieces had been tooled to fit into each other with different degrees of firmness. The short one joined tightly with the receptacle in the Gimmick; the middle piece loosely at its inner end with the first piece and securely at its outer end with the third piece.

But before he could join the pipes together, Longman had to break out the front window. Irrationally, it bugged him, made him feel like a vandal. He hesitated with the butt of his gun poised, then struck several times, until only a few tiny shards clung to the frame. Ryder had been emphatic: "Absolutely no glass or it could wreck the illusion." So, scraping with the gun barrel, Longman cleared all the small pieces out of the frame.

RYDER

Northward from the emergency exit, Ryder paced off about three hundred feet. There he went down on his knees beside the inside express rail. He took one of the grenades from his pocket, then paused to peer intently along the roadbed. In the distance he saw the hulking shadow of a train. He nodded, as if in acknowledgment of a judgment confirmed. With meticulous care he covered the lever of one grenade and taped it beneath the lip of the inside rail. Then he moved to the outside rail and repeated the procedure with the second grenade. When he was satisfied the grenades were firmly in place, he pulled the pins. The grenades were now fully armed. Without a backward glance Ryder trotted back to Pelham One Two Three. When the wheel of a train struck, the lightly taped grenades would be dislodged, automatically releasing the levers. The grenades would explode in five seconds.

Steever was standing guard at the rear door. Ryder nodded to him, but walked past the dirty red sides of the car to the front. Longman looked out at him through the glassless window from which the middle length of pipe already protruded. Longman passed him the third length of pipe. He screwed it tightly into the middle one, with the end angled toward the tunnel wall.

Now, when Longman, standing outside, pushed the pipe construction inward toward the train, the controller would be shoved clockwise through switching into series position. At that point the bulk of the cast-iron weight would prevent it from moving farther. A sharp pull backward would then disengage the two outside pieces of pipe, leaving only the short first piece, which would not be visible from outside the train.

For the rest, Ryder was banking on illusion: on the power of assumption to triumph over actuality. People didn't really *see* glass, and so they would *assume* it. Accepting the fact that a train could not move without a motorman, the police would *assume* the presence of a motorman in the darkened cab. Ryder acknowledged that some observer, hurdling the psychological barrier, might perceive the truth, but even so it would be met with official skepticism long enough for them to make their escape.

When he had checked the arrangement of pipes to his satisfaction, Ryder hauled himself up into the car and entered the cab.

"I wish we were getting started," Longman said impatiently.

"As soon as Command Center says the track is clear."

"I know," Longman said. "It's just that I'm getting itchy."

Ryder estimated that Longman had about ten minutes before he went to pieces. Well, in ten minutes they should be home free.

WELCOME

Joe Welcome was fed up. For one thing, the bright light had cooled him on the chick. Still a hot chick, sure, but the mileage was showing. And he was beginning to get uptight about the operation. There wasn't enough action. The best part had been back when he'd unloaded on that fat guy on the tracks. That was how he liked it—fast and tough. Ryder was a brain, even little Longman was a brain, but they were too fancy. You want to get out of someplace? Come out fast, and come out zapping. Sure, there was cops, but they had four fast shooters, didn't they?

And the SMGs—that was another one of his beefs. He didn't agree when Ryder said they would have to ditch them. The tommy gun's firepower was why everybody lay down and rolled over for you. With one submachine gun he'd take on a *thousand* cops.

BOROUGH COMMANDER

"They're sitting right there," the borough commander said, pointing under the limousine. "If the street collapsed we'd land on top of them. It's the closest I've been to them since the whole thing began."

Union Square lay to their right. A block to the south on the left was S. Klein, the department store that had been a discount house long before anyone used the term. The crowds that normally thronged the sidewalks were beginning to coagulate around the swarm of police cars. Traffic was piling up.

"If the street collapsed," the commissioner said, "it wouldn't be such a bad idea. The whole city sinking down and disappearing. It's not such a bad idea."

The commissioner's pessimism was as much a surprise to the borough commander as his joke had been. But he said nothing.

"The people," the commissioner said. "Subtract the people from the scene and it would be easy to catch crooks."

"You know what I'd like to do, Mr. Commissioner?" The borough commander wrenched his eyes away from the park. "I'd like to slip down one of those emergency grates and shoot the hell out of them."

"Haven't we been over that before?"

"I'm just talking. It makes me feel better."

The radio crackled. "Communications to PC. Come in sir."

The borough commander answered. "Come in, come in."

"Sir, the hijackers are being told that the track is clear."

"Okay, thanks." The borough commander looked at the commissioner. "Wait, or get started?"

"Get started. For once we'll be a step ahead of them."

RYDER

"Command Center to Pelham One Two Three."

"Pelham One Two Three here. Report."

"The track is cleared. Repeat, the track is cleared."

Longman was pressed against Ryder, his breathing a succession of deep sighs that sucked his mask into his mouth. Ryder glanced at him and thought, He'll come to grief. Whatever happens, however well it comes out, Longman will fail. Then he spoke into the mike. "Is the track cleared all the way to South Ferry? Confirm. You know the penalty if you're lying?"

"I want to tell you something. You're not going to live to spend that money. I have a strong hunch. Do you read me?"

"We're starting the train now," Ryder said. "Over and out."

"Mark my words—"

Ryder switched the radio off. "Let's go," he said to Longman. "I want the train to be moving in thirty seconds."

He opened the latch and nudged Longman through the cab door. Ryder took a final look at the Gimmick and followed. The door clicked, locking behind him.

288

The emergency brake cord hung just behind the motorman's cab. It looked like a skipping rope, with a red wooden handle dangling about six inches below the ceiling. Tom Berry watched the small hijacker reach up with long, thin scissors and cut the cord. The wooden handle rolled as it hit the floor. The heavy man at the other end of the car cut the second cord and put the handle in his pocket.

The small man made a hand signal, and Berry saw the heavy man acknowledge it with a nod before he opened the rear door, crouched, and dropped out of sight to the track. The small man, moving with awkward speed, slid by the leader, who was covering the passengers with his tommy gun, and pulled the front door open. He sat down before dropping to the track. The leader nodded crisply to the man in the center of the car, who started to turn, paused, and blew a kiss to the girl in the Anzac hat. Then he trotted jauntily to the rear. He opened the door and, barely bending his knees, jumped down.

The leader was looking at the passengers, and Berry thought, He's going to make a farewell speech, tell us what a great bunch of hostages we've been.

"You will remain in your seats," the leader said. "Don't try to get up. Remain seated."

He felt behind him for the handle and slid the front door open, and as he moved out Berry thought, Now is the time, whip out your gun and plug him. . . . The leader dropped from view. Just before the door slid shut, Berry caught an oblique view of the small man on the tracks. He was holding what seemed to be a length of pipe, and Berry, with a sudden flash of insight, knew what was going to happen to the train, and how they proposed to throw off pursuit and, as the press would surely refer to it, make their brilliant and daring escape.

He didn't believe what he was doing. He could not really be running in a crouch with his drawn gun in his hand. The train started with a shattering jerk, and the momentum carried him almost to the rear door. He found the handle and slid it back. He

stared at the tracks fleeing backward beneath him and thought, You were a parachutist, you know how to make a landing; and then he thought, There's still time to go back and sit down.

He jumped, sailed, and felt an agonizingly prolonged moment of sickening pain before he blacked out.

GRAND CENTRAL TOWER

When the red blips on the model board at Grand Central Tower indicated that Pelham One Two Three was moving, Marino was passably cool. "They're on their way," he said.

In a matter of seconds the information was broadcast from Police Headquarters to all cars.

Simultaneously with Marino's announcement, Mrs. Jenkins, in her quiet voice, was saying to Lieutenant Garber at Jay Street, "Pelham One Two Three is presently about a hundred feet south of its former position."

All TA foot patrolmen and cars were alerted, and the entire pursuit, aboveground and below, surged southward as if attached by invisible strings to Pelham One Two Three.

RYDER

Longman had been overanxious and had stumbled after pushing the pipe. But he had kept his grip on it as he recoiled when the train started, and it came away in his hand. Ryder pulled him off the track into the shelter of the tunnel wall and braced an arm across his trembling chest as the car rumbled by—a towering, terrifying bulk. Then he took the pipe from Longman's unresisting hand and tossed it across the track. Steever and Welcome were waiting for them close to the tunnel wall.

"Let's move," Ryder said. He trotted southward and waited in the white glare of the light marking the emergency exit as the others straggled after him. "Keep it lively," he said sharply. "You know the drill."

"I thought I saw something fall out of the end," Steever said. "The end of the car."

Ryder looked down the track. "What did it look like?"

"Could be a person. But I'm not even sure I saw it."

Welcome said, "If anybody fell out of the end of that car, he's for the embalmer." He hefted his machine gun.

Ryder looked down the track again. There was nothing visible. The car was already out of sight. He glanced at Steever. Battle nerves? He had seen tension conjure up ghosts many times before, and in men as self-contained and unimaginative as Steever.

"We're wasting time," Ryder said. "Let's get started."

Longman said, "You're sure it's clear up there?" He tilted his chin toward street level. "Sure the cops will take off?"

"Yes. They'll follow the train." Ryder heard the rasp of impatience in his voice. "I'm going to give the commands." The precision drill had been a matter of necessity, not choice. In rehearsal, with each man on his own, one or another of them kept slipping up, so he had devised a simple by-the-numbers routine. He had also decided against entering the chamber of the emergency exit at this point, in case some passerby looking through the grate might see or hear them.

"Submachine guns," Ryder said crisply. He put his gun down on the roadbed. Steever and Longman followed, but Welcome still held his, fondling it possessively.

Steever said, "Come on, Joey, you need two hands to work."

Welcome said, "Who in hell are you?" But he put it down.

"Hats and masks," Ryder said.

The reappearance of their faces came as a shock, and Ryder thought, These seem less real than the masks. It surprised him, when Welcome spoke, to hear his own sentiments echoed.

"Tell you something, you all looked better with them on."

"Disguise," Ryder said.

He had removed the wads from his face before putting his mask on, and Longman had removed his eyeglasses. So it remained only for Steever to take off his white-haired wig, and Welcome to strip off the mustache and curving sideburns.

"Coats," Ryder said. "Remove, turn, put back on."

The navy raincoats were all reversible—Welcome's to a light beige poplin waterproof, Steever's to medium gray with a black

fur collar, Longman's to tan herringbone, his own to a Donegal tweed. He watched closely as each buttoned his coat up over the bulging money jacket.

"Hats."

They took their hats from their pockets. Welcome's was a powder blue low-crowned golfing hat with a narrow red and navy blue band, Steever's a gray with a short, upturned brim, Longman's a gray astrakhan Russian hat, his own a sporty brown cap.

"Gloves." They peeled their gloves and dropped them.

"Handgun in coat pocket? Check." He waited. "Okay. Wallets. Show the ID card and shield."

He hoped they would have no reason to use them, but it was conceivable that a cop or two, remaining on the scene, might question them. If so, they were to say they were part of the force stationed in the tunnel and present police credentials, which had been even more expensive to obtain than the submachine guns.

"Can't you go a little faster?" Longman said.

"This character is scared of his own burps," Welcome said.

"Almost finished," Ryder said. "Pick up guns, detach magazine, put in pocket. Put guns down again." He didn't want any armed submachine guns left behind.

All four bent for their guns. Three removed magazines.

"Not me," Welcome said, smiling. "I'm taking mine along."

GRAND CENTRAL TOWER

Marino, his voice ringing in the stillness of the Tower Room, said, "Pelham One Two Three just passed Fourteenth Street."

"Any idea of the speed?"

"Well, I would guess it's in series."

"What does that mean?"

"About thirty miles an hour. Can the police cars keep up with them through the traffic?"

"We don't have to do that. We've got cars in position all along the route. They pick up as the train hits their area."

"It's now about halfway between Fourteenth and Astor Place."

"Okay. Keep talking to me."

CLIVE PRESCOTT

At the desk trainmaster's console at Command Center, Prescott gave up trying to contact Pelham One Two Three. He listened to Mrs. Jenkins' voice reporting to Garber over the squawk box.

". . . continuing downtown, estimated to be in series position speed."

It made no sense, Prescott thought. Inch by inch their position was monitored, so how could they hope to evade pursuit? It was dumb. And yet, so far, they hadn't made a single mistake.

He tried again. "Pelham One Two Three. Command Center calling."

ANITA LEMOYNE

In exactly one minute, Anita Lemoyne thought, I'm going to get hysterical. *Can't the stupid jerks count?* Everyone was babbling about the hippie who had jumped out.

"All that momentum," the old man was saying. "He couldn't be alive."

Someone else said, "What made him do it?" and then answered himself. "Bombed out. They *do* crazy things like that."

"You think they'll let us go soon?" the mother said.

Anita jumped up, screaming, "Don't you clods know what you saw? All four of them got off. There's nobody *driving* this train!"

The old man seemed startled for a moment, then shook his head and smiled. "My dear young lady, if they all got off, we would be standing still. One of them has to be on to drive it."

Anita's eyes went wildly from one uncertain face to another and rested on the mother's. She must have been doing some simple arithmetic, Anita thought, she's getting the message.

The mother screamed on a sustained ululant note. And that, Anita thought, ought to make believers out of the rest of them.

TOM BERRY

Young Tom Berry's father was bawling him out for some crime he hadn't committed, scourging him with that cold voice that could draw blood. His mother was pleading for him, but her voice

was strange. It sounded like a man's. He opened his eyes, and pain drove his dream away, though the voices continued.

He was lying against a pillar, off the roadbed, and he was hurt. His head, his shoulders, his chest . . . He put his hand to nose and mouth; they felt pulpy and wet. He probed his head and found a huge lump. The voices worried him. He lifted his head an inch and found their source.

He could not judge the distance, but he could see them clearly enough, all four of them. They were ranged against the wall, and they were undressing. They no longer wore their stocking masks, and their faces under the naked bulb marking the emergency exit were erratically lit: brightly on the prominence of nose and ears, hollowed by deep shadows on the flatter planes. The leader was doing most of the talking. Gradually Berry began to realize what they were up to. Their hats and coats were different, they were disguising themselves. In their new clothing and with the police in wild pursuit of the train, they would come up through the emergency exit and simply mingle with the crowd.

His gun. It had been in his hand when he jumped. He raised himself on his elbow to look for it, then, in a sudden panic, huddled behind the pillar. They might see him, the whiteness of his face might give him away. But he couldn't look for the gun if he kept his faced pressed into the tunnel floor. The hell with the gun. He could get another gun, but not another face. He groaned, then hastily muffled it. Why was he here? Why had he jumped from the frying pan? Where was his head?

The four hijackers were arguing. No, two of them. He placed the angry voice as belonging to the stud. The cold, uninflected one was the leader's. The other two were silent, looking on. Thieves falling out? Would they now proceed to slaughter each other? If they did, he wouldn't hesitate to crawl over there and collar them.

"You men—dead though you may be—are under arrest. You are entitled to one phone call each, and I hereby notify you of your rights according to Supreme Court decision. . . ."

Where is my gun? He began to scrabble with his hand on the grimy tunnel floor.

Through the window of Woodlawn One Four One, the faint rectangle of light that marked Pelham One Two Three wavered. DCI Daniels rubbed his eyes.

"They just begun to move," the motorman said.

"Well, what the hell are you waiting for!" the DCI shouted.

"For your signal. You're killing my arm, Cap'n, I can't drive no train that way."

The DCI loosened his grip. "Get going. Not too fast."

"*They* sure as hell ain't dawdling," the motorman said as the train began to crawl forward. "See how fast those green signals turned red? You sure you want me to go all this slow?"

"I don't want them to see us."

"This speed they sure won't see us. Nor us see them."

"Then go faster, damn it, if that's your judgment."

"Faster," the motorman said. "That's my judgment."

He nudged the controller to series position and the train shot ahead, but only for a moment. The forward wheels made a faint metallic sound, and then the entire tunnel seemed to explode. The rear of the car hung suspended for a split second before crashing back on the roadbed, swaying and bouncing crazily as the motorman applied his brakes, coming at last to a stop in a haze of dust and overheated metal.

Beside the motorman, the DCI was holding his head. His eyes were crossed, and a thin stream of blood trickled out of his hairline. He pushed past the motorman and out of the cab. There, leaning against the door to steady himself, he surveyed the car. Everyone seemed to be shouting. Cops and weapons were strewn about on the floor. One man was rolling from side to side, crying in oddly controlled gasps, clutching at his kneecap.

"Help that man," the DCI said. He was going to say something else, but lost the thread. He felt the bloody place on his head.

"Are you hurt, sir?" It was a burly sergeant, speaking very calmly. "What happened, sir?"

"Booby-trapped," the DCI said. "Tell your men to sit down, Sergeant. I'll reconnoiter." His mind drifted. He went into the

cab. The motorman was sitting on his metal stool shaking his head from side to side.

"Report the incident, Sergeant," the DCI said. "Find out how soon the corps of engineers can get us back—"

"What you mean, *Sergeant?*" the motorman said. "You a little shook up, Cap'n?"

"Don't argue, Sergeant. Get on that radio and report."

He went to the front door and slid it open. As he was crouching to jump, one of the men said, "Can we help you, sir?"

The DCI smiled. Funny new breed of cops, spoiled by cars and partners and computers. They didn't realize that the old-timer walked his beat alone and unafraid, and beware the miscreant who trifled with him. He dropped to the tracks. Then, hands behind his back, eyes moving slowly and watchfully from side to side, he began to walk his beat.

RYDER

Ryder said mildly, "Disarm your gun, Joe, so we can get out of here."

"Me and the gun is going out together," Welcome said.

"You can't take it," Ryder said, still mildly.

"My friend goes with me. The old firepower, you know, if the fuzz turns up."

"The whole point of the escape plan is to walk away unnoticed. You can't do that if you're carrying a submachine gun." The argument was a replay. It had come up several times, but Welcome had eventually conceded—or so it seemed.

"Not *carry* it. I slip it under my coat."

The old record played on, Ryder thought. "A submachine gun can't be hidden under a coat."

Longman said shrilly, "This is crazy. We have to get going."

Steever's face showed neither annoyance nor partisanship. Welcome, smiling, was watching Longman sweat.

Ryder said, "Will you leave your gun?"

"Hell, no, General."

He was still smiling when Ryder, firing through his pocket, shot

him in the throat. The shot was soundless, overwhelmed by a shattering explosion northward in the tunnel. Longman sagged against the tunnel wall and vomited. Welcome lay on his side, his legs twitching, his left hand clawing at his throat, his right still holding the submachine gun. Ryder kicked it loose, removed the magazine, and put it in his pocket. Then he crouched for a close look at Welcome. His eyes were shut; his breathing was shallow. Ryder put his automatic against Welcome's head. He looked at Steever.

"He might last just long enough to talk," he said, and pulled the trigger. He looked again into Steever's expressionless face. "Get Longman straightened out."

When he stood up again, he had Welcome's money jacket in his hand. To the north in the tunnel he saw a moiling cloud of smoke and dust.

Steever supported Longman with a hand around his waist, and wiped off the front of his coat with a handkerchief. Longman looked ill. His face was drained of color, and his eyes were red-rimmed and weeping.

"Take off his coat," Ryder said.

When Ryder moved toward him with the jacket, Longman looked terrified. "Me?" Longman said. "Why me?" and Ryder realized that his fear had passed beyond the rational and that he was afraid of everything.

"You're the thinnest. Two jackets won't show on you." He secured the jacket on Longman and buttoned up his coat.

Steever said conversationally, "The train blew good."

"Yes," Ryder said. He looked Longman over. "All right. I think we're ready to go upstairs."

BOROUGH COMMANDER

"That short move they made to Union Square," the borough commander said. "It wasn't in the script. It's got me worried." They were speeding downtown, the siren wide open.

The commissioner was pursuing a path of his own. "They know we can follow every move the train makes. They know we're

covering them every inch of the way on the surface. They're not stupid. So they may be very clever."

"Yes," the borough commander said. "They said they moved to get away from the police staked out in the tunnel. But they knew we were in the tunnel before, and didn't seem to mind. Why now?"

"Well, why?" the commissioner said impatiently.

"This time they didn't want us to see what they were doing."

"What were they doing?"

"They don't care that we're following them—right? In fact, stretching the point, you could say they want us to follow them all the way downtown—right?"

"If you have a theory, spit it out," the commissioner said.

"My theory is that they aren't on the train."

"That's what I thought your theory was. But how can the train move if they're not on it?"

"That's the catch. Except for that, it makes sense. The whole pursuit flows south, but they stay near Union Square and pop up through an emergency exit. How about this—three get off and one stays on to drive the train?"

"You ever meet a self-sacrificing crook, Charlie?"

"No," the borough commander said. "A more logical tack— suppose they figured out some way to make the train go with nobody in the cab?"

"If they did that," the commissioner said, "they're dead ducks. Daniels is following on the express track."

"They might be able to conceal themselves until he went by." He shook his head. "That short move. That unexpected move."

"Well, Charlie? You want to play your hunch?"

"Yes, sir," the borough commander said. "With your permission." The commissioner nodded. The borough commander leaned forward to the driver. "Turn back to Union Square."

The radio broke in. "Sir. The motorman of DCI Daniels' train has reported that they were blown off the track. By an explosive."

The commissioner asked about casualties and was told that one policeman was hurt, not seriously. "That was the purpose of

the short move," he said to the borough commander. "They didn't want anybody around when they mined the track."

"Never mind turning back," the borough commander said to the driver. "Go on as you were."

OLD MAN

The old man, calling on ancient memory, activating disused impulses, held up his hand (that hand that once was a scepter, demanding obedience at home, subservience in the shop) and said, "Quiet down. Everybody quiet down a minute." He stood up and held on to a strap. "My friends, the situation is not so bad as it looks."

The black man gave a snorting laugh into his bloody handkerchief (*My* handkerchief, the old man thought), but the rest became attentive. "In the first place, we don't have to worry about the hijackers anymore. As the young lady pointed out, they are off the train. Good-by and good luck."

"Then who's driving it?"

"Nobody. Some way, they got it started."

"We'll all be killed!" An agonized scream from the mother.

"Not so," the old man said. "I admit that right now we are on a runaway train, but that's purely temporary."

The car entered a curve and careened wildly, the wheel flanges grinding, bumping, as they resisted the pull of the car to follow the curve off the tracks. The old man, clinging desperately to the strap, was half lifted from the floor. The black man reached up and steadied him. The train straightened out.

"Thank you," the old man said. The black man ignored him. "Ladies and gentlemen." The old man held up his hand again. "I happen to know something about the subway, and I tell *you* it's not too much to worry about. This is the safest railroad in the world, like they call it. They got these things on the track, trippers. Whenever a train goes through a red light, the trippers come up automatically and stop the train!" He looked around him in triumph. "So. Soon we will run into a red light, the trippers will come up, and presto! The train will stop."

"Pelham One Two Three is now passing Canal Street station. Still proceeding at the same speed."

In the reverberant stillness of the Tower Room, Marino savored the unhurried, professional steadiness of his tone.

"I read you," Lieutenant Garber said. "Keep talking."

"Roger," Marino said crisply. "Four more stations, and then they're at South Ferry."

TOM BERRY

With the first impact of the explosion, Tom Berry curled into the fetal position and sustained another minor injury in the process. His knee struck a heavy object and went numb. Nursing his knee, he raised his head an inch or two and saw one of the hijackers lying on the roadbed. It was the lover boy, and Berry concluded that the explosion had felled him. Then he saw the leader slapping at his coat and realized that the explosion had been something separate, that the leader had shot him through the pocket of his coat.

Suddenly, with wild hope, Berry thought of the object his knee had struck. He patted the grimy floor frantically, and found his gun.

He rolled over on his stomach, still in the shelter of the pillar, and propped the short barrel of the .38 on his left wrist. He looked for the leader through the sight, but he had disappeared. Then he picked him up bending over the body. Berry heard him fire and then saw the leader remove something from the body. The money belt. He watched him slip it onto the small man's shoulders and tie it in place.

He was having trouble with his vision. He shut his eyes, squeezing them hard to rupture the film that obscured them. When he opened his eyes, the little man was disappearing through the break in the tunnel wall. The heavy man was behind him. Berry put his sight on the broad back and squeezed off. He saw the heavy man convulse and topple backward. He shifted the revolver quickly to find the leader, but he was gone.

ANITA LEMOYNE

Anita Lemoyne swayed to the front of the car. Behind her the old prophet was still holding forth. Anita braced herself against the sway of the car and stared through the window. The tracks, the tunnel, the posts were swept up in the rush of the train as if by some powerful vacuum cleaner. A station whipped by, an oasis of light, crowds of people. Two names. Brooklyn Bridge–Worth Street? Three or four more to South Ferry, the last stop. And then what? The old guy could be right about that tripper jazz. She strained her eyes looking for red signals. They sailed past Fulton Street and back into the tunnel. Ahead, as far as she could see, the signals were all bright green.

TA PATROLMAN ROTH

Patrolman Harry Roth phoned headquarters as soon as the train flashed by the Fulton Street station.

"She just whizzed by."

"Okay. Thank you."

"Listen. You want to know something funny? I didn't see anybody driving the train."

"What the hell are you talking about?"

"The front window is busted out, I think, and nobody is in the cab. I was right close at the edge of the platform, and I didn't see anybody. I'm sorry, that's what I saw."

"Don't you know trains can't drive all by themselves, because of the deadman's feature?"

"Okay. I'm sorry."

"You really thought there was nobody in the cab?"

"Maybe he was bending down."

"Oh, bending down. Over and out."

I know what I saw, Patrolman Roth said to himself.

RYDER

The pillar was a defensible position, but defense was not one of Ryder's options. The man who fired the shot had to be killed, quickly, if he was to make it back to the emergency exit.

He had acted instinctively when the shot was fired, sensing that he couldn't get by Steever and into the emergency exit without drawing a second shot, and so had taken off on a crouching run to the nearest pillar. The shot had come from the south, and since he had seen no one on the roadbed, he assumed that the enemy, too, was hidden behind a pillar.

He glanced at the exit. Longman was framed in the opening, staring at him. Urgently he pantomimed climbing, a series of rising hand-over-hand gestures. Longman only stared. He repeated the gestures decisively. Longman then turned toward the ladder. Steever lay where he had fallen. He had crashed onto his back with a shattering force. His eyes were open, moving, and Ryder was certain that he was paralyzed.

He put both men out of his mind and returned to his problem. The enemy knew precisely where he was. And there was no way he could flush out the enemy, except by taking a risk. He checked his automatic, then deliberately stepped out from the shelter of the pillar. The shot rang out at once, and Ryder fired at the muzzle flash, then twice more before withdrawing back of the post. He strained for some sound, but heard none.

He had no way of knowing if he had scored a hit, and now he must pile risk upon risk. There was no time for maneuver. He ran forward to the next pillar. No shot. Either he had hit the enemy, or the enemy was waiting for an unmissable shot. Again he ran. No shot. He had closed the distance by a third. And now he could see the enemy. He was sprawled on the track, only his legs still in the shelter of a pillar, and Ryder knew he was hurt. He was still conscious, trying to raise his head—but you didn't expect gifts, you were satisfied with an advantage. That was what Ryder had now, and it remained only to exploit it.

He stepped out from behind his pillar and walked down the center of the track. The enemy stretched out his right hand, and Ryder saw his gun, lying on the roadbed a few inches beyond the extended fingers. The enemy saw or heard him, and tried to crawl toward the gun.

But it was beyond his reach.

OLD MAN

As Pelham One Two Three ran by the Wall Street station, the passengers became agitated again and crowded around the old man. "Where are the red lights?" "We're not stopping!" "We'll all be killed!"

"There will be a red light," he shouted. "There *must* be." He turned toward the girl, keeping watch at the front of the car. She shook her head.

"The train will stop," the old man said falteringly, and knew that his life was over. The others would die in an accident; he was already dead of failure.

TOM BERRY

The first slug had hit under Tom Berry's upraised right arm, and his revolver flew away. The second had seemed to strike in front of him and then skid into his body, below the chest. The impact threw him to his left, onto the roadbed, where he came to rest in a wetness his mind refused to identify as his own blood. Losing his revolver was getting to be repetitious.

He watched the leader approach—calm, unhurried. What's his rate of speed? That's exactly how much more time I have to live. The leader could have stopped, taken careful aim, and finished him off, but, Berry thought, he was a compulsive perfectionist. He would administer the *coup de grâce* in the traditional way, gun to temple, as he had with his late colleague. No fuss and no muss. Just a single instant of monstrous red explosion, and after that, peace. What was so good about that kind of peace?

He was sobbing when the leader paused above him, and he had a view of sensible, unstylish black shoes. The leader was starting to bend. Berry shut his eyes. *Will she weep for me?*

Somewhere in the tunnel, someone was shouting.

PATROLMAN SEVERINO

At Bowling Green station Transit Patrolman Severino was so close to the edge of the platform that Pelham One Two Three actually brushed him back, leaving an imprint of dust and grime

on his uniform. He looked directly into the cab, and his report, when he radioed headquarters, was so concise it left no doubt of its plausibility.

"Nobody in the cab. Repeat, nobody in the cab. Window busted out and nobody in the cab."

DCI DANIELS

The scene kept shifting in DCI Daniels' head, the way it did when you were catnapping. One moment he was back on Ie Shima with the Seventy-seventh, and the Jap navy was bombarding the hell out of them. Next moment he was in a subway tunnel. But mostly he was walking his old beat. Third Avenue, in the Thirties, it was. Still plenty of Irish around, but the Armenians predominated. Like Menjes, the grocer. No, Menjes was a Greek. . . . He put his hand up to his head. He was bleeding. Nothing serious, didn't even hurt. Jap gun butt had grazed him?

A man was walking along the street in front of him. He was in the tunnel, and ahead of him a man walked slowly southward between the local tracks. He knew every last soul on the beat by sight. Didn't recognize this man. Didn't like the way he walked. Not doing anything suspicious, but the old cop's instinct smelled trouble. Catch up and check him out.

Man on the tracks. Holding something. A gun? He slipped his own gun out of the holster. Saw the man stop. Look down. Start to bend over somebody. . . .

"Hey! Freeze right there! Drop that gun!"

The man whirled, in a crouch, and the DCI saw muzzle flash. He returned fire, and the thunder of the gun through the silent midnight streets cleared his head. He was shooting it out with the man who had broken into Paulie Ryan's saloon. . . .

RYDER

Ryder had no last thoughts. He died instantaneously, with a metallic taste on his tongue, from a .38-caliber round that entered just below his chin, smashed his teeth and palate, and curved upward through the roof of his mouth into his brain.

DCI DANIELS

Some shooting, DCI Daniels thought, good as thirty-five years ago, when he killed the armed man who tried knocking over Paulie Ryan's. His first commendation for it. Funny that he had just done it all over again. And what was he doing in a subway tunnel?

He moved up on the fallen gunman, who lay face up, his eyes open and staring at the tunnel roof. There wasn't much to see— a dead, neatly dressed man with a ruined, bloody face.

He turned to the victim, poor thing. Bloody, too, but alive. Lustrous blond hair down to the shoulders, bare toes in open sandals a bit grimy, but that was the city for you. He knelt and said in a gentle, comforting voice, "We'll have an ambulance along in a jiffy, miss."

The face screwed up, the lips parted, and the DCI bent closer to catch a whisper. But instead of words there was laughter, surprisingly booming to come from such a young girl.

CLIVE PRESCOTT

Prescott didn't understand how a train could be driven without a motorman's hand on the deadman's feature, but he did understand the urgency of the message. He ran to Correll. "Nobody driving the train!" he screamed. "Have to stop it!"

Correll said, "A train can't drive all by itself."

"It *is* driving itself. They doped the controller somehow; it *is* driving itself. Don't argue. It's nearly to South Ferry, and it'll loop back to Bowling Green and smash into the rear of the train that's standing in the station. Can you turn a signal red and trip it? Hurry, for God's sake!"

"Tower can trip it if there's time," Correll said. He whirled toward the console, and just then Nevins Street Tower came in on the squawk box.

"Pelham One Two Three just cleared South Ferry station, going strong at about thirty, headed toward loop."

Prescott groaned. But Correll, unaccountably, was suddenly grinning and waving his hands in the air. "Don't worry. I'll stop it.

Presto! Pelham One Two Three, the desk trainmaster commands you to stop!"

Prescott threw himself at Frank Correll and began to choke him. It required all four of Correll's dispatchers to pry his fingers from Correll's neck, and reinforcements to bring him down and pin him to the floor. Then, with three men sitting on him, he was told about the time signal.

"There's a timer in the loop," one dispatcher said calmly. "If a train hits the curve too fast, like this one just has, the signal turns red and activates the trippers and the train brakes and stops. Frank knew that, of course. He was just making a little joke."

Prescott's rage was not quite extinguished. "That's why I tried to choke him," he said. "I can't stand his little jokes."

BOROUGH COMMANDER

"Controls doctored, nobody in the cab?" The borough commander yelled back at the radio voice, repeating its message.

"Yes, sir. That's correct, sir."

The borough commander leaned toward the driver. "Back to Union Square. Open it up, break the speed laws."

As the car cornered on two wheels he said to the commissioner, "Shouldn't deny a hunch. They're back there."

"Were," the commissioner said. "They took us in, Charlie."

"Speed. More speed," the borough commander yelled.

"There'll be a dozen cars there ahead of us," the commissioner said. "They'll be too late, too."

The borough commander smashed his fists together, spraining his left wrist and shattering two knuckles.

ANITA LEMOYNE

Somebody was cursing the old man, and by the time Anita Lemoyne looked back from the window to see what was happening, most of the passengers had broken for the rear of the car. Not the old man. He was sitting in his seat with his head bowed, his lips trembling. What the hell was he crying about, him and his no-show red lights—he'd had a long enough life! Next to him the

militant black was sitting very straight, his chin up, his long legs crossed, and one foot casually swinging. Okay. At least he would go in style. Him and me, a proud, doomed black stud and an aging white whore. Oh, yes, and the old wino, still asleep, still drooling. Some trio.

The car swept through South Ferry station, past the yelling, fist-shaking people on the platform, and on into the dimness of the tunnel. Now what? Ahead she saw the tunnel wall curve, and she *knew* what—they were going too fast to make it. The wheels would leap off the track, the train would smash into the wall. She braced her feet wide apart, and directly ahead was a red signal. The old man was right, after all. But it was too late, they were hitting the curve. . . .

She felt a terrific drag under her feet and she was thrown forward against the window. There was a hissing sound, and screams from the rear of the car as it lurched to a stop.

From stunned silence the car exploded into a hysterical chorus of joy, and Anita thought, Well, folks, we'll all live to love another day. She turned and sagged against the door. The old man was looking at her, trying to smile.

"Well, young lady, didn't I say we would stop?"

The militant put the bloodstained handkerchief into the old man's hand. "Burn it, dude, it's nigger blood."

The wino lady belched. " 's Forty-secon' Street?"

Punch line, Anita thought, the old bum came up with the punch line. She opened her purse and dropped a ten-dollar bill in the spread lap with its layers of wildly mismatched clothing.

LONGMAN

Longman edged up on the ladder and pushed at the grate with both hands. The grate squealed on rusty hinges and a cloud of grit showered down on him. But he held fast and pushed it up. When his head reached sidewalk level, he heard shots below him. He froze for an instant, then stepped out to the street beside Union Square.

Facing the park wall, his back to the sidewalk, he lowered the

grate slowly to the ground. Several passersby glanced at him, but none looked twice. The famous New York indifference, he thought exultantly, crossing to the east side of the street and merging into the stream of pedestrians flowing past Klein's. A block ahead, near Seventeenth Street, he saw a police car. It was double-parked, and a man was leaning on the window, talking to the cops. Keeping his eyes straight ahead, he turned the corner into Sixteenth Street. He forced himself to slow down as he walked eastward. At Irving Place he turned left. Ahead was the grillwork fence and stripped trees of Gramercy Park. He thought of Ryder, and remembered the shots he had heard as he climbed the ladder. Ryder would be okay, he told himself, and with an odd reluctance to dwell on the matter, put it out of mind. He walked east on Eighteenth Street past Second Avenue, with the massive pink buildings of Stuyvesant Town in view.

Then he was at his own building, the drab stone tenement with the grayed-down façade and, at the windows, people and dogs gazing out, wistful and bored. He climbed the stairs to the second floor, fumbled for his keys, opened the three locks in order from bottom to top, went inside and locked the door, top to bottom. He went to the kitchen and turned on the tap. While he was waiting for the water to run cold, a glass in his hand, he suddenly let out a shout of wild and abandoned triumph.

CLIVE PRESCOTT

Prescott left at six thirty. It was dark, with that washed-down air the city sometimes wore in crisp cold weather. He had doused his head in water, but it was no relief for his exhaustion. He looked up at the great dignified buildings the Borough of Brooklyn had inherited from its past, glowing palely with night-lights.

On Fulton Street the stores were closed or closing, and soon the whole shopping area would be deserted, too. The department stores were barricaded, their watchmen alert, their burglar alarms set for intruders. A newspaper vendor, a weathered woman of fantastic durability, was closing up her stand. He averted his eyes from the giant newspaper headlines.

A black boy thrust something in his face. "Panther paper, brother."

He shook his head and moved on. The boy fell in step. "Come on, man, get to know what it's all about. You want to go on being Charley's field hand?"

Prescott pushed the paper away roughly and walked on, then stopped. "I'll take one."

"Right on."

He tucked the paper under his arm. I am sick, Prescott thought, sick of cops and criminals and victims and bystanders. Sick of anger and of blood. Sick of what happened today and will happen tomorrow. Sick of white and of black, of my job and my friends and my family, of love and of hatred. Above all, I am sick of myself, sick of being sick at the imperfections of the world that nobody would try to fix up even if they knew how.

If only he had grown three inches taller. If only he had had a good outside shot. If only he were white. Or truly black.

The one thing nobody could ever take away from him was the way he had been able to drive. He was fearless coming down the middle with the ball, contemptuous of the big men who lay in wait to clobber him when he was in the air, suspended, with the ball already arching toward the basket. BOOM! But he came in every time, loping into the wall of waiting big boys. . . .

He crumpled the Panther paper into a crude ball, crouched, wheeled, drove, and released a graceful hook shot at a storefront sign. Two points. A derelict, leering, clapped his hands, then shoved out a grimy palm. Prescott pushed by.

Tomorrow he would feel better because there was no way he could feel worse.

DETECTIVE HASKINS

Detective Second Grade Bert Haskins, who, his Englishy name to one side, was one-hundred-proof Irish, had once regarded detective work as the most glamorous available to man. For about a week. Then, disabused of every notion he had ever entertained about brilliant reasoning and matching wits with masterminds, he

buckled down to the real job of criminal detection: plodding and patience. Detective work was climbing stairs, ringing doorbells, dealing with frightened, belligerent, closemouthed, or dunderheaded citizens. It was following a hundred blind leads for one live one. You plugged. And plugged. And plugged.

The Transit Authority files had already yielded more than a hundred names of employees who had been discharged for cause, and the delving would continue into the night. Mostly the cause had nothing to do with criminal activity. Nevertheless it had to be assumed that any discharged employee might be disgruntled. But disgruntled enough to hijack a subway train?

Three of the hijackers had been shot. A quarter of a million dollars each had been recovered from money jackets worn by two of them. That left one hijacker and half a million dollars. No official identification had yet been made of the dead hijackers. One of them might turn out to be a former TA employee. That still didn't eliminate the missing fourth man.

Haskins and Slott, his partner, and eight other teams of detectives had been assigned to this aspect of the case, and unless somebody got lucky, it would take days to check out the complete list. They had divided up the names and set forth, after a passionate exhortation from their chief.

They had slapped shoe leather for more than four hours now. It was an axiom of the trade that nine out of ten people you had to track down lived in walk-ups. It figured. Poor people committed more crimes than rich ones. Or, more accurately, more crimes that violated the criminal code.

A half hour ago he had told Slott, who had an ulcer and whose bitching was getting on his nerves anyway, to go home. He could handle the three remaining names himself. Then he went into a small dry-cleaning store operated by an ex-TA platform guard who had been fired six years before for spitting on passengers. In response to Haskins' question he said he had been in a dentist's chair all afternoon having his gum sliced to ribbons and a couple of roots dug out by brute force. Dr. Schwartz was the name of the butcher, and his phone number was . . .

Haskins made a note to call Dr. Schwartz and then checked his list. He was equidistant from Fitzherbert, Paul, residing on Sixteenth Street west of Fifth Avenue, and Longman, Walter, Eighteenth east of Second. Which first? Too tough a question to handle without coffee, but luckily there was a joint right at the corner. He would drink his coffee, maybe eat a piece of apple pie, and then, the inner man fortified, the brain stoked up, he could make the big decision a detective (second grade) was so well equipped to handle.

LONGMAN

Longman couldn't bring himself to turn on the radio. He had seen criminals in the movies too often give themselves away by buying all the papers or clipping out stories. Of course nobody would hear his radio if he turned it low, but still he wouldn't do it. If Ryder had been killed, what was his hurry to find out?

But at six o'clock, without thinking about it consciously, he had turned on the television news. The hijacking was the top story, and the camera coverage was remarkable. When they showed "the sector of the tunnel where the shoot-out took place" and swung around to the spot where Steever had fallen, Longman winced, not wanting to see any bodies or, for that matter, any bloodstains. There were dark areas that could have been bloodstains, but there were no bodies. Later, though, the cameras were on hand when three bodies on stretchers were brought out by cops. He felt no emotion, not even for Ryder.

Next, there were interviews with police brass, including the commissioner. Each one referred to it as a "heinous" crime. Questioned by the reporters about the missing hijacker—Longman felt a hot flush sweep through his body—the commissioner said that a very large number of detectives had been assigned to the case and would work long shifts until the criminal was apprehended.

There was no mention of checking the files of ex-TA employees. He remembered when Ryder had brought that matter up how the idea had alarmed him. "They don't have to find me," he had said. "I can stay at your place."

"I *want* you to be at home. They'd otherwise be suspicious."

"I'll have to work out an alibi."

Ryder shook his head. "They'll check alibis carefully. *Most* of the people they see won't have an alibi, you'll be lost in the crowd. Simply say you spent part of the afternoon taking a walk, part of it reading a book or taking a nap, and don't be the least bit precise about when you did what."

"I'll give it some thought—what I'm going to say."

"No. Don't rehearse it or even think about it. Remember, you'll just be one in a very long list of names."

"You make it sound easy."

"It is easy," Ryder said.

"Still, I'd like to give it a little thought."

"No thought," Ryder said firmly. "Not now, or afterwards."

Actually, this was the first time he *had* thought about it. Ryder was right. It was strictly routine for the cops, and he was just another ex-TA employee among hundreds of others. He could handle it. He listened to the chief of detectives admit under questioning that descriptions of the missing man were sketchy, but that a number of passengers were going through the picture files at Police Headquarters. Longman almost smiled. He had no record; there would be no pictures of him. He switched off the set.

He went into the kitchen and made tea. Sitting at the kitchen table, still wearing his coat—he hadn't been able to bring himself to take it off—he ate graham crackers and smoked a cigarette. Then he decided to lie down for a while, and felt a dull pain in his chest. It took him a long moment to realize that he wasn't having a heart attack, that it was the weight and pressure of the money jackets. He got off the bed and went to the front door, checked all three locks, and returned to the bedroom. After pulling the window shades down as far as they would go, he at last took off his raincoat and then the money jackets. He placed them carefully on the bed, side by side, in precise alignment.

Walter Longman, he said to himself, you are worth half a million dollars. And then another uncontrollable scream raced up his throat. He clapped his hand over his mouth to muffle it.

FRANK CORRELL

After Prescott left, Frank Correll had gone back to his own console and worked it like (as *Transit*, the employee paper, had put it once in a feature article) "a man possessed, body and soul dedicated to making the railroad run as smooth as ice cream." He screamed a great deal, whirled in his chair to shout instructions to his dispatchers, swept coffee off his desk in a wide flail of his arm when somebody in misguided kindness brought him some. In constant consultation with the yard, with Operations, with Maintenance, with tower rooms, with motormen, he organized new flexes, discarded old ones, worked miracles of manipulation until, at eight twenty-one p.m., A Division was back on schedule, all trains running on time.

"Okay," Correll said to his relief. "I'm giving you back your railroad." He stood up, put his jacket on, pushed the knot of his tie up to his bruised throat, and slipped into his topcoat.

His relief, sitting down in his place, said, "Good job, Frank."

"I have only one regret," Correll said. "That I was not able to get the road straightened out before rush hour."

"No human being could have done that, in the circumstances," the relief trainmaster said.

"In that case, I wish I wasn't human." Turning abruptly, his hands plunged deep into his pockets, Correll strode off.

The relief man said, "He makes a nice exit."

At the Communications Desk, Frank Correll paused and listened. ". . . and full service restored at eight twenty-one."

It would be picked up by the media. One line, he thought. Service restored at eight twenty-one. So much for blood, sweat, and tears.

TOM BERRY

The senior resident in surgery accompanied Tom Berry's stretcher down from the recovery room.

"Where am I?" Berry said.

"Beth Israel Hospital. You've just had two bullets removed."

He hadn't meant to say where. "I mean *how* am I?"

"Okay," the resident said. "We issued a bulletin saying that your condition was fair."

"I rate a bulletin? I must be dying."

"The media wanted to know. You're in good shape." The resident looked out the window. "Nice view. Looking right down into Stuyvesant Park."

Berry explored himself. His arm was bandaged from the shoulder to the elbow, and there was a fat dressing in the approximate center of his torso. "How come no pain?"

"Sedation. You'll feel some, don't fret."

"Was I shot in the gut?"

"You weren't shot anyplace in particular. Missed the important things by a millimeter here, a hair there. Luck of a hero. I'll drop by later on. Terrific view."

Berry wondered if he was lying, if his condition was critical. They never told you; they didn't trust you to understand something as complicated as whether you were going to live or die. He shut his eyes and dozed.

Voices woke him. Three faces were looking down at him. One was the resident. The other two he recognized from pictures— His Honor, the mayor, and the PC. So—he was a hero.

"I believe he's awake now," the resident said.

The mayor smiled. He was wrapped in a huge coat, a voluminous muffler, and an astrakhan hat with earmuffs. His nose was red and his lips looked parched. The commissioner was smiling, too, but not very well. He just wasn't a smiling man.

"Congratulations, Patrolman, ah . . . Barry," the mayor said. "You performed an act of extraordinary valor. The city is in your debt."

He put out his hand, and with some effort Berry shook it. It was icy cold. Then he shook the commissioner's hand.

"Splendid work, Barry," the commissioner said.

They were both looking at him expectantly. Of course. The modesty bit. "Thank you. I was lucky. I only did what any man in the department would have done."

The mayor said, "Get well soon, Patrolman Barry."

The commissioner tried to twinkle. He wasn't a twinkling man, either. "We look forward to your recovery, *Detective* Barry."

Surprise and modesty, Berry reminded himself. "Thank you, sir, thank you very much. I only did what any—"

But the mayor and the commissioner were already leaving. As they went through the door, the mayor said, "He looks better than I do. I bet he feels better, too."

Berry dozed again. When he woke, it was because the resident was saying, "There's a girl to see you." Deedee was standing in the doorway and the resident said to her, "About ten minutes."

She was solemn and on the verge of tears. "That doctor said you weren't badly hurt. Tell me the truth."

"Mere flesh wounds."

A few tears spilled out of her eyes. She took her glasses off and kissed him on the lips.

"I'm all right," Berry said. "I'm glad you came."

"Why *wouldn't* I come?" She frowned.

"How did you know where I was?"

"How *wouldn't* I! You're all over the radio and telly. Is there much pain, Tom?"

"Heroes never feel pain."

She kissed him and left tears on his face. "I can't stand the idea of your hurting."

"I don't feel a thing. They're taking terrific care of me. Look out the window. Some view!"

She picked up his hand and put her cheek against it. She kissed his fingers and then released his hand. She seemed indecisive for about a fifth of a second, then said, "I must say you risked your life in an unworthy cause."

I'm not up to it, he thought, and tried to divert her. "A little while ago the mayor and the police commissioner were here to see me. I'm promoted to detective. Third grade, I guess."

"You could have been killed!"

"It's my job. I'm a cop."

"Killed to save the city a million dollars!"

"There were people involved, too, Deedee," he said gently.

"I won't argue with you now. I can't fight with you when you're hurt."

"But?"

"But when you get better, I'm going to make you promise to quit the pigs."

"And when I get better, I'm going to make you promise you'll quit the movement. No. Don't make a speech. I know you've got beliefs, but so do I." He reached for her hand. She drew back, then surrendered it to him. "I like the work. Not all of it. Some parts of police work are lousy. I haven't figured out the proportions yet."

"They took you in." Her eyes darkened, but she didn't relinquish his hand. "You bought the whole bundle."

He shook his head. "I'm going to stay with it until I know how I feel. Then I'll either buy the whole bundle or get out."

The resident appeared in the doorway. "Time's up. Sorry."

"I guess we better stop seeing each other," Deedee said. She walked quickly to the door, then stopped and looked back at him.

He thought of some winning things he might say to her, but he didn't say them. The game was over, the exasperating, amusing, but, finally, childish game they'd been playing for months. The issue was real. It had to be faced.

"Just one thing—Deedee," he said. "Think it over first."

He didn't quite see her leave because the resident was blocking his view. "In about ten or fifteen minutes you might start to hurt a little," the resident said.

Berry looked at him suspiciously, then got it straight. What the resident was talking about was physical pain.

LONGMAN

Longman finally turned on the radio at nine o'clock. The news was a rehash. There was only one reference to the missing hijacker —the police were bending every effort toward his apprehension. He switched off the radio and went into the kitchen, for no particular reason except that he was restless and had been doing a lot of moving from room to room. He was wearing the money

317

jackets again—the bed didn't quite seem the place for half a million dollars—and had put his raincoat on, partially to conceal the jackets, partially because it was chilly in the apartment; as usual, they were chintzy with the heat.

He looked at the linoleum on the kitchen table and for the first time appreciated how ugly it was, how badly worn. Well, he could afford new linoleum now. He could afford to live somewhere else, any part of the world, for that matter.

Half a million. It was too rich for his blood. So was a quarter of a million. He smiled, for what must have been the first time in a week. But the smile disappeared when he suddenly remembered the three bodies being brought out of the tunnel. Three dead and one survivor—Wally Longman, of all people. He thought of them laid out on a morgue slab. Two animals—and Ryder. In Ryder's death he had lost—what? Not a friend, really. Colleague, maybe? He had had a great deal of respect for Ryder: his reserve, his courage, his coolness. Above all, Ryder had been kind to him, and not too many people had been that.

What would Ryder be doing if he had been the sole survivor? Well, he would certainly be calm, relaxed, probably just sitting and reading. He wouldn't be sweating out the police—what with no record, no description of him, no live confederates who could give him away. Well, Longman thought, even though he was nervous where Ryder would be glacially cool, he was sitting pretty, too.

He experienced a rush of pleasure and jumped to his feet. He felt so full of energy that he began walking around the table to work it off before he started letting out any more whoops.

He was still loping around when someone knocked at the door. He froze, terrified, and the hot flush surged through his body.

There was a second knock and then a voice: "Hello, Mr. Longman? Police Department. I'd like to talk to you."

Longman looked at the door, its surface half covered by a garage calendar featuring a pretty girl in hot pants and no top, looking down cross-eyed at herself. Three locks. Three strong locks no cop could open. Ryder had instructed him to answer the

cops' questions. But Ryder had not anticipated his own death and the fact that the money was *here* instead of cached away in Ryder's apartment, as planned. Why hadn't he thought about the damn money before? He was *wearing* it! Still, it was well concealed and he could justify the coat because the apartment was so cold. But how could he justify ignoring the first two knocks? Not answering was a giveaway. He had blown it.

"It's just a minor matter, Mr. Longman. Would you mind opening up?"

He was standing next to the window. The window. The three locks. It was quiet on the other side of the door, but he was sure the cop was still there. He turned silently to the window, gripped the sill, and slowly raised it. He ducked through the window onto the fire escape.

DETECTIVE HASKINS

You were supposed to stand clear of a closed door, so that somebody shooting through it would miss you. But the heavy silence inside and the indifferent fit of the door with the jamb were too inviting. So Detective Bert Haskins pressed his ear to the crack and heard the distinctive squeal of wood against wood. A little soap rubbed on the runners, he thought, as he started down the stairs, and he might have got away with it. On the other hand, if Slott hadn't taken his ulcer home, this guy would have been a dead duck anyhow, because one of them would have covered the back way out.

In the detective dodge you did pick up a few useful aptitudes— the gumshoe bit, for instance. You also learned to case a joint on arrival, so you knew there was a door under the stairwell that led outside to the rear of the building. Haskins opened just enough of the door to accommodate his body, slipped through, and closed it quietly. He was in a small courtyard. He eased into a shadow and looked up.

The man—Walter Longman—was almost directly above him, fiddling with the bracket that hooked the ladder to the guardrail of the fire escape. Forget it, Longman, Haskins said to himself,

those things are always rusty. Just let it be and drop from the bottom rung.

Longman made a last effort to release the bracket, then gave up. Haskins watched him lift one leg awkwardly over the guard-rail. Good, Haskins thought, now the other . . . excellent. Longman was no acrobat, in fact he moved like an old man. He was dangling now, his hands clenched tightly around the rusty metal of the bottom rung, reluctant to let go. Shame on you, Haskins thought, a vicious hijacker afraid of a little four-foot drop?

Haskins watched the white knuckles. As soon as the fingers opened, he took a single step out of his shadow. He was perfectly placed. Longman dropped, and Haskins caught him neatly. Longman's head whipped around, presenting a pale, crumpled face and startled eyes.

"Surprise," Haskins said.

John Godey

Morton Freedgood is his real name and one thing about him is a surprise. His spare, fast-paced novel, *The Taking of Pelham One Two Three*, reads like the work of a tough, talented man in his twenties. Mr. Freedgood is a gentle, talented man in his sixties. Otherwise he is exactly what the creator of this book would have to be: the authentic New Yorker and the complete professional writer. "That's all I am," said Mr. Freedgood, as though it weren't enough.

Born in Brooklyn, brought up in the Bronx, moved to Manhattan, he loves the city and its teeming, grimy, resourceful, cussing, lively, deadpan millions, doing their jobs everywhere from Gracie Mansion to the motorman's cab on the Lexington Avenue subway. And he laughs at the city as only a native New Yorker is allowed to and only a lover can.

He began writing early—serious short stories for the literary "little magazines." He then moved into the slicks with mysteries and thrillers. For many years he did movie publicity for Paramount, Twentieth-Century Fox, United Artists; and his first novel, about the industry, was *The Wall-to-Wall Trap*. When the idea of hijacking a subway car first came to him, he shelved it as not being possible. Then, like his hero, he suddenly saw how it could be done, and he began spending a lot of time underground, talking to railroad personnel, to the tower people, to the Transit and New York police—and of course to the Federal Reserve Bank. Result: a best-selling novel, and a forthcoming movie.

If John Godey is happy in his city and happy in his work, he is evidently equally so in his family. His wife is an artist. She has recently done a book about American art history. Their daughter is now a graduate student at Harvard. It was while she was growing up that the family tried living in Connecticut. Now the Freedgoods are, inevitably, and for good, back in Manhattan.

"But," says Mr. Godey, "I've given up riding subways."

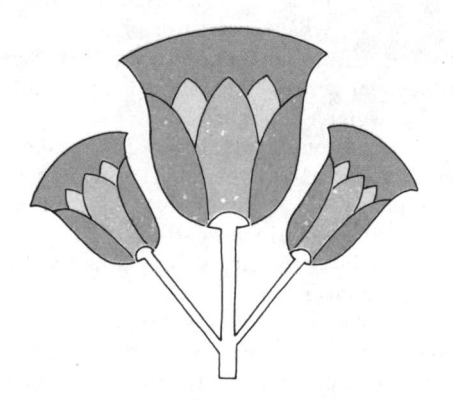

*Would the man Judith loved sacrifice the living
to appease the ancient guardians of the
treasures of the dead?*

THE CURSE OF THE KINGS

A CONDENSATION OF THE BOOK BY

Victoria Holt

ILLUSTRATED BY JOE ISOM

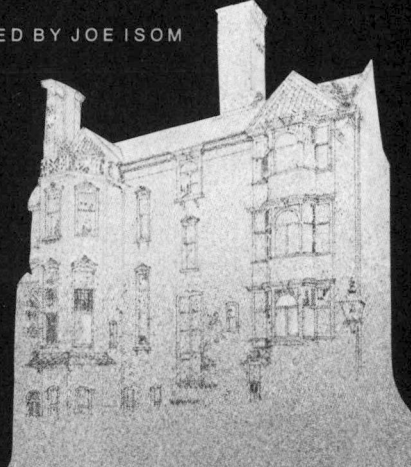

At home in Cornwall it was easy for Judith to make light of prophets of doom. She, like all sensible people, considered the odd rumors about Sir Edward Travers' mysterious death in Egypt little more than superstitious imaginings.

And when she had the good fortune to join her husband's expedition to the tomb Sir Edward had attempted to explore, Judith expected it to be the most exciting time of her life.

But on the banks of the Nile, the promise of adventure soon gave way to the dark threat of disaster. Curiosity was slowly paled by fear. And at last there seemed no way out of the unthinkable danger into which she, and those she loved, had been cast.

The author of *The Secret Woman* has written a new novel that suspensefully combines romance with intrigue as she tells a haunting story that deftly entwines the lives of English gentry with the ghosts of the ancient kings of Egypt.

Prologue

*W*HEN Sir Edward Travers died suddenly and mysteriously there was consternation and speculation, not only in our neighborhood but throughout the country. One newspaper headline ran: SIR EDWARD TRAVERS VICTIM OF CURSE? Another reported: SUDDEN DEATH OF EMINENT ARCHAEOLOGIST BRINGS ABRUPT END TO EXPEDITION.

A paragraph in our local paper stated, "The death of Sir Edward Travers, who recently left this country to carry out excavations among the tombs of the pharaohs, has caused us to wonder if there is any truth in the ancient belief that he who meddles with the resting places of the dead invites their enmity."

SIR Ralph Bodrean of Keverall Court, our local squire and Sir Edward's closest friend, had given financial aid to the expedition, and when, a few days after the announcement of Sir Edward's death, Sir Ralph had a stroke, it was hinted that his misfortune was the result of the same curse.

I was at the time companion to Lady Bodrean, Sir Ralph's wife. It was a post which did not suit my nature but which my financial needs had forced me to take. When Sir Edward's body was brought back to England for burial in our churchyard I accompanied Lady Bodrean to the funeral service. There I could not

take my eyes from Tybalt Travers, Sir Edward's only son, who had already attained some distinction in his father's profession. He was, of course, chief mourner.

I had loved him, foolishly and hopelessly, from the time I had first seen him. He seemed to me to possess all the masculine virtues. He was tall and lean and had the brow of a scholar, yet there was a touch of sensuality about his mouth. His gray eyes were deep-set and veiled and one could never be certain what he was thinking. He was aloof and mysterious. I often told myself that it would take a lifetime to understand him. And yet what a stimulating voyage of discovery that would be!

A few days after the funeral I took Lady Bodrean's dogs for their daily walk and went, out of habit, to Giza House, the home of the Traverses'. I stood at the wrought-iron gate, looking at the house which had always fascinated me. At that moment Tybalt came out, and to my embarrassment it was too late for me to turn away because he had seen me.

"Good afternoon, Judith," he said. "You must come in."

He smiled at me, which made me feel ridiculously happy. It was absurd. Sensible, proud Judith Osmond, to feel so intensely about another human being! How had I ever fallen into such a state?

He led me up the path through somewhat overgrown shrubs and pushed open the door. The carpets were thick at Giza House, so that footsteps were noiseless. We went into the drawing room, where the heavy midnight-blue velvet curtains were fringed with gold and the carpet was also deep blue with a velvety pile. This was the Chinese room, but the grand piano which dominated it bore the flavor of Victorian England.

We sat down and Tybalt said, "We're planning another expedition to Egypt to the place where my father died."

"You think that wise?" I asked.

"Surely you don't believe these rumors about my father's death, do you, Judith?"

"Of course not."

"I am certain he was on the verge of a great discovery. The day before he died he said to me, 'I believe shortly I am going to prove

to everyone that this expedition was very much worthwhile.' He would say no more than that. How I wish he had."

"I understand there was an autopsy."

"Yes, but they were unable to find the cause of his death. He was a healthy man, and suddenly he was struck down. It was very mysterious. However, I am going back, and I shall attempt to find out what it was my father was on the point of discovering and if that had anything to do with his death."

"When will you leave?" I asked.

"It will take us three months to get ready."

The door opened and Tabitha Grey came in. Like everyone at Giza House she interested me. She was beautiful in an unobtrusive way. And I was fascinated by her air of resignation, her acceptance of life. I had never been quite sure of her position; she was a sort of specially privileged housekeeper.

"Would you like some tea, Judith?" Tabitha asked.

I declined with thanks, explaining that I should be going back without delay. Tabitha smiled sympathetically, implying that she understood Lady Bodrean was no easy taskmistress.

Tybalt walked back with me, talking all the time about the expedition. I was fascinated by it.

"I believe you wish you were going with us," he said.

"With all my heart."

"Would you be prepared to face the curse of the pharaohs, Judith?"

"Yes, I certainly should."

He smiled at me. "I wish," he said earnestly, "that you *could* join us."

I went back to Keverall Court bemused. I scarcely heard Lady Bodrean's complaints. He *wished* that I could join them. Only by a miracle could I do that.

Then Sir Ralph died and there was more talk of the curse. The man who had led the expedition and the man who had helped to finance it—both dead! There must be more than coincidence in this.

And then my miracle happened. It was like something from a dream. Cinderella was to go—not to the ball—but with the expedi-

tion to Egypt. I could only marvel at the wonder of it, and I thought constantly of everything that had led up to this.

It really began on my fourteenth birthday when I found the piece of bronze in Josiah Polgrey's grave.

Chapter I

MY fourteenth birthday was one of the most eventful days of my life, because on that day I not only found the bronze shield but I learned some truths about myself.

It was a hot July afternoon. The house was quiet, for neither Dorcas, Alison, the cook nor the two maids were anywhere to be seen. I suspected that the maids were exchanging confidences in their attic bedroom; that the cook was drowsing in the kitchen; that Dorcas was in her garden; that Alison was mending or embroidering, and that the Reverend James Osmond was in his study pretending to prepare next Sunday's sermon and, in fact, dozing in his chair.

I was in the churchyard watching Pegger, the sexton, dig a grave. I was fascinated by the cemetery. Often I would get out of bed, kneel on the window seat and look down at the burial ground. In the mist it would seem very ghostly indeed, and the gray tombstones were like figures risen from the dead; in the bright moonlight they were clearly gravestones, but they lost none of their eeriness for that. Sometimes it was pitch-dark, and the rain would be teeming down, the wind howling through the branches of the oaks and buffeting the ancient yews; then I would imagine that the dead had left their graves and were prowling around the churchyard just below my window.

My morbid interest probably started when Dorcas first took me to put flowers on her sister Lavinia's grave, which we did every Sunday.

On this hot July afternoon Pegger paused to mop his forehead. He looked like an Old Testament prophet, with his mane of white hair and beard. He regarded me sternly. "This be the last resting

place of Josiah Polgrey, Miss Judith," he said. "He's lived his three-score year and ten and now he's to face his Maker." Pegger shook his head gravely, as though he did not think highly of Josiah's chances in the next world.

"How many graves have you dug in your whole lifetime?" I asked.

"More than I can say, Miss Judith."

"And your son, Matthew, will dig them after you. Just think of that."

"If it be the Lord's will I'll dig a few more yet."

"You must dig all sorts and sizes. You wouldn't need the same size for little Mrs. Edney and Sir Ralph Bodrean, would you?"

This was a ploy to bring Sir Ralph into the conversation. I found our squire fascinating. When he passed in his carriage or on one of his thoroughbreds I would bob a little curtsy, and he would nod and raise a hand in a quick imperious gesture. Some had said of him—as long ago someone had said of Julius Caesar—"Hide your daughters when he passes by." Well, he *was* the caesar of our village. He owned most of it; the outlying farmlands were on his estate. As long as the men touched their forelocks with due respect and the girls did not deny him their favors, he was a good master, which meant that men were assured of a roof over their heads and that any results which might ensue from his dallying with the maidens were taken care of. There were plenty of "results" in the village now and they were always granted extra privileges.

But to Mr. Pegger the squire was Sin personified. Because of my youth he could not talk of our squire's major qualification for hellfire, so he gave himself the pleasure of touching on his lesser ones.

There were house parties at Keverall Court almost every weekend; the guests came to hunt foxes, otters and stags, or to shoot pheasants, or merely to make merry in the baronial hall. They were rich, elegant, often noisy—people from Plymouth and sometimes from as far away as London. I thought they brightened the countryside, but in Mr. Pegger's estimation they desecrated it.

I considered myself very lucky to visit Keverall Court every day except Saturday and Sunday. The squire's daughter and nephew had a governess, Miss Graham, and were also taught by Oliver

Shrimpton, our curate. Because I was the rector's ward, Sir Ralph had graciously allowed me to join his daughter and nephew in their schoolroom to profit from instruction. This meant that every school day I passed under the old portcullis into the courtyard and entered the great hall with its minstrel gallery. There I mounted the wide staircase as though I were one of the lady visitors from London; passed along the gallery, where all the dead—and some living—Bodreans looked down on me, and went into the schoolroom, where Theodosia and Hadrian were usually already seated.

This afternoon I was interested to learn that the squire's current sin was, as Mr. Pegger said, "putting in his nose where God hadn't intended it should go."

"And where is that, Mr. Pegger?"

"In Carter's Meadow, that's where. He wants to set up digging there. Disturbing God's earth. Filling the place with heathen ideas."

"What are they going to dig for, Mr. Pegger?" I asked.

"It's digging up the past, they say. They reckon they're going to find bits and pieces left behind by them as lived here in St. Erno's years and years ago."

"It's all very respectable, Mr. Pegger. It's called archaeology."

"What it's called makes no difference. If God had intended 'em to find these things He wouldn't have covered 'em up with His good earth."

"Perhaps it wasn't God who covered them up."

"Then who?"

"Time," I said portentously.

He shook his head and started to dig again. "Let the dead bury their dead, I say."

"Well, *I* think it would be interesting if we found something very important here. And it's not a sudden fancy of Sir Ralph's. He's always been interested in archaeology. Perhaps that's why his nephew is named Hadrian."

"Hadrian!" thundered Mr. Pegger. "And the young lady too. Theodosia. They're not good Christian names."

"Not like your Matthew, Mark, Luke, John, Isaac, Reuben and the rest. But did you know, Mr. Pegger, that Theodosia means

divinely given? So you see it *is* a Christian name. As for Hadrian, he's named after a wall and a Roman emperor."

"They're not good Christian names," he repeated.

"Lavinia," I said. "I wonder what that means."

"Ah. Miss Lavinia," said Mr. Pegger. "It was a pity."

"It was very sad, wasn't it, to die so young?"

"With all her sins upon her."

"I don't think she had many. Alison and Dorcas speak as though they loved her dearly."

"Every mortal man has sins," declared Mr. Pegger. "As for women, they can have ten times as many."

"Not Lavinia," I said.

"Lavinia! She were the prettiest of the rectory girls." Mr. Pegger put down his spade to mop his brow once more. "This be one of the hottest days the Lord have sent us this year." He stepped out of the hole and I peered down into it. Poor Josiah Polgrey, who beat his wife and had his children out working on the farm at five years old. On impulse I jumped down into the hole.

"What be doing, Miss Judith?" demanded Mr. Pegger.

"I just want to dig a bit, to see what it feels like to be a grave-digger." I dug the spade into the earth as I had seen Mr. Pegger do. I repeated the operation several times before my spade struck something hard.

"I've found something, Mr. Pegger," I cried. I stooped and picked up the object. "What is it, do you know?"

Mr. Pegger bent down and took it from me. "Piece of old metal," he said. I gave him my hand and he pulled me out of Josiah Polgrey's grave.

"There's a sort of engraving on it," I said.

"I'd throw that away—sharp about it," said Mr. Pegger.

But I did no such thing. I went back to the rectory carrying the piece of what appeared to be bronze with me. It was oval-shaped and about six inches in diameter. I didn't give much thought to it, because talking about Lavinia had made me think about her. How sad it must have been when the news was brought that Lavinia, beloved daughter of the Reverend James Osmond and sister of Ali-

son and Dorcas, had been killed on the train which was taking her from Plymouth to London.

"She was killed outright," Dorcas had told me one day as we pruned roses at Lavinia's grave. "It was a mercy in a way, for she would have been an invalid for the rest of her life had she lived. She was twenty-one years old."

"Why was she going to live in London, Dorcas?" I had asked.

"She was going to take up a post as governess. Lavinia had been staying with a distant cousin, so she took the train from Plymouth, and then there was this terrible accident. We were heartbroken."

"That was when you decided to take me in and bring me up to take Lavinia's place."

"You have a place of your own, dear. And you're not in the least like her."

"She was quiet, I suppose, and gentle; and she didn't talk too much, probe or be impulsive or try to order people about—all the things I do."

"No, she was not like you, Judith. But she could be very firm."

"So then because she was dead and I was an orphan you decided to take me in."

"And you are related to us, Judith. A sort of cousin."

"A distant one, I suppose. All your cousins seem to be so distant."

"Well, we thought it would help us all—and you too, of course."

So Lavinia had had a marked effect on my life, and I fell to wondering what would have happened to me if she had not decided to take that particular train to London.

On a table in the stone hall of the old rectory stood a great bowl of buddleia, lavender and roses. The rectory had been built in the early days of Elizabeth's reign and had been the residence of rectors for the last three hundred years. Their names were inscribed on a tablet in the church. The rooms were large and some beautifully paneled, but dark because of the small leaded windows.

I went up the staircase to my room to wash the ornament. I was drying it with cotton wool when there was a knock on the door.

"Come in," I called. Dorcas and Alison entered, looking so solemn that I cried out, "Is anything wrong?"

333

They exchanged smiles. "We were listening for you to come in," said Dorcas. "We have been making up our minds to speak to you for some time. As it is your birthday and fourteen is a sort of milestone, we thought the time has come."

Alison drew a deep breath and said, "Well, Judith, you have always been under the impression that you were the daughter of a cousin of ours. This is not the case." I looked from one to the other. Alison cleared her throat. "You were on the same train as Lavinia."

"In the accident?"

"Yes, you were in the accident—a child of one year or so."

"My parents were killed, then."

"It seems so."

"Who were they?"

"They . . . they must have been killed outright. No one came forward to say who you were."

"Then I might be anybody!" I cried. "Perhaps I'm the long-lost heiress to a great estate. My parents may still be searching high and low for me. . . ."

Alison and Dorcas were smiling again. I had further food for my flights of fancy. "Perhaps I'm a foreigner. French, or Spanish. I do look rather like a Spaniard. But then lots of Cornish people do."

"Well, all ended well. You came to be as our very own and that has been a joy for us."

"It's rather exciting not to know who you are. Just think what you might discover! I might have a sister or brother somewhere. Or grandparents. Perhaps they'll come and claim me and take me back to Spain."

"Oh, Judith, you romance about everything," said Dorcas.

"I'm glad she's taken it like this," added Alison.

"What other way should I take it?"

"So you don't feel that you were . . . deserted?"

I said, "It's a very exciting birthday surprise. Now look at this. I think when it's cleaned up it will be rather unusual."

"Where did you find it?"

"In Josiah Polgrey's grave. Mr. Pegger was digging it and I had a go, and lo and behold, my spade struck this."

"I've seen something like this before," said Alison. "I think it may have some significance."

"What do you mean, Alison? *Significance?*"

Dorcas and Alison exchanged looks. Alison said, "I think, Judith, that you should take it along to Keverall Court and ask if you may show it to Sir Ralph."

I was excited. Now that there was talk of digging up Carter's Meadow, how interesting it would be if I had been the first to find something!

"I'll take it right away," I said.

"I should wash first—change your dress and comb your hair."

I smiled at them. I may have stumbled on something important from centuries ago, and they were worried about my changing my dress and making myself presentable to see Sir Ralph!

I RAN under the portcullis, into the courtyard, and then into the great baronial hall of the Bodreans. The heavy iron-studded door creaked as I pushed it open. How silent it seemed inside!

I wondered what Hadrian and Theodosia were doing and thought of the fun I would have tomorrow when I told them what I had found. I had already magnified it into something priceless. The greatest archaeologists in the world would shake my hand: "We are so grateful to you, Judith. We have been digging for years and never have we found anything quite so wonderful as this."

I heard the scraping of a chair behind me. I had not noticed Derwent, the footman, dozing there.

"Oh, it's you," he said.

"I want to see Sir Ralph immediately. It is a matter of the utmost importance."

He looked at me superciliously. "Now, miss. This is another of your tricks, I know."

"It's no trick. I have found something of great value." I hugged the piece of metal against me and faced him squarely.

"He's taking tea with her ladyship."

"Go and tell him I am here," I said imperiously.

Within five minutes I was in the library, that fascinating room

335

full of Sir Ralph's collection of exotic pieces. I laid the metal on the table, and immediately knew that I had made an impression.

"Good God," said Sir Ralph. He used oaths of which, I reflected, Dorcas, Alison and the Reverend James would not have approved. "Where did you find this?"

I told him that it was in Josiah Polgrey's grave.

His bushy eyebrows were lifted. "What were you doing there?"

"Helping to dig it."

He had two kinds of laughter—one a wild sort of roar and the other inward, when his chin shook, and I think that was when he was most amused. He was amused in that way now.

"It's important, isn't it?" I said.

"Bronze," he said. "Looks prehistoric. If you find anything more bring it to me."

He nodded in a way which I realized meant dismissal, but I had no intention of being dismissed like that.

"You want me to leave you my . . . er . . . bronze?" I asked.

He narrowed his eyes, and his jaw wagged slightly. "Yours!" he bellowed. "It's not yours. This belongs to the nation."

"Is it of interest to archaeologists?"

"What do you know of archaeologists?"

"I know they dig and find all sorts of wonderful things. Roman baths and lovely tiles and things like that."

"And that's what you'd like to do, is it?" He laughed then—the wild roar. "You fancy archaeologists are constantly finding jewels and Roman villas. You've got a lot to learn. Greater part of the time is spent digging for things like this—the sort of things that have been found times out of number."

He laid a hand on my shoulder and led me to the door.

"You'd like to know what this is, wouldn't you?"

"Yes. After all, *I* found it."

"I'll let you know when I get the verdict on it. Meanwhile, if you find anything else you'll know what to do with it, won't you?"

"Bring it to you, Sir Ralph."

He nodded and shut the door after me. I went slowly down the stairs and out into the courtyard. I had lost my piece of bronze, but

it was pleasant to remind myself that I had contributed to the knowledge of the world.

Although my find was identified as part of a shield, possibly of the Bronze Age, and many of its kind had been found before, it brought about several important changes.

In the first place it sent up my prestige in the schoolroom. When I arrived for lessons both Hadrian and Theodosia were far more respectful than they had been before. I had always thought Theodosia rather a silly little thing—although she was about a year older than I, and Hadrian was slightly older still. They were both fair, Theodosia rather fragile, with innocent blue eyes and a chin that receded a little. In spite of the fact that they lived in this mansion and I came from the rectory, I was the leader and was constantly telling them what they ought to do.

I spent the morning explaining how I had found the object, and drove poor Miss Graham to despair. I whispered that we should all dig in Carter's Meadow, because that was where they thought there was a lot of treasure. That afternoon we found spades in the gardeners' sheds and set to work. We were discovered and reprimanded; but the result was that Sir Ralph decided that we might learn something about archaeology and ordered the long-suffering Miss Graham to give us lessons. Poor Miss Graham did her best. I was fascinated—far more than the others. When Sir Ralph learned this his interest in me seemed to grow.

Then Sir Edward Travers and his family came to live in the old dower house. The Traverses were friends of the Bodreans' and had visited Keverall Court many times. Sir Edward was connected with Oxford University in some way, but was constantly engaged on expeditions. His name was often in the papers and he was very well known in academic circles.

After the Traverses moved in, the dower house became Giza House.

"Named for the site of the Pyramids, I believe," said Dorcas.

Now that the dark old house with the overgrown garden was inhabited, I could no longer so easily scare Theodosia with stories that it was haunted or dare her and Hadrian to run up the path and

look through the windows. It lost none of its strangeness, though. "Once a house is haunted," I told the nervous Theodosia, "it's haunted forever."

We learned that Sir Edward was a widower and had two children—a son, Tybalt, who was grown up and at the university, and a daughter, Sabina, who was about the same age as Theodosia and myself and was therefore to share our lessons.

It was some time before I saw Tybalt, but I decided to dislike him before I set eyes on him, largely because of the way Sabina spoke of him. She did not so much love as adore him. According to her he was godlike.

"I don't believe anyone is as good as that," I said scornfully.

"Nobody but Tybalt," insisted Sabina, who talked constantly, whether anyone was listening or not. I told Hadrian this was because she lived in that strange house with her absentminded father and those odd servants, two of whom were Egyptians named Mustapha and Absalam. They wore long white robes and sandals, and moved about stealthily, so that you never knew whether or not they were spying on you.

Sabina was pretty, with fair curls, big gray eyes and a little heart-shaped face. Theodosia, who was quite plain, very soon adored her, and their friendship strengthened the alliance between Hadrian and myself.

Through Sabina we learned of life in Giza House. How her father would shut himself in his room for days and silent-footed Mustapha or Absalam took his meals to him on trays. Sabina often had her meals alone or with her companion housekeeper, Tabitha Grey, who gave her lessons at the piano. She always referred to her as "Tabby," and I christened her "Grey Tabby," which amused them all. I pictured her as middle-aged, with graying hair. I was very surprised eventually to meet a striking-looking younger woman.

We could hardly wait for Tybalt to come down from Oxford. Sabina was exalted. "Now you will see for yourselves." Then one morning she came into the schoolroom in tears, because Tybalt was going up to Northumberland on a dig with Sir Edward rather than coming home.

Instead of Tybalt we had his friend Evan Callum. He was going to ground us in the rudiments of archaeology in order to earn a little money before going back to the university.

I threw myself into my new studies with fervor. I was much more interested in the subject than the others. Sometimes in the afternoons I would go down to Carter's Meadow with Evan to get experience in the practical side of the work. Once I saw Sir Ralph there and he came over to speak to me. "Found any more bronze shields?"

"No. I haven't found anything."

He gave me a little push. "Finds don't come often." His jaw wagged in his amused way, and I had a notion that he was rather pleased to see me there.

Our lessons with Evan Callum were taken in the afternoons, because the mornings were spent with Miss Graham or Oliver Shrimpton learning reading, writing and arithmetic. In addition, Theodosia, Sabina and I had to do needlework three mornings a week. The alphabet had to be embroidered, a proverb, our names and the date. Naturally we chose the shortest proverb we could find, but even so the task was laborious. We had to make horrible little cross-stitches on a piece of cotton, and if one stitch was too large or too small it had to be unpicked and put right.

We had strummed on the piano under Miss Graham's supervision, but now we had Grey Tabby it was decided that she should give the music lessons. So we had teachers from three sources—Miss Graham from Keverall Court, Grey Tabby and Evan Callum from Giza House and Oliver Shrimpton from the rectory.

I was fascinated by Giza House. There was something sinister about it. In the first place it was dark. There were many rich velvet curtains—not only at windows but over doors and alcoves. And it was so thickly carpeted that you rarely heard people come and go.

There was a strange old woman who lived in an apartment at the top of the house. Sabina referred to her as "old Nanny Tester."

"Who is she?" I demanded.

"She was my mother's nanny, and then Tybalt's and mine."

"But you don't want a nanny now, surely."

"We don't turn servants out when they have served us many years," Sabina said haughtily.

"I believe she's a witch. She spies on us. She's always peering out of the window and dodging back when we look up." Every time I went to the place I glanced at the top window for Nanny Tester.

I was intrigued by the sessions with Evan Callum, and I became particularly fascinated by Egyptian culture. I loved hearing about the old civilization—the gods, the dynasties, the temples that had been discovered. I caught my enthusiasm from Evan. "There's a treasure stored in the hills of the desert, Judith," he used to say.

Evan told us of some recent Egyptian discoveries in which Sir Edward Travers had been involved, and he also gave us insights into the history of that country. He explained that the great gods of the Egyptians possessed all the strengths and virtues of men, but in addition they each had one attribute of an animal, and this animal was their particular sign. For example, Horus was the hawk because his quick eyes saw all.

But I think what interested me most were the accounts of burials. When the important dead were embalmed and put in their tombs their servants would often be buried with them, so that they might serve them in the new life as in the old. Treasure also was stored in their tombs, that they might not suffer poverty in the future.

"This custom, of course," Evan explained, "has led to many of the tombs being robbed. Throughout the centuries men have plundered them, although it is said that the curse of the pharaohs descends on those who disturb their eternal rest."

I was very interested in the embalming process. Evan explained that it was perfected three thousand years before the birth of Christ, and no one has ever really discovered how the ancient Egyptians did it so expertly.

Sabina said she had seen a mummy. They had had one at Giza House. "It was in a sort of coffin," she said.

"A sarcophagus," Evan corrected.

"We've still got it," said Sabina. "But the mummy has gone." She shuddered. "I'm glad. It was horrible."

"It is interesting," I cried. "Just imagine. It was somebody who actually lived thousands of years ago!"

I couldn't get the thought of the sarcophagus out of my mind, and a few days later when we went for our music lesson I decided that I was going to see it. When Theodosia was at the piano Sabina led Hadrian and me to that strange room which the servants wouldn't enter alone.

The sarcophagus was in a corner. It was like a stone trough. I knelt down and examined the rows of hieroglyphs on the top.

"My father is trying to decipher them," explained Sabina. "That's why it's here."

I touched it wonderingly. "Just imagine, thousands of years ago people made these signs and someone was embalmed and laid inside there. Don't you think that's wonderful? Oh, how I wish they'd left the mummy!"

"You can see one in the British Museum. It's just like someone done up with a lot of bandages."

I stood up and looked about the room. I said, "There's a strange feeling in this room."

"You're just trying to frighten us," Sabina said.

"It's because the tree outside the window makes it dark," said Hadrian.

During the next few days I became obsessed with ancient burials and wanted to know exactly what it felt like to be laid to rest in a sarcophagus. Hadrian and I found two old sheets, cut one of them into strips and hid them in the summerhouse. When next we went to Giza House for our music lessons, Hadrian and I contrived to have ours first and then went into the garden to retrieve our supplies. We went into the room where the sarcophagus was. I put the sheet over my head—having cut a hole in it for my face—and made Hadrian bind me up. We took off the lid, and I got inside and lay still. Hadrian left.

It was a tremendous, exciting joke. I thought I was very brave to lie in that sarcophagus, for I felt that I might arouse the wrath of the gods at any moment.

It seemed a long time before the door opened. Sabina said, "Oh,

why do you want to keep looking at it?" And I knew Hadrian had brought them in as we had arranged. Then they saw me.

There was a bloodcurdling scream as I struggled out of the cold troughlike receptacle. Theodosia, seeing this thing rising from the dead, as she believed, had begun to scream. She slid to the floor in a faint.

I heard Hadrian shout, "It's all right, Theodosia. It's only Judith. It's not a real mummy."

"You've killed her!" said Sabina.

Then I saw the stranger in the doorway, and for a moment I thought he was one of the gods come for vengeance. He looked angry enough. He stared at me. What a sight I must have looked— my bandages hanging about me, the sheet still over my head. "What *are* you doing?" he said, and picked Theodosia up.

"Judith dressed up as a mummy," squealed Sabina. "She's frightened Theodosia."

"How utterly stupid!" he said, giving me a look of contempt. Then he walked out of the room with Theodosia in his arms.

I scrambled out of the bandages as Sabina came running back into the room. "They're all fussing round Theodosia," she informed us, and added rather gleefully, "They're angry with you two."

"She's all right?" I asked anxiously.

"She's sitting up now, but she looks pale and she's gasping. People can die of fright."

"Well, she isn't going to," I said.

Tybalt came into the room. He still looked angry. "May I have an explanation?"

I looked at Hadrian, who waited as usual for me to speak. "I was only being a mummy," I said.

"Aren't you a little old for such tricks?"

I felt small and bitterly humiliated.

"You didn't think, I suppose, of the effect this might have on those who were not in the joke?"

"No," I said, "I didn't think."

"Actually, it's quite a good habit. I should try it sometime."

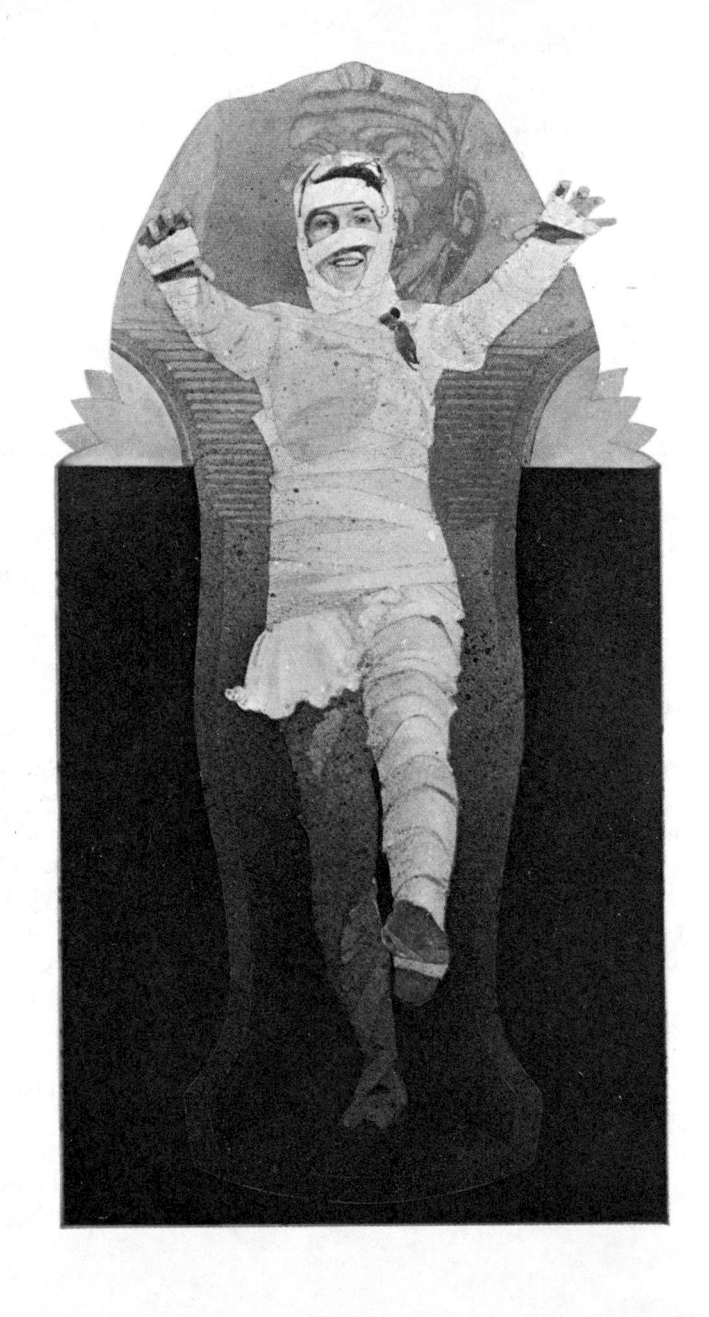

If anyone else had said that to me I should have been ready with a pert answer. But he was different. Right from the beginning I knew it.

THERE *was* trouble. Hadrian was beaten and I was confined to my room for two days.

After that ordeal Tybalt was frequently at Giza House, but he scarcely noticed me.

Eventually Hadrian went off to the university to study archaeology. Then Evan Callum graduated and took a post in one of the universities. Miss Graham and Oliver Shrimpton continued to teach us, and Dorcas tried to teach me a few of what she called "home crafts," which meant showing me how to make bread and preserves, but I was not very good at that.

"You'll need it one day," she said, "when you have a home of your own. Do you realize you're nearly eighteen, Judith? Why, some girls are married at that age."

I knew that she and Alison hoped I would marry—and I knew whom.

We all liked Oliver Shrimpton. He had an enthusiasm for his work, and for the last two or three years, since the Reverend James seemed to get more and more easily tired, he had practically carried the parish on his own shoulders.

He and I had always been good friends, but having lived under the same roof with him for so long I regarded him as a kind of brother. I sometimes wondered, though, if I had never seen Tybalt I might have been reconciled to the idea of marrying Oliver and going on in the rectory. It had been my home all my life, and it was a foregone conclusion that when the Reverend James retired or died Oliver would come into the living.

I could not talk to anyone of my feelings for Tybalt. They were absurd anyway, for surely it was ridiculous to feel this intense passion for someone who was hardly aware of one's existence.

But our relationship did undergo a change and he began to be a little aware of me. Tabitha Grey was very kindly and noticed how despondent I was when Evan Callum ceased to teach us archae-

344

ology. As I grew older she seemed to grow younger. I suppose at fourteen anyone of twenty-four seems very old; but when one is nearly eighteen, twenty-eight seems almost young. Tabitha was Mrs. Grey, so she had been married.

I had tried to find out from Sabina exactly what her position was in the household.

"Oh, she just manages everything," Sabina said. "She looks after the servants—and Nanny Tester too, and she knows quite a lot about Father's work. He talks to her about it—so does Tybalt."

That gave us something in common and I had one or two talks with her after our music lessons. She told me that on one occasion she had been a member of Sir Edward's party when they had gone to Kent to work on a Roman excavation.

She also lent me some books, and late one afternoon when I went to Giza House to return them, I heard music coming from within. I glanced through a window and saw Tabitha seated at the piano playing a duet with Tybalt. As I watched, they turned to each other and smiled. How I wished he would smile at me like that.

Then they both saw me. I felt rather ashamed for being caught looking in, but Tabitha motioned for me to come inside.

They met me at the door. "Oh, you've brought the books back. I've been lending these to Judith, Tybalt."

Tybalt looked at the books and his eyes lit up. "What did you think of them?"

"I was fascinated."

"We must find some more for her, Tabitha."

We went into the drawing room and talked . . . how we talked! I had not felt so *alive* since Evan Callum had left.

Afterward Tybalt walked to the rectory with me, carrying the books, and told me of his adventures. He said good-by at the door and mentioned that we must have another chat. "In the meantime, go on reading. I'm going to tell Tabitha what to give you."

"Oh, thank you!" I said earnestly and went inside.

Dorcas must have seen us from one of the windows. "Wasn't that Tybalt Travers?" she asked, as I started to ascend the stairs. "I've heard that they hope for a match between him and Theodosia."

I felt sick.

"Well," went on Dorcas cautiously, "it's to be expected. The Traverses and the Bodreans have been friends for years."

No, I thought. Never. Silly little Theodosia! It wasn't possible.

THE next week Evan Callum came down to stay at Giza House with the Traverses. During his stay he was invited quite often to Keverall Court. He also called at the rectory to see me and we had a very interesting talk. He told me I had been his most promising pupil and it was a great shame that I had not been able to take up the subject in earnest.

Miss Graham found another post and left, and so our lessons were over. Life was quite changed for me now. I did some of the parish visiting with Dorcas and Alison. I read to those whose eyesight was failing; I took food to the bedridden and went off to the town to shop for them in the little trap we called the jingle.

I was becoming the typical rectory daughter. That Christmas I went carol singing, and when we called at Keverall Court we were invited in for saffron cake and a sip from the great wassail bowl. I saw Theodosia and Hadrian in the great hall and felt a nostalgia for the old days.

Soon after that we had a frosty snap—rare with us. The trees were white with hoarfrost and the children could skate on the ponds. The Reverend James caught a cold which was followed by a heart attack, and within a week he was dead.

And so the rectory blinds were drawn down and the day came when bells tolled and we lowered the Reverend James Osmond into the grave which Mr. Pegger dug for him. We then went back to the rectory to eat cold ham and to mourn.

Fear of the future mingled with the grief of Alison and Dorcas; but they looked to Oliver and me for the obvious solution. They wanted me to marry Oliver, who now would become the rector. We could all go on living under this roof as before.

Oliver was as kind as ever to us; but, of course, as Dorcas said to Alison, unless something was *arranged*, they and I would have to move out. Quite suddenly something was arranged.

346

Oliver called us together and said, "I want to talk to you. I'm thinking of marrying."

Dorcas' eyes shone and Alison was looking at me reproachfully. You might have told us! she was implying.

Oliver went on. "Miss Sabina Travers has promised to marry me."

We congratulated him—I wholeheartedly, Dorcas and Alison in a bewildered way. As soon as I went to my room they joined me, dismay and anger on their faces.

"To think that all this time he was deceiving us."

"You are not being fair," I protested. "How has he deceived us?"

"Leading us to think—"

"But he did no such thing. And I think Sabina will do quite well as the rector's wife."

"She's far too frivolous. I don't think she's capable of carrying on a serious conversation."

"She'll be wonderful with the parishioners. She'll never be at a loss for words and she'll be able to listen to all their troubles without really hearing them. Think what an asset that will be."

"Judith, you don't seem to *care!*" cried Alison.

I burst out laughing. "Listen to me, both of you. I wouldn't have married Oliver if he'd asked me. He's been too much like my brother. I'm fond of him; I like Sabina. Do believe me when I say I could never have married him, convenient as it would have been."

Then I went to them and hugged them both, the way I used to do when I was younger. "Dear Dorcas and dear Alison, I'm so sorry. It's the end of the old life. We've got to leave the rectory. But even if I had been willing, Oliver had other plans, hadn't he?"

They were touched by my demonstrations of affection. "Oh, it's not that," said Dorcas. "We were thinking of your happiness."

"And that could not be here," I said. Then I added, "Just think. Oliver and Sabina! Why, he'll be Tybalt's brother-in-law!"

They looked at me in surprise, as though to say, What has that to do with our predicament?

Then Alison said, "Well, what we have to do is to start making plans at once."

The Reverend James Osmond had left his daughters very little

347

money, but if they could find a reasonable cottage they could just about manage to exist.

As for me, I promised myself that as soon as they were settled in their new home I would go and find a post. I was uneasy—not at the prospect of working, but of leaving St. Erno's. Should I become a governess like Miss Graham? Or perhaps, as I had had a classical education more advanced than most rectory girls, I might teach. It would be less stultifying than working in some household where I could not mix with the family and yet was a little bit above the servants so that it would be impossible for them to accept me.

Sir Ralph came to the rescue. There was a cottage on his estate which was vacant and he would allow the Misses Osmond to have it for a peppercorn rent. They were delighted. The arrangement solved half the problem, but Sir Ralph was determined to be our complete benefactor. Lady Bodrean needed a companion and he thought that I might be suitable.

Alison and Dorcas were delighted. "After our disappointment everything is working out so well," Dorcas said. "We have our cottage, and it would be wonderful if . . . er . . . you could get along with Lady Bodrean."

"Ah, there's the rub," I said lightheartedly. But I felt far from that, and not without reason. On the rare occasions when I had seen Lady Bodrean I had been met by frosty stares. She always reminded me of a ship, for with her voluminous petticoats and skirts which rustled as she walked she seemed to sail along without being aware of anyone in her path.

I had never tried to ingratiate myself with her, being conscious of a certain antagonism. Now I was in a different position.

Two days later she received me in her private sitting room. The chairs were covered with needlepoint worked by Lady Bodrean herself. The frame with a new piece stood close to her chair and she was working at this when I was shown into her room.

She did not look up for quite a minute. It might have been disconcerting if I had been the timid sort. Then she said, "Oh, it's Miss Osmond. You've come about the post. You may sit down."

I sat, my head high, the color in my cheeks.

"Your duties will be to look after my engagements, both social and philanthropic. You will read the papers to me each day. You will care for my two pomeranians, Orange and Lemon." At the mention of their names two dogs reclining on cushions raised their heads and regarded me with contempt. "Now I should like to hear you read."

She handed *The Times* to me. I started to read of the resignation of Bismarck and the plan to cede Helgoland to Germany, and I was aware of her openly scrutinizing me through her lorgnette. The sort of treatment one must expect when one was about to become an employee, I supposed.

"That will do," she said in the middle of a sentence. "I should like you to start immediately. I hope that is convenient."

I said I should need a day or so to settle my affairs, and she graciously conceded that I might have the rest of that day and the next in which to prepare myself.

On the way back to the cottage (which had the delectable name of Rainbow Cottage) I told myself that while I was going to hate being employed by Lady Bodrean, I now would have many opportunities to see Tybalt.

Chapter II

MY ROOM at Keverall Court was close to that of Lady Bodrean's, in case she should want me at any time. It was a pleasant room and from the window I could see the roof of Giza House, which comforted me.

I had not been in the house long when I came to the conclusion that Lady Bodrean disliked me. She would ring quite often after I had retired and would tell me peevishly that she could not sleep. I must make tea for her, or read to her until she dozed. She was never satisfied with anything I did. If there was nothing of which to complain she was silent; if there was she would refer to it over and over again.

Her personal maid, Jane, commiserated with me. "Her ladyship

seems to have it in for you," she admitted. "I've seen it before. A regular servant's got dignity. But companions and suchlike—that's up another street."

I suppose some natures could have borne it better than mine, but I had never been one to accept injustice. In the old days when I had come to this house I had come on equal terms with Theodosia. It was very hard to accept the new position, but the only alternative was to leave St. Erno's, and so I stayed on at Keverall Court.

I didn't see Tybalt during this time, for he and his father had gone on an expedition into the Midlands, but Tabitha always had books for me. Reading, visits with her at Giza House and the knowledge that Dorcas and Alison were happily settled provided the only brightness in my life at that time.

I saw Theodosia now and then. She would have been quite pleasant to me if her mother would have allowed it. There was nothing malicious or proud about Theodosia. She would never be actively unkind, but at the same time she did little to alleviate my position. Perhaps she remembered the past, when I had been inclined to bully her.

I went to Rainbow Cottage to see Dorcas and Alison as often as I could. It was an interesting little place, about three hundred years old, I think. It had been built in the days when any family who could build a cottage in a night could claim as their own the land on which it had been erected. It was the custom in those days to collect bricks and tiles and to start building as soon as it was dark, and work through the night. Four walls and a roof constituted a dwelling and that could be done by morning. After that, the place could be added to. That was how Rainbow Cottage was built. Now it boasted a moderately good kitchen, where Dorcas baked the most delicious bread I had ever tasted.

I hated leaving them and going back to Keverall Court and my onerous duties. But Orange and Lemon turned out to be blessings, for they needed daily exercise and this gave me the opportunity to slip over to Giza House and have a chat with Tabitha.

One day I called and knew immediately that something exciting had happened. She told me that Sir Edward was planning an

expedition to Egypt and she hoped to accompany the party. "Now that Sabina is married, there is no need for me to stay here."

"You will have some job to do?"

"Not an official job, but I can housekeep if that should be necessary and I can be useful in a fetch-and-carry sort of way."

I looked at her ecstatically. "How I envy you! Will Tybalt be accompanying his father?"

"Indeed yes. It's going to be a very important mission. Of course you know that Sir Edward is one of the greatest archaeologists in the world."

I nodded. "And Tybalt is following in his footsteps."

"He is his father all over again," she said. "Men like the Traverses have one great passion in their lives—their work. It's something that those about them must always remember."

"Did you know Lady Travers?"

"At the end of her life, yes."

"It wasn't a very happy marriage, was it?"

She looked startled. "Well, they had little in common, and as I said, men like Sir Edward perhaps don't make model husbands."

I was certain that she was warning me. Then she said brightly, "You remember Evan Callum."

"Of course."

"He's coming to visit us, and I hear that Hadrian will be returning also. They'll be interested to hear about Sir Edward's expedition."

I stayed talking, although I knew I shouldn't. I wanted to glean all I could. Tabitha was quite animated.

"It would be wonderful if you could come," she said. "I am sure you would prefer it to looking after that not very agreeable lady."

"Oh, if only I could."

"Never mind. Perhaps someday . . ."

I went back to Keverall Court in a daze. I dreamed that Tabitha was taken ill and couldn't go on the expedition. Someone must take her place, Sir Edward said. "I know," cried Tybalt. "What about Miss Osmond? She was always interested." How ridiculous and how unkind I was to wish an illness on Tabitha!

Lady Bodrean destroyed my daydream. "I am surprised, Miss

Osmond," she said. "I have been ringing my bell for half an hour."

"I'm sorry. I forgot the time."

"Forgot the time! You are not here to forget time, Miss Osmond. You are not paid for that, you know."

She reminded me far more than was necessary that I was a servant. She curtailed my liberty whenever possible. If she could humiliate me she did; and she found many opportunities.

I shall never forget the day she told me that there was to be a ball at Keverall Court. "Of course, a young lady in my daughter's position must be brought out formally. I am sure you realize that, Miss Osmond, because although you yourself are not in the same position, you did learn something of gracious living when you were allowed to take lessons here."

"Graciousness is something that I miss nowadays," I retorted.

She misunderstood. "You were very fortunate to be allowed to glimpse it for a while. *I* always think it is a mistake to educate people beyond their stations."

"Sometimes," I said, "it enables the sons and daughters of erudite churchmen to be of use to their betters."

"I am glad to see you take that view, Miss Osmond. I have to confess you do not always show such becoming humility."

She was an exceedingly stupid woman. I had learned that Sir Ralph had married her for her fortune. Why he should have done so was beyond my understanding, since he was a rich man in his own right. But I could understand why he had acquired his reputation for seeking consolation elsewhere.

"Now," she went on, "there will be a great deal for you to do. You've no idea, Miss Osmond, what giving a ball like this entails."

"I shall do my *humble* best," I replied.

ONE afternoon Jane, Lady Bodrean's personal maid, invited me to tea. She had a little spirit lamp in her room, which she had made very comfortable. I sat down and she poured.

"My word, she's got it in for you."

"I gather my company doesn't give her much pleasure. I wonder she doesn't allow herself the treat of being rid of it."

"She's enjoying herself. I've seen it happen before. The nursery governess before Miss Graham. Nice spirited sort of girl, she was. But she hadn't been here long when things started to happen. Sir Ralph had his eyes on her and when Lady Bodrean got to work . . . my word, she changed. In the old days Sir Ralph, he were a one. No woman safe from him. The fur used to fly. Many times I've heard—being in the next room, you know."

I could picture her, ear to keyhole, while a younger Sir Ralph stood accused before his wronged wife.

"After a while Lady Bodrean seemed to make up her mind that there was nothing she could do about it. But she got to be more of a tartar every day."

I said, "I should get out, I suppose."

Jane moved toward me and whispered, "You could find a better place. What about Miss Theodosia?"

"What of her?"

"This ball . . . well, it's a sort of coming out. All the fine rich gentlemen of the neighborhood will be invited. Then they'll have balls and suchlike goings-on, and before long they'll find a husband for Miss Theodosia. You're her friend . . . so . . ."

"I, her friend. Please don't let Lady Bodrean hear you call me that. I'm sure she would be most indignant."

"Now you're getting bitter. You have to be clever. You and Theodosia were together as children. You could become friends with her again and when she marries . . . you see what I mean? Madam Theodosia wants a companion, and who better than her old friend? What do you think of it?"

"Machiavellian! Suppose Theodosia doesn't marry?"

"Theodosia not marry! Of course she will. They've got the man for her already. I heard Sir Ralph talking to her ladyship about it."

"Oh?" I said faintly.

"I wouldn't mind taking a bet with you, Miss Osmond, that before the year's out the engagement will be announced. After all, there's a title. Money, well, I'm not sure what he has, but Miss Theodosia will have enough. When her father dies she'll be one of the richest young ladies in the country."

I said, although I knew the answer already, "So for Theodosia they've chosen—"

"Mr. Tybalt Travers. Oh, yes, he's the one."

Soon after Sir Edward and Tybalt returned to Giza House they came to dine at Keverall Court. I contrived to be arranging some flowers in the hall when they arrived.

Tybalt said, "It's Miss Osmond, isn't it?" As though he had to look twice to make sure. "How are you?"

"I'm the companion now, you know."

"Yes, I heard. Are you still reading books on archaeology?"

"Avidly. Mrs. Grey is so helpful."

"Good. Father, this is Miss Osmond."

Sir Edward gave me a vague look.

"She's the one who dressed up as a mummy. She wanted to know what it felt like to be in a sarcophagus. She's read several of your books." Now Sir Edward's eyes twinkled. I think the mummy adventure amused him.

At that point Lady Bodrean appeared at the top of the staircase. "My *dear* Sir Edward . . . and Tybalt!" She swept down the stairs. "I thought I heard you talking to the companion."

I went to my room then and stayed there all the evening. I pictured them at the dinner table, Theodosia looking pretty in pink satin—gentle, amenable, and with an immense fortune which would be so useful in financing expeditions to exotic places.

I don't think I ever felt quite so hopeless as at that moment, and I asked myself whether I should offer my resignation without delay. But of course that was not my nature. Until he was married to Theodosia I would continue to dream—and hope.

Not long afterward I walked the dogs over to Giza House, and as I arrived Evan Callum came down the walk.

"I heard you were coming back," I said. "It is so good to see you."

"And how is everything with you?"

"You know that Oliver married Sabina, and I am now companion to Lady Bodrean."

He grimaced.

"Ah," I said with a smile, "I see you have an inkling of what that means."

"I am sorry. You were the best of my pupils. You had such enthusiasm, and that is one of the greatest assets in our profession. Poor Judith. But this is just a phase. They come to all of us. Theodosia's at Keverall, and she would never be unkind, I'm sure."

"No, but I see little of her. I am always kept so busy dancing attendance on her mama."

He gave me a compassionate look. "I shall hope things change for you. We must meet—often."

"There will be barriers between us, because when you visit Keverall Court you will come as a guest."

"I should soon leap over any barrier they put between us," he assured me.

I was greatly comforted by Evan's return to St. Erno's.

HADRIAN arrived at the end of the week. I was in the garden when he called to me. He had become good-looking—or perhaps he had always been so and I had not noticed before. There was something inherently pleasant in Hadrian, and a twinkle was never far from his blue-gray eyes. I felt that he was one of the people on whom I could rely.

"You've become a scholar, Hadrian," I said.

"You've become a flatterer."

Just then Theodosia came into the garden. She was in a white muslin gown with pale blue dots and she wore a white straw hat with blue ribbons. She'd grown quite pretty, I realized.

"I was thinking that it's like old times, now we're all together," said Hadrian. "Evan and Tybalt . . ." I noticed that Theodosia blushed slightly, and I thought of Jane's words. It was true, then.

AFTER Hadrian returned Theodosia saw far more of me than she had before. It seemed that she wanted to make it up for previously having avoided me. But the only time her mother was the least bit affable was when she talked of Theodosia's coming-out ball.

"You might go along to the sewing room," she told me one day, "and give Sarah Sloper a hand. There are fifty yards of lace to be sewn onto my daughter's ball gown."

Sarah Sloper was too good a dressmaker to allow me to put a stitch into her creation, but Theodosia was there for a fitting so I helped her get into the dress, a froth of blue chiffon. She looked lovely in it, I thought with a pang. I could imagine her floating around the ballroom in the arms of Tybalt.

"Do you like it, Judith?" she asked.

"The color is most becoming."

"I love dancing," she said.

She waltzed around and I felt we were back in the schoolroom. I went to her and bowed. "Miss Bodrean, may I have the pleasure of this dance?"

She made a deep curtsy, and then we danced around the room while Sarah Sloper watched us with a grin. Suddenly Sarah jumped to her feet and curtsied, for Sir Ralph was standing in the doorway watching us.

Our dance came to an immediate halt. I wondered what he would say to see the companion dancing with his daughter.

"Rather graceful, didn't you think, Sarah?" he said.

"Why yes, sir, indeed, sir," stammered Sarah.

"So that's your ball dress, is it?"

"Yes, Father."

"And what about Miss Osmond, eh? Has she a ball dress?"

"I have not," I said.

"If you had one, what color would it be?"

"It would be green, Father," said Theodosia. "It was always Judith's favorite color."

"That's said to be unlucky," he replied. "Or it was in my day. But I'll swear Miss Osmond's not superstitious." Then he went out, his chin wagging.

Theodosia looked at me with raised eyebrows. "Now why did Father come in here?"

"You should know more about his habits than I do."

"I believe he's quite excited about my ball. Judith, Mrs. Grey was

saying that you were reading some books on archaeology. I wish I knew more about it. I think I'll start reading too."

I understood, of course. She was desperately anxious to be able to talk knowledgeably to Tybalt.

THE invitations had been sent out; I had listed the guests and ticked them off when the acceptances came in. I had helped arrange flowers and chosen the dance programs with their pink and blue pencils, and for the first time Lady Bodrean seemed pleased.

Two days before the ball I emerged from her apartment and was about to go for my daily walk when I found Theodosia in the corridor. She looked excited.

"Judith," she said, "I've something to tell you."

My spirits sank. This is it, I thought. Tybalt has asked her to marry him.

She slipped her arm through mine. "Let's go to your room," she said. "You will never guess what it is."

I thought, I can't bear it. I'll have to go away—at once. I'll get a post far away and never see any of them again.

I stammered, "I know. You . . . you're engaged."

She stopped short and flushed hotly, so I knew that although this might not be the surprise she had for me now, it was coming soon. "You always thought you knew everything, didn't you? Well, clever Judith is wrong this time."

We went into my room and she opened the cupboard door. Hanging there was a green chiffon evening dress.

"It's your ball dress, Judith."

"Mine!" I felt the lovely soft material, then took the dress down and held it against me.

"It's absolutely right," declared Theodosia. "Put it on. I long to see you in it."

"First, how did it get there?"

"Oh, do try it on first and I'll explain."

"No. I must know."

"Oh, you're maddening! Father said you were to have it."

"But . . . why?"

"You remember when he saw us dancing. That day he said to me, 'That girl, Judith Osmond, is to go to the ball.' I said, 'Mama would never hear of it,' and he said, 'Then don't tell her.' "

I saw myself at the ball dancing with Tybalt. "But it's impossible. She will never allow it."

"She won't dare go against Father."

"What an unwelcome guest I should be."

"Only to one. The rest of us all want you to go. Myself, Evan, Hadrian, Tybalt. We're all going to have a lot of fun hiding you from Mama."

I began to laugh.

"I knew you'd enjoy it. The dress was a secret. I chose the material and Sarah used me as a model. You're a bit taller than I and just a little thinner. But I'm absolutely sure it's a perfect fit. Do put it on now."

I did so. The transformation was miraculous. It was indeed my color. I let down my thick dark hair, and with my eyes shining and color in my cheeks I would have been beautiful, I thought, but for my nose, which was too large. Hadrian always used to laugh at my nose. "It's a forceful one," he said. "It betrays your character."

Theodosia said, "Your hair ought to be piled high on your head and you should have a Spanish comb. I wish it were a masked ball. Then it would be so much easier to hide you from Mama. But she will say nothing, at least not at the ball. She wouldn't want a scene there. The storm will come later."

I didn't care. I was going to the ball. I should have a little dance program and I would keep it forever, because I was certain that Tybalt's initials would be on it.

THE night of Theodosia's debut came. Thank heaven Lady Bodrean was too busy with Jane helping her dress to be bothered with me. So I was free to dress myself in the green satin sheath over which were yards and yards of flowing silk chiffon. When I went to my room I found that Theodosia had laid a Spanish comb on my dressing table. I felt that I really had friends in the house now.

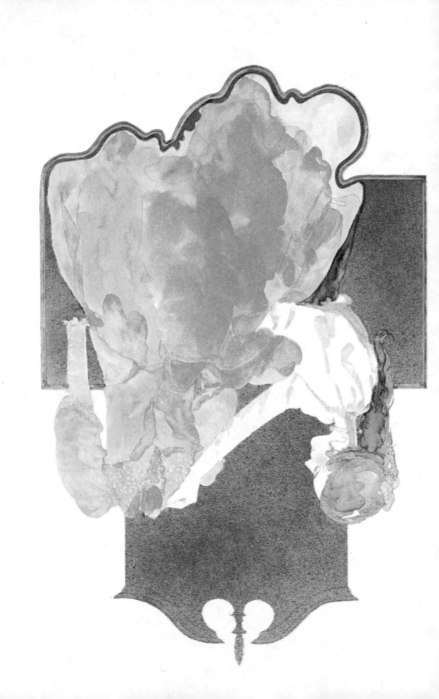

Sir Ralph and Lady Bodrean stood at the head of the great staircase to receive their guests. I did not present myself, but what fun it was to mingle with the guests, who were so numerous that I was sure I could escape Lady Bodrean's eye.

I danced first with Hadrian, who had always been my friend. As we waltzed he said, "You love the old house, don't you?"

"It seems like part of my life. Don't forget, as a child I was here almost every day."

"I feel the same. Theodosia's lucky. It'll be hers one day."

"You sound envious," I said.

"I sound as I feel. You see, I'm a bit of a charity boy myself."

"Oh, no, Hadrian. You're Sir Ralph's nephew, almost a son."

"Not quite."

"Then I tell you what you should do," I said lightly. "Marry Theodosia."

"My cousin? You don't think she'd have me, do you? I fancy her gaze is fixed in another direction."

"Is that so?"

"Have you noticed her being eagerly intent every time anyone mentions archaeology? She's so excited about this expedition. You'd think she was going on it."

I couldn't bear to talk of Theodosia and Tybalt, so I said quickly, "Don't you wish you were going out to Egypt?"

"I'd enjoy it in a way. I was talking to Evan about it. We both would have been flattered if we'd been asked to join the party, even in a minor capacity."

"And Tybalt?"

"Well, he's the great man's son. And he has the same passionate absorption as his father."

When the orchestra stopped Hadrian led me to a seat sheltered by pots of palms. Evan came up with Theodosia and they sat with us.

"You are enjoying the ball, Judith?" Theodosia asked anxiously.

I assured her I was. Then Tybalt appeared. I thought he had come to claim Theodosia, but instead he sat down. Evan then said that he believed Theodosia had promised him this dance.

They went off, and Hadrian said he had a partner to find; that left Tybalt and me alone.

"You will be gone very soon," I said. "How you must be longing to set out."

"It's a most exciting project, of course."

"Tell me about it."

"We'll go by ship to Port Said and overland to Cairo. We shall stay for a while and then make our way toward the ancient site of Thebes."

I clasped my hands ecstatically. "Do tell me more about it. You're going to the tombs, aren't you?"

He nodded. "My father has been preparing for this project for some time. He was out there several years ago, and he had the impression that he was on the verge of a great discovery."

"Have you been there before?"

"Yes, with my father. His party discovered a tomb which must have been prepared for a great nobleman. It had been robbed, thousands of years ago. It was very disappointing, as you can imagine. All the hard work, the excavating, the probing, the hopes . . . I'm getting carried away with my subject, but it's your fault, Miss Osmond. You seem so interested."

"I am, tremendously so."

"I can hear it in your voice and see it in your face. But now I am sure you would like to dance."

It was like a dream come true. There I was, dancing with Tybalt. I longed for the music to go on and on, but it stopped, of course, and we went in to supper with Theodosia, Evan and Hadrian.

I could not help noticing how insignificant Hadrian and Evan were in comparison with Tybalt. When Tybalt was talking of archaeology he glowed with an intense and single-minded passion which I was sure only a man who could feel deeply would experience. I believed then that if ever Tybalt loved a woman it would be with the same unswerving devotion which he gave to his profession.

Hadrian was telling us about a fishing expedition he had en-

joyed in the Scottish Highlands when Lady Bodrean walked past our table in the company of several other guests. She raised her eyebrows in astonishment and there was a silence which seemed to go on for a long time. Then Lady Bodrean recovered herself and made introductions, leaving me until last. "Miss Osmond," she said, making my name sound almost obscene.

After some polite conversation she and her party went on.

"Oh, dear!" said Theodosia, very distressed.

"I somehow felt it would happen," I said, trying to pretend I was not perturbed. "I really shouldn't be here. I may well be sent packing tomorrow morning."

"Surely not," Tybalt said. "Your company has made it such an interesting evening." That made everything worthwhile. I felt absurdly happy, yet Tybalt looked concerned.

Hadrian put his hand over mine. "Don't worry, Judith. You'll weather tomorrow's storm."

"In any case," I said, "trouble is for tomorrow. At the moment it's a beautiful night and the company is invigorating, so what more could we ask?"

"Mama can be very fierce," said Theodosia.

Tybalt leaned toward me and said, "You live in the moment."

"It's the only way to live. Tonight I'm a kind of Cinderella. Tomorrow I return to my ashes."

"I'll be Prince Charming," said Hadrian. "Let's dance."

We laughed, danced and joked; but my ability to live in the moment was only with me when Tybalt was there. I hoped to see him again, but I thought it advisable to return to my room before all the guests had departed.

I WAS wrong in thinking that the storm would break the next morning. Lady Bodrean had no intention of allowing it to wait.

I was still in my ball dress when the bell rang vigorously. I went along to her room. She had not changed for bed, and her violet-colored velvet gown looked quite regal.

"Well, Miss Osmond, what have you to say for yourself?"

"What do you expect me to say, Lady Bodrean?"

"What I do not expect is insolence. You were at the ball tonight. How dared you intrude?"

"Sir Ralph gave instructions that I was to go to the ball."

"I do not believe it."

"Perhaps your ladyship would wish me to call him." Before she could reply I had pulled the bell rope, and in a moment Jane was there. "Lady Bodrean wishes you to ask Sir Ralph if he will come here—if he has not already retired."

Lady Bodrean was spluttering with rage, but Jane had hurried off to call Sir Ralph.

"I have never in all my life been subjected to such . . . such . . ."

I was intoxicated with happiness still. I had danced with Tybalt; he had talked to me; I had conveyed to him my interest in his work. He had said, "Your company has made it such an interesting evening." So how could I care for this foolish old virago?

Her husband appeared in the doorway. "What the—" he began. Then he saw me. "What's Miss Osmond doing here?"

"I sent for her. She had the temerity to mingle with our guests tonight."

"She was one of them," he said shortly.

"You invited this young woman without consulting me?"

"I did."

"Miss Osmond is under the impression that because she was allowed to have a little education, and some of it under this roof, she is entitled to special treatment. I tell you I will not allow this. She came here as a companion and shall be treated as such."

"Madam," said Sir Ralph, "you will do as I say. . . ."

I saw the blood color his face; he reeled slightly. I rushed forward and helped him to a chair. Jane hurried away again and shortly came back with Blake, Sir Ralph's personal servant.

Blake loosened Sir Ralph's collar, and taking a small tablet from a box put it into his employer's mouth. Sir Ralph lay back in the chair; his face, which had been a suffused purple, became gradually paler. Blake looked at Lady Bodrean. "I'll get him to bed now, my lady."

Sir Ralph rose shakily to his feet and leaned heavily on Blake.

He nodded at me and a shadow of amusement came into his face. Then Blake led him away.

When the door shut Lady Bodrean turned on me. "Go back to your room," she said. "I will talk to you tomorrow."

I went back, but I did not think of her. I had so many memories to brood on.

AT THE end of that month Sir Edward and Tybalt left for Egypt with their expedition. Evan went back to the university, Hadrian went to Kent to do some work on a Viking burial ship and I returned to the monotony of serving Lady Bodrean.

There were no more walks to Giza House, because Tabitha had accompanied the party. But I called often at Rainbow Cottage, where there was always a welcome. And Theodosia sought me out. She liked to talk about the books she was reading, and I could see she was making a great effort to learn about archaeology.

She would invite me to her room and it sometimes seemed as though she were on the verge of confidences. Once she pulled open a drawer and I saw a bundle of letters tied up with blue ribbon. How like Theodosia to tie up her love letters with blue ribbon! Yet somehow I could not imagine Tybalt's writing love letters to Theodosia!

"How is Mama behaving these days?" she asked me idly.

"Very much as usual."

"Poor Judith!"

"Oh, we all have our problems."

"Yes." She sighed, then said, "Judith, have you ever been in love?"

I felt myself starting to flush uncomfortably, but she went on. "It's wonderful," she said, "and yet . . . I'm a little scared."

"Why should you be scared?"

"Well, I'm not very clever, as you know."

"If he's in love with you?"

"If! Of course he is. He tells me so every time I see him . . . every time he writes. . . ."

I half wanted to escape, half wanted to stay and be tortured.

"I really find archaeology rather boring, Judith, and of course it's his life. I've read the books, but they're mostly about tools for digging and all those boring pots and things."

"If you're not interested perhaps you shouldn't pretend to be."

"I don't think he expects me to be. I shall just look after him. That's all he wants. Oh, it will be wonderful, Judith. But I'm worried about my father. He won't like it."

"Won't like it! But I thought he was anxious for you to marry Tybalt."

"Tybalt! I'm not thinking of Tybalt." There was singing in my ears. "Tybalt!" She repeated his name with a sort of horror. "Why, I'd be scared to death of him. I'm sure he thinks I am quite foolish."

"He's serious, of course, which is much more interesting than being frivolous."

"Evan is not frivolous."

"So it's Evan!" I began to laugh. Then I hugged her. "Oh, Theodosia, I'm so happy . . ." I had the presence of mind to add, "for you."

"You thought it was Tybalt, and that's what Father wants. He's always been a great admirer of Sir Edward and interested in everything he does. And he would have loved me to be like you and able to learn about all this stuff. But I'm not like that, and how could anybody want Tybalt when there's Evan!"

"Someone might," I said calmly.

"Judith, you like Evan, don't you?"

"Of course I do, and I think you are ideally suited."

"That's wonderful. But what do you think Father will say?"

"There's a way to find out. Ask him. He may be delighted."

"He won't be. He's fascinated by the Traverses. I believe he would have gone to Egypt if he'd been well enough."

"What does Evan say?"

"He says that we're going to be married, whatever happens."

"You may be cut out of your father's will."

"Do you think I care for that? I'd rather have Evan and starve."

"It won't come to that. He has a good job at the university,

hasn't he? Even if you don't inherit a vast fortune you will be a professor's wife."

"Of course. I don't care about Father's money." She hugged me. I was so happy. How pleasant it is to work for someone's happiness when doing so contributes to your own!

THEODOSIA had been right when she said that her father would not be pleased. After her talk with him she came to my room in tears. "He won't have it," she said. "He's furious."

"Well, you have to stand firm if you really want to marry Evan."

"You'll help me, won't you, Judith?"

"With all my heart," I said.

She was greatly comforted and stayed in my room while we made plans. I told her that the first thing she must do was write to Evan and tell him the state of affairs.

"I shall tell him that you know, Judith, and that we can count on you."

The next day I was surprised to receive a summons from Sir Ralph. When I went to his apartments he was in a dressing gown and seated in an armchair.

"Sit down, Miss Osmond."

I obeyed.

"I have the impression that you are interfering in my daughter's affairs."

"I know that she wishes to marry," I said. "I cannot see that I have interfered."

"Indeed! Didn't you tell her to come and deliver her ultimatum to me?"

"I told her that if she wished to marry she should tell you so."

"And perhaps ask my permission?"

"Yes."

"And if I did not give it, to defy me?"

"What she will do is entirely for her to decide."

"I guessed it," he said. "You've been propping her up. You know that this fellow is penniless and my daughter will be a very rich woman one day. Do you still think she should marry this man?"

"If she is in love with him."

"Love! I didn't know you were sentimental, Miss Osmond."

"In my opinion marriage is something which should be decided on by the partners concerned."

"And my daughter's marriage does not concern me?"

"Not as closely as it does her and her future husband."

"You should have been an advocate. Instead of which I believe you have a fancy for the profession of the man my daughter would marry—if I permit it."

"It's true."

"I believe you know that I wanted another marriage for my daughter."

"There has been a certain amount of speculation."

"You don't think it's a bad idea that my daughter chose this man? In fact, Miss Osmond, aren't you a little pleased about it?"

"I don't know what you mean."

"Don't you? You're a wily one, Miss Osmond." He lay back in his chair, laughing, his face suffused with color.

A few days later Sir Ralph declared that he would permit an engagement between his daughter and Evan Callum.

EVAN and Theodosia were married on Christmas Day, and Oliver Shrimpton performed the ceremony. I sat at the back of the church with Dorcas, Alison and Sabina.

When the bride came down the aisle on her husband's arm Sabina whispered to me, "It'll be your turn next." I noticed that her eyes went to Hadrian.

Good heavens! I thought. Is that the way some people are thinking?

As for myself, I had always looked upon Hadrian as a brother. I laughed to think of what Lady Bodrean would have to say if she knew that. She would think it highly presumptuous of her companion to consider Sir Ralph's nephew as a brother.

After the bridal pair left, Sir Ralph sent for me and said that Lady Bodrean would not require my services for a few days and therefore I might read the papers to him.

So each morning I sat with him for an hour or so and read *The Times;* but he would never let me get very far. I realized that he really wanted to talk.

He told me about the expedition, and I was able to talk of it intelligently to him because of the little knowledge I had acquired.

"It's a pity we couldn't send you up to the university. You'd have done well, I think. Always had a feeling for it, didn't you? I always had it myself, but was never anything but an amateur."

I said that there was a great deal of pleasure to be found in being merely an amateur.

"With Sir Edward it's a passion. Tybalt will be another like his father. Very difficult man to live with, is Sir Edward. His wasn't a very happy marriage. There are some men who marry a profession rather than a wife. Always up and off somewhere. When at home, buried in his books or his work."

"I suppose she wasn't interested in his work."

"His work came first. With that sort of man it always does."

"Your daughter has married an archaeologist."

"That fellow. He'll be talking in a classroom all his life, and when his day's work is over he'll go home to his wife and family and forget all about it. There are men like that—but they're rarely the ones who rise to the top of their profession. Would you like to see some reports of what is happening in Egypt?"

"Oh, I should enjoy that."

I read some of the reports to him and we discussed them. How those hours flew! I had slipped into a new relationship with Sir Ralph. His interest in me had become the basis of a friendship which I should never have thought possible.

Chapter III

IT WAS not until early March that the news came of Sir Edward's mysterious death. Sir Ralph was deeply shocked and this shock resulted in another stroke, which impaired his speech. It was then that rumors circulated about the curse of the pharaohs,

for it was known that he had backed the expedition financially. He was unable to attend Sir Edward's funeral, but a few days later he sent for me and when I went to his room I was surprised to see Tybalt there.

It was pitiful to see the once robust Sir Ralph the wreck he now was. He indicated that he wished us to sit on either side of him.

"Ju . . . Ju . . ." he began, and I realized he was trying to say my name.

"I'm here, Sir Ralph," I said, and when I laid my hand on his he took it and would not release it.

His eyes turned toward Tybalt, who placed his hand in Sir Ralph's other hand. The old man smiled and drew our hands together. I looked into Tybalt's eyes and I felt a slow flush creeping over my face.

Sir Ralph's implication was obvious. I withdrew my hand, but Tybalt continued to look at me. Sir Ralph had closed his eyes. Blake tiptoed in and said, "I think it would be better, sir, if you and Miss Osmond left now."

We went out of the house together, and when we had walked a little distance Tybalt said, "He's right, you know. We should."

"I . . . I don't understand."

"Why, Judith. He was telling us that we should marry."

"He was wandering in his mind."

"I don't think he was. I think it has been his wish for some time."

"I don't understand this. Do you mean that you will marry me because Sir Ralph has implied that he wants you to?"

"That's not the only reason, of course."

"Tell me some others," I said.

"You have always been interested in my work, haven't you—vitally interested?"

"Why, yes."

"You see, we should get on very well. My mother was bored by my father's work. It was a very dismal marriage. It will be different with us."

"Even that does not seem to me an adequate reason for marrying. If love came into it . . ."

Then he laughed and drew me close. "Do you doubt that it does?"

"I should like some sort of declaration."

"First let me have one from you, because I'm sure you will do better than I. You're never at a loss for words. I'm afraid I am—often."

"I suppose you know that I have been in love with you for years. Sir Ralph knows it, I believe."

"I had no idea I was so fortunate! I shall be the most arrogant man in your life."

"There are no others of any importance—and never have been. I shall spend my life convincing you of that."

"So you agree to share it with me?"

"I would die rather than do anything else."

"My dearest Judith! I love you," he said.

"Say it again. Keep saying it. I have so long dreamed of your saying those words. I can't believe this is really true."

He took my hand and kissed it fervently. "I don't deserve you," he said. "I have not your gaiety, your spontaneity, everything that makes you so attractive. I can be dull, far too serious...."

"One can never be too serious about the important things of life."

"I shall be moody, preoccupied. I shall neglect you for my work."

"Which I intend to share with you, including the moods and the preoccupation, so that objection is overruled."

"I am not able to express my feelings easily. I shall forget to tell you how much I love you. You alarm me. You think too highly of me. You hope for perfection."

I laughed as I laid my head against him. "I can't help my feelings," I said. "I have loved you so long. I only want to be with you, to make your life smooth and easy and just as you wish it to be."

"Judith," he said, "I will do my best to make you happy."

"If you love me, if you allow me to share your life, I shall be that."

He slipped his arm through mine and gripped my hand tightly.

We walked on and talked of the future. He would like our marriage to take place as soon as possible. We were going to be very busy with plans for the next expedition. Would I mind if after the ceremony we stayed at Giza House and plunged straight into our arrangements?

Would I mind? I cared for nothing as long as I could be with him. The greatest joy which could come to me was to share his life forevermore.

THERE was astonishment at Rainbow Cottage when I told Dorcas and Alison my news. They were glad that I was to be married but a little dubious about my bridegroom; Oliver Shrimpton was so much more eligible in their opinion.

"You'll be Lady Travers," said Alison.

"I hadn't thought of that."

Dorcas shook her head. "You're happy. I can see that."

"Oh, Dorcas, Alison, I never thought it possible to be so happy."

"But you hope for too much," said Dorcas. "You think everything's going to be perfect."

I laughed at her. "In this marriage," I said, "everything will be."

I SAID nothing at Keverall Court about my engagement. It hardly seemed appropriate with Sir Ralph so ill. And the next day he died.

I don't think anyone missed him as much as I did. My great joy was overshadowed by grief. But at least, I thought, he would have been pleased. He had been my friend, and during the weeks before his death our friendship had meant a good deal to me, as I believed it had to him.

Lady Bodrean talked to me and to Jane about Sir Ralph's virtues, but I sensed that the lull in her hostility to me was momentary. Little did she know the blow I was to deliver. I was to be married to the man whom she had wanted for her daughter—her poor companion would soon be Lady Travers.

When Hadrian came home I told him the news. "It's not of-

ficially announced yet," I warned him. "I shall wait until after the funeral."

"Tybalt's lucky," he said glumly. "I reckon he's forestalled me. If you'd had a fortune, Judith, I'd have laid my heart at your feet."

"Biologically impossible," I told him.

THAT night Sir Ralph's lawyers asked me to be present at the reading of his will. When I called at Rainbow Cottage and told Alison and Dorcas of this they looked at each other in a most embarrassed fashion.

"Is anything wrong?" I asked.

"There is something we think you ought to know," said Dorcas. She bit her lip, looked at Alison, then said, "It's about your birth, Judith. You are our niece. Lavinia was your mother."

"Lavinia! Why didn't you tell me?"

"Because it was rather an awkward situation."

"Lavinia was the eldest," went on Dorcas, "and Father doted on her. It was a terrible shock when we heard she was going to have a child. We smuggled her away to a cousin in London who had several children of her own. Lavinia could look after them and keep her own baby there. It was a good arrangement. About a year after your birth she brought you to see us, but of course she couldn't come here. We all met in Plymouth. We had such a pleasant time—and then we saw her off on that train."

"There was an accident. She was killed and I survived."

"And what was going to happen to you was a problem. So we said you were a cousin's child and brought you home."

"Well, you are in fact my aunts! But who was my father? Do you know that?" They looked at each other for a moment and I burst out, "Can it really be? It explains everything. Sir Ralph!"

Their faces told me that I had guessed correctly.

"I'm glad. I was fond of him." I went to them and hugged them. "At least I know who my parents were now."

"We thought you might be ashamed to have been born . . . out of wedlock."

"Do you know," I said, "I believe my mother must have been the one love of Sir Ralph's life." I thought of the way he looked at me, the amused twinkle in his eyes. He was saying to himself, "This is Lavinia's daughter."

"Now, Judith," said Dorcas, "the reason you are expected to be at the reading of the will is because he has left you something. It will come out that you are his daughter and we didn't want it to come as a shock to you."

THEY were right. I was mentioned in Sir Ralph's will. He left a quarter of a million pounds to the Archaeological Research Fund to be used in whatever way Sir Edward or Tybalt Travers thought fit. He left an income for life to his wife; to Hadrian, one thousand a year; to Theodosia, his heiress, the house on the death of her mother and one half of the remainder of his estate. The other half was to go to his natural daughter, Judith Osmond. In the event of the death of one of his daughters, her share of his fortune would revert to the survivor.

It was astounding. I had acquired a fortune so great that it bewildered me to contemplate it. I should not go penniless to my husband, as I had thought. I remembered Sir Ralph's taking my hand and Tybalt's and placing them together. I wondered if he had told Tybalt of our relationship and of what he intended to do. I then felt my first twinge of uneasiness.

THE truth of my birth was now known throughout the village. Some people had guessed, they said—being wise after the event. Alison and Dorcas were alternately pleased and ashamed. Alison said that she was glad her father had not had to face this scandal. At the same time I was now a woman of means whose future was secure. The scandal would die down, the benefits remain.

When I went to see them after the reading of the will they looked at me as though I had become a different person. I laughed at them. "You foolish aunts!" I cried. "The fact that I'm going to be rich doesn't change me at all! And let me tell you, there is going to be no cheeseparing in this house again. You are going

373

to have an income that will enable you to live in the manner to which you have been accustomed."

It was a very emotional moment. Alison's face twitched and Dorcas wept. I embraced them both. "Just think of it," I said. "You can leave Rainbow Cottage. You can sell it if you wish" (for Sir Ralph had left it to them) "and go and live in a lovely house with a maid or two. . . ."

Alison laughed. "Judith, we're quite happy here and it's our very own now. We shall stay."

Dorcas dabbed her eyes and said, "Judith what about *him?*" They both looked at me anxiously. "We . . . we wondered whether he knew that you . . . er . . . were coming into this money."

"Aunts!" I cried sternly. "You are very wrong. Tybalt and I were meant for each other. I'm passionately interested in his work."

Alison said, with a touch of asperity, "I hope he's not passionately interested in your money."

I was angry with them. "This is monstrous. How could he be?"

"Now, Judith, we are only concerned for your good," said Dorcas.

My anger melted. It was true. All their anxiety was for my welfare. "Listen," I said, "I love Tybalt. Do you understand that? I always have. I always will. Do you doubt it?"

"We were wondering about *him.*"

"Of course," I said, "he doesn't show his feelings as I do. He may seem aloof and cool—but he's not."

"It would break our hearts if you weren't happy, Judith."

"There's nothing to be afraid of. Your hearts are going to remain intact."

I COULDN'T help enjoying most of my inevitable interview with Lady Bodrean. A day or so after the will had been read I presented myself to her.

"So," she said, "you have come to hand in your notice."

"Certainly I have, Lady Bodrean."

"You know by now that you were *forced* on me."

"Then you will have no objection to my leaving immediately."

"I hear you are shortly to be married," she said, her lip curling.

"You have heard correctly," I told her.

"I must say I was surprised until ... er ..."

"Until?" I said.

"Sir Ralph confided a great deal in Sir Edward. They were close friends. I've no doubt he told him the position."

"You are suggesting that Sir Tybalt Travers has asked me to marry him because I am Sir Ralph's daughter?"

"I know that Sir Ralph was eager for a union with that family. Of course, he would have preferred his *true* daughter to have made the match—instead of which she went off with a penniless schoolteacher."

"I must remind you that Professor Callum is far from penniless. He holds a good post in one of the country's foremost universities, and the term schoolteacher is hardly the correct one to apply to a lecturer in archaeology."

"He was not the man Sir Ralph wished his daughter to marry. She was foolish and flouted us—and it seems to me that Sir Ralph then decided that he would offer her chance to you."

"My future husband is not a prize packet to be offered around."

"One might say that there was quite a prize to be offered to him. I am surprised at the manner in which my husband has left his fortune. It is a victory for immorality and extravagance."

I would not let her see that she had scored with her suggestion that I was being married for my money. When I left Lady Bodrean I returned to Rainbow Cottage, which would be my home until my marriage.

THE next day I presented myself at Giza House. It seemed different now that it was to be my home. Tabitha welcomed me warmly and told me how pleased she was that Tybalt and I were to marry. "I am sure you are the one for Tybalt." She pressed my hand. "I shall never forget how you used to come and borrow books. Your stay at Keverall Court was not very happy for you, I fear."

I told her that nothing that had gone before was of importance anymore. In the last weeks life had given me all that I had ever hoped for.

"You must understand Tybalt. At times you may feel that he neglects you for his work."

"It's going to be my work too. I'm going to join him in everything he does. I'm as excited as he is about all this."

"That's as it should be," she said. "I hope when you become mistress of Giza House you will not wish me to leave."

"How could I? We're friends."

"I have always been a close friend of Tybalt and his father. If I may continue here as housekeeper I should be very happy. On the other hand, if you should prefer—"

"What nonsense!" I cried. "I want you to be here. You're my friend too."

"Thank you, Judith."

Tabitha then showed me the house and introduced me formally to the staff. Emily, Ellen, Jane and Sarah were the maids, so like others of their kind that it took me some time to know which was which. I had seen the two Egyptian servants, Mustapha and Absalam, several times before. They were strange, alien and, I had heard, even sinister.

Tabitha explained that Sir Edward had liked them to cook him exotic dishes. He had employed them on digs in Egypt and for some reason had taken a fancy to them and brought them to England. She said they had been desolate but fatalistic about his death. They were certain it had come about because he had incurred the curse of the pharaohs.

"They are very concerned because Tybalt plans to carry on where his father left off. I think if it were possible for them to dissuade him they would do so." When I was presented to them they eyed me with suspicion, but I was prepared for that.

Janet Tester was another matter. She was the old woman who had been nurse to Tybalt and Sabina and remained with them after Lady Travers' death. I had seen Nanny Tester at a distance on one or two occasions and had thought her a peculiar old woman,

but she did not seem so unusual in Giza House as she would have in more ordinary surroundings.

"I must explain Janet Tester to you," said Tabitha, before she took me up to introduce us. "She is quite old now. She came as nurse to Sir Edward's wife, to whom she was devoted. She stayed on to look after Tybalt and Sabina, but when Lady Travers died Janet was almost demented with grief. We have to be a bit careful with her and treat her gently. Her apartment is at the top of this house. Janet keeps to herself, although, of course, we keep an eye on her."

"What an unusual arrangement."

"You'll find you're marrying into an unusual family."

We mounted the stairs to Janet Tester's apartment.

I was unprepared for the white-haired, gentle-looking woman who opened the door when we knocked. She wore a crisply laundered sprigged-muslin blouse and a black bombazine skirt.

Tabitha said, "Janet, I've brought Miss Osmond to see you."

She looked at me, her eyes misty with emotion. "Come in, come in," she said.

It was a charming room with a sloping roof and it was prettily furnished, with handmade rugs on the floor and many embroidered cushion covers. There was a fire burning and the kettle on a hob was beginning to sing.

"You'll take some tea with me," she said, and I replied that I should love to. "Tybalt told me about you and I said, 'Now you tell me what she's like, Tybalt,' and all he could say was, 'She's enthusiastic about the work.' How like him! I've often seen you tearing about down in the gardens when you were a child. What a one for mischief you were! I'll make the tea."

"Shall I do that," asked Tabitha, "while you and Miss Osmond have a chat?"

The expression in the gentle old face changed startlingly. The eyes were almost venomous. "I'll make my own tea in my own room," she said.

While she was making it she said to me, "I always stir it and let it stand five minutes. It's the only way to get the right brew."

When she poured the tea she said, "Well, I hope you'll be happy, my dear. Tybalt used to be such a good boy."

"*Used* to be?" I asked.

"When he was a little one he was always with me. He was his mother's boy then. But when he went away to school and started to grow up he turned to his father."

She stirred the spoon around and around in her cup. I could sense an uneasy atmosphere. "And now you're going to marry him," she said. "How time flies. It seems only yesterday I was playing peekaboo with him."

The thought of Tybalt's playing peekaboo was so funny that I couldn't help laughing. "He's come a long way since then," I said.

"I hope it's not on the road to ruin," said Janet Tester, stirring fiercely.

I looked at Tabitha, who had lifted her shoulders. I decided then that Tybalt's profession was not a happy subject, so I returned to his childhood.

That pleased her. "He was a good boy. He didn't get into all that much mischief. Miss Ruth—Lady Travers—doted on him. He was her boy, all right. I've got some pictures."

I reveled in them. Tybalt sitting on a furry rug all but in the nude; Tybalt a wondering two-year-old; Tybalt and Sabina.

There was a picture of Tybalt standing beside a rather pretty woman with a lot of fluffy hair who was holding a baby on her lap. "There they are with their mother. Oh, and here's Tybalt at school." He was holding a cricket bat. "He wasn't good at sports," said Nanny Tester in a disappointed voice. "His life became all study. And then Sir Edward, who'd scarcely noticed the children before, started to prick up his ears."

She conveyed her feelings by so many gestures—the tone of her voice, a contemptuous flick of the hand, a turning down of the lips. I had been with her a very short time, but I had learned that she disliked Tabitha and Sir Edward; she had adored Miss Ruth, and while Tybalt the child had qualified for her devotion, I was not so sure how she regarded the man.

I sensed Tabitha's relief when we could politely leave. Tabitha

378

went on ahead, but Janet caught my hand in hers. "Come again, Miss Osmond," she whispered. "Alone."

Later I thought a good deal about that meeting. I wondered why Janet Tester felt so strongly—and her attitude had betrayed to me that she did—about Tabitha.

Chapter IV

THE weeks before my wedding were flying past. Dorcas and Alison wanted quite a celebration. They seemed so relieved that they no longer had to preserve the secret of my birth that they were like children let out of school. Moreover, anxieties for the future had been swept away. The cottage was theirs; I was going to give them an allowance, and my future was settled.

However, there had been a little friction between Tybalt and the aunts over the wedding. This, Alison had said firmly, could not take place until a "reasonable" time had elapsed after the deaths of Sir Edward and Sir Ralph.

"You should wait at least a year," said Dorcas.

I had never seen Tybalt express his feelings so forcibly.

"Impossible!" he cried. "We shall be leaving for Egypt in a matter of months. Judith must come as my wife."

I agreed with him. I was ready to agree with him on anything. When I was with him I forgot all my misgivings. Although he was by no means demonstrative, he would look at me in a way which sent me into a state of bliss, and I knew that he was contemplating our future with the utmost pleasure. He took me into his confidence completely about his plans.

When he talked of ancient Egypt a passion glowed in him. I had never seen him so enthralled by anything as he was by his work, but I used to tell myself that our marriage was going to be the most important thing that ever happened to either of us. I would see to that.

My aunts shook their heads over me. I was besotted; and they were sure that to let a man see before marriage how much

379

you adored him was wrong. Afterward, yes. Then it was a wife's duty to submit to her husband in all ways. But before the marriage one did not "make oneself cheap."

They were excited, though, for after all a wedding in the family was an event. They talked about the reception and worried because Rainbow Cottage was too small, although the bride's house was the necessary place for it.

I could laugh at them, but I sensed their uneasiness. They had not wished me to wait so much for convention but because they thought it would give me time to see clearly, as they called it. The fact was that Tybalt did not appeal to them at all.

Then Dorcas caught a cold—something she invariably did when she was anxious; and her colds had to be nursed because they often turned to bronchitis.

One afternoon Tybalt came hurrying over to Rainbow Cottage, his eyes glowing as he took my hands in his.

"A most exciting thing has happened, Judith. A workman in Dorset has unearthed some Roman tiles. It seems very likely that this is going to lead to a great discovery. I've had an invitation to go along and give an opinion, and am leaving tomorrow. I want you to come with me."

"That's wonderful," I cried. "Tell me all about it."

We walked in the garden, talking. After he left I went in to tell the aunts that I was leaving next day, and I was astonished at the opposition.

"My dear Judith!" cried Alison. "What are you thinking of? How can you—an unmarried woman—go off with a man?"

"The man I am going to marry."

"It wouldn't be right," said Alison firmly.

"Dear aunts," I said, "in Tybalt's world these little conventions don't count."

"Judith, many a girl has anticipated her marriage to her own bitter cost. She trusts her fiancé, goes away with him and discovers that there are no wedding bells."

"At one moment you are suggesting Tybalt is marrying me for my money and at the next that he plans to seduce me and then

discard me. Really, you are being absurd." I went to my room and started to pack for the trip.

That evening Alison came to my room. Her face was strained. "I'm worried about Dorcas. I do think we should have Dr. Gunwen at once."

I went to fetch him.

When he came he said that Dorcas' cold had developed into bronchitis. Alison and I were up with her all night.

I knew the next day that I could not go to Dorset and leave Alison to nurse Dorcas alone, so I went over to Giza House to explain to Tybalt. We went into the garden, but before I could speak he began to tell me that the finds were even better than had at first been thought. I interrupted him. "I'm not coming, Tybalt."

He stared at me incredulously.

"My aunt Dorcas is ill. I must stay. She has these turns and it is rather frightening. Please understand, Tybalt. I want to be with you, but I just can't leave Rainbow Cottage now."

"Of course," he agreed, but he was very disappointed.

Tabitha then joined us in the garden.

"I can't go to Dorset," I said. "My aunt Dorcas is ill and Alison needs me here to help."

"But of course," said Tabitha.

"Would you come in Judith's place?" asked Tybalt. "I'm sure you'd find it of paramount interest."

Paramount interest. Was that a reproach? Did he feel that I should have found it of *paramount* interest?

Tabitha was saying, "Well, since Judith must stay, I will go in her place."

Tybalt pressed my arm. "I was looking forward to showing you this marvelous discovery. But there'll be plenty of time—later."

"The whole of our lives," I said.

In a few days, much to our relief, Dorcas began to recover. She was touched that I had stayed behind to help nurse her and comfort Alison. I heard her say to Alison when she thought I

couldn't hear, "However impulsive Judith is, her *heart's* in the right place."

I knew they talked about me and my coming marriage. I did so want to reassure them, but that seemed impossible. I was greatly looking forward to the day when I would leave Rainbow Cottage, naturally because I longed to be Tybalt's wife, and in addition I wanted to escape this atmosphere of distrust and to prove to them that Tybalt would be the most wonderful husband in the world.

Tybalt and Tabitha were away for two more weeks, and when they returned they were so full of what they had seen that they talked of little else. I was filled with chagrin because I could not join in their conversation.

Tybalt was amused. "Never mind," he said. "When we're married you'll go everywhere with me."

Our wedding day was almost at hand. Sabina had said that we might have a discreet reception at the rectory. After all, Dorcas had been ill and Rainbow Cottage was small and the rectory had been my home and she was Tybalt's sister. "I insist on it," she said. "And Oliver insists. You'll be married in *his* church and we'll have just a few friends in."

It did seem a good idea; and even Dorcas and Alison accepted it, though they insisted that in view of the recent deaths it must be a quiet family affair.

When I discussed the matter with Tybalt he was rather vague. He wanted us to be married, he said. When and how were unimportant. Besides, he had a surprise for me.

"We'll have a honeymoon. You won't want to go straight back to Giza House."

"That," I murmured, "is immaterial to *me*. All I ask is that I am with you."

With an unusually tender gesture he took my face in his hands. "Judith," he said, "don't expect too much of me."

I laughed aloud—I was so happy. "Why, I expect *everything* of you."

He held me against him. "I'm afraid of this high opinion you have of me. You are too imaginative, Judith. You get an idea and

it's usually something you want it to be and then you make every-thing fit into that."

"It's the way to live. I shall teach you to live that way."

"It's better to see the truth."

"I will make this my truth."

"My darling Judith, there is no one like you."

"Of course there isn't! I am myself. Reckless and impulsive, the aunts would tell you. So *you* must not have too high an opinion of *me*."

Tybalt said, "I came to tell you about our honeymoon. I'm going to take you to Dorset. We are all so excited about this discovery. I long to show it to you."

I said that was wonderful; but it did occur to me that there would no doubt be a great many people there and a honeymoon on our own might have been more appropriate.

THERE was so much to do in preparation even for a "discreet" wedding, including sessions in Sarah Sloper's cottage which went on for hours. One morning while I stood in my white satin gown, with Sarah kneeling at my feet adjusting the hem, she said, "Well, fancy it coming to this. He was for Miss Theodosia, you know, and she gets the little professor and you get *him*."

"You make it sound as though it's some sort of lottery, Sarah."

"They do say marriage be a lottery, Miss Judith. And you being Sir Ralph's girl and all. I always guessed that. Why, he had a real fancy for you. And Miss Lavinia. Pretty as a picture she were, but I'd say you took more after Sir Ralph."

"Thank you, Sarah."

"Oh, I weren't meaning it *that* way, Miss Judith. You'll look pretty enough in your bride's dress. Brides always do. That's why there's nothing I like making better. And is it to be orange blos-som? I had orange blossom when I married Sloper. I've still got it put away in a drawer. I look at it now and then and think of the old days. You'll be able to do that, Miss Judith. It's a pleasant thing to do when things don't turn out just as you'd fancied." She sighed and went on fervently. "Well, let's pray the sun'll shine

on your wedding day. They do say, 'Happy be the bride the sun shines on.'"

I laughed, but this assumption that my marriage would be a perilous adventure was beginning to irritate me.

ON A rather misty October day I was married to Tybalt in the church I knew so well. I came down the aisle on the arm of Dr. Gunwen, who had offered to give me away.

A fellow archaeologist and friend of Tybalt's was his best man. He was named Terence Gelding and would be going to Dorset, and would accompany us to Egypt. On the night before the wedding Tybalt had gone to the station to meet his friend and bring him back to Giza House. Tabitha told me that they had all stayed up very late, talking. I felt that vague tinge of jealousy which I had begun to notice came to me when others shared an intimacy with Tybalt.

But as I made my vows before Oliver, and Tybalt put the ring on my finger, I was more completely happy than I had ever been.

It was disappointing that as we came into the porch the rain should begin to pelt down.

"You can't walk out in that," said Dorcas at my elbow.

She was right, of course. So we stood there, and I heard the whispers behind us.

"What bad luck!" someone said. "Not wedding weather by any means."

A gnomelike creature came walking up from the graveyard. As it approached I saw that it was Mr. Pegger, carrying a spade to which the brown earth still clung. When he saw us he pulled up short and his fanatical eyes took in Tybalt and me in our wedding clothes. He looked straight at me. "No good 'ull come of such indecent haste," he said. "It's ungodly." Then he nodded and walked past the porch with a self-righteous air.

I heard Theodosia whisper, "Oh, Evan, how unpleasant. It's like an ... *omen*."

I looked up at the lowering sky and I seemed to hear Sarah Sloper's reedy voice: "Happy be the bride the sun shines on."

AFTER A FEW MINUTES the rain stopped and we were able to pick our way across the grass to the vicarage. There was the familiar drawing room decked out with chrysanthemums and starry Michaelmas daisies. A table had been set up at one end of the room and on this was a wedding cake and champagne.

I cut the cake with Tybalt's help. Hadrian made a witty speech and Tybalt responded very briefly. I kept saying to myself, "This is the supreme moment of my life."

Theodosia was beside me. "Oh, Judith," she said, "I'm so glad we're sisters. Isn't it odd that Father got his wish that his daughter marry Tybalt?" She was gazing across the room at Evan. "I'm so grateful to you...."

"Grateful...?"

She floundered a little. Theodosia had never been able to express her thoughts gracefully. "Well, for marrying Tybalt and making it all come right."

Then Sabina joined us. "Isn't this *fun?* The three of us, all married. And doesn't Tybalt look wonderful?" She gazed at him with that adoration I had seen so many times before. "Fancy Tybalt's being a bridegroom! We always thought he would never marry! He's married to all that *nonsense*, Nanny Tester says. And now your dreams have come true, Judith. Isn't it a wonderful *fairytale* ending?"

"It's not an ending," said Theodosia soberly. "It's really a beginning. Evan is so pleased because he's been invited to join the expedition."

"Has he really?" cried Sabina. "That's a great honor. When he's away you must come and stay."

"I'm going with him," declared Theodosia fiercely. "You don't think I'd let Evan go without me!"

"Has Tybalt said you may? Papa never liked wives around, unless they were workers themselves ... but you're not, Theodosia. I daresay that now he's a married man Tybalt has sympathy for others."

"He has said I may go," Theodosia said.

"How wonderful! You'll be company for Judith. Tabitha's

going. Of course, she's very knowledgeable. There she is talking to Tybalt now. She's beautiful, don't you think? She always seems to wear the right things. That silver gray now . . . It's just *right!* You'll have to be careful, Judith," she added playfully. "She's young really. About a year, possibly two years older than Tybalt, that's all. Of course, she is always so quiet, but it's the quiet ones you have to be wary of, so they say. . . . Oh, Judith, you're quite disturbed, I believe. As if I meant it. Tybalt will be the most *faithful* husband in the world! He's too busy anyway to be anything else. The wonder is that he married at all. I'm sure you're going to be wonderfully happy."

"Oh, doesn't she run on," I said to Theodosia. "No one else gets a chance."

"You're only silent because it's your wedding day," said Sabina. "If you weren't thinking of Tybalt you would never have allowed me to have the floor for so long."

"Trust you to make the most of your opportunities. Look, here's Hadrian."

"Hello," said Hadrian. "A family gathering."

"We were talking about the expedition," said Sabina. "Among other things."

"Did you know Evan and Theodosia are coming?" I asked.

"I had heard there was a possibility. We shall all be together—all except Sabina and Oliver."

"So you're going too, Hadrian."

"It's a great concession. Gives me a chance to escape my creditors."

Dorcas hurried over to me. "Judith, do you realize that the carriage will be taking you to the station in less than an hour? I think it is time you changed."

I slipped away with my aunts and we went to the room which Sabina had set aside for me. There hung my silver-gray grosgrain coat and skirt. Silver gray. So elegant. Yes, when worn by a woman like Tabitha.

"You look lovely," cooed Dorcas.

"That's because you see me through the eyes of love," I said.

"There'll be someone else who will be looking at you in the same way," said Alison quickly.

I went out to the porch. The carriage was there and Tybalt was waiting for me. Everyone crowded around as Tybalt and I drove away on our honeymoon.

WHAT shall I say of my honeymoon? At first it was wonderful, and the wonder lasted for two nights and a day. Then Tybalt was all mine. We had broken our journey to Dorset and stayed at a little inn in the heart of the moors.

I shall never forget that little inn: the big feather bed in which we lay together; the sign creaking just outside our window; the sound of the nearby waterfall sending its sparkling water over the craggy boulders.

There was a fire burning in the grate, and as I watched the flickering shadows with Tybalt's arms about me I was completely happy.

Breakfast was served to us in the old inn parlor, with its brass and pewter on the shelves and hams hanging from the rafters. Hot coffee, bread straight from the oven, ham and fresh eggs, scones, and homemade strawberry jam with a bowl of Devonshire cream the color of buttercups. And Tybalt sitting opposite, watching me with a look of wonder in his eyes. If ever I was beautiful in my life I was beautiful on that morning.

After breakfast we went out onto the moors and walked for miles over the short spring turf. The innkeeper's wife had packed a little hamper for us and we picnicked by a tiny trickling stream. We saw wild moorland ponies; but the only human beings we encountered on that day were a man driving a cartload of apples and pears who raised his whip to us and called a greeting, and another on horseback who did the same. A happy idyllic day, and then back to the delicious duckling and green peas and afterward the cozy bedroom and the flickering fire. The next day we caught the train to Dorset.

Of course I was fascinated by the Roman site, but I wanted only one thing in my life at that time and that was to love and be

loved by Tybalt. The hotel at which we stayed was full of people who were with the working party, which made it rather different from our Dartmoor haven. Although it was brought home to me that I was an amateur among professionals, I was as eager as ever to learn—a fact which delighted my husband.

The day after we reached the hotel, Terence Gelding arrived. He was tall and rather lean, with the same serious and dedicated expression I had noticed among so many of Tybalt's associates. He and Tybalt would talk animatedly for long periods, and try as I might to follow their conversation, it was not always easy.

When there was a possibility that an amphitheater might have existed close to the site the excitement was great. After that Tybalt was often at the site with the workers, and sometimes I went with him. I talked to the more humble members of the party; I studied maps; I even did a little digging, as I had in Carter's Meadow. I watched first-aid methods in the restoration of a plaque on which was engraved the head of a caesar. I was fascinated—but I longed to be alone with Tybalt. Interested as I was in this absorbing subject, I *was* a bride on her honeymoon.

We were two weeks on the Roman site, and I believe Tybalt was reluctant to leave. He spent our last evening closeted with the director of the expedition. He came in just after midnight and sat on my bed, his eyes shining.

"It's almost certain that there's an amphitheater," he said. "What a discovery if we're right!"

"I'm sure you are, Tybalt."

"Oh, but one can't be sure—not unless there is absolute proof. Why are you smiling?"

"Was I?" I held out my arms to him. "Perhaps because I was thinking that there are other exciting things in life."

He came to me at once and for a few moments we embraced. I laughed softly. "I know what you're thinking," I said. "Yes, there are more exciting things. But I imagine the tombs of the pharaohs win by a head."

I amused him. My frank enjoyment of our love was something which I am sure would have completely shocked Dorcas and

Alison. But then many people would have considered me bold and brazen. I wondered if Tybalt did. "You see," I explained to him, "it has always been impossible for me to pretend."

He said, "I don't deserve you, Judith."

"You can always try to be worthy," I suggested.

I was happy. So was he. Then we returned to Giza House.

IT WAS a gloomy afternoon in November when we arrived. The weather was warm and damp, and the October gales had stripped the trees of most of their leaves. As we pulled up at the wrought-iron gate of Giza House, Tabitha came out to greet us.

"Not a very pleasant day," she said. "You must be chilled. Come in quickly and we'll have tea."

I stepped into the hall and, in the shadows, saw Mustapha and Absalam, their dark eyes fixed intently on me. They would be remembering me, of course, as the rowdy child and afterward the companion from Keverall Court who came to borrow books. Now I was the new mistress.

Tabitha showed us to our room. I stayed to freshen up while she returned to the drawing room with Tybalt. When I had washed I went to the window and looked out. The thick shrubs and trees made the garden dark. In the room the curtains were deep blue edged with gold braid in a Greek key pattern. The bed was a large canopied four-poster. The carpet was thick. Book-shelves lined one wall; some of the books I had borrowed and read. It occurred to me that this had been Sir Edward's bedroom, and I wished that a different room had been chosen for us. Then I remembered that I was the mistress of the house and if I did not like my room I could say so.

I changed my traveling clothes and went down to the drawing room. Tybalt and Tabitha were sitting side by side on the sofa, examining some plans. As soon as I entered, Ellen wheeled the tea wagon in and stood by while Tabitha poured. Tybalt then began a long description of the Roman site.

"You must have had a very interesting time, Tybalt," said Tabitha, smiling. "I trust Judith found it equally so."

She looked at me slightly apprehensively, and I assured her that I had enjoyed our stay in Dorset very much.

"And now," said Tybalt, "we must begin to work out our plans in earnest. It's astonishing how the time flies when there is so much to do. I want to leave in February."

So we talked of the trip, and it was pleasant sitting there in the firelight while the afternoon darkened into evening.

"I'm happy," I assured myself. "I've achieved my dream."

MY FIRST night in Giza House was strange indeed! One of the maids had lighted a fire in the bedroom and the flickering flames threw their shadows over the walls. How different from those of the Dartmoor cottage! These seemed like sinister shapes which would assume life at any moment. There was a door behind a blue velvet curtain. I opened this and saw that it led into the room where the sarcophagus had been.

I had gone up to bed in advance of Tybalt; and the room in firelight, with only two candles burning in their tall candlesticks on the dressing table, seemed alive with shadows.

I wondered why Tybalt was so long. Was he talking to Tabitha, telling her things which he did not want me to know? What an idea! I must not be jealous of the time he spent with her.

When Tybalt finally came into the room the sinister shadows receded. Candlelight, I remembered, was becoming.

"What were you doing in that room?" he asked.

"I found this door. It's the room where the sarcophagus was."

"You weren't thinking of dressing up as a mummy, were you . . . to frighten me?"

"You . . . frightened of a mummy! I know you love them dearly."

"Not," he replied, "as dearly as I love you."

On the rare occasions when Tybalt said things like that, my happiness was complete.

"Do YOU like the room I had prepared for you?" asked Tabitha next morning. Tybalt had gone to his study; he had some correspondence to deal with.

"It's a bit ghostly," I said. "I always thought there was something rather haunted about Giza House."

"It's all those trees and shrubs in the garden, I daresay. Would you like to change your room?"

"No, I don't think so."

"Judith, anything you want you must do, you know. You're mistress of the house now."

"I can't get used to being the mistress of anything."

"You will in time. You're happy, aren't you?"

"I have what I've always wanted."

"Not many of us can say that," she replied with a sigh.

"And you, Tabitha?"

I wished that she would confide in me. I was sure there were secrets in her life. She was still young—a widow, I supposed. Life was by no means over for her—and yet there was about her a resignation, a subtle secrecy, which could have been one of the reasons why she was so attractive.

She said, "I have had my moments. Perhaps one should not ask for more than that."

Sabina said we must celebrate Christmas Day at the rectory, and she insisted on my aunts' joining us, though I think they believed we should have gone to them at Rainbow Cottage.

Tabitha and I decorated Giza House with holly and mistletoe. "It was something we never did before," she said.

The maids were delighted. Ellen told me that it was more like a house since I'd come home. They liked me and seemed to take pleasure in addressing me as "my lady," though it invariably startled me.

It was at the beginning of December when the first uneasy situation occurred.

It was afternoon and dusk was beginning to fall. I had gone to our bedroom and on my way saw that the door which led from the corridor into the sarcophagus room was ajar. I thought perhaps Tybalt was there, so I looked in. Mustapha was standing silhouetted against the window.

I went in, and as I did so I found Absalam standing between me and the door.

I felt the goose pimples rise on my skin. I said, "Mustapha . . . Absalam . . . is anything wrong?"

There was a brief silence. Then Absalam said, "My lady, we are your most humble slaves."

"We don't have slaves here, Absalam."

They bowed their heads. Then Mustapha spoke. "It must not be, my lady," he said, shaking his head gravely.

"What?" I asked.

"Stay here, my lady," Absalam said. "You tell Sir Tybalt he must not go. A husband listens to his beloved."

I began to grasp their meaning. They were afraid to go back to Egypt, the scene of the tragedy which had overtaken their master.

"I'm afraid that's impossible," I said. "Plans are going ahead. They couldn't be altered now."

"It is death there. There is a curse. . . ."

Of course, I thought, they would be very superstitious. I said, "Have you spoken to Sir Tybalt?"

They shook their heads in unison. "No use," Absalam said. "No use to speak to his great father. So he die. The curse comes to him and it will come to others."

"It's a legend," I said, "nothing more. It is good of you to be so concerned, but there is nothing I can do."

"It is death . . . death."

They looked at me with great sorrowing eyes and shook their heads mournfully as I slipped through to the bedroom.

THAT night as we lay in bed I said to Tybalt, "The Egyptians spoke to me today. They believe that if we go to Egypt there will be disaster."

"If they feel that, they must stay behind."

"They asked me to speak to you. They said a husband loves his beloved and would listen."

"They are very superstitious."

"Sometimes I'm a little frightened."

"You, Judith?"

I clung to him. "Only because of you," I assured him. "What if there is something in this curse?"

"My dear Judith, you don't believe *that*."

He laughed in the darkness. And that was all.

WHAT dark days they were before Christmas. There was a great deal of rain and the fir trees glistened and dripped; the southwest wind moaned outside the windows.

Theodosia and Evan came to stay with Lady Bodrean at Keverall Court. Sabina, Oliver, Tybalt and I were invited for Christmas Eve. Hadrian was there too and was going to stay until we left for Egypt.

It had long been a custom to sing carols in the Keverall Court ballroom on Christmas Eve, and many of the people from the neighborhood joined the company. After the singing, Lady Bodrean's guests went to the hall for a supper of squab, mutton and beef pies; and, of course, hot Cornish pasties. We drank Keverall Punch, which was served in an enormous pewter bowl. The recipe, known only to the steward of Keverall, had been handed down through the last four hundred years.

Lady Bodrean was all charm when we met. "It is a pleasure to see you, Lady Travers," she said. I felt myself giggling inwardly as I graciously acknowledged her greeting.

After we had partaken of the pies and punch, we went to church for the midnight service and then strolled home in the early hours of Christmas Day. It was all done as it had been many times before, and I felt it was good that all the friends of my childhood were gathered together.

Christmas Day at the rectory was pleasant too. Sabina presided at the table where once Alison had sat. There was turkey with chestnut stuffing, and later flaming plum pudding was ceremoniously carried in. Then we played charades and childish guessing games, at which I excelled and Tybalt did not. Dorcas and Alison looked on and applauded my success.

Afterward, as Tabitha, Tybalt and I walked the short distance

from the rectory back to Giza House, I found myself wondering whether there would always be the three of us together. Was it because when Tabitha was with us Tybalt's attitude toward me seemed to change? Sometimes he seemed almost formal, as though he were afraid to betray to her that affection which more and more he was beginning to show when we were alone.

JANUARY was with us. There was a cold snap, and the hoarfrost glistening on the shrubbery gave the gardens the look of a fairy-land. One morning, at breakfast, Tybalt was going through the mail when he frowned and made an exclamation of disgust. "These lawyers!" he complained.

"What's happened?"

"Sir Ralph's will is taking a long while to settle. It seems as though it's going to be months before everything is clear."

"Does it matter so much?" I asked.

"The trust he has left will make a great deal of difference to the expedition. We have to employ possibly a hundred workmen. They have to be paid; they have to have living quarters. That's why one cannot begin such an undertaking until all these tiresome financial matters are taken care of."

"And you can't touch this money until the will is proved?"

"Oh, it will be all right. With such a sum made over to us we shall be able to anticipate our income. But there will be legal formalities. I daresay I shall have to go to London."

He then told me that he believed his father had discovered the way into an unbroken tomb. "He was so excited. I remember his coming to the house. He had rented the Chephro Palace from Hakim Pasha, one of the most influential men in Egypt. He was interested in our operation. The pasha is still eager to help and we shall use his palace again.

"Father was a man who rarely showed his feelings, but he seemed exuberant when I saw him come into the courtyard that night. I thought I would wait until he had changed and had had a light meal, which Mustapha and Absalam always prepared for him. Then I would go down and wait for him to tell me. I was of

the opinion that only some tremendous discovery could have made him excited on that day.

"When I went down I found him ill. He complained of pains and I saw that his limbs trembled. I suggested to Absalam and Mustapha, who were very upset, that we get him to bed. That night he died, but before he did I was sent for. As I knelt by his bed his lips moved. I was certain he was saying, 'Go on.' That is why I am determined."

"But why did he die at precisely that moment?"

"There was talk of the curse, which was absurd. Why should he be cursed for doing what many had done before him? He may have eaten tainted food. That, I can assure you, has happened more than once."

"But to die so suddenly."

"It was the greatest tragedy of my life. But I intend to carry out my father's wishes."

DURING the cold spell Nanny Tester caught a chill which turned to bronchitis. I helped nurse her, and I think she liked to have me there, which was fortunate, for she had what seemed to me an unreasoning dislike for Tabitha.

In February, Tybalt went to London to make further arrangements about supplies and to see the lawyers. I had hoped to go with him, but he had said that he would have so much to do that he would be able to spend little time with me.

I waved him off at Plymouth station, and I couldn't help thinking of Lavinia's going on that same journey with her baby in her arms. And then an hour later she was dead. To love intensely was a mixed blessing. I was completely happy only when Tybalt was safe beside me. When he was absent I imagined all kinds of horrors which could befall him.

That evening as I sat with Tabitha I told her of my fears. She smiled at me gently. "Sometimes it is painful to love too well."

I wondered afresh what her life had been and why she never spoke of it. Perhaps she will one day, I thought, when she knows me better.

Then we spoke about Nanny Tester. Tabitha thought she was recovering very well.

"But these attacks always leave her a little more feeble. Her mind wanders quite a bit," Tabitha said.

I had noticed that. I noticed too that my presence seemed to soothe her, so I used to take up her food and sometimes I sat with her. I would take a book and read or do needlework.

One day I was sitting by her bed when she said, "Watch her. Be careful."

I guessed she was wandering in her mind and said, "There's no one here, Nanny."

"I could tell you some things," she murmured. "I was always one to keep my eyes open."

"Try to rest," I said.

"Rest! When I see what's going on in this house. It's him and it's her. She eggs him on. Housekeeper! Friend of the family! What is she? Tell me that. You don't see. That's how it often is. Those it concerns most don't see what's under their very eyes."

"What do you see, Nanny?"

"I see the way things are between them. She's sly. We can do without her. There's nothing she does I couldn't do."

That was hardly true, but I let it pass.

"I never knew housekeepers like that one. You'd think she was the mistress. Then he goes away and what happens? She's called away. Oh, it's some family affair. What family? You watch out, my lady," she murmured. "You're nursing a viper in your bosom."

The term made me smile; and when I thought of all Tabitha did in the house and how charming and helpful she was, I was sure that the old woman had an obsession, probably because she was jealous.

THE house seemed different without Tybalt. A fire was lighted every night in the bedroom and I lay there watching the shadows. I often fancied I heard noises in the next room, and one night I got out of bed to see if anyone were there. The books, the table at which Sir Edward had often worked looked ghostly in the faint

light of the crescent moon. I went back to bed and dreamed that I went into the room and the sarcophagus was there. From it rose a mummy, and then the wrapping suddenly disintegrated to show Mustapha and Absalam. They advanced, pointing to me and saying, "Stop him. A man listens to his beloved. The curse of the kings will come upon you."

I awoke shouting something and sat up in bed. I thought, When we come back I will change this house. I will have the dark shrubs taken away; I will plant beautiful flowering shrubs, lovely blue and pink hydrangeas and red fuschias dripping their bells from the hedges. We will replace the darkness with the brightest of colors. In that mood I slept.

NEXT morning Tabitha had a letter in her hand when I went down to breakfast. "Oh, Judith. I'll have to go away for a few days. A relative of mine is ill. I think I ought to leave at once."

"Today?"

"Yes. I'll get the ten thirty for London and go from there to Suffolk."

She left the table hurriedly. She seemed very embarrassed, I thought. Within the hour Jenner, the coachman, drove her in the jingle to the station.

I watched her go and I kept thinking what Nanny Tester had said. "He goes away and . . . she's called away."

I went upstairs to Nanny's apartment. She was standing by the window, her old-fashioned flannelette dressing gown wrapped about her.

"So she's gone," she said, "eh, my lady. Didn't I tell you?"

"How did you know?"

"Oh," she said, "I've seen it. I knew it was coming. She's the one he wanted. He took you for your money. That's it. And what for? So that they can go and dig up the dead. It's not right."

"Nanny," I said, "you're not yourself. Let me help you to bed."

"To bed . . . why to bed? It's for me to put you to bed, my precious."

"Do you know who I am, Nanny?"

"Know you. Didn't I have you from three weeks after you were born?"

I said, "You're mistaking me for somebody else. I'm Judith, Lady Travers—Tybalt's wife."

"Oh, yes, my lady. You're my lady all right. And a lot of good that's done you. I'd have liked to see you wife to some simple gentleman who didn't think more of digging up the dead than his own young wife."

I said, "Now I'm going to bring you a hot drink and you're going to sleep."

"You're good to me," she said.

I went down to the kitchen and told Ellen to prepare some hot milk for me to take to Nanny, who wasn't feeling well.

"You'd think she'd be better, now Mrs. Grey's gone," said Ellen. "Goodness, my lady, she does seem to hate Mrs. Grey."

On her way back to Giza House, Tabitha had to go to London. Tybalt was ready to return, so they came together.

I was uneasy. There were many questions I wanted to ask; but it was wonderful to have Tybalt back and he seemed delighted to be with me. He was happy and contented. The financial problems had been straightened out and we would leave for Egypt in March.

"Now," he said, "we shall be very busy. We must prepare to leave in earnest."

He was right. There was nothing to think of but the expedition.

Chapter V

The Chephro Palace stood majestic, golden-colored, aloof from the village. I was astounded that the great Hakim Pasha should have put so much magnificence at our disposal.

Several members of the working party had gone on ahead of us, taking a good deal of the equipment along. Hadrian, Evan and Theodosia, Terence Gelding and Tabitha had sailed from South-

ampton with Tybalt and me, but as Tybalt had some business to settle in Cairo, he and I had left the ship at Port Said.

I had read and imagined a great deal about Egypt; yet none of my fancies could compare with the reality, and the impact upon me was exhilarating, exciting beyond my dreams.

It was a golden land, dominated by a sun which could be merciless. One was conscious of thousands of years of antiquity. When I saw a goatherd in his long white robes I could believe I was far back in the days of the Old Testament. The country held me spellbound; I knew that here anything could happen—the most wonderful things, the most fearful. It was both beautiful and ugly; it was stimulating, thrilling and sinister.

We had stayed at a small hotel which looked out onto the Nile. From my window I could see the riverbank and the golden Muqattam Hills; the men in their white robes and sandaled feet; the disdainful camels picking their dainty ways. I listened in wonder when I first heard the muezzin from the top of his minaret calling the people to prayer; and I was amazed to see them stop wherever they were and pay homage to Allah.

I shall never forget the day Tybalt took me into the *suqs*. I was constantly aware of the scrutiny of the dark-eyed people, the jostling crowds, the mingling smells of dung and perfume, the side-glances from veiled dark eyes.

The shops were like huts open to the street. We paused at one where a man worked, cutting and engraving stones. On a shelf inside the hut was an array of rings and brooches.

"You must have a scarab ring," said Tybalt. "It'll bring you luck in Egypt." He selected one. "This is tourmaline," he said. "The carved beetle was sacred to the ancient Egyptians."

The eyes of the shopkeeper shone at the prospect of a sale. I listened to him and Tybalt as they bargained over the price, while several small children came around to watch. They could not take their eyes from Tybalt and me. I suppose we appeared very strange to them.

Tybalt showed me hieroglyphs delicately carved around the beetle. He translated: "'Allah be with you.' There could not be

greater good luck than that. It is what every man should give to the one he loves when she first comes to this land."

I slipped the ring on my finger. There were delighted cries of approval from the children. Tybalt paid the shopkeeper and we went on our way with his blessings.

Tybalt looked at my ecstatic face and pressed my hand with the ring on it. "If you could have a wish, what would it be?" he asked.

"That I could be as happy as this every day of my life."

THE next day we went out to the Pyramids—one of the remaining wonders of the ancient world. Mounted somewhat precariously on my camel, I felt exhilarated, and I could see how much Tybalt enjoyed my excitement. One hundred thousand men had toiled for twenty years to achieve the Pyramid of Cheops, Tybalt had told me; the stone had been quarried from the nearby Muqattam Hills and dragged across the desert. I felt, as everyone else must on witnessing this fantastic sight, speechless with wonder.

When we dismounted I entered the Pyramid of Cheops and followed Tybalt up the steep passage to the burial chamber, where the pharaoh's red granite sarcophagus was displayed. Then we returned, perched high on our reluctant beasts of burden.

That night we dined at a small secluded table. I had piled my dark hair high on my head and wore a green velvet gown which I had had made by Sarah Sloper before I left home. I kept touching the pink tourmaline ring on my finger, marveling afresh at the wonderful thing that had happened to me. Tybalt had told me later that it was the gift of a lover, that good fortune might preserve in a strange land the one he loved best. But there flashed into my mind the thought that even if my fortune had been a deciding factor in Tybalt's wishing to marry me, I didn't care. I would make him love me for myself alone.

Tybalt leaned forward and took my hand. "What are you thinking, Judith?" he asked.

"About the wonder of everything. You look suddenly sad, Tybalt. Are you?"

"Only because you won't go on being excited about everything. You'll become blasé. I shouldn't like that."

"I don't believe I ever would."

"Familiarity, you know, breeds contempt—or at least indifference. I feel since we have been together in Cairo that things which I have seen before seem fresh, more interesting, more wonderful. That's because I'm seeing them through your eyes."

It was indeed an enchanted night.

The kabobs served by the silent-footed men in their long white robes tasted delicious. I couldn't believe they were simply pieces of lamb on skewers which had been grilled over charcoal. The *tahina* sauce into which the meat was dipped was made of sesame seeds, oil, white sauce and a hint of garlic.

Afterward we ate *esh es seraya*, which was a delicious mixture of honey, bread crumbs and cream. We drank rose water and grenadine with fruit and nuts in it, called *khoshaf*.

It was an evening never to be forgotten. After dinner we sat on the terrace and looked out on the Nile, while we drank Turkish coffee and nibbled Turkish delight.

The stars seemed to hang low in that indigo sky, and before us flowed the Nile down which Cleopatra had once sailed in her royal barge. I wished that I could hold those moments and go on living them again and again.

Tybalt said, "You have a great capacity for happiness, Judith."

"Perhaps," I answered. "If so, I am fortunate. It means that I can enjoy to the full the happiness that comes my way."

And I wondered then if just as I felt this intensity of pleasure I could feel sorrow with an equal fervor. I would not brood on it, though—not on this night of nights on the romantic banks of the Nile.

THE next day we arrived at the Chephro Palace and found the rest of the party already settled in. I stood in the entrance hall and gazed with wonder at the beautiful staircase in white marble. The floor was covered in mosaics of the most exquisitely blended colors, and the stained glass in the windows depicted the sea

journey of the dead through hideous dangers until they came under the protection of the sun-god Amen-Ra.

Tabitha came to welcome us. She looked at Tybalt with shining eyes. "I'll take you to your room," she said to me. "Then you can explore the rest of the palace—and I daresay you will want to look at the site, Tybalt."

"You're right," Tybalt said.

"You'll have a meal, then. Mustapha and Absalam are working in the kitchens, so they will mix a little English cooking with the Egyptian." She led the way up that imposing staircase and we went along a gallery, the walls of which were decorated with mosaic patterns similar to those in the floor of the hall. These were figures, always in profile, usually of some pharaoh giving gifts to a god. On the ceiling was engraved Amen-Ra; his symbols were the hawk and the ram. Below was his son Osiris, god of the under-world, who judged the dead when they had made their journey along the river. Isis was there, the great goddess beloved of Osiris, and their son Horus.

"The figures are beautifully done," I said.

"It would be an insult to the gods if they had not been," added Tybalt. He slipped his arm through mine and we went into the room which had been prepared for us. I stared at the enormous bed standing on a platform. Mosquito nets festooned over it from the ceiling like flimsy cobwebs.

Tabitha showed us an antechamber with a sunken marble bath in the center of which was a statue; on the walls were mosaics depicting nude figures. A many-sided mirror reflected my image, and the frame of the mirror was studded with chalcedony, rose quartz, amethyst and lapis lazuli.

I laughed. "It is very grand. We shall feel like royalty."

"Hakim Pasha has given instructions to his servants that any of our complaints will be met with dire punishment. He regards his servants as slaves and expects absolute obedience from them."

"What happens to offenders?"

"Their bodies are probably found in the Nile. Or they may be deprived of a hand or an ear."

I shivered.

"That's Egypt," said Tabitha, laying her hand on my arm. "Now perform the necessary ablutions and come down to eat. Then I expect Tybalt will want some sort of conference."

When we were finally alone Tybalt said, "Well, what do you really think of it?"

"I'm not sure," I replied. "I wish it were not quite so grand, and the pasha does sound rather diabolical."

"He's quite charming. He and my father became good friends. You'll meet him soon and can see for yourself."

"Where does he live, then, since he has given us his palace?"

"My dear Judith, this is but *one* of his palaces. It may well be the most grand, but he would consider it quite ill mannered not to give it up to us. Now let's get cleaned up. I can't wait to hear what's been going on."

THE dining room with its heavy curtains was lighted by a chandelier which held about a hundred candles. We sat at the big table—Hadrian, Evan, Theodosia, Terence Gelding, and others whom I had not previously met but who were all practiced archaeologists, deeply interested in the task ahead. Tybalt sat at one end of the table, and I at the extreme end. Hadrian was on my right and Evan on my left.

"Well, here you are at last, Judith," said Hadrian. "What do you think of this *köfte?* Personally I prefer the roast beef of old England, but don't let anyone know I said that. Osiris might not grant me admittance to heaven when my time comes."

"You are very irreverent, Hadrian, and I advise you to keep such thoughts to yourself."

"There speaks our Judith," said Hadrian. "She has just arrived and is already telling us what we should do."

"What *have* you been doing while you were waiting for Tybalt?" I asked.

"Going over the site, getting the workmen together, arranging for this and that. You wait until you go out there and see the hive of industry we've created. And we do face difficulties," said

Hadrian. "You see, many of the diggers remember Sir Edward's death and believe that he died because he went where the gods did not wish him to."

"There is a certain amount of reluctance to continue?"

"It's there, don't you think, Evan?"

Evan nodded gravely. I looked along the table where Tybalt was deep in conversation with the men around him. Tabitha was sitting near him. I noticed with a pang of jealousy that occasionally she threw in a remark which was listened to with respect. I felt I had lost Tybalt already.

After the meal Tybalt went out to look at the site, and I was permitted to accompany the party. There was a fair amount of work going on in spite of the hour. The full moon and the clear air made it quite bright; it was easier to work at this hour than under the heat of the blazing sun.

Tybalt left me with Hadrian, who smiled at me cynically. "Not quite what you expected?" he said.

"Exactly," I said.

"Of course, you're a veteran of Carter's Meadow."

"I suppose it is rather similar, although there they were merely looking for Bronze Age relics; and here it's the tombs of the dead. It's really exciting."

"You have to learn to be cautious in this game. As a matter of fact, there are lots of things you have to learn."

"Such as?"

"Being a good little archaeological wife."

"And what does that mean?"

"Never complaining when your lord and master absents himself for hours at a stretch."

"I intend to share in his work."

Hadrian laughed. "Evan and I are in the profession, but I can assure you we're not allowed to share in anything but the more menial tasks. And you think that you will be?"

"I'm Tybalt's wife and I shall certainly learn all I can. I hope I shall be able to take an intelligent interest—"

He laughed at me. "You'll do that. But in addition to an in-

telligent interest, take equally intelligent heed. That's my sound advice."

"I don't really need your advice, Hadrian."

"Oh, yes, you do. Now! You're looking for Tybalt, I can see. He'll be hours yet. He might have waited until morning and devoted the first night in the Chephro Palace to his bride. Now had I been in his place—"

"You are *not* in his place, Hadrian."

"Alas! I was too slow. But now let me take you back to the palace. You must be ready to sink into your bath of chalcedony. I wonder what Lady Bodrean would think of it?"

"I should love her to see me in my state apartments—especially if she had lesser ones."

"That shows a vengeful spirit, Cousin Judith. You *are* my cousin, you know."

"The thought had struck me. How are your affairs?"

"Affairs? Financial or romantic?"

"Well, both, since you raise the question."

"In dire straits, Judith. The former because that's their natural state and the latter because I didn't know in time that you are an heiress."

"You don't think I would have allowed myself to be married for my money, do you?"

"Women who are married for their money don't know it at the time. You don't imagine the ambitious suitor begs for the honor of sharing a girl's fortune, do you?"

"Certainly it would have to be done with more subtlety than that."

"Of course. Come on, I'll get you back to the palace."

When we arrived Theodosia came into the hall. Evan was at the site, she told us, and Hadrian remarked that he would have to go back. "You can depend upon it, it will be the early hours of the morning before we return. Tybalt's a hard taskmaster."

Hadrian left, and I followed Theodosia. The room she and Evan shared was large and dark, and the floor was covered by a Bokhara carpet. She shut the door and faced me.

"Oh, Judith," she said, "I don't like it here. I hated it from the moment we came. I want to go home."

"Why, what's wrong?" I asked.

"You can *feel* it. It's eerie. But I can't tell Evan. Why can't they let the pharaohs stay in their tombs?"

"But my dear Theodosia, the purpose of archaeology is to uncover the secrets of the past."

"It's different finding weapons and Roman floors and baths. It's this tampering with the dead that I don't like. I dreamed last night that we found a tomb and there was a sarcophagus just like the one in Giza House. And someone rose out of it with bandages unraveling. . . ."

"I can't live that down, can I?"

"I cried out in my dream, 'Stop it, Judith.' And then I looked and it wasn't you; it was me. I thought it was a sort of warning."

"You're getting fanciful, Theodosia."

"But anyone could get fancies here. There's a sort of shadow of the past everywhere. This palace is centuries old. All the temples and tombs are hundreds and thousands of years old. Oh, I'm glad you've come, Judith. It'll be better now you're here."

I said, "Are you worried about Evan?"

She nodded. "I often think of what happened to Sir Edward."

I said, "Of course we get anxious, because we love our husbands. If we could only take a calm rational view we should see how foolish all this talk is."

"Yes, Judith, I suppose so."

"Why don't you go to bed?" I said. "You're not going to sit up and wait for Evan, are you?"

"I guess not. Goodness knows what time they'll come in."

I smiled at her, said good night and left her. I went along the gallery. How silent it was! The heavy velvet gold-fringed curtains shut me in and my feet sank deep into the thickly piled carpet. I stood still, suddenly tense. I was not alone.

There was the softest footfall behind me. I turned sharply.

"Absalam!" I cried. "Mustapha!"

They bowed. "My lady," they said simultaneously.

Their dark eyes were fixed on my face and I asked quickly, "Is there anything wrong?"

"Wrong?" They looked at each other. "Yes, my lady. But it is still not too late."

"Too late?" I said falteringly.

"You go home. You ask it. You are new bride. He cannot refuse his beloved."

I shook my head. "You don't understand. This is Sir Tybalt's work . . . his life."

"His life . . . It was Sir Edward's life, and then his death." They looked at me with deeply sorrowing eyes.

"Good night," I said. "I shall retire to my room now."

It was two o'clock in the morning when Tybalt came in. I cried out in pleasure at the sight of him and sat up in bed.

He came to me and took my hands in his. "Why, Judith, still awake?"

"Yes, I was too excited to sleep. I was wondering what you were doing out there on the site."

He laughed. "They've just been marking out the proposed areas and making general preparations."

"You are going on where Sir Edward left off?"

"I'll tell you about it sometime. Now you should be asleep."

But I was not ready for sleep. Nor was Tybalt. We lay awake talking for an hour.

"Yes," he said during the course of the conversation, "we are exploring the same ground which my father did. You know he was convinced that there was an undisturbed tomb in the area. Of course, the majority were rifled centuries ago."

"I should have thought they would have tried to keep the burial places secret."

"Up to a point they did, but there were so many workmen involved. Imagine hewing out the rock, and then all the transport that would be needed to bring the treasures into the tombs."

"And then the robbers came," I said. "It's odd that they were not deterred by the curse."

"Perhaps they were, but the fabulous riches found in the tombs might have seemed a worthwhile reward for damnation after death."

"Yet Sir Edward, who was working for posterity and not for personal gain, was struck down."

"My father's death had nothing to do with a curse. It was due to natural causes."

"Which no one seems certain about."

He kissed my forehead. "Foolish Judith!" he said. "I'm surprised at you."

We were silent for a while and then I said, "I have seen Mustapha and Absalam. They said I should persuade you to go back home."

That made him laugh. "It's such nonsense. The curse was a tale put about to frighten off robbers. But it didn't, you see. Almost every tomb that has been discovered has been tampered with. That's why it's the dream of every archaeologist to find a tomb which is just as it was when it was closed thousands of years ago. I want to be the first one to set foot in such a burial place. Imagine the joy of seeing a footprint in the dust which was made by the last person to leave the tomb, or a flower offering lying there, thrown down by a sorrowing mourner. Oh, Judith, you've no idea of the excitement this could give."

"We must try to see that your dream is realized."

"My darling, I'm so happy to have you here with me. You're going to be the perfect wife."

"It's strange that you should say that. Did you know that Disraeli dedicated one of his books to Mary Anne, his wife? The dedication said to 'a perfect wife.'"

"No," he said, "I'm an ignoramus—apart from one subject."

"You're a specialist," I said, "and knowing so much about one thing, you couldn't be expected to know about others. He married her for her money, but when they were old he would have married her for love."

"Then," said Tybalt lightly, "it must indeed have become a perfect union."

I thought, If that happened to me I should be content.

Then he started telling me of ancient customs, and I asked why the Egyptians had made such a fine art of the burial of the dead.

"It was because they believed that the life of the spirit went on after death. Osiris, the god of the underworld and judge of the dead, was said to be the first ever to be embalmed and this embalming was performed by the god Anubis. When a man died he became identified with Osiris, but to escape destruction he had successfully to traverse the mythical River Tuat, which was said to end where the sun rose in the kingdom of the sun-god, Amen-Ra.

"This river was beset by dangers, and no man could navigate it without the help of Osiris. The horrors of the river increased as the flimsy craft, in which the soul of the deceased traveled, progressed. Great monsters rose to threaten him; the waters boiled and were so turbulent that the boat was in danger of sinking. Only those who had led good lives on earth and were valiant and strong could hope to survive—and they only with the help of Osiris. For those who lived on, the tomb was their home. Their ka, which is the spirit that cannot be destroyed, would pass back and forth between the afterworld and the mummy lying in the tomb. That is why it was considered necessary to make these burial chambers worthy of their illustrious inhabitants, so that they might not miss the jewels and treasures they had enjoyed during their sojourn on earth."

I said, "I can understand why they would not be very pleased with intruders."

"They?" he said.

"There must be many people who believe in these gods. I think people like Mustapha and Absalam believe that Osiris will rise up and strike anyone who intrudes into his underworld."

"Superstition. My dear Judith, we are employing about a hundred men, and some of them are very poor. These excavations are a godsend to them."

"You take a practical view, Tybalt."

"You must too."

"I would, of course, if you weren't involved."

He said a strange thing then. "You love me too much, Judith. It's not wise."

It was the time of Sham El-Nasim, which celebrates the first day of spring. At home it would be Eastertime, I thought, and I pictured Dorcas and Alison helping Sabina decorate the church with daffodils and other spring flowers.

The days since my arrival had disappointed me because I had seen so little of Tybalt. He spent every possible moment at the site. I longed to accompany him, but he explained that although when there was work which I could do I should be allowed to participate, that time was not yet.

Theodosia and I were together a good deal and we often took drives in the little horse-drawn traps called *arabiyas*. Sometimes we were driven away from the town and we saw the fellahin working in the fields with oxen and buffaloes.

Other times we would go shopping together in the *suq*. One day we came upon a shop where a young girl sat, bent over a piece of leather on which she was embossing a design. We paused, and she stopped work to regard us intently out of enormous eyes made to look even larger by the heavy application of kohl.

She said in tolerable English, "You ladies like?" She indicated a row of slippers, bags and wallets into which the soft embossed leather had been made.

We tried on the slippers and studied the bags, and the outcome was that I bought a pair of oyster-colored slippers with a blue pattern and Theodosia a bag with a pale red pattern.

The girl was delighted with her sale, and after that we often stopped at her shop. We learned that her name was Yasmin and that she had a friend who dug for the expedition.

Whenever I passed the shop I always looked for her slight figure bent over her work. For me she was part of the life of the *suq*.

In the early mornings or late afternoons we would take a trip in one of the boats up the Nile and see the women washing their clothes and chattering together. We often marveled at the way

a woman could gracefully carry a great jar of water on her head without spilling a drop.

It seemed that in a very short time the scene had become familiar to me. I was frustrated, though, to be shut out from the main work. I wrote some of Tybalt's letters and kept some accounts, and had to be content with that, but I was determined that it should be only temporary.

Sham El-Nasim was a public holiday, and Theodosia and I strolled down to the *suq*.

The shops were closed, and the streets were different without the sounds and smells and activities of the vendors. Many people were making their way to the mosque. They were dressed in their best clothes, and although the women kept to their black, some of the men wore bright colors.

We paused to watch the snake charmer. We never failed to be astonished at the sight of the snake rising from the basket as the music drew it out. On this day of Sham El Nasim we noticed a soothsayer squatting on his mat near the snake charmer.

As we passed he cried, "Allah be with you. Allah is great and Muhammad His Prophet."

I said to Theodosia, "He is asking to tell our fortunes. Come on. Let's see what the future holds for us."

Two mats were set out on either side of the soothsayer. He beckoned to us, and rather self-consciously we sat down. I was aware of a pair of piercing hypnotic eyes fixed on my face.

"English ladies," said the soothsayer. "Come from over the sea."

There was nothing very remarkable in his knowing that, I thought; but Theodosia was pink with excitement.

He darted a look at her and said, "From over seas you have come, back over seas you must go." He lowered his eyes. "I see much that is evil. You must go back . . . back across the seas."

"Which one of us?" I asked.

"You both must go. I see men and women weeping, I see a man lying still. His eyes are closed, there is a shadow over him."

Theodosia had turned pale.

I said, "Who is this man you see? Describe him."

411

"There are men and women. They are underground . . . they disturb the earth and the resting places of the dead, and over them is the shadow. I see it clearly now. You are there . . . and you, lady. And now it is near you, and now it is over you."

Theodosia was trembling.

"The sun is bright overhead," went on the soothsayer. "And the shadow is gone. You are on a big ship, you sail away. There. I have seen two pictures. Allah is good. The choice is free."

"Thank you," I said, and I put coins into his bowl.

"Lady, you come again. I tell you more."

"Perhaps," I said. "Come, Theodosia."

He reached for the bowl in which I had dropped the money. As his bare arm emerged from his robes I saw the sign on it. It was the head of a jackal. That was the sign of one of the gods, I knew; but I could not remember which.

"The blessing of Allah fall on you," he muttered, and sat back on his mat, his eyes closed.

As TYBALT was at the site with several of the party, I went to bed early and was asleep almost at once. An hour or so later I awoke. I started up in terror because I saw a shadowy shape looming up beside my bed.

"It's all right, Judith."

"Tabitha!"

The candle which she carried shone with a faint light. "It's Theodosia. She's had some ghastly nightmare. I wish you'd come in and comfort her. She seems quite distraught."

I leaped out of bed and put on a dressing gown, and we went along to Theodosia's room. She was lying on her back, staring up at the ceiling. I sat down beside her bed. "What on earth happened, Theodosia?"

"I had an awful dream. The soothsayer was there and there was something in black robes, like a great bird with a man's face. It was the angel of death."

"It was that old fortune-teller," I said to Tabitha. "He was just trying to frighten us."

"What did he say?" asked Tabitha.

"He talked a lot of nonsense about a dark shadow hovering over us. Theodosia took it all too seriously."

"You shouldn't, Theodosia," said Tabitha. "They do it all the time. And I don't mind betting that he said Allah was giving you a choice."

"That's exactly what he did say."

"He's probably envious of someone who is working for us. This often happens. When we were here last there was a man who was uttering evil prophecies all the time. We discovered that his greatest enemy was earning more working on the site than he was himself. It was pure envy."

This seemed to comfort Theodosia. "I shall be glad when we can go home," she said.

"These surroundings grow on you," prophesied Tabitha. "People often feel like that at first. I mean those who are not actually involved in the work."

She began to talk as she used to when I visited her at Giza House, and so interesting was she that Theodosia was considerably calmed. Tabitha told us how last time she had been here she had seen the celebration of Moulid en-Nebi, which was the birthday of Muhammad.

She went on to describe the occasion, and as she talked I noticed Theodosia's eyelids closing.

"She's asleep," I whispered.

Outside the door Tabitha paused and looked at me. "Are you sleepy?" she asked.

"No," I told her.

"Come to my room for a chat."

I followed her. Her room was beautiful. There were shutters at the window, and she opened these wider to let in the warm night air. Then she turned and lighted a few candles. "Now, tell me, Judith," she said, "does all this come up to expectations?"

"In many ways, yes."

"But not all?"

"Well, I thought I should probably have more work to do."

"It's a very skilled occupation. At the moment it is mainly work-men who are needed, but Tybalt was telling me that you are a great help in many ways."

I felt suddenly resentful that Tybalt should discuss me with her. She seemed to sense my feelings, for she said quickly, "Tybalt does confide in me now and then. It's because I'm such a friend of the family. You are of the family now, and because of this I was saying to Tybalt that you should know the truth about me."

"What should I know about you?" I asked.

"What only Tybalt and his father knew in their household. When I took the post of companion to Sir Edward's wife, we thought it best that I should be known as a widow. But that is not the case. I have a husband, Judith."

"But . . . where is he?"

"He is in a mental home."

"Oh, I see. I'm sorry."

"You will remember that I went to Suffolk before we left. I had had a call because my husband had taken a sudden turn for the worse."

"He died?" I asked.

A hopeless expression came into her eyes. "He recovered," she said.

"It must be a great anxiety for you."

"A perpetual anxiety. He is well cared for, in the best possible hands. But it is futile to visit him. He does not know me. It brings no pleasure to him and only great unhappiness to me."

"I'm sorry," I said.

She brightened. "Well, they say we all have our crosses to bear. Mine has been a heavy one. But since I came into the Travers household I have been happier than I ever dreamed of being."

"Thank you for telling me. Was it always so, from the time you married him? You cannot have been married so many years. You are very young."

"I am thirty," she said. "I was married at eighteen. It was a marriage arranged for me. My people thought it was a great chance for me because my husband was wealthy compared with

415

my family. Even at the time of our marriage he was a dipso-maniac. It grew steadily worse, and when he became violent he was put away. I had met Sir Edward when he lectured on ar-chaeology to amateurs, and we became friendly. Then he offered me a post in his household as companion to his wife. It was a great help to me."

"You will stay with us?"

"As long as I am allowed to."

"That will be as long as you wish."

She came to me then and kissed me on the forehead. I was moved by the gesture; and as I drew away from her I saw the brooch at her throat. It was a scarab in lapis lazuli.

"I see you have a scarab brooch."

"Yes, it was given to me by . . . a friend . . . when I first came to Egypt." I saw that her fingers were trembling as she touched the brooch.

When I went back to my room I could not sleep. Memories from the past intruded into my mind. I remembered walking over to Giza House when I was a companion to Lady Bodrean and seeing Tabitha and Tybalt at the piano. I thought of their arriving home together after she had been called away; and echoes from Nanny Tester's revelations kept coming back to me. I wondered who had given her the scarab brooch. Was it Tybalt? Then a hor-rible thought crept into my mind. If Tabitha had been free, would Tybalt have married me?

A FEW days later Theodosia and I visited the Temple of Thebes, taking a donkey-drawn carriage and rattling on our way over the sandy soil. Here had been the center of an ancient civilization which had crumbled away, leaving only the great burial cham-bers of long-dead pharaohs to give an indication of the splendor of those days.

In the temple we examined with wonder the lavishly carved pillars, each capped with buds and calyxes. Wandering among them, we came face-to-face with a man who was clearly European. He said, "Good morning." His eyes were a tawny color

and his skin was tanned. He wore a panama hat pulled down over his eyes as a shield against the sun.

"What a fascinating spot," he said. "Do you live here?"

"No. We're with a party of archaeologists working on a site in the valley. Are you visiting?"

"In a way. I'm a merchant and my business brings me here. But I am very interested to hear that you are with the expedition."

"My husband is leading it," I said proudly.

"Then you must be Lady Travers."

"I am. Do you know my husband?"

"I've heard of him, of course. He's very well known in his field." He lifted his hat. "We may meet again."

NEXT morning Theodosia and I sat on the terrace overlooking the Nile and talked. After a while she said to me, "Judith, I think I am going to have a baby."

I turned to her excitedly. "Why, that's wonderful news!"

A frown puckered her brow. "Fancy having a baby . . . here."

"Well, you wouldn't, would you? You'd go home. Besides, if you're not sure, it must be months away."

"Sometimes I feel we shall be here forever."

"Oh, Theodosia, what an idea! It'll be a few months at the most."

"But suppose they don't find this . . . whatever it is they're looking for."

"Well, this is a very costly business. I'm sure that if they don't succeed in due course, they'll know they aren't going to and then we shall all leave."

"But I'm frightened, Judith. I wish we could go home. I just long to see the rain. There's no green here and I want to be among normal men and women."

I laughed at her. "Yasmin would think the people in the *suq* were more normal than us, I do assure you. It's a simple matter of geography. You're just a bit homesick, Theodosia."

But she continued to fret; and when it was affirmed that she was indeed pregnant, I could see that this caused her concern.

Chapter VI

IT WAS the time of Ramadan—the month of fasting and prayer. I learned that this was the most important event in the Muhammadan world and that the date varied because of the lunar reckoning of the calendar, so that it was eleven days earlier each year. Tybalt told me that in thirty-three years Ramadan passed through all the seasons of the year successively; but originally it must have taken place during a hot season, as the word *ramada* in Arabic means hot.

It began with the rising of the new moon; and until the waning of that moon no food must be eaten between dawn and sunset. Only soldiers, babies and invalids were allowed food.

The aspect of the place changed with Ramadan. A quietness settled on the narrow streets. There was a three-day holiday, although the fasting went on for twenty-seven more days. Five times a day twenty shots were fired as a call to prayer. Ramadan meant that I saw more of Tybalt.

"One must never offend them on a religious issue," he told me. "But it's galling. I need these workers desperately at the moment." We went through some papers, and then he put an arm about me and said, "You've been so patient, and I know it isn't quite what you expected, is it?"

"I had such absurdly romantic ideas. I imagined myself discovering the entry to a tomb, unearthing wonderful gems, discovering sarcophagi."

"Listen, Judith, I'm going to take you to the site, tonight. I'm going to show you something rather special."

"Then you have made a discovery!"

"Not exactly. What I do think is that we may be on the trail of something important; maybe not, but I'm going to take you into the secret. We'll go down after sunset. Ramadan Moon is nearly full, so there'll be enough light, and the place will be deserted."

"Tybalt, it's so exciting!"

He kissed me lightly. "Not a word to anyone. They would think I was being indiscreet, or such an uxorious husband that I was carried away by my wish to please my wife."

I felt dizzy with happiness. When I was with him I wondered how I could ever have doubted his sincerity.

THE moon was high in the sky when we left the palace. The stars looked solid in the indigo velvet, and no slight breeze stirred the air; it was delightfully warm—a relief after the torrid heat of the days. We took one of the boats up the river and then an *arabiya* took us to the site.

Tybalt led me past the mounds of earth over the brown hard soil to an opening in the side of the hill.

He said, "My father opened up this tunnel." He took a lantern which was hanging on the wall and lighted it. Then I could see the tunnel, which was some eight feet in height. I followed him and at the end of the tunnel were a few steps.

"Imagine! These steps were cut centuries ago!" I said.

"Two thousand years before the birth of Christ, to be exact."

"How thrilled your father must have been!"

"It led, as so many discoveries have led before, to a tomb which was rifled probably three thousand years ago. He came through here into this chamber. Look at the walls," said Tybalt, holding the lantern high. "See those symbols? That is the sacred beetle— the scarab—and the man with a ram's head is Amen-Ra."

"I recognized him and I am wearing my scarab now. It will preserve me, won't it, in my hour of danger?"

He stopped still and looked at me. In the light from the lantern he seemed almost a stranger. "I doubt it, Judith," he said. Then his expression lightened and he went on. "Perhaps *I* can do that. I daresay I would manage as well as a beetle."

I shivered.

Tybalt said, "It's so awe-inspiring. We all feel that. The man who was buried here belonged to a world whose civilization had reached its zenith when in Britain men lived in caves and hunted for their food in the primeval forests."

"Who was the man who was buried here?"

"We couldn't discover. There was so little left. The mummy itself had been rifled. The robbers must have known that often valuable jewels were concealed beneath the wrappings. All that my father found here when he reached the burial chamber was the sarcophagus, the mummy, which had been disturbed, and the soul house, which the thieves thought was of no value."

"I haven't seen a soul house," I said.

"I hope I will be able to show you one, one day. It's a small model of a house, usually with colonnades in white stone. It is meant to be the dwelling of the soul after death."

We came to another flight of steps.

"We must be deep in the mountainside," I said.

"Look at this," said Tybalt. "It is the most elaborate chamber, and it is a sort of anteroom to the one in which the sarcophagus was found."

"And this is the tomb which was excavated by your father."

"Months of hard work, expectation and excitement, and this is what he found—just another empty tomb! But he discovered something else, Judith. I'm certain of it. That was why I came back. He must have found that there was another tomb here."

"Wouldn't you see the entrance?"

"It could be cunningly concealed. We could find nothing here that led beyond. But somewhere in this tomb, I felt sure, there was a vital clue. I may have found it. Look! You see this slight unevenness in the ground? There could be something behind this wall. We are going to work on it . . . keeping it as secret as we can."

"Do you think that because your father discovered this he was murdered?"

Tybalt shook his head. "That was a coincidence."

"It seems strange that he should die at such a moment."

"Life is strange, Judith." He held the lantern and looked down at me. "How many of us know when our last moment has come?" He put his free hand to my throat and touched it caressingly. "You are cold." He was standing very close to me. "What are you afraid of, Judith? Of the curse of the pharaohs, of *me* . . . ?"

"I'm not afraid," I lied. "I just want to be out in the air. It's oppressive in here."

"Judith . . ." He placed his hand over my mouth.

"Listen," he whispered. Then I heard it distinctly in the silence of that place—a light footfall.

"Someone is in the tomb," whispered Tybalt. He stood very still, listening. "Who is there?" he called. His voice sounded strange and hollow. There was no answer.

"Keep close to me," he said. We mounted the staircase to the chamber, Tybalt holding the lantern high above his head. There was no one there.

As we passed through the door into the warm night air my legs felt numb, and I was trembling visibly.

Tybalt turned to me. "Poor Judith. Come on. We'll get the *arabiya* and go back to the palace."

Everything was normal now—the river, with its strange beauty and its odors, the palace and Tybalt.

I could not understand what had come over me in the depth of that tomb. Perhaps it was the strangeness of the atmosphere, the knowledge that three thousand years or so before, a dead man had been laid there; perhaps there was something in the powers of these gods which could even make me afraid of Tybalt.

ON THE river side of the palace was a terrace. There I would find a spot in the shade and idly watch the black-clad women chattering together as they washed their clothes. One late afternoon just after siesta Hadrian came out and sat beside me. "It seems ages since we've had one of our little chats," he said.

"Where have you been all the time?"

"Your husband is a hard taskmaster, Judith."

"It's necessary with slothful disciples like you."

"Who said I was slothful?"

"You must be or you wouldn't complain. You'd be all agog to get on, as Tybalt is."

"He's the leader, my dear Judith. His will be the kudos when the great day comes."

"Nonsense. It will belong to you all. And when is the great day coming?"

"No one knows. By the way, did you know that we are to have a visit from the pasha?"

"No."

"He has sent word. A sort of edict. He will honor his palace with his presence and dine with us."

"That is interesting. I suppose I shall *have* to entertain him."

"You flatter yourself. In this world women are of small importance. You will sit with hands folded and eyes lowered and speak when you are spoken to—a rather difficult feat for our Judith."

"I am not an Arab woman and I shall certainly not behave like one. When is the great man coming?"

"Very soon. I've no doubt you will be informed."

A SUBTLE change had crept over the palace because the pasha was coming. One heard excited voices in the kitchens; floors were washed with greater vigor, and brass was polished until it looked like gleaming gold. The servants of Hakim Pasha knew that the tolerant reign of his guests was temporarily at an end.

Tybalt told me what we must expect. "He is the governor of these parts, one might say. He owns most of the land, and it is because he has lent us his palace that we are treated so well. He has made it easy for us to get workmen, and they know that to work well for us is to work well for the pasha. He was of great assistance to my father. I remember my father's taking him on a tour of the site. I expect I shall do the same. He was completely fascinated by everything he saw."

"And what will my role be?"

"Just to behave naturally. He is a much traveled man and does not expect our customs to be the same as his. I think you will be amused by his visit. Tabitha will tell you about it. She will remember when he came here to see my father."

I asked Tabitha and she told me that they had been apprehensive, but they need not have been, for the pasha had been goodness itself and as eager to please them as they to please him.

One day Tabitha and I went to the *suq*, and as we were walking back to the palace we saw Hadrian and Terence Gelding sitting on the hotel terrace. With them was the man whom Theodosia and I had met in the temple. Hadrian hailed us and we joined them.

"This is Mr. Leopold Harding," said Hadrian.

"We have met already," I said.

"Indeed we have," replied Mr. Harding. "It was in the temple, when we were sight-seeing."

"You two must be in need of refreshment," Terence said.

Tabitha and I ordered mint tea, and Mr. Harding told us that he was very interested in the excavations because his business was antiques.

"Are you interested in archaeology?" I asked.

"Only as an amateur, Lady Travers," Mr. Harding replied. "Handling objects—some of which are, mostly wrongly, said to have come from the tombs of the pharaohs—arouses an enormous interest. I wonder whether there is a chance of my being allowed to look round the excavations. Sir Tybalt has high hopes of discovering a hitherto undisturbed tomb, I believe."

"All archaeologists hope for that," replied Hadrian. "But it's going to be a long hard exercise. I feel in my bones that we are doomed to failure."

"I don't believe Tybalt could be mistaken," I said hotly.

"You are his doting wife," replied Hadrian.

I wanted to stop Hadrian from talking in this manner before a stranger so I changed the subject. "Have you really dealt with articles which were discovered in tombs, Mr. Harding?"

"One can never really be sure," he answered. "You must do me the honor of visiting my little storeroom. I haven't a great deal there, but some of my pieces are interesting."

We said we should enjoy that, and with an *au revoir* we left him sitting on the terrace of the hotel.

THE pasha's arrival was magnificent. He traveled in a carriage drawn by four beautiful white horses, preceded by a train of camels with bells around their necks.

He dismounted at the gate, where Tybalt, with some of the senior members of the party, greeted him. He was then taken into the inner courtyard, where he was seated on a special chair which was inlaid with semiprecious stones.

Several of the servants were waiting with sweetmeats and glasses of tea. Three glasses must be drunk—the first very sweet, the second even more so and the third with mint. The glasses were filled to the brim, and it was a breach of etiquette to spill any of the tea. We women did not take part in this ceremony, but out of respect for our European customs were allowed to sit at table. I was even accorded a place beside the great pasha.

He was clearly delighted with his reception and rather pleased to see the women. He studied us intently, and I think we all pleased him—Tabitha for her undeniable beauty, no doubt; Theodosia for her femininity—and myself? I certainly hadn't Tabitha's looks or Theodosia's fragile charm, but I did possess a vitality which neither of them had, and perhaps this appealed to the pasha, for of the three he seemed most taken with me.

Dinner went on for several hours. I noticed the expressions of fear on the faces of the servants as they proffered the kabobs and *köfte* to their master. He was served first, and I was appalled by the large quantities he ate.

The pasha led the conversation. He spoke glowingly of our country, our queen, and the boon that the Suez Canal had brought.

"Think of this great achievement," he said. "A canal one hundred miles long flowing through Lake Timsah and the Bitter Lakes—from Port Saïd to Suez. It has brought the British in force. People come here as never before. You British—what a flair for trade! Your Thomas Cook with his steamers up the Nile . . ."

I said that Egypt had much to offer the discerning visitor. Its ancient civilization was one of the wonders of the world.

"And who knows what else may be discovered!" he said, his little eyes alight with joy. "Let us hope Allah smiles on your endeavors."

When Tybalt expressed his gratitude for all his help, the pasha said, "Oh, it is right that I should place my house at your disposal.

My ancestors have amassed great wealth, and there is a story in the family of how we began to build up our fortunes." He turned to me. "Would you like to hear it?"

"I should very much like to," I told him.

"It will shock you. It is said that long, long ago we were tomb robbers!"

I laughed.

"That is the story that has been handed down for hundreds of years. Now I must expiate the sins of my fathers by giving to those who would open tombs for posterity."

"One day the whole world will be grateful to you," said Tybalt.

"So I continue to placate the gods," said the pasha. "I have even taken for my family sign the head of Anubis, who embalmed the body of Osiris when his wicked brother Set murdered him. Osiris rose again and I honor his sacred embalmer, and he gives my house its sign."

The pasha regarded Tybalt seriously. "The good Sir Edward suffered a great tragedy," he said. "This gives me much unhappiness. But you, Sir Tybalt, I know will find what you seek."

"It is good of you to say so," replied Tybalt.

"And then you will leave us, and take away with you these beautiful ladies." He bent toward me. "Why I could wish that you do not succeed." Then he talked to me about my impressions of the country. We had quite an animated conversation, and it was clear that although a few of my answers to the pasha's questions might have been somewhat unconventional, I had made a success.

The pasha was to continue his journey to another of his palaces by moonlight, as it was too hot to travel by day. Before he left Tybalt would take him to inspect the site.

While they were preparing for this there was a scream from without. I hurried into the courtyard and saw one of the pasha's servants writhing in agony. He had been bitten by a scorpion, and I shall never forget the terror in his face—whether for fear of the scorpion's sting or for having called attention to himself during the pasha's visit.

Before I had left England, Dorcas had supplied me with many

homemade remedies which she insisted were good for all the dangers I might encounter in a hot dry land. One was an antidote for wasp stings and adder bites, and I determined to try it on the scorpion's poison. I brought my pot of ointment and as I applied it I noticed the man had been branded on his arm with a sign I had seen before. He immediately grew calmer, and I am sure he thought there was some special healing power in that jar.

The dark eyes of his fellow servants regarded me with awe, and I felt like some occidental witch doctor. The pasha nodded and smiled approvingly. He thanked me personally for what I had done for his servant.

Half an hour later the pasha walked to the boat which was waiting to take him and Tybalt upriver to the site. The boatmen had decorated it with flags and flowers, and many people had assembled to watch. It was clear that not only the servants of the palace but the fellahin of the neighborhood lived in terror of the powerful pasha.

IT WAS not until early morning that Tybalt returned. I awoke at once, and he sat on a chair and stretched out his legs.

"You must be tired," I said.

"I suppose so, but quite wakeful. I had to make sure that all went as it should."

"I hope I was adequate."

"So much so that I believe he thought you would be an admirable addition to his harem."

I giggled. "Did you show him the new discovery?"

"It was necessary to do so. There had to be some explanation about why we were working from inside those subterranean passages. He was most interested, of course, and asked to be informed as soon as anything is revealed."

"Do you think that will be soon, Tybalt?"

"I don't know. We have found an indication that there is something beyond the walls of one of the chambers. Because of the inevitability that robbers would attempt to break into the tombs, one burial chamber was sometimes hidden behind another—the

theory, as you know, was that the robbers having found one tomb would believe that was all to be discovered and fail to find the more important site behind it." He frowned. "There was one rather disturbing incident during the tour. You remember when we heard a footstep in the passageway?"

"Yes, I do." The terror which had overtaken me then came back to me clearly.

"It happened again," said Tybalt, "although we saw no one."

"Someone might have hidden in the deep pit under that rather fragile wooden bridge you've put up. Did the pasha hear it?"

"He said nothing. He probably thought it was one of the party."

"What happened to the young man who was stung by the scorpion?"

"He seems to have made a miraculous recovery, thanks to you. You'll have a reputation as a sorceress if you're not careful."

"What a success I am! The pasha contemplates offering me a place in his harem, and I am possessed of strange powers which I keep enclosed in a jar. I can see I'm a wild success. I hope I find the same favor in the sight of my true wedded lord."

"I can give you complete assurance on that point."

"So much so that I may one day be allowed to share in your work? I mean the *real* work, not letters and accounts."

"I know you always imagined yourself being in the thick of everything. It can't be, Judith. Not yet."

"What of Tabitha?"

"What of her?"

"You seem often to talk of your work to *her*."

There was a brief silence. Then he said, "She has had some experience. She worked a great deal with my father. Be patient, my dearest."

When he used that term of endearment my happiness overcame my frustration. If I was indeed his dearest I was content.

"How long shall we be here?" I asked briskly.

"Are you tired of it already?"

"Indeed not. It grows more fascinating every day. I was thinking of Theodosia. She longs to go home."

"She is too timid for an expedition of this sort. In any case, she can go home at any time."

"And Evan?"

"His job is here. He's a good archaeologist, really—though inclined to theorize rather than practice."

"And you do both?"

"Of course."

Soon I fell asleep, but I doubt whether Tybalt did. I suspect he lay awake thinking of the day he was going to break through into a tomb undisturbed for three thousand years.

IN THE early morning Theodosia and I went into the *suq*. Her desire to go home was becoming an obsession, as were her fears of bearing a child. I did all I could to comfort her.

"Where would you go?" I asked. "To Keverall Court and your mother?"

She grimaced. "Well, at least there wouldn't be this frightful heat; and Sabina would be there."

Sabina was going to have a baby too, but her reactions were quite different from Theodosia's, according to her letters. It seemed that she was delighted and so was Oliver. Sabina had written that Dorcas and Alison were wonders. "They seem to know *everything* about babies—although why they should is a bit of a puzzle, except, of course, that they had you when you were little." I felt a twinge of nostalgia as I thought of them all.

Theodosia and I went past the shop where Yasmin usually sat, but in her place was a young boy working the leather.

"Where is Yasmin today?" I asked.

He looked up. His eyes were furtive and it was clear he could not understand me.

"I daresay," I said to Theodosia, "she is taking a day off."

We walked on, and as we passed the soothsayer murmured, "Allah be with you." He looked so hopeful, and the bowl in which payment was placed was empty. So once again we sat on the mats beside him.

He shook his head and said, "The shadow grows big, my ladies."

"Oh, yes," I replied lightly, "you told us about that before."

"It flies overhead like a bat, a big black bat."

"Sounds rather unpleasant," I said.

He turned to Theodosia. "And my lady has been blessed. My lady is fertile. Go back to the green land, lady. There you will be safe."

Theodosia was very upset by this and rose, and the soothsayer leaned toward me. His brown fingers gripped my wrist like claws. "You great lady. You say go and they will listen."

I looked down at his arm and there I saw the brand again—the head of the jackal. I said, "You tell me nothing but of this big bat who hovers around. Is there nothing else?"

"Allah offers much. Great joy, many sons and daughters, a big fine mansion, but in your green land. Not here. The bat is very close now. It can be too late for you . . . and for this lady."

I put money in the bowl and thanked him.

Theodosia was trembling. I slipped my arm through hers. "It's a pity we listened to that nonsense," I said.

Chapter VII

TYBALT was certain he was on the right track. Those working inside the tomb had found indisputable evidence that there was another chamber behind the wall which they were now excavating.

"It will be a bitter disappointment," he said, "if someone has already been there."

"But if it has been hidden behind the other tomb, can they have been?"

"There may be another entrance. Unfortunately, there'll be a delay for the Feast of the Nile, which is imminent. There is no definite date for the feast. It will depend on the state of the river."

"Why?"

"Well, because it's a sort of placating ceremony. It dates back thousands of years to when the Egyptians worshipped the river. They believed it had to be pacified so that it would not overflow

and carry whole villages away. This has happened frequently and still does."

"Do they really think that if they perform this ceremony the river will stay within its bounds?"

"It's become a custom, a reason for a holiday. In the past there was a human sacrifice. Now they throw a doll into the river, often a life-size, beautifully dressed doll. This represents the virgin who used to be thrown into the river in the old days."

ON THE day of the feast the banks of the river were very crowded. There were *arabiyas* everywhere. Some people traveled on camels, whose bells tinkled gaily, as had those on the necks of the pasha's beasts.

In the *suqs* most of the shops were closed, but there was the smell of cooking. There were for sale little flat cakes made of fried flour and honey, *herisa* loaves, and mutton or beef sizzling over a fire of camel dung. There were the lemonade sellers in red striped gowns, and stalls where glasses of mint tea were sold. The beggars had come in from far and wide. They often raised their eyes to heaven, their begging bowls before them, calling out for baksheesh and asking Allah to bless those who did not pass them by.

Our party viewed the colorful scene from the highest terrace of the palace. I sat beside Tybalt, with Evan and Theodosia on my left. Soon Hadrian joined us. I thought he looked a little strained and wondered if he were finding the heat oppressive.

The river looked red because it had swallowed some of the rich land upstream. The people shuddered as they pointed out the blood color. Was the river in a vengeful mood?

From the minaret rang out the voice of the muezzin: "Allah is great and Muhammad His Prophet."

There was an immediate silence as men and women stood where they were, heads bent in prayer.

Then we watched the procession wend its way to the river's edge. Banners were held aloft, and in the midst of the crowd was a carriage in which reclined the life-size doll which represented the sacrificial virgin.

I stared at the doll. She was lying back in her carriage seat, her eyes closed, exactly like a young girl, with a yashmak hiding the lower part of the face. About her wrists were silver bracelets, and she was dressed in a magnificent white robe. I could not believe that she was not a real girl; and there was something familiar about her too. The procession passed on.

"What a lifelike doll," said Hadrian.

"It has to be as realistic as possible, I suppose," I said. "It reminds me of someone. I know! Little Yasmin, the girl who made my slippers."

"Of course," said Theodosia. "That's who I was thinking of! Look."

We watched as the doll was lifted high and thrown into the seething waters of the Nile. It was tossed about, and when it finally sank there was a long-drawn-out sigh. The angry god had accepted the virgin. Now we could expect the river to keep within its banks. There would be no flooding of the land.

GIFTS arrived at the palace—a tribute from the pasha and an indication of his goodwill. For me there was an ornament—in the shape of a lotus flower made of pearls and lapis lazuli. Both Theodosia and Tabitha had received similar ones.

Tybalt laughed when he saw them. "Yours is the most elaborate," he told me. "You are obviously the favored one. That's the sacred flower of Egypt and symbolizes the awakening of the soul."

"I must write a fitting letter of appreciation," I replied.

Theodosia's was of feldspar and chalcedony. "I wish he hadn't sent it," she said. "I fancy there is something evil about it."

Poor Theodosia was having a miserable time. She felt ill every morning, but it was the ever growing homesickness that was most alarming. Evan told me that as soon as this expedition was over he would try to remain at home. It seemed to him that Theodosia was indeed getting into a state of melancholy when a gift appeared evil to her.

As we took our usual walk to the *suq* she explained to me that Mustapha had been horrified when he saw the ornament.

"Oh, dear, they are not going to start that 'Go home, lady' talk again, I hope."

"He was afraid to touch it. He said it means something about your soul waking up, as it can only do when you're dead."

"What nonsense! The fact is that those two servants want to go back to Giza House. So they're trying to frighten us into persuading Tybalt to go home."

"Tybalt would rather see us all dead as long as he could go on looking for his tomb."

"That's an unfair thing to say."

"Is it? He drives everyone hard. He hates the festivals and holidays because they interfere with work. He just wants to go on and on . . . like a man who's sold his soul to the devil."

"What nonsense! They're following a clue inside the tomb. There's a possibility that they're going to make the greatest discovery of all time."

"Oh, I want to go home." She turned her pale face toward me and I was touched with pity for her.

"It won't be long," I said soothingly. "Stop brooding and seeing evil in everything. Enjoy the strangeness here. You must admit it's very exciting."

"I hated that river ceremony. I couldn't get it out of my mind that it was Yasmin they threw into the river."

"How could it have been? We'll go and see her now and you can tell her how the doll reminded you of her."

We wended our way through the crowds until we came to the leather-goods shop. A man was seated in the chair usually occupied by Yasmin. He rose, seeing us as prospective customers. I guessed that he was Yasmin's father.

"Allah be with you," he said.

"And with you," I replied. "We were looking for Yasmin."

A look of terror passed across his face. "Please?" he said.

"Yasmin. She is your daughter?"

"No understand."

"We used to talk to her almost every day. Why is she not here anymore?"

But he would only shake his head. I took Theodosia's arm and we walked away, and I thought of the doll which had been flung into the seething waters of the Nile.

WHEN we returned to the palace it was to find that letters had come for us. I took mine to the bedchamber, and while I was reading them there was a knock on the door. Tabitha came in holding a letter in her trembling hand.

She looked at me as though she were scarcely aware of me. "Tybalt . . ." she began.

"He's at the dig, of course."

"I thought perhaps . . ."

"Is anything wrong, Tabitha? Is it bad news?"

"Bad . . . I don't know whether one would call it that. It has happened . . . at last. My husband's dead."

"Oh, dear!" I jumped up and went to her. "Come and sit down. You've had a shock." I led her to a chair. "I suppose," I said, "it's what they call a happy release."

"He could never have recovered. Oh, Judith, you don't know what this means."

I said gently, "I understand. Let me get you some mint tea."

I rang the bell and in a moment Mustapha appeared. I asked him to bring the tea, and in a very short time it came. We sat there sipping the refreshing beverage, and she told me of the long and weary years when she had been a wife, yet not a wife. "It is more than ten years ago that he had to be put away, Judith," she said. "And now . . ." Her beautiful eyes were luminous. "Now," she added, "I'm free."

SHE was longing to talk to Tybalt, but there was no opportunity for that when he came in. He and the others had stayed late at the site and dinner was ready when they arrived. Immediately the meal was over Tybalt wanted to go back to the site. I watched Tabitha. She wanted to break the news to him privately.

She was waiting for him when he came home that night. It was past midnight. I watched him come in, but he did not come up to

our room. I guessed Tabitha had waylaid him. An hour passed and still he did not come.

I asked myself why it should take so long for her to tell him what had happened. Insidious little thoughts like niggling worms, and as obnoxious, crept in and out of my mind. I kept thinking

of Nanny Tester's ominous words. She had been rambling in her mind, but they *had* come back together on that occasion. I remembered seeing them at the piano. They had looked like lovers then, I had thought. But if Tybalt had been in love with Tabitha why had he married me? Because Tabitha was not free?

A wild rage rose within me. I loved Tybalt absolutely. My life had no meaning without him.

I heard a footstep outside the door and then Tybalt came in. I closed my eyes, feigning sleep, because I could not trust myself to speak. I was afraid that if I confronted him with my doubts and fears I might find them confirmed.

He sat down in a chair and remained deep in thought. It must have been an hour that he sat there. And I knew he was thinking, Tabitha is free.

WHY does everything seem different with the rising of the sun? It only had to appear, and fears which had seemed overpowering by night began to evaporate.

How foolish I was! Tybalt loved me. He had made that clear. But at the same time it was possible for him to have affection for others, as he undoubtedly had for Tabitha. She had been a member of his household before I had, a friend of the family, so naturally her affairs would be of deep concern to him.

I could see it all clearly in daylight and I laughed at myself.

Theodosia was not feeling well that day, and Tabitha offered to walk with me into the *suq*. Naturally we talked about her news.

"It seems wrong to feel this relief, but I can't help it," she said. "It was no life for him in any case."

"I don't think you should blame yourself for being relieved," I assured her.

"One does, nevertheless. One wonders if there was anything one could have done."

I glanced at her. She looked different—younger. We passed the shop where Yasmin used to sit. The old man who was now in her place looked up and saw me, then dropped his eyes to his work.

The soothsayer spoke as we passed, and Tabitha sat down on a

mat beside him. "A great burden has been lifted," he said. "You are happy as not for a long time."

He looked up at me and touched the other mat.

"You are loved," he said to Tabitha. "You should go away, far away to the land of the rain. You should go, and live in great joy, for you are loved and the burden has dropped from your shoulders."

Tabitha's color deepened.

I thought, He means Tybalt. Tybalt loves her and she loves Tybalt and she is free . . . though he is no longer.

The soothsayer's eyes were on me. "Go back, lady," he said. "The bat hovers over you like the great hawk. He is waiting."

"Thank you," I said. "My future is always the same." We put our money in the bowl and walked away.

EVAN came while I was sitting on the terrace late that afternoon. I always enjoyed watching the sunset. It fascinated me how the sun would be there one moment and then darkness would descend almost immediately, so unlike the long twilights at home.

Evan said, "I'm glad I found you alone, Judith. I wanted to talk to you about Theodosia."

"How is she today?" I asked.

"She's very depressed. I begin to think it might be best for her to go home."

"Couldn't you go with her?"

"I doubt whether Tybalt would be prepared to release me."

"I see."

"I suppose if it were imperative he would, but it's hardly that."

"Would she be willing to go home and wait for you?"

"I don't think she would want to go back to our university quarters. She could go to her mother, but you know Lady Bodrean never really approved of our marriage. I think Theodosia wouldn't be very happy at Keverall."

"Perhaps she could stay at Rainbow Cottage with the aunts, or with Sabina at the rectory."

"That's an idea. I know she doesn't want to leave me . . . but I will ask her." He seemed a little more cheerful after our talk.

THE NEXT DAY I was in the courtyard when a voice whispered, "Lady."

As I looked around a young Arab slowly emerged from the shrubbery.

"Lady," he said, "you have magic in jar." He held out his hand, which was bleeding slightly.

I took him into a little room which opened onto the courtyard and told him to wait. When I returned with Dorcas' ointment he said, "I am Hussein. I come because I want to talk with you."

I looked intently into his frightened dark eyes. "What do you want to say, Hussein?"

"I want to speak of Yasmin. You very kind to her. Now she is gone. I pray to Allah to bless her soul."

"You mean she is dead?"

A look of infinite sorrow crossed his face. "She was taken away. I loved her."

"Tell me what you know of Yasmin's disappearance."

"Lady, we love. But her father say no. She is for the old man who keeps many goats and sells much leather. But love is too strong, and we meet. Oh, this I dare not say. We have offended the pharaohs."

"Oh, come, Hussein, I daresay the pharaohs had a few love affairs in their time."

"I work inside the old tomb. I know when there will be workings, and when there are not we meet there—in a secret place."

"I understand. But you are bold, Hussein."

"The night the great pasha comes we are to meet. But Sir Travers says to me, 'Hussein, you are to take a message to Ali Moussa. He is a man who makes tools, and you are to bring back what I ask. I will give you paper.' So I must obey and I cannot go to the tomb. Yasmin went alone . . . and I never saw her again."

"But you talk of her as though she is dead."

"She is dead. She was thrown into the river on the day of the feast. To the sacred crocodiles."

"Crocodiles!" I cried. "Why do this awful thing?"

"It is because she is in the sacred tomb. It is the curse of the

437

pharaohs. Lady, you see pictures on these walls of the prisoners the pharaohs bring from their wars."

"I have seen men tied upside down to the prows of ships on these pictures, and others without a hand or an arm or leg."

"You have seen, lady, what happens to those who offend the pharaoh. They are given to the crocodiles. Sometimes they take only an arm, a leg . . . and the captive lives on."

"Now you are afraid that they will take you too?"

He nodded.

"I don't think so, Hussein. They would surely have done so by now. I think somebody who was there on the night she went to the tomb alone killed her. You should say nothing to anyone of your relationship with her."

"No, I do not. It was our secret. It is for this reason we choose such a place for our love."

"I am glad you came to me," I said. "Come again if you learn anything more."

He nodded again. "I knew you wise lady," he said.

I COULD scarcely wait to see Tybalt. But it was late afternoon when he came back to the palace. He went straight up to our room, and I found him sitting, staring dejectedly at the tips of his boots.

"Tybalt," I cried, "Yasmin is dead."

"Yasmin?" he repeated vaguely.

"She's a girl who made leather slippers in the *suq*. She was thrown into the river at the Feast of the Nile."

He looked at me in a puzzled way and I realized that he was not giving me his attention.

I cried out angrily, "A girl has been killed and you don't seem to care. Yasmin was in the tomb the night when the pasha came and—"

"What?" he said. I thought in exasperation, One only has to mention the tomb and he is all attention!

I said, "One of your workmen has been to see me. They had a meeting place in the tomb and the girl has died."

"A meeting place in the tomb! They wouldn't dare."

"The point is that the girl is dead. She was thrown into the river on the day of the feast."

Tybalt said, "They throw a doll into the river nowadays."

"This time they threw Yasmin. I thought I recognized her. Tybalt, what are you going to do about it?"

"My dear Judith, this is just a tale someone has told you. These people love drama. The storyteller in the *suq* always makes up stories of lovers who die for love."

"I'm sure he wasn't making this up. What can we do about it?"

He looked at me warily. "We are not these people's judges. Some of their customs seem strange to us, even barbaric, but we come here as archaeologists and consider ourselves lucky that we are allowed to do so. One of the cardinal laws is No Interference."

"In the ordinary way, yes. But this—"

"It sounds absurd to me. Even in the old days, when a girl was thrown into the river as part of the ceremony she had to be a virgin. It seems to me that your Yasmin was not likely to be that."

"Someone wanted to get rid of her."

"There are many ways of disposing of bodies other than such an elaborately public one."

"I think it was a warning."

He passed his hand wearily over his forehead.

"Tybalt, I don't think you are really paying attention."

He looked at me and said, "We have completed the excavation on which our hopes rested, and it has led us to a chamber which is a blind alley. It must have been put there to trick robbers."

"Tybalt!"

"Yes, all our efforts and all the money we have put into this have been wasted."

I wanted to comfort him; I wanted to put my arms about him and rock him, and there was nothing I could say which would not seem banal.

"So," I said coolly, practically, "this is the end."

I knew that he had completely forgotten Yasmin, indeed that he had scarcely given her a thought. He was scarcely aware of me. There was nothing on his mind but failure.

Chapter VIII

ALL next day everyone talked of going home. It had been one of the most expensive expeditions ever made and it had led to nothing—a blind alley in an already depleted tomb!

Theodosia was unfeignedly overjoyed. The thought of going home was a tonic to her.

Hadrian said, "Our great adventure shall soon be at an end. Has it cured you, Judith? You were so crazy to come out here, weren't you? And it wasn't quite what it seemed."

"I have found it fascinating."

"And you haven't minded being an archaeological widow?"

"I have always understood that Tybalt would have to be working most of the time," I said.

He came closer. "I wouldn't have neglected you like that, Judith. And all for nothing!"

I turned on him angrily. "A loyal supporter of your leader, I see."

He grinned at me. "You and I were always good friends, weren't we?" Then he was serious suddenly. "If ever you needed me—"

"*Needed* you!"

"Yes, my dear cousin. Even the most self-sufficient of us need others at times."

I thought, He *knows* something. I said sharply, "You had better explain yourself."

He seemed then to decide that he had gone too far. "There's nothing to explain. I'm just being my nonsensical self once again."

But he had planted seeds of uneasiness in my mind.

A few days later there was great excitement. Tybalt had picked up another trail. He talked to me jubilantly about it. "I have this notion that we have been working in the wrong place. There's something behind the wall which we have yet to probe."

"What if it's another blind alley?"

"I've got to try it," he said. "I won't give up until I have."

The effect on everyone was startling. People like Terence

Gelding and the senior members of the party were delighted. So was Tabitha. But poor Theodosia! She was so disappointed. So was Evan, I believed, but solely on Theodosia's account. He was a husband first, I thought, archaeologist second. And I knew that secretly I was making comparisons.

TABITHA told me that Theodosia's melancholy was upsetting Evan. "Tybalt is quite concerned. He says Evan is not concentrating on his work because he is continually worrying about his wife."

Why should my husband talk to Tabitha about this? Although I knew he talked to her about a great deal and I had come upon them more than once in earnest conversation, I felt resentful.

Tabitha, always energetic in smoothing the way for Tybalt, had the idea to make up a little party and go for a tour of inspection. "Let Theodosia see for herself how interesting it is," she said.

Tybalt gave his permission, and to my surprise Theodosia agreed to join the party. She genuinely wished not to worry Evan and was determined to put on a bold face in spite of her fears.

Leopold Harding was very interested in what was happening at the site. He had been sympathetic when we thought the expedition had failed, and had told Hadrian how pleased he was that hopes had been revived.

"He is longing to have a real look round," said Hadrian.

Hadrian and I had gone together to his storeroom. Some of his pieces were very valuable, and he had glowed as we admired one after another. He told us about the difficulty of getting goods shipped to England, and how glad he was when he was able to acquire jewelry or small pieces which he could carry himself.

Now Tybalt agreed for him to come. Terence Gelding was in charge, and the party also included Hadrian, Evan, Leopold Harding, Tabitha, Theodosia and myself. We went to the site in the evening, when the workmen were not there. I could never enter the subterranean passages without a thrill of excitement, so I guessed how Theodosia would be feeling. She was now noticeably pregnant and leaned on Evan's arm; but she seemed prepared to enjoy the adventure.

441

Terence lifted his lantern high and pointed out pictures of the gods and the pharaohs. I recognized the ram-headed Amen-Ra, and Horus, the hawk. There was Anubis, the jackal, which reminded me of the mark on the arm of the man whose wound I had dressed. I had also seen it on the soothsayer's skin.

Terence said, "This was the tomb of a minor potentate—a man of wealth, though, because even a secondary tomb cost a great deal. It could even be that several people were buried here."

"And made a sort of syndicate to pay for it?" asked Harding.

"Wouldn't they have been dead?" asked Theodosia.

"No," said Terence. "Long before their deaths, work was started on their tombs. In the case of a pharaoh, building went on for years and only stopped at the time of his death."

"So the longer he lived the better his tomb," Hadrian added.

We proceeded carefully along the narrow passageway, then into a chamber. "This is not the burial chamber," said Terence. "That would be farther on. This pit you see here might have contained something which was removed when the tomb was robbed. The wooden bridge was put up by us, to be used when we needed to cross the pit to get into the passage just beyond."

Theodosia, I believe in an endeavor to show Evan that she was unafraid, started to cross. Just then the bridge crumpled and Theodosia fell, taking part of it with her into the pit.

There was a terrifying silence. Then I heard Hadrian cry, "Good God," and Evan scrambled down, a drop of some twelve feet.

Terence took charge, gave orders and then climbed down and knelt with Evan beside the prostrate form of Theodosia.

It was like a nightmare—the gloom, the silence—and everything seemed to take such a long time. We improvised a stretcher, but bringing Theodosia out of the pit was no easy matter. I did all I could to comfort Evan. He kept saying, "It's my fault. I should never have let her come here."

When we finally got Theodosia back to the palace her child was born—dead—a five-month girl. Theodosia remained unconscious, and Tabitha stayed with her while I sat with Evan in an adjoining room, trying to comfort him.

"If she comes through this," Evan said, "I shall never bring her away from home again. You know how frightened she was. She *sensed* disaster. It's my fault."

Tabitha came to the door and beckoned us to come in. I looked at Theodosia's pallid face, clammy with sweat, and I knew she was going to die. Evan knelt by the bed, the tears running down his face, and Theodosia opened her eyes.

"Evan," she said.

"My love," he answered, "my dear, dear love."

"It's all right, Evan. I . . . I'm not afraid. . . ."

Then she was aware of me. "Judith. My . . . sister. It's right over me now . . . the black bat. . . ."

I heard Evan whisper, "O God."

And then Tabitha's hand was on my shoulder. "It's all over, Judith," she murmured.

The effect of Theodosia's death was dynamic.

Had not Sir Edward died? And now another death. This was the curse of the pharaohs! I had rarely seen Tybalt so affected. "I have set up an inquiry," he told me. "We have to find out how such an accident could have happened. The bridge had been strong enough to hold men and a certain amount of heavy equipment. Why should it have broken when a young woman attempted to cross it? There has to be a logical explanation."

The verdict of many was that the curse had made the bridge fall apart. It was the work of the angry gods. But if the gods were angry, why should they have chosen to wreak their vengeance on Theodosia, who had done nothing to offend?

Evan was beside himself with grief. He could not concentrate when one spoke to him. His eyes would fill with tears; sometimes he would talk of Theodosia and his happiness with her and the hopes they had shared for the future of their child. It was unendurable, and I spoke to Tybalt about it.

"Evan will have to go home. He can't stay here."

"We need him here," said Tybalt.

"Not in his present state, surely."

"It might be good for him to immerse himself in work."

"Everything here reminds him of what he has lost. He must go home at once."

"He will only mourn for his wife there. Work will help him to overcome his grief."

"I daresay you would find it difficult to understand Evan's feelings for Theodosia."

He looked at me oddly.

"Yes," I said, "I know you would. But *I* understand. At the moment he is dazed by his grief. We have to help him, Tybalt. He has lost what is most dear to him, more dear than anything you can understand. Work cannot save him. Nothing can save him."

My voice broke, and he patted my shoulder. I went on. "This is not a matter of archaeology. This is a matter of human decency, human kindness. I have to look after Evan . . . if others won't."

"Well, naturally we want to do what is best."

"Yes, I know, the work must go on. But I am going to write to my aunts and ask them to take him in."

I had not been able to cry until the moment I wrote that letter. Then the tears started to fall down my cheeks onto the paper, smudging the ink. I put down my pen.

If only Theodosia had never set foot on that bridge. But then it would have been someone else. What if it had been Tybalt! My heart missed a beat. Since we had come to Egypt my idyllic dreams had become tinged with doubt and fear.

I had always felt that Tybalt withheld some part of himself, while I had revealed myself entirely to him. Did he lack human warmth, and that need for others which makes us all so vulnerable and perhaps lovable? How much did he depend on me? How much did he need me?

Why was I tormented by these doubts—I, who had always believed wholeheartedly in my ability to mold the pattern of my life? Why was I failing now, when I had everything I had always longed for? The answer was that I suspected his feelings toward me and the motives which had led him to marry me. I believed that his work came before anything in his estimation, before me. Before Tabitha? I finally admitted that I was jealous.

445

I picked up my pen and finished writing. I knew Alison and Dorcas too well not to expect an immediate response.

When it came, Evan did not protest or express surprise. He seemed like a man in a dream . . . or a nightmare.

And so he left us and went to Rainbow Cottage.

AFTER the death of Theodosia, Leopold Harding attached himself to our party. Tybalt gave permission for him to look around the work site. He asked intelligent questions and evidently had read up on the subject or cross-examined Hadrian. He and Hadrian were constantly together and we all saw him quite frequently.

Soon Tybalt's depression vanished. He was sure that beyond the wall of the old tomb was the way into another and that success was imminent.

I heard often from home. Then one day I had a letter from Aunt Dorcas that disturbed me:

> Evan talks a little about it now. He is certainly better than he was on his arrival. . . .
>
> A memorial to Theodosia is being set up in the church. There was a service for her. People are talking as they did when Sir Edward died. Oh, dear, I do wish you would come home.
>
> Lady Bodrean asked us to Keverall Court for tea. She said it was odd how you, her companion, had now become a woman of considerable wealth. She was referring to the fact that you will have all, now that Theodosia is dead.

My heart began to beat fast. I had not thought of that clause in Sir Ralph's will until now. I had twice as much money as I had before, and Keverall Court would be mine on the death of Lady Bodrean. But I often wished I had never inherited a fortune. Then I could have been assured that I had been married for myself.

TYBALT had said that we must behave as though the tragedy had not taken place. It was the best way to quell the rumors. When we went out, though, people looked at us furtively. They thought we were mad to brave the curse of the pharaohs.

One day Tabitha suggested we go together to the *suq*, and I agreed. As we walked we spoke, as we always seemed to, of Theodosia.

"Don't brood, Judith," she said. "I have to stop myself doing that. Remember, I was the one who suggested the tour. If I hadn't . . . she would be here today."

A silence fell between us. I thought, Suppose it were not an accident? Suppose someone wanted to kill Theodosia? Who would gain from her death? I was the one who had become twice as rich.

When we came to the open market square there was noise and color everywhere. A flame swallower was about to perform and a crowd of excited children hopped around him; the snake charmer was sitting half asleep, his snakes in their baskets. We went across the square and into that now familiar maze of streets, past the leather shop where Yasmin sat no more, past the meat on sticks and the caldron of hot sauce—and there was the soothsayer.

He eyed us slyly. "Allah be with you."

I wanted to move on, but Tabitha hesitated. He knew, of course, of Theodosia's death.

"The little lady," he said, "she heed not my warning."

Tears pricked my lids. I could imagine Theodosia so clearly sitting on the mat beside him.

"I see it," he said. "It hovered. It hovers still." His eyes were fixed on me.

"I do not wish to hear," I said almost petulantly.

He turned from me to Tabitha. "A burden has dropped from you," he said. "There is happiness now. The obstacle will go and there is the reward if you are wise enough to take it."

I was about to put money into his bowl, but he shook his head.

"No. Not this day. I do not want baksheesh. I take only payment for service. I say, lady, take care."

When we walked away I was shivering. "He was right about Theodosia, and now he is warning me. You are the lucky one. You, it seems, are going to get your reward when you have removed the obstacle. Or is it already removed?"

"They talk," said Tabitha. "It's a kind of patter. But we must

447

not let them see that we are disturbed. That would be the very way to increase the rumors."

But I *was* disturbed, deeply.

When we returned to the palace I sat on the terrace alone for a while. Then I remembered that I had left Dorcas' pot of ointment in the little room which led off the courtyard. I went to fetch it, and when I came through the door I heard voices and paused.

Tabitha was speaking. "Oh, yes, it's a great relief to be free. If only it happened before. And now, Tybalt, it's too late. . . ."

I stood absolutely still. There was a ringing in my ears; the courtyard seemed to recede and I felt faint.

Too late! I knew too well what that meant. I had suspected for some time. Now I knew. I turned and ran to my room. There I lay on the bed hoping Tybalt would go back to the site. I did not want to see him—not yet—not until I had decided what I must do.

I remembered so many incidents. The manner in which he had looked at her when she sat at the piano; the warning words of Nanny Tester; the time when she had gone to see her husband, and Tybalt had discovered that he must be away at the same time.

She was beautiful and poised and experienced. She was the one he loved, the one whom he would have married had she been free.

Why had he married me? Why had he not waited for her?

It was all becoming very clear, too clear for comfort. His proposal had been sudden. He had asked me because he knew that I had inherited money from Sir Ralph. Now Theodosia's death had made me a very rich woman. Theodosia's death! Oh, no, I would not accept such absurdly wicked thoughts. And yet if I were gone Tybalt and Tabitha could marry, and who would inherit a rich wife's fortune but her widower!

I wondered how often he was with Tabitha when I believed him to be working on the site. I pictured them together. I couldn't bear these imaginings and yet I could not stop myself from creating them.

I felt young and inexperienced. I did not know what I could do. And of whom could I ask advice? I thought of Hadrian. We were fond of each other in a cousinly way, although he had hinted at

stronger feelings. We had protected each other when we were children; yet I could not tell even him of my fears, because I could not bear to discuss Tybalt even though my imaginings were becoming fantastic.

Chapter IX

FROM that time I began to feel that I was often followed. I was afraid to be by myself in a lonely part of the palace; footsteps began to sound stealthy, and in the silence I would find myself looking over my shoulder furtively. I had teased Theodosia, but now it seemed I had inherited her terrors as well as her money.

Yet I had an irresistible urge to come face-to-face with my fears. At the back of my mind was the thought: It is Tybalt. He wants to be rid of me. And on the heels of that thought was another: That's a lie. He loves another woman, but he would never harm you. You know that.

It was in this mood that I took an *arabiya* to the temple, alone. I told my driver to wait for me. As I entered the temple I was aware of the stillness all about me. I tried to give my entire attention to the carvings, but I was not really concentrating. I kept listening for the sound of footsteps, for the sudden swish of robes. I had a strange sensation that something evil was close to me.

I fancied I heard the sound of deep breathing, and I felt my heart thundering. The pillars of the ancient ruined temple were close together like trees in a forest. Someone could be standing close to me, yet I would not see him. At any moment murderous hands could seize me. I could be buried here in the sand. And the driver of my *arabiya?* A little money exchanging hands and not a word would be said about the lady he had brought out to the temple. It would be very simple.

Yes. Someone *was* close. A tall shadow had fallen across my vision. Someone was stalking me, but the pillars protected him from my view. Suddenly his hands would be about my throat and I would look up into his face. Tybalt's face?

I started to run, and when I emerged from the shadow of the pillars into the open I almost fell into the arms of Leopold Harding.

"Why, Lady Travers, what's wrong?"

"Oh . . . nothing. I didn't see you."

"I saw you come rushing out of the temple. I was just about to go in. Would you like to take a walk round with me?"

"Thank you, but I think I'll go back to the palace. I was a little overcome by the heat. My *arabiya* is waiting for me."

"I shall not allow you to go back alone," he said.

I was glad of his company on the ride back. He talked about practical matters, such as his arrangements for the dispatching of his goods. "It has been a very successful trip," he said. "Of course, one buys a lot of stuff which we call run-of-the-mill. But occasionally there are real finds."

"Have you any this time?"

"I think so . . . yes, I think so."

When we arrived at the palace I went to my room and lay on my bed. The fear still hung over me. Had I really been in danger? Or was I imagining this because I had discovered that my husband loved another woman and wanted to be rid of me?

DURING the last few days I had neglected the paper work I did for Tybalt. I did not want him to know that anything was wrong so I decided to put everything in order. There were papers which he had left for me to put away. I always filed his notes in a brief-case so that he could find what he wanted easily. He had told me that this particular case, which was of very fine sealskin, had belonged to his father. It was lined with black corded silk.

I had noticed sometime before that the stitching of the lining had come apart, and I decided to mend it now. As I thrust my hand inside the lining I realized that there was something there. I drew it out and saw that it was part of a letter:

. . . an expensive project even for you. Yes, I'll subscribe. I wish I could come with you. I would but for this heart of mine. Come round tomorrow. I want to talk to you about that plan of ours. I'm

leaving a tidy sum to your cause on condition that your son
marries my daughter. Those are the terms. No marriage, no money.
I've set my heart on this. Tell the boy what depends on it. A
daughter of mine and a son of yours! What a combination we'll
have for the grandchildren. See you tomorrow.   Ralph B.

I stared at the letter. "A daughter of mine and a son of yours!"
He had meant Theodosia at the time, but when Theodosia had
wished to marry Evan, Sir Ralph had offered me as the bride. He
would have explained to Tybalt: "Judith is my daughter. The will
stands if you take her." Tybalt had had to be bribed to marry me.
I had loved him for years. I loved him no less now. But I had had to
learn that he was ruthless where his profession was concerned.
And where his marriage was concerned too?

Oh, no. I was being ridiculous. Many people married for money;
loving one woman, they married another. But they did not murder.
There. I had faced it. Could I really suspect Tybalt and Tabitha
of such a criminal deed? Theodosia's premonitions of disaster
had proved to have substance. What of mine?

I could not stay in my room and decided to go down and sit on
the balcony. On the stairs I met Tabitha. "Oh, hello, Judith," she
said. "I was looking for you. I took a walk in the market and what
do you think the soothsayer told me this time? 'You will have your
bridegroom,' he said. 'It will not be long now.'"

"No black bat for you, then?"

"No, a husband, no less."

"Who is the bridegroom to be?"

Tabitha laughed and lowered her eyes. Then she said, "It is a
little premature to say. No one has asked me. Perhaps that's to
come." She was smiling as she passed on upstairs.

I DID not tell Tybalt about the letter. I hid it in a little box of
embossed leather which I had bought from Yasmin some time before. I mended the case and filed the letters in order.

Leopold Harding came to say good-by, and Tybalt told him that
he must visit us in England.

"I shall take you up on that," was the reply.

There was to be a conference at the hotel. I gathered that funds were getting low and it had to be decided whether the expedition could be continued.

While Tybalt was at the hotel one of the servants came to tell me that a worker from the site had hurt his hand and wanted me to dress the wound with my now famous salve.

When I went down to the courtyard I found Yasmin's lover. I took him inside. His hand was not badly hurt and had perhaps been grazed purposely.

He had something of importance to tell me. "Lady, you do not know why Yasmin was thrown into the river. Because she was found where she should not be, she was taken away and killed. I now have confession from the man who did it. He dared do nothing else. It was the order. And then there came another order, to cause an accident. There must be a warning because it is important to some that you go away."

"I see," I said. "And who gave these orders?"

The boy began to tremble visibly.

"Your secret will be safe with me," I said.

"I dare not tell," he said. "His servants are everywhere. Even in this house. You see their mark—"

"The jackal?"

"It is the sign of Anubis—the first embalmer."

I said, "The pasha?"

The boy looked so frightened that I knew I was right.

"So," I said, "he gave orders that Yasmin should be killed, and then that one of us should have a fatal accident on the bridge."

As I tied the bandage he said, "I tell you, lady, because there are orders that there should be more accidents, that all may know the curse is alive, and the kings are angry with those who defile their resting places."

I said, "Thank you for telling me."

"You will tell the sir and go away, and then you will be safe."

I said, "I will tell him."

I felt sick with horror. I went to my room to be alone, to think.

The pasha wanted us out of the way. Why? I thought of his sitting at the table, eating, paying compliments, assessing our feminine attributes. He had lent us his palace. Why, if he did not want to help us? To have us under his eyes; that was why. His servants waited on us and reported everything we did. It was becoming very clear.

I remembered suddenly that the soothsayer had the brand of the jackal on his arm. So he too was the servant of the pasha. Was it his task to predict death and disaster, to drive us away?

All the servants were the pasha's servants. There were only two we had brought with us, Mustapha and Absalam. And what of them? I must find out.

I rang the bell, and when Mustapha came I asked him to bring me mint tea.

I stood beside him as he laid it on the table. I said, "There is an insect. Oh, dear! It's gone up your arm." Before he could move I drew up his loose sleeve. The brand would be on the forearm, where I had seen the others.

My little ruse told me what I wanted to know. On Mustapha's forearm was the brand of the jackal. When he left I sat there sipping my tea and thought that if Mustapha was the pasha's man, Absalam must be also.

Sir Edward had died in the palace. He had eaten food prepared by Mustapha or Absalam and he had died. Now Tybalt was in danger as his father had been. We were all in danger. Sir Edward had discovered something in the tomb which had necessitated his immediate death. So far it seemed that Tybalt had not found what his father had, as no attempt had been made on his life. But if Tybalt were to make that discovery . . .

I began to shiver. I must see him. I must make him listen.

How quiet the palace seemed. I went to my favorite seat on the terrace, and as I sat there waiting for the conference to end I saw someone coming up the steps toward me. To my surprise it was Leopold Harding.

"I thought you had gone," I said.

"No, there was a slight hitch. Business, you know. I have just come from the hotel. I have a message from your husband."

I stood up. "He wants me to go there?"

"No. He wants you to meet him at the site."

"Then the conference is over?"

"I don't know, but he asked me to give you this message, as I had a few hours to spare before leaving. I said I would take you there. He told me the exact spot."

I said, "I'm ready. I'll come now." He led the way to the river, and we took a boat and went to the site.

The valley looked grim under the glare of the late afternoon sun. In spite of the windlessness there always seemed to be a fine dust in the air. The site was deserted because the men were awaiting the outcome of the conference.

We came to the opening in the hillside which was the way into the tomb, but to my surprise Leopold led me past that and into what looked like a natural cave. To my amazement there was a hole in the side of this cave.

He said, "Let me help you through here."

"Are you sure?" I began. "I have never been here before."

"Your husband has just discovered it. Give me your hand."

I stepped through and was surprised to find myself at the top of a flight of steps. "There are lanterns here," Leopold said. "I will light them and then we can have one each."

"Is this place connected with the tomb?"

"Oh, yes, but I don't think it was considered worth exploring until now." He handed me a lantern and I could see steps which had been cut out of the earth. I descended the steps, turned, and there facing us was a door.

"This is the spot," said Leopold Harding. "I'll go ahead, shall I?"

We were in a small chamber not more than eight feet in height. I saw that there was an opening ahead and I went toward this. I mounted three or four steps and called, "Tybalt, I'm here."

I went through a doorway into another chamber; this one was larger than the other. It was very cold. Then the first shadow of alarm touched me. "Tybalt," I called. My voice sounded shrill.

I said, "Mr. Harding, there is nobody here."

I looked over my shoulder. I was alone. I went down the steps, back to the smaller chamber. Leopold Harding was not there. I went back to the opening. The door was shut.

I called, "Mr. Harding. Where are you?"

There was no reply. I could see no handle, no bolt, nothing with which to open the door. I pushed it, then tried to pull it, but it remained fast shut.

"Where are you? Mr. Harding, where are you?"

No answer. Only the hollow sound of my own voice.

I knew then what it meant to have one's flesh creep. The awful realization had come to me. I was alone and only Mr. Harding knew where. Why? Who was he? Then I remembered my suspicions of Tybalt. Could it be that he had had me brought here to . . . to rid himself of me? Oh, this was madness.

I set down the lantern and banged my fists on the door. It did not give. How was it shut? How had it opened? All Leopold Harding had appeared to do was to push it and we stepped inside.

Tybalt must be here somewhere. It was better to look, to assure myself before I allowed this creeping terror to take a grip on me. I picked up the lantern and walked resolutely toward the steps, ascended them and was in the larger chamber. I must explore this. There might be a way out.

I held my lantern high and examined the walls of the chamber. I saw an opening and went through this into a corridor.

"Tybalt," I called. "Are you there, Tybalt?"

No answer.

I saw that the walls had been decorated. Rows of vultures were depicted there, their wings stretched as though they hovered. I reached yet another chamber and examined it with care. There seemed to be no outlet from this one either. I had come to the end of my exploration.

I felt my legs trembling and I sank down onto the floor. Now I knew a fear that I had never known before. All the warnings I had received, all the premonitions, they had some meaning. I should have heeded them.

But why should Leopold Harding wish to trick me? Why had he lied to me? I remembered coming out of the temple and running straight into that man. He had been the one who had stalked me there. He had meant to kill me. Oh, but this was a better idea!

Had Tybalt ordered him to do this—and who was he that he must take his orders from Tybalt?

I was sure something moved overhead. Something was looking down at me. I held up the lantern and saw a great bat, with enormous wings, carved on the ceiling. Its eyes were of obsidian and the light of the lantern made them seem alive.

I stared up at it, hideous, malevolent, and I said to myself, "What is to become of me? What does it mean? Why have I been brought here?" I fancied I could hear the soothsayer's voice: "The bat is hovering, waiting to descend."

I was so cold. Or was it fear that made me shiver so violently? I must move. I stood up unsteadily. I examined the walls. There *must* be a way out of this place. Now I could see the drawings on the walls more clearly. There were pictures of ships, and men tied upside down on their prows. Men without one or more limbs. And there was the crocodile who had maimed them, sly, ugly, with a necklace about his neck, and earrings hanging from his ears.

I thought, There is little air in here; I shall use what there is in a short time. The thought inspired me with courage. I would not sit here quietly and wait for death. I would find the way out if it was to be found.

I picked up the lantern and examined the walls again. I now saw some significance in the drawings. They were meant to depict the progress of a soul along the River Tuat. There was the boat on a sea from which rose hideous monsters, snakes with double heads, waves which enveloped the vessel; above was Osiris, god of the underworld and judge of the dead. He was giving his protection to the traveler in the boat and would conduct him through the turbulent waters of the Tuat to the kingdom of Amen-Ra.

Then I saw an alcove in the wall. As I examined it my foot touched something. I stooped down and saw a gleaming object.

A matchbox! A small gold box. What a strange thing to find in

such a place. It was no antique piece. I turned it over in my hand and I saw the name engraved on it: E. TRAVERS.

Sir Edward's matchbox! I felt dizzy with this discovery. Sir Edward had been murdered because he had been here. I was certain of that now. It would have been by the order of Hakim Pasha, but why did he want our expedition to end in failure? If the pasha were really interested in archaeology, why should he kill rather than allow discoveries to be made?

Because *he* wished to make them? I recalled vividly the pasha's plump face, his lips greasy from the food he was eating. He had looked sly as he murmured that there was a legend that his family founded its fortune on robbing tombs.

Could it possibly be that he continued to build up his fortune in this way? If that were so he would not be very friendly toward archaeologists who might expose him. Was that why he offered his palace, why his servants waited on us, why they had orders to frighten us away?

I knew I had the answer. I clutched Sir Edward's golden matchbox as though it were a talisman.

The lantern light grew dim. What should I do when the oil ran out? Would I be dead by then? How long could one survive in such an atmosphere?

"O God," I prayed, "help me. Show me what to do. Let Tybalt come and find me. Let it be that he wants me to live, not to die."

I could see the old church now with the tower, and the headstones tottering over some of the graves. "You can't read what's on them." That sounded like Alison's voice. "I think that they should be removed . . . but you can't disturb the dead."

"You can't disturb the dead." It was as though a thousand voices were chanting that over and over.

This was delirium, but I welcomed it. It took me away from this dark and fearsome place. It took me to the graveyard where old Pegger was digging a grave.

"And who's that for, Mr. Pegger?"

"It be for you, Miss Judith. You was always a meddler and now look where it 'as brought you . . . to the grave . . . to the tomb."

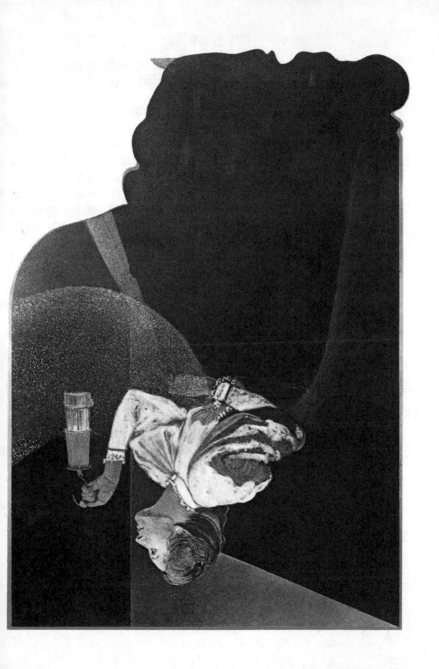

There were the echoing voices again. "To the tomb"—and I was back in this cold place of death and terror.

"O God, help me. Let Tybalt find me. Let him love me. Let it have been a mistake." I tried to get up, and as I stood I kicked something. It was the matchbox, which I had dropped. I picked it up, and as I did so the wall seemed to move. There was an opening, and I fell through it and was in a dark passage, facing a door. I banged on this door. I kicked it. I tried to open it. But it did not move. I stumbled along the passage. It was short and came to an abrupt end. I went back and sank down beside the door. There was nothing I could do—nothing but wait for death.

I lost consciousness for a time. Then in sudden panic I rose again. I cried, "Help me. Help me. God, Allah, Osiris, anyone . . . help me." I was half sobbing, half laughing, and I kicked and kicked with all my strength. And then . . . the miracle happened. There was an answering knock from the other side of that blessed door. Now I could hear noises beyond that wall. Someone knew I was here. Someone was coming to me.

I sank back. The noise increased. The door trembled. I sat watching it, the tears falling down my cheeks. Had I ever known such exaltation? Only when one is about to lose it does one realize how sweet life is.

The door moved. Then I was no longer alone. "Judith . . . "

It was Tybalt, as I had known it would be. He was holding me in his arms and I thought, I did not die of fear, but I shall now die of bliss.

"My love," he said. "Judith, my love."

Chapter X

DURING the days that followed I lived in a kind of daze. There were times when I was not sure where I was and then Tybalt would be holding me in his arms, reassuring me.

I had suffered a severe shock, and I was constantly told that everything was all right. I would lie still, clinging to his hand. But

when I dozed I would often awaken to find myself crying, "Help. Help. God . . . Allah . . . Tybalt . . . help me."

There could be few who had been buried in one of the tombs of the pharaohs and come out alive.

Who had done this to me? That was what I wanted to know. Where was Leopold Harding? And why had he taken me down into that underground vault and left me there?

Tybalt said, "We shall know in time. He has disappeared. But we shall find him."

"Why did he do it, Tybalt? Why? He said he was taking me to you. He said you had asked for me to come."

"I don't know. It is a mystery to us all. We are trying to find him. All you need think about now is that you are safe and I shall never allow you to be lost again."

"Oh, Tybalt," I said, "that makes me happy."

ONE afternoon Tabitha came to sit by my bed.

"I want to tell you something, Judith," she said. "You've been talking a great deal. Tybalt and I were shocked to know what was in your mind. You thought that we were lovers. My dear Judith, I love Tybalt, yes—I always have—as I would love a son if I had one. I came to the household, as you know, when my husband was put into a home. Sir Edward's wife was alive then, but ill. Oh, I know it was wrong, but Sir Edward and I loved each other. Nanny Tester knew it and spied on us. She was devoted to Sir Edward's wife and she hated me. When Lady Travers died she all but suggested that I had murdered her. Afterward, as you know, I accompanied Sir Edward on some of his expeditions. We would have married had I been free. But I was not, until it was too late. . . ."

"I understand now," I said.

"My dearest Judith, Tybalt realizes how lucky he is. He confided to me long before he asked you that he wanted to marry you. That was when you were Lady Bodrean's companion. . . ."

"I can see," I said, "that my wild and foolish imagination built up the situation."

"It was not a real one. It did not exist outside your imagina-

tion, remember that. I've something else to tell you too. Terence Gelding has asked me to marry him."

"And you've accepted?"

"Not yet. But I think I shall."

"You'll be happy, Tabitha. At last."

"And you will be happy too. I never saw Tybalt work so hard or so fervently as when they were pulling down that door. I have never before seen that purpose, that desperate need. . . ."

I laughed. "I do believe I must be of greater importance to him than a pharaoh's undisturbed tomb after all."

"I am sure of it," said Tabitha.

Later Tybalt said to me, "As soon as the doctor has seen you we are going home. I have asked Dr. Gunwen to come out and make sure that you are fit to travel."

"Then is the expedition over?"

"It's over for me."

"My poor Tybalt."

"Poor. When you are here, alive and well."

Then he held me against him. "At least," I said, "I found happiness that I never dreamed possible."

I DID not understand why Hadrian had not come to see me and so asked Tybalt to send for him. He arrived late in the afternoon, and I had never seen him so sober before.

"Judith." He took my hands, kissed me on both cheeks. "That! To happen to you. It must have been frightful."

"It was."

"The swine!" he said. "The utter swine. Better to have put a bullet through your head than that."

"Why did he do it, Hadrian?"

"That we shall have to find out. Thank God the conference ended when it did. About the time you and Harding entered that place they had agreed that there was to be an extension of a few more weeks. When we came back to the palace, one of the servants reported that he had overheard Harding telling you that Tybalt wanted him to take you to the site and that you had gone off with

him. Tybalt was alarmed. I think he has been more uneasy than he has let us know about a lot of things. We went to the site and searched for you. We began to think it was hopeless, but Tybalt wouldn't give up. And finally we heard the knocking."

"What *could* have been his motive? I believe he tried to kill me in the temple one day."

"But how could your death possibly profit him? There was Theodosia. Do you think that was Leopold Harding?"

"No, that was the pasha and his servants," I said.

"The pasha!"

"One of the workmen—that boy, Yasmin's lover—warned me. Yasmin was discovered in the tomb and they killed her. She was there on the day the pasha came to us. You remember the Feast of the Nile."

"Good God, Judith!"

"The bridge was tampered with because the pasha wanted a victim. It didn't matter who."

Tybalt came in and sat on my bed. He regarded me anxiously.

"You've been tiring Judith," he accused Hadrian.

I insisted that I was not tired. I told him we had been talking of Leopold Harding and looking for a reason why this attempt had been made on my life.

"Tybalt," I said, "I wonder if Yasmin's lover knows anything. It was he who told me that the pasha wanted to drive us away."

"We'll send for him," said Tybalt.

"On some pretext," I warned. "No one must know that he is suspected of helping us."

WHEN the boy stood before us I asked what he knew of Leopold Harding.

"He is friend of the pasha. Pasha give him beautiful things. Jewels, stones, furniture . . . all kinds. Leopold Harding goes away and comes back to the pasha."

"He is a servant of the pasha, then?"

The boy nodded.

"Thank you," I said. "You have served me well."

DR. GUNWEN ARRIVED. He said I was strong-minded and had suffered few ill effects, but that I should "get away from these foreign parts for a bit." I was well enough to go home.

Tybalt came to share the good news with me, and as I lay against him I thought of green fields. It would be autumn now and the trees would be turning golden brown. The apple tree in Rainbow Cottage would be laden with russets, and the pears would be ready for gathering.

I felt an inexpressible longing for England. I would turn Giza House into the home I wanted it to be. Darkness should be banished. I would have bright colors everywhere.

I said, "It will be wonderful to be home with you."

The next day, as I began making our preparations, I learned more of what had happened.

Mustapha and Absalam had disappeared. Had they heard that I suspected the pasha? There was more than that. The narrow passage which I had stumbled into was evidence that there was something beyond. It was the greatest discovery of the expedition and it was clear that Sir Edward had been aware of this on the night he died.

Tabitha told me that Terence was taking over the leadership because Tybalt had decided to come home with me.

I said, "No. I can't allow it." I stormed into our bedroom, where he was putting some papers together. "Tybalt, you're staying."

"Staying here?" He wrinkled his brow.

"Did you know that they are probably on the verge of one of the greatest discoveries in archaeology? That passage leads somewhere. You know it. It leads into a very important tomb."

"I think that maybe they *are* on the verge of a great discovery."

"Which was the purpose of this expedition that you had been planning ever since your father died."

He nodded.

"And he died because he got too close. He was there in that place where I was."

"And because you were there we have been led to this."

"Then it wasn't in vain."

464

"My God, I'd rather never have found the way."

"Oh, Tybalt, I believe that. But you're going to stay now."

"I'm getting ready to leave with you."

"I will *not* have it," I said. "I will *not* let you go now. You are going on. It's *your* expedition. When finally you reach that tomb, when you see the dust there undisturbed for three thousand years . . . and perhaps the footprint of the last person to leave . . . *You* are going to be the first. Do you think I would allow Terence Gelding to have that honor?"

It was a battle of wills. I simply refused to go. I could not be happy if we left at this stage. I made Dr. Gunwen agree with me and I finally won the day.

IT IS well known what happened. That was *not* the discovery of the century.

Tybalt's expedition found the tomb before the pasha's men, working from a different part of the hill, reached it.

What treasures there would have been! It was clearly the burial place of a great king. The pasha had been working toward it for some time; he knew that there was a way in through the chambers in which I had spent those terrifying hours; that was why when Sir Edward discovered it he had been murdered.

Alas, for Tybalt's great ambition. There was the sarcophagus, the mummy of the pharaoh, but robbers—perhaps the pasha's ancestors—had rifled the tomb two thousand years before.

WHEN we came back to England there was great rejoicing at Rainbow Cottage. I had asked that the aunts should not be told of my adventures, because, as I said to Tybalt, we shall go off to other places together and they would fret all the time and say, "I told you so."

A few days after we had arrived home there was a paragraph in the press about an Englishman, a successful dealer in Egyptian antiquities, who had been found drowned in the Nile. His name was Leopold Harding. Whether his death was due to foul play was not certain.

It was clear that he had been one of the pasha's servants. Harding disposed of priceless objects which the pasha may have taken from tombs. If there were jewels, they would have to be broken up and sold separately—and the transactions would be carried out under cover of legitimate business.

The pasha had been hoping to make the discovery of a lifetime. Sir Edward had found the trail, so he had died through Mustapha and Absalam. Then Tybalt had arrived to take up where his father had left off, and Theodosia had died as a warning. Because we remained, Leopold Harding had been ordered to kill me. He had failed. The pasha did not like failures, so Leopold Harding had been murdered.

The adventure was behind me. Leopold Harding had attempted to take my life and had instead taken away my fears. But for Leopold Harding and the Egyptian expedition, I might have gone on for years doubting Tybalt's love for me, for he could never have expressed in words what he did when he came to get me, and when he was ready to give up his life's ambition just as he believed it to be within his reach.

"My poor Tybalt," I said, "I did want you to make the great discovery."

"I made a greater one."

"I know. Before, you thought you wanted more than anything in the world to find the greatest treasure ever known to the world."

"But I did that," he said. "I discovered what you meant to me."

So how could I but be grateful to all that had gone before? And how could I not rejoice when I looked forward to the richness of the life we would lead together?

Victoria Holt

Victoria Holt has an innate feeling for the drama and romance of history. Her strong sense of the past is enhanced by her travels, and on her frequent trips she gathers much of the background material for her books. She has set her novels in France, in England, in tropical islands, and now in Egypt, a country which has long fascinated her.

Miss Holt says, "When I first saw the Valley of the Kings I was completely entranced. To drive between the stark hills and step into the chilling passages which led to the tomb of Tutankhamen was an experience I shall never forget. The blind alleys, the carvings on the walls, and most of all the indefinable atmosphere of antiquity filled me with a great excitement. I knew that I was going to use this fantastic setting for a book."

Victoria Holt lives in a London flat which looks out on a lively street on one side and Kensington Gardens on the other. She spends her summers in Cornwall, overlooking rolling hills and a rugged coastline. In either home she spends about five hours a day on her writing. She began writing novels nearly twenty-five years ago, and uses a pen name in order to keep her identity secret and to avoid being distracted from her work.

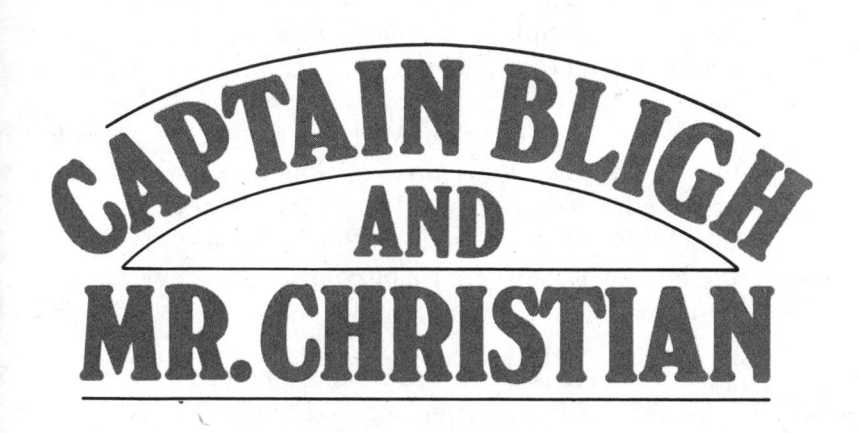

CAPTAIN BLIGH AND MR. CHRISTIAN

AND

A condensation of the book by
RICHARD HOUGH

•

Illustrated by Chris Maygar

Their conflicting destinies
were charted not by honor,
but by the mysterious passions
of the human heart

Richard Hough, a distinguished naval historian, has taken a completely new look at the most celebrated mutiny of all time. His search for truth took him on prolonged journeys to the Pacific islands where the mutiny, Bligh's miraculous open-boat escape and Christian's lonely death occurred. His exploration of these dramatic events inevitably led him to confront the dark places of the human heart where jealousy, pride and envy had sown the seeds of disaster.

"Mr. Hough is a scrupulous reporter and a superb maritime writer, and his account of this haunting adventure is a model and a delight."
—*New Yorker*

"The author has provided a new depth of insight into the characters of all the principals in a tragedy of truly classical proportions. . . . A true adventure story long to be remembered."
—Denver *Post*

"A fascinating book . . . made up of flesh-and-blood people acting out a terrible drama."
—Omaha *World-Herald*

Prologue

"THE PEOPLE ARE RIPE FOR ANYTHING"

A FEW minutes before 4:00 a.m. on April 28, 1789, Midshipman George Stewart felt his way down the main hatchway of His Majesty's Armed Vessel *Bounty*. The ship was creaking gently, like the bones of a tired old man, as Stewart went below to rouse his friend Fletcher Christian, now acting lieutenant. There had been little wind, and the air on the lower deck was humid and rank with the smell of sweat, damp timber, soiled clothes and old cooking.

Christian, who was to have the next watch, occupied a berth a few steps forward from the ladder, on the starboard side, behind a canvas screen. A lantern hung there, and when the screen was lifted Christian could just make out Stewart's silhouette. Stewart, at twenty-three, was a year younger than Christian—shorter and leaner, too. They had been together for more than nineteen months.

Christian did not need to be awakened. If he had slept at all since he had climbed into his hammock, it was only fitfully. On the previous evening, in desperation, he had lashed the two masts lying in the ship's launch to some planks to make a crude raft. He intended to desert ship here in the middle of the Pacific and paddle to one of the Friendly Islands, through which the *Bounty* was sailing.

It was a suicidal plan. Only three days earlier a party from

the *Bounty* had been molested while collecting water on one of the Friendly Islands. A man coming ashore alone, without the awe-inspiring presence of a great ship anchored close by, was likely to meet a violent end. Yet Christian had determined to go through with his plan, and had risked divulging it to several others, including Stewart. He had even managed to stow provisions and articles for trading in preparation for his escape.

Stewart leaned over Christian's hammock to call him to his watch and found, as he related later, that his friend was "much out of order." He begged him to abandon his plan, knowing that conditions on board the *Bounty* without the second-in-command would become intolerable for all. Christian, a master's mate, provided both a release for their captain's uncertain temper and a link between the officers and the restless crew. With "the people" (as the enlisted men were called) Fletcher Christian was popular.

"When you go, Christian," Stewart pleaded quietly, "the people are ripe for anything."

Christian was in no condition to evaluate the implications of this information. When Stewart left, he pulled himself up the ladder through the main hatchway and came on deck. There was a light swell and a faint breath of wind from the east, hardly enough to fill the sails. The new moon had long since set and it was still dark. However, an active volcano on an island less than thirty miles away intermittently lighted the sky.

During the first few minutes of his watch another midshipman appeared. Christian recognized Edward Young at once by his walk and burly build. He was tough, ruthless, and a close friend. He, too, had heard of Christian's plan to desert ship and was as anxious as Stewart had been that he should not carry it out, though for different reasons.

Young *wanted* a mutiny and had to be certain of Christian's support, since his good relations with the lower deck were a priceless asset in a rebellion. So he quietly repeated Stewart's information that the men were "ripe for anything." But Young went further, and his plan was simple. While everyone was asleep below, he and Christian should seize the ship. There was no need for

bloodshed, though they would need control of the arms chests. The captain and his clerk, John Samuel, and midshipmen Hayward and Hallett would be seized and cast adrift in the ship's small cutter. They had a better chance (though they did not deserve it) of reaching an island than Christian would in his makeshift raft. Leaving Christian with these fearful thoughts to contemplate, Ned Young went below.

The next step was Christian's. But he remained inactive for some time, struggling between the temptation to desert and the infinitely more fearful yet intoxicating temptation to incite mutiny.

Two of his friends had now independently told him of the mutinous state of some of the people, and he had seen evidence of it himself, for they were always ready to confide in him. They only awaited a leader. Not only was he the only man on board who could prevent a mutiny, he was also the only one who could successfully lead one. But Christian understood the price of mutiny. At worst, disgrace for his family, and death at the end of a rope for him. At best, fear and guilt for the rest of his life, since the man who must be deposed, cast adrift, almost certainly to die, was one to whom Christian owed his advancement to acting lieutenant and whom he had loved and admired—his captain, William Bligh.

Chapter 1

"A FATAL TURN TO THE AFFAIR"

IN APRIL 1789 Lieutenant Bligh, captain of the *Bounty*, was thirty-four years old. He came of good yeoman stock. The Blighs were minor landowners in Devonshire; some went to sea, others, like William's father, Francis, into the civil service. William's own career was never in doubt. He would go to sea. His home city, Plymouth, had been on the threshold of great nautical events for centuries, and when William Bligh was a boy of thirteen, James Cook in the *Endeavour* cleared Plymouth Sound on the first of his three great voyages to the Pacific.

Francis Bligh took a great deal of trouble over his only son's education. By the time the boy was fifteen he had a good knowl-

edge of science and mathematics, could express himself well and drew with clarity and imagination. He first went to sea at sixteen as an able seaman. Knowing that he had to show both a good record and exceptional skills if he was to win promotion—he lacked the patronage of anyone influential—he decided to specialize in navigation, hydrography and cartography. He had his warrant as a midshipman within six months, and his passing certificate for that rank before he was twenty-one.

Then in 1775 there occurred a series of events that would later bring together William Bligh and Fletcher Christian. Bligh was on board a small and (as he described it) "very leaky" sloop, HMS *Ranger*. The American Revolution had just broken out, and the *Ranger* was given the chore of searching suspect ships for contraband in the Irish Sea. She spent much of her time in the port of Douglas in the Isle of Man owing to her unseaworthy condition. During one of these long periods of shore leave Bligh met the Betham family, and fell in love with their daughter, Elizabeth.

The Bethams were influential, rich, and accomplished in the arts and commerce. When Bligh first met Elizabeth Betham, he found her intelligent and understanding. She was not especially beautiful, but she had charm and liveliness. Elizabeth liked the crisp, clever, self-confident young midshipman, with his definite ideas and determined ambition, and before the *Ranger* left Douglas for the last time early in 1776 the young couple had "come to an understanding."

Elizabeth and William knew that it would be a long time before they met again. News of Bligh's exceptional skill as a navigator and hydrographer had reached the ears of James Cook himself, and on March 20, 1776, Bligh had received his appointment as sailing master on HMS *Resolution*. He would sail with the world's most famous explorer, who was soon to embark on his third great voyage.

The main purpose of this expedition was to discover (no matter how many had failed before) a northwest passage from Europe to India through America. The British government had now offered a £20,000 reward for the first man to find a way. James Cook

was determined to be that man. He spent a year in the South Pacific and planned to make his attempt to find the passage eastward from the Pacific instead of westward from the Atlantic.

As sailing master, William Bligh was Cook's right-hand man. He also became directly involved in the subsequent events that led to Cook's death.

It was January 1779 when Cook had reluctantly brought his two vessels, *Resolution* and *Discovery,* south from Alaska after a valiant but unsuccessful struggle to find a way through the ice. He planned to winter in the Sandwich Islands while he prepared for a second attempt. On January 16 he made out a small indentation in the coast of Hawaii, and as usual, the sailing master was sent to reconnoiter in the *Resolution*'s pinnace.

Bligh explored the bay with his usual care, taking soundings and drawing a rough chart. It was, he learned, called Karakakooa Bay and was some three miles across at its entrance, with two villages, Kowrowa on the western shore and Kakooa in the center. That night Cook wrote in his journal: "Mr. Bligh returned and reported that he had found a bay in which was good anchorage and fresh water tolerable easy to come at. Into this bay I resolved to go to re-fit the ships and supply ourselves with every refreshment the place could afford." It is the last entry contributed by Cook.

When the Englishmen took their vessels into Karakakooa Bay, every native who could find room in a canoe came paddling as fast as he could toward the two sloops. They clung to the gunwales of the ships' boats, climbed up the sides of the *Resolution* and *Discovery,* packing the decks, the masts and yards so tight that the *Discovery* began to list from their weight.

There did not appear to be any menace in them, though they purloined everything removable in the usual Polynesian manner. Yet nowhere in the islands—though the sailors had experienced everything from warm hospitality to downright hostility—had there been such a feeling of tension and emotionalism. The Karakakooans seemed to be on the edge of a nervous breakdown.

During the weeks that followed, relations between the excitable

natives and their exasperated guests became increasingly difficult. Yet repairs were effected and Cook's ships stocked with vast quantities of foodstuffs. Outwardly, harmony was maintained between the leaders of both sides. Then, on February 14, when the *Resolution* was anchored less than half a mile from the northwest shore of the bay, the captain received the ominous news that the *Discovery's* large cutter had been stolen during the night.

Cook was furious. He determined to go ashore at once with a party of marines and bring the native chief back to his ship as hostage. He had used this method of retrieving items stolen by islanders before with unfailing success. He gave orders also for a boat from each ship, one of them commanded by William Bligh and the other by Lieutenant Rickman, Bligh's junior by several years, to patrol the entrance to the bay. They were to prevent any of the natives from escaping. Nothing was said about opening fire if the need arose; Cook detested violence and avoided it whenever possible.

There was no good landing place for a boat at Kowrowa, and Cook had to use a rocky promontory as a jetty. He clambered out onto the slippery rocks and made for the village, with Lieutenant Phillips, the marines officer, following with his men. They found Chief Terreeoboo in his hut. The fat old man appeared bewildered by the early call, and Cook was soon convinced that he knew nothing of the theft of the cutter. When the captain invited him on board his ship, the chief readily agreed to come, and they began to walk toward the shore.

At about this time there was heard the distant sound of musket fire from the bay. Immediately all signs of friendliness and respect from the natives dissolved, and they began arming themselves with stones and spears.

It was clear that they suspected Cook's designs on their king. Accordingly Terreeoboo was permitted to remain, and when the natives saw that he was safe they allowed the marines to return to the shore without him.

At this delicate moment, with Cook and Phillips some thirty yards from the shore, the mob's fury was suddenly reenergized by

news brought by runner of slaughter out in the bay. Bligh had fired at one large canoe which had attempted to escape.

Stones now began to fly about the beleaguered party. A young warrior lunged at Phillips with his dagger. Phillips deflected the blow. Another came at him from behind. Phillips turned, discharged a ball and killed him instantly.

The screaming mob closed about Cook. The marines on the shore fired one volley, then a second. The front ranks of the natives were decimated. The rest came on, running over the bodies, and the marines were overwhelmed. As they struggled in the shallow water their brains were beaten out against the rocks.

Cook had already been knocked down by one stone. Beside him Phillips had drawn his sword and was seen holding back the mob for several seconds. Then, as Cook rose, he was rushed and stabbed from behind. When he fell a second time the nearest warriors pounced on his body in a frenzy of eagerness to share in the glory of the assassination.

Phillips could do no more. Still using his sword to great effect, he retreated across the rocks, dived into the water and swam to the boat. Too late the *Resolution*'s guns roared. The smoke drifted across the bay as if to salute the death of the great navigator, a death that everyone agreed to be the direct result of Bligh's impetuous firing on the canoe—an action, according to a fellow officer, which had given "a fatal turn to the affair."

As soon as he had navigated the *Resolution* back to England, Bligh made his way to the Isle of Man. There he married Elizabeth Betham on February 4, 1781. She, like her husband, was twenty-six years old. She was clever and talented, and her support in the troubled years ahead was unswerving. The marriage also secured him a wide range of connections, all powerful and potentially valuable.

For the next two years England was still at war. Within ten days of his marriage Bligh was appointed master of the captured French frigate *Belle Poule*, in which he saw action for the first time at the bloody but indecisive engagement at the Dogger

Bank. Then, as a junior lieutenant, he took part in the relief of Gibraltar. He reached England again on November 14, 1782, just in time for the birth of his first daughter, Harriet Maria.

For nearly five years he did not have another naval appointment, and half pay was a mere two shillings a day, hardly enough for a growing family. Bligh settled down with Elizabeth and their baby in their modest home in Douglas, and began inquiries among his wife's relatives for work.

Elizabeth's mother's uncle, Duncan Campbell, was a prominent West Indian merchant and shipowner. He quickly showed his confidence in Bligh by appointing him to command one of his merchantmen, and later to be his agent at Port of Lucea, Jamaica, for several months. Now well paid, Bligh brought his family to London. While he was bringing shiploads of sugar and rum across the Atlantic, Elizabeth gave birth to two more daughters.

Then, in the late summer of 1785, Bligh received a request from old family friends of Elizabeth's for a berth for Midshipman Fletcher Christian on Campbell's fine new ship, the *Britannia*. Aware that to sail under William Bligh would provide priceless experience, Christian also wrote to him direct. "Wages are no object: I only wish to learn my profession, and if you would permit me to mess with the gentlemen, I will readily enter your ship as a foremaster, until there is a vacancy among the officers. . . ."

That seemed to Bligh to be the right spirit, and he responded that Christian would be welcome on these terms.

There was no strong maritime tradition in the Christian family, yet at eighteen Fletcher made the surprising decision to join the navy. He took readily and happily to life at sea, the privations as well as the boisterous company and the delights of new places and peoples. He got on well. His good education, his lively mind and manner, ensured that. In 1784, as a twenty-year-old midshipman on the homeward passage from his first voyage to the Far East, he was given a watch in HMS *Eurydice*. This was unusual for a young man with only two years' service.

The next year he sailed with Bligh on the *Britannia*. He was five feet eight inches tall, dark-haired, handsome, strong and well built.

He was also—fatally—as emotional, passionate and mercurial as Bligh himself.

For most of the time Christian was a lively and amusing companion, but he was also subject to moods of depression. These bleak periods did not usually last for long and his resilient spirit soon would reassert itself. Ashore, he was the first to attract the women. They loved the combination of his swashbuckling self-confidence and his seeming vulnerability.

During his second voyage on the *Britannia* he was promoted from gunner to second mate. This and other special favors aroused resentment in Edward Lamb, the mate of the *Britannia*. Seven years later, when Bligh was under fierce attack, Lamb wrote to Bligh: "When we got to sea I saw your partiality for the young man. I gave him every advice and information in my power, though he went about every point of duty with a degree of indifference that to me was truly unpleasant; but you were blind to his faults and had him to dine and sup every other day in the cabin, and treated him like a brother in giving him every information."

By now Bligh's success in the service of his benefactor, Duncan Campbell, had attracted the attention of many people. The most important of these was Sir Joseph Banks, scientist and explorer, naturalist and visionary, a man of great wealth and influence who had sailed with Cook on his first Pacific voyage and was now president of the Royal Society.

Like Campbell, Banks had substantial financial interests in the West Indies, and for more than a decade the cost of feeding the slaves working on the sugar plantations there had been a constant worry. The main problem was that most of their food had to be imported from North America.

As long before as 1775 the Society for West India Merchants had offered to underwrite the expense of importing a cheap food-yielding plant into the "West India Colonies"; and in its turn the Royal Society offered its prestigious gold medal to the first person who succeeded in conveying "six plants . . . in a growing state." The plant that the merchants and the Royal Society were chiefly interested in was the breadfruit, a prolific, tough, doughy plant

that grew readily all over Polynesia. It could be made into a dura-
ble paste, for use during the few months that it was not in season;
and from the fiber beneath its bark a useful cloth could be made.

A contemporary historian wrote: "If a man plants ten of them in
his lifetime, which he may do in about an hour, he will completely
fulfil his duty to his own and future generations as the native of
our less temperate climate can do by ploughing in the cold winter,
and reaping in the summer's heat."

Early in 1787 Banks and Lord Sydney, one of King George III's
principal secretaries of state, began discussions on the transport
of some breadfruit plants from Polynesia to the British West Indies.
Formal authority for the voyage was given in May 1787.

The vessel was to proceed by way of Cape Horn to Tahiti for
the collection of upward of one thousand breadfruits, thence to the
West Indies. Time was short if the worst Cape Horn weather,
which began around April, was to be avoided, and urgent consideration was given by Banks and Lord Sydney to the choice of vessel, of master to command her, and of a botanist to supervise the
horticultural aspects of the voyage.

The selection of botanist was no problem. David Nelson was
Banks's man. Quiet, unassuming and diligent, he had sailed with
Cook on his last voyage, had successfully collected plants and seeds
and knew how to look after them at sea. He had already been to
Tahiti and even had a fair smattering of the language. When the
call came, he gladly gathered together his plant presses and drying papers, his wooden boxes and casks. For his assistant he chose
twenty-five-year-old William Brown from Kew.

Banks had no doubts about the choice of commander either, and
Bligh heard the first official news of his appointment on August 5.
It was the greatest honor that could have been paid to the thirty-
three-year-old lieutenant. He wrote to Banks: "I have heard the
flattering news of your great goodness to me, intending to honour
me with the command of the vessel which you propose to go to the
South Seas, for which, after offering you my most grateful thanks,
I can only assure you I shall endeavour, and I hope succeed, in
deserving such a trust."

Bligh's vessel had been chosen in his absence. She was the *Bethia,* a three-masted merchantman built two and a half years earlier, ninety-one feet long overall on the upper deck, handsomely ornamented with a figurehead of a woman dressed in a riding habit.

Modifications to the *Bethia* for her unusual new function were put in hand without delay. "The difficulty of carrying plants by sea is very great," Banks emphasized. "A small sprinkling of salt water or of the salt dew which fills the air even in a moderate gale will inevitably destroy them if not immediately washed off with fresh water. It is necessary therefore that the cabin be appropriated to the sole purpose of making a kind of greenhouse . . . and that in case of cold weather . . . a stove be provided by which it may be kept in a temperature equal to that of the inter-tropical countries."

The whole of the lower deck from a point midway between the main and mizzen masts and the stern, normally the most comfortable area in a ship, was sacrificed to the greenhouse, with rows of pots to accommodate over one thousand plants. This meant overcrowding, on a voyage that was certain to last nearly two years, for the ship's complement of no fewer than forty-seven. There could also be no accommodation for Royal Marines, either for punitive measures ashore or to give edge to the captain's authority on board. The ship's commander would have to fend for himself.

Honored and flattered as he was at this appointment, Bligh was from the beginning alarmed that he was to have no marines on such a long and hazardous voyage, nor any commissioned officer to share his responsibilities and support him.

During September the *Bethia,* now more appropriately named the *Bounty,* was fitted out. Provisions for the voyage consisted largely of the basic—and notorious—ship biscuit, tough and weevil-ridden; salt pork and beef in casks; dried peas; grog (rum), beer and wine. In addition there were supplies of the marvelous new portable soup. This concoction was regarded as an acceptable substitute for fresh vegetables, and therefore antiscorbutic. It was made by boiling vegetables until finally the remaining juice solidified, when it lasted forever. (There is a piece in the National Mari-

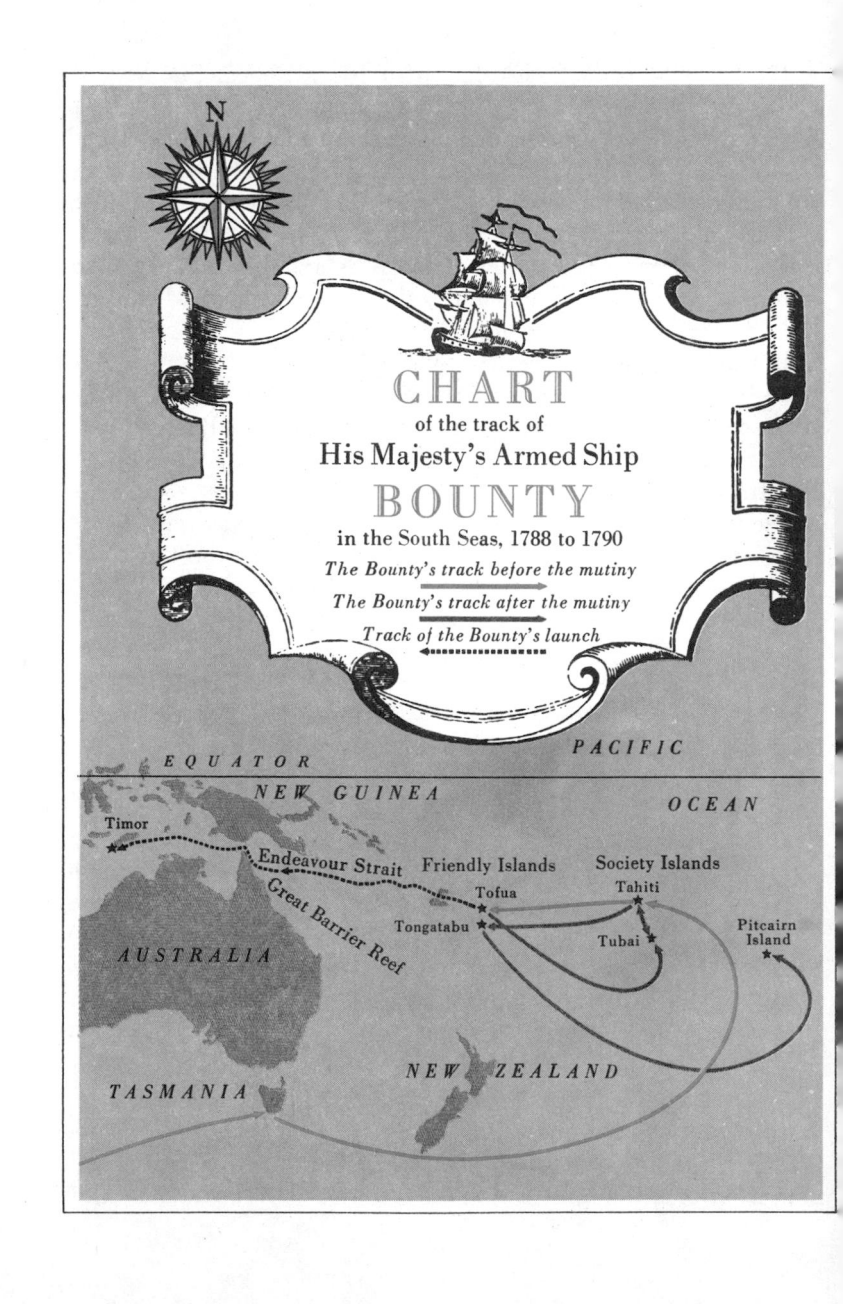

time Museum, Greenwich, today.) The carpenters had also built four cases on the forecastle for a dozen hens, some pigs and half a dozen sheep.

The *Bounty*'s mission was regarded primarily as a trading one. Accordingly, to buy 1000 breadfruit plants Bligh obtained no fewer than 2800 steel blades of various kinds, 1000 knives with wooden handles and sheaths, several thousand nails, 48 saws, and numerous hatchets, gimlets, rasps and files—all beloved by the Polynesians and worth a king's ransom in local currency, though a mere £125 in England. Those old favorites, mirrors and colored beads, were included, along with six dozen coarse shirts for special presents. In addition there were one hundred gold ducats for more sophisticated trading places, like Batavia or Java, for the replacement of lost plants en route—if any could be found—and for purchasing provisions.

Besides this provisioning, Bligh's most important task was the selection of his officers and men. Except for the gardener and his assistant, all were selected by Bligh personally. One of the first chosen was fourteen-year-old Peter Heywood, son of a close friend of the Betham family, a lively boy whom everyone liked. When Elizabeth's father wrote recommending this "ingenious lad," Bligh willingly complied.

Elizabeth herself had already staked a claim for John Hallett, brother of an old friend. And the Bethams also asked Bligh to include Tom Hayward.

Then there was Edward Young, a saturnine young man, reputed to have West Indian blood in his veins, whose mother could trace her lineage back to Queen Mary Stuart. Bligh had once been entertained by his family in the Orkneys, and thought Edward "had the look of a stout able seaman."

These, then, were the midshipmen, all young, all enthusiastic for the adventure that lay ahead, all seemingly able.

Bligh also knew, either personally or by reputation, most of the warrant and petty officers—William Peckover, for instance, the gunner, who had sailed on all three of Cook's Pacific voyages, and the quartermaster, John Norton. John Fryer, the *Bounty*'s master,

was unknown to him, but he came with a good reference, and Bligh told Banks that he was confident that he was a good man.

The surgeon, Dr. Thomas Huggan, was grossly overweight and appeared to be a very steady drinker. However "the doctor has a good character," Bligh wrote cheerfully to Banks.

There was no shortage of enlisted men to choose from, and Bligh believed that when he had sorted through all the candidates he had chosen well. The captain was insistent on having a musician in the ship's company, both to cheer the men and to provide the music for dancing. He knew how slack the men could become on a long voyage, especially when the trade winds blew steadily day after day and there was little to do. There was some difficulty in finding a fiddler prepared to face the rigors of a two years' long circumnavigation, and in the end he had to make do with Michael Byrn, who was nearly blind.

Fletcher Christian's master-pupil relationship with Bligh had developed into something deeper. Now twenty-two years old, a first-class navigator and promoted to master's mate, he was one of the first to know that he would be sailing to the South Seas.

The only officer holding the king's commission was Bligh. Christian and the other midshipmen—really apprentice officers—were classed as enlisted men (and could therefore be flogged) but messed separately and had other privileges.

Bligh received his orders to take the *Bounty* from London to Spithead on October 15, and sent his family ahead of him so that he could spend his last days with them at Portsmouth.

It was a terrible passage down the Channel. Nevertheless the captain found little to complain about. The men worked well together, and Bligh thought that he would soon "have them all in very good order." His final sailing orders were needlessly delayed until November 24. By then the weather had changed for the worse, and when at last he did make sail into the Channel he was beaten back again. His only consolation was that he was able to spend a little time longer with "my dear little family." It was not until two days before Christmas that a fair east wind blew, and he was able to set sail.

Chapter 2

BLIGH's orders were to sail from England to Tahiti, a distance of over twelve thousand miles, stopping only at the Canary Islands. He was to arrive in Tahiti in late March or April 1788, when the breadfruit would be ripe for transplanting. This timing was already in jeopardy, as rounding the Horn would now require a great deal of luck as well as good seamanship. Yet Banks considered that it was worth taking the risks, as it would mean getting cheap food for the plantation slaves a year earlier.

For the twenty days of their passage to the Canaries the men learned one another's ways, the habits and weaknesses of their officers, and above all watched their commander, on whose discretion their well-being and their lives were going to depend, perhaps for several years. There were things about him that were already causing a measure of uneasiness—the uncertain nature of his temper in particular. They were all used to bad language. There was nothing shocking about that. But Bligh never seemed to stop, even when he was talking conversationally. They had never heard anything like it before.

THEY sighted the Canaries in cloudy, heavy weather on the morning of January 5. Twenty-four hours later the *Bounty* moored off Santa Cruz de Tenerife, a neat, trim little Spanish town, all church spires and straight roads flanked by low houses.

It took four days of hard work to take on board fresh provisions and water. Bligh complained at the high prices of everything, but with no other port on his route, he had to pay out. As it was unlikely that there would be another chance of writing home, Bligh left behind at Santa Cruz reports to be taken by the next ship bound for England saying all was well. Only the surgeon gave cause for complaint. Fat Dr. Huggan lurched about the ship, forever swinging a bottle. The *Bounty* herself was "the completest ship I believe that ever swam, and she really looks like one fit to encounter any difficulties."

Once clear of Tenerife, Bligh called together the ship's company and read an announcement. Its terms have a direct bearing on much of what happened later. "We are proceeding to Otaheite [Tahiti] without stopping and by way of Cape Horn. But because of the delays in England the season is now far spent and we may be defeated in our efforts to reach the South Sea by this short route. But I am determined to try. If I fail in the attempt I shall put about to the Cape of Good Hope and proceed by the easterly route to the Society Islands. In either event, it is necessary to be careful of our provisions, especially our biscuit. I shall therefore now reduce the allowance to two-thirds, all other provisions remaining at full rations."

The ship's company was to be put on three watches. This meant that the men would work four hours on watch and eight off, instead of four hours on and four off. The men were also told that the evenings would be laid aside for their amusement and dancing. As to the watch keepers, the master and gunner would be in charge of watches as before. For the third watch, Mr. Christian would be in command.

What an oddly uneven announcement this was! On the one hand it showed caution, care and consideration for the men. The common crew—"the people"—were generally treated as slaves. Cook, however, was of a new enlightened school of commanders which recognized that the survival of the ship's company during a long voyage depended on the health and well-being of each man. Bligh had witnessed Cook's success, and his own concern for a rigid economy of victuals, a careful regard to a balanced diet, and compulsory dancing and games in the evenings made good sense.

On the other hand, Christian was no better qualified to be the officer of the third watch than the other master's mate, Will Elphinstone, or Midshipman Tom Hayward. Bligh's choice showed the same favoritism as he had shown in the *Britannia,* where it had led to resentment. Already Christian was being invited to Bligh's cabin in the evenings, and soon after this he was shot up to the rank of acting lieutenant and into the position of second-in-command, over the head of Fryer—the master to whom he had been mate.

Only midshipmen Hayward and Hallett, and Bligh's dour clerk, John Samuel, disapproved. Fryer himself showed no resentment at the time; yet he certainly felt the injury, and his relations with Bligh became increasingly touchy, until the two were scarcely on speaking terms.

It took the *Bounty* more than four weeks to reach the Equator—some seventy-five miles a day—through fair but humid weather. Though the ship was aired whenever possible and washed down below with vinegar, everything was quickly covered with a fine white mold.

According to Bligh's log, and the journal he published later, those first weeks were happy. On the crossing of the line there was much dancing, hilarity and tipsiness. Three bottles of rum were shared out, and each man had half a pint of wine as well. But had there been troubles, it would hardly have been in Bligh's interest to recount them. James Morrison, the bo'sun's mate, in *his* journal, wrote of discontent within a few days of leaving Santa Cruz. First there was the matter of the missing cheese. Bligh ordered a cask to be opened in front of the ship's company, as was the custom, to prevent any suspicion of malpractice. Two cheeses were missing. "They have been stolen," Bligh declared angrily.

"This cask has been opened before, sir," said the cooper, Henry Hillbrant, daringly. "It was opened by the order of Mr. Samuel at Spithead and the cheeses were sent to your lodgings."

Bligh turned on Hillbrant. "I'll give you a damned good flogging if you say any more of this." Then to the ship's company: "The allowance of cheese for the officers as well as the people will be stopped until this deficiency is made good."

The matter of the missing cheeses was followed some three weeks later by the pumpkin affair. With the temperature in the eighties, pumpkins Bligh had bought at Santa Cruz began to go bad. To avoid waste and consume them quickly, Bligh ordered Samuel to issue them instead of biscuit, one pound of pumpkin for two pounds of biscuit. The men refused with one voice.

When Bligh heard of this near-mutinous protest, "he came up in a violent passion," declared Morrison, "and called all hands."

"You damned infernal scoundrels!" Bligh shouted at them. "I'll make you eat grass or anything you can catch before I have done with you!"

THE voyage continued with fair winds from the Equator until the *Bounty* had the first taste of Horn weather nearly six weeks later. During this leg, slackness and dirt were Bligh's first enemies. The men scrubbed themselves down daily, and every afternoon they combined exercise with hygiene by pouring water down one pump to the bilge and pumping it up again with the second pump. The captain was satisfied only when the water coming up was pure as the water poured down. Bligh equated a sick man with personal failure, and he recorded with satisfaction that the *Bounty* survived the tropics with no serious sickness.

The first southern gale struck the *Bounty* at the entrance of the Strait of Magellan, but the wind died quickly, and two nights later, in bright moonlight, the mountains of Tierra del Fuego, the first land they had seen since the Canaries, emerged in the southeast. Bligh ordered a sheep to be killed to celebrate. "It gave them a pleasant meal," he recorded.

James Morrison told this story differently, too. The sheep, he said, had died of starvation, and they had to throw most of it overboard. Moreover, it was a substitute for the day's ration of meat, not a supplement.

On March 24 Bligh noticed the sky "very much streaked and appearance of wind." But the ship's long ordeal did not begin in earnest until the night of March 28. A westerly gale brought strong, slanting rain, and the seas often broke over the deck—"it exceeds any I have seen," Bligh noted in his log. He knew what he was up against, and his respect for the power of the elements was as massive as his determination to prevail. His weapons were his ship and his men, and he nursed them both devotedly.

Day after day, as he tacked and wore, gaining a few miles in a few days and losing them all and more in a few hours; as he took his observations lashed to the mast, watched every change of the weather from hail and snowstorms to squalls and brief periods of

moderating gales; ordered the sails furled, or reefed, or set according to the constant changes in direction and strength of the wind—all this time, sodden, half frozen and weary himself, his first thoughts were for the welfare of his ship and men.

This was William Bligh at his best, gladly agreeing to the men's request for unwatered grog to keep out the cold, deputing two men from each watch to supervise the only fire below to dry out the clothes and the hammocks of the others, ordering hot soup for all and hot breakfasts of boiled wheat and sugar, and a pint of decoction of ground malt once a day.

The *Bounty* and her company both reacted stoutly, and for two weeks of this battering the ship showed few signs of the strain she was undergoing. Then "she begins to be a little leaky," Bligh noted flatly, and ordered the men to the pumps every hour. He gave attention to his men by sacrificing his cabin at night, which allowed more room between decks and "rendered those happy who had not dry beds to sleep in."

By the middle of April, Bligh was beginning to lose hope. Because of the sails' weight and stiffness from snow and ice, the weakened men found it well-nigh impossible to haul them up and furl them. When they came down from the yards they were unable to speak and scarcely able to stand. Still, no ship's company could have been more loyal, determined and tenacious.

On April 13 Bligh wrote: "It is now three weeks since we came round Staten Land, a time we have spent with much fatigue and almost constant bad weather. Few ships could have gone through it as we have done, but I cannot expect my men and officers to bear it much longer."

Eight days later, with nine men out of action, the *Bounty* badly leaking and no sign of the weather easing, Bligh knew that he had been defeated. Just before five in the afternoon he called all hands aft and told them that he was going to put over the helm and bear away for Africa. "You have endured much and I congratulate and thank you all." The whole crew—until that moment close to despair—spontaneously burst into three cheers for their commander.

Bligh had proved himself an unsurpassed captain in a time of

adversity. To have survived those weeks of Horn weather without the loss of a man, of a spar or even a yard of canvas, was a stunning achievement.

The *Bounty* made good speed across the South Atlantic, running at up to nine knots with a strong westerly wind. But the weather remained consistently foul and it was not until they were almost in sight of Table Mountain that it at last eased. On May 24 the *Bounty* came to anchor in False Bay, Cape of Good Hope. It was the crew's first sight of other human beings in eighty-six days.

The *Bounty* remained at Cape Town for thirty-eight days. The ship was in poor shape after her Cape Horn battering. The carpenter and his crew had a lot of repairing to do, and every day the boats plied between the shore and the ship, bringing a mass of miscellaneous stores. These included apple-tree saplings and all sorts of seeds for Nelson, the botanist, to plant on Pacific islands.

Although it was midwinter in Cape Town, rainy and cool, the crew thrived on the diet of fruit and vegetables, fresh meat and real bread instead of ship biscuit. Bligh noted with approval the neatness and cleanliness of the town, but deplored the condition and treatment of the slaves. "One could not fail," he wrote, "to reproach the owners of a want of decency and compassion in not relieving such a degree of wretchedness."

At four o'clock in the afternoon on July 1 the *Bounty* weighed anchor. Ahead lay the longest leg of the voyage, across the Indian Ocean for well over six thousand miles to Tasmania, which was still thought to be the southern tip of Australia.

It seems almost miraculous today that after forty-nine days a navigator equipped only with suspect charts, a compass, a chronometer, nautical tables and a sextant, could make accurate landfall not just on a coast but on a particular rock—the Mewstone off Tasmania. But then Bligh was a peerless navigator, and on August 19, he worked the *Bounty* carefully—noting every detail for future navigators—into Adventure Bay.

Christian took a party ashore for wood, others took casks in the launch to fill with water, some of the men fished and Christian succeeded in shooting a few birds for the pot. Although they were

curious about the natives, the islanders always retreated silently inland before they could be approached with gifts. David Nelson collected soil and specimens, and planted some fruit trees, vegetables and seeds in a clearing. (In afteryears Bligh claimed to be the progenitor of Tasmania's apple industry.) On September 4 they set out on the last leg of their journey to Tahiti.

At sea the first major trouble with one of his officers occurred, significantly, on the day with "the wind as steady as a trade," the temperature at a mellow sixty degrees Fahrenheit and the weather fair. On the morning of October 9 there were clerical formalities to be carried out—monthly expense books to be signed both by the commander and the master. Bligh examined the books, signed and sent them to Fryer for his signature. But Fryer, a petulant, uneasy man who had made no trouble when passed over for promotion, now would not add his signature unless Bligh himself signed a certificate confirming Fryer's own good behavior during the passage: something for the record in case of trouble later.

Bligh was livid and turned up all hands. Then, with Fryer at his side, he read aloud the Articles of War, with all their hints of dire retribution. His clerk, Samuel, produced the books and Bligh held them out to Fryer. "Now sign them books," Bligh ordered.

Fryer took the pen, and in a voice so loud that none would miss his words, he said, "I sign in obedience to your orders, but this may be canceled hereafter." And he did so. According to Morrison this was only one of several rows between commander and master before they reached Tahiti.

Bligh's relations with Surgeon Huggan also were going from bad to worse. One of his able seamen, James Valentine, had been taken ill in Adventure Bay, and in accordance with usual practice had been bled from the arm by Huggan, who neglected to look after it properly. The arm became inflamed, and Valentine retired to his hammock. The captain visited him and found him in a very poor condition. A few days later Valentine died.

Bligh was very put out, because he had hoped to complete his voyage without a casualty—an impressive confirmation of his quality as a commander. But as the *Bounty* sailed into the tropics

and the temperature and humidity rose daily, more men were taken ill. Huggan said it was scurvy. Bligh was outraged. Only inferior commanders, with dirty ships and dirty men eating a poor diet, experienced this dread disease among their crew. Bligh examined the men with care. "It appeared to be nothing more than the prickly heat," he wrote in his log.

Nevertheless, more fell ill, and Bligh became very worried. He asked for the full sick list from Huggan and was astonished to discover that only one name appeared on it. Huggan was obviously unable to carry out even the simplest duties. The captain ordered the sick men off all salt provisions and gave them flour and a daily dose of essence of malt instead.

Under Bligh's care the health of the men improved as Huggan's condition grew worse. On October 24 Bligh discovered that his surgeon had been lying on his bunk in an alcoholic stupor for four days. Disgusted, he ordered his cabin to be cleaned out and his stock of liquor removed and hidden. Huggan was later seen lurching about the ship searching for his bottles. He failed in his quest and eventually returned, thwarted, to his cabin.

Two days later the doctor's condition had so improved that Bligh felt that he was capable of carrying out one last important duty before they landed. Cook had been accused of allowing his men to spread venereal disease among the innocent natives. "To free us from any ill-founded suppositions," Bligh ordered every officer and man to report to Huggan for venereal inspection. That night Bligh wrote with satisfaction: "Every person is totally free from the venereal complaint."

Early on the evening of October 25, 1788, dead on course as always, Bligh sighted the towering green volcanic peaks of Tahiti. The sky was clear, a favorable and gentle trade wind fanned them, the temperature was seventy-eight degrees. It was ten months since they had left England, and they had sailed more than 27,000 nautical miles.

The *Bounty* drew close to the island during the night, and by the following morning they could make out deep valleys, thick, rich forests, coconut palms along the sandy shoreline and groves

of breadfruit trees. Here and there they could pick out natives' huts arranged in small groups. It truly appeared the paradise on earth of which they had all heard such extravagant accounts.

THE *Bounty's* welcome was characteristically Polynesian. As Bligh worked the ship through a break in Tahiti's reef and into the clear calm of Matavai Bay, hundreds of long canoes came out from the shore. In them were the most attractive people the crew of the *Bounty* had seen on all their voyage. Tall young women held armfuls of fruit. Their hair, woven with hibiscus flowers, fell to their shoulders and half across their breasts. Their skin was a rich olive in color, their eyes were as black as their hair.

Tahitian men and girls swarmed from the canoes up the sides of the *Bounty*, cluttering the upper decks. They climbed the rigging, scuttled down the ladders, chattering, laughing, shrieking, insatiably curious. "Where is the great Cook?" they asked. (They pronounced it Toot.)

Bligh had warned his men that they must not refer to the assassination, since Captain Cook had already become a legend to the Tahitians. "Here is the son of Cook," David Nelson told them in their own tongue, pointing to Bligh.

Soon they were busily trading, and the minor chieftains exchanged gifts of hogs and fruit for hatchets and mirrors. The coconut harvest was at its peak and the crew all drank deeply of the restorative milk as they bartered and made their choice of the girls who showed off their bodies with uninhibited enthusiasm.

At this stage there was little thieving, to Bligh's surprise and relief. When one native was caught stealing, a chief flew into a rage and drove the culprit overboard into the sea. Then, as the sun went down, the native men were ordered ashore. Only chosen girls, sometimes two to a man, were allowed to remain, sharing hammocks or lying with their lovers on deck through the hot night.

After the discomforts, the harsh discipline, the celibacy of the past ten months, there now began a long, lazy period of self-indulgence that wrought great changes in the crew. The *Bounty* began to look like a small village, with the womenfolk settling in

Chris Manger

comfortably, stowing the hammocks at dawn, folding the bedding, fetching and preparing the food, gossiping among themselves and making love to their men.

The person most changed by this new life was Bligh himself. From October 26, 1788, to April 4, 1789, Bligh became the benevolent autocrat of northern Tahiti, the honored viceroy of King George III, instead of the stern commander of a ship at sea. Bligh had watched at close quarters how Cook time and again had succeeded in acquiring the affection and respect of the Polynesians with firmness and kindness. Bligh had learned his lessons well—above all he remembered the results of his own fatal impetuosity at Karakakooa Bay.

David Nelson had given Bligh lessons in Tahitian on the passage out, and from the moment when the *Bounty* dropped anchor in Matavai Bay the captain set about "cultivating a friendship with the natives." First he sought out the one man on whom would depend the success of his whole breadfruit enterprise. This was Teina, the ruler of this area of northern Tahiti, a fine, sturdy figure of a man, six feet four inches tall, a stern authoritarian among his people. It is clear that he became deeply attached to Bligh, and not only for what he could cadge from him. He was saddened as well as chastened when Bligh was angry with him and transparently delighted when he was reinstated in his esteem.

Teina's wife, Queen Itea, was an equally formidable figure, a veritable giantess. Bligh described her as "a very resolute woman, of a large make, and has great bodily strength." They had four children under six years; the eldest boy, in accordance with local custom, was made nominal king at birth. Teina would reign as regent until his son became a man.

Bligh, a sentimental man with those who showed him affection, returned the friendship of the muscular ruler and his massive wife with ardor. The two men would talk for hours on end about Polynesian and English manners and customs, and especially about life in the royal palaces in England. Teina could not hear enough about King George III.

Bligh, however, was horrified by some of the Polynesian sexual

practices—what he called "numerous sensual and beastly acts of gratification"—and to hear that the queen shared her bed equally with her husband and his servant. Clearly promiscuity was also accepted as normal within families, and brothers freely slept with each other's wives. Outside the family it was something different, and while Bligh was at Matavai there were cases of knifing for infidelity outside the family.

But not for one day did Bligh forget the main purpose of his visit to Tahiti. The first thing he had to do, after establishing cordial relations with Teina, was to raise the subject of breadfruit tactfully. On a warm rainy day in November they sheltered in a hut and Bligh talked to the regent. "You have many good friends in England," he said, "including King George. When ships come again to Tahiti they will bring more presents for you."

Teina, "much pleased and satisfied," urged Bligh to stay at Matavai. "Do not go to the other islands. I will gladly send any presents King George might prefer—hogs, plantain, bananas, coconuts, breadfruit—"

"Breadfruit is a very good idea," said the captain. "King George will like that." And so the matter was concluded. The minor chiefs were informed by Teina that King George was to be presented with as many breadfruit saplings as the ship could carry, and the following day Bligh went ashore with Nelson and his assistant, Brown, to locate the most suitable place for a nursery garden.

They found it at Point Venus, the northern extremity of the Tahitian coastline, where one of Tahiti's biggest rivers meets the sea. David Nelson chose a spot close to this river for his garden. Today full grown breadfruit trees rise here, two-hundred-year-old memorials to this determined gardener! From that time until the *Bounty*'s departure the area was forbidden to the natives. To reinforce security Bligh made Christian commander of a shore-based establishment. Peter Heywood, Peckover, the gunner, and four armed men provided the defense force.

So, once again, Christian had been given a situation of comfort and privilege, and he settled down happily to a life of indolence. Like all the *Bounty*'s men, he had many girls to choose from and

for a time lived a promiscuous life. Then he found a real *taio,* the daughter of a chief, called Mauatua, whom he renamed Isabella. In the eyes of the men of the *Bounty* all the Tahitian girls were beautiful, but there was something especially radiant about Isabella. Christian also acquired, as many of them did, a male *taio*— a servant and friend.

The *Bounty's* enlisted men were allowed ashore on leave two at a time and were free to do as they liked so long as they adhered to Bligh's rules of conduct, which adjured them "to study to gain the good will and esteem of the natives." There was not in fact very much to do ashore, and since officers and men alike admired the tattooing with which all the natives adorned themselves, the *Bounty's* company, almost without exception, were tattooed to pass the time. And they soon vied with one another for the most elaborate design.

On shore or on shipboard, on watch or off, the demands made on most of the men were very light. One or two were kept busy. Peckover, for example, was responsible for trading; and Bligh encouraged the armorer and the carpenters to meet the natives' needs. The natives brought to them the precious iron tools and toys which they had acquired from Cook, now in need of repair. It all helped good relations.

From Morrison's and Bligh's journals we can visualize the scene on a December evening, with the *Bounty* anchored a mere hundred yards from the beach. Bligh would be ashore with Nelson, and most of the *Bounty's* company would be on deck, lying about with their *taios,* chatting or fishing with lines over the side. Earlier the women had prepared food in the galley below—fish, pork, breadfruit, plantains, bananas and other fruit. Now the air was still, the bay calm, the temperature in the lower eighties.

On one side the mountains rose dark against the starlit sky, toward the open sea the breaking rollers on the reef cast a white line separating the lagoon from the Pacific. The natives, as usual, were out fishing, each canoe and the sea about it illuminated by a splash of yellow light from a burning reed bundle.

As always, the beating of the surf on the reef was the predomi-

nating sound. The other sound that was with them day and night, however calm the lagoon, was the creaking of the *Bounty*'s timbers. Byrn struck up a tune on his fiddle; the women chatted among themselves and later drifted off with their men.

Even now, however, Bligh's command was a lonely one. If he had wanted a female *taio*, it would not have conformed to his dignified status to take one. He kept himself occupied with study of the Tahitian people. He entertained Teina, his wife and their large family, and kept anxious watch over the progress of the breadfruit plants. Indeed, on December 5 the whole transplantation, and even the *Bounty* herself, was placed in jeopardy when a tropical storm struck Tahiti.

That afternoon the seas broke over the reefs, converting Matavai Bay from tranquil lagoon into boiling caldron, "threatening us with instant destruction." The rain came down in torrents, and Bligh had to draw on all his skill to ride out the storm.

Ashore, the river burst its banks, and Nelson and Brown struggled to save their breadfruit by digging a trench to divert the floodwater. Mercifully the rain eased off later in the day, the river subsided, and in the end few plants were damaged.

Matavai Bay was clearly no ideal anchorage. Bligh found a better one six miles west of Point Venus at Oparre. There he discovered a little bay of sufficient depth, better protected from the sea and the trade winds. Over Christmas the encampment on Point Venus was dismantled, and over seven hundred potted breadfruit plants were transported in the ship to Oparre.

The young breadfruit plants flourished in their new garden, as did the seeds of the mutiny. It was on the brief voyage to Oparre that the extent of the decline in spirit and efficiency among the ship's company became evident. As the *Bounty* entered the bay, her forepart ran firmly aground. Using both the bower and kedge anchors, Bligh was finally able to have the ship drawn from the reef and refloated. But the two anchors and their cables became fouled, and it took more than twenty-four hours to free them.

Bligh was exasperated with his officers. The men whom he had chosen with such care now became victims of his foul tongue and

fitful temper. "If I had any officers to supersede them," he wrote, "or was able to do without them, considering them as common seamen, they should no longer occupy their respective stations."

Fletcher Christian suffered most. Bligh saw him less frequently now that Christian lived ashore with Isabella, and so meetings—not always private—only occurred as a result of Bligh's displeasure at some actual or imagined failure in the acting lieutenant's duties.

Things were no better among the seamen. The frequency of floggings began to rise steeply—for insolence, disobedience and neglect of duty. Huggan had continued to drink himself senseless every day since their arrival and died on the evening of December 10. But one of the last duties he had been able to perform was checking "the venereal list." Eighteen officers and men had to apply to the surgeon for a venereal cure; and, incidentally, be fined. The spread of venereal disease in the crew led Bligh to the conclusion—since confirmed—that gonorrhea was rife among the Tahitians long before the arrival of the Europeans.

Worse trouble was to come. Between midnight and 2:00 a.m. on January 5, able seamen Muspratt and Millward, and Charles Churchill, the master-at-arms, stole a complete arms chest, climbed into the small cutter and deserted ship. This was not difficult as Hayward, mate of the watch, was asleep as usual. The theft was discovered when the watch was relieved at 4:00 a.m. Bligh was not informed until half an hour later. He ordered Hayward confined below in irons, and the hunt began at dawn. When the men were recaptured the ship's company was mustered, and Bligh read out the Articles of War. He publicly rebuked Hayward, and then ordered twelve lashes for Churchill and two dozen each for the others. The three men were confined in irons until February 4, when they were brought up and the punishment was repeated.

The *Bounty* was becoming a slack ship. On January 17 Bligh had ordered the sail room to be cleared and the sails taken on shore to air. Among them, rotten and mildewed, were unused spare sails which had previously been reported in good order. So his officers were liars and slackers. "Scarcely any neglect of duty can equal the criminality of this."

As the *Bounty's* long stay in Tahiti drew to a close with the strengthening of the breadfruit plants, the final breakdown in order and discipline approached, and the other Bligh—the fair-weather commander—began to emerge more clearly. His first failing was lack of imagination. For more than five months, amid the seductive delights of one of the most beautiful islands in the world, he left his men to the supervision of his officers and cursed them when he discovered they had failed him. But they were failing a commander who himself had failed the severest test: to lead when things seem to be going smoothly.

On February 27 Bligh wrote that "the plants are in a very fine state and Mr. Nelson thinks they will be perfectly established in the pots in the course of a month." In the early days of March he began to give serious attention to the state of the ship.

The last days at Oparre were chaotic, crowded and moving. There was chanting and dancing, eating and drinking and love-making, all on a glorious scale. For the women it was considered a triumph to conceive a half-European child, and they were as open in their appetites as in their sentiments, lamenting the imminent severance of long friendships.

Somehow, amid what Bligh described as "a vast excess of grief," the delicate task of ferrying over one thousand breadfruit plants to the ship was completed without a casualty. Below decks aft the *Bounty* took on the appearance of a floating conservatory.

On the evening of April 3 the crew said a last farewell to their *taios,* and the canoes paddled slowly away with many cries of sadness. Only Teina, his sister and brother and the queen, were allowed to remain on board as a special privilege, grateful for one more evening with Bligh.

"May God bless and protect you for ever and ever," were Teina's last words as he went over the side to his waiting canoe. He had with him Bligh's last and highly prized presents—two muskets, two pistols and four thousand rounds of ammunition. This once obscure regent of a part of northern Tahiti was now the richest and most powerful ruler in the whole of the Pacific.

The crew lined the side of the *Bounty* and gave Teina and his relatives three cheers in Royal Navy style. At 6:30 a.m. on April 4 anchors were weighed and the *Bounty* set sail on a west northwest course. The three weeks' long passage of the *Bounty* from the tranquil waters of Tahiti to Tofua was most curious. Bligh's uneven temper, his parsimony, his relentless demands for perfection, his lack of self-control, his weakness for publicly humiliating his officers—all show that he was at the end of his tether.

The *Bounty* needed an iron hand. Every crew member had been affected by the relaxed time ashore. But the pressure should have been applied evenly and with justice, not with abuse, empty threats and histrionics followed by a sudden return to familiarity as if nothing had happened. "Which of the young gentlemen will dine with me tonight? Mr. Christian . . . ?"

Christian's own agonized summary of his state of mind during these weeks was that he was in hell. "Whatever fault was found," reported one witness later, "Mr. Christian was sure to bear the brunt of the captain's anger."

But why? It could be explained easily if we knew—but we never shall for sure—that Bligh and Christian had a homosexual relationship going back to their first voyages together, when the *Britannia*'s mate had seen Bligh's "partiality for the young man." In the navy of that time, intimate friendships were often made on the long, lonely voyages. So long as they were not damaging to discipline they were accepted as a normal part of shipboard life. As for Bligh and Christian, all we know for certain is that Bligh's friendship with him was both intimate and long lasting, and that at Tahiti, when Christian shared his bed with a particularly beautiful young woman, it was broken. Was the renewal of their relationship in the confined quarters of the *Bounty* especially hard for Christian to bear? Certainly, from his behavior, it seems that Bligh was experiencing jealousy.

IN SPITE of the long-drawn-out and emotional farewell, there were few regrets among the men at leaving Tahiti. Only a handful of them had developed "strong connections" with the native

girls—perhaps only Christian and a few able seamen had remained with the same girl for most of the time. For the rest, "everybody seemed in high spirits," according to Morrison. They talked of home, predicted the length of their passage and calculated the wages that would be owed to them.

At first it seemed good to be on the move again, but the hard work, slim rations and the irascibility of their commander soon changed all this. Bligh had reinstituted his daily inspection for cleanliness. Most of the men were found wanting and had their grog stopped. On April 12 a seaman was given twelve lashes for neglect of duty. On another day during exercises Bligh and Christian fell out about some real or supposed failure. The captain cursed him roundly in front of the crew. Christian responded mildly. "Sir, your abuse is so bad that I cannot do my duty with any pleasure." Bligh then berated him again.

There was to be one stop for wood and water before the ship made for the notorious Endeavour Strait, north of New Holland, as Australia was then known. This was to be at Nomuka in the Friendly Islands some 1800 miles west of Tahiti. Bligh sighted the outlying islands on April 22. Although he claimed to know Nomuka well, he had difficulties in finding the most convenient and safe anchorage. When he went ashore he gave the chiefs presents generously and was dissatisfied with the *quid pro quo*—a number of coconuts, of which the *Bounty* already had sufficient.

The next morning, a nasty dark day of spitting rain, Christian went ashore with eleven men carrying casks for the collection of water from a pond a quarter mile inland. Will Elphinstone took four men with axes and saws for felling and cutting up timber. Christian's orders from Bligh were curious. He was to take arms ashore but they were to be left in the boat because he said they would be "much safer on shore without them."

Christian met with trouble the moment he landed, and the natives harassed his men all the way through the woods to the pond. Under conditions of great danger, with the natives "poising their clubs or spears with a menacing look," Christian managed to bring off two boatloads of filled casks. He returned to the *Bounty* with

the second boatload and reported to his captain that he was having great difficulty carrying out his duties.

"You damned cowardly rascal!" shouted Bligh. "Are you afraid of a set of natives while you have arms to defend yourselves?"

"But the arms are of no use while your orders prevent them from being used," Christian replied.

Bligh did not change the order, and Christian continued with his duty. When the captain later sent Fryer ashore in the large cutter with a reinforcing party, merry hell was going on at the beach. Soon children were in the water all around the cutter, climbing on the oars, trying to get over the gunwale, shrieking and laughing, half in fun, half in hysteria. One of the sailors, fearful that the cutter would drift on shore, threw out the grapnel. Quick as a flash, some children cut the small anchor's rope and made off with it. Still, amid this pandemonium, Christian managed to hoist the remaining casks aboard the launch and get away without injury.

Bligh was beside himself with fury when he heard of the loss of a grapnel. "God damn your blood," he shouted at Christian, "why did you not fire—you an officer?"

At last the *Bounty* slowly moved out to sea. Little progress was made in the light winds. Bligh was not seen on deck next morning, and the *Bounty* was at peace.

The captain remained below until noon, when he emerged from the hatchway and made his way along the deck to his own personal pile of coconuts bartered from the natives. Suddenly he swung around to call for the master. "Mr. Fryer," he said accusingly, "don't you think these coconuts have shrunk since last night?"

Fryer looked at them carefully. "Sir, they are not so high as they were," he admitted, "but I think the pile may have been flattened by the men walking over them during the night." This could well have been the case but, convinced that he was the victim of a robbery, Bligh ordered every coconut stowed below brought on deck. Everyone had traded for a supply, and it was some time before the men stood beside their individual piles as if on inspection parade, some bewildered, some angry, all apprehensive at this fresh demonstration of their captain's eccentric behavior.

Christian bore the brunt of Bligh's attack. "Damn your blood, you have stolen my coconuts," Bligh addressed him.

"I was thirsty," Christian answered, at once confessing to his crime. "I took one only, and I am sure no one touched another."

"You lie, you scoundrel." He shook his fist in Christian's face. "You must have stolen half of them."

Then he turned from Christian and confronted the rest of his officers and men, shrieking and waving his fists. "There never was such a set of damned thieving rascals under any man's command before. . . . I suppose you will steal my yams next. But I'll sweat you for it, you rascals. I'll make half of you jump overboard before you get through Endeavour Strait."

He turned to his clerk, standing at his side, and in a loud voice so that all could hear, said, "Mr. Samuel, stop these villains' grog and give them but half a pound of yams tomorrow. The officers' coconuts will be stowed aft, and no one will touch them." At that, he turned abruptly away and went down to his cabin.

In the eyes of the officers Bligh was committing robbery not only of their coconuts but of their grog and the food to which they were entitled. No wonder, as Morrison observed, "the officers then got together and were heard to murmur much at their treatment."

But Bligh had not yet finished with Christian. That afternoon Bligh came on deck again. When he spotted Christian he reopened his attack, calling him a thief and a scoundrel. When Christian managed to get away from his tormentor, he came forward, tears coursing down his cheeks. In spite of all he had suffered, it was the first time any of the men had seen him brought to this condition.

"What is the matter, Mr. Christian?" asked William Purcell, the ship's carpenter and one of the few warrant officers.

"Can you ask me, and hear the treatment I receive?"

"Am I not as badly treated as you?" Purcell suggested. There was a measure of truth in this. Purcell had been one of Bligh's most long-suffering victims.

"You have something to protect you," Christian said, referring to Purcell's privileges as a warrant officer. "But if I should speak to him as you do, he would probably break me, turn me before the

mast, and perhaps flog me. If he did," he continued in a desperate voice, "it would be the death of us both, for I am sure I should take him in my arms and jump overboard with him."

Others overheard, and as the evening advanced, rumors circulated through the hot oppressive night that the second-in-command was contemplating desertion. There was real concern among many of the crew. They were genuinely fond of Christian, who was easy on discipline, made them laugh and helped to make life endurable. What would it be like without him?

There was not a man on board who expected soft treatment at sea. Many had suffered under harder men than Bligh and served in ships where flogging took place much more frequently than on the *Bounty*. Neither did flogging in itself create disaffection. It was one of the accepted unpleasant aspects of life at sea, like weevils in the bread or a squall off a lee shore.

The restlessness now stirring stemmed from two causes: the widespread resentment at the recent injustices and real fear for the future. The notorious dangers of Endeavour Strait, to which Bligh frequently referred—its shoals, its hidden coral reefs, its rocks and islets—all stoked the fires of anxiety in the men's minds. It was a hazardous passage. Under a commander who seemed to have lost control of his senses, the prospect was fearful.

As the light faded a volcanic eruption on the island of Tofua— they had seen its smoke as far distant as Nomuka and it had never since been out of sight—brightened into a flickering flaming torch that lit up the surrounding sea.

Christian was in his berth going through his possessions when he received a message that the captain desired his company at supper. An invitation to supper was not unusual after a row, but was surprising after today's events. In any case, Christian was completing arrangements that would result in his never seeing Bligh face-to-face again. "Tell Mr. Bligh that I am indisposed, and give him my compliments."

Having failed with Christian, Bligh sent to the "young gentlemen's" mess. Would any of them care to sup with their captain? Only Tom Hayward accepted, and as he left, his fellow midship-

men booed him. The captain's supper invitation was not his only peace overture of the evening. During Fryer's first night watch Bligh came up on deck and began chatting cordially.

Fryer commented conversationally, "There is a fair breeze springing up, sir, and we had a new moon earlier. That bodes well for our arrival off the coast of New Holland."

"Yes, Mr. Fryer," Bligh answered. "It will be lucky for us to arrive on that coast with a good moon."

Bligh then gave instructions for the night and returned to his cabin, from which he was to emerge a prisoner six hours later.

Chapter 3

"CONSIDER WHAT YOU ARE ABOUT, MR. CHRISTIAN"

So IT was that at 5:00 a.m. on April 28, 1789, Fletcher Christian reached his agonizing decision to lead a mutiny rather than desert ship. He went forward to approach Matthew Quintal and Isaac Martin, two able seamen of his watch whom he judged to be riper for rebellion than anyone else. Quintal was a stocky, violent man of twenty-one; Martin, the only American in the crew, was nine years older, tall, lean and tough. Christian told them he intended to take the ship—"but there is to be no murder." Already by that step he was fatally committed, incitement to mutiny being a capital offense. He asked for their support and for their opinion on who would join them. Quintal showed immediate enthusiasm, Martin was less certain but at length agreed. That made four mutineers, counting Ned Young. How many more?

They could certainly count on Charles Churchill, one of the toughest men in the *Bounty*. Despite the price he had paid in January for deserting, he was a near-certain ally. Then there were Quintal's friend Will McKoy, Matt Thompson, a hardy veteran of forty, Alex Smith, Jack Williams. They had all shown disruptive intentions in the past and were among those flogged for insolence or disobedience. That would make nine.

There was a figure standing at the stern. They could just make out his silhouette against the first gray light now stealing over the

horizon—Charles Norman, the carpenter's mate, an odd fellow at the best of times. He was staring at the sea. Not quite right in the head, not a reliable ally.

Christian decided to ignore him. Instead he sent Quintal below to raise those they had selected, while he took aside in turn the other men in his watch whom he thought he could trust.

The first act in the conspiracy ran smoothly. Quintal disappeared quietly down the forward main hatchway. He roused the chosen men, whispering, "Christian is seizing the ship. Are you with us?" Each man rolled from his hammock and climbed up on deck, at first numbed, then excited at the prospect. By good chance one of these men had the keys to the arms chests. Fryer as master would normally have kept them, but, weary of being disturbed by men on watch who would often take a fancy to shooting a bird or a shark, he had recently handed them over. But for Fryer's slackness there could never have been a mutiny.

It was at this point that Christian made an alarming discovery: two of the four men they intended to seize were asleep on top of the arms chests—John Hallett below, Tom Hayward up on deck.

The situation was restored by Christian's decisiveness. He went below and brusquely roused Hallett, ordering him up on deck to attend to his duties. As soon as he had gone, Christian opened the chest and ordered Thompson to stand guard over it and to hand out arms. Christian himself took no half measures, arming himself fully, in the style of a pirate, with musket, fixed bayonet, a pistol, a box of cartridges and a cutlass.

Up on deck again, he discovered that Hayward had risen and disappeared. (In fact he had been shaken awake by Charles Norman, who wanted to show him a shark—a common enough sight in these waters.)

The first crisis had been overcome. It was 5:15 a.m. The sun would rise in an hour and a half. By then the ship would be in Christian's hands. It was astonishing that the mutiny could gather so many followers without the knowledge of a single nonparticipant. On deck Christian already had Quintal, Martin, Churchill, McKoy, Thomas Burkitt and Williams—all seamen with either a

cutlass, or a brace of pistols, or a musket with a fixed bayonet.

Able seamen John Sumner, Alex Smith and Henry Hillbrant appeared from the hatchway, all equipped with arms handed out by Thompson, who followed them on deck. There was still no sign of Ned Young.

Midshipman Hallett had disappeared. Hayward was still out of sight at the stern, watching the white trail of the shark with Norman, and remained unaware of what was going on until he turned at the sound of men approaching him. Christian was in the lead, a wild sight with his long dark brown hair falling loose to his shoulders.

Hayward walked bravely forward to meet him. "What is the cause of this act?" he demanded of his senior officer.

"Hold your tongue," Christian told him curtly.

Christian deputed Martin as armed guard over Hayward and also over Hallett, who had now reappeared and was standing, helpless and terrified, by the side of the older midshipman.

With control of the upper deck established, Christian led a party down the ladder to the after cockpit. Bligh's cabin door was ajar and he was asleep on his bunk. Fryer, his cabin opposite, had his door closed. Christian, followed by four others, stepped into the six by seven foot cabin. There it would have been hard to raise, let alone aim, their muskets. Bligh was roughly awakened and instantly pulled from his bunk.

"What's the matter? What's the matter?" he demanded.

"Hold your tongue, sir," Christian told him.

Suddenly the full danger and horror of the situation struck the captain and he called out at the top of his voice, "Murder!" over and over again.

His cries were heard from one end of the *Bounty* to the other. The ship's company responded instantly, and in different ways. Some imagined they were being attacked by native canoes, and raced up on deck to repel boarders. Others thought one of their number had gone berserk. For some minutes the *Bounty* was in a state of confusion and uproar. Men running up the ladders collided with those coming down, shouting news of the mutiny. One

or two hotheads threw in their lot with the rebels and were given arms. But most stayed neutral, warily watching the tide of events.

Bligh could not understand why no one came to his aid. He felt sure that only a handful of men were concerned in this mutiny. What of Fryer, the ship's master, for instance?

John Fryer had been asleep when Sumner and Quintal burst into his cabin. He attempted to rise, but was held down and was "so flurried and surprised" (he said in court later) that he forgot all about the pistols he always kept in his cabin.

"You are a prisoner," he was told. "Hold your tongue, sir, or you are a dead man." There was no doubt that they meant it.

Fryer lay still, listening to the sounds of tumult. Through the glass panel of his door he could see figures struggling up the ladder, among them his captain, dressed only in his shirt and nightcap, hands bound behind his back. The tail of Bligh's shirt had been caught in the knot, exposing his buttocks.

"What are you doing with the captain?" he said.

"Damn his eyes!" said Sumner. "Put him into a boat and let him see if he can live on three-quarters of a pound of yams a day."

"Into the boat? What boat?"

"The small cutter," answered both Sumner and Quintal.

"Good God! The small cutter's bottom is almost eaten out with the worms."

"Damn his eyes! The boat is too good for him." And the two mutineers divulged the rest of the plan. With Bligh were to go John Samuel, Hallett and Hayward. Fryer now asked to be allowed up on deck to speak to Captain Bligh. Shouted messages passed between the master's cabin and the upper deck. Christian, rightly judging that the master would be another disruptive influence in an already dangerously confused situation, said no at first, then relented. Sumner and Quintal escorted Fryer up the ladder.

At the moment when Fryer appeared on the upper deck the sun, deep red and larger than life, heaved itself out of the eastern seas. The scene it lit was even more chaotic than anyone below could have imagined. Everybody was making a noise, either cursing, jeering or just shouting, for the reassurance it gave them.

Bligh was the central figure on this crowded stage, shouting the loudest, threatening and demanding to be released, as full of violent spirit as ever. He stood abaft the mizzenmast; Christian held the end of the cord that tied his hands, his guards had muskets cocked and aimed at him. "I dare you to fire at me!" he shouted at them, and they lowered the barrels and uncocked them. It was a small but notable victory.

Standing near Bligh and Christian on the quarterdeck were the hard-core mutineers Churchill, Quintal, McKoy, Martin and Burkitt. Forward on the forecastle deck some ten men were at the booms assisting in hoisting out the cutter.

"Mr. Christian, consider what you are about," Fryer said, appalled by the scene.

"Hold your tongue, sir. *Mămōō!*" *Mămōō*—silence—was one of their most frequently used Tahitian expressions.

Fryer persisted, raising his voice. "Mr. Christian, let Mr. Bligh go down to his cabin and I have no doubt that we will all be friends again in a very short time."

Christian said, "Hold your tongue! Not another word or you are a dead man. You know, Mr. Fryer, that I have been in hell for weeks past."

Christian's eyes were "flaming with revenge," as Morrison described later. But Fryer did not retreat. For the first time that anyone could remember, he showed real courage. He begged Christian at least to give the captain a chance of getting ashore, and reminded him of the state of the small cutter.

"No, that boat is good enough," Christian answered.

Fryer edged closer to his captain and, speaking softly, suggested that he should stay on board in the hope of retaking the ship.

Bligh replied with a bellow as loud as before, "By all means stay, Mr. Fryer. Isaac Martin is a friend," he said, indicating the American, who was standing aft among the hen coops and who had earlier given Bligh a glance which he had mistakenly interpreted as friendly. Then Bligh began to shout hysterically, "Knock Christian down! Knock Christian down!"

No one moved. Christian ordered Quintal and Sumner to take

Mr. Fryer back to his cabin and they quickly led the master away. At the hatchway Fryer spoke to James Morrison, eager to learn of any who were not committed mutineers. "I hope you had no hand in this business?"

Morrison answered that he knew nothing about it. "If that's the case," Fryer said quietly, "be on your guard, there may be an opportunity of recovering the ship."

Morrison's reply was unencouraging. "Go down to your cabin, sir, it is too late for that."

On deck Christian still held the line that tied Bligh's wrists; in his other hand he held a bayonet. Whenever Bligh started to shout at them, McKoy, Churchill and Christian repeated the word *mămōō* and threatened to run him through or blow his brains out. For a time it seemed as if the mutiny was nothing more than an excuse for exchanging obscenities. At length Bligh appeared to be running out of words and stood with a furious expression on his face, licking his parched lips. One of his guards stepped forward and fed him a newly peeled pomelo. Soon Bligh's voice regained its full force.

Christian caught sight of John Smith, Bligh's servant and cook, and ordered him below for bottles of rum from the captain's cabin to serve out to all the crew under arms. "And also bring up the captain's clothes," he added.

Before Smith carried out his bidding he untucked his master's shirttail from the knot binding his wrists, making him a more decent figure. Then he went below and returned with Bligh's trousers and jacket, and a tray of glasses, tin mugs and bottles of rum.

There was a lull in the uproar as Smith helped his captain on with his trousers and put the jacket over his shoulders. Then he took up the tray and served the mutineers. His task completed, he went below.

On deck the drinking continued. Every man with a musket also had a mug or glass of potent navy grog in his hand. Bligh watched hopefully. Much more of this and the mutiny might turn into a drunken orgy, which could have one of two results: a quick end for him, or the chance of a counterattack. Bligh looked from one

familiar face to another. Some were blackly hostile, others uncertain, some hid their fear. There were surely more than enough who would follow him, but the mutineers did not relax their guard.

At 7:00 a.m., one and a half hours after Bligh had been dragged from his cabin, the small cutter was at last got into the water. It at once began to sink. One might as well throw Bligh and his cronies straight into the water as into that boat. Also it now became clear that it was no longer a matter of casting adrift the captain and three others. At least twenty of the crew, including William Cole, the bo'sun, and William Purcell, the carpenter—both valuable men—were loyal to Bligh and determined to leave the ship with him. Christian had seriously miscalculated. If he kept behind by force those who wanted to leave, there would be the constant threat of a countermutiny. Reluctantly he ordered the large cutter to be lowered into the water, but there was scarcely room even in this.

"You must give us the launch, Christian," Cole demanded.

Purcell, too, spoke in an agonized voice. "Mr. Christian, I want to see my native country. Let us have the launch and do not make a sacrifice of us."

Young chose this moment to appear from hiding with a musket and fixed bayonet. He resolved Christian's dilemma by indicating assent to Cole's demand.

"Hoist out the launch, Mr. Cole," said Christian.

The launch was twenty-three feet long, and six feet nine inches in breadth. It could be rowed, and two masts could be stepped. There were six seats for the oarsmen and a five-foot seat along each side in the stern. Fifteen men would be its normal maximum capacity. As soon as it was in the water, the men who had chosen to follow Bligh hastened to collect their possessions and any supplies they could lay their hands on. Purcell demanded his tool chest. Christian at first refused, and then yielded to Purcell's pleas.

Some of the men were already in the boat, receiving and stowing their gear with frantic speed. At every additional item the launch rode lower in the water. Christian was trying to stem the flow of goods, waving his bayonet, threatening and calling out,

"Carry nothing away!" No one took much notice. Morrison (though no one was certain which side he was on) had dropped a towline and grapnel into the launch; and Cole went up onto the quarterdeck after a compass, despite the armed opposition.

When Quintal saw the bo'sun trying to get the compass from the binnacle he exclaimed, "I'll be damned if you have it! What do you want with a compass with the land in sight?"

Cole protested boldly. "Quintal, it is very hard you'll not let us have a compass when there are nine more in the storeroom." Burkitt was the only man near, ferocious and armed to the teeth. To Cole's surprise he spoke up for him. "Quintal," he said, "let Mr. Cole have it." Cole hastened away with the precious compass.

Bligh's clerk was economical in collecting his personal possessions, just a few shirts and stockings in a pillowcase. He was more concerned with his master's box of surveys, his timekeeper, log and journals. Churchill intercepted him and seized all but the last two. To Bligh's vehement protests he replied savagely, "Damn your eyes, you are well off to get what you have!"

Amid this tumult two men remained outside the mainstream of the mutiny. Incredibly, the shark was still attracting the attention of Charles Norman, who remained leaning over the stern rail as if nothing had happened. The blind fiddler, Michael Byrn, sat in the rejected large cutter, crying in fear and bewilderment.

By eight o'clock several loyalists already on board the launch were attempting to create order. On the quarterdeck Christian was still beside Bligh, as he had been now for almost three hours. His agony of mind was reflected so clearly in his dark face that even the most frightened men remembered it long after. Several of those present, including Bligh himself, considered that he might take his own life at any moment.

Christian turned to midshipmen Hayward and Hallett. "You are to go into the launch now," he said. Bligh's wrists were then untied, and he was hustled toward the gangway. He appeared utterly exhausted. Christian said, "Come, Captain Bligh, your officers and men are now in the boat and you must go with them."

Bligh looked earnestly into Christian's eyes. "Consider what you

are about, Mr. Christian," he said. "For God's sake, drop it. I'll give my bond never to think of it again if you'll desist." Christian made no reply. "I have a wife and four children," Bligh pleaded.

"It is too late. I have been in hell."

"It is not too late," said Bligh.

"No, Captain Bligh, if you had any honor, things would not have come to this, and if you had had any regard for your wife and your family you should have thought of them before and not behaved so much like a villain."

Amid the growing impatience of mutineers and loyalists alike, they continued their dialogue. For a second it seemed that there was a chance of Christian weakening. Then Ned Young appeared, musket in hand. He seemed to emerge from nowhere whenever events reached a critical point. Bligh looked at him accusingly. "This is a serious affair, Mr. Young," he warned.

"Yes, sir," said Young, "it is a serious matter to be starved. I hope this day you get a belly full."

Christian, energized by the presence of Young, made some quick decisions. He saw that he could not work the ship in any sort of emergency with the men left to him. He wanted no troublemakers, but he did want skilled men. He called Joseph Coleman, the armorer, and McIntosh and Norman of the carpenter's crew to come back from the boat, but not the carpenter himself.

Bligh, seeing that the launch would not survive a day with so many on board, added his own voice, suddenly reassuring and hearty. "You can't all go in the boat, my lads. Some of you must stay in the ship. Never fear, my lads, I'll do you justice if ever I reach England." The three men climbed up the gangway. Fryer for his part was trying to persuade Christian not to put him in the boat, claiming that the mutineers would need him to sail the ship.

"We can do very well without you, Mr. Fryer," said Christian.

Bligh broke in, this time in contradiction: "You are to remain on board the *Bounty*, Mr. Fryer."

Nobody seemed to want the ship's master. But Christian had the last word, backed by a threatening cutlass. "By God, sir, go into the boat or I'll run you through."

That left only Bligh. He turned to Christian and asked, "Do you consider this treatment a proper return for all the friendship I have given you in the past?"

Christian was visibly upset and uncertain how to answer. What was there to say? Their relationship, once so deep and so passionate, had been shattered. In the words Christian spoke he showed again how deeply disturbed he was. "That—Captain Bligh—that is the thing—I am in hell—I am in hell!"

Bligh walked down the gangway in dignified silence and stepped unaided into the launch, where a place had been cleared for him in the stern. He was followed a few moments later by one of the mutineers carrying Christian's own sextant and nautical tables.

Christian said, "There, Captain Bligh, this is sufficient for every purpose. You know the sextant to be a good one." They were the last words he spoke to his captain.

"Mr. Christian, send me down some muskets, for God's sake," Bligh cried out.

The mutineers had been momentarily subdued during the captain's disembarkation, but on hearing this demand the wilder elements gave vent again to curses and threats. Churchill, however, did lower four cutlasses at the end of a line.

Cole gave orders to cast off. As they drifted astern last messages were called from the *Bounty*'s quarterdeck. Charles Norman, his shark now forgotten, was in tears, as were several others. "I wish I could go with you to see my wife and family," he cried. "Remember me to them."

The launch rubbed along the *Bounty*'s hull, slipping by degrees toward the stern quarter. It was nearly ten o'clock, the sun already very hot. What little wind there had been earlier had died, and the sea was gently undulating. Bligh and Cole got the men to the oars and the gap between the two ships began to widen. They could faintly hear Christian's voice calling for the topgallant sails to be loosed aboard the *Bounty*. It was like eavesdropping on a world they would know no more.

If the sea remained calm, the nineteen loyalists, including the captain, had a good chance of making Tofua, the volcanic island

which had offered them such pretty lights the night before. But after Tofua? The nearest European settlement was thousands of miles away; their launch was no longer than four men stretched out; the distance between gunwale and the water less than the length of a man's hand; and they had food and drink for no longer than one week.

Chapter 4

"PUT UP THE HELM, MR. FRYER"

As THE *Bounty* bore away slowly to the northwest, Cole and Fryer created some sort of order in the launch. Bligh sat silently in the stern contemplating their situation. As always, he was filled with the comforting knowledge that he had done no wrong, that he was a victim of villainy and circumstances beyond his control. Clearly, as he wrote in his log shortly after, Christian and his fellow pirates had never intended to leave Tahiti, with "its allurements of dissipation."

Typically, however, even as he was consoling himself that he was innocent, Bligh was preparing to recoup his fortunes. First he must make his way to England, then he must clear his name, regain the favors of his patron, exact revenge on those who had injured him and complete the breadfruit mission. Nothing less than this would satisfy him.

Through the hot afternoon, with six men at the oars, the launch made slow progress toward the steep black volcanic cliffs of Tofua. It was already dark when they finally drew near the shore. Hearing the rollers beating on the rocks, Bligh decided to stand off through the night and keep two men at the oars. To warm and give his men cheer, Bligh served them all half a pint of grog, about one third of their total supplies. It was the last generous ration of any kind they were to enjoy for seven weeks.

The island was an inhospitable place five miles long and four miles wide. The present eruption of its volcano was a mild one, more like a slow leak in the earth's crust. In the morning Bligh took the launch along the coast and discovered a small cove. But

517

the men who waded ashore found only some fresh water. That afternoon they worked the launch south till they spotted some coconut trees high on the cliff tops. A small party got ashore through the surf, climbed the cliffs and collected twenty coconuts. That night they each had a coconut and made themselves as comfortable as they could in the boat.

Next morning Bligh led another shore party in the hope of collecting provisions. After issuing a morsel of bread and a teaspoon of rum to every man, he scrambled over the side, taking two cutlasses and his precious log.

This time the party found lengths of vine hanging down the cliffs, clearly provided to assist climbers. It was their first proof that the island was inhabited. Bligh led the way boldly to the cliff top, and later discovered a cave at the head of the cove, where they spent the night.

The following morning some friendly natives appeared, and the sailors exchanged buttons torn from their jackets for plantains and breadfruit. Bligh explained that their ship had been wrecked and that they were the only survivors. The natives showed no signs of either joy or sympathy. Toward evening, Bligh wrote in his log in the cave, "I saw with peculiar pleasure that we had increased our stock of provisions, and that at sundown the natives left us."

Now confident that this island might supply them with the provisions they would need to survive the long open boat voyage he was planning—of which his men still knew nothing—Bligh sent parties inland to trade. More canoes, some from other islands, began to appear, and gradually the first familiar signs of hostility began to creep into the conversation. Out of the corner of his eye Bligh saw a party of natives moving toward the line securing the launch to the shore. They seized the line and attempted to drag it ashore. Bligh recognized the need for immediate action. His only weapons were the two cutlasses, and his men were outnumbered by more than ten to one.

Bligh rushed at one of the chiefs, holding his cutlass over him and demanding that his men should let go of the line. The chief gave the required order, and the natives retreated.

By noon the situation on the beach had formed a familiar pattern. Trading continued, but it seemed now more like a ritual prelude to violence. In the early part of the afternoon the signs of hostility increased. A strong and threatening body of natives lined the shore, ostentatiously separating Bligh and his party from their launch. With superb insouciance, Bligh settled down in the cave to write up his log so that the world might know one day how he had died. When he had finished, he gave the book to Peckover. "Get it to the boat if you can," he told him, "and tell Mr. Fryer to keep her well in on the beach when he sees us breaking out."

Peckover walked boldly down the beach, pushing his way through the crowd, the book under his arm. He broke through, waded out to the launch and delivered the message and the log.

Several chiefs now came up to Bligh's cave. "Will you not stay the night?" asked one.

"No, I always sleep in my boat," answered Bligh. "But in the morning let us do more trading."

"You will not sleep on shore," said another. It was a statement which suggested he would not leave it either. "We will kill you!"

Bligh seized one of their number by the arm, holding his cutlass in his other hand as a sign that he would strike if an attack were made. Then he led his party down from the cave, across the beach "in a silent kind of horror," as he described it.

It was a repetition of that nightmare scene in Karakakooa Bay just ten years earlier. Between his party and the launch were two hundred warriors. Bligh walked straight toward them as if they were urchins at a street corner. Something in his demeanor served to hold back the massed natives until the last of his men had scrambled safely into the launch. Then the chief in Bligh's grip broke free. At once another chief raised his hand as an order for an all-out attack. Bligh saw this signal and ran into the sea, struggling through the waves toward the launch.

Bligh's courage inspired his men. Not one panicked. Six were at the oars, ready to row as soon as their captain was on board. The *Bounty*'s hefty quartermaster chose this moment to match his captain's gallantry and leaped into the surf to tackle the natives single-

handed. In a second he was hurled to the ground and beaten to death with stones. Dark figures struggled for the possession of his trousers as he died.

Fryer helped to haul his captain into the launch. The stones were flying thick and fast, many of them wounding the men. Other natives had waded into the surf, some seizing the stern. Bligh slashed at the natives' arms until they released their grip.

The fleeing launch was still no match for the natives that pursued them out of the cove. Again and again their canoes closed on it; they released salvos of stones like broadsides. "Come back for the man you have left behind!" they taunted.

Bligh realized that soon his men would all be stunned or dead, and the launch overwhelmed. "Throw over your clothes!" he ordered. It was like throwing raw meat to a pack of wolves. At once the natives dived into the water, struggling to be the first to reach these prizes. Now using sail, the launch put on speed, and with darkness falling and the sea rising, the Tofuan coastline faded into the distance.

The horrible death of the quartermaster proved a blessing to his shipmates, for John Norton had been the weight of two men. His absence meant five percent more food for every man, five percent more room in the packed little craft.

It was almost dark, the sea was choppy, and they were taking in water as they began tacking south into the rising wind. Bligh told his crew they were heading for Tongatabu, an island he had visited with Cook. Here, he said, they were sure of acquiring all they needed. Mr. Cole, the bo'sun, said, "Sir, I would rather trust to Providence and live even on an ounce of bread a day than to go to Tongatabu, for I believe the natives would take everything we have, then cut us to pieces."

There was a murmur of agreement. Then Peckover spoke up. "Could we not make Timor, sir?" The gunner's suggestion found instant and excited response from the men because they knew there was a long-established Dutch settlement on the island. It was as if in a few days they would be walking up the quay at Kupang to a warm welcome.

Bligh recognized the dangers in this euphoric mood, and warned them of what lay ahead. In a twenty-three-foot open launch they would face storms and the danger of shipwreck. They had not a single map. They might die insane from the heat and from thirst. The food would be rationed severely. They had on board one hundred and fifty pounds of biscuit in bags, some of it already spoiled by seawater, twenty pounds of pork, a few coconuts and breadfruit, the last moldy. For drink, they had twenty-eight gallons of water, five quarts of rum and three bottles of wine. That was all.

"Well, my lads, can you live on two ounces of bread and a gill of water a day?"

There was a chorus of agreement. Bligh was still not satisfied and asked each individually if he was prepared to face stringent rations. "Aye, sir!" "Aye!" There was not a voice of dissent.

"Then in God's name put up the helm, Mr. Fryer."

The launch swung around and scudded before the wind at a fine pace. "Let us give thanks for our miraculous preservation," Bligh began the prayers that night. "Oh Lord, we have faith that you will continue to offer us your gracious support."

THE skill, courage and endurance of the launch's crew were put to severe test within hours of their decision. By the middle of the next morning they were being driven before a full easterly gale. For the next two days they constantly had to bail for their lives. Even during their worst sufferings, Bligh continued to plot their progress, taking readings at noon whenever the sun could be seen. When the sea was rough the only way he could do this was by standing in the center of the boat, steadied by a man on each side. He continued to record all the new land he discovered, including twenty-three of the Fiji Islands.

On the evening of May 6 the launch passed close inshore of several of these attractive islands. The men could see clearly the streams pouring down the cliffs from the mountains while they eked out their ration of stale water, and ate their two ounces of moldy bread within full sight of plantains, yams and bananas. It

was hard to bear, but there were no protests. The islands were obviously inhabited, and in their weak condition and without fire-arms, the risks of being seized were too great.

On the following day rain came down, heavily and continuously. By spreading a sail they were able to collect thirty-four gallons in one night, and this probably saved their lives. As Bligh wrote, "I consider the general run of cloudy and wet weather to be a provi-dential blessing to us. Hot weather would have caused us to have died raving mad with thirst."

As the launch continued on its westerly course, through recur-rent gales and downpours of tropical rain, the men weakened day by day. Bligh resorted to a variety of makeshift methods to pre-serve their health and spirit. He had them make a patchwork Un-ion Jack out of a bundle of old signal flags which had been thrown into the boat. He encouraged them to throw out fishing lines, which were a subject of endless speculation, though they never brought a fish on board. In the evenings he would lead his men in songs, rousing the weak or reluctant until all were singing, the brave sound reaching far out over the lonely surrounding sea.

An elaborate ritual grew up around the simple process of con-suming a few ounces of food each day. Bligh himself always broke his bread in small pieces and mixed it with his water ration in a coconut shell, "taking care never to take but a piece at a time so that I am as long at dinner as at a more plentiful meal!"

After twenty-one days at sea he discovered that there was enough bread on the present allowance for only another twenty-nine days. Already all the men were showing signs of weakness. "Our appearances were horrible," wrote Bligh, "and I could look no way but I caught the eye of some one in distress." He hardened his heart. That evening he told his men there would have to be a fifty percent cut in their basic food. He wrote in his log that it had been "like robbing them of life."

As a token that Providence might finally favor them, boobies and noddy terns were sighted, a sure sign that land was not too far distant. At noon the next day one of the men caught a noddy in his hand and killed it. Bligh, who described this noddy as the

size of a small pigeon, divided it—entrails, bones and all—into eighteen parts. In accordance with naval tradition, one man stood with his back to the launch's company while another pointed in turn to the spread-out parts, calling, "Who shall have this?" The first man answered each time with a name until all the bird had gone.

Exactly one month after he had been cast adrift with no more than a sextant, an old quadrant and a book of tables, Bligh caught his first glimpse of Australia and brought the launch to within sight of the Great Barrier Reef.

The only European who had sailed and charted these waters was Cook. He had only just escaped destruction on the 1500-mile-long reef, but he had reported gaps through which a ship could enter into the island-studded calm water beyond. To penetrate this reef in a launch, manned by a crew in the last stages of weakness, was hazardous indeed. One touch of that razor-sharp coral, and their boat would be torn to splinters.

The next day it was Fryer who spotted a possible gap. At first it looked too narrow. Then as they ventured nearer it seemed to open before their eyes. With the wind behind them, and assisted by a fast current, the launch shot through into the calm waters beyond.

Late in the afternoon Bligh ran in to a fine sandy beach on an island which he named Restoration Island: both for the anniversary on this day of the restoration to the throne of King Charles II in 1660, and to commemorate their own salvation. When the moment came for the crew to step ashore, many of them could scarcely make their way through the water to the beach. Cramped for so long, starved almost to death, they were, remarked Fryer, "like so many drunken men."

At Restoration Island the men's speedy recovery was matched by the rapidity with which they reverted to their old ways. Within twenty-four hours, when their bellies had been filled with berries and oysters, the grumblers began to grumble, the slackers to slack, and Bligh himself to hector and nag, curse and threaten.

On the second day Bligh ordered his men off to search for oysters and settled down in the shade to write up his log. It was a repeti-

tion of the situation in Tahiti, with Bligh absenting himself from his men, appearing only occasionally and then to upbraid them. By now everyone was in a bad temper, for besides the reaction to their ordeal, most were suffering from stomach pains from the unaccustomed food. Also they were anxious again for their safety. Natives in great numbers had been sighted on the mainland, waving their spears threateningly.

That evening they embarked again to search for another temporary home. At Sunday Island, named for the day of the week they landed, matters got worse and there was almost another mutiny. Again the dispute was over food. Bligh sent out foraging parties in different directions about the island, then claimed that all the food gathered was in his charge. Purcell resisted this hotly. Bligh cursed him and said, "If I had not brought you here you would all have perished."

"Yes, sir," Purcell replied sarcastically. "If it had not been for you we should not have been here."

This was too much for Bligh, who seized his cutlass, sliced the air above Purcell's head and ordered him to fetch another cutlass to defend himself.

Fryer now stepped between the men. "No fighting here," he told them.

Bligh turned on Fryer. "If, sir, you interfere with me in the course of my duty, you will certainly be the first person I shall put to death." This silenced the master. Bligh ordered the parties away again on a further search, and they obeyed reluctantly. The risk of rebellion was ended. Bligh ordered a small fire that night, but Fryer made one of his own, which got out of hand. For fear the natives would attack, Bligh then ordered the launch to sail the next morning.

Once they were again at sea a remarkable change came over the men. Although they were back on rations little better than before—just a few dried oysters or clams to add to their bread allowance—for a time everyone was full of confidence and good spirits. The grumbling ceased and Bligh again became undisputed commander.

Just before dawn on June 3 they reached the feared straits north of Australia. As they would need daylight to negotiate the hazards of uncharted reefs and unpredictable currents, it was not until noon that Bligh ordered the helm to be put over. The route he took was the narrow, dangerous channel—separating Prince of Wales Island from the continent—known as Endeavour Strait. But Bligh safely negotiated shoal water, rocks, sand banks and reefs, like the peerless navigator he was.

By evening they were free from the worst dangers, and open sea lay ahead. It had a tonic effect on all hands. This bright optimism, however, was short-lived. The strength they had gained from their few sustaining meals among the islands did not last long. After only four days the men became lethargic and slept much of the time. They had to be awakened for their bite of food.

On June 10 Bligh considered that more than half of them were showing signs of "an approaching end to their distresses." However, he did not yield an ounce on the rations, though there still remained enough for another fifteen days and there were already signs of land ahead. Strict economy had become his obsession.

By the following day everyone was at the last extremity. Never had their prospects seemed lower. Bligh looked at their swollen legs, their "hollow and ghastly countenances," observed their extreme weakness, and wondered what had come over them. Cole regarded his captain and observed, "I really think, sir, that you look worse than anyone in the boat."

This brought Bligh back to reality. He laughed and returned him "a better compliment."

Yet, though Bligh might appear as bad as anyone, he was the only one who still remained confident that the boat would reach its destination. At noon he calculated that they were less than one hundred miles from Timor. When he passed this information to his men they showed "a universal joy and satisfaction."

The island was finally sighted soon after 3:00 a.m. on June 12. Even the weakest among them rose from the bottom of the launch and broke into hoarse cheers of relief; then, led by Bligh, they knelt down in prayers of thankfulness for their deliverance.

Chapter 5

"A GREAT ROCK"

AT MIDDAY on April 28, 1789, the *Bounty* was a ship without a commander, its company stunned by the sudden breakdown in law and order. Only Christian had his wits about him. Haunted though he was by the last sight of the packed, wallowing launch, he knew that these men, the guilty and the nonguilty, were his responsibility. Still, he was not going to propose himself in command. Others must do it. They did so, eagerly and unanimously.

Christian now acted briskly. If they were to survive, there must be discipline again. He ordered the midshipman George Stewart, a nonmutineer and a severe taskmaster, to command the second watch. Then, just as he had made the appointment of the *Bounty's* new captain a democratic decision, so he consulted his men about their long-term plans.

"Where will you sail to now, lads? Remember that if the launch reaches a port there will be an immediate search for us. And they will look for us anyway later when the ship does not return."

"Carry us wherever you think proper, sir," one man spoke, and there appeared to be general agreement with him. Tahiti, the mutineers knew, was out of the question as a permanent home. It would be the first place that any searching vessel would make for. They needed a remote island, and Christian told his men that he had chosen Tubai, some three hundred miles south of Tahiti, noted but not landed on by Cook. It was far from the likely route of any traffic of searching vessels, and had a single harbor with difficult access. Cook had written of the natives that "their countenances express some degree of natural ferocity"; but they could hardly be worse than those on the Friendly Islands.

Everything was made shipshape on board for the long voyage east. The piles of fruit which had covered the decks under Bligh's regime were tidied up. All but a few of the breadfruit plants were hurled into the sea. Christian then moved into Bligh's cabin, and with a complement of only twenty-five they all enjoyed less

cramped conditions. However, discipline was no less severe than under Bligh, but no one was inclined "to dispute the superiority of Mr. Christian."

Tubai was sighted a month after the mutiny, a typical volcanic Polynesian island some five miles long. Dozens of canoes were launched from the beach and soon the *Bounty*'s decks were thick with natives, scrounging and thieving for all they were worth. Christian had difficulty getting rid of them without violence, and it was obvious that they would be back in greater strength.

The next morning's assault was executed with cunning. First eighteen nubile young women, the pick of the Tubaian girls, came out to the ship. All were well versed in seduction, and while they were busy at work, the main attack came. Fifty canoes, all manned by warriors with spears, approached, and the baying of conch shells filled the bay with an insane, threatening chorus. Christian ordered the *Bounty*'s four-pounders to be fired into the packed canoes at point-blank range. The result was devastating. A dozen died in the attack, many more were wounded, and the rest—men and girls—screamed and fled.

Christian named their anchorage Bloody Bay. Later he went ashore with an armed escort to survey the island. In spite of the catastrophic start, he remained convinced that he could dominate these people. The land was ripe for cultivation, and in the unlikely event that a searching ship might arrive there, it would be an easy place to defend. It would make an ideal settlement, but first they needed livestock, women, and native men to serve them. All these were unavailable.

"We lacked women, and remembering Tahiti, where all of us had made intimate friendships, we decided to return there, so that we could each obtain one." So wrote the mutineer Alex Smith, who now revealed that this was an assumed name, and reverted to his own name, John Adams. The *Bounty* sailed back again to Matavai Bay on June 7, 1789.

There was enormous excitement among the natives on Tahiti when the *Bounty* was sighted, and Christian watched the canoes coming out to meet them with complete equanimity. He had an

ingenious story ready, built on Bligh's earlier tale that Cook was still alive.

They had met Captain Cook, Christian told the chiefs, and Captain Bligh had gone on board with some of his men, taking with them the ship's launch and all but a few of his plants. Cook and Bligh had then sailed off together to a settlement in New Holland which Cook had been sent to establish by order of the king. As soon as possible, Christian continued glibly, Bligh would come back to Tahiti with more gifts for his old friends.

All this was believable to the Matavaians, and when Christian told them that their beloved Cook would like food, livestock and native helpers for his new settlement, they fell to with a will. Soon the *Bounty* began to look like Noah's ark—460 live hogs, fifty goats, chickens, a bull and cow originally left at Tahiti by Cook, and for good measure some dogs and cats. The crew had less success recruiting natives, who showed a disappointing reluctance to leave their families. Finally only Jenny, Mary, Sarah and Isabella, who still regarded themselves as the wives of Adams, McKoy, Quintal and Christian, agreed to remain on board, together with seventeen men and boys and one young girl. But at the last minute seven more women were tricked into sailing with the ship.

By now Christian had realized the cardinal mistake he had made in not disposing of his nonmutineers. They knew all his plans and no matter how many promises they made, nor how good their intentions, if they were allowed to remain at Tahiti, the news that the *Bounty* had gone to Tubai would leak out sooner or later. The only way to avoid this risk had been to prohibit shore leave to all the ship's company and forbid them, under the threat of the most savage punishment, from talking to the natives about their plans. Like it or not, they must now all stick together.

The *Bounty* sailed out of Matavai Bay on June 16, 1789, and anchored off Tubai a week later. Conforming to colonizing practice, Christian led his mixed party ashore and started work on a fort without further delay. It was to be a magnificent affair, nearly one hundred yards square, with earthen walls eighteen feet thick at the base, surrounded by a twenty-foot-deep moat, and entered

by a drawbridge. On each corner one of the *Bounty*'s four-pounders was to be mounted, and the ship's swivel guns were to be placed along the walls. Within this fort they would be secure from both native uprisings and attack from the sea. Above it, even while it was under construction, the Union Jack flew bravely.

A halt to the promising start of this new settlement was brought about by two forces, one from within, one from without. The Tubaians, submissive after their earlier bloody defeat, became increasingly anxious. They watched the moat being dug, and told one another that they were to be exterminated and this was to be their mass grave. But the more serious source of conflict stemmed from the colonists' continuing shortage of women. The men became increasingly reckless in their efforts to persuade some of the local girls to join them, and several times on these hunting expeditions they were ambushed, stripped of their clothes and beaten.

Like any good colonial governor, Christian tried to conciliate the chiefs, but violence was inevitable. Woundings, abductions and killings culminated in a minor colonial war—muskets against spears—in which sixty-six natives were killed. The Englishmen suffered only two injuries, but Christian's brave plans were shattered. He gathered his men about him for a discussion of their future. Sixteen out of twenty-five voted to return to Tahiti.

Christian accepted the decision gracefully. "Gentlemen," he said, "I will carry you wherever you please. I desire no one to stay with me. But I have one favour to request—that you will grant me the ship, tie the foresail and give me a few gallons of water, and leave me to run before the wind, and I shall land upon the first island the ship drives. After what I have done I can not remain at Tahiti. I will live nowhere where I may be apprehended and brought home to be a disgrace to my family."

This speech, its emotional overtones, its frankness, were all typical of the man. His great enterprise had failed; they did not need him any longer. But his old friend Young spoke up. "We shall never leave you, Mr. Christian!" Other voices joined his. "We will never leave you!" Eight in all.

The men put their plans into immediate effect. Everything that

had been brought ashore was taken back to the *Bounty*. Christian also had Brown collect some of the finest fruit plants he could find and stow them in the great cabin. Then on September 18 all embarked, together with some local natives who had linked their fortunes so closely with the white men that they feared for their future on the island. The *Bounty* put to sea.

Christian never knew how close to discovery they had been at Tubai. A month before they left the island, the brig *Mercury* had passed within two miles of Tubai at night and had observed only the lights on shore. In daylight she could not have failed to spot the *Bounty*. Nor did he know that Bligh had now reached Timor safely and had already dispatched reports of the mutiny, with a detailed description of every one of those who had remained on board the *Bounty* so that "the pirates" might be identified and apprehended.

THE *Bounty* arrived off Tahiti for the third and last time on September 22, 1789. There had been no further disagreement among the crew. Christian was to have the ship and the eight hard-core mutineers who had agreed to stick with him: Young, Mills, Quintal, McKoy, Adams and Williams, the American Isaac Martin and William Brown, the assistant gardener from Kew. With the help of two Tubaian natives, who had sworn everlasting loyalty, and some more men they hoped to persuade to accompany them from Tahiti, Christian reckoned that he could work the *Bounty* safely. Isabella, Mary, Jenny and Sarah would of course remain with their *taios*. The other men would find their own women.

Midshipmen Stewart and Heywood, Byrn, Coleman, Norman and McIntosh, who had taken no part in the mutiny, felt safe enough to set up home at Matavai. Here they would remain until they could take passage on board a passing vessel, or were picked up by a searching British ship. Besides these six men, ten others preferred to risk discovery at Tahiti.

Christian went ashore with the first of the Tahiti party. He was anxious to be away quickly. He was filled with unease, trusting

neither his companions nor the Matavai chiefs, who must now soon learn the truth about Bligh and the mutiny, either from his ship-mates or the natives who had been abducted to Tubai earlier and were now returning to their homes.

The news that met him on shore only increased his anxiety. A great ship like the *Bounty* had only recently left. The ship's master, Captain John Henry Cox, had been puzzled by Teina's tale of the *Bounty* returning under a new captain and leaving again loaded with livestock for a place where Captain Cook had built a new settlement. Captain Cox had explained to Teina that Cook had been dead for years, and to prove it had presented him with a dramatic picture of the assassination. The chief was furious at the deception that had been perpetrated on him. Christian had wanted to fill some of his casks with water, but now he thought that even this was too risky.

The last picture the world had of Fletcher Christian for more than eighteen years was of him standing on the black volcanic sandy beach of Matavai Bay, the cutter drawn up ready to take him to the *Bounty* anchored a half mile out. He was in earnest discussion with Stewart and young Heywood, giving them both hope and warning. A ship would certainly come.

"When it does, give yourselves up at once," Christian told them. "Do not attempt to hide. You are both innocent. No harm can come to you, for you took no part in the mutiny."

Then he took Peter Heywood aside and asked him to deliver messages to his own family. Christian recapitulated in detail the events connected with "that unfortunate disaster" as he wanted his family to know them: "Tom Hayward was asleep, John Hallett not yet on duty, and it was then that the idea of taking the ship first entered my head. I alone was responsible for this act." He was determined that no one else should be implicated. It was his mutiny, his alone.

ALMOST everyone believed that the *Bounty* would remain at anchor for two more days to take on wood and water, and that evening there were numbers of natives on board, supping and

drinking with the remaining mutineers. When darkness fell and while the festivities continued below in the forecastle, Christian and Young silently cut the anchor cables, hoisted sail and stood out past the reef. It was the only way they could be sure of having enough women this time. Without them Christian knew that their settlement, wherever it might be, was doomed before it began.

Next morning Christian and Young took stock of their spoils. In all they had eighteen women, only four of whom were on board of their own free will, and six men. Two of the men were the Tubaians, the other four were victims of Christian's trick. All were regarded by the Englishmen as manservants—slaves, really—to help with the heavy work. All passed muster for this role. Unfortunately the same could not be said for all the women. These included six who, although somehow included in the evening's festivities, were past their best childbearing years. Later next day, when the *Bounty* was passing the neighboring island of Mooréa and a canoe put out from that island, Christian had the six surplus women "who were rather ancient" taken off. The other kidnapped women watched them leave the ship with envy—if only they too were old and fat!

Christian now conducted the important business of pairing off the women, the white men being given a range of choice. Only one of the natives had a wife of his own.

That accomplished, the *Bounty* continued before the wind through the Cook Islands searching for a spot that met their needs. The island must be remote, harborless and uninhabited. The last requirement was the most important. An inhabited island meant not only possible trouble at the hands of the Polynesians, but also communications. The word of a white settlement would travel at the speed of the natives' great ocean-sailing, twin-hulled canoes. At one island after another it was the same story. They would approach, examining it through the glass to judge its coastline and interior, draw near it with caution and expectation; then they would spot dark figures on the beach, and canoes putting out; and Christian would order the helm put over and they would run out to sea again.

Gradually Christian's naturally cheerful nature, scarred by guilt, turned dour. There was now no gaiety on board the *Bounty*. With tempers fraying, the ship continued its restless voyage until she left the waters of eastern Polynesia far behind and was back among the Friendly Islands.

Here Christian was forced to anchor, collect water, barter for food and make a final decision about their future. The trading was conducted peacefully, and at the end of two days Christian had made up his mind. He had already studied Bligh's charts, and among books he had consulted was a volume of Hawkesworth's *Voyages*. On page 561 he read of Carteret's voyage:

> We continued our course westward till the evening of 2d July [1767], when we discovered land to the northward of us. Upon approaching it the next day, it apeared like a great rock rising out of the sea: it was not more than five miles in circumference, and seemed to be uninhabited; it was, however, covered with trees . . . it having been discovered by a young gentleman, son to Major Pitcairn of the marines . . . we called it Pitcairn's Island.

This sounded highly promising to Christian. Its only drawback, as far as he could calculate, was that it was so distant—almost three thousand miles east, and against the trades all the way. Young and the others agreed that they should make the attempt, and on November 15 the *Bounty* made sail and headed southeast.

Two discouraging months passed before the "great rock" at last broke the horizon ahead of the *Bounty*'s bows. Carteret had been two miles out in his reckoning, but there was no mistaking it— the silhouette matched exactly the careful engraving in Hawkesworth's book. The date was January 15, 1790. Nine months after the mutiny Christian had found the home for which he had searched for so long.

There was no sign of life, only seabirds wheeling about the cliffs. The island was thickly wooded, two miles long by perhaps one mile wide. The land rose precipitously on the southern and western sides, and with only a few breaks in the cliffs along the

northeastern coastline as well. There was little level ground, but the gentler slopes on the eastern side of the island offered the prospect of farming.

Three days later, when the wind slackened enough for Christian to bring the *Bounty* closer inshore, the large cutter was hoisted out. Christian and three others, with three natives, rowed across what was to become known as Bounty Bay, were picked up by a rolling breaker and hurled onto a beach—no more than a dozen yards wide—at the base of a steep cliff.

They struggled up the cliff three hundred feet to a ridge. Christian was soon satisfied that the beauty of the place was peerless, the soil rich, the fruit abundant, the climate benign. Here, on this level strip of land above the beach, their dwellings built behind the thick banyans would be invisible from the sea.

On the following day the *Bounty* was brought in closer to shore, and the ship's company, together with the livestock, were ferried onto the narrow beach. There was much to be done just to tide them over—a sailcloth was rigged for a roof the first nights, and they built open fires to cook their meals, but they survived all this stoically. In their new element, after four months of wandering, cheerfulness and relief predominated. Above all, Christian himself was a happy man again. One of the men told of his "joyful expression such as we had not seen on him for a long time past."

Chapter 6

"PANDORA'S BOX"

ON HIS arrival at Kupang in Timor, Bligh dined in the house of the second-in-command of this Dutch settlement, the governor being indisposed. He left the table as soon as it was polite to do so, and retired to his room. Above food and drink, it was peace that he wanted. Here, alone for the first time since the night of the mutiny, utterly weary in mind and body, he lay down to rest and give thanks to Almighty God, "Who had given us power to support and bear such heavy calamities, and had enabled me at last to be the means of saving eighteen lives." As soon as he had

rested he wrote to his wife, ending with blessings to "the little stranger"—the infant who had been born after he left England. In fact there were twin girls, making five in all so far. Later, Bligh prepared a complete account of all his troubles for Sir Joseph Banks. He knew well that if he was to survive at all in the navy, it could only be with the support of his patron. In the accompanying letter he wrote: "In this, you will find, sir, the misfortunes of a man, who pledges his honour to you, which could not be foreseen or guarded against, whose conduct will bear the test of the minutest enquiry, and who only regrets that you should see him so unsuccessful."

As to the rest of the survivors, all at first seemed to recover wonderfully under the care of the Dutch settlers, and Bligh was given a large house for himself and his shipmates. It would be pleasant to report that this was a happy establishment, but from the time the *Bounty*'s survivors recovered their strength until Bligh at last got away from them, their life together was filled with petty squabbles.

To Bligh's troubles was added the sudden loss of his friend, David Nelson. This ever-enthusiastic gardener caught a chill, and he died of "an inflammatory fever" a few days later.

Since a ship was not expected at Kupang for some time, Bligh determined to go to Batavia, where there were more frequent ships returning to Europe. He therefore bought, with money he could raise on the strength of his rank, a schooner which he named HMS *Resource*. It was only eleven feet longer than the launch, but it was properly decked and a good deal more comfortable.

The *Resource* got away from Kupang on August 20, towing the *Bounty*'s launch and escorted by two armed native boats for protection in the pirate-infested waters. This last voyage of the *Bounty*'s survivors was one of incessant grumbling, misery and contention, but they arrived without serious incident at Batavia some four months later. The last days together of the *Bounty*'s survivors were no happier than the previous weeks. The monsoon had arrived, the climate was wretchedly uncomfortable and unhealthy. Bligh caught a bad dose of malaria, and four others died of it.

The next ship for Europe would sail in two weeks, and Bligh learned that there were accommodations on board for only three. He reserved these for himself, his clerk and his servant. Meanwhile, the others reasonably asked, how were they to keep themselves until they, too, could get home?

Bligh was the only person who could help them, but Thomas Ledward, acting surgeon since Huggan's death and hitherto a stout supporter of his captain, wrote home to his uncle: "The captain denied me, as well as the rest of the gentlemen who had not agents, any money unless I would give him my power of attorney and also my will, in which I was to bequeath to him all my property, this he called by the proper name of security. . . . In case of my death I hope this matter will be clearly pointed out to my relations."

Ledward at length obtained a berth in the *Welfare*, which did not live up to its name and was lost en route with all hands.

BLIGH landed at Portsmouth on March 14, 1790. He hastened to London, presented himself at the Admiralty, and word of the mutiny then spread quickly. The *Gentleman's Magazine* echoed the general feeling that "the distresses he has undergone entitle him to every reward. In navigating his little skiff through so dangerous a sea, his seamanship appears as matchless as the undertaking seems beyond the verge of probability."

King George received Bligh and he was entertained at a series of adulatory banquets. At the Royalty Theatre a "fact told in action" spectacular entitled *The Pirates!* drew great crowds. It included a Tahitian dance, and "An exact Representation of the Seizure of Captain BLIGH in the cabin of the *Bounty*, by the pirates." His account of his misfortunes, sent to Sir Joseph Banks, had had the desired effect. Sir Joseph was already busily engaged in persuading the lords commissioners to prepare another breadfruit expedition—again to be commanded by Bligh. And as further proof of his confidence in his protégé, Banks saw to it that the House of Assembly in Jamaica granted Bligh a gratuity of five hundred guineas in appreciation of his efforts.

United with his beloved Betsy and his girls at Lambeth, Bligh spent much of the summer of 1790 writing up his narrative, based on the log he had retained through all his adventures. It was an instant success, and everyone accepted that Bligh was a victim of a plot and was in no way to blame. In October a token court-martial found that "the *Bounty* was forcibly seized by the said Fletcher Christian, and Lieutenant Bligh is honourably acquitted of responsibility for the loss of his ship."

Events seemed at last to be flowing in Bligh's favor. The promotion he had sought for so long came to him rapidly, first to commander and a few weeks later to post captain. His family life was joyous and serene. A sixth child—yet another daughter—was born on February 21, 1791.

And a twenty-four-gun frigate, the *Pandora,* had been dispatched to the Pacific to search for the *Bounty* and her mutineers. She carried a strong party of marines, and Tom Hayward and John Hallett among the officers. Their eagerness to settle accounts with Christian and their familiarity with Tahiti and with the ways—as well as the looks—of their old shipmates, were reckoned to be priceless assets in the search. The commander of the *Pandora* was a truly ferocious martinet (beside whom, it was said, Bligh was a lamb), one Captain Edward Edwards, forty-eight years old, survivor of a mutiny of his own which he had put down with consummate ruthlessness.

Finally Banks's efforts to get away a second breadfruit expedition proved successful. This time Bligh took no chances. He insisted on two ships, a brand new West Indiaman, the *Providence,* and a supporting brig, the *Assistant.* He took endless pains over his officers, too, choosing only those with the best records. In addition he had on board a lieutenant of marines, two corporals, a drummer and fifteen marine privates.

On August 3, with the blessings of the king, his patron and the whole nation, "Breadfruit Bligh" (as he had come to be nicknamed—by some affectionately, by others ironically) sailed again for Tahiti. There must be no more trouble. He knew that he would not be forgiven a second time.

THE FIRST NEWS Captain Edwards heard when he arrived at Tahiti on March 23, 1791, was that the *Bounty* had sailed away, its destination a secret, six months earlier. On board had been Fletcher Christian and eight mutineers.

Of the sixteen members of the *Bounty*'s company who had settled on Tahiti, two (Churchill and Thompson) were dead. The intention of most of the remainder was to give themselves up without delay as a demonstration of their innocence.

Their eagerness was so great that it became something of a race to reach the English man-of-war. The winner was the armorer, Coleman. Even before the *Pandora* had dropped anchor, Coleman was in the water swimming out. Peter Heywood was next. He found a canoe and paddled eagerly out and climbed aboard. He was met on the quarterdeck by Lieutenant Larkin, the ship's first lieutenant.

"I suppose you know my story, sir?" Heywood began. Receiving no answer, he went on, "I belong to the *Bounty*."

Larkin again made no comment. The young men, under armed guard, were taken below to the captain's cabin.

Hearing that his old friend Tom Hayward had miraculously survived and was on board, Heywood asked eagerly for him, "supposing he might prove the assertions of our innocence." But Heywood's hopes were soon dashed, for Hayward "received us very coolly, and pretended ignorance of our affairs!"

His old messmate's failure to support him was an especially savage blow. Then "appearances being so much against us," Heywood later recounted, "we were ordered to be put in irons, and looked upon,—oh infernal words!—as *piratical villains*." It had become horribly clear that Edwards intended to treat them all as guilty of mutiny until they had been proved innocent.

On the following day, Edwards dispatched Tom Hayward to round up the handful of mutineers who had decided to make a stand in the mountains. His men had a hard time of it among the steep gorges and dense forests, but a good intelligence service was on their side. The natives quickly forgot old loyalties and guided them toward the runaways' hideout. When finally dis-

covered and surrounded, the mutineers decided they had no alternative but to put down their arms. Their hands were bound behind their backs and they were sent down to the boat under a strong guard. Thus was the *Bounty's* crew on Tahiti apprehended.

THE *Pandora* remained at Matavai for five weeks, while Edwards did his utmost to extract from Teina and his chiefs the likely whereabouts of the *Bounty*. In this he was unsuccessful. Christian had told no one his destination for the good reason that he had not known it himself.

On the *Pandora's* quarterdeck a cell was built for "the pirates." It was entered by a scuttle in its roof and ventilated by two nine-inch-square scuttles. Inside, each of the fourteen prisoners had his legs in irons, his wrists handcuffed. One of them described how these were secured: "The first lieutenant in trying the handcuffs, took the method of setting his foot against our breasts and hauling the handcuffs over our hands with all his might, some of which took the skin off with them, and all that could be hauled off by this means were reduced and fitted so close that there was no possibility of turning the hand."

"Pandora's Box" was the name the prisoners gave this black cell. "The heat of the place when it was calm," wrote Peter Heywood, "was so intense that the sweat frequently ran in streams to the scuppers, and produced maggots in a short time. . . . These troublesome neighbours and the two necessary tubs which were constantly kept in the place helped to render our situation truly disagreeable."

While they were in Matavai Bay they were at first allowed to see their *taios* and their children, conversation being conducted through the vents. Stewart's marriage had been romantic and blissfully happy. Years later a missionary to Tahiti was told of its ending. "A beautiful little girl had been the fruit of their union, and was at the breast when the *Pandora* arrived. The interview was so affecting and afflicting that the officers on board were overwhelmed with anguish, and Stewart himself, unable to bear the heartrending scene, begged that she might not be admitted again

on board. She was separated from him by violence and conveyed on shore in a state of despair and grief too big for utterance." Stewart's Peggy died of a broken heart two months later.

The prisoners remained in Pandora's Box for four months longer, while the *Pandora* sailed from island to island in the Pacific, searching for Christian and the *Bounty*. By the middle of August, Edwards had to admit defeat and set course west for the long passage home.

Edwards was no navigator. He was, in short, as incompetent as he was wickedly cruel. He approached the Great Barrier Reef at a point where there are few breaks, and the result was that the *Pandora* was wrecked.

As she filled, preparations were made on deck for abandoning ship. Meanwhile the prisoners, tumbled together in one corner of Pandora's Box, became increasingly anxious. In desperation they at last broke their leg irons, to give themselves at least some chance of swimming if the hatch was ever unlocked so that they could escape.

This is how Morrison described what happened next: "As soon as Captain Edwards was informed that we had broke our irons he ordered us to be handcuffed and leg-ironed again with all the irons that could be mustered, though we begged for mercy."

Later Coleman, Norman and McIntosh, whom Bligh had named as being forcibly detained on board the *Bounty,* were released to work at the pumps. Byrn also was released. The rest could only resort to prayer, until in the last panic-stricken minutes when the captain had already abandoned ship (he was by no means the last to leave), the master-at-arms dropped them the key to their irons. There was one moment of heroism in this dismal episode. At the very last, a Will Moulter, the bo'sun's mate, risked his life by pausing to unbolt the scuttle. The prisoners who had been able to release their irons fought their way out through the narrow gap and plunged into the sea. But four were still manacled and they went down in the ship—John Sumner, Dick Skinner, Henry Hillbrant and Peggy's beloved George Stewart.

During their period of recovery on a nearby island, the pris-

oners were kept apart from the others, firmly tied and deliberately deprived of any shade from the tropical sun. On the long journey that ensued they were kept bound hand and foot in the bottom of the open boats. Kupang was reached on September 17, and they were placed at once in prison, in stocks. A week later when the Dutch surgeon made a routine visit, the stench and filth were so awful that he refused to enter until the place had been cleaned out by slaves.

This ill-treatment continued all the way back to the Cape of Good Hope, where Edwards transferred them to the man-of-war HMS *Gorgon*. It says much for their physical and mental resilience that any survived. The worst of their ordeal was now over. They were treated humanely on the *Gorgon*, and their condition had much improved by the time they reached Spithead. There they were removed to HMS *Hector*, to await their court-martial. According to Morrison, "we were treated in a manner that renders the humanity of her captain and officers much honour, and had beds given us and every indulgence that our circumstances would admit or allowed."

MEANWHILE, on Pitcairn, Christian's first favorable impressions had been confirmed. Rolling land accounted for about a third of the island's 1200 acres. The island's plentiful timber was ideal for building and for making canoes. The seas were rich in red snapper, mackerel, gray mullet and lobster. The red colluvial soil produced fine vegetables and fruit, and many brilliantly colored flowers like hibiscus and bougainvillea.

Besides all these rich advantages Pitcairn enjoyed a mellower climate than Tahiti. Some eighty inches of rainfall a year were spread out evenly; and the temperature in winter rarely fell below sixty-five, or in summer rose above eighty degrees.

Christian remained in command for the first week. He had no intention of taking on the responsibility of governing the island, but everyone recognized the need for a strong organizing hand until they became settled. After that they would see. Isabella made herself responsible for the women's affairs.

By midday on January 23, 1790, the work of unloading the *Bounty* was finished. The ship herself had been stripped of her masts and spars, her stocks of cord and rope, the cabin fittings, the ladders and companionways, the rails and the decks. Never again would the settlers have the opportunity of acquiring ready-sawed and matured timbers on this scale, nor—of almost greater importance—the nails that secured them.

Now the men stood about on the forecastle deck, drinking mugs of rum from the last barrel still on board. Quintal and McKoy, notorious for their tippling, had been at it all through the morning as they worked.

Christian appeared from below, stripped to the waist, and, like the other mutineers, almost as brown as the natives. "Well, lads," he asked, "are we to run her ashore now?" There was much talk, and feelings were not unanimous.

One or two favored keeping the *Bounty* at anchor for a while longer; others were for destroying her at once—before minds could change, before perhaps the natives might form a conspiracy to sail away with the women. The middle course was to run her on shore where she could later be dismantled.

None of them saw Quintal disappear below. Suddenly they heard above the sound of the pounding surf cries of alarm from the women on the shore. Christian looked around; there was smoke rising from the main hatch, increasing in volume every moment, and he could hear the dread crackling sound of fire.

Everyone ran aft, but they were helpless. The fire was growing fast, whipped up by the onshore wind. All buckets, even the pumps, had been sent ashore the previous day.

"It's no good, lads, into the cutter," Christian shouted. Only then did Quintal appear aft, a lurching figure, drunk as a lord, a sly expression on his face.

"Where have you been, you scoundrel?" shouted Christian.

"Best be done with her," Quintal answered, "or the Indians would have had her." And, as the roar of a sudden new gust of flame sounded behind him like an explosion, he was over the side before any of them.

Even down on the water they could feel the heat, as the flames shot half as high as the masts had once stood. Christian steered the cutter toward the beach, riding in high on a wave. The women waded out to meet the boat, clutching at the gunwale, all wailing in a chorus of grief, some tearing their hair and beating their fists against their temples.

With the coming of darkness the spectacular but melancholy scene caused many of the white mutineers as well as the natives to cry in chorus with the women. Voluntary exiles the white men may have been, but the end of the *Bounty* was like the slamming of a prison door; while for the conscripted natives and most of the women it was the end of any hope of returning to their Tahitian homes.

By midnight the *Bounty* was burned to the water. Only one or two of her ribs still rose, scarlet and curving, above her corpse. These remained flaming a while longer like torchlights above a ceremonial funeral carriage, before they collapsed with a hiss into the waters of the bay that was to bear her name forever.

No one seems to have thought of punishing Quintal for burning the *Bounty*. McKoy believed that his friend had done the right thing. The opinion of the others, led by Christian, was that this was no time to fall out among themselves. Besides, there was too much to do. It would be easy enough to survive here like animals; but if they were to create a civilized community there must be order, and this required a lot of hard work.

The first and most difficult task was to drag their stores to the small plateau above the bay, where they intended to build their dwellings. Ropes and pulleys were used, and by the end of February all but the heaviest lengths of timber had been hauled up the three-hundred-foot cliff.

Christian had surveyed the island, and he put it to the other white men that the land in the center, with its shallow valleys and good natural drainage, should be divided into nine equal parts, each a private estate for one of them. Here they would grow their own crops, sharing between them the services of the six native men. The arrangement was agreed to without fuss. Some

545

men were better off than others, but the merits and the demerits worked out fairly evenly. On an island so richly endowed it seemed unnecessary to quarrel about small advantages.

For what now happened at Pitcairn we have to rely on Jenny's reminiscences nearly thirty years later, the stories handed down to the children and grandchildren of the original settlers, notably Quintal's son Arthur, John Adams's accounts given to several visitors before he died, and traditional legends—sometimes unexpectedly fresh—to be heard still on the island today.

There is a good deal of disparity between the recorded times of events but a surprising unanimity on what happened and in what order. There is no reason to doubt that the main outline of the story of life—and death—on Pitcairn is true.

During these first months they were all too busy to give much thought to the confined nature of their environment, or to the potentially dangerous injustices of their community. Homemaking is an absorbing occupation, and there was no time for brooding. The families built their houses in clearings chopped out from the trees on the plateau, using as material both timbers salvaged from the *Bounty*'s wreck and trees they felled on the sites. The standard pattern was two rooms, one above the other, the lower raised a foot or two off the ground, the upper reached by a ladder. The pitched roof was covered with thickly-matted palm leaves, and along the sides ran a wooden gutter to catch the rain, which was fed into one of the *Bounty*'s casks. Advice was proferred from family to family, but no rules were laid down. All that Christian insisted on was that the houses must be invisible from the sea, and a long line of banyan trees was left on the seaward side of the community like a permanently drawn curtain.

By the middle of the year—it was winter but the drop in temperature was scarcely discernible—the village was beginning to assume an orderly aspect. Jack Williams, who had often acted as armorer's mate to Coleman, had set up the forge; and the new farmer-sailors had begun to clear their land and plant yam and sweet-potato seeds, and sugarcane, banana and plaintain plants, which they had brought from Tahiti and Tubai.

The chickens scratched about the village, and the evocative sound of the cock crowing provided the white men with a morning reminder of home. But the hens were not willing layers in this climate, and it was this failure to provide eggs that led to the community's first tragedy. Seabirds nested thickly on the cliff faces, so the women went out daily to collect their eggs. In October, Jack Williams's wife slipped and fell to her death. It was their first loss—but by no means the last on these dangerous cliffs—and Williams took it hard.

A few days later Isabella gave birth to the first native-born Pitcairner. She and Christian named him Thursday October Christian. Then one woman of the three shared by the Tubaians fell ill with a growth on her neck and died within a few weeks. So now the six natives had only two women between them.

Still, by the end of 1790 the community had settled into a routine. The women did the cooking and housework, washed the clothes and made new ones from the *Bounty*'s sails. When they wanted meat the white men went out and shot hogs which ran wild like the other livestock they'd brought from Tahiti. The native men lived at peace with one another, and relations were good with most of the white men.

Quintal and McKoy—whose violence was uncontrollable when they were drunk, and bad enough when they were sober—had little to do with the others. Jack Williams, Pitcairn's only widower, was unhappy and increasingly resentful. He kept himself occupied at his forge, mending and making tools, converting cutlasses into billhooks and keeping an edge on the axes.

The other mutineers formed two main groups. In one were Adams and Young, who had adjoining gardens and houses and lived closely with the natives; they were judged by the others to exchange wives freely with each other and the native men. In the second group were Christian, Martin, Mills and Brown.

Fletcher Christian's friendship with Ned Young had died a slow death since the mutiny. The growth of Christian's regret and remorse was matched by his feeling of resentment toward the man who had incited him, until he began to believe, with some reason,

Chris M Jager

that the tragedy would never have occurred but for the malevolent intervention of this dark intriguer. For his part Ned Young,
a highly educated and articulate young man, felt he was being
treated shabbily and detested Christian's piousness and moodi-
ness. It was not he who had acted violently. His motive in suggesting that they should rid themselves of their tyrannical commander was to relieve his friend of the burden hanging from his
neck—to show him the way out of his private hell. In Young's eyes
it was Christian's decision alone which had started the mutiny.

The women now began to show signs of restlessness. Even those
who had come of their own free will felt an acute longing for the
wider spaces, the gossip and familiar faces of Tahiti. Once the
community was established, Christian allowed his authority as
leader to diminish. He would disappear for long periods, and
would sit in the cave—known today as Christian's Cave—high above
the cliffs, staring out to the sea. He always went armed with a
musket, perhaps to blow out his own brains, or perhaps in fear of
what was about to happen.

During the next eighteen months the decline in the spirit of
the Pitcairn community continued, although several more children
were born. Then, some time in the middle of 1792 Jack Williams,
deciding that he had had enough of celibacy, confronted Christian
and the other white men. Surly and defiant, he told them that he
intended to take by force one of the natives' wives. Christian was
outraged. "They have but two women for six. This can only lead
to violence," he said.

"Then I shall take the cutter and seek a woman elsewhere,"
Williams said. "I would rather be captured and taken back to
England in irons than remain on this island any longer."

Christian and the others suddenly realized that Williams was
in a strong bargaining position. He was the only man who could
handle the forge. Without him they would be condemned to a
primitive existence. Christian spoke quietly to the others, then
turned to him. "Who is it you will have?"

Williams, truculent in his moment of triumph, spoke sharply.
"Nancy or Mareva. Either will do."

"We shall draw, then," said Christian decisively. He said to Brown, "Will, take two sticks, one short one for Nancy and one long one for Mareva."

Brown presented his two fists, the ends of the sticks projecting above his thumbs. Williams drew out the shorter of the two.

NANCY and her native man, Talaloo, were eating their evening meal when they saw Christian leading the eight white men, armed with muskets, toward their house.

"Nancy, you are to live with Jack Williams," said Christian. "He has been without a woman for too long."

Nancy had long wanted to leave Talaloo for the lonely white man. Like Mareva she felt of a lower caste than the other women with their white-skinned men. She nodded and went willingly with her new mate.

The next day all the community went about their business in the normal way, except that the white men carried their pistols in their belts and tended to keep together more than usual. Talaloo had left his house and was hiding at the west end of the island, the natives reported. Brown and Christian, whose gardens adjoined at the west end of the village, talked apprehensively of what might now happen. If it came to civil war, only Menalee, who regarded himself as Christian's *taio*, might remain loyal. The muscular Tetaheite and his friend Oho, both from Tubai, had long since turned surly and distant. Timoa and Nehow—from Tahiti— went about their daily duties silently and inscrutably.

Nothing happened for several days. There was still no sign of Talaloo. Then one evening at the very end of September, when the women were together preparing food for their men, Isabella overheard Nancy singing a Tahitian song quietly, as if to herself. It was a simple, extemporized song such as the natives often sang, but Isabella picked out this warning: "Why do the men sharpen their axes? To cut off the white men's heads."

She slipped away and hastened to her husband with the message. Christian acted instantly. Loading his musket, he hurried to the house where the native men always gathered in the evenings

and burst in on them. They were all there except Menalee. Talaloo had come back, no doubt to organize the massacre. As further confirmation of Nancy's warning, there were axes lying about.

There was pandemonium in the little room, and in the confusion Talaloo, followed by Timoa, fled toward the entrance. Christian pulled the trigger at point-blank range, but the musket misfired. Then he, too, fled.

He reached his house without injury. Later Menalee told him that the natives had indeed conspired to attack the white men as they lay asleep, that their hate was boundless, and that Talaloo and Timoa had fled into the hills. Oho had also fled, armed with an axe and swearing vengeance.

Three days of armed truce passed, during which there was no communication between the white men and the native men except through Menalee. On the fourth day Timoa and Talaloo, armed with axes, surprised the women fishing from the rocks of Bounty Bay, seized Nancy and disappeared.

When the white men heard of this kidnapping, they decided that only with the death of Talaloo could there be peace again on Pitcairn. Menalee was given the role of agent provocateur. He was to pretend that he had changed sides. Isabella would cook three puddings. One would be poisoned. Menalee, armed with a concealed pistol, must go up into the hills with these puddings and seek out Nancy and the two Tahitians.

"You must say to them, 'I have brought you food to sustain you,'" Christian instructed his *taio* carefully. "Then you must say, 'Soon we will rise and kill all the white men.' Then you must give Timoa and Nancy each a pudding, and the third pudding to Talaloo. If he does not die, you must shoot him."

The next evening Menalee returned with Timoa and Nancy. Timoa told Christian and Brown what had happened. "Menalee brought three puddings, and he said they were for us as we must be hungry. He told us that all the natives, the men and the women, would rise up against the white men. But I knew that this was not true and that Menalee had been sent by you. Menalee made Talaloo take one of the puddings."

Nancy said, "But Talaloo would not eat his pudding. He threw it in the bushes and ate mine instead. Menalee asked, 'Why do you throw away your good pudding?' But Talaloo did not answer."

"So Talaloo still lives?" said Christian.

"*Mămōō, mămōō*, master," said Menalee impatiently. "This is not the end of the story. Next I pulled out my pistol and held it to the back of Talaloo's head and pulled the trigger. But there was only a little sound, not a big sound. It did not fire. Talaloo turned and saw the pistol in my hand. He looked at me with fear in his eyes and ran into the forest. I ran after him."

"He ran fast," broke in Nancy.

"I ran like the wind," Menalee cried proudly. "I caught him and together we rolled on the ground striking at each other. Talaloo was calling to his wife for help."

"Talaloo did not know how much I hated him," said Nancy. "I took up a stone and beat at my husband's head."

"We beat his head until he was dead," boasted Menalee.

"This is only the first killing," Christian said to Brown. "The blood will flow fast on Pitcairn now."

It was a quiet evening and for once there was no wind. The seabirds were silent, the tall palms along the cliffs stood upright and still. One of the babies was crying somewhere, but otherwise the village was quiet. Nancy had slipped back to Williams's house. The smoke from the cooking rose straight up into the darkening sky as Christian and Brown, Mills, Martin, Williams, Quintal and McKoy talked together softly in Christian's house.

"We must sleep with our muskets loaded," said Brown, "and we must trust no one. Not even one another. Do not trust me. And certainly not Ned Young. He is too much with the natives."

"We should have killed them all long ago," muttered Quintal.

"We have been soft with them," added McKoy. "Kill Oho now. He is out there somewhere still. That one is a plotter."

There was a strong feeling that Oho must go. He was their greatest danger. Perhaps Tetaheite, too. But certainly Oho.

"Send Menalee again," Martin suggested. "He is a good killer."

553

Someone else added tartly, "He needs a woman with him to help."

At length it was agreed that Christian should send his *taio* out on the hunt again the following day. If he succeeded, they would trust him in future. If he failed, he would be shot as a traitor.

On the next morning, Christian carried out the plan as agreed except that he sent Timoa, too, as support. The two men found Oho alone, hungry and frightened. They pretended to commiserate with him, pledging revenge on the white men. Then at a moment when Oho's back was turned Menalee drew out his pistol and killed him with one shot in the head.

AFTER this second murder it seemed that the natives had been cowed into submission. But even after six months without further bloodshed, trust was not reestablished—neither between natives and white men, nor among the men of the same race. Young and Adams took no part in their old shipmates' affairs, while Christian, Brown, Mills and Martin were increasingly watchful of the natives—even of Menalee.

McKoy and Quintal were more or less drunk all the time now. They had reached the end of their share of the *Bounty*'s wine and spirits, but McKoy, who had once worked in a whisky distillery, succeeded in making a brew from the root of the ti plant which grew freely everywhere on the island. It was even more potent than navy rum.

The women now despised their fellow countrymen and—except for Isabella, who remained loyal to the end and was expecting a third child—had also lost respect for the white men. These were no longer the mysterious white-skinned masters who had once so strongly attracted them with their fine clothes, their possessions, their ardent passions. The white men rarely washed. Their clothes had long since worn out and they dressed like the natives, with no more than a belted skirt about the waist and a hat to keep off the sun. They, too, went barefoot, and their manners had become increasingly brutish.

Plotting began again in September 1793. This time the natives succeeded in keeping the plot a secret. Menalee was not included,

except as a possible victim. This time they would have firearms. Musketry did not come easily to them, but Young and Adams had instructed them how to shoot birds and hogs.

On the morning of September 20 the white men were out in the fields. Menalee was helping Mills. The other native men, too, began the day by working on the plantations. Then, one by one, the three of them—Tetaheite, Nehow and Timoa—stole away and made for the village. Unnoticed by the women, each succeeded in stealing a musket and ammunition.

The natives crept up first on Jack Williams, the man who had started all the trouble. He was repairing his fence where some dogs had got through. They shot him in the back of the head as he was leaning over to secure a post, and he died instantly.

Among those who heard the shot was Isaac Martin. Assuming that Brown or Mills was out hunting, he called across the valley to Christian, who was invisible but within earshot, "Well done! We'll have a feast today."

Next, the natives saw Mills and Menalee working together. Tetaheite decided to split this potentially dangerous combination. "We have shot a great hog," he called to Mills. "We need Menalee to help us carry it."

Mills released Menalee from his work, and Menalee strode off toward Williams's garden. He was almost on top of the body before he saw it. Then he saw the three natives.

Menalee turned as if to run away. But Tetaheite, who was as strong as two men, held him and whispered threateningly, "*Mămōō!* Be with us or you will die. All the white men are to die!"

By unhappy chance, Menalee's own *taio* was to be the next victim. Knowing that to sound a warning would lead to instant death, Menalee remained in agonized silence as they crept up behind Christian, who was digging yams.

Tetaheite fired into the back of Christian's head, carrying out the execution with speed and skill. Christian died almost instantly. But as he lay on the newly tilled soil, he called out—not very loudly, not in a tone of agony or anger—simply, "Oh, dear!"

Two white men heard Christian's death cry, for McKoy had

come into Mills's plantation to ask him something. Now alarmed by this second shot and the sound of the voice that had followed it, McKoy said to Mills, "That was surely some person dying?"

"I think it was only Isabella calling her children to dinner," Mills replied.

A moment later Menalee appeared in the clearing. He was panting as if he had run far, and he spoke in a tense voice. "Your house is being robbed by Tetaheite and Nehow. Go there quickly!"

McKoy, now acutely alarmed, ran down the valley. Before he reached his house a third shot rang out. It came from inside, and the ball whistled past his head. So Menalee had tricked him. All four natives had risen in revolt.

McKoy ran back up the hill. He was a fast runner in spite of his drinking and easily outpaced the heavier Tahitians. He made first for the spot where he believed Christian to be working. Instead he found his corpse; the blood from his head wound soaked the soil. Another shot sounded, scarcely a hundred yards away. Menalee had acquired a pistol and had run up to Mills as if to warn him of the danger. Mills, unsuspecting, had gone to meet him and was shot in the face at point-blank range.

Now McKoy ran to give the news of Christian's death to Isabella. Shortly after Christian had left for his work, she had gone into labor. When McKoy burst into her house, she was already giving birth to her third child, with Nancy as midwife.

Menalee had now run amok. He saw McKoy leave Christian's house and guessed that he would make next for the house of his friend Quintal. He ran through the trees to get there first, picking up a large stone on the way since he did not know how to reload the pistol.

McKoy and Menalee reached Quintal's house together. McKoy yelled, "Mat, get to the woods with your musket!" When Quintal came out he saw the two men struggling on the ground beside his pigsty, and McKoy was proving the stronger of the two. As Quintal raced to help him, he saw McKoy lift Menalee up bodily and hurl him over the fence into the sty among the pigs, where he

lay still. Quintal grabbed another musket for McKoy and told his wife, Sarah, to warn the other white men; they then made off into the hills to await the outcome of this day of murder.

IsAAC MARTIN had heard the shots and shouts but he had heard no word of warning. So when he saw three armed natives coming across his land, he awaited their arrival, unsuspecting—he knew Young and Adams were in the habit of lending the natives muskets. Tetaheite and the others came straight up to him. They were laughing and put the barrels of the muskets to Martin's belly as if this were a practical joke; they loved practical jokes.

"Do you know what we have been doing this morning?" Tetaheite asked. "We have been doing the same as shooting hogs"— and two of the natives pulled the triggers together.

There were two clicks. Martin joined in their laughter. It was like old times. They had often laughed together at simple jokes.

Tetaheite and Nehow recocked their muskets and, still laughing, again pulled the triggers. This time both muskets fired. By some miracle the shots did not kill Martin. Clutching his stomach, he ran off, not to his own house, but to Brown's. He got there before his pursuers, and collapsed on the floor.

Menalee was the first native to arrive. As he burst in he seized one of the *Bounty*'s sledgehammers from a hook on the wall and beat out Martin's brains as he lay on the floor. He turned next to Brown, who was frantically trying to load his musket. Brown then burst past him, racing for the entrance, dodging past Nehow and Tetaheite.

Then an odd thing happened. Timoa was outside, musket reloaded and raised. For some reason Timoa had taken a fancy to Brown—or perhaps it was only sudden pity. No one would ever know. But as Brown dashed past, Timoa said in English, "Fall when I fire."

Brown ran, and when he was a dozen yards from his house he heard a shot and at once fell to the ground, feigning death. This did not satisfy Menalee. He ran up to Brown, striking him a terrible blow on the head.

557

Brown rose to a sitting position, calling out for mercy. "If you are going to kill me, let me see my wife first," he begged.

Menalee first allowed him to go, but then snatched a musket from Nehow, and shot Brown dead.

FIVE white men were already dead. But the natives could no longer hope to finish their business as stealthily as they had begun it. Down in the village pandemonium had broken out. Calls of warning and shouts for help reached as far as the hills and echoed back from the forests. There was no telling now who was killing whom, where the next shot might be fired or who might die.

Jack Adams, who was working in his field, heard Sarah Quintal call out to warn him of the danger. He put down his tools and made for Brown's house. He saw no bodies. But the four natives were standing about the entrance, leaning on the butts of their muskets as they had often seen the white men do. Adams regarded them all as his friends and was not put out by the sight of the four muskets.

"What is the matter?" he called out.

They all turned together, threateningly, raising their muskets at the same time. Adams did not linger. He ran off into the forest, making for his own house. He was hastily filling a bag with some yams when all four natives burst in. Menalee fired across the room as Adams struggled to escape through the window. The ball struck him in the back of his shoulder and passed out through his neck, sending him tumbling to the ground outside.

Menalee raced around the house and hurled himself onto the wounded man, beating him again and again with the butt of the musket. Tetaheite was the next to arrive. His musket was still loaded and he held it to Adams's body and pulled the trigger. But again it misfired.

Adams was a strong man and there was plenty of life in him yet. He struggled to his feet and ran fast inland, leaving a trail of blood but easily outstripping his pursuers.

Timoa got nearest to Adams in the race and he called out to him to stop. "It's all right," he shouted.

At a safe distance and from a safe height above the natives, Adams paused. He needed to stanch the flow of blood. He turned back and looked down at them.

"Why is it all right?" he called to them. "You want to kill me."

"No," replied Timoa. "We do not want to kill you. We forgot that Mr. Young told us to leave you alive for his companion."

Adams considered his situation carefully. He badly needed attention to his wound. If they were determined to kill him, they would get him in the end. There was little to lose by putting his trust in them, for what it was worth. So, holding some palm leaves to his neck, Adams walked slowly back to the four natives, and together they made their way, as if by a prearranged plan, to Christian's house.

Here an orgy of grief was taking place. Isabella lay on her bed nursing her new child, a baby girl. Young sat in a chair Christian had made, as though it were the throne to which he had succeeded. No one present realized that this one white man, around whom they were gathered, had brought about this massacre; that he had briefed and incited the four native men, just as he had earlier spurred on Christian to take the *Bounty*. As before, he had absented himself discreetly while the cruel deeds were done.

Into this crowded little house Jack Adams was led, pale from the effects of his wounds, bewildered by the size of the gathering, shocked and in pain. "Why did you do it?" Adams asked, talking quickly in English so that the women would not understand.

"They would do it one day themselves. This island is like Tofua, always erupting. Soon it would have gone up in a great explosion. It is better to control an explosion as I have done."

Young was quite calm about it. Now there would be no shortage of women. He had already planned to have Isabella as a second wife. He had always admired her looks. He would have Nancy, too, making three in all—a small harem.

Although Young would wait a few days before putting these plans into effect, he spoke now of Adams's likely choice, thinking it might cheer him. Quintal and McKoy were not yet dead, but what of their handsome wives, Sarah and Mary?

SARAH SUCCEEDED in rejoining Quintal in the hills. There he and McKoy built themselves a shelter in a good tactical position and awaited the inevitable attack by the four natives. It was not long coming.

The natives' attack was a brief and abortive business. They fired a few shots without effect, and when the fire was returned fled back to the village, where they were severely rebuked by Young for lack of courage.

The wave of violence ran its course, bringing new jealousies in its backwash. Only one week after the massacre, in the evening when the natives were gathered in the center of the village, Menalee became jealous of the attention Timoa was showing one of the women and took up a musket and shot him dead. Tetaheite and Nehow then attacked Menalee, who fled from the village with his musket.

Menalee made his way to the hideout Quintal and McKoy had built. They seized their weapons and were about to fire at him.

"I have come to be your *taio*," he called out. "Do not kill me."

"Put your musket down on the ground," Quintal ordered. "Then you may come to us."

Keeping the native covered with his musket, Quintal told Sarah, "Go to the village. Ask Mr. Young why Menalee has come to us."

Sarah returned later with a letter from Ned Young. It told how Menalee had killed Timoa, and recommended that they should kill him if they valued their lives. He himself intended to arrange for the death of Nehow and Tetaheite.

Menalee's was an easy execution. McKoy shot him in the back with his own musket. But now McKoy and Quintal believed that Young might have laid a trap for them in the village, so they remained clear of it.

Three days passed. Then Young's wife, Susan, appeared from the village with a message that the two natives were dead and they could come back to Young.

When they asked for proof, they did not have long to wait. Susan returned with a bag; inside it were the severed heads of Tetaheite and Nehow.

"You see they are dead," she told them triumphantly.

So McKoy, Quintal and Sarah returned to the village with Susan, believing that their troubles were at last over.

Now that the number of men had been reduced to four, only the original wives remained all the time in the same house. The others moved from bed to bed as their fancy, and the men's fancies, took them. But with peace and security and the end of the racial struggle, the women soon became restless again. In April 1794 Jenny told Young that the women were going to build their own boat, and to ram home her point she began dismantling the timbers of one of the houses. Young and Adams discussed this new challenge to their authority with some anxiety and decided to humor the women. A boat of sorts was completed, and on August 13, 1794, it was launched in Bounty Bay. "According to expectation she upset," noted Ned Young dryly in his journal.

In one last desperate attempt to get away, the women conspired to murder the white men and leave in the *Bounty's* cutter. The plot was disclosed in time by one of their number, but the men went through another period of fear and suspicion before they were satisfied that they were out of danger. Time was the best cure for the women's restlessness—time and the community's fecundity. By early 1795 the population had so increased that even Jenny could see that they could never all pack into the cutter with their children, even if they did succeed in killing the remaining white men.

Even without violence at the hands of the women, tragedy on this unhappy island struck again and again. In 1796 McKoy's body was discovered at the foot of the cliffs below Christian's Cave. He had evidently bound his own hands and feet, tied a weight about his neck and leaped to his death.

The death of McKoy had a fearful effect on Quintal. He drank as heavily as ever and led a life separated from the rest, with his wife, Sarah, whom he beat mercilessly. One day in 1799 Sarah, too, was found dead at the bottom of the cliffs. Quintal said that she had gone searching for birds' eggs. He demanded Jenny in

her place, threatening Jack Adams and Ned Young with instant death if she was not handed over.

The two men realized that Quintal had lost his reason, just as McKoy had, from the raw alcohol he brewed from ti roots, so they battered in his head while he lay in his house in a stupor.

THIS final murder on Pitcairn had a profound reforming effect on Young and Adams. First they forbade all alcohol. Then they suddenly gave themselves to the Christian faith with the zeal of early evangelical missionaries. Shame for their past misdeeds must have been one reason for this conversion. But there was another. Young had been unwell for some time. He was losing weight, had long suffered from asthma and now knew he was dying.

Jack Adams, brought up among London's docks, was scarcely literate. Knowing that Ned Young would soon be dead, leaving him the father of this flock of women and children, he took reading lessons from his companion every day, so that he would be able to officiate at divine service and lead their hymn singing after Ned was gone. Consequently, when Young finally died in 1800, Adams rose to his responsibilities splendidly. He was warmly supported by the womenfolk and older children, to whom, at the age of thirty-three, he was already like an aged prophet, their undisputed temporal and spiritual leader. The community remained at peace, soothed by prayer and the new spirit of love.

FOR years the outside world remained ignorant of all this. The women grew fatter and middle-aged, and their children began to cast about for wives. In 1807, Thursday October Christian, now a man, surprised everybody by asking McKoy's widow, Mary, to marry him, and in 1808 she gave birth to a child, her fifth, nearly twenty years after her first on Tahiti.

In the same year a sail was sighted.

Captain Mayhew Folger of the sailing ship *Topaz* of Boston, Massachusetts, was one of the first sealers ever to pursue his prey in the southern Pacific. On September 28, in acute need of water and fresh provisions, he dropped anchor in Bounty Bay. Within

half an hour an outrigger canoe had come alongside, and Folger could look down from the bows of his vessel to see three young men waving their paddles above their heads. To his astonishment the tallest of the three canoeists called out in English, "Where do you come from?"

"Come on board, we will not harm you," Folger replied. The young men climbed up on deck and stared about them in wonder. They were tall and muscular, dusky rather than brown-skinned, with full lips and wide-set black eyes.

"What is the name of this island?" Folger asked.

"Peetcairn, sir."

"Were you born here, are you English?"

"Yes, we are English." The eldest answered, and then asked, "Are you English?"

"No, we are American." They seemed to be relieved at this.

Like his companions, the tallest youth wore a cloth around his waist with a knife stuck into the belt. He also wore a straw hat decorated with cocks' feathers. Now he introduced himself as Thursday October Christian, the others as his brother Charles, and James Young. "We were born here. But not our mothers and fathers. They came here a long time ago in a ship as big as this."

"Where are your mothers and fathers?"

"Our fathers are dead. They died long ago. I am the oldest man," said Thursday proudly. "Except for Mr. Adams, of course."

"Who is Mr. Adams?"

"He is a very old man. He teaches us about God. He would like to see you if you are not English."

Folger went ashore with them and was led up a steep cliff track. There were children everywhere, all half-breeds who spoke an odd dialect in which he could recognize English words. Then he saw older women standing outside their houses, fat and dark and handsome, pure Polynesian, smiling and waving shyly.

Folger was brought at last to a middle-aged man sitting outside his house with two women beside him. He was pure European, a stout and stooping figure, with long gray hair falling over his shoulders. His features were fine, with a long nose and steady

brown eyes. There was a pale, wrinkled scar on one side of his neck. His shoulders, chest and legs were covered with tattoos.

The man rose and extended his hand in greeting when Folger approached. "I hear you are from our old English colonies in America. My name is John Adams. We are glad to welcome you to our island."

On that day Adams related to the American the story of the *Bounty* and her men since she had last been seen sailing out of Matavai Bay nineteen years before, from the early days of earnest endeavor, through the decadence of the mid-1790s, to the death by murder or suicide of all but two of the male community. Then he spoke proudly of their conversion to the word of God. "We are happy today. May God preserve us as we are."

Later Adams learned with amazement and relief that Bligh and many of his men had survived to return to England, and that those who had chosen to remain on Tahiti had been brought back to a court-martial. Some had been hanged, Folger remembered, but he could not remember their names or how many.

Folger then reembarked, taking casks of water and as much fresh food of all kinds as his long boat could carry. "We will return to you in eight months," were his last words to Adams.

The consequences of this sealer's chance call at Pitcairn were surprisingly slight. The *Topaz* never returned, and life continued its uneventful course. Folger had, however, corrected the calendar for Adams: in Christian's long search about the southern Pacific he had failed to allow for the *Bounty*'s crossing the date line, so ever since they had lived one day behind, holding the Sabbath on a Saturday. This was now corrected, and Christian's first-born son, Thursday October, changed his name to Friday.

The story of the fate of the *Bounty* mutineers was not heard in England for another five years. Folger's sealing voyage was a long one, and the War of 1812 cut off most communications between England and the United States. When at last a letter from Folger arrived at the Admiralty in 1813, the lords commissioners were too busy with more important things to be bothered with some doubtful tale about a long-forgotten mutiny.

Among the Admiralty's problems at this time was the American frigate *Essex*, which had been seizing British whalers off the coasts of South America. Two frigates were sent from England to destroy her. En route to Valparaiso, they sighted Pitcairn.

The arrival in 1814 of two warships flying the British flag caused consternation on the island. The women and older children had long known that their leader was a hunted man. They also knew that it was only his authority that held their community together.

Friday Christian and one of Ned Young's boys went out in a canoe to greet the ships' commanders. The sons of two mutinous midshipmen faced the Royal Navy's authority for the first time, determined to protect the last of their fathers' shipmates.

They need not have worried. The officers were kindly men who harbored no vengeful feelings about the remote event in the Royal Navy's history. One of them wrote of Friday October: "A tall fine young man, about 6 feet high, dark black hair, a countenance extremely open and interesting." He found Young, too, "a very fine youth."

After being assured that the Royal Navy intended no harm, Christian and Young took the two commanders ashore. They talked at length to the man who long ago had held Captain Bligh at bayonet point in his cabin. His piety and the Christian simplicity of the life he had created on the little island convinced them that it would be "an act of great cruelty and inhumanity" to arrest him and take him home to inevitable court-martial and execution. So they left him there, with the Royal Navy's blessing.

Jenny, above all the women, longed to return to Tahiti and her family. She got her way in the end, too. But not until 1817. In that year the American ship *Sultan* called at Pitcairn, and she persuaded the commander to take her on board.

By the time she reached her home the first Christian missionaries were at work on Tahiti, and to one of these she gave her first account of the events since she had left the island in 1789. It was published in the Sydney *Gazette* on July 17, 1819.

Ten years later "Reckless Jack" Adams, as he had once been known, died, deeply mourned by his wife and mistresses, children

and grandchildren. He remains today the most honored figure in Pitcairn's history. His grave—set alone among orange, lemon and banana trees, close to his original home—is tended with special care and always decorated with flowers. The example of his piety had saved Pitcairn when it was so nearly too late.

Chapter 7

"THE WORST OF SERPENTS"

THE court-martial that assembled on board HMS *Duke* in Portsmouth harbor to try the ten officers and men of the *Bounty* was a great British *cause célèbre* of the autumn of 1792. Those who stood trial were Midshipman Peter Heywood, armorer Joseph Coleman, bos'un's mate James Morrison, carpenter's mate Charles Norman and his assistant, Tom McIntosh, and five able seamen— Tom Ellison, Tom Burkitt, John Millward, Will Muspratt and blind Michael Byrn. Under the presidency of Lord Hood, eleven Royal Navy captains sat in judgment on the prisoners.

At that time Bligh himself was at the other end of the world. He had arrived at Tahiti in April, and was soon away again with his supply of breadfruit plants—twice as many as before. He would land with them in the West Indies in January 1793, to general acclaim and a reward of one thousand guineas.

However, when later he wrote with seeming truth that, "This voyage has terminated with success," he was sadly unaware of two bitter and ironic consequences. The first was that when his breadfruits matured and fruited, the slaves would not eat them. The second was that while he was away, many influences in England were at work against him in the matter of the court-martial. His absence reduced the power of the prosecution; it was held to be a travesty of justice that the court-martial should sit at all without the chief prosecuting witness. And both the Heywood and Christian families had powerful connections and could destroy the good name of Bligh, who lacked such support.

The Heywoods were a large family, and Peter Heywood was the apple of the family's eye. His father had died just two months

before Bligh had returned to England in 1790, and when his grief-stricken mother wrote anxiously to Bligh asking for news of her son, he had replied:

Madam:
    I received your letter this day, and feel for you very much, being perfectly sensible of the extreme distress you must suffer from the conduct of your son Peter. *His baseness is beyond all description,* but I hope you will endeavour to prevent the loss of him, heavy as the misfortune is, from afflicting you too severely. I imagine he is, with the rest of the mutineers, returned to Otaheite.
I am, Madam,
Wm. Bligh

Certain that Peter could never have committed the crime of which Bligh accused him, Mrs. Heywood wrote to all her friends and relatives with naval connections. Peter's uncle, Commodore Thomas Pasley, was in Portsmouth when the prisoners arrived in 1792, and he took the trouble to seek out Fryer, Cole, Purcell and Peckover, all of whom confirmed Heywood's innocence. He also closely interrogated the young man himself and was able to reassure his family that he was confident that Peter had played no active part in the mutiny; and he arranged for him to get the best possible legal advice.

This was not a time of soft justice in England, least of all to mutineers and pirates, but as stories of Bligh's behavior before the mutiny spread, people began to think that there was more to the notorious case than met the eye. Also, Captain Edwards's treatment of the prisoners had become widely known and tended to bring public sentiment around in favor of Heywood and the others and against Bligh.

The trial began on September 12, 1792. From the outset it was evident that Coleman, Norman and McIntosh would be acquitted, since Bligh had left behind the statement that they were forcibly detained. It was also pretty clear that four of the seamen who had been seen bearing arms during the mutiny—Ellison, Burkitt, Millward and Muspratt—had little hope of escaping the gal-

lows. The interest in the trial, apart from the usual morbid fascination, lay therefore mainly in the fate of Heywood and Morrison, especially Heywood.

On the morning of September 18 Lord Hood announced the court's verdict—"that the charges have been proved against the said Peter. Heywood, James Morrison, Thomas Ellison, Thomas Burkitt, John Millward and William Muspratt, and I do adjudge you and each of you to suffer death by being hanged by the neck." He went on to "humbly and most earnestly recommend the said Peter Heywood and James Morrison to His Majesty's royal mercy." The rest went free.

The Heywood family were thus condemned to another period of agonizing doubt, but all was well, both for Heywood and Morrison. A free pardon was sent two weeks later. On Commodore Pasley's recommendation Lord Hood himself offered to take Heywood on his flagship, *Victory*.

To acquit, and at once to reinstate, an officer who had been one of Bligh's chief targets was a public rebuke to the absent captain, and everyone recognized it as such.

Morrison, too, had no difficulty in finding a ship. Of the four mutineers condemned to death, Will Muspratt eventually won his freedom on a legal technicality; and so, of the twenty-five who remained behind in the *Bounty* only three met the common fate of every mutineer.

THE eighteen months' long period between William Bligh's return from Jamaica and his next employment in the Royal Navy was one of anxiety and unhappiness for him. As soon as the court-martial was over, fierce contention had broken out among the families involved; and the Heywoods and Christians relentlessly set about the destruction of Bligh's reputation. Especially damaging was the publication by Fletcher's brother, Edward Christian, of the minutes of the court-martial, with a long, cleverly written appendix of his own. Although Britain was now at war with France, and his contemporaries were gaining distinction in battles and adding to their fortunes with prize money, Bligh was kept

on half pay, an embittered and penurious officer with few people except his loyal wife prepared to support him.

His chance came at last, when the controversy was dying down, in April 1795. He was appointed to the command of the *Calcutta*, which was ordered to join the fleet of Admiral Adam Duncan in the North Sea, blockading the Dutch fleet.

In the following January he was given the command of the much larger *Director*. Dull blockade duties occupied the *Director*'s company for many months. In March 1797 Bligh was aware of a dangerous spirit running through the ship. Six men refused or neglected their duties. Bligh served out lashes to them all, and to five more a few days later. The running of the ship became more and more difficult, and Bligh soon realized that this was no passing restlessness. He took the *Director* to Sheerness, and there, at 9:00 a.m. on May 19, 1797, he was for the second time ordered off his ship by mutineers.

This time Bligh was in good company. For the whole command of the Royal Navy at Nore had risen up against their officers, demanding improved pay and conditions. Bligh took an active and responsible part in the closing stages of this "Mutiny of the Nore."

By this time Bligh was nearing the end of his active service in the Royal Navy. His reputation as a navigator and hydrographer, as naturalist and scientist, was untarnished. He was now a Fellow of the Royal Society and had been presented with its gold medal. His family life remained blissfully happy, and there was no more loving and anxious father. Yet his professional life was rarely free from discord, and Betsy seemed to be forever involved in defense of his reputation.

In 1804 there was yet another court-martial. At this time Bligh was commander of the *Warrior*. He had a good deal of trouble with his second lieutenant, John Frazier. Then Frazier had an accident. He fell between casks loaded in a launch and claimed afterward that he was unable to keep his watch. Bligh, considering him a malingerer, had him charged with "contumacy and disobedience." On the surgeon's evidence, Frazier was acquitted. The lieutenant wasted no time in pushing home his advantage

and reported that Bligh "publicly on the quarter deck . . . did grossly insult and ill treat me . . . by calling me rascal, scoundrel and shaking his fist in my face and that . . . he behaved towards me and other commissioned, warrant and petty officers in the said ship in a tyrannical and oppressive and unofficerlike behaviour."

When the news of this accusation reached the Admiralty, it was decided to court-martial Bligh in turn. The *Warrior* court-martial, as it came to be called, was the last, inglorious event in Bligh's naval career. This was no public *cause célèbre*, but the outcome was humiliating. His officers might, as Bligh complained, "turn out to be the worst of serpents," but the court-martial's considered opinion was that "the charges are in part proved, and we do therefore adjudge Captain William Bligh to be reprimanded and to be admonished to be in future more correct in his language."

Bligh was restored to his command and wrote without delay to Banks, complaining about everything—the court-martial, the findings and his officers. "Instances of my doing good," remarked Bligh to his patron, "and rendering service are numerous since my youth to this moment. I defy the world to produce one act of malevolence or injustice."

Once again the powerful hand of Sir Joseph Banks offered him a new and seemingly golden opportunity to end for the time being his long period of misfortune. Banks's offer was the governorship of New South Wales, with a salary of £2000 a year, and a pension of £1000 a year. It was an opportunity that Bligh could not pass by. The one serious drawback was that he would have to leave behind his beloved Betsy and his children. As he explained sadly to Banks in his reply, her nerves had so suffered on account of her husband's troubles that she could not possibly undertake such a long sea voyage. "The sound of a gun or thunder" was unbearable to her, and even when Bligh's ship was in port she could remain on board only a few hours.

In February 1806 he bade his wife and five of his daughters farewell. His daughter Mary accompanied him. She had married a naval officer, John Putland, who had agreed to act as Bligh's lieutenant during his governorship of the colony.

Bligh found conditions in New South Wales far worse than he could have dreamed possible—a corrupt, violent, drunken and immoral community, controlled by a ruthless military junta, the New South Wales Corps. The settlers, the farmers and the convicts, with few exceptions, had all succumbed to alcoholism. Women sold their bodies, men their land and their stock, for rum. The officers of the corps saw that they got it—at a price.

The governor, Bligh discovered to his chagrin, was regarded as no more than a cipher. He fought valiantly but unskillfully against this gangster regime, but he was quite out of his depth in this world of chicanery and corruption.

Here, in this remote outpost, without the support of law, military strength or influential friends, Bligh was more helpless than he had ever been in the past. There was no Betsy, no Banks, to support him. His daughter could do nothing, his son-in-law was dying of consumption. The small company of friends he had made when he had first arrived soon dissolved.

On January 26, 1808, there was a military coup. Major George Johnston, the corrupt commanding officer of the New South Wales Corps, went to arrest Bligh in Government House. The manner of his arrest is the most controversial event in the notorious Rum Rebellion. All that is known for sure is that he took a lot of finding and that he was eventually discovered in a back room underneath a featherbed, wearing his naval uniform and a gold medal he had earned in battle. Was it cowardice that sent him there, or did he hope that the soldiers might eventually look for him elsewhere, thus enabling him to escape?

Bligh, as so often before, is his own stoutest defender: "For twenty-one years I have been a Post-Captain, and have been engaged in services of danger, not falling within the ordinary duties of my profession. . . . Was it for me then to sully my reputation and to disgrace the medal I wear by shrinking from death, which I had braved in every shape?"

After suffering numerous humiliations and vicissitudes, Bligh sailed from New South Wales on April 27, 1810, and arrived in London six months later.

After this ordeal, the last of so many, Bligh applied for promotion to flag rank; and his request was granted. He never hoisted his flag, never went to sea again, but at least he could retire from his turbulent public career as William Bligh, rear admiral of the Blue, who had fought alongside Nelson and was one of the greatest navigators and explorers of his day. Bligh's devoted and dedicated wife fell ill, and she died in April 1812. Bligh died in December 1817, some twenty-four years after the man who was once his close friend and who became his greatest enemy.

Epilogue

"A CRIME OF SO BLACK A NATURE"

THE solution to the mystery of the *Bounty* mutiny lies somewhere in the passage between Tahiti and Tofua. To understand what may have happened it is necessary to look far back at a little considered side of life in the Royal Navy.

At the end of the eighteenth century the moral standards in the Royal Navy had never been lower. To reduce the dangers of "indecent conduct" the navy encouraged natives abroad—as well as wives at home—to come on board whenever the ship was in port. No one can say whether, on balance, these tactics were successful, but the reports of courts-martial reveal numerous cases of "gross indecency." For every case brought to court, there were certainly many hundreds which went unpunished.

Those who attempted to bring about moral reform in the navy had no doubt that the encouragement of prostitution on shipboard actually encouraged "indecent conduct" at sea too. One pamphleteer angrily demanded, "What can be more *unnatural*, more contrary to all the feelings of our common nature, than the open, undisguised, unblushing, promiscuous concubinage, which now takes place on board His Majesty's ships of war?"

From many such protests we can judge how widespread "intimate friendships" were in the navy at that time. The ship's commander, with his own cabin and the privilege of privacy, and with special responsibilities such as Bligh had for the "young gentle-

men" on his voyages, was in a special position to enjoy such relationships.

Bligh's friendship with Christian, as we have seen, was most intimate and long-lasting. This was their third voyage together, and it is clear that Christian was singled out for special favors in the *Britannia* and later in the *Bounty*. He had the key to Bligh's liquor store and when standing watch would often send down one of the men to fetch him a tot. He is reported as having had supper with Bligh every other night.

There were disputes between the commander and his protégé before they reached Tahiti, but they were few and not very violent. At Tahiti the close relationship was broken. Christian lived with a native woman, while Bligh, with Cook as an example, lived an abstemious life.

Let us look back to early April, 1789. Bligh is angry at the state of the ship and the slackness of officers and men. If he had been experiencing jealousy, which is extremely likely, then his first target for vengeance would obviously be Christian. And it is at this time—according to all accounts—that Fletcher Christian's ordeal began.

The days between Matavai Bay and Tofua reveal a commander who was at the end of his tether, behaved violently and irrationally, showed extreme possessiveness and a truly fearsome venom toward his officers, and toward Christian in particular. After refusing to spend the evening with Bligh for the last time, Christian, in a deeply disturbed state of mind, determined on a step so dangerous that it amounted to suicide. He was foiled, was offered an alternative course of action which at any other time he would not have contemplated—and which he almost instantly regretted. "It is too late," was his *cri de coeur* to Bligh. "I have been in hell."

If it seems odd that in the heat of the court-martial and its aftermath no one made an accusation of "indecent conduct" against Bligh, there are three possible explanations. The first is that no one knew for sure. The second, that it might implicate others. The third, that it was an especially dangerous accusation to make against a commanding officer.

In any case, I believe that the solution of the *Bounty* mystery lies somewhere in this forbidden darkness.

Bligh and Christian were both highly strung. Bligh's qualities and weaknesses as a leader are now clear to us: an unsurpassed foul-weather commander who revealed his lack of self-confidence only when the going was good; courageous, dutiful, a superb seaman and navigator, but fretful, impatient and seriously lacking in imagination. Shrewd people who met him for the first time would see the short, stout figure with wide-set mariner's legs, small, bright, angry, blue eyes set against a wax-pale complexion, and would think, There is a difficult man! Christian, on the other hand, exposed shamelessly his insatiable appetite for affection, and Bligh, who pretended to himself that he was above such things, fell under the spell of Christian's charm and liveliness.

Bligh promoted this weak, moody, temperamental and senti-mental young man above his ability. Where Bligh had moments of magnificence as a leader, Christian had none. Just as he de-stroyed the community of the *Bounty* with an explosion ignited by pent-up despair, so he later brought about the destruction of the community he had founded on Pitcairn by a failure to rise to the re-sponsibilities of leadership. There was just not enough fiber in him to endure the harsh treatment and the humiliation he suffered under Bligh.

Was all this enough to drive Fletcher Christian to mutiny? Not at first perhaps. Knowing him as we do, we are not surprised that he preferred to slide out of his crisis. It needed a Ned Young—the *Bounty's* Iago—to put steel into Christian's resolve, and to bring about the most celebrated mutiny of all time.

A Letter from the Author

The new documentary material that has enabled me to shed fresh light on the exciting events of the mutiny and its aftermath stems mainly from my researches in the Naval Library and Public Record Office in London, and in the Mitchell Library in Sydney.

There is, however, one major source which is respected by all present-day *Bounty* scholars and which necessitates some comment—James Morrison's *Journal*. This *Journal*, which claims to be a day-to-day account, has all the marks of authenticity. At the same time, it seems incredible that Morrison could have kept it up-to-date (or indeed kept it at all) through those five months in "Pandora's Box," the shipwreck and all that followed. The likeliest explanation is that it was impounded or destroyed by Captain Edward Edwards and that Morrison rewrote it while awaiting the court-martial. This would account for the hints that the author is writing with the advantage of hindsight.

At Pitcairn, however, the events enter a parable stage and it is here that I have had to rely on two less trustworthy sources—the reminiscences of Jenny (John Adams's *taio* on Tahiti who became Isaac Martin's wife on Pitcairn) and the accounts of John Adams himself, which he gave to several visitors before he died.

Throughout the rest of the book, most of the dialogue is verbatim. I have occasionally modified the punctuation, the spelling and sentence construction in ships' logs, narratives, journals and other reports.

I owe a special debt of thanks to His Royal Highness the Duke of Edinburgh, and to Rear Admiral R. J. Troubridge, Flag Officer Royal Yachts, for inviting me on board HM Yacht *Britannia* when, by happy chance, it sailed in the wake of the *Bounty* in the early weeks of 1971. I should have felt very much less adequately equipped to write this book if I had not sailed the Cape Horn waters where the *Bounty* took such a beating, made my way into Matavai Bay, eaten breadfruit on Point Venus and landed on that tiny beach on Pitcairn Island.

ACKNOWLEDGMENTS

Page 2: *The Cornell Farm,* oil painting on canvas by Edward Hicks (1936), is from the National Gallery of Art, Washington, D.C., gift of Edgar William and Bernice Chrysler Garbisch. Used by permission.

Page 482: Chart by Paul Bacon.